Acclaim for Lauren K. Denton

"A poignant and heartfelt tale of sisterh[ood, motherhood, and]
Hurricane Season deftly examines the ro[le]
past plays in creating a hopeful future. Rea[d]
hurricanes—both literal and figurative—t[he]
—KRISTY WOODSON HARVEY,
AUTHOR OF *SLIGHTLY SOUTH OF SIMPLE*

"Inspiring and heartwarming fiction that will please many a heart. Lauren Denton has done it again. In *Hurricane Season*, Denton delivers emotional depth while examining the many types of 'storms' that cause havoc in our lives. After making us love her characters and feel every ache of their journey, she brings us full circle through a beautiful story, reminding us all that *this too shall pass*."
—JULIE CANTRELL, *NEW YORK TIMES* AND *USA TODAY*
BESTSELLING AUTHOR OF *PERENNIALS*

"It's true what they say. There's no place like home. And reading a Lauren Denton book feels like coming home. With characters you'll want as friends, a setting you can step into, and a poignant story of sisters and family ties and all the messiness of a wonderful life, Denton has penned another tale that will settle in deep and stay awhile, long after the last page is turned."
—CATHERINE WEST, AUTHOR OF *WHERE HOPE BEGINS*,
FOR *HURRICANE SEASON*

"An engaging, lyrical story of sisterly love. *Hurricane Season* is sure to add to Denton's growing fan base."
—RACHEL HAUCK, *NEW YORK TIMES* BESTSELLING AUTHOR

"Denton's *Hurricane Season* feels like home. Through sisters Jenna and Betsy you will recognize which sister you are, the sister you could be, and the sister you yearn to become—the woman you hope to become. It's an absolutely lovely story of love, loss, and the hope of new beginnings."
—KATHERINE REAY, AUTHOR OF *DEAR MR. KNIGHTLEY* AND
THE AUSTEN ESCAPE

"Denton's delicious debut [*The Hideaway*] is a treat for the senses and the heart. Her exquisitely lyrical writing and character-driven story is a must-read."

—LIBRARY JOURNAL, STARRED REVIEW AND DEBUT OF THE MONTH

"*The Hideaway* is the heartwarmingly southern story about the families we are given—and the families we choose. Two endearing heroines and their poignant storylines of love lost and found make this the perfect book for an afternoon on the back porch with a glass of sweet tea."

—KAREN WHITE, *NEW YORK TIMES* BESTSELLING AUTHOR

"This debut novel is the kind of book you want to curl up with on a rainy day or stick in your beach bag for your next vacation. It is poetic and compelling, emotional and full of life. Its haunting beauty will linger long with readers."

—RT BOOK REVIEWS, 4½ STARS, TOP PICK! FOR *THE HIDEAWAY*

"In this fine debut, Denton crafts a beautiful, heartbreaking story of true love that never dies. This book will please inspirational, contemporary, and historical fans alike."

—PUBLISHERS WEEKLY, STARRED REVIEW OF *THE HIDEAWAY*

"Denton's first novel charms readers with her idyllic settings and wonderful cast of characters . . . *The Hideaway* is a deeply satisfying exploration of family, friendship, and the meaning of home."

—BOOKLIST

"From the opening of *The Hideaway*, the reader is captured by the voice of a woman who has for too long kept a story that must be told, one the reader wants to hear. Denton has crafted a story both powerful and enchanting: a don't-miss novel in the greatest southern traditions of storytelling."

—PATTI CALLAHAN HENRY, *NEW YORK TIMES* BESTSELLING AUTHOR

"*The Hideaway* is a delightful tale of secrets, past regrets, and second chances. You will fall in love with these characters, and their intriguing stories will keep you reading long into the night! A lovely debut novel!"

—CATHERINE WEST, AUTHOR OF *WHERE HOPE BEGINS*

Hurricane Season

The Hideaway

Two Novels in One Volume

Also by Lauren K. Denton

Glory Road

Hurricane Season

The Hideaway

Two Novels in One Volume

Lauren K. Denton

THOMAS NELSON
Since 1798

Hurricane Season © 2018 by Lauren K. Denton
The Hideaway © 2017 by Lauren K. Denton

Published in Nashville, Tennessee, by Thomas Nelson. Thomas Nelson is a
registered trademark of HarperCollins Christian Publishing, Inc.

Interior Design: Mallory Collins

Thomas Nelson titles may be purchased in bulk for educational, business,
fund-raising, or sales promotional use. For information, please e-mail
SpecialMarkets@ThomasNelson.com.

Publisher's Note: This novel is a work of fiction. Names, characters, places,
and incidents are either products of the author's imagination or used
fictitiously. All characters are fictional, and any similarity to people living
or dead is purely coincidental.

ISBN 978-1-4041-1181-3 (custom)

Printed in the United States of America
19 20 21 22 23 LSC 5 4 3 2 1

Contents

Hurricane Season

For Kate and Sela
and for Matt

one

Betsy

She usually stayed in bed until at least six, but this morning she was restless, like animals get when the barometric pressure drops before a storm. It wasn't the cows, or the approaching hurricane season, or even the milk prices, which had dipped lately. It was something else, something she couldn't quite name. She felt like she needed to both run a mile and go back to sleep for the next three hours. It was energy and lethargy, anticipation and dread. Anna Beth would likely diagnose it in a heartbeat, but Betsy had always been good at pretending everything was just fine.

She kicked her legs out from under the sheet, her feet searching for a cool spot in the bed Ty had just vacated. Even with the windows closed and the AC pumping, heat still seeped in, filling the cracks and crevices of her old house with thick Alabama heat. The meteorologists on the news last night had been in a frenzy as they pointed out heat waves radiating across the country. It was only mid-June, but two tropical waves had already rolled off the shores of Africa. Thankfully, they'd fizzled out before reaching land.

"We likely won't be so lucky later in the summer," the forecasters thundered, striking terror into the hearts of all those living near the coast, including those in Betsy's small town of Elinore, fifteen miles north of the Gulf of Mexico. "The most active hurricane forecast in two decades," NOAA predicted with eager excitement.

El Niño this, La Niña that, everyone had a handy explanation for the coming tide of heat and storms that promised to pummel south Alabama and surrounding coastal areas, but Betsy had her own ideas. This summer she'd turn thirty. Not as big a milestone as forty, but it was a milestone nonetheless. The idea of thirty had always felt maternal, heavy with maturity and substance. While everyone else was talking about the fanfare of an active season— every word punctuated by an exclamation point!—all she felt was a slow hiss of air. It leaked gradually, lazily, not so quickly that anyone else would notice, but she felt it. Like a slow but steady lightening.

Downstairs, the toe of Ty's boot beat out a rhythm on the kitchen floor as he waited for the coffee to finish dripping. She heard his jumbo-size metal coffee mug scrape across the shelf and thunk down on the counter. The coffee pouring into the mug, the carafe sliding back into place on the hot pad. She imagined Ty's face, prickly with the night's passage. His hands, big and warm, knuckles sticking out from his long, sturdy fingers. His brushed-silver wedding ring.

When the screen door thudded closed, she swung her legs over the side of the bed. She grabbed a clip from her nightstand and twisted her long brown waves up into a bun, then pulled her light cotton robe around her shoulders and padded into the kitchen. At the window over the sink, she brushed aside the curtain to peek into the backyard. Ty made his way across the dewy grass to the barn. Only the curves of his shoulders were visible in the moonlight.

The coffee was good and hot, scorching her throat on the way down. After pulling her breakfast casserole out of the fridge and popping it in the oven, she opened the back door. Damp morning air met her face with a whisper. On the porch Etta was curled up in a tight ball in her favorite spot on the couch. Betsy couldn't stand the layer of fur Etta always left behind, but the cat was too cuddly to stay mad at for long.

She reached down and scratched Etta's chin and behind her ears. When she pushed open the screen door, Etta jumped down from the couch and slid between Betsy's feet. By the time Betsy reached the bottom of the porch steps, the cat was already halfway to the barn to check for spilled milk.

Crossing the yard, she inhaled the aroma of damp grass, earthy hay, and fresh sawdust coming from the henhouse. It was the same henhouse generations of Ty's family had used on this property. She and Ty had repaired as necessary and added extra space a few times to accommodate more hens, but the house was basically the same. Not a typical box made of wood and screen. It had a shingled roof, weathered wood siding, even a screened porch. A trumpet vine covered in long red flowers climbed one corner post, and a gravel walkway snaked around the side. Some mornings, when dewy fog hung heavy over the farm and everything was blurry and half erased, Betsy imagined the henhouse as a home for fairies or hobbits.

The hens got anxious if she robbed them of their eggs too early in the morning, so she crept in quietly, eased the door closed behind her, and locked it to keep the determined hens from making a quick escape. The interior was full of quiet clucking. The hens were mostly content, but Betsy knew from experience that exasperation at her intrusion wasn't far off.

"Good morning, little mamas," she murmured as she pulled out eight brown eggs, lightly speckled, two yellow, and one as blue as a robin's egg. "Worked hard this morning, didn't you?"

She placed the eggs in the basket hanging by the door, then scattered a few scoops of feed across the ground. The hens fluttered down from their perches to dine, all indignities forgiven.

With the henhouse door locked tight behind her, she paused before turning back to the house. It often stopped her, the beauty—almost perfection—of their little space on this earth. Franklin Dairy Farm, the land Ty had worked and shaped and brought to life. The sky was now streaked with bold purples and blues, bright pinks and yellows. Oaks and hickories—tall, thick, and majestic—dotted their five hundred acres. She could hear the steady *whoosh whoosh* of the milking machines even out here in the yard. Faint strains of Chris Stapleton's "Tennessee Whiskey" floated out of the speakers Ty and Walker had jiggered up in the nooks and crannies of the barn.

Through the steadily increasing light, she could just make out Ty's outline as he stooped over a cow hooked up to a machine. Ty was thick but not overweight. Just solid, as if he could carry the weight of the world on his shoulders and not buckle or even protest. She'd liked that about him when they first started dating, and it hadn't changed.

She thought about going out to the barn and kissing him good morning. It would surprise him, delight him. She closed her eyes and could feel his lips, warm and soft, faint prickles at the edges. He'd still smell like sleep, but also like oats, grass, and good outside air.

She opened her eyes, lips tingling, and grabbed the basket of eggs off its hook. The eggs clattered against each other but didn't break.

Instead of turning toward the barn, she retraced her steps back to the house, keeping her head down to avoid the two ant beds that always magically reappeared, always in the same place, the morning after she'd poured vinegar and boiling water over them. It was amazing—they had the most industrious animals, even insects, on their property. Ants that did nothing but work, just as they were supposed to. Cows overflowing with maternal milk. Hens that offered eggs each morning without fail, their bodies giving forth life as they should. Even Etta had once offered them a litter of kittens, much to their surprise. It seemed every *body* on the farm consistently obeyed God's natural order of things, producing and giving life, working and contributing as they should.

Betsy sidestepped the ant mounds, and when she looked up, the first thing she saw was the swing, moving slowly in the breeze. The swing hung from the lowest branch of the sweeping oak tree in the backyard. The tree was like something from Grimms' fairy tales—it sat in the middle of an otherwise treeless yard, its limbs extending twenty, thirty feet from the trunk, arms of Spanish moss swaying in the breeze, fingers of ivy trailing up and across the limbs. The shade underneath was thick and dark, always at least fifteen degrees cooler than the heat-saturated yard.

It was the kind of tree Betsy and her sister, Jenna, would've loved to have had in their backyard growing up—a backdrop to their adventures, even if most of their adventures were only in their minds.

Under the swing was a dirt patch where broods of kids—including Ty—had swung, their feet trailing in the dirt and stomping out the grass. That swing was the first thing Ty had showed Betsy when he brought her to the farm their senior year of college. They'd been together for about a year, but it wasn't until she saw this place that she understood who he really was and what a life with him would look like. When he had pointed out the swing, she was confused at first.

"The swing?" she asked him. "You want to take over your grand-father's farm because of a wooden swing?"

"No, not the swing. The farm will be profitable. I can make a few changes and get this place running smoother than lake water. It's gonna be great." Then he put his hands on her shoulders and turned her so she faced the swing directly. "Tell me what you see there."

"Wood. Dirt. A tree."

"I see children," he said. "I hear laughter. I see a childhood spent outside in the heat and air and light. I see our future."

Staring at that swing now, Betsy took a deep breath and squeezed her eyes closed, then opened them again. The swing swayed back and forth on an invisible breeze. With her free hand, she brushed back a lock of hair that had escaped her clip and started for the house. On her way past the swing, she raised her leg and gave it a swift, hard kick.

two

Jenna

The babysitter was late, Addie and Walsh were flying around the house in superhero capes yelling the Batman theme song—"Da-na-na-na-na-na-na-na Batman!"—and Jenna had just poured a mug of coffee when Walsh bumped into her from behind, spilling hot liquid down the front of her black Full Cup Coffee T-shirt.

"Walsh, please!" She set the coffee mug down and pulled her damp shirt away from her skin.

"Sorry, Mommy." Walsh's brown eyes were wide. She crept backward, then turned to run but stopped to grab a dish towel off the kitchen table first. "Here." She dabbed at Jenna's shirt with the towel, itself too damp to do the job.

Jenna took the towel from Walsh and kissed her cheek. "Thank you," she whispered. Walsh grinned and took off, her cape flying behind her.

After wiping her shirt as well as she could—she'd be wearing an apron over it anyway—Jenna leaned against the counter and took a long swallow. She still didn't understand how she could make coffee all day long, then drink the stuff at home. But at least she believed in what she was selling. Full Cup did make a good cup of coffee.

She sighed. Where was Kendal? Her head hurt and she had ten minutes to get to the coffee shop, a drive that usually took twenty with traffic. She thanked her lucky stars she wasn't opening today—as manager, she had the ability to pencil someone else into those early-morning slots—but it meant getting home later.

As Addie and Walsh zoomed through the kitchen and wound around her legs like cats, part of her wanted to call in sick and stay home with the girls all day, but another part of her wanted to get in the car and drive away. Maybe not come back for a while.

She squeezed her eyes closed and raked her hands through her hair. Then the doorbell rang and there was Kendal, her stand-in babysitter for the next two weeks until summer daycare began for the girls. With red, puffy eyes and a trembling voice, Kendal explained that she and her boyfriend had broken up the night before.

"But don't worry, Miss Sawyer, I'm fine. I brought my craft box for the girls. We'll have a blast." With one more messy sniff and a swipe at her eyes, she dropped her bag in the foyer and attempted a smile.

Jenna sighed and pushed the door closed. With her long blonde hair and killer legs, Kendal was Jenna a decade ago, except Jenna never would have allowed herself to wallow in misery over a boy. If anything, it had been the boys miserable over her. Back then, she always left before they did.

But no sense thinking about those old days—Kendal was here and she was a mess. Jenna wasn't super comfortable leaving Addie and Walsh with her, but what else could she do? She'd already been late to work this week—car troubles, a lost stuffed hippo, long story—and she couldn't afford to lose this job. It paid for the girls' school, offered surprisingly good insurance, and on good days, it made her feel like she was contributing something to the world, even if it was only a perfect heart in milk foam. Not quite the artistic contribution she'd had in mind all those years ago, but it was something, and it was all she had.

"Addie? Walsh?" she called. "I'm heading out."

Small feet pounded on the hardwood floors, then two tornados of early-morning energy slammed into Jenna's legs, their arms squeezing her tight.

She knelt in front of them. Addie's blonde curls were a tangled mess, but her blue eyes were bright and her mouth curved into a smile. Walsh's still-pudgy wrists were covered in every plastic bracelet in their dress-up box and a few of Jenna's. Walsh reached up for a hug, her breath soft and sweet in Jenna's ear. "Bye, Mommy," she whispered.

Jenna smiled. Thoughts of running evaporated like steam over a cup of French roast. She pulled the girls close and kissed their foreheads. "Listen to Kendal, okay? I think she brought some fun things for you to do today. I'll be home after work, and we'll have something yummy for dinner."

"Breakfast! Can it be breakfast for dinner?"

As both girls chanted, "Pan-cakes! Pan-cakes!" Jenna kissed their cheeks one more time and slid out the door.

In her car she exhaled a rush of air. Through the front window of her tiny two-bedroom East Nashville house—once crisp white but now faded to a light gray begging for a new coat of paint—she could see the girls still bouncing, the sparkles from their princess pajamas visible from the driveway.

Kendal pushed her hair back from her face, offered a bright smile, and led the girls into the den, out of Jenna's sight. Only then did Jenna remember her almost-full coffee mug sitting on the kitchen counter.

Traffic was lighter than usual and she skidded into the small side parking lot with a minute to spare. Just enough time to shove her purse into a locker in the back, grab her apron, and put on her best smile.

She checked the time. Eight fifteen. She switched her phone to silent and slid it in her apron pocket. She was setting out a stack of CDs a local songwriter had dropped off when a customer burst through the door. Jenna looked up to see Lisa Rich, CEO of Trust Partners, a well-known accounting firm with an office down the block. Purse dangling from her elbow, Bluetooth in place on her ear. Obnoxiously complicated drink order. Notoriously bad tipper.

Jenna slipped behind the counter and tapped the barista on the shoulder—the new girl, Melissa, already bracing herself for Lisa's deluge. "I got this," Jenna whispered.

"Thanks," Melissa whispered back before cowering behind Jenna.

"Hi, Miss Rich," Jenna said, despite the obvious fact that Lisa was talking to someone on her Bluetooth.

"It's *Mrs.* and I'm in a hurry."

"I'm so sorry," Jenna said, discreetly pulling a Post-it off the underside of the counter by the register. "We'll have your order out to you in a moment."

Lisa reached up and pushed a button on the contraption stuck to her ear. "Wait—I haven't given you my order."

"Would you like your regular?" Jenna's voice was innocent.

The woman's right eyebrow rose just a millimeter. Probably all the Botox would allow. "Yes. My regular."

"We'll have that right out." Jenna turned and handed the slip of paper to Melissa.

Melissa eyed it with suspicion, then looked back up at Jenna. "You're a genius."

"I know."

Melissa grinned and reached for the fat-free milk. "Does this even taste good?" she whispered.

"I have no idea and no desire to find out."

As Melissa worked on the grande double shot, four pumps sugar-free peppermint, nonfat, extra-hot, no foam, light whip, stirred white mocha, Jenna walked the counter and checked the three other baristas working hard to fill drink orders. She was able to get a pack of napkins for Mario and open a sleeve of cardboard cup sleeves for Jensen before Melissa had the drink ready.

"I'll let you do the honors." Melissa handed the drink to Jenna like it was gold plated. "Think it'll do the trick?"

"Nah," Jenna muttered. "Probably nothing will. Mrs. Rich?"

Mrs. Rich pressed the button again on her Bluetooth and clicked her heels across the tile floor. She stared at Jenna before taking the cup. "The peppermint's sugar-free?"

"Yes, ma'am."

"Extra hot?"

"Extra hot."

"Stirred wh—"

"It's just like you like it. If not, it's on me."

The woman hesitated, then put her mouth to the edge of the cup and took a dainty sip. Jenna could almost feel Melissa's nervousness buzzing behind her. But Mrs. Rich just swallowed and gave a slight nod, her bright-red lipstick smudged onto the lip of the cup. After swiping her credit card and signing, she shouldered her massive Louis Vuitton bag and turned without a word. When she pulled open the glass door, a breeze of warm air floated in, and she clicked up the street to begin her day.

Jenna turned to Melissa and rolled her eyes. Melissa bit her lip to hold in her laughter.

A few minutes after nine, Mario poked her in the side. "Your date is here." He grinned.

"Shut up. He's not my anything, and it's not a date."

"It happens every morning. It's a date."

"Not every morning," Jenna said, working to make a latte "extra foamy" for a woman in white Nikes and a wide-brimmed straw hat about to set out on a downtown walking tour. "He skips Fridays because he meets a buddy to run in Riverfront Park."

"See, you even know his schedule."

Jenna rolled her eyes. "It's not a date."

"Whatever it is, he's waiting for you. And looking extra cute today, I might add."

Jenna looked over her shoulder. Sam always looked cute. Cute wasn't his problem.

After handing the woman her extra-foamy latte, she ducked out from behind the counter. "Be back in ten," she said to no one in particular. Other than Melissa, who was still training, the baristas on shift this morning were the A-team. She could be gone an hour and come back to smooth sailing, but ten minutes was all Sam would get.

She slid into the chair across from him and smoothed a loose curl away from her face. He smiled and nudged her coffee toward her. Black, double shot, and not a drop of syrup. "Thanks," she said. Then she smiled too.

"You're welcome. It's nice to see you." He started every conversation with her the same way. He'd been doing it for the two months they'd been having this almost-daily nondate. From anyone else, it would be annoying, but coming from this guy, it was close to endearing.

"You always say it like it's a surprise. All you have to do is open those doors any morning, Monday through Friday, sometimes Saturday, and you'll see my smiling face."

"I know. That's why I come here. You know, I tried the Starbucks around the corner before I settled on this place."

"Oh yeah? What made you switch?"

"The manager didn't like me." He leaned back in his chair and stretched his long legs out to the side of the table. "I thought I was charming, but she never gave me anything for free."

"I never give you anything for free."

"Except the ten best minutes of my day."

"I think I know why that manager didn't like you. She saw right through your whole charming act."

"Nah, not possible."

She laughed.

"Did you see *Mrs. Rich* this morning?" he asked.

Jenna nodded, sipping her coffee.

"That woman is . . . Well, let's just say she makes me think of opening my own accounting firm every day. Many times a day."

"Why don't you do it?"

"Open my own firm? Let's see, money, office space, clients . . ."

He counted each barrier off on his fingers. "It could happen one day. But I'm not there yet."

She nodded again, watched him over the rim of her cup. The first day Sam Oliver walked into Full Cup, he was just another guy in a button-down and khakis with a cell phone pressed to his ear. But then he hung up when he got to the front of the line where a barista was waiting to take his order. He ordered a large coffee, no frills. Then he smiled at the girl and added a tip onto his receipt.

Jenna had been wiping down tables and fielding requests from customers scattered among the tables. When he sat down to wait for his coffee, she couldn't resist. "You may be the only person this morning who's ordered a plain coffee. Maybe the only person this week."

"My coffeemaker decided to quit on me this week. I haven't had a chance to get out and buy another one, so I'm just trying to get a shot of caffeine to my brain." He smiled. He had a nice smile. "Plain coffee is all I need."

"So you make coffee at home and you drink it straight up? You sure aren't our typical coffee shop customer." She swiped the towel across a just-vacated table, then turned back for the counter.

"What's your favorite coffee then?"

"Kind of a personal question. I only just met you."

He smiled, slow and amused. "If you don't tell me, I'll just come back tomorrow and ask again."

She looked at the clock above the counter. "See you then." She took her place behind the counter and resisted the urge to look back at him.

That first quick conversation was nearly two months ago, and he'd yet to buy a new coffeemaker. They'd progressed from exchanging a few words while he waited for his coffee to spending her ten-minute break at a table in the back. Every day except Friday.

"How are Addie and Walsh?" he asked now.

"They're fine. Addie is learning to write her name, and Walsh spends most of her time upside down in one form or another."

"My sister did gymnastics her whole childhood. Always flipping around, turning cartwheels, and whatnot. Maybe Walsh is destined to be a gymnast."

Jenna smiled. "I wouldn't be surprised."

"And Addie will be something studious. A teacher maybe."

"Or a therapist. A psychiatrist maybe."

"You think?"

Jenna shrugged. It was tempting to think Addie, at almost six years old, was too young to understand a lot of things. But lately, it seemed every time Jenna assumed something would go over her older daughter's head, it instead went right in her ears and came back later in the form of a pointed, intelligent question.

She fiddled with the cardboard sleeve on her cup. Sam watched her for a moment before speaking. "Are you ever going to let me take you on a real date? Somewhere you don't have to wear an apron, where we can talk for longer than ten minutes?"

Jenna bit her bottom lip, glanced at the clock over the counter.

"Don't do it," he said, hanging his head. "You just sat down."

"It's a busy morning. Melissa's new. I need to get back up there."

He sighed. "I'm just going to keep asking. I'm like a bulldog when I put my mind to something."

"So what does that make me? Your chew toy?" She smiled as she stood, retying her apron strings into a tidy bow.

"No. You're the girl I can't stop thinking about every time I leave this place."

She paused behind her chair. This had gone on long enough. "Sam . . ." He waited, ever patient. "Look, I'm not right for you. My life is . . . complicated."

He shrugged. "People are complicated. Our lives are too."

She glanced around before continuing. "I work all the time because I have to. I have to make money to pay for daycare, for insurance, for rent. Any free time I get I spend it with Addie and Walsh." She swiped her thumb over a drop of coffee on the table. "You could have any girl you want. I'm not the one you need to be chasing. Trust me." She could have given him a hundred more reasons, but she figured this would be enough.

"The only thing I know I want right now is a chance. With you." He leaned forward on his elbows. "That's not going to change unless you tell me to get lost. I may be persistent, but I can take that kind of hint."

She smiled in spite of herself. "Guess I'll see you tomorrow then."

Though Full Cup was one of the busiest coffee shops in the city, lulls occurred during the day. Midmorning and midafternoon were for the college students, white earbuds snaking up to their ears, laptops open, concentration intense. They could be demanding—too much caffeine made them impatient and snappy—but this afternoon the line at the counter was short, giving Jenna a chance to work on the shift schedule. Alexandra had just planned an impromptu surprise party—in the Bahamas, no less—for her sister and needed five days off at the end of the month. As the "cool" manager, the one people actually wanted to work for, Jenna had no choice but to rework the schedule.

She wedged herself, the store laptop, and the big scheduling binder into a booth in the back where she could see most of the store but was out of the way enough that she might be left alone for a few minutes if she was lucky. The back of the store was known as the gallery. A few times a year they asked artists in town to submit art to hang on the walls. Any type of art was accepted, even a few pieces she knew Addie—or for that matter Walsh—could do better.

As she opened the laptop and waited for it to power up, she focused on the fishing line–clock face–teddy bear conglomeration suspended from the ceiling. If it was art, she was Superwoman. Back in the day, she would have been willing to call most anything art, as long as it made the viewer *feel* something. Today, all that teddy bear nightmare made her feel was annoyed. But then again, that was something.

She slid her eyes left to an eight-by-ten photo hanging on the wall. Black and white, Ilford Galerie paper, skinny black frame, white mat. Simple, understated, nothing to draw the eye except the face in the photo. The old woman had her eyes closed, her lips curving upward, her head tilted back to catch the last rays of the sun as it dipped below the mountains in the west. Of course, you couldn't see the mountains in the photo, but Jenna remembered the smell of the crisp air, the sting of the cold on her cheeks as she clicked the shutter, the way the wind funneled through the mountain pass. The photo was eight years old. Could Rickie, the woman Jenna had befriended out west, still be alive?

Finally, the laptop chugged to life and she dove into the job of figuring out how to get her best, most popular barista to the Bahamas for a week and balance the remaining baristas' school schedules, family obligations, and need for shifts in her absence.

Between helping customers, cleaning up the mess from a

flushed diaper in the bathroom—seriously? Who does that?—and searching for a missing bottle of raspberry-peppermint syrup, she finally finished the schedule. As she closed the laptop and stood, her phone buzzed with a text. She pulled it out and saw she'd missed several texts, all from Max.

I have news. Call me.

Then: I know you keep your phone on you at work. I need to talk to you.

The last one said: Now's not the time to ignore me.

Before she could punch the button to call him, the phone buzzed again, this time with a call.

"I'm not ignoring you," she said before he could unload on her. "I'm at work. What's going on?"

"You got in."

"Got in where?" She gestured to a waving Mario that she'd be just a minute.

"Halcyon."

Jenna sat back down in the booth and leaned her head against the wall behind her. Mario held his hands up in frustration.

"How?" She ignored Mario's well-practiced drama.

"A spot opened up and you got it. I may have pulled some strings, but I didn't have to pull many. They loved what you sent."

"But they were just shots of the girls . . . and trees . . ."

"Doesn't matter. It got you in."

"What about the money? I felt like an idiot even applying, knowing I couldn't afford it."

"All you have to do is get yourself here. Everything else is paid for."

"How in—?"

"Believe it or not, there are wealthy art patrons who love to pay for people like you to go on retreats like this. Don't ask too many questions. Just get yourself here by Friday. And don't forget your camera."

three

Jenna

Two hours later, Jenna was on her way home, the scent of roasted coffee beans and vanilla syrup saturating her clothes and skin. She propped her elbow on the edge of the open window and dug her fingers into her hair. Max was nothing if not abrupt. To the point. It was one of the things she loved about him. Well, loved or hated, depending on the situation.

Max was the head of the photography department at Belmont University and the only person who really knew her passion for photography. She'd met him at the Botanical Gardens in Nashville a couple years back. She noticed him watching her as she stooped over a pile of leaves, craning to catch the edge of a ray of sunlight.

"Can I help you?" she asked without looking up.

"Just wondering who taught you to get low like that. Under the light, I mean. It's not how most people would do it."

Jenna pulled her face away from the camera and shrugged. "I'm just playing around."

"Not what it looks like to me."

22

Since then, they met every month or so at the gardens and other places around town to take photos together and discuss her "creative future," as he called it. They always went somewhere the kids could come, which limited their excursions to an hour, tops. They'd met at the downtown library a few times. At the top of the atrium stairs, they used Addie and Walsh as their models, capturing the flood of light from the windows on their faces. Old enough to be her father, Max had become her friend, and their excursions were her sole creative outlet.

Three months ago, he'd blown in the door of Full Cup, marched to the counter, and slapped a flyer down in front of her as she counted money in the register. He stared at her until she looked up.

"You made me lose count," she told him.

"This is more important." He jabbed the flyer with his finger. "You need to do this."

She stuck the money back in the register, closed the drawer, and glanced down at the piece of paper.

Halcyon Artist Retreat is a calm refuge hidden
in the pristine and protected Singer Creek
Nature Preserve near the Gulf Coast of Florida.
We offer the gift of time, space, and beauty to
pursue the art that makes you feel alive.

"You're kidding, right?"

"Do I look like I'm kidding?" He arched a thick gray eyebrow, his mouth set in a straight line.

"I'd never get in."

"Lucky for you, I'm on the advisory committee. But you won't need my help—your work will speak for itself." She held up her hand but he continued. "Before you ask, they offer scholarships, and being on the committee means I have input regarding who gets them." He tapped his finger on the flyer. "This is a great opportunity for you."

She glanced back down at the flyer. The bold print at the bottom said artists could stay as long as they wished—as briefly as two weeks all the way up to the full eight weeks. Eight weeks of solitude? Too heavenly—too terrifying—to even consider. Not to mention impossible.

"You've been looking for a way to get back into your photography, and this is a solid chunk of time of nothing but that. Plus you'd have a photography mentor there. I know him. He's good. Little rough around the edges, but that might not bother you."

"This sounds amazing, but if you remember, I have two small people to take care of. What would I do with them for even one week?"

"Details." He waved his hand in the air. "We can work all that out. Look, just go to the website, read what people say about Halcyon. It doesn't get better than this. And you have to drive through Alabama to get there—isn't that where your sister lives?"

Jenna nodded absentmindedly. One photo on the flyer showed a lake at dusk, cabins in the distance, a ring of people sitting around a small campfire. Sparks like fireflies shooting up in the air. Dark trees reaching toward the sky. Another showed a woman standing before a huge canvas set against a backdrop of thick oaks dripping with Spanish moss. It all reminded her of another life. But that was a lifetime ago.

"I don't think so." She pushed the piece of paper back across the counter.

He stared at her without taking it. "Jenna, you have the best, most natural untaught talent I've ever seen, and I've seen a lot. It's time to get back to it. Drawing hearts in milk foam doesn't count as art."

A loud horn from behind jolted her from her thoughts. In her rearview mirror, she caught the rude gesture from the driver behind her and held her hand up in apology. Her speedometer told her she was going thirty in a fifty, annoying everyone around her. She sped up and shook her head to clear away Max and his insane ideas. Just before turning onto her street, she heard a *ding*, her car's polite way of telling her she was low on gas.

"You've got to be kidding me," she murmured.

She'd had to pay for the girls' summer extended-day programs this pay period and her next paycheck wasn't until Friday. She dragged her free hand through her hair. She felt like one of those hamsters on a spinning wheel, going faster and faster but never actually going anywhere. No fancy art retreat would fix that.

At home Jenna opened the front door expecting Walsh's thirty pounds to careen around the corner and into her arms as she did every day, but today it was quiet. Kendal sat on the couch, wiping her nose, her eyes still red and puffy as pillows, her cell pressed to her ear. *Pull yourself together,* she wanted to tell the poor girl.

"Kendal?"

Kendal jumped up. "Oh, Miss Sawyer, I didn't hear you." To her boyfriend, she said, "I gotta go. I guess I'll just see you around." Ex-boyfriend, apparently.

As Kendal gathered her things, Jenna dropped her purse on the table and found Addie on the floor in her bedroom surrounded by a pile of pink and purple Legos.

"Mommy! Will you help me put this castle together?"

"In a minute. Where's your sister?"

Addie shrugged. "She was in here but she left to find more Legos."

Jenna's heartbeat picked up as she went room to room looking for Walsh. She pulled back the shower curtain and peeked behind the couch, checking all the normal hiding places. In her tiny house, it only took a few seconds to realize Walsh wasn't inside.

"Kendal, where's Walsh?"

"I— She's not with Addie?"

"No. When's the last time you saw her?" Jenna tried to keep her voice from rising.

"I don't know," Kendal said, panic creeping into her own voice. "It's been a little while. I thought they were both in Addie's room."

"I've told you, you have to know where Walsh is all the time."

"Mommy, what's wrong?" Addie stood in the doorway to the kitchen, her brow scrunched in worry, a familiar sight on her older daughter's sweet, sensitive face.

Jenna crossed the room and threw open the front door, calling Walsh's name. Again. Again. She checked the bushes around the side of the house where Walsh liked to look for ladybugs and the tree next door that she liked to pretend she could climb. After a few minutes, she was walking up and down the sidewalk yelling Walsh's name. Finally, she heard Walsh's voice.

"Mommy!"

Jenna whirled around to see Walsh running toward her. Delores was walking with her, trying to keep up as well as she could with her bad hip. Walsh ran straight into Jenna's legs.

Jenna knelt so she was eye to eye with her youngest. "Where have you been?"

"Playing with the puppy," she said, as if it were the most normal thing in the world.

Jenna's pulse thudded in her ears. Delores held up her hand and jogged toward them, out of breath. "I'm so sorry, Jenna. I was making my dinner when I saw her out on my patio playing with Greta. I was going to call, but I figured I'd just bring her back over before you started to worry."

Jenna swiped at a tear at the corner of her eye.

"Oh dear," Delores said. "I suppose I'm a little too late."

Jenna held Walsh to her chest and tried to slow her breathing.

There were times when she wished Addie and Walsh had been lucky enough to be born to someone else, someone with a more solid, together life—a happy, All-American, dog-in-the-backyard, cookies-in-the-oven family. Sometimes she longed for that life for herself, missed it as though it was something she'd once had and let slip through her fingers.

Other times she wished she was still Jenna Sawyer, girl on the run. An old boyfriend had called her that once. Never sticking around too long, always chasing the next bright, shiny possibility. Things were different now, though there were times—like this one—when she wished she could still run. Leave before it started to hurt.

But the reality of Jenna's world, in all its terror and beauty, stared back at her on the sidewalk. She brushed Walsh's hair back from her face and kissed her forehead.

That night, after a dinner of pancakes and scrambled eggs, a serious talk with Walsh about not leaving the house by herself, and four bedtime stories, the girls were finally asleep. Jenna stood by the stove finishing the cold eggs. She was exhausted and still rattled from the afternoon. Even though Kendal should have been more responsible, Jenna felt the weight of it on her own shoulders.

She pulled a bottle of red off the counter and poured a few inches in two wineglasses, then settled down on the couch to wait. A few minutes after eight, Delores gave her customary three soft knocks and let herself in. "Hey there." She closed the door behind her. "Girls to sleep okay?"

"Yes, ma'am. Haven't even heard a peep from Walsh."

Delores laughed as she sat on the other end of the couch. "That little girl's gonna run you ragged. Good thing she's so cute."

"It's always something. The daycare hours change, the baby-sitter has boyfriend problems, customers think their skinny latte is the most important thing in my life. Then Walsh goes missing."

Delores patted Jenna's knee. "She wasn't missing. She was just at my house. It's a familiar place for her. She probably didn't realize she was doing anything wrong."

"I know. You're right. But not knowing where she was? It was terrifying. All I could think about was some guy in a wife-beater cruising the street in a van with dark windows." Jenna rubbed her eyes.

"Well, you can't let yourself go there. Walsh is fine, safe and sound in bed, and all is well. It was just a little hiccup." Delores reached for the wineglass on the coffee table. "Don't mind if I do. Doctor says a little bit is good for my heart."

Jenna smiled. Delores said the same thing every night.

"Did that cute boy come to see you today?"

"As always."

"It tells me something that he comes to see you every morning on his way to work."

"Tells me something too. He has too much time on his hands."

Delores shook her head. "That's not it and you know it. Why won't you let him—?"

"It won't work."

"And why not?"

"Because . . . he's just not my type."

Delores narrowed her eyes over the top of her wineglass. "And what does that mean?"

"He's too . . . innocent. And he's smart—he's probably never made a bad decision in his life."

"Honey, everyone makes bad decisions and he's no different. Plus, you're too young and too smart to shut down all romantic interests before they even get off the ground."

Jenna shifted on the couch and settled deeper into the soft pillows behind her back. As she did she glanced at her friend. Delores had been "popping over for a quick visit" almost every night now for months. She usually stayed just long enough to have a glass of wine. And long enough, Jenna suspected, to ward off some of the loneliness that crept in at night.

Her husband, Willard, died a year ago, a day after their fiftieth wedding anniversary. Jenna's love life was always a hot topic of conversation when Delores visited. But they talked about other things too—the best way to make a perfect cup of coffee, Delores's dismal attempts to fit in with the "Silver Sneakers" crowd at the local gym, Jenna's once-promising photography dreams.

As if reading her mind, Delores nodded toward the wall across from the couch. "I love those photos, you know."

Jenna nodded. "Me too. But I was such a mess then."

"All new mothers are."

She'd taken the series of photos soon after Walsh was born. Jenna had been a postpartum wreck—trying to keep a two-year-old alive on her own while nursing an infant who wanted to nurse round the clock, breasts like hot rocks in her chest, her brain a sleepless blur. In her fog, she'd pulled her camera from the back of the closet, popped in some film, and started shooting.

Walsh, with her olive skin and head full of dark hair, was asleep, temporarily paused in her constant quest for more milk, her eyelashes hints of color on her pale cheeks. Addie sat on the floor with a basket of wooden blocks, her blonde hair hanging in perfect round ringlets. Jenna took photo after photo, not knowing how they would turn out, but not really caring either. What mattered was that her fingers had found freedom, her hands and legs moving in familiar motions as she twisted to focus, kneeling to capture the light on Walsh's cheek, bending to catch the whirl of hair at the back of Addie's perfect head.

Even now she could still remember how the fog had lifted, the cobwebs cleared. Her fatigue—an almost tangible beast in the room with her at all times—crept off into a corner and gave her a few minutes of peace and clarity. Behind the camera, she hid herself from reality and escaped to a place where at the click of a shutter, she could make everything perfect.

When she met Max, their monthly excursions were a breath of fresh air, but not the same as diving full into that creative river and letting it flow without thought or care, trusting the current would take her to just the right shots.

"Do you remember that artist retreat I mentioned a while back?" Jenna turned to Delores. "The one Max wanted me to attend?"

Delores nodded. "You told me you didn't think you were going to apply."

"I didn't plan to, but then I did, even though I knew there was no way I could afford it, much less take time for the trip. It was mostly to get Max to stop hounding me."

"And?"

"I found out today I got in. And it's paid for."

Delores sat up. "So you're going?"

"I don't know." As she said the words, she knew what she wanted the answer to be. But even if she was able to take time away from work, kids, the house, laundry, babysitters, all the things that kept her away from that creative river inside her—which was more like a trickle these days—would it all come back?

"What do you mean, you don't know? Seems like it was just handed to you. You tell them yes."

"What would I do with the girls?"

Delores tapped her fingernail against the edge of her glass. "Well, you know they love coming to my house." She smiled.

"Delores, I can't leave my rowdy kids with you for a week. They'd wear you out."

"I can handle kids, my dear. I have four of them."

"But they're grown adults. When's the last time you bathed a squirming three-year-old or made dinner for a picky five-year-old?"

"True. What about family?" Delores already knew about Jenna's parents. Her mom had died six years ago, and her dad, never all that involved in the child-raising aspect of parenthood, became even less so after his wife's death. He was still in Birmingham, intent on working until he was too old to hold his arms up before his orchestra, poised and ready for action. "Your sister?"

Jenna shrugged, but the truth was, she'd already thought about Betsy. The idea made her nervous though. It had been a little while since they talked—really talked—and telling Betsy she wanted to go off and do nothing but take photos for two weeks would come out of left field.

"They live on a farm, right? Do they have kids?"

"Nope. Little sister gets the kids. Big sister gets the perfect husband."

"That man is not perfect, I guarantee it. The question is, would your sister and her imperfect husband be willing to keep the girls while you go?"

Jenna drained the rest of the wine in her glass, then set the glass back on the table. "I don't know. Maybe? But seriously, how could I do this? Even if she did keep them, I can't take time off from my life and go do something like this. It's too much."

Even as she spoke, she thought of the savings account she'd set up after Walsh was born. She'd been tucking money into it each month with the intention of planning a surprise vacation for the three of them. Maybe a couple of weeks at the farm could be like a vacation for the girls. It wasn't Disney or riding horses on the beach in Georgia, but she wouldn't have been able to afford something like that anyway.

Delores shifted in her seat so she faced Jenna. "You know about the oxygen masks on airplanes, right?"

Jenna stifled a smile. "Yes, I've heard of them."

"They always tell passengers if the masks come down, put the mask on yourself before you try to put it on anyone else. It's the same with kids, honey. You have to take care of yourself so you can go and take care of your kids. I see how you are over here. I know it's hard."

"They're good kids. I can't just—"

"Of course they're good." Delores put her hand on Jenna's knee. "They're good because of you." Jenna shook her head but Delores continued. "You need to be good to yourself too. Look, I wasn't a single parent like you, but with Willard's work schedule, I was on my own a lot. More than I thought I would be. I loved those kids, still do, but there were times I wanted to turn left instead of right into our neighborhood. Just drive off into the sunset—not forever, just for a little while. Just to breathe without four other little people taking all my air. Maybe this would be a chance for you to breathe for a little while. On your own."

Delores glanced at her watch and rose from the couch amid a chorus of protests from her ankle and knee joints. "It's almost my bedtime. I'll keep an eye on my back patio tomorrow in case Walsh comes over for more playtime." At the door she paused. "You need to do this, Jenna. Call your friend and say yes."

After Delores left, Jenna remained on the couch, her mind running through possible scenarios. The logistics made her head hurt, but part of her wanted to jump in the car and be free of it all. To pretend, just for a little while, that she was like she used to be—on her own, untethered. That she wasn't living with two beautiful, innocent consequences of a failed relationship and mistakes. That at twenty-eight, she wasn't a woman who had put her own desires and goals on the back burner to be drop-kicked into single, working motherhood.

Her eyes were growing heavy, but she pulled her old laptop out of the drawer in the coffee table and turned it on. On her bank's website, she entered her password to be directed to her accounts. Her checking account was perilously low—that was to be expected this close to payday—but the total in her savings account filled her with a delicate hope. It wasn't a gold mine, but it could cover bills and rent for a short time.

The AC clicked on and she pulled a blanket off the back of the couch. She shivered, whether from the cold or anticipation, she wasn't sure. She thought of Betsy and Ty's farm, basically a five-hundred-acre playground for kids, with an assortment of animals added in for good measure. The girls would have a blast—like summer camp. Betsy and Ty would probably love the entertainment.

Before she could change her mind, she grabbed her phone and scrolled until she found Betsy's number.

"She won't mind," she whispered.

But she put the phone down without calling and rested her head against the back of the couch. She pulled the blanket up to her chin and closed her eyes. Mornings were a better time for favors. New mercies and all that.

four

Ty

Ty Franklin's mornings began hours before everyone else's. Every night before bed, he set his alarm for 4:30 a.m., an hour he once thought was only for late-night bar hoppers and graveyard-shift workers. When he became a dairy man, he saw that the darkest hour before the sun rose was actually one of the most beautiful in the entire twenty-four-hour masterpiece. He now considered himself a lucky man, awake to the day's first sighs and stretches.

With coffee in hand he pushed open the barn door. It stuck a little, as it always did. He muttered to himself, annoyed that he'd forgotten to buy another can of WD-40. It was the hinge, just the hinge, but it made sliding the door open louder than necessary. He liked to disturb the girls as little as possible before they shuffled to their places in the milking line.

Walker was already in the barn, attaching tubes and lines. The kid tried hard, but he was just so young. He wanted to be a dairy farmer too, and his daddy, the owner of a neighboring farm, insisted that he get a job in another barn to learn the ropes. A little arrogant,

Ty thought, but he didn't have a teenage son so he couldn't judge another man's parenting choices. He just tried to teach the boy all he could while keeping him from overturning milk buckets and scaring the cows.

"Morning, Mr. Franklin."

Ty nodded. He leaned over Walker's shoulder. "Rework that line. See that kink there? It'll keep the milk from flowing. The cow will kick at it and hurt herself."

"Yes, sir." Walker fumbled to untwist the cap and straighten the line.

Every morning.

Ty took his cap off, rubbed his forehead, and jammed it back on his head. He made his way through the barn to his small office on the side. Every day he carefully wrote out the details from each milking. The dusty file cabinet in the corner held a stack of yellow legal pads, the pages covered in his tiny, neat script. He knew what Excel was and he knew punching in numbers on a spreadsheet could take the place of him hunching over legal pads every morning. But he liked the security, the familiarity of paper. He'd rather not entrust his life's work to an invisible cloud.

At five o'clock he and Walker swung open the gate and stood back. The girls shuffled out of one side of the barn into the other. They knew exactly where to go, so all the men had to do was stay out of the way. As number 013 passed by, she paused and swung her head toward Ty. He reached out and rubbed the top of her soft, black-spotted nose. The cows could be as affectionate as a dog—a Labrador even. Nothing quite compared to a fifteen-hundred-pound Holstein sidling up to you, cud breath and all. It made you feel a certain something inside.

Especially if this cow, and two hundred like it, were your ticket to a glorious retirement, as they were for Ty. He wouldn't be purchasing any thirty-foot fishing boats or houses on Ono Island, but he wouldn't have wanted that anyway. He imagined himself kicked back on the porch in a rocker with Betsy next to him. Iced tea at their elbows, a bucket of snap beans, or maybe pecans, at their feet.

That was all he'd ever hoped for, ever since he first laid eyes on her their junior year at Auburn. It was as if he skipped all the in-between life and his mind went straight to the end—the two of them in rockers, hands together, enjoying life. At one point, he assumed a few towheaded kids would be there frolicking in the front yard, but the way he saw it, he had 218 cows in his barn and a handful of rowdy farmhands to corral. He had just about as much mischief as he could handle.

Once the girls were all hooked up, happily munching oats while their milk flowed, Ty walked to the barn door to dump out a bucket of water. While shaking it to get the last drips out, he saw his wife up by the henhouse. He usually kissed her good-bye when he wrenched himself out of bed, but this morning he hadn't. He wasn't even sure why. She'd been curled up on her side, facing away from him, the outline of her body visible through the thin sheet. Her knees were pulled up, her hands together in front of her face like she was fending off the world.

He traced a light finger down her spine. When her defenses were down—when she was asleep or lost in a fog of thought—that's when he could tell the shadows were still there, tangled in her hair, grasping at her elbows, yanking on her heart.

Sometimes he wondered if maybe Betsy would've been better

off marrying one of those fraternity boys at Auburn. She could have had anyone, and she picked Ty. He still didn't understand it. He told her when they started dating that he'd do anything for her. He meant it then, when they'd known each other for all of five minutes, and he still meant it now. But what if the one thing he longed to give her, he couldn't? It went against the core of who he was—this *not* being able to give her what she wanted.

Instead of disturbing her that morning, he'd just let her sleep, praying she was in the middle of a good dream—something soft and warm and easy. But seeing her up by the henhouse, staring at the swing he used to play on when he was a kid, he wished he'd taken the two seconds to kiss her. To remind her that he loved her, that they'd be okay.

She talked so breezily about how she was looking forward to the summer, making day trips to Orange Beach, maybe booking them a night somewhere nice. But her armor wasn't strong enough to fool him. Sometimes he wondered if his was strong enough to fool her.

five

Betsy

When the rush of the morning milking was over, the men came to the house and ate her breakfast and drank her coffee like it was the last oasis before a cross-desert journey.

Betsy pulled up a kitchen chair and sat with her knees tucked under her chin, her arms around her legs. She loved to hear Ty in the midst of friends, joking and poking fun as only a group of men-boys could.

"Mrs. Franklin, have you heard anything from Quincy's?" Walker asked.

"Still working on it. I talked to the owner's wife again yesterday. She says they're getting close to a decision."

Quincy's was a market up in Dadeville that had been hemming and hawing for months over whether they wanted to stock Franklin milk. As the one responsible for all the marketing and publicity for the farm, Betsy had long been working on the deal. Quincy's had spread from Dadeville to six different towns, all in areas without major chain grocery stores.

"It'd be a big step, getting Franklin milk on those shelves," Ty said.

"If you need me to, I can make the drive up there one afternoon," Carlos said. "See if I can't convince them in person."

"And how would you do that?" Ty asked. "Nothing but your charm?"

"Hey, I'm great with little old ladies."

On the counter by the coffeepot, Betsy's cell phone dinged, alerting her to a new e-mail from Bankston Detention Facility. The director said the group of twenty boys, aged twelve to sixteen, would arrive at ten for their tour of the milking barn.

Another e-mail had slipped in unnoticed. This one was from Valerie, the head of the children's program at Elinore Methodist. For years, Betsy had been a regular face on the rotating schedule of nursery volunteers, but last fall she quietly took her name off the list.

Betsy typed out a quick reply to Valerie's request for more help. "Sorry I can't be there this Sunday." With any luck Valerie would take the hint and stop asking.

When the guys finished eating, they lined up at the sink to rinse off their plates and place them in the dishwasher like dutiful schoolchildren. Betsy stood to help, but Ty put a hand on her shoulder.

"Let them do it." Betsy smiled and sat back down. He stood next to her and wrapped his arm around her shoulders.

"Oh, I'm meeting Anna Beth for lunch today," she said. "Leftovers from dinner last night are in the fridge if you want them for lunch."

"What's all this?" Carlos asked. "Grown man and your wife has to make your lunch?"

"No, I'm a man who's lucky enough that his wife thinks of him and leaves lunch for him. Not that you'd know about that."

Betsy shushed Ty, but Carlos laughed. "*Ay, mi hombre.* You just wait. Gloria will come around. Latino women don't like their men to get soft." He jabbed Ty's stomach.

Ty laughed and slapped his hand away. "I'm not soft, man. You ready to go?"

Carlos hopped off the stool. "Ready, Boss."

The phone rang before the guys made it out the door. Ty backpedaled and picked up the receiver from the kitchen wall. After a moment, his face changed and he looked over at her. He held out the phone. *Your sister,* he mouthed.

She took the phone. "Jenna?"

"Hey, Bets. How are you?"

"I'm good. Everything okay there?"

"Yeah, everything's great."

After a last glance over his shoulder, Ty followed the men toward the barn. Betsy sat back down. "Really?" she asked. Jenna's voice was a notch too chipper, a glaring sign that something might not actually be that great.

"Really. Things are good."

"Addie and Walsh?"

"They're into everything, driving me crazy half the time," Jenna laughed. "But they're fine."

It had been almost a year since Betsy had seen Jenna's daughters. Addie would turn six in December and Walsh, the baby, was three. Betsy had only seen Walsh a few times in her short life, the most recent being last summer when Betsy drove to Nashville—seven hours in Ty's truck with a busted AC—for a visit. What she'd hoped would be a bonding weekend with her sister had turned into an unexpected babysitting gig while Jenna took on extra shifts at the coffee shop.

"I actually . . . ," Jenna began. "I need a favor. Do you have a minute?"

Twenty minutes later, Betsy replaced the phone in its cradle. Two weeks with Addie and Walsh. She should have checked with Ty first, but when it came down to it, Betsy could never say no to Jenna. She thought of long-ago days, lying under the bed with her little sister, eating pudding with plastic spoons and trying to keep her from crying. She'd do anything for Jenna—then and now.

A sigh ached to escape her lips, but she bit it back. Who was she to judge Jenna's life choices? From what she knew of Addie and Walsh, they were happy kids, and that spoke to Jenna's abilities as a mother. Good thing, because if Betsy had to give her any wisdom about how to be a good mother—much less try to be one herself— she wouldn't even know where to begin.

At ten on the nose, the battered gray school bus from Bankston Detention pulled up out front, and twenty teenage boys shuffled off, hormones and pent-up energy swirling around them like almost visible steam. Whether it was a group like this, a well-behaved homeschool co-op, or a YMCA camp group, Betsy knew from experience that the educational part of the field trip had to be as exciting and hands-on as possible. If she dared to talk about farming practices and environmental threats—vital concerns in the lives of dairy farmers but boring to anyone not making a living from farming—she risked mutiny.

Betsy had started the farm's educational program a couple of years ago. It had been an expensive endeavor, renovating the barn to accommodate touring facilities, but thankfully, it took off quickly.

During the school year they hosted field trips from schools all across Mobile and Baldwin Counties. In the summer most were from day camps and playgroups around the area. Bankston came every week.

As soon as the teachers had gathered the group outside the barn, Betsy positioned herself front and center and held her hand up. After a few outbursts, the boys quieted down. With that raised hand she pointed out three children who she knew needed the most attention. The first, a tall kid with linebacker shoulders and a cocky smile, sauntered to the front of the group. The other kids laughed and slapped him on the back. Catcalls echoed off the barn walls.

"What's your name?" Betsy asked him.

"Whatever you want it to be," he said with a smirk.

Gigi, one of the Bankston staff members whom Betsy had learned not to get on the wrong side of, clapped her hands once, hard. "Jerome!"

"Sorry, sorry. Yeah, it's Jerome, but my boys call me the Juice."

"Farmer Juice." Betsy put her hands on her hips. "I like it."

The other kids laughed and Jerome did a little jig, spinning around in a circle and bowing, much to the delight of the group. Gigi clapped her hands again.

"Welcome to Franklin Dairy," Betsy said. "I have a lot to show you. Most of the cows have already finished their first milking of the day, but there's plenty more work to do and I'm going to need your help with something special."

She put her hand on Jerome's shoulder and led him into one of the pens, then motioned for the rest of the group to follow. Jerome's friend punched him on the shoulder. "Boy, get ready! You gonna be pulling on some . . ." He cut his eyes to Betsy. A sly grin crossed his face.

Betsy willed herself not to smile. "Teats. They're called teats."

"No, sir, I'm not." Jerome turned to Betsy. "I'm not putting my hands on those . . . things." He peered into the barn where a pregnant Holstein was undergoing a routine checkup. "That's just dirty. And wrong."

"They're not dirty. That's how the milk comes out. You like cold milk with your cookies?"

Jerome and his friend nodded.

"Cheese?"

Nodded again.

"Yogurt? Ice cream? Cake? None of that can be made without milk. Or if it is, it's not very good." She lowered her voice to a whisper. "But don't tell the anti-milk crusaders I said that."

The kids looked confused, but it squeezed a laugh out of Gigi.

"But no, Farmer Juice, that's not what I need your help with. I need help with this."

In the side pen was a calf, only six weeks old and cute as a puppy.

"I need you to feed her." Betsy handed Jerome a bottle Ty had already prepared. It looked like a regular baby bottle, only bigger.

Bankston often sent the hardest-to-crack kids to the farm because of the bottle feeding. In some mysterious way, the gentle, nurturing act did something to the kids. Sure, they walked through the viewing room and learned how dairy farming contributed to their daily life, but it was the bottle feeding they loved. Anytime Ty had a new calf on the farm, Bankston was the first group Betsy called. They always scheduled a trip and brought the roughest and toughest of their kids.

These kids—Jerome, his friend, and the others—passed the bottle back and forth between them, wiping the calf's chin when milk bubbled out and smoothing the hair on her back and head.

It seemed the act of taking care of another small life calmed them, soothed their agitation and restlessness. By the time they piled on the bus an hour later, all the kids high-fived her, and a few gave her hugs.

"Can we come see her again?" Jerome asked, one hand on the bus door. "Maybe when she's a little bigger. Or if another baby cow comes along."

"I'm sure there will be more calves, but you know what? I hope the next time I call Bankston, they tell me Farmer Juice has moved out and is living his life, working hard at school, and doing well."

Jerome smiled and pulled himself up the steps of the bus. Gigi was the last to step onto the bus. "You have kids?" she asked.

Betsy raised her eyebrows and shook her head no. They'd never talked about anything more personal than what percentage of fat they liked in their milk—Gigi skim, Betsy 2 percent.

"You planning on it?"

Betsy let out a laugh, awkward and too loud. "That's getting a little personal, don't you think?"

"All I'm sayin' is, you should. Women like you are who we need raising kids in this world. Raise them up to be respectful and hardworking." The woman nodded. "Farm kids are what you need."

Betsy knocked on the glass door and waved at the driver. "I do have farm kids, Gigi, a bunch of them. You bring them to me every Friday morning."

Gigi grunted and heaved herself up onto the bus. The engine roared to life, and the bus pulled out of the small grass parking lot, arms sticking out of windows on both sides of the bus, waving to her.

She waved until the bus disappeared around the curve in the driveway. The sounds of children's laughter and conversation died away as quiet fell on the farm again.

six

Betsy

"Anna Beth?" Betsy checked the clock on the oven and cringed: 11:58. She was supposed to meet her friend for lunch at noon.

"Girl, where are you?" Through the phone, Betsy heard the murmur of lunchtime conversation. "I'm halfway through my first mimosa, and before you ask, yes, I did say 'first.'"

"I didn't say anything. Although it is a tad early, even for you."

"School is out, the little monsters are gone, and I have a three-week break before I have to woman the front office. I'm enjoying my time off. Now, where are you?"

Betsy grabbed a damp rag from the sink. She squeezed the water out and wiped breakfast crumbs from the counter as she spoke. "I'm so sorry, but I'm going to have to miss lunch. My sister called this morning. She's driving down tomorrow and dropping the kids off with us for a little while."

"What?" Anna Beth screeched. "How long's a little while?"

Betsy squeezed one eye closed. "Two weeks?"

"Girl, you are crazy. And very nice."

"Anyway, I thought I'd be able to swing lunch, but I just finished up with Bankston, I'm dirty, and I have a million things to do before they get here."

"Well, I'm not having lunch by myself. Lucy and Jackson are squared away at friends' houses, so I have the afternoon. Tell you what. Why don't I bring lunch to you? I can help you with your million things."

"Oh, you don't need to—"

"Hush. I'll get some chicken salad to go and I'll be there in twenty."

Betsy exhaled and tossed the rag in the sink. "Thanks."

"No problem. And let's see . . ." Anna Beth's acrylic nails tapped the tabletop.

"What is it?"

"This is Jenna you're talking about, right? Wild child, boyfriends, the whole bit?"

That described Jenna's younger days to a T, but now? Betsy shook her head. "She's not like that anymore. She can't be—she has Addie and Walsh."

"But she's all of a sudden leaving them with you for two weeks?"

"Well . . . yeah. I'm fine though."

"Mm-hmm. I'll stop at the Pig on the way. I'm bringing you a bottle of wine. Sounds like you may need it."

Betsy took a quick survey of the house: The casserole dish from this morning's farmer breakfast still in the kitchen sink. Two baskets of laundry on the couch waiting to be folded and put away. The back porch coffee table covered with printouts of Excel files, results of Ty's and her last financial "state of the union" meeting. She glanced out the back window just in time to see Ty climb onto the seat of the tractor and crank it up. Carlos stood by directing him between the fence posts into the back field.

She should go out and tell him about Jenna's imminent arrival with the kids—especially since she hadn't asked him first. In this case though, it seemed asking for forgiveness might be easier than asking for permission.

Upstairs, the guest room was already made up with crisp sheets and an empty water carafe on the bedside table, ready for Ty's parents in case they decided to come for an overnight visit. Uninterested in having any part in the family farm, they rarely did. Down the hall, she poked her head into the empty room. It had remained bare all these years except for a double bed with a sky-blue iron headboard salvaged from an estate sale, an old white dresser with glass knobs and an attached mirror, and a white rocking chair from Betsy's grandmother. Addie and Walsh would need more than this.

She rummaged through the hall linen closet and pulled out a set of sheets with tiny roses set against a white background. Roses always reminded her of Jenna. As sullen as she had been as a teenager, Jenna had helped their father tend his rose garden in the backyard with scientific precision.

She also found the cream-colored cable-knit blanket her grandmother knitted for her before she was born. Betsy had draped that blanket across every bed she'd ever slept in, from her childhood home to Auburn then to Elinore. She couldn't remember when or why she'd folded it and put it away. She held it in her hands now, thick stitches of cotton as soft as the fingers that made it.

Her grandmother spent decades knitting, her nimble fingers purling and plaiting in ways Betsy never had a desire or inclination for. Spending weeks at her house during summer breaks with

Jenna when their parents worked long hours, Betsy grew familiar with the vocabulary and shape of stitches, even if she didn't pick up the knitting needles herself. As the older, calmer granddaughter, the one more concerned with making others happy, she was the one who sat and kept their grandmother company while she knitted. Jenna ran free on their grandparents' four acres, laughing with kids from neighboring houses, sneaking kisses and cigarettes.

Even if she never purled on her own, Betsy knew the significance of a dropped stitch. It would start with a little puff of air from her grandmother's nose, a slight shake of her head, then her fingers quickly working backward to recover that disobedient stitch. She'd go back to just before things fell apart and make the necessary change to prevent the same thing from happening again.

Betsy unfolded the blanket on the double bed and held it by the ends, gently flapping it to settle it across the sheets. Her grandmother's stitches had held tight all these years, not a dropped stitch in sight. She smoothed her hands across the blanket, straightened the corners, and imagined the room holding two little girls after holding nothing but dreams and damaged furniture. She sat on the corner of the bed, across from the antique dresser, then reached over and ran her thumb across the crack in the top drawer.

"Hey, girl," came Anna Beth's voice from downstairs, then a slam of the back door. "I ate some of this chicken salad on the way over here. Hope you don't mind." Her feet thudded up the staircase. "I was starving since you left me high and dry for lunch."

Her friend appeared in the doorway to the empty room, fanning her damp face. "It's hot as two cats in a wool sock out there. And you wouldn't believe the line at the Pig. They've got their chicken legs on sale ninety-nine cents a pound, and it's brought out all the bargain shoppers. You know there's nothing I hate more than bargain shoppers with their coupon binders. Now, how are you?"

Betsy smiled. Anna Beth was always in a frenzy about something—the blazing heat that blanketed their part of Alabama for at least eight months out of the year, beachgoers invading Elinore for its "charming" dining and shopping, or how parents in their district always disregarded the deadlines for signing kids up at the elementary school. She was the school registrar and had to deal with the latecomers who insisted their child be registered, even after class lists had been posted. Talking to Anna Beth, you'd think those parents were late for tea with the queen.

"I'm fine," Betsy said. "Thanks for bringing lunch."

"Mm-hmm." Anna Beth glanced through the bedroom. "Your nieces'll sleep in here?"

Betsy nodded. "It's not much. I need to pick up some coloring books or something for them."

"I'll bring a few things over. I have some toys up in the attic, and we still have a ton of books."

"Thanks, but I'm sure Jenna will pack some of their toys."

Anna Beth snorted. "From what you've said, Jenna might not come prepared. You'll need something if it rains. Kids go stir-crazy when it rains. At thirteen and fifteen, mine still go crazy when they're stuck inside all day, despite a whole world of electronic doodads all over the house."

Anna Beth turned toward the stairs. "You ready to eat? I got the chicken salad you like—the kind with all the grapes and nuts in it."

"That sounds great. I just need to grab one more thing."

She opened the top dresser drawer and pulled out *Henderson's Book of Fanciful Flowers*. Written by Albert Henderson in 1918, the back cover was held on by threads and the corners were jammed and bent, but the pages inside were still crisp and flat. She'd bought the book years ago at a used bookstore, the first and only time she'd let herself buy something to decorate the room she hoped would one day be her nursery. Back then, she was in her garden every day weeding, pruning, and fighting off aphids. She used to love it—getting her hands dirty, seeing her hard work result in color and life popping up from the soil—but it had been a while since she'd visited. The garden was mostly full of dandelions and crabgrass now.

The *Book of Fanciful Flowers* may not have been a true children's book, but the dreamy watercolor loops and swirls, depicting everything from sunflowers and roses to peonies and forget-me-nots, seemed whimsical and childlike. Along the edges of each page, Mr. Henderson had written, in careful ink, descriptions of each flower.

A peony bush full of flowers brings good luck, but if the flowers fade or fall off, prepare for disaster.

While known to signify everlasting union, dahlias can also symbolize betrayal and dishonesty. Use caution when gifting dahlias to a beloved.

Her plan had been to cut out the pages and frame them, but the pages remained between the covers, and the book had been shut up inside that dresser drawer since the day she threw it in there and slammed the drawer closed with enough force to splinter the wood. She ran her hand across the fragile cover, like reintroducing herself to an old friend, and propped it against the mirror.

Anna Beth leaned forward and peered at the cracked drawer. "Gorilla Glue will take care of that. That's what I love about antiques like this. You never know what troubles they've been through." She patted the top of the dresser. "But it makes 'em tough."

Downstairs, they spread their lunch out on the table. While Betsy dragged one of the two laundry baskets from the couch over to her kitchen chair, Anna Beth retrieved two wineglasses from the cabinet and poured cold pinot grigio.

"I don't know, AB," Betsy said, already bringing the glass to her lips. "It's a little early for happy hour."

"Psshhh," Anna Beth muttered. "Cheers." She clinked her glass to Betsy's. "Oh, this reminds me. I'm having a little get-together at my house on Wednesday for some new neighbors. I'd ask you and Ty to come, but we're having margaritas and tapas from El Gato. Not exactly kid-friendly."

"What about Lucy and Jackson?"

"They'll spend the night with Tom's parents in Elberta. They'll eat a pound of Cheetos, drink a gallon of sweet tea, and come home with three kinds of stomachache, but it'll be worth it for a night off." She took a sip of her wine and looked pointedly at Betsy. "So what's up with Jenna? Does she always make plans at the drop of a hat like this?"

Betsy smiled. She was used to Anna Beth's express train of thoughts, swerving and veering all over the place. "She's spontaneous—or at least she used to be—but she just found out yesterday she was accepted at the retreat. I think she told me as soon as she could."

Anna Beth narrowed one eye. "How close are y'all, really?"

Betsy hesitated, tapped her fingernails on her wineglass. "I don't know. We were close once, but it was a long time ago. When I left for Auburn, she still had two years at home with our parents, which didn't go over very well. They never appreciated her free spirit. Always wanted her to calm down, behave, sit still."

Betsy picked a pair of Ty's socks out of the basket and folded them together. She passed them back and forth between her hands before tossing them back in the basket. "It was probably hard for her to be there without me. When I was home, I was sort of the mediator between her and my parents. Without me there . . . well, Jenna's not naturally submissive."

"Who is?" Anna Beth asked around a bite of food. "Give me that." She leaned over and pulled the laundry basket to her. "I already ate half a basket of bread at the restaurant waiting on you. You eat, I'll fold."

"Yes, ma'am." Betsy popped a grape in her mouth. "Anyway, Jenna moved around a lot after her stint in college, had some boyfriends here and there. We just have different lives. But she does have those two sweet girls."

"How'd she let that happen? Seems she wouldn't want to be tied down by kids."

"Oh, I don't think having kids was her intention. She just . . . got lucky. Or unlucky depending on how you look at it."

"Humph." Anna Beth folded a pair of blue jeans, then sat back in her chair, her eyes on Betsy.

"What?"

Anna Beth pursed her lips, then shook her head. She reached forward and grabbed a T-shirt.

Betsy looked down and pushed the chicken salad around the plate with her fork. It had always been easy for others to dismiss Jenna because of her wildness, her disregard for rules, but Betsy never could. Jenna was her sister, after all. No one else had been through their particular childhood. Not that it was especially bad—in fact, it should have been pretty close to perfect.

Their parents, Drs. David and Marilyn Sawyer, were models of professionalism in their respective fields—David as conductor of the Birmingham Symphony Orchestra and Marilyn as the head of the UAB Cancer Research Center. Having had children much later in life, they were dedicated to their work with a single-minded passion and focus. They threw themselves into civic causes and charity work, were devoted to organizations that helped better the world, and generally tried to be good stewards of their money and influence. All good, noble things, but models of how to be an attentive, involved parent? How to cherish and encourage? Not exactly.

With their parents always focused on their careers, it had been Betsy and Jenna against the world. Huddled together under Betsy's bed. Hunched over rocks in the backyard looking for cicada shells and long, wiggly worms. Lying in bed together at night listening to their father's concertos on the stereo downstairs, Betsy whispering fairy tales to Jenna into the wee hours. Betsy never asked to be pushed into the mother role, but it was a role she learned early to play.

It had been a long time since Betsy had had a need—or a desire—to mother Jenna, but even so, she always felt the deep-down urge to defend her sister.

"Jenna loves her daughters. I think she's just still trying to figure out her place in the world."

"If you ask me, at twenty-eight and two kids, you're long past the time of figuring things out," Anna Beth said. "Best get your butt in gear."

Betsy shifted her chair to move out of a sharp ray of sun and caught sight of Ty standing just outside the barn doors, laughing at something she couldn't see. It was always a treat to see him laughing and carefree. He was often so reserved, so focused on the task at hand, but when he laughed—cheeks stretched wide, blue eyes squinted, shoulders shaking—it was a gift.

Anna Beth followed her gaze out the back window. "You two are such lovebirds. Big house, great farm, tons of room for kids. Life already figured out."

"We don't have everything figured out." She finished her last bite of chicken salad and reached for a shirt to fold. "Who does?"

"Tom does. And Ty does too. Tell me your husband isn't doing exactly what he wanted to do with his life. No farmer gets caught up in a life of farming, whether it's cows or crops. You're only in it if you chose it. Maybe you and I got caught up in it, but we did it willfully when we married these boys. They have it figured out."

Betsy glanced back at Ty again. He pulled off his cap, revealing his blond hair damp with midday heat, and threw it at Carlos. Carlos picked it up and dropped it in a bucket, causing Ty to shout. He pulled his cap from the bucket and wrung water out of it.

"You're probably right," Betsy said. "I think he does have things pretty much figured out."

"Of course I'm right. That's why you love me."

seven

Ty

At 8 a.m. EDT, a tropical storm warning
has been issued for the south and southeast edges of Puerto Rico in the Caribbean
Sea. Interests elsewhere in the central
and eastern Caribbean should closely monitor the progress of this system.

Ty sat in his office, his grandfather's old black radio tuned to the
AM station that sent out a constant flow of crop stats, animal
prices, and weather reports. That crackly radio usually made him
feel like a real farmer, but today the steady stream of numbers and
words annoyed him. He fiddled with the dial, turned it all the way
to the right hoping for even a hint of real music—country, rock,
something—but all he got was static.

He turned it back to the left, slowly. Maybe he'd find that
same music his grandfather used to play in the barn—wordless

melodies, a river of gospel, bluegrass, folk. But even at the lowest end of the dial, there was nothing but politicians and rural Baptist preachers.

He was about to turn the thing off when a computerized weather report crackled through. "Tropical Storm Bernard has taken a northwesterly turn," said the robotic voice. "It is expected to continue to the north . . ."

Ty swiped at the Off button, leaned forward, and rubbed his temples with his thumbs. The radio wasn't the problem, and neither was Bernard. A tropical storm this early in the season wasn't anything to get worked up about, especially one that would no doubt curve back out into the Atlantic. He'd been tracking storms long enough to know when to worry. But the alarming predictions about this year's hurricane season—not to mention its similarities to another season years ago—had him on edge.

The summer he turned fifteen was predicted to bring an especially severe hurricane season. Ty had spent every summer since he was nine working on the farm with his grandfather—along with any weekends he wasn't busy playing baseball—and this one was no different. By August, his grandfather's old radio had sent out so many alarms and beeps, cautions and warnings that it had become background noise. So far, none of the storms had affected the farm directly—just fallen limbs and debris and a few short power outages. As a result, Ty paid little attention to the reports about Hurricane Louis that came through the radio, and even brushed off his grandfather's concerns and extra efforts to secure the farm.

Louis roared through Baldwin County a few days later, damaging everything in its path and chastening Ty for having the nerve to doubt his grandfather's ability to sense coming danger. Ty had always known his grandfather was a good man, but waiting up with

Granddaddy as the storm blew through, seeing how worried he was about the farm, the land, and the house, changed his view of him forever.

"Hurricanes have come and gone every season since my father built this place," Granddaddy said by candlelight after the power had blinked off. Wind rushed and moaned outside, and lightning forked through the eerie gray-green sky. His grandfather was on edge, waiting for the winds to die down so he could get outside and survey his property. "Lord willing, the farm will be here for many seasons to come. And one day it can be yours. It's a big responsibility. Are you up for it?"

Ty nodded. "Yes, sir. It's what I want."

"I know you do, son. Your daddy didn't want the farming life, but I see it in you. So be it. Franklin Dairy will pass on to you."

Later, after the worst of the storm had passed, Granddaddy pulled on his boots and opened the back door. He turned to Ty. "You comin'?"

Together, they stepped through the debris in the yard and dodged tree branches still swaying in the wind. Everything looked okay until they passed the barn.

"Oh no. No, no." Granddaddy took off running to the fence that was supposed to have kept the cows safe in the field during the storm. Instead, one large section had fallen, the old wooden boards snarled and splintered at the ends. Thirty-two of Granddaddy's 150 cows had escaped through the gash in the fence. Even at his young age, Ty knew the rules of the game: a loss of cows meant a loss of milk, which meant a loss of money. It was a hard hit for the farm.

Ty might have started the summer still a boy, but he took an important step toward manhood the night of that storm. Now, more than fifteen years later, he still remembered what it felt like to know Franklin Dairy would one day be his. It was an intimidating but welcome weight of responsibility. A weight that had only increased over the years.

He heard a knock at the door and glanced up. Carlos leaned against the doorframe, beating dust from his blue jeans with his faded Crimson Tide ball cap.

"What's up, man?" Carlos asked, not really looking for an answer, just someone to shoot the breeze with for a minute.

Ty leaned back in his chair, springs and metal squeaking. "Checking numbers. The usual." He nodded to the hat in Carlos's hand. "I'll help you with the stalls if you leave that cap off."

"Nuh-uh." Carlos set it firmly back on his head. "Hat stays with me."

While the men forked fresh bedding into each of the cow stalls, Ty relished the peace that came with doing a job well and quietly. With the herd in the fields and the music off, the only sound came from industrial fans on either end of the barn and the swishing of their pitchforks into bags of sawdust. Ty's mind was free to roam, although today, his mind wasn't going anywhere easy. It shifted from memories of his grandfather to the broken pump he and Carlos would have to fix later to the phone call that came this morning.

Jenna. He didn't even have to see her to feel the thorn digging into his flesh.

Carlos could only stand to work in silence for so long, and after a few minutes, he broke it. "Something under your skin? You're shoving that pitchfork mighty hard there. Remind me not to get in the way."

"I'm good. Just . . . distracted."

"What did Dr. Evans say about 186?"

They'd lost a cow yesterday, a female soon to have a baby. Ty hadn't been sure what it was, but the thought of infection—something that could spread to the rest of the herd—had worried him.

"Undetected heart condition, no infection. He couldn't say specifically what it was, but he offered to do an autopsy to be sure." Ty patted down the last layer of sawdust and moved the bag down to the next stall.

"For a pretty penny, I bet."

"Bingo."

"Good there's no infection. Nothing that'll affect the rest of them," Carlos said. "So if it's not the cow, what is it? Tell me to mind my own business if you want, but I'll just ask you again later." He grinned.

Ty shoved a fork-load into the stall. Patted it down. Lather, rinse, repeat.

"It's nothing, man. Just heard a weather report earlier is all. Tropical storm down in the Caribbean."

"Yeah, I heard it too. Staying out in open water, don't you think?"

"Probably. Can't let our guard down though. That's the same as begging the thing to come and unleash destruction. We have some boards left over from last summer. I'll see about getting more. May have time later today to make a run to the Feed and Equipment."

"You like to be prepared for everything, don'tcha, Boss?"

"I can't prepare for everything. But this farm's been here a heck of a lot longer than I have. It's not going to be blown to bits on my watch."

Ty paused and ran his free hand over his head, then picked the fork back up again. Maybe he was being too hard on Jenna. Betsy tried to take care of her. He should probably try to do the same. But her calling meant she needed something, and Ty wasn't sure Betsy had anything to give. Not money, not energy, certainly not another chunk of her heart. Last summer was the last time, as far as Ty was concerned.

Betsy had been so confident that first procedure would work. He'd hoped it would too, of course, but he knew it was usually better to expect the worst. Not as hard of a fall that way. Betsy, on the other hand, had expected the best, even planned for it—she'd use the weekend in Nashville to give the good news to Jenna. It didn't pan out that way though.

After they got the call that the test was negative, Ty had expected Betsy to bail on the trip, but she didn't. Putting five hundred miles between her and the double glass doors of South Alabama Fertility Specialists would feel good, she'd said. Give her something else to focus on. And anyway, Jenna had asked her to come, and Betsy would do whatever she could for her sister.

He still kicked himself for letting Betsy go, but at the time, he didn't have the heart to say no. When she pulled up the driveway at the end of the weekend, both she and the truck were on their last legs. She hadn't gotten the rest and peace she'd gone to Nashville to seek. Jenna had been a sour taste in his mouth ever since.

So the phone call? It was the same as the leaves swirling in the wind, the animals all jittery in their pens, the weathermen loosening their top buttons and rolling up their shirtsleeves. Everyone knew something was coming.

eight

Betsy

It was a long day, as Ty had predicted. Betsy didn't see him before the afternoon milking, which took him through the early evening. He blew in the back door as lightning bugs floated around the backyard and cicadas in the trees chirped out their scratchy melodies. He wolfed down a bowl of spaghetti, then ducked back out the door.

"Sorry, babe," he said. "Broken pump. Carlos and I have to fix it before tomorrow."

It was well after ten before she heard the back door open and his footsteps, heavy with fatigue, on the stairs. She was propped up in bed reading.

"Everything okay?" she asked when he trudged into their bedroom.

He shrugged, unbuckling his blue jeans and stepping out of them. He pointed to the bathroom. "Shower."

Ten minutes later, he entered the bedroom, smelling of musky soap. She'd planned to tell him about Jenna and the girls as soon as he came out of the steamy bathroom, but then he collapsed onto the bed next to her, flung his arm over his eyes, and groaned.

"That bad?"

"It's working again, but I don't know how long it'll hold up. It's the second time we've had to rig it. Wish I could have called Chuck."

For years Ty had used Chuck Panter anytime a piece of equipment broke or malfunctioned, but with the closing of several dairy farms in south Alabama, there wasn't enough broken machinery to keep him in business. At one time there had been twelve dairy farms in his territory. Now there were three, and Franklin Dairy was the biggest by far.

After a moment, Betsy reached over and turned off the lamp. In the semidarkness she had the nerve to ask, "What about us? How are we doing?" She knew the numbers, but numbers only told half the story. Many times their numbers had been down but Ty said not to worry, that the next season would bring them well into the black, and it always happened.

But he didn't immediately dismiss her concerns, which made her concerns feel that much more real.

"I was thinking about calling the principal at the elementary school," she said. "See if he'd be interested in setting up some more field trips for next school year. And I talked to the head of the summer program at the Y. They're adding us into their weekly camp schedule this summer."

"That's great, Bets."

She turned her face toward him. He stared up at the ceiling, one arm behind his head.

"The field trips help," he finally said. "They really do. The renovation set us back, but it'll pay off. We'll be okay." He reached over and pulled her toward him. She scooted close enough to feel the heat radiating off his body, slid one leg between his, and nestled her head under his chin.

He sighed. "We always make it work, don't we? When something doesn't go our way, we try something else."

"What are we trying this time?"

"We'll be creative, how about that?" He pulled his head back and smiled at her. His face, weathered from spending hours of every day of the year outside in the elements—heat, cold, rain, wind—bore straight white lines between his eyes and temples. He said he couldn't be outside in the sunshine without his sunglasses on or his light-blue eyes would scald right off his face. She reached up and traced the line to his ear.

"Maybe it's time for that vacation you've been talking about," he said. "A long weekend. What about Destin? Or New Orleans? You could take me to that antique shop you like on Magazine Street. Walker and Carlos could keep an eye on things here for a few days."

"How can we do that when we can't pay to fix a broken pump?"

"We *can* pay to fix it; I'm just choosing to fix it for free."

"Hmm." She pressed her cheek into his chest. His heartbeat was as steady and insistent as the metronome that used to sit on top of her parents' Steinway. "That would be nice." A vacation would be good for them. Help them reconnect, away from the responsibilities of the farm, from the distraction of the milking schedules. The veterinarian visits and field trips.

He rolled onto his back again, keeping one arm tight around her. "So what's up with Jenna?"

"Things are good. She's getting ready to go on a two-week art retreat. It's a big deal, I think. Something she didn't want to turn down. It's in Florida."

"Two weeks at the beach? Sounds right up her alley."

"It's . . . I don't think it's actually on the beach. And maybe it'll be good for her. She's wanting to get back into her photography, and this will give her a chance to get away and focus on it. She used to be really good."

"What about Addie and Walsh?"

Betsy paused a moment too long. Ty turned to her with wide eyes. "Betsy?"

"I told her I'd run it by you, but I said I thought we might be able to keep them here."

"And when is this retreat?"

She took a deep breath and bit her lip. "It starts tomorrow."

Ty lifted his shoulders and peered down at her. "Tomorrow? As in twelve hours, tomorrow?"

Betsy nodded.

He sat up and leaned his elbows on his knees. "You've got to be kidding me."

"It's two weeks. Nothing at all. It'll be mostly me taking care of them anyway. I know you'll be busy. And I should have asked you earlier."

He laughed, almost a grunt. "You think?"

She put a hand on his back. "I'm sorry. Really. I just . . ." How could she explain the deep-down kernel of need inside her—the need to protect, defend, shelter her sister? Even when Jenna made rash, spur-of-the-moment decisions, even when she infuriated Betsy like no one else could.

Betsy closed her eyes. Jenna had once begged her parents to let her attend some kind of photography program the summer after her freshman year at Alabama. Betsy made it clear she thought her parents should let Jenna go, but they said no. They hadn't even considered it.

"Jenna was always happiest when she was behind a camera. If this is her shot at trying photography again, I want to give it to her. And I can't shake the feeling that something else is going on with her too, but I don't know what it is."

Ty turned and looked at her over his shoulder. "I don't know if you believe all that or if you're just saying it to make things sound better." He sighed and lay back against the pillows. "I love you for taking care of your sister. I don't love the situation, but it'll . . . It's fine. You're right though—I won't have much time for visiting. Or helping you with the girls."

"It's okay. I don't expect you to change anything. I'll take care of it all."

Ty exhaled through pursed lips and rubbed the top of his head. "I wish she'd given us a little more of a heads-up before we become babysitters."

"I know." Betsy's chest squeezed at the thought of little feet pounding up and down the stairs of the old farmhouse. Laughter in the hallways. She hoped she hadn't made a big mistake in saying yes.

Outside, the faint sound of lowing cows, content in the barn, crossed the expanse of grass and yard and crept inside the house. The sound was strangely comforting.

Ty's arm around her tightened. "You looking forward to seeing Addie and Walsh?"

She nodded. "Yeah, I am. It's been over a year. Walsh was still a baby last summer."

"I remember last summer."

Betsy squeezed her eyes closed, shutting out the memory. She swallowed. "Things are different now, you know that. We've moved on. It'll be easier."

Ty was quiet. After a moment, Betsy propped herself up on one elbow to peer down at him. "I'm fine."

"Good. Because I'd rather them not come at all if it's going to be hard for you."

Betsy leaned down and kissed him on the lips. "Thank you for worrying about me. But I'm a big girl. I can handle it."

He pulled her to him again, his arm tight around her back. He nuzzled her cheek with his nose and kissed her, soft but pressing, urgent. She gave in for a moment, the familiar and pleasant ache rising in her belly, but when his hand slipped down to the waistband of her thin cotton pajama bottoms, she inhaled and pulled her lips away, just a fraction of an inch, so small she almost hoped he hadn't noticed.

But he dropped his head back against his pillow. She put her hand on his chest and lay her head on the pillow next to his, her forehead pressed into his cheek. "Another night?" she whispered.

She felt him nod. In minutes he was asleep.

Long after Ty nodded off, Betsy lay awake. The half-full moon shining through a hazy film of cloud made a soft glow on the bedroom walls. The clock on her nightstand glowed red numbers—1:24.

Nashville last summer had been hard. At first she'd expected it to be a chance to celebrate good news of a positive pregnancy with her sister. Then after the nurse had called with the results, she hoped it'd be a chance to rest, lick her wounds, and get her feet back underneath her. It wasn't until she dropped her bags in Jenna's cozy little house that she learned Jenna had been offered the chance to pick up extra shifts at Full Cup and would be working for much of the weekend, starting with the late shift that night.

All Betsy had said to Jenna about the doctor visits was that she was "having some tests done," making sure things were running normally. Nothing to indicate any real problem. Still, Betsy had hoped that Jenna would have somehow read between the lines. Used some sisterly wavelength and instinctively known Betsy needed her. Not walk out the door the minute Betsy arrived.

"You don't mind hanging with the girls, do you? I know they'd love to spend some time with Aunt Betsy without boring old Mom around," Jenna said.

"I don't know, Jenna, I kind of thought . . ."

"Please? This is good money for me. And I'll be in and out. I'll have a break between shifts around lunch tomorrow, then you and I can catch up on Sunday."

"I have to leave Sunday. I have a field trip lined up for Monday morning."

"Oh. Well . . ."

Betsy exhaled. Thoughts of bonding, reconnecting, evaporated. "It's fine." What else could she do? "The girls and I will have a great time." She imagined a protective layer, like bubble wrap, creeping up the walls of her heart.

Betsy spent the weekend building sheet tents in the cramped living room, making pizzas with the meager offerings in Jenna's kitchen, and making up fairy tales about mermaids and seahorse princes. When Jenna arrived home after her Sunday-morning shift, Betsy pulled her suitcase, now stuffed with crayon drawings and a pink feather boa Addie insisted Betsy take with her, out to the truck. She turned to say good-bye to the girls.

"I wish you could stay longer." Tears slid down Addie's cheeks.

Betsy's heart filled with a potent mixture of longing and anger she'd never felt. She bent down so she could talk to Addie at her eye level. "How about this?" she whispered. "What if we make plans to see each other again real soon? Maybe you can even come to the farm and get to know the cows."

"Can I ride one?" Addie asked, her bottom lip still trembling.

Betsy laughed. "We don't usually ride the cows, but I don't think Uncle Ty will mind. He'll pick out the perfect one for you to ride."

That perked Addie up enough for Betsy to leave without dissolving into tears herself. Before she climbed into the truck, she cupped Walsh's plump cheek in her hand, then turned to Jenna.

"Thank you." Jenna's arms were tight around Betsy's neck. "This has been a huge help. And I'm sorry we didn't really get a chance to catch up."

It was now mid-June and that bright July morning last summer was the last time Betsy had seen Jenna or the girls. She FaceTimed with Addie and Walsh often, but whenever Jenna got on the phone, she kept the conversation light and easy—what the girls were learning, funny things they'd said recently. Anytime Betsy asked about anything more personal—whether Jenna was satisfied with her job, if she'd met anyone nice, if she was happy living in Nashville—Jenna would change the subject.

Maybe the act of keeping the girls here for a little while would somehow bring her and Jenna closer. There were so many conversations Betsy wanted to have with Jenna, about so many things, but there always seemed to be some sort of dividing wall between them. Betsy didn't even know how it got there. Things used to be so different with them.

She wished Jenna could stay even just one night at the farm. She imagined the two of them sitting up late on the porch, talking and laughing as they did when they were much younger, before real-world problems invaded their make-believe universe.

nine

Betsy

Betsy was waiting on the front porch when a car turned off Highway 35 onto the gravel driveway. It was a moment before Jenna's small blue Honda appeared from the tunnel of trees that lined the drive. Betsy smiled when the driver's side door opened and Jenna's blonde curls popped out.

"Hey there," Betsy called on her way down the steps. "Welcome to the farm." She enveloped her sister in her arms and squeezed, breathing in the strawberry scent of her shampoo. After a moment, she pulled back, her hands still on Jenna's shoulders. "Your hair is shorter."

Jenna put her hand to her head. "It's easier this way. I still can't control it, but at least it's out of my face."

"It looks great." Whenever she thought of Jenna, it was usually as the wild, defiant teenager she once was. But here she was, an adult. A mother. The reality always caught her off guard. "It's really good to see you. I wish you could stay."

"I know. I have to be there tonight though. They do this big welcome thing, I don't know." She looked past Betsy to the house. "This place is gorgeous, as always. Addie's been talking about the cows since we crossed into Alabama. Did you tell her she could ride one?"

Betsy was about to explain when a knocking came from the backseat, loud and insistent. They both turned to see Addie's face pressed up against the glass.

"Let me get them out," Jenna said with a laugh. She ducked her head into the backseat. Addie had already unbuckled her seat belt and clamored around Jenna to hop out of the car. Jenna pulled a sleeping Walsh from her seat, then stood.

Addie took a few cautious steps toward Betsy, then stopped and turned back to Jenna.

"It's okay." Jenna ran her hand down Addie's hair.

Addie moved toward Betsy, then ran the last few steps, knocking into her knees and burying her face in her legs. "Aunt Betsy!" she said, her voice muffled by Betsy's shorts.

Betsy closed her eyes for the briefest moment, then smiled big. "Well, hello to you." She pulled Addie's face up so she could look at her. "You've grown about a foot since I saw you last. And your hair—it's so long!" Addie's blonde curls reminded Betsy of Jenna as a child, her curls almost taking on a life of their own, especially in the summer.

"And here's my baby." Jenna switched Walsh to her other hip. Betsy knew mothers often called their youngest child their "baby," but there was nothing baby about Walsh. Not anymore. Her dark hair hung to her shoulders in gentle waves, her small upturned nose was flecked with tiny freckles, and her rosebud lips were a deep magenta.

Betsy's heart ached as if Walsh were her own child and she'd missed her growing up. She reached over to Walsh clinging to Jenna's shoulder. Walsh tucked her chin and hid her face in Jenna's neck. Betsy tickled Walsh's cheek with the tip her fingernail, just enough to see the girl's cheeks stretch into a grin.

"There it is," Betsy said. "I knew a smile was in there somewhere." Walsh giggled and Betsy turned to Jenna. "Y'all come on in."

Addie ran ahead of them into the house. Inside, her eyes darted here and there to take it all in. "Wow," she breathed.

Addie's reaction was similar to how Betsy felt when Ty brought her to the farm when they were dating. The house wasn't grand or huge, but it was comfortable. Broken in. Even with his grandmother's collection of ancient weaver's looms standing in the corners and orange-and-yellow afghans covering every piece of furniture, it had felt like a place of welcome.

Now, deep slipcovered couches had replaced the looms, and fabrics in a mix of ticking stripes and faded flowers had replaced the afghans, but it still felt like a haven, a place for rest.

Walsh squirmed and Jenna set her down. "Be careful." Jenna ruffled Walsh's hair. "Don't mess anything up."

"Don't worry about it," Betsy said. "We don't have anything they can mess up. If they could, Ty would have already dropped something on it or broken it."

The girls scrambled into the window seat and stared out at the fields and the faded red barn in the distance.

Jenna breathed in deep. "It's so peaceful." She stretched her fingers out, then squeezed them closed. Was Jenna itching for her camera? There'd been a time—years ago in high school—when Jenna rarely went anywhere without it. She'd had a talent, somehow always able to capture just the right angle or shadow to make the viewer see her subject—whether a child at play or a leafless tree in winter—in a different light. She'd even carried that talent for artistry to Wyoming where she took photos and served as a yoga instructor at a remote artists' colony. Thankfully, that was before Addie and Walsh.

Betsy took two glasses from the cupboard and filled them with ice. "I'm excited about your retreat." It wasn't a lie, exactly. Just an extension of the truth.

Jenna sat on a stool at the kitchen counter. "Thanks. I am too. I think."

"What do you mean?" Betsy poured iced tea into the glasses and passed one to Jenna.

"I don't know. It was all so quick. Two days ago, I was making the schedule for work, penciling myself in for a full week, and now I'm leaving the girls with you and headed to who-knows-what."

Betsy nodded. Two days ago, she was planning a month of field trips, some marketing for the farm, and a meeting with a farmer's market in Foley. Now she was wondering what she'd do with two young kids for half a month.

"But impulsive decisions are my trademark, right?" Jenna smiled, but it was halfhearted.

Betsy tightened her hands around her glass. "Do you think if you'd taken more time to think about it, you would've decided not to go?"

Jenna shrugged. "I probably would've talked myself out of it, but . . ."

"But what?"

Jenna kept her eyes down and swirled her tea in her glass. "Things like this don't come my way very often. Or ever. If I'd said no, who knows when I'd have a chance to get away and do something like this again?"

Etta zipped through the kitchen then, the girls following just behind her.

Betsy finished her tea, then set the glass in the sink. "Hey, you two," she called. "How about those cows? Want to go see them?" She looked at Jenna. "Is that okay?"

"Of course. They'll love it. As long as Ty's okay with it." She bent down to help the girls with their shoes.

"He's in the middle of the second milking, but we can see the cows already out in the pasture." She turned to Addie and Walsh. "Maybe later on he'll let you try milking one of them."

Addie's eyes widened. "Does it hurt them?"

Betsy laughed. "You don't have to do it if you don't want to, but no, it doesn't hurt them. It'll hurt them if we don't milk them." She ushered them out onto the back porch and down the steps. The openness of the yard was too much to contain Walsh's excitement. She wriggled out of Jenna's arms and burst into a run. Addie ran a couple of steps, then stopped and looked back at Jenna.

"I'll stay with you, Mommy."

"It's okay, baby. Go ahead and run."

Addie waited another second, then took off. "Walsh," she hollered. When they reached the wooden fence, they peered through the slats and pointed at the cows in the distance.

"That's some love," Betsy said as she and Jenna picked their way across the prickly grass that had grown inches since Ty last cut it.

"Sometimes I don't even know how it happened. I look at them and think, Where did you little girls come from? I know that sounds crazy."

"Not too crazy. But they seem happy. Look at them."

Addie held Walsh around the middle from behind, Walsh's legs kicking and reaching for the bottom rung of the fence. As soon as her feet connected with the rung, she grabbed onto the top of the fence to get a better view of the cows beyond. Addie supported her little sister from behind.

"You must be doing something right," Betsy said.

Jenna shrugged. "I think they're just glad to be away from our house for a bit. This will be good for them."

Addie and Walsh's chatter grew quiet, and Betsy turned to see Ty walking toward them from the barn.

"Hey there," she called to Ty. "They're here."

"I see that." He unlocked the fence and pushed it open wide, then knelt in front of the girls. "Hello," he said formally.

"Hi," Addie said. "I like your cows."

"Thank you. I like them too." He tousled Walsh's hair, then stood up. "Hey, Jenna. It's good to see you."

"You too, Ty." Her voice was hesitant, but she relaxed when Ty held out an arm and gave her a quick hug.

"Sorry to run, but I need to get back out there." He rubbed the creases on his forehead. "I just wanted to say hey. I'll be back up as soon as I can." He looked at Betsy and she nodded, then he was gone, headed toward the barn. His mind, Betsy knew, was wrapped around pumps, quotas, and the two weeks ahead.

Jenna raised her eyebrows. "Is he okay?"

"He's fine. Just busy."

Back inside, Betsy pulled out crackers and strawberries for Addie and Walsh, then cut two thick slices of buttery pound cake. "Milk, right?"

"Of course," Jenna said.

Betsy placed the slices of cake on blue-and-white transferware plates and handed one to Jenna.

"Are these Nana's plates?"

Betsy nodded, her mouth full of pound cake.

"I wish I'd had the sense to say I wanted some of her things when she died. I was too wrapped up in my own teenage dramas to care." She ran her thumb along the edge of the plate. "The girls would love to eat off their great-grandmother's china."

"I have twelve of these," Betsy said. "I can wrap up half of them and send them home with you."

"No, I wasn't . . . I didn't mean that. I just . . . You've had your head on straight for a long time. I wish I was more like that."

While the two women ate, the girls took a couple bites, then darted off to one part of the house or another, exploring and chasing the cat. Betsy pulled out a pad of paper and a pen to jot down the girls' schedules, but Jenna laughed.

"I just want to make sure I know what to do. Remember, I have no experience with this."

"If I figured it out, you can too, and probably better than me. That reminds me . . ." She fished an envelope from her purse and held it out to Betsy.

"What's this?"

"Just a little money. I wanted you to have some extra on hand to cover the girls' food and incidentals while I'm gone."

"You know you don't have to do this. We can take care of it."

"I know, but it'll make me feel better. Just take it."

Betsy hesitated, then took the envelope from Jenna's hand.

When they finished going over everything about the girls' routines and particular challenges, Betsy cleaned up the kitchen, wiping spills and dribbles that didn't usually appear in her kitchen. Jenna walked through the house, picking up framed photos, books, and other knickknacks, then absently placing them down again. She was so lost in thought, Betsy just let her roam. When Jenna's phone rang in her bag, she checked the screen, then moved toward the back porch.

"I need to take this, but I'll just be a minute." She opened the door as wind blew against the house, pulling the screen door on the porch wide open, then slamming it shut.

Betsy peered out the window above the kitchen sink. Dark purple spread across the sunlit sky. "Guess that storm decided to come on in." Thunder cracked and a bolt of lightning skittered across the sky. A flock of doves took flight from the side pasture and zipped to the east. *I'll check on the girls for you,* she mouthed to Jenna.

She found Addie and Walsh in the empty room, lying on their backs, staring at the ceiling and talking. Betsy stopped in the doorway and knocked on the jamb. "Mind if I come in?"

"Sure." Addie sat up. Walsh rolled over onto her stomach.

"What are you girls chatting about? Still playing a game?"

"We're looking for clues."

"Oh yeah? What kind of clues?"

"Just clues about the house. What kind of place it is."

Betsy raised her eyebrows. "Well, what did you find out?"

Addie looked around her. "We like the house. A lot. And the cows. And Uncle Ty. I think we could stay here for a while. Maybeeee . . . about four years."

Betsy laughed. "Four years, huh? That's a long time. I think you'd miss your own home by then."

"Yeah," Addie said. "Probably." She pulled down Walsh's pant leg where it had stuck up above her knee. "But this house just feels good. And we packed my favorite princess dress and Walsh's blanket, so we can stay as long as we want!"

She jumped off the bed and ran to their small pile of bags in the corner. She reached her hand into an old University of Alabama duffel bag, then tossed a well-loved blanket to Walsh and laid out the dress for Betsy to see.

"Very pretty," Betsy said.

Walsh pulled the blanket over her face and folded her knees up under her belly. "Find me!" she yelled to Addie.

Addie giggled. "I can still see you, silly."

As the girls began a game of hide-and-seek, Betsy stepped out. Rain was falling hard now, splattering the windows and turning the world outside steamy and blurred.

Jenna stood in the kitchen, leaning against the counter with her phone to her ear. She was smiling and chewing on her bottom lip. "Okay. Max told me it was a single cabin. It's just me, so that's fine." She glanced at the clock on the microwave. "Yes, I can make it by then, but don't worry about saving any dinner for me. I'll grab something on the way."

Betsy tiptoed back up the stairs. Jenna called her just as she reached the empty room. She sat on the bed and tried to look like she hadn't been eavesdropping. Addie and Walsh stood by the window peering at a honey bee buzzing on the other side of the glass.

Jenna tapped on the door. "Hey, you two."

"Mommy, there's a huge bee in the window. Come see," Addie said. Walsh's face was pressed to the glass.

"Hmm, wow." She leaned down and looked over their shoulders. "That's a big one. Come sit with me a minute." She pulled the girls to her.

As Jenna talked to them, giving them a list of dos and don'ts while staying at the farm, Betsy stepped out of the room to give them privacy. In the hallway she leaned back against the wall. Photos of the farm, left over from Ty's grandparents, clattered behind her.

"It sounds like you've already made up your mind," Betsy had said to Jenna on the phone the day before.

"No, it's not like that. I'm asking you before I tell them anything. But I have to give them an answer soon. Like . . . today. This is . . . Oh, Betsy, please say yes."

Betsy walked out into the backyard and breathed in the warm morning air as the two weeks swirled in her mind.

"Look, I understand if it's not going to work," Jenna said. "I'm sure I can figure something else out."

Betsy exhaled. "Of course they can stay here. That's not the problem. I'm just . . . I'm trying to understand you. It's a quick decision, dropping the girls off with barely a heads-up. Have you thought this through—your job, money, bills while you're gone? What about—?"

"Betsy, I've thought about it from every angle. Trust me. You don't have to worry about me. Or the girls. I know I used to be . . . irresponsible, but I'm not now. I can't afford to be—not with two kids who are stuck with me as their mom."

"They're not *stuck* with you."

"You know what I mean. They only have me. I have to do things right. And that's part of the reason why I want to do this retreat. To let them see me pursuing something that matters to me. To see me working toward a goal. I appreciate your concern, but this is something I need to do on my own. Can you let me do that? You're my sister, my friend. We're partners, right? Isn't that what we always said?"

Betsy nodded. "Yeah. We did."

"It's not like I'm leaving them with strangers. And as far as kids go, they're a breeze. They sleep late in the morning, they love Curious George, and they can drink their weight in apple juice."

Betsy smiled, in spite of her frustration.

"Oh, and Addie has to sleep with her stuffed elephant or she stays awake all night. Don't forget that."

Betsy gave a small laugh. "I think we can handle it."

"It'll be great. They'll probably want to stay forever."

Twenty minutes later, Betsy stood by Jenna's car, already cranked with the AC blasting. The storm had pushed through quickly, leaving behind a blanket of thick humidity. Kneeling, Jenna hugged the girls tight. "Listen to Aunt Betsy, okay? I want her to tell me how well you're behaving when I check in later."

"Will you miss us?" Addie asked.

"Oh yes," Jenna said. "I will miss you tons. But I'll take some pretty pictures and when I get back, I'll need you to tell me if they're any good. I'll need your help too." She poked Walsh gently in the stomach.

Jenna stood and wrapped her arms around Betsy. "Thank you," she whispered. "And sorry again for the late notice. I'll make it up to you."

"Just be safe. Let us know when you get there."

"I will." She climbed into the car. "Love you girls," she called as she ducked her head.

Betsy thought she saw tears in Jenna's eyes, and her arms ached to hold her little sister one more time. She stepped closer to the car, but when Jenna rolled down her window and turned her face to them, her eyes were dry. A little red, but no tears.

Wet gravel crunched under the tires as Jenna pulled away. Betsy and the girls waved until the car disappeared around the curve of the driveway. Then she put her hands on their backs and guided them up the steps. The afternoon sun was just beginning to peek out from behind the dark clouds.

One afternoon when she was fifteen, Betsy visited her mother's office and stood in the dim light of the quiet lab, all the other techs gone for the day. Her dad had picked her up from school and dropped her at her mom's office on his way to the Alys Stephens Center for a symphony performance. She and her mom would pick up Jenna at school in half an hour. Jenna had detention. Again.

Betsy stared at the wall. Faces stared back at her from photographs. Mostly young people, children, babies even. Some were photographed in light moments—laughter, a smile, or at least a hint of one. Playing, working, cooking, living life. But a few were taken toward the end—faces barely suppressing the pain that raged inside them. Eyes full of the knowledge of the truth about their lives.

She scratched the back of her leg with the laces of her tennis shoe, then reached out and touched one of the photos. A teenager wearing a backward ball cap grinned loosely, as if all was right with the world. His arm was flung around the shoulders of a tall girl whose eyes were closed in laughter. "Mom, tell me about him."

Her mom crossed the room. Her lab took up most of the eleventh floor of the UAB Cancer Research Center. It smelled musty—like damp newspaper or old dirt—with a hard edge of Lysol mixed in. This lab was where really smart people—scientists, doctors, technicians—made groundbreaking discoveries in the field of brain cancer research, and Betsy's mom was the head of it all. Her black orthopedic shoes padded across the floor, her rumpled white lab coat billowing behind her.

She grazed her fingers across the teenager's face. "Brian McLaurin," she said, her voice low and reverent. "He was only seventeen. Bone cancer that spread to his brain. He was a stand-out basketball star on his high school team before the pain started." She moved to her right and nodded toward the next photo on her "inspiration wall," as she called it. "Cynthia Graves. Left a young family behind. Juanita Powers, the lead in her middle school play."

She kept going, calling out the names of each face on her wall. Her mother hadn't always focused on cancer of the brain, but it was always something horrible and tragic. Betsy was only fifteen, the same age as some of the people on the wall, and she couldn't imagine someone choosing to devote her life to something so depressing, even if it did save lives.

She tuned out her mom's words but kept watching her. The way she touched each photo, a gentle smile on her face, a little laugh when she noted something funny about the person in his or her precancer life. She knew every detail about them—their hobbies, families, jobs. Where they went to school, what sport they played, what their dreams and hopes had been. Somehow that careful attention didn't extend to remembering that Betsy didn't like green beans. That at the age of twelve, Jenna still wanted the nightlight on in the hallway outside her bedroom. That the two girls in her own house needed a mother who paid attention to the small things.

Her mom wiped a tear away and sniffed, then strode back to her desk on the other side of the room. Betsy followed her. Her mom's desk was empty of any personal items—no photos of her or Jenna, no calendars with puppies or exotic islands. "Why do you keep those photos up on the wall if they make you so sad?"

"They remind me why I'm doing all this." She waved her arm around at the lab. "They inspire me to pour all I have into finding cures. Not for them—it's too late for them—but for their families, friends, children. The ones they left behind." She gazed back up at the wall. "They're why I do everything."

Her mom said plenty, but it was the unsaid words that cut the deepest. They left an empty pocket, a vacuum that sucked a hole in the center of Betsy's chest. It was the first time she realized with utter clarity that her mom actually wished those kids had been hers. Maybe even instead of Betsy and Jenna. It was the way her constant tension slipped away for a moment, the way her smile became real, not forced and tight. She was a better mom to these poor dead kids than she was to her own fully alive children.

Betsy looked at her watch—a yellow-and-green Swatch her favorite babysitter had given her two years before. "Mom, we've got to go. It's almost five."

"Mmm?" Her mom kept her gaze on the paperwork on her desk.

"Jenna. Detention. It's over in five minutes."

Her mom looked up, her eyes hazy, faraway. "Detention," she said, as if it were a foreign language. Which it kind of was. If it wasn't related to cancer or her lab or grant money, it was an unknown concept. She straightened the papers on her desk and clipped them with a black binder clip, then gave Betsy a sad smile. "What would we do without you?"

ten

Jenna

Google told her the drive from Elinore would take six and a half hours, but she figured if she pushed it, she could make it in less than six. Singer Creek Nature Preserve. Halcyon Artist Retreat. Two weeks of solitude, a chance to stretch creative muscles that had once been brimming with promise.

It wasn't the first time she'd tried to get away to chase her dreams. Sometimes she wondered what would have happened if her parents had said yes to the artist's residency the summer after her freshman year of college. If they'd believed in her art, trusted that she had something to say through her camera, something she couldn't find a way to say with words, or even a paintbrush or pencil. Could attending that summer program in Seattle have changed her whole life? Set her on a straight path toward creative fulfillment? Toward good decisions, respectable boyfriends, satisfying jobs? Maybe not. But maybe.

Instead, that spring night when she had driven back home to Birmingham from Tuscaloosa to talk to her parents about it, they'd glanced at each other and shared one of those quick looks that meant, "What in the world are we going to do about Jenna?" Part of her thought they might be happy she'd not only found something she was good at but was pursuing it. Pushing for it, asking for it.

"I think it's great," Betsy, who was home from Auburn for the weekend, had said when Jenna explained that the opportunity was offered to only a handful of students in her photography class and she was one of them. It was expensive, but it would offer her a furnished apartment for the summer, daily workshops with professional photographers, and priceless instruction from the famed but elusive Theodore Griffs.

"Photography as a hobby is great—something to do with your extra time." Her mom set her fork down next to her plate. "But it's just not something you can pursue as a regular, dependable job. It's not something that will make you any money."

"Who's talking about money? Maybe she just wants to have fun with it," Betsy said.

"Fun? Fun is taking photography as an elective. Using it as a creative outlet outside your regular classes. Maybe you could even set up a side business taking photos at birthday parties or events. That'd be fun. Going clear across the country to work with a man who looks like a serial killer is not my idea of fun."

Nothing is your idea of fun, Jenna thought. And she regretted her decision to pull up the photographer on Google earlier to show her parents that he was a real, well-known—if a little scary-looking—photographer.

"So you're going to let this guy's looks scare you off? He's a big deal—did you read what it said about him? Spending a summer learning from him could be huge for Jenna. Why can't she go?"

Betsy always stuck up for Jenna—it was part of the unspoken code of their sisterhood, as ingrained as their hair or eye color.

"Betsy, it's fine." Jenna wiped her mouth with her napkin and pushed back from the table. "You don't have to—"

"No, wait a minute. Y'all let me go clear across the globe for my semester in England two years ago. This isn't half as far or nearly as expensive. I don't get it."

"That was different. It was—"

"Girls." Their father was known for his silence and calm demeanor, so when he spoke, and with force as he did this time, they listened. "That's enough. Your mother has given her answer." He turned to Jenna. "If you want to pursue your photography on your own, that's fine. Anything in the arts is a worthy endeavor, as far as I'm concerned. But you spending a summer across the country with no supervision is out of the question."

Jenna's cheeks flamed. His voice had been steady, but she heard the emphasis on *you* anyway. It was as clear to her as the roof over her head or the hard chair she sat on—if it had been the other sister asking, the answer would have been different. But she was Jenna, ever dependable if solely as the disappointment. She'd proven that with lackluster grades, unsuitable boyfriends, and questionable after-school activities. Disappearing behind the camera was the only thing she was good at.

She left the dining room but paused unseen in the kitchen when she heard their conversation pick back up.

"I get that I don't have any sway here," Betsy said. "I just think you could give her a shot. She never asks to do anything and this one thing, you won't let her do."

"Jenna asks to do plenty, it's just not often for very smart reasons. We're thinking of her future, Betsy," her dad said. "She needs to concentrate on her grades, not some summer getaway with a bunch of friends in Seattle."

"Dad, I think it's more—"

"Her grades are already hanging by a thin thread," her mom broke in, "and that's without the distraction of this summer fling. She needs to focus, maybe even take some summer classes—*on* campus, *real* courses—and think about what she wants to do with her life." Jenna peeked around the edge of the door just in time to see her mom smooth her hair and brush imaginary crumbs off the front of her blouse. "Anyway, no telling what kind of trouble she'd get into in Seattle, of all places. Isn't that where those grunge people are? She'd probably end up on drugs. Or pregnant."

Jenna pulled back to avoid being seen, her stomach clenched as if her mother's words had been a physical blow.

"Jenna's a little wild, but she's not like that." Jenna heard the exasperation in Betsy's voice. "Why can't this be a way for her to figure out what she wants to do in the future? You let me do it, and it's not even like someone would hire me just because I worked at a marketing firm in England for a semester."

"Maybe not, but it shows that you challenged yourself, that you're determined to succeed, that you value hard work and dedication."

"Really? I think it shows I found the one semester-abroad program that let me combine my major with quaint English pubs and British guys with cute accents."

Dad scoffed. "That's not why you went and you know it."

"Why do you always think it's Jenna who does things for the wrong reason? Why do you automatically expect me to do the right thing? The good thing?"

"That's just the way you are, Betsy." Their mother's voice was maddeningly calm. "It's what you do. Jenna, on the other hand . . ." She cleared her throat.

I what? Jenna screamed in her mind. *What am I?*

Betsy stood, her chair scraping against the floor. "I think you're making a big mistake by not letting her go."

Alone now in her car, driving toward a mysterious destination that promised similar space and time to pursue her art and sharpen her skills, Jenna wondered at the prophetic nature of Betsy's comment. It was sort of true, wasn't it? Her parents' refusal to allow her to go to Seattle almost ten years ago had been the beginning of a downward spiral that dumped her out with two kids, a job filling recycled cardboard cups with fancy coffee, and a handful of abandoned dreams. Part of her wanted to blame it all on her parents, but she was old enough to know that was a weak excuse. She'd made her own choices.

Instead of the interstate, she stayed on small highways and two-lanes. Signs with happy names like Seaside, Rosemary Beach, and Sunnyside slid past her windows. Panama City, Port St. Joe, and Apalachicola, then national forests and wildlife management areas. Everything green and lush, full of life. As she drove she twisted the bracelet on her wrist until her skin grew sore. The bracelet—purple and blue pipe cleaners twisted together—was a gift from Addie the night before.

"Here, Mommy," Addie had said. "You can wear this on your trip."

Jenna slipped it over her hand and onto her wrist. "I'll keep it on the whole time."

"To remind you of me?"

"I don't need something like this to make me think of you. You're in here." She tapped her chest, over her heart.

Addie beamed, then frowned. "Wait. How am I in there if I'm right here?"

Jenna rolled down the windows and inhaled the warm, salty air. When she felt the magnitude of what she was attempting—going fourteen days without seeing her kids, resurrecting a long-dormant passion—she pushed the anxiety back and focused on the road. In her little blue car hurtling east, then south, she smiled as the air through the windows whipped her curls. She rolled up the window and cranked the AC. Freedom, light and elusive, won out over the panic and set her fingers tapping on the steering wheel.

The woman Jenna had spoken to on the phone warned her not to use GPS to get to Halcyon. Those instructions would send her to Chopper's Alligator Farm, the owner of which would not be amused by another misguided artist showing up at his front gate and asking for directions. So when Jenna saw the first sign for Singer Creek Nature Preserve, she took the woman's advice and ignored the blue dot, trusting that the signs would point her to her destination.

She didn't know much more about Halcyon than what she saw on the flyer Max had shoved across the varnished coffee shop counter three months ago. She'd been too afraid to read much about it, to hear about artists who'd left there full of new ideas, determination, purpose. The way she saw it, it was better not to get her hopes up. But now it was happening. The space that had opened up for her felt too good to be real. More than she deserved.

"All art begins as a passion, an idea set deep inside the soul of a person," the flyer had read. "Often, all that person needs is space *to bring the idea to fruition. Halcyon is this space. It is a refuge to pursue the art that makes you feel alive."*

Not until now did Jenna have a spark of memory about "halcyon." She was probably thirteen or fourteen and had walked into her father's office on the second floor of their house without knocking. He was hunched over his desk, scratching out music notes and drawing new ones on a score. Treble clefs, bass clefs, 3/4 counts.

"What are you working on?" she'd asked.

He glanced over his shoulder, then turned back to the sheet music before him. "I'm writing a new piece for my summer concert series. It's called 'Halcyon Days.' It's going to be beautiful if I can just figure out this coda . . ." And with that, he retreated again to the space in his mind where no one could reach him. Later, he explained to her the story behind "Halcyon Days." The beautiful widow. The kingfisher. The unusual calm.

When she pulled off the highway at the sign for Singer Creek, her hurriedly scrawled directions told her to drive ten miles south on a thin two-lane road, then turn off onto another road for a few miles. Her directions didn't mention that this road was white sand instead of asphalt and just wide enough for her car. Leafy tendrils and vines encroached along the edges and tall trees lined the road, meeting above to form a canopy that blocked out the last of the daylight.

This must be wrong, she thought. But as she inched forward, just past a sprawling oak with Spanish moss drooping down to brush the top of her car, a driveway opened up. Not even a driveway really, just a blip of space carved out between trees. She pulled in. Down the path, her headlights illuminated a sign hung on a tree, suspended from a scrolled arm of iron and squeaking back and forth in the breeze. *Welcome to Halcyon.*

⌒

"Don't worry," a voice behind her said. "You're in the right place."

It was full dark now, and constellations of stars popped out bright against the heavy sky. Jenna had just climbed the steps to the screened porch on the front of the dining hall where the schedule—if it could even be called that, loose at it was—had told them to meet.

The woman who spoke to her was bent over at the edge of the porch in a triangle pose, legs in a V, one arm reaching down to her blue yoga mat, the other stretched up high. Despite her obvious confidence, her body was at the wrong angle over her lead knee. Jenna was tempted to tell her she needed to realign her torso to get the most benefit from the stretch, but she kept her secret to herself.

"Were you expecting a classroom?" The woman straightened up, stretching her arms over her head.

"No, I . . . Well, I don't know what I expected. Definitely not a campground."

On the walk from her cabin—small, clean, comfortable—to the porch of the dining hall, Jenna had passed a lake ringed by other cabins like hers, each with its own small deck extending over the water. A fire pit was situated at the edge of the lake, and before darkness fell, she spied a couple of small buildings—studios, she presumed—up the hill past the dining hall. Halcyon was like its own little world in the middle of the wild jungle of the nature preserve.

"Good guess," the woman said. "That's exactly what this is. Or was. It used to be a summer camp for children whose parents wanted them to be future environmentalists or something. A group of philanthropists bought it back in the nineties, dumped a bunch of money into it, and invited artists to come play. I'm Casey, by the way." She extended her hand and Jenna took it. "You're Jenna Sawyer from Nashville, right? Former photographer, now coffee extraordinaire?"

Jenna stared at her, unsure if she was the butt of a joke she wasn't aware of. "How'd you know that?"

"We're selective about who gets in. We have to be. Hundreds apply for each session. We only take ten. And anyway"—she gestured to the camera hanging around Jenna's neck—"you're the only photographer we have this session. I figured you'd be pretty easy to pick out."

Jenna fidgeted with the camera strap that suddenly felt like it was biting into the skin of her neck. "Calling me a photographer is probably a stretch."

"You are. Otherwise you wouldn't be here. The whole point of Halcyon is to reconnect, right? Dive back in. Like I said, you're in the right place, like it or not. Now, if you'll excuse me for a minute . . ." She grinned, then greeted someone else approaching the porch.

"Hundreds apply for each session." Must have been some mighty big strings Max had pulled to get Jenna in. She already felt way out of her league.

Quiet conversation and laughter floated all around her on the porch where a handful of lamps lit the space in a comforting glow. Palm branches pressed against the outside of the screened walls. A ceiling fan whirled above, disrupting cigarette smoke rings and rustling pages of open sketchbooks. A handful of artists had scattered around the room, some seated on deep couches, some on the floor leaning against the porch rails.

Artists all had a certain look, Jenna had always thought. It didn't matter if they were painters, photographers, writers, whatever. It was something "other"—a little different, little off-kilter, often out of step with the world around them. She'd had that look at one time, but she figured it'd been swallowed up by life and spit out in some vague, bland form.

She'd just settled on a metal glider when Casey walked to the center of the porch and cleared her throat, halting the hushed talk.

"I hate to break up the camaraderie, but I wanted to go over a few things before everyone goes their separate ways. I'm Casey Malone, one of the mentors here this summer. My drug of choice— that is, my art of choice—is the physical arts: yoga, Pilates, Barre." She put one hand up around her mouth. "And for my own personal plug—I do yoga three times a day—a five-thirty sunrise session, eleven o'clock before lunch, and a six o'clock evening session. Anyone is welcome to join me, but I won't be offended if no one does. End of plug." Everyone laughed and she took a small bow.

"Now, your other mentors are Lane Michaels, oil and acrylic painting. Denise Trimm, creative writing. Yannick Bello, charcoal and pencil drawing." As she said each name, the mentors raised their hands and smiled. "And our last mentor is Gregory Galloway." She looked around, eyebrows raised. "It seems our resident photographer is missing. Big surprise." Nervous laughter rose in the room. "If he shows up, I'll just let him introduce himself." Casey was smiling, but the undercurrent of annoyance wasn't buried deep.

"You may have already figured this out as you've been chatting, but all of you are here for varying lengths of time, something that sets this retreat apart from others like it. Halcyon exists for eight weeks every summer. Some of you are here for just a couple of weeks and a few of you are staying the entire two months as a sabbatical. Regardless of the length of your own personal retreat, I know I speak for all the mentors when I say we're excited to have you here.

"Unlike most of your real lives, there's not much of a schedule at Halcyon. You're free to do your thing however and whenever you want. The preserve is magnificent and you may find all the inspiration you need right here. However, we're only a few miles from the coast, so if you need more, don't be afraid to venture out.

"We do encourage you to come here to the porch every evening at seven. It's where we discuss our work, what we did or didn't accomplish during the day, or any problems we're having. It's a workshop atmosphere where everyone is respectful and encouraging. We're here to support and offer constructive feedback, and most people find this is the most helpful part of the retreat."

Then she asked everyone to tell their names and what they hoped to get out of the week. Jenna always hated icebreakers like this. They reminded her of the week in college when she lost her mind and thought she might actually want to join a sorority. Five grueling days of prim parties, saccharine conversation, and ridiculous icebreakers where one by one, girls explained through tears how their future happiness depended on having a certain arrangement of Greek letters tied to their name. All except for Jenna, of course. After the second day, she called her mom and told her she'd have to accept having just one daughter follow her footsteps into sorority life. And it wasn't going to be her.

There were no tears in this group, but even still, everyone had a good answer. Most of them had a specific goal for their time at Halcyon—work on a novel, learn how to use a new medium, finish an MFA thesis. As each of the other artists spoke, Jenna thought about Addie and Walsh and what they thought of her. What they'd think of her when they were teenagers, then grown women. How she'd measure up. She thought of how sometimes she wished she'd made different decisions, decisions that had taken her to other places, other lives.

"Jenna?" Casey prompted.

Jenna looked up. It was her turn. She opened her mouth to say something—anything—but then she noticed a man standing at the top of the stairs, just on the other side of the screened door. He hadn't been there a moment ago, and judging by the rest of the faces turned in her direction, she was the only one who saw him.

"Anything?" Casey asked.

"Yeah, I, uh . . ." She glanced back at the door where he still stood. His gaze sliced through her protective layers like a scalpel and made her forget everything. "I'm not sure why I'm here," she finally said.

While a few people in the room smiled, some looked at her with scrunched eyebrows, concern crossing their faces.

"We appreciate the honesty," Casey said. "And I have to say, figuring out *why* you're at Halcyon might be the whole point to your time here." She turned to the rest of the group. "I want each of you to remember, not everyone gets a chance like this. You're the lucky ones, so soak up all you can. The time goes fast."

As she spoke, the man pulled open the screened door and climbed the last step onto the porch. Wearing black jeans, a white T-shirt, and a black leather jacket despite the heat, he looked as out of place as Jenna felt. At the top of the steps, he crossed his arms and leaned against the porch railing.

"Gregory Galloway, everyone," Casey said.

He nodded, arms still crossed. The dull roar outside from cicadas and tree frogs seemed even louder for how quiet the porch was. A single sheet of paper blew off a table and coasted to the floor. No one moved to pick it up.

"So we just wrapped up introductions." Casey spoke into the awkward silence. "Sorry we didn't wait for you, but I'm sure you can catch up with folks later on and get to know everyone."

He nodded again. "I heard what I needed to."

"Care to add anything?"

He took a deep breath. "Actually, I do have one more thing. I didn't hear anyone talk about why we call this place Halcyon. If you don't mind . . ."

Casey held out her hands. "Be my guest." She stepped out of the center of the group and sat on the floor.

Gregory stayed where he was, leaning against the rail with ease. "The name *halcyon* comes from the ancient Greeks. It was their name for a small, brightly colored bird called a kingfisher. Legend tells us that these birds built floating nests on the sea. There on the water, their nests tossed around by winds and waves, the females realized they needed calmer waters for their eggs to have any hope of hatching."

His words were slow and deliberate, as if to make sure everything soaked in. Jenna was lulled by his voice, his presence. The glow from the lamps caught the strong edge of his jawline, making him appear chiseled out of something hard. But his eyes were bright as he looked around the room. Even though she knew the story from her father, she hung on every word.

"So these tiny birds"—he held his thumb and forefinger up a few inches apart—"they charmed the god of the winds, who allowed a period of temporary calm while the babies in the eggs grew and developed. This physical peace and calm, which we now call halcyon, surrounded the nests until the eggs hatched and the babies flew away, able to live and thrive on their own.

"Here at Halcyon, our gift to you is this calm—separation from your life and its chaos and responsibilities—so you can grow and develop as an artist. Your gift to the world is who you become while you're here."

He paused a moment, looked around at the faces peering at him, then crossed the room and pulled open the door into the darkened dining hall.

"That's it, folks," Casey said. "You're on your own. Breakfast is at seven in the morning."

The artists stood and stretched, resuming conversations from earlier and collecting their belongings. Along with their mentors, they all left the porch, several smiling in Jenna's direction as they passed, but most absorbed in conversation about the work they'd begin tomorrow. Already she felt herself removed from the group, set apart. But she wasn't concerned. She kind of liked it that way.

Alone on the porch, she pushed back with her foot, sending the glider into gentle movement. The cry of a bird, the sound foreign and strange, echoed above the other nighttime noises. She twisted the pipe-cleaner bracelet around her wrist again in soothing circles, the fuzz tickling the delicate skin on the inside of her wrist. Off in the distance, thunder rumbled.

She'd called Betsy earlier before coming to the dining hall. With no reception on her cell, she'd placed a long-distance call on the landline in her cabin.

"They're having a blast," Betsy said when Jenna asked about the girls, partly expecting Betsy to tell her to get in the car and drive back to Elinore. "They spent the day exploring every corner of the house and yard. Maybe tomorrow we can get them into the barn."

"Are you sure y'all are going to be okay?" She hated to think that she'd shoved her kids off on her sister just so she could be alone with her camera. "Maybe if I—"

"Jenna," Betsy broke in. "We're fine. Really. Try to enjoy yourself."

Before they got off the phone, Jenna gave Betsy the address

of the retreat and the official phone number. There was a front desk with a landline in the main studio. Surely someone would be around to answer the phone in case of an emergency.

She dug her hand into the pocket of her rain jacket and pulled out her cell to check the time. Eight thirty. With any luck Betsy would already have the girls in bed. Jenna could check in quickly to make sure the evening had gone well. She didn't want to call so much that Betsy would think Jenna didn't trust her, but she was dying to hear whether the girls missed her, whether they'd been scared going to sleep. If Betsy had remembered Addie's stuffed elephant.

But when she swiped her thumb across the screen and scrolled to find Betsy's name, she noticed her phone still wasn't getting any service. She held it up a little higher in the air—the very thing she always made fun of other people for doing—keeping an eye on the screen to see when things kicked back into gear. Nothing.

"Great," she muttered.

Behind her, the door from the dining hall creaked, humidity making it stick as someone on the other side tried to open it. When it finally released, Gregory walked through the doorway, a small bowl of something dark in his hand, and pulled the door closed behind him. He didn't see her.

"Hey," she said.

He turned, his fork halfway to his mouth. "I thought everyone was gone," he said, his face hard.

"I was just trying to make a phone call."

"Don't bother. This metal roof is like a force field. Nothing gets through." He pointed to the ceiling with his fork.

Jenna glanced up. "Is it any better outside?"

He shook his head as he took a bite. "Service is terrible everywhere around here. You can try, but we usually have to drive outside the preserve if we need to make any important calls. For some reason, texts seem to work better. Sometimes."

Jenna watched as he took another bite.

"It's chocolate bread pudding. The good stuff comes out late." He raised his fork in a small wave and headed for the porch door. She smelled cigarette smoke and rich chocolate as he passed her. She surprised herself by speaking, not wanting him to walk out into the night just yet, leaving her alone.

"You left out part of your story earlier."

"Oh yeah?" He stopped with his hand on the door. "What'd I miss?"

"Alkyon," she said, her voice surer than she felt. "The widow who threw herself into the sea when she found out her husband had died in a shipwreck."

He paused a beat before speaking. "Where'd you learn that?"

"The gods turned her into a kingfisher and renamed the bird after her. Somewhere along the line Alkyon was changed to Halcyon."

He watched her for a moment in silence, making her stomach churn. He was older than her—midforties maybe—with bits of gray sprinkled into his dark hair. With a scruffy beard, tan skin, and crow's-feet, he looked like someone who'd lived a good life outside, in sunshine and warm breezes.

"Do you always tell that story to the new people?" she asked.

"Yep. And you're the first to correct me. Or to have any prior knowledge about the legend."

Jenna shrugged. "Just thought you might want to know the rest of the story." Rain began to fall, the drops hitting the metal porch roof like pebbles. He pulled his gaze away from her and peered out into the damp night.

She stood and tugged on her raincoat.

"You going out in this?" he asked.

"It's just water. It won't hurt anything."

He grinned. It was so fast, she'd have missed it if she hadn't been looking. The quick smile cracked the hard edges of his face, softening it and deepening the creases at the edges of his eyes. Then it was gone. He pushed the screened door and held it open. "After you."

At the door, she zipped her raincoat up over her camera and started down the steps. At the bottom she inhaled deeply. The scent of rain mixed with salty air, Spanish moss, and sandy dirt was almost intoxicating.

"*Petrichor,*" Gregory said behind her. The rain hitting his jacket made a soft *pat-pat-pat*.

"Excuse me?"

"It's the name of what you're smelling. That scent when rain first starts to fall. It's Greek. The smell of the fluid that flows in the veins of Greek gods."

"You sure do know a lot about Greek mythology." Jenna pulled her hood closer around her face.

"I like figuring people out. Even better if they're not around to tell me I'm wrong." He kept his gaze on her, making her shuffle her feet and readjust her camera strap.

"So I guess you're my mentor."

"It would appear so."

"I'm not so hard to figure out. Not much to analyze."

He cocked his head. "We'll see." He regarded her a moment longer, then shoved his hands in his pockets. "You know where you're going?" He tipped his head to the dark expanse in front of her.

She looked toward the general direction of the cabins. At least she thought it was the right direction. She was turned around now that everything was inky dark except for the porch above. Everyone else had disappeared. "No idea."

He took a few steps and stood next to her. "The cabins are down there." He pointed through the trees to a faint glow. "Follow this path, two hundred yards that way. And watch out for deer. They like to come out when it rains." He turned and headed up the path away from the porch in the opposite direction. "I'm sure I'll see you around."

"Thanks," Jenna called.

He didn't answer.

She started down the sandy trail. The rain was still light, making a chorus of drips and drops on the branches around her. She reached up and pushed her hood back, letting the warm rain hit her face and hair, and followed the glow through the trees.

eleven

Betsy

Betsy was in the kitchen cleaning up from the girls' dinner when Ty came in that evening, a little earlier than usual. The girls were upstairs in the empty room playing with My Little Ponys. He kicked his boots off on the porch, then crossed the kitchen to kiss her cheek. "How'd the afternoon go?" He reached into the fridge for the pitcher of tea.

"Good, I think." She wiped the last of the spaghetti sauce from the table. "They explored the house, I took them to see the hens, then Anna Beth brought by some toys, thank goodness. They brought a couple things with them, but I don't have much here for them to play with."

"They don't need much, right? We live on a farm. There's plenty for them to do outside."

"I guess so. That's what I'm hoping anyway."

Ty drained his glass and nodded. "They'll be fine. The hens and cows should keep them occupied. Just make sure to keep them out of the way during milkings. Don't want anyone to be trampled." He set his glass in the kitchen sink. "I need a shower."

"I'll walk up with you. I closed the other doors upstairs, but Walsh seems to be pretty industrious. I found her standing on the counter in the bathroom earlier, eating toothpaste."

Ty laughed and rubbed his hand over his face. "This is going to be interesting."

Upstairs, he poked his head in the girls' room. Addie was still busy with the ponies, making them "talk" to each other. Something about a parade and wearing crowns and high heels. Walsh was lying across both pillows at the top of the bed, already fast asleep, her dark hair covering half her face.

"The little one's wiped out," Ty whispered. He backed away from the door and headed for their bedroom.

"You don't want to say good night to Addie?" Betsy whispered.

He shook his head. "I'll catch her tomorrow." He crossed into their room and closed the door behind him.

Part of her wanted to follow him in there, protected behind the closed door, but she turned back to the girls. "Let's get you kiddos ready for bed."

"Can I sleep with the ponies?" Addie asked quietly.

"Sure. We can tuck them in right next to you and Walsh."

"Are we both sleeping in this?" She gestured to the double bed.

Betsy nodded. "Is that okay? I don't have two beds for you."

Addie scratched her chin and looked at Walsh. "I think that's a good idea."

Betsy picked up a limp Walsh and carried her into the bathroom with Addie close on her heels. Addie showed Betsy where she'd lined up their toothbrushes on the bathroom counter, then reminded her that they both had to use the potty before bed. Betsy brushed Walsh's teeth as well as she could, then helped her sit on the toilet. The child barely woke up, her head drooping to one side, her thumb lodged in her mouth.

Back in the bedroom, Betsy folded down the blanket and laid Walsh on one side of the bed. Addie climbed up into the other. She nestled down in the bed and pulled the blanket up to her shoulders, her stuffed elephant under her chin.

"Are you going to be okay in here?" Betsy asked. At this point, she was fairly certain a hurricane wouldn't wake Walsh, but Addie seemed almost too calm. "It must feel strange not to be in your own bed. If you need me, I'll be right downstairs."

"Where do you sleep?" Addie asked.

"In that room right across the hall." She pointed to her closed bedroom door.

Addie nodded and turned onto her side, facing Walsh. When she closed her eyes, Betsy stood, not sure of the right thing to do. She turned off the lamp next to the bed.

"Don't worry," Addie said in the dark. "I'll take care of Walsh."

Betsy stood in the doorway a moment before she pulled the door closed behind her. Then she opened it back up a couple of inches. Wouldn't hurt to let in a little light.

Betsy and Ty waited until they were in bed before they talked about the day. It was always like that—they might spend two hours together downstairs, looking for something to watch on TV or sitting on the back porch, but if they had something important to discuss, their unwritten rule was to wait until they were in bed before bringing it up. It was as if the darkness softened the hard edges, blurring any anger, frustration, or annoyance until it was easier to manage, easier to pull out into the open.

Betsy slipped between the cool sheets while Ty was still in the bathroom. The lights were off, but the moon was bright, and it filtered through the windows, the curtains casting thin shadows across the floor and bed.

"So, we're parents for the next two weeks," Ty said as he climbed into bed. "I always thought we'd be here, but not like this." He stretched and yawned. "How are we supposed to know what to do? What if one of them gets sick? Or baths—how does that work?"

"We'll figure it out. I do know a little bit about kids." She smiled. "And you probably know more than you think."

"I doubt that. My only experience with kids was the one time I babysat a neighbor's nephew while she went to work. The kid jumped out his bedroom window and ran to a friend's house four streets away while he was supposed to be napping."

"You never told me that story."

"Why would I? Doesn't sound too good, having a kid escape on my watch."

Shadows darted and danced across the ceiling as the fan swirled. Ty shifted his leg so it pressed against Betsy's. She could feel his gaze on her cheek, but she didn't turn her head.

"Maybe this is our chance to see if we have what it takes to be parents." She gave a little laugh, but her throat felt funny. Too tight.

Ty rolled up onto his elbow, his face above hers. "I have no doubt—not even a hint of a doubt—that we have what it takes to be parents. We have buckets of it. Acres of it." He kissed her, then lay back again. "Anyway, the thing about having kids is that they usually start out as babies. It'll be a different ball game practicing with two kids raised by a single mother who works all the time. No telling what life is like for those three."

Betsy rolled to her side and punched her pillow into shape beneath her cheek. She thought of Addie and her fierce protection of her little sister. "The girls are fine."

Sometime during the night, Betsy awoke to an unfamiliar sniffling, then a small moan. It was quiet, muffled, but it was enough to bring her out of a dead sleep. She sat up in bed, flung the sheets away, and patted the bed until she found Ty's arm.

"Ty? Ty! Someone's—"

Then she remembered. They weren't alone in the house.

"Which one is it?" he mumbled.

"Go back to sleep. I'll check."

She tiptoed across the hall, her eyes adjusting to the darkness. Walsh's side of the bed was still and quiet, but as Betsy stood watching, unsure of what to do, another sniffle came from Addie's side. She knelt next to the bed and patted the small lump under the covers until she reached Addie's face, her damp cheeks. "Addie? What's wrong, honey?"

"I had a bad dream. A scary one."

"There's nothing to be scared of," she said, cringing as the words left her mouth. She had terrible night terrors as a child—much later than most kids had them. She still had them at nine, ten years old, old enough to remember the sheer terror and fear that accompanied those awful nights. Her parents always told her there was nothing to be scared of and that she should just go back to sleep, the worst words they could have said.

She tried again. "Tell me what scared you."

"It was Mommy. She was leaving. She was driving away in a big school bus."

"That must have been sad. But you know what? Your mommy isn't in a big school bus, and she's coming back very soon."

"And she'll bring me a treat?"

"That's what she said, isn't it? I bet she'll find you something wonderful."

Addie nodded, sniffled again. "Could you sleep with me? Just for a little bit?"

"I don't know if I—"

"Please? I'll be quiet and I won't move a muscle."

Betsy smiled in spite of herself. "Okay. But just for a little bit."

Addie scooted toward Walsh, leaving a space of about eight inches for Betsy to squeeze into. Betsy scooped the parade of My Little Ponys onto the floor, then stretched her legs out and pulled her grandmother's blanket up over herself. When she settled, the girls' scents filled her senses. Was it possible to get light-headed over the smell of sleeping children? She inhaled. It was sleep, a little sweat, lingering cinnamon from the snickerdoodles she'd given the girls after dinner, and something else she couldn't quite name.

Addie had been still a couple of minutes, not moving a muscle, just like she said, when Walsh grunted in her sleep and flopped over, one arm flinging against Addie. Addie giggled, then stopped. "Sorry."

"It's okay," Betsy whispered. "Did that hurt?"

"No. She does it all the time," Addie whispered back.

"Do you and Walsh sleep together at home?" Betsy remembered the girls being in separate bedrooms last summer.

"Sometimes. When Mommy has to work late, Walsh usually comes into my room after the babysitter puts her to bed."

"You take good care of Walsh, don't you?"

"I do."

She couldn't see Addie's face, but she could almost hear the smile.

❦

Betsy woke to Ty standing over her next to the bed. "Are you okay in here?" he whispered.

She tried to sit up, but Addie's arm had pinned her in place. In her sleep Addie had curled up next to Betsy's side. Walsh lay partially on top of Addie, her plump arm draped across her sister and onto Betsy's right shoulder. All three of them filled half of the double bed; the other half was empty.

"You're like a magnet," Ty whispered, grinning. "Look at them. They can't get close enough to you."

In the midst of that tangle of warm skin and sleepy breaths, dreams she'd packed away into a tiny space in her heart flooded back. She lifted Addie's arm and slithered out from underneath it inch by inch.

"You don't have to get up," Ty whispered as Betsy tried to free herself without disturbing the girls' sleep. "I just got up to go to the bathroom and saw you weren't in bed."

"It's okay. I can't . . ."

Addie whimpered as Betsy pulled herself free. "Aunt Betsy, please don't go."

"It's okay," Betsy whispered. "Uncle Ty is going to lie down with you for a few minutes." She turned to Ty. "Please stay with her."

She was already out in the hallway when Ty caught up to her. "Wait, where are you going?"

"Addie had a bad dream and needs someone to lie with her. Just please do it for me."

She closed her bedroom door and leaned against it, relishing the stillness of the air, the empty bed, the familiar, unchildlike scents of her space. She stretched out in bed—her side cool, Ty's side still warm—and put a hand over her thumping heart.

It's just two weeks.

Then guilt, like a heavy tide of truth, washed over her, soaking her spirit and her soul. It didn't tell her anything original. It just confirmed what she already knew: she'd make a terrible mother. Her own mother had been distant and distracted—how could Betsy possibly hope to make a good one?

The truth that had come to her inch by inch over the last two years now blazed with certainty. If Betsy had kids, she'd mess them up in a million small ways, and if God had a hand in it, and she figured He probably did, then He was doing the only natural thing a father would do—protect those kids. Protect them from her. It was the only thing that made sense.

twelve

Ty

Ty's internal alarm clock buzzed at four thirty as usual, even though he was still in Addie and Walsh's bed, nudged to the very edge by Addie's poky backbone. He pushed himself up on his elbow. Walsh was curled up next to her sister, both their faces relaxed in easy slumber.

He was used to sharing a bed, but not like this. Betsy and Ty often lay in bed together, legs and arms entwined, but when the light went out, they pulled apart, no skin touching. It had always been like that—no offense meant or taken, just two people who wanted to sleep free and undisturbed. These two girls knew nothing about that. For hours, they'd either slept on top of him, hung arms over his head, kneed him in the stomach, or dug toes into his legs. They were completely and blissfully unaware.

He crept into his bedroom, brushed his teeth in the dark, and pulled on blue jeans and a clean shirt. He grabbed socks and his belt and tiptoed to the door, the taste of coffee already on his tongue.

"Babe?" Betsy's whisper floated to him from the bed.

He turned and crept back to the bed. "Sorry. I tried to be quiet." She shifted and he sat on the edge of the mattress. Her sleepy warmth curled around him, poured into his bones. "You okay?"

"I'm good." She yawned. "Have you heard anything from the girls yet?"

"Not a peep. I just left their room and they didn't even move when I got up."

"You stayed the rest of the night?"

He nodded. "They had me in a vise grip."

She smiled and let out a small laugh, just a puff of air, really. But it was something.

"Were you okay last night? With the girls?"

"Yeah," she said with a shrug. "I was fine. Why?"

"You just seemed a little edgy."

"It was nothing," she said, as he knew she would. But then she inhaled and paused, as if thinking of the right words. She bit her bottom lip.

"What is it?" *Steady, Ty.*

She shook her head. "I think I'll make pancakes for breakfast. Think they'd like that?"

He hesitated, watched her face for . . . for what? It wasn't like she was depressed. Or angry. Or volatile. She was his Betsy. His sensitive, funny, private, and beautiful wife. What would he even be looking for?

He smiled. "They'll love it."

When Ty pulled open the barn gate, he was sixteen minutes late to the morning milking. The first round of forty were already in place in line, their udders plugged into the machines, the soft *whoosh* of milk filling the pumps and flowing into metal tanks. Such a beautiful sound, the sound of milk and money.

He walked through the line, checking tubes and attachments, pleased to find Walker had done a better job than usual. Maybe he was finally learning something.

"Wild night, Mr. Franklin?" Walker pushed the wide broom near Ty's feet.

"Watch yourself, kid." Carlos straightened up from underneath number 039. "That's your boss you're talking to."

"Right, I'm sorry. I didn't mean anything by it," Walker sputtered, his cheeks pink and awkward. He backed away and took the broom to the other side of the barn.

"But seriously," Carlos said. "You're never late. How wild was it?"

"As if I'd tell you anyway."

"Come on, man! Throw a boy a bone here."

Ty shook his head. "You need to take that up with Gloria." He reached over and adjusted a milk line, then ran his hand down the bristly back of lucky number 040.

"I'm in the doghouse." Carlos sat on a stool and pulled off his boot. Dumped it upside down and two pebbles fell out. He kicked them to the door of the barn. "I missed our anniversary a few days ago. She let me get all the way until ten o'clock that night before saying anything about it. Just kept her anger pent up all day. It's a wonder that woman doesn't implode with all the things she doesn't tell me."

Ty patted 040 once more, then strode to the back office to make a note to call the vet about a possible bruise on her hoof. He kicked at Carlos's foot as he passed by. "You need to take care of that, my friend. I heard Ollie's Meat-and-Three is having a buy-one-get-one-free night. Maybe you should take Gloria out for an apology dinner."

Carlos was still laughing when Ty reached the privacy of his office. He grabbed a notebook and pencil off the desk and sat on the couch, but he didn't open the notebook. Carlos's words had cut a little close. "Woman troubles," is what Carlos would call it, which was why Ty rarely confided anything real to him. His marriage, his life with Betsy, seemed too private, too covered in nerve endings to even talk about. But the idea of imploding under the pressure of things left unsaid—that touched something raw in him.

He'd had a girlfriend named Summer his first year at Auburn. It was the perfect name for her. She was perky and pink, with a light splatter of freckles across her nose. Always happy. If he did something nice for her—brought her a bunch of daisies he'd bought at Toomer's Drugs or waited for her after one of her classes in the Haley Center—she'd grin bigger than the moon, wrap her arms around him, and kiss him, front and center, unafraid of anything or anyone watching. If something got under her skin, she'd talk to him about it, work out the issue, then leave it behind. She wasn't the type to say, "Fine," when she meant anything but.

In the end they broke up but remained friendly, because things with her could never be anything but friendly, and he'd breathed a sigh of relief. It wasn't that he wanted someone dark or angry or hard to read, but something about Summer's open-faced honesty and the easy way she talked about her feelings and desires made him feel less like a man than he was comfortable with.

Ty heard the clang of number 026 kicking at the machine. She always got antsy at the end of her milking, ready to be released to the field.

"Time's up, Boss," Carlos called. Ty scratched out the note to call the vet and tossed the notebook back on his desk.

Out in the barn Carlos was halfway through unhooking the cows from the machines. Ty started at the far end of the line, releasing udders and dabbing on a thin coat of Bag Balm to prevent irritation.

When they finished the line, the cows shuffled into the field to graze for their breakfast. Walker opened the gate to allow the next forty into the milking parlor, then he, Carlos, and Ty went through the line, dipping the udders into antiseptic, hooking them into the milking machines, and checking each cow for potential problems.

While they waited the few minutes it took to milk the group, Carlos poured a cup from the Mr. Coffee sitting on top of a plastic barrel and leaned against the wall next to Ty. "So, Ollie's. Think that'd work?"

Ty glanced sideways at Carlos, judging his seriousness. "Man, no. Don't take her there. I was kidding."

"Why? They have a great catfish plate."

"Sure they do. But do you really want to take Gloria to a backwoods diner for an anniversary dinner? When you're already trying to climb out of a hole?" Ty shook his head.

"Well, what do you suggest, Mr. Romance? There's not much else around here."

"We're twenty miles from beachside dining at sunset. Start there."

Carlos gulped his coffee and grunted. "This stuff is terrible." He tossed the half-empty cup into the trash barrel, but it bounced and sent coffee up the wall. He muttered a string of obscenities under his breath and grabbed a rag to wipe down the wall. "You been married, what, ten years?"

"Eight." Ty leaned over and felt number 080's udder. Just another minute or so to go.

"I've been married fif—sixteen years. How'd you get so smart about women?"

"Good luck, I guess."

"Nah. You probably just give Betsy whatever she wants." When Ty didn't correct him, Carlos chuckled. "So, what Betsy wants, she gets. I see who wears the pants around here."

Ty looked at his friend. "You're an idiot." He grabbed the damp rag and wiped some coffee Carlos had missed.

When the second group of forty was done, they began the process over again and Ty took a knee next to number 096. Smack in the middle of the line. He knew it'd get Carlos all messed up—he liked to go through the line in order—but Ty didn't care. Number 096 was Rosie, and Rosie was special.

As he cleaned her and hooked her up, he thought back to his junior year at Auburn when he first saw Betsy. She jogged by the ag field every day in her little running shorts and tank tops, her hair bouncing. Even from the barn, he could hear her friend's constant chatter, but Betsy was usually quiet, her eyes glued to him. He could feel her gaze without even turning his head. It sank into his shoulders, the back of his neck.

When they started to see each other officially—no longer separated by a wood and metal cattle fence—he discovered that different was good. While she wasn't the exact opposite of his old girlfriend Summer—she wasn't gloomy or irritable or depressed— she wasn't a spoonful of sugar either. When she'd get worked up about something, she'd occasionally vent to him about it. She'd rant and rave and he'd watch, pleased to see a real woman let herself feel her anger. But most times she'd clam up, and he had to use superhuman powers to decipher her mood.

That generous dose of mystery, the unknown depths, made

him feel like a man. Like it was his job to spend his days plumbing those depths, deciphering her particular brand of hieroglyphics.

He'd still choose her now. Of course he would. Even if he suspected that, as with Carlos's wife, there were volumes of words Betsy was leaving unsaid.

thirteen

Jenna

Though Halcyon focused on freedom and a lack of structure, Jenna slipped into a routine in her first couple of days. Breakfast, camera, woods. No yoga. Then the same thing after lunch. And she did it all alone. Some of the other artists teamed up and worked together—painting, drawing, building—but the thought of forced politeness, of awkward camaraderie, of other people asking her opinion and waiting for her deep, philosophical answers made her squirm with discomfort. No thanks.

She did, however, wish she had a little more mentor input. Other artists meandered around the preserve with their mentors deep in conversation or with their heads together, looking over the day's work. With her mentor mostly MIA, she couldn't help feeling left out.

It was late afternoon on the third day. She'd called Betsy that morning from the cabin so she wouldn't have to worry about the call dropping. When she'd again apologized for the retreat, for the kids, for her and Ty's messed-up plans, Betsy had come close to scolding her.

"Jenna, you're there. You made the decision and you need to stick with it. It'll all be wasted if you don't actually *do* something while you're there." Funny that she echoed the exact words running through Jenna's mind. "Let it go. We are fine. The girls are completely fine. Don't worry about us. Just . . . go do your thing. We'll all be here when you finish up."

Jenna had exhaled, long and deep. Betsy was right. She'd made the decision, and she needed to trust her sister—and her own choices. Right or wrong, she needed to stick by them. She thought of Delores's words about airplane oxygen masks the night she found out she'd gotten into Halcyon: *"Sometimes you have to take care of yourself so you can take care of your kids."*

Buck up. Do what you came to do.

With the reassurance that her children were well taken care of, she longed to sink back into her creativity, to find it waiting for her, ready for her eye and fingers and steady breathing, but every single photo she'd managed to take was worthless. She couldn't put her finger on it, but something was off in all of them. There was no focus, no purpose.

Before kids, her photography focus had usually been people. Bodies at rest, bodies in motion. When she picked up her camera after having Addie and Walsh—on her excursions with Max to the Botanical Gardens or Centennial Park, or just playing with the kids in the front yard—she tried to broaden her focus into the natural world, but her favorite subjects were always people and their expressions. Desires and fears splashed across their faces.

At Halcyon, alone for the first time in she didn't know how long, she had no idea where to start. Trees, moss, sand. Murky

ponds, skittery birds, strange animals—was that what she was supposed to be capturing? That's all there was out in this "pristine and
protected" nature preserve, as the flyer had said. That and heat.

Her phone, tucked into her camera bag, had buzzed with a
text message earlier in the day. She'd brought it with her in case
of an emergency—either hers or Betsy's—but the service on it had
been next to nothing every time she checked it. The buzz—the first
non-nature sound she'd heard since leaving the dining hall after
breakfast—startled her. She unzipped the bag and checked her
phone, thinking of everyone it might be—Betsy, Max, maybe even
Delores checking in on her. But she didn't recognize the number.

> Missed you this morning. The guy behind the counter—the
> really chatty one—told me you'd skipped off to the beach.
> Lucky girl. He gave me your cell number. Hope it's okay
> I used it. Also hope you're having fun and relaxing. You
> deserve it. Sam

She thought of Sam arriving that morning at Full Cup, searching the line for her as he always did. The tall black coffee he probably
ordered for her before Mario gave him the news that she wouldn't
be joining him for their nondate.

It wasn't like she'd had any way to let him know she hadn't just
"skipped off to the beach," as Mario put it. They hadn't exchanged
phone numbers, their only contact being the ten minutes a day
when she could partially let her guard down. Even with Sam
though, she never could let it down all the way. She hadn't wanted
to hurry his inevitable realization that she was too much, too risky,
too . . . something.

She tried to send a text back—Thanks for checking in. Not

having too much fun yet, but better than making drinks for Mrs. Rich.—but service had dropped back to zilch. It was probably part of the master plan of Halcyon: get a bunch of artists out in the middle of nowhere, cut off their lines to the outside world, and see what happened. So far for Jenna, what had happened was a whole lot of nothing.

Occasionally, she held her camera out and scrolled through the images. Halcyon provided a large-format Epson printer, and she had the option to print any images she wanted and discuss them with the group during the evening workshop. So far she'd avoided that, not ready for complete strangers to talk about her work like they could better explain what she was trying to say with it. And what was it with everyone here going on and on about what they were trying to *say* with their work?

Why do I care? She knelt to the ground, one knee pressing into wet dirt and soaking her jeans. *It's their art. Who am I to do anything but appreciate it?* At least they were making progress. She, on the other hand, was at least half a mile away from the retreat center, alone except for two hawks circling above and huge fox squirrels rustling in the trees. The beauty around her was so new, so savage and raw, but she couldn't capture it in a way that felt real. She was spinning her wheels, missing her girls, and waiting for inspiration to strike. And sweating.

Enough. She zipped her camera into its bag and headed back for dinner.

⌒

The dining hall was abuzz with chatter when she entered. Artists and mentors mixed together at tables in the long room and the screened porch at the front. By now she was used to not having her own mentor at her elbow like the others. It was fine. Everyone already had food on trays, so Jenna hurried to the buffet tables at the back and picked up a tray, filling a plate with grilled shrimp, wild rice, roasted asparagus, and salad. At the end of the line was a platter of brownies. It wasn't chocolate bread pudding, but it would work.

Standing alone with a tray of food and a glass of iced tea in her hand, she felt like she was in high school all over again. All the cool kids were already seated at tables, talking, smiles on their faces. She found an empty spot at the end of a table and set down her tray. Before she could even sit, Casey appeared before her. Clad in different but equally as strappy and trendy yoga gear, she sat on the bench across from Jenna. "How are things going for you?"

"Good, they're good." Jenna arranged her food and drink and sat. "I mean, I'm still trying to find my footing, I guess." She took a sip of tea.

Casey nodded. "I totally get it. It can take a little while to get used to the quiet and lack of distractions. We're so wired for noise and activity that when life does slow down, we can feel a bit . . . disoriented. Does that sound about right?"

Jenna had paused with her glass in her hand. "Sure. Yeah. That's it."

"Mm-hmm," Casey murmured, her chin in her hand, then sat up a little straighter. "I've noticed you haven't said much in the workshops at night. We'd love to hear how you're feeling, what you've learned so far. You may think it's nothing, but even small steps are forward progress, you know?" She squinted and nodded, a perfect combination of pretension and encouragement on her face. Jenna wondered if she practiced that look in the mirror.

Just over Casey's right shoulder, Jenna saw Gregory at a table with Yannick, the mentor she had seen hunched over a large sketch pad and a box of charcoals in various parts of the preserve. They were deep in conversation, but as Jenna watched, Gregory glanced her way. He paused for a brief moment, then turned his attention back to Yannick.

"Right, I know." Jenna fiddled with her napkin. "I may. It's just . . . Sometimes things make more sense in my head without me trying to mess it all up with words. Does that make sense?"

"Sure, absolutely. Just remember, we're all in the same boat here. We're all trying to connect to the passion, to that internal drive." She stood and adjusted her slim black tank. "I look forward to hearing your insights whenever you're ready."

Then she glided away, her footsteps quiet and graceful. Jenna had met people like Casey before, back in Wyoming when she taught yoga at the colony, commune, whatever Betsy had called it. It was a place for creative, enlightened people to feel at home. They preached all the same things—connect to your passion, find your inner light, blah blah blah. While she'd loved being there—far from her family's disapproval and lack of understanding—she always felt like she was standing on the rim of something deep, peering over the edge but unable to jump in like everyone else. Even as she taught yoga and heard herself say the words that went along with it, she felt removed, set apart from the hive-mind. She only jumped in deep when she was alone with her camera.

After dinner, everyone gathered on the porch with their work of the day. Canvases, notebooks, sketch books, and laptops filled the space not occupied by artists and their mugs of tea or glasses of wine. She found a seat close to the door, comforted by the nearby escape route. As everyone pulled out their work, Jenna stared down at her camera. She wanted to be assured by its presence, this little black box that served as her ticket to spend a couple weeks away with these people, these true artists, when she felt like a fake.

Max had said she had rare, untaught talent. Put the girl in the wild, he must have thought, and she'll blossom into the photographer, the artist, she's meant to be. But instead, the camera had done nothing but block her out. Fend off her attempts to create something worthy, as if her fingers on its buttons and dials were clumsy blocks of wood.

They went around in a circle, each person speaking of his or her experience of the day, how it shaped the art they put before the group. As a woman a few feet away from her wiped away tears, explaining how she had broken through her month-long writer's block and cranked out fifty pages of her Great American Novel, Jenna stood and opened the screened door a few inches, just enough to squeeze through but not enough to make it creak. After closing it behind her, she exhaled and descended into the comforting dark.

The night air was thick, saturated with scents of pine needles and damp earth. By now Jenna could make her way through the dark to the cabins. She'd left the lamp on in her own cabin, and as she trudged down the path, the glow from her front window drew her like a magnet.

She'd said to Casey on the first night that Halcyon seemed like a campground, and she wasn't too far off in that initial estimation. Everything was built from logs and thick planks of wood, but the buildings were somehow sleek too, as if the place had been built for discerning adults as well as kids. The cabin—hers, at least— was small and tidy, outfitted in smooth, fragrant cypress and cedar. Downstairs was a mini-kitchen and bathroom, while the loft upstairs contained a twin bed, comfortable side chair, and small dresser. Just the basics, but all she really needed.

Inside, she set her camera on the tiny kitchen counter. What she wanted to do was take it outside and throw it into the lake. Instead, she climbed the ladder to the bedroom and lay down across the bed's patchwork quilt. Having just been here a handful of days, she was surprised by how at home she felt in the small space. She could stay here a while, holed up in the woods, leaving only for food and dips into the lake. But her camera, sitting alone on the counter downstairs, would beckon. It wouldn't leave her alone for long, that much she knew.

She exhaled and willed the tension to leak out of her shoulders and neck. She held her hand up and prodded the space between her thumb and forefinger where a sandspur had pricked her earlier in the day. It was still sore, the prick a tiny red dot on her skin.

She turned her hands this way and that in the dim light. Small palms, short fingers. She had her mother's hands. Even her fingernails were shaped the same—thin ovals with deep crescents. How she knew that, she wasn't sure. It wasn't like she and her mom had ever bonded over manicures. They hadn't bonded over anything.

Jenna pressed her fingertips to her forehead, remembering how the phone call six years ago had come so out of the blue. She'd only spoken to her mother a handful of times since she'd left Tuscaloosa and moved away, first to Wyoming, then to Asheville, North Carolina. Each time they spoke it was clear they didn't agree on what Jenna should be doing with her life. That morning though, it was Betsy on the phone, relaying bits of information in staccato bites. Their mom, the totaled car off the edge of Highway 31, the sheet of stationery on her desk at home with the meager beginnings of a letter. *Dear Jenna, I wish . . .*

Jenna pointed and flexed her toes, then pointed them again to stretch her legs as far as they'd go. She had the letter. Not with her now, but it lived in the bottom drawer of her bedside table at home. She hadn't looked at it again since the day her dad said she should keep it, but those four words were imprinted on her brain.

She pulled off her shoes and dropped them to the floor with a satisfying *plunk*. Sometimes she liked to imagine what the rest of the note from her mom would have said, had she taken the time to finish it before she left for work that day. Before she lost control of her car when another driver crossed the median into her lane.

Dear Jenna, I wish things between us had been different.

Dear Jenna, I wish I could tell you how much I love you.

Dear Jenna, I wish you knew how extraordinary you are.

But Jenna was a realist, not that kind of dreamer. More likely it was along the lines of *Dear Jenna, I wish you were more like your sister.*

fourteen

Betsy

After that first day, when she ended the evening in bed, emotionally depleted and physically spent, Betsy roused her sea legs. Up before the girls in the mornings, she made breakfast, helped them get dressed, and took them outside. Inside the house, their sweet routines and innocent sleepy movements pulled at her loose threads, threatening to unravel all her determination. Outside was easier. Fresh air, space to breathe.

Walsh loved the hens and eggs the best, having overcome her initial fear of the shadowed henhouse, but Addie loved tending to the cows. With Ty's supervision she'd choose one and brush her with the stiff-bristled brushes he kept in a wooden box by the barn door. After a thorough brushing, Addie fed her as many apple cores, banana peels, and chunks of stale bread as she could before Ty caught on.

"Why can't I give them treats?" Addie asked one day after Ty gently pried the bag of bread from her hands. "Treats make

126

everyone happy, even cows. You should know that, Uncle Ty. You're a cow farmer."

Ty glanced up at Betsy and bit back a laugh. "Yes, I am. And you're right, they do like treats. But we can't spoil them. They'll get sick like kids who eat too much candy." He patted the cow on the rump and steered Addie out of the barn.

Both girls loved to run through the fields, darting between the silent cows chewing grass and clover. When they tired of running and dodging steaming patties, Carlos or one of the other guys would hoist them up onto a tractor and take them for a short ride. Addie laughed every time she caught sight of the honey wagon out in the fields. Ty had painted a huge bee on its side in white and black paint, leading Addie to think the long, tube-shaped container was full of honey.

Addie stopped laughing when she realized what it actually carried, even more so when she learned that what was inside the honey wagon went straight back into the fields, helping to grow the grass and grain that fed the cows. Ty tried to explain the importance of the cycle of nutrition, but she wrinkled her nose and gave the honey wagon a wide berth.

Jenna finally called again on Wednesday, just as Betsy was wiping the girls' faces with a damp washcloth and getting them into pajamas. Betsy gave the phone to Addie so she could say good night, but the call dropped just after Addie said hello.

"Mommy, I'm here, I'm here," Addie repeated, pressing the phone tighter to her ear and shouting.

Betsy pried the phone out of her hands and tried calling Jenna back. It went straight to voice mail. Addie stormed off and threw herself onto the bed, a rare flash of anger. Walsh's eyes grew big and her bottom lip trembled. Jenna texted later and said cell service was spotty and that she'd try again when she could. Betsy tried to explain about phone coverage and dropped calls, but both girls went to bed with tears in their eyes.

The next night Jenna called again, but it was after nine o'clock. The girls had been in bed for almost two hours.

"Sorry to call so late," Jenna said. "I've had no service bars on my phone all day. This is the first time the call has gone through."

"It's okay. I wish you'd been able to call earlier though. The girls are dying to talk to you. I'd get them up, but . . ."

"No, no, don't worry about it. I'll call again soon. They're doing okay?"

"They miss you, of course, but they seem to be pretty happy. What about you? Have you been able to take a lot of pictures?"

Jenna paused before speaking. "Yeah, I have. I'm out all day with my camera, and there's plenty of time for whatever I want to do. The schedule is super loose. And it's beautiful here. Palm trees, Spanish moss, ponds with tree frogs and geckos. Everything is lush and overgrown."

"That sounds beautiful." Betsy pulled back the quilt on her bed and climbed in. Ty was still downstairs catching the last few minutes of a Braves game.

"Yeah . . . ," she began. Then she was quiet for a moment.

"Everything okay?"

"I've just been thinking about Mom a little. Do you remember when we used to drag our blankets under your bed and hide?"

Betsy smiled. "Sure. That's where we kept our stash of chocolate pudding cups."

"That's right. Mom never understood why they disappeared so fast. I guess she never noticed the empty containers in your garbage can. You used to tell me stories of what it would be like to be a grown-up, all the jobs we could have. Whatever we wanted to be. You were going to work at Prescott Branding. Do you remember that? All those summer internships practically guaranteed you a job there."

Betsy stretched her legs under the sheet. "Oh, I remember." Her onetime goal of being an account exec at Birmingham's top ad agency seemed like a lifetime ago. "You always wanted to be an actress and a vet and a photographer."

"And you told me I could do it if that's what I wanted."

"Yep. It's probably the same thing you tell Addie and Walsh. That they can be whatever they want to be."

"That's what we tell them, but . . . we can't just *be* anything, you know? Sometimes it just doesn't work out. I mean, look at you. You were supposed to be cranking out genius ad campaigns for big companies, but instead you married a farmer and live with a bunch of cows. No offense, it's just not what you planned way back when." Jenna took a breath. "All that time, we thought we really could just go and do and be and things would fall into place, but it doesn't always happen that way."

Betsy stilled her legs. She could have said a million things about what had and hadn't worked out in her own life, but she focused on her sister instead. "What's going on with you, Jenna?"

"Nothing. Just that . . . we can't always get what we want." She paused. "Sorry, that's stupid. And I've always hated that song."

"What do you want that you're not getting?" Even as she said the words, she imagined a long, winding list of things Jenna probably wanted. Or maybe Betsy was just thinking of her own list, the one that swirled around her head, out the window, and up into the still night air.

"I just . . . I wonder if maybe coming here was a bad idea. I've already given up my photography. Why try to force it to work again?" She paused, then her next words were soft. "What do you think Mom would say about me being here?"

Betsy closed her eyes and spoke carefully. "I think she would be glad you're pursuing something you feel passionate about."

"Really? That's what I was trying to do with Wyoming. And even before that with the program in Seattle. What makes you think she'd feel any different this time?" Jenna laughed, small and tired. "She said I'd either end up on drugs or pregnant. She always did have such high hopes for me."

"Oh, Jenna, she didn't mean . . ." But she stopped. That had been one of the things about their mother that sometimes hurt the most—she always said exactly what she meant and she never minced words. And in Jenna's case, her words cut deep.

"No, it's okay. It's fine. I mean, one of her worst fears for me has already happened. I'm not planning on doing any drugs, so what else can go wrong?"

Betsy sat up and leaned forward, as if her sister were sitting right in front of her. "Look, what Mom would think about you going to Halcyon doesn't matter anymore. You're older now and . . . I don't think going there was a bad idea. Last weekend you were so excited about it. It's got to be hard to get yourself back into that . . . creative place, but it's in you. I know it is. Just give it time." What was she saying? Trying to convince her sister to try to be *more* artistic, *more* free-spirited? She was glad Ty wasn't there to overhear her.

"Mom definitely wouldn't want you to give up, regardless of what she thought about you going there in the first place."

Silence. "Maybe you're right." Jenna sighed. "I'm sorry. It's late. I'm probably keeping you and Ty from going to bed. Have the girls been waking up early?"

There she went again. When conversation got too personal or raw, Jenna always changed it to something easier. But then again, so did Betsy. It was better than focusing on the things that hurt. She sighed. "Not too early. Walsh usually wakes up first, then she wakes Addie up with her singing. Then they both come downstairs."

Jenna chuckled. "Are you and Ty surviving?"

"We're fine. The girls will be happy to see you though when you get back."

Jenna inhaled, then exhaled into the phone. "I'll let you go then. I'll call again soon."

"You sure you're okay? If there's anything else bothering you . . . I'm here if you want to talk again." It used to be so normal, so natural—confiding in each other. At one time, they were the keepers of each other's secrets.

"I know. Thanks. I'm good."

Then she was gone. Betsy tossed her phone down and lay back against the pillows.

She had been ten when she spotted a lofty, regal bed in a magazine and asked her parents to prop her bed up on casters. When they said no, she begged. Finally, one Saturday afternoon before her dad had to be downtown to conduct his orchestra, he brought in a box of casters. Clothed in his tuxedo and gold cufflinks, he slithered under her bed and lifted each corner, one leg at a time, and slid the casters into place. When he finished, he was covered in a thin scrum of dust and her bed was six inches higher. She beamed; he searched for a lint roller.

From that afternoon on, the pocket of space under Betsy's bed became her and Jenna's refuge from the world. They colored, listened to the radio, ate their pudding, and told wild, far-fetched stories filled with mermaids, dragons, dark enemies, and handsome princes. Good always won, evil was always defeated, and dreams always came true.

Later, that private sanctuary was where Jenna first revealed her love of photography to Betsy. Betsy already knew Jenna was artistic—she could draw anything, painted with quick and sure brushstrokes, and sometimes stayed after school to help clean paintbrushes in the art room. But until then, Betsy hadn't known how much Jenna loved to take pictures.

One particular day in seventh grade, Jenna slid under the bed and told Betsy in angry whispers how she'd swiped their mom's Nikon—the one she used to take photos of cancer patients for her inspiration wall—and taken black-and-white photos of trees and leaves to use in a presentation about her favorite artist.

"That's awesome, Jenna," Betsy had said. "Mom will kill you when she finds out you used her camera, but I bet your pictures look great."

"They did, but it didn't matter. Mrs. Lipscomb gave me a D because I didn't use the right kind of poster board for the presentation. But it wasn't my fault! By the time I got Mom to take me to buy some, all they had left was plain yellow. Mrs. Lipscomb wanted white trifold."

"That's it? She gave you a D for yellow poster paper?"

Jenna sighed. "I was supposed to use a certain kind of tape on the photos. I used the Scotch tape from the kitchen drawer."

Betsy handed Jenna a plastic spoon and a cup of pudding. "I'm sorry." At fifteen, Betsy already knew chocolate could fix most problems. Or at least dull their sting.

Jenna peeled the lid off and licked the pudding from the back of the shiny foil. "She also said Ansel Adams wasn't a real artist. Or at least not the kind we were supposed to focus on. She said if I wanted to study photography, I could wait until high school and take a photography class."

Betsy scraped her spoon around the edge of the cup to get the last bit. "Well, of course you'll do that. You'll probably be a better photographer than the teacher. You're good, Jenna. Just keep practicing. Maybe Mom will let you use her camera more."

Jenna shook her head. "I dropped it when Mr. Barton's dog barked behind me. Cracked the lens."

Betsy closed her eyes. That was always the way it was for Jenna. She had good intentions, but somehow she always screwed up the follow-through. So much for dreams coming true.

Now, lying in bed in her grown-up house far away from that secret shelter, Betsy wondered about all those stories she used to tell Jenna. Were they really just lies? Real life held plenty of good and evil, battles and rescues. And if you worked hard, you really could be anything you wanted to be. Right?

Maybe it was only partly true.

Some dreams were too far-fetched—the short kid who wanted to slam dunk, the chubby girl who had a crush on the prom king, the painfully shy kid who wanted the lead in the school play. Then there was the young girl who wanted to take pictures, but only heard that she hadn't chosen the right dream and that her methods of achieving her goal were wrong. Betsy's first and deepest instinct was to tell that young girl to keep pressing ahead, to fling aside doubts and naysayers, to pursue her desire with a single-minded focus.

But what about Betsy's dream? She'd pressed and prayed and

pursued as much as she was able, but nothing had happened. At what point did pursuing the dream become futile? Was there a point at which the dreamer should just let it go? But what were you supposed to do when the dream felt fundamental to the fabric of your being, of your soul? What then?

fifteen

Betsy

"Can we go see the cows?" Addie asked the next morning as Walsh darted out of her chair to follow Etta into the den. "Do you think they're awake yet?"

"They've been awake for hours." Betsy had just poured her second cup of coffee. "We can go see them when they have their breakfast, but I have an idea. Let's get dressed and go see the hens first. We can see how many eggs they have for us, then we'll check on the cows."

Addie's eyes grew wide. "Will there be any baby chicks?"

"Probably not today. But you can help me pull the eggs out of the nests."

Walsh ran around the backyard while Addie tiptoed into the henhouse. She was hesitant at first, but curiosity and the anticipation of speckled eggs got the best of her. Betsy showed her how to feel underneath the hens for the eggs and place them in the basket. Addie sprinkled a scoop of chicken feed on the ground, then darted

135

out the gate to join Walsh on the swing. Betsy gave the hens one more scoop and locked the gate behind her.

By the time they made it to the barn, most of the cows had been turned out to pasture. A few, those with any hint of ailment or problem, were still in the side pen for a closer inspection. Ty looked up when they entered the barn. "Well, good morning," he said to the girls. He drew close to Betsy, snaked his arm around her waist. "And good morning to you," he whispered.

Addie pulled on Betsy's hand. "Aunt Betsy, did you know Uncle Ty snores?"

"Hey now." Ty squatted down and looked in her face. "That's supposed to be our secret."

Betsy laughed. "It's not a secret, Addie. I think the neighbors down the street know Uncle Ty snores. The cows know for sure."

Addie giggled.

"What's on tap for today?" he asked as Addie stepped away from him and Betsy to explore the barn. Walsh ran headlong into a bench, tumbled over it, then righted herself and knelt down to peer at something on the floor.

"You're looking at it. The girls wanted to see the cows. Addie keeps saying she wants to ride one."

Addie whipped her head back around to Ty when she heard that.

"Hmm," he said, scratching his chin. "I have to go see Roger about a part for the tractor, but Walker owes me, so I think he's your guy."

Walker's head popped up from the other side of a cow lingering in the milking line. "What's that, Mr. Franklin?"

"I need someone to show these little ladies around the barn. Since you ditched me early last Saturday to visit your girlfriend, you can help out for a little while longer today, right?"

In addition to his weekday work, Walker also helped with the milking and cleaning on Saturday mornings. His daddy wanted him to work as much as possible while he was out of school for the summer.

"Oh, uh, sure," Walker said, his Adam's apple bobbing. "I mean, I'm supposed to meet Erin . . ." He caught the look in Ty's eye. "But yeah, I can help."

Ty clapped his hands together. "Great. Why don't you take Addie and Walsh to see Rosie?"

Betsy smiled. Rosie was her favorite out of all 218 cows. Her face was kinder than the rest, if that was possible. Breeding attempts had so far been unsuccessful with her. Ty suspected she was sterile, but Betsy had high hopes for her.

Addie and Walsh followed Walker to the side pen. She turned to follow them, but Ty caught her arm. "How do the girls seem to you?"

Betsy shrugged. "I think they're okay. Neither of them has mentioned Jenna today."

Ty nodded, bit the inside of his cheek. "Two weeks is a long time to leave your kids."

Betsy inhaled, watching as Walker led the girls into the pen where Rosie stood, munching grass.

"I bet she misses them," he said. "I hope she misses them. I mean, look at them."

Addie stood in front of Rosie's face, rubbing the top of the cow's nose. Then Walsh held her face against Rosie's huge fuzzy cheek. She closed her eyes and smiled. Rosie kept munching, unconcerned about the two small people petting her.

Betsy nodded. After all these years, she could still read her sister's face like fingers on Braille. And what she'd seen on Jenna's face when she left the previous week spanned the entire spectrum of emotion, from the delight of sudden freedom to the terror of someone letting go. Which of those faces came closest to the actual truth?

∽

"We can't eat these."

"You can't eat grapes?" Betsy had just set a lunch of grilled cheese and grapes in front of the girls on the back porch. "Why not?" Had Jenna forgotten to tell her the girls were allergic to grapes?

"Mommy always cuts our grapes in half. If we eat them like this, they could get stuck in our throats and make us choke."

Of course. Betsy got a knife from the kitchen counter and returned to the porch. "Note to self: cut grapes in half," she said as she cut. "Got it."

Addie pulled Walsh's hand back when she tried to grab a grape as Betsy sliced them. "Careful," she said.

After lunch—during which thankfully she hadn't made any other mistakes—she left Addie on the porch love seat with a stack of Anna Beth's books while she tucked an already half-asleep Walsh into bed upstairs. When she returned, Addie was asleep too, as Betsy suspected. The girls had played hard all morning with every animal they could find, be it cow, cat, barn mouse, or annoyed hen.

As she straightened the kitchen, gathering cups and shoes, Ty returned from Roger's place. Betsy thought of the meager amount of food he sometimes kept in the barn office for days when he couldn't make it up to the house to eat lunch. It was nothing more than a few bags of chips. Maybe an apple. She deposited the cups in the sink and the shoes by the back door. After a quick check on Walsh upstairs, she ducked out the back door, a Tervis cup of iced tea in one hand and a pimento-cheese sandwich in a brown paper bag.

She spotted him out by the back fence shielding his eyes from the bright sun. The tractor moved slowly out in the field, and three men stood close to it in a group, peering at the ground as if it were a crystal ball. As she drew closer, Ty turned and walked back into the barn from the other side, his stride purposeful and quick. She entered the doors and smiled. "Hi," she called. She crossed the floor and met him near his office.

He looked up and grinned. A sheen of sweat covered his top lip and brow. She reached up and brushed a few specks of grass out of his hair. His hair was still as thick and blond as it had been in college, except now he had patches of gray at his temples. She loved that gray as much as she loved the crease in his forehead.

"Whatcha got in that bag?" he asked.

She held it out to him. "I brought you a sandwich. And tea." She passed the glass to him and he drank half of it in two gulps.

"You're an angel. Thanks." He took the bag from her hand. "Whatever this is, it's much better than what I would have been eating."

"What's going on with the tractor?"

"Belt's worn out. It made it through spring planting, but we have to fix it before harvest when we're dodging storms. Speaking of, Roger's bringing some extra plywood when he brings the spare part for the tractor. I want to cover some of the upper windows of the barn."

"Already? There's not a storm out there, is there?" Betsy usually paid close attention to the weather reports, but in the chaos of the last couple of days, she'd forgotten to check. She'd never admit it to Ty, because big storms meant a possible loss of milk, but she always felt a rush of excitement when tropical storms rolled in. Hurricanes, not so much. But it was possible for a tropical storm to bring nothing but strong breezes, cooling rain, and an excuse for Betsy to hole up with a book in the front window. She was almost embarrassed by how much she liked them.

He shook his head. "Doesn't hurt to go ahead and have everything in place though. Things could get ugly later in the summer. The Gulf waters are heating up early."

Betsy peered at him, trying to detect the level of his nerves. The hurricane he went through with his grandfather years ago was always in the back of his mind, pushing him to do all he could to keep the farm safe. "Warm water isn't a good sign."

"Nope." He rubbed the back of his neck, then took another swig of tea. "The girls in the house?"

"They're both asleep. The morning wore them out."

He glanced back out the door of the barn.

"I'll let you get back to work then." She backed away, but he reached out and tugged her hand.

"Come here." He pulled her to him.

"What?" she asked, but she already knew. His eyes always gave him away.

"Seeing you out here earlier this morning, all I wanted to do was this, but we had those extra little eyes around." His lips met hers. A little salty, but warm and familiar. His hand went to the small of her back, pulling her hips toward his.

"Ty." She looked over his shoulder. Walker was just outside the barn, his fingers dancing across the screen of his iPhone. He was oblivious to anything except the message he was typing, but Carlos and the others could return any minute.

"Don't worry about them. They'll be out back until Roger gets here." He kissed her again, the prickles around his mouth bothering her, but only a little bit. "Right about now, I'm pretty glad we decided to put that couch in the office."

She pulled back and opened her eyes. "You aren't serious." One corner of his mouth pulled up. She thumped him on his chest. "You're crazy. No way."

"I'll be quick." His cheeks reddened when she smiled. "We can be fast. Discreet." He raised his eyebrows.

Betsy bit her lip. "I don't think so. I'd rather not shock the cows." She looked over his shoulder again. "Or Walker."

Ty kept his gaze on her, his mouth and eyes caught somewhere between hope and disappointment. Finally, he looked down at his boots, scuffed one on the ground. "Definitely wouldn't want to shock anyone. Maybe . . ." He took a breath.

"What?" She pulled close to him again, her stomach twisting into a tight ball of desire and embarrassment.

He shook his head, then kissed her cheek. "Nothing. I'll see you later."

Etta bounded into the barn and twined between Betsy's legs. Betsy reached down and scratched her head, then turned toward the door, Etta in step next to her.

"Betsy?" Ty called.

She turned to face him.

"Thanks for the lunch," he said after only the briefest hesitation.

Betsy had fallen in love with Ty's neck first. The back of it, to be specific. Then his forearms—thick, strong, blond hair fuzzing freckled skin. She didn't even know his name at first. He was just a guy—an ag student, she later learned—feeding cows in a field she jogged past. That was back when she jogged for exercise, and even then it was really just a chance to hang out with friends and hope they'd pass the football team on its way to practice.

Farmers weren't her thing—the only ones she knew of in Birmingham were at the Pepper Place Farmer's Market on Saturday mornings—but then she saw him, his arm outstretched, feeding an enormous bull from the palm of his hand. The skin on the back of his neck was tan and soft-looking. As her friend babbled about her date the night before, Betsy had to fight the urge to hop the fence and lay her cheek against that soft skin.

They passed the field, but she turned around for one last look. His calm, confident stance, the way his hat sat on his blond hair, the way his jeans sat on his hips. She imagined a life with him before they'd even said hello. They married a year and a half later, the summer after they graduated, and spent the next two years working hard on the farm.

The days were long, sweaty, and demanding—getting the fields ready for their first full harvest in two years, organizing the cattle, meeting the farmhands who'd worked for his grandfather, and deciding who else they needed to bring on. Betsy put her marketing degree to work and got Franklin Dairy on social media, joined various dairy associations in the Southeast, and began talks with stores and markets across the area. She quickly fell in love with the farm and the ways they could contribute to the life of the community and the region as a whole.

But the physical work was unending—hammering, hoeing, seeding, herding, feeding. She worked as hard as Ty did and used muscles she didn't know she had. Occasionally she wondered what in the world she'd gotten herself into, but then he'd cross the barn to kiss her, his lips salty and sweet. He'd catch her eye from across the room and her legs would melt. He'd find her hand under the table at a dairy association meeting and she'd remember why she chose him and this life. *Their* life.

At the end of each day, they collapsed in bed, exhausted but happy. Happy with the farm, with each other, with the years that lay ahead and all the life that would fill those years. Back then, she wouldn't have been so shocked by what Ty had suggested in the barn. The thought of making love there, especially with the other guys so close at hand, made her cheeks burn now, but back then, she might have been the one to suggest it.

Betsy tiptoed up the back steps and eased open the door, but her stealth was unnecessary. Addie was sleeping hard, her mouth open slightly, her cheeks pink in the afternoon heat. Betsy reached up and pulled the chain to turn on the ceiling fan. When the breeze lifted strands of Addie's hair, Betsy slipped into the house, pressing the door almost closed behind her. Upstairs, Walsh was still asleep as well. Betsy had no idea how long they were supposed to nap. Just one of the many things she hadn't thought to ask Jenna before she left.

She entered the coolness of her own bedroom, the fan still spinning, the bed still unmade. Instead of tidying up as she normally would have, she kicked off her shoes and lay down on the bed, arms and legs starfished out to the sides. Then she reached up and pulled Ty's pillow to her, hugged it close.

Would things ever go back to how they used to be, back when she had no problem letting go? Ty would tighten his grip on her hips, his mouth an inch away from her own, and her legs would turn to water, bone and sinew dissolving to nothingness. The air between them crackled with anticipation and desire. It used to be so easy to let herself go—like drifting into the Gulf, the warm, languid water covering her skin and holding her tight.

But that was *before*—before the poking and prodding, before all that captivating mystery and spontaneity and optimism was reduced to circled numbers on a calendar and biweekly dates with a nurse practitioner in pink polka-dot scrubs. Back when things between them were fun and easy, fresh and new.

Somehow Ty had been able to move past it all, compartmentalizing the facets of his life into neat pockets with clearly defined boundaries. Betsy, however, was stuck somewhere in the in-between, twisted and twirled into a messy, tangled knot she didn't quite recognize. A close match, but not the real thing. And if this Betsy didn't work the way God and nature intended, how was she supposed to offer herself up for pure pleasure or even accept the offer? It seemed too bold. Too easy after such an upheaval.

Dr. Fields, however, seemed to think that part wouldn't, or shouldn't, be an issue.

"Spontaneous pregnancy can happen," he'd said. "So you two need to keep at it. Try to enjoy yourselves."

Those were his parting words, tossed out like a consolation prize as they stood to leave his office. Just before that, they had listened as he rattled off all the things that could be wrong since he'd yet to find a single thing that was definitely wrong. The usual course of action—intrauterine insemination, two words Ty could barely make his mouth say—hadn't worked for them, even though they'd tried the relatively easy process three times. The doctor had suggested four, but three negatives seemed like enough.

"So there's . . . Is there anything else we can try?" Ty had asked.

Betsy lifted her eyes. Ty hadn't been eager about visiting the fertility specialist in the first place, so she was surprised he'd ask about more treatment.

"Oh, there's always something," the doctor said. "I think IVF would be an appropriate course of action for you."

"Would it work?"

The doctor paused. "There's always a chance."

It was the pause that did it for Betsy.

For Ty, it was the money.

The cows gave them a nice life, a fine life, but they wouldn't pay for something like IVF. The financial advisor at the clinic went over payment plans with them, ways they could finance the procedure and the drugs, not to mention the various tests, scans, and other related steps that went along with the deal. All told, they would be out of pocket way more than they could imagine spending. They had insurance, but it laughed in the face of voluntary fertility treatment.

Yes, it was an investment in their future children—as the advisor had repeated—but what kind of future would they have if they mortgaged their house, barn, and cows to give them life? What would they have left to raise those children with, other than their wits and love?

Ty had shaken his head, his mind made up. Betsy knew they'd talk about it that night in bed, the lights off, legs together. He'd hear her out, let her cry, maybe shed a tear of his own at the thought of saying good-bye to such a longing. But facts were facts. That kind of treatment was out of the question. Time to move on.

That's when the doctor had mentioned natural pregnancy. "You could also try praying," he'd said, a helpful afterthought.

That was five months ago, in early January, a particularly

raw way to start the new year. The doctor's words echoed in her brain at all hours—*"anything is possible"*—but she just didn't see any way through that vast, gaping hole between what she wanted and their actual reality: unexplained infertility. Plain old infertility she could have dealt with—diagnose the problem, fix it. It was the unexplained part that was so hard to swallow. Nothing was actually wrong with them? All his parts worked and so did hers, but they weren't working together? How was that possible?

Weeks of going round and round like this in her head made her feel like a children's carousel she couldn't stop, so on a dreary day in March with spring just around the corner, she stuck her leg out and stopped the spinning. She wrapped her grandmother's yellow crocheted baby booties in tissue paper and hid them in her closet. Threw away the marked-up calendar from the previous year. Shoved her book of fanciful flowers to the back of the dresser drawer in the room that was to have been the nursery. Moving on was the only choice she had, so she did.

She always thought she'd be done having kids by the time she was thirty. She thought by now she'd be happily absorbed in the living and raising part. And here she was, approaching her thirtieth birthday with two little girls sleeping in her empty room—they just weren't hers.

sixteen

Jenna

Jenna stood in the middle of a rickety bridge that stretched over a bayou ringed with needlcrush, cattails, and huge, knobby cypress knees poking out of the water. A patch of lily pads covered one side of the water, and on one, a frog sat in the bright sunshine. With elbows perched on the railing, her eye fixed to the viewfinder, she tried to get a shot of him before he jumped away, but the harsh light washed everything out.

She'd been at Halcyon for seven days. Casey and Gregory had both explained that the solitude and quiet—and the lack of real structure—were meant to encourage deep focus and hard work. They were right. The lack of structure—not to mention the absence of the photography mentor—meant Jenna could go days without seeing anyone if she wanted. She ate meals in the dining hall, of course, but she'd managed to miss the nightly workshops with no repercussions.

However, the solitude also meant no one knew she'd yet to produce anything of worth. She was surrounded by beauty she'd never seen before—murky swamps, bright-yellow croaking frogs, palm trees with lime-green fruit, towering pines, and scrubby oaks covered in Spanish moss—yet every time she tried to capture that beauty, it came out flat. Like she was trying too hard.

It was nice to have no one checking up on her, tapping her on the shoulder and asking to see her work, but somewhere around the middle of the week, she'd started to panic. For once, she'd had an incredible opportunity dropped in her lap and now it was sliding through her fingers. No way did she want to go home with nothing to show for her time here. She hadn't left her kids for that.

Behind her, something moved in the trees on the other side of the bridge. She peered into the shadows, but the glare made the shade appear deeper. It was all tree trunks and leaves until she noticed one trunk was moving toward her. Not a trunk. A man.

"Sorry. Didn't mean to startle you," he called. It was Gregory, this time without the leather jacket, which would have been ridiculous in this heat, but still in the beat-up jeans. Camera around his neck, tripod under his arm.

"I'm just glad you're not an alligator."

"An alligator?"

"Yeah." Jenna shaded her eyes as Gregory approached. "Don't they have those in Florida?"

"True, but you're more likely to see a fox or an armadillo. I've seen a couple of gators around here, but they don't seem to be too interested in humans."

"Good to know."

"How's it going?" Was that a smirk on his face? Yes. It was small but it was there.

"Awesome." She held up her camera. "I think these are going to be great."

He raised an eyebrow. "Good, that's good. Think you'll be ready for the workshop tonight?"

Jenna exhaled, blowing air out in a rush. Now he was doing his job? "I don't know. I'm not much for public displays of embarrassment."

"What's so embarrassing? We're all here to learn, right? To connect to our passion?"

She tried to hold it back but she couldn't. Her eyes rolled almost involuntarily.

Instead of the glare she expected, Gregory laughed. "I know what you mean. It can get a little repetitive. And annoying."

He stepped up to the railing and propped his elbows on the edge. A cloud floated in front of the sun, relieving the brightness of the light for a moment.

"So do you have other jobs going on other than here at Halcyon?" She leaned back against the railing and shot a glance at him. His eyes were on the water. "I assume you're not just hanging out at the beach all day." Heat crept up her cheeks and she closed her eyes for a second. Since the very first night at the dining hall, something about his swagger brought out a defense mechanism in her. She needed to be more careful. She didn't know this man well enough to be sarcastic.

"I'm not sunbathing, that's for sure. I'm a working photographer. Magazines, journals, some textbooks. I go where the job takes me. Which is why I've been a little absent these last few days." He cut his eyes to her. "I've been told I'm not always the most attentive mentor." If she expected an apology—which she halfway did—she didn't get it. "Anyway, right now I'm working on something I'm hoping *National Geographic* will pick up. It's on forgotten places in Florida. Unseen angles and views. This mentor gig at Halcyon is perfect because I needed to be down here anyway. Kill two birds, you know?"

"What kind of forgotten places? This preserve doesn't seem too forgotten to me. It's crawling with artists."

He nodded. "You're partly right. But the cool thing about places like this is that you can be in a populated area, but two or three hundred yards away is a little slice of swamp that's true wilderness. Untouched. In fact . . ." He pointed to their right, in the deeper woods behind the creek. "That's where I'm headed. I found something last week on the rare occasion I didn't have my camera on me. You can come with me, if you want. I'll show you what I'm talking about."

At the end of the bridge, they stepped off the wood onto a sand and dirt path just wide enough for one person. The shade deepened the farther they walked into the trees.

"This is like another world," Jenna said. Limbs stretched overhead, making a canopy that dimmed the light. All around them were sounds and stirrings of unseen animals and birds. "Not like the Deep South I know, that's for sure."

"Geographically, we're in the Deep South, but that's about it. It almost feels prehistoric, doesn't it? Like maybe this was how it looked billions of years ago. Dark and wet. Strange noises. Creatures around every bend."

"Okay, you're creeping me out a little bit."

Gregory laughed. "Sorry. I get a little excited when I'm in places like this. That's why I love my job. The world is my office."

As they walked he pointed out various trees and plants. Black gum and coastal plain willows. Pond and bald cypresses. Leggy banyans. And the birds: egrets and night herons. White pelicans and roseate spoonbills. Even a mangrove cuckoo, which apparently was a rare find. He seemed to know a little about everything.

"This cypress here—judging by its size, it's at least a couple hundred years old. The forest has probably looked just like this for all those years. No real change other than everything getting bigger and fuller."

She thought of that proud cypress, growing year after year toward the sunlight, unconcerned with the pace of anything around it.

"Okay, we're close. Look here." He guided her off the trail to the left, into a dense thicket of tall grass and hanging vines.

From somewhere came the sound of running water. With the sun behind clouds and the thick trees overhead, everything was dim, blues and greens fading into each other, until the tangle of foliage opened into a hidden cove of clear water surrounded by boulders. Water trickled down the face of the rocks, creating a waterfall ten feet high that splashed into the pool below. A thin creek—narrow enough to step over—ran away from the pool, winding off through the trees.

"It's not Niagara, but it's a rare find in Florida." Gregory set his tripod and camera down on a bed of dry leaves. "Not much elevation change anywhere, but there's just enough here to create this little pocket of water."

"Where does it come from?" Jenna knelt and peered into the water. It was so clear, she could see straight to the bottom. It tapered from the shallow edges to deeper waters in the center. "Everything else around here is murky and still. I've yet to come across water that's moving. Nothing like this creek."

"Singer Creek, to be exact. Legend says an Indian woman who stayed behind when her people were run out would sit here and sing to her lost children. She was known as 'the singer.' I guess someone thought it had a nice ring to it, and they named the creek and the preserve after her."

Jenna dipped her fingers in the water. It was crisp and cold. Gregory leaned over and did the same thing.

"Some say this comes from an underground spring straight from the Appalachians," he said. "I have my doubts, of course. The closest Appalachian foothill is up in Alabama, a long way from the Florida marshes. But who knows? Maybe this water has traveled underground all that way. Just to spit out in these rocks."

He sat on a dry patch of rock and pushed a smattering of leaves away to make room for Jenna. With her camera still hanging around her neck—no way was she going to trust it sitting alone near all this water—she sat next to him. After pulling her shoes off, she dunked her feet in the cool water.

"Nice, huh?"

"Very." She leaned over and cupped her hand and poured water over her calves, up to her knees. Sweat on the back of her neck evaporated, leaving her with a chill.

They sat in silence a moment, the only sound the trickling water and movement all around them in the forest.

"Now your turn," Gregory said, his voice low, as if to leave the peace undisturbed. "Tell me about you. Have you figured out yet why you're here at Halcyon?"

"Not really. Maybe my epiphany is still coming."

"Okay. Well, tell me about your photography then, what you do with it at home."

She shook her head. "I don't do much with it at home. I don't have time."

"Sure you do."

"What? How do you know?"

"We make time for things that are important."

"But isn't that what this place is about? Time to connect to our art—time and space that's not in our regular lives? It's all I've heard about since I got here."

"Sure, sure, that's what we say." He reached down and flicked water into a school of minnows. "And it's true to an extent. But I stand by the idea that if something is important enough, you'll squeeze it in. In the margins. Here, the margins are stretched, but when you get back home, everything goes back to normal. The passion, the drive has to be there. You get it?"

She nodded. He didn't know anything about her life. Of course a man would think it was as easy as just picking up the camera. But it was never that simple.

Then he reached over and lifted her camera from around her neck. She grabbed on to the strap. "What are you doing?"

"May I?"

She let go and averted her eyes. She didn't want to see his expression as he scrolled through the images she'd captured over the last handful of days.

After a moment, with her eyes still on the water, she sensed rather than saw him shake his head. "These are crap," he murmured.

"Excuse me?"

"You're taking shots you think you need to take." He scrolled through her images. "Sun shining on the water, palm branches, a pretty little mound of wildflowers. This is amateur. I'm just guessing here, but I'd say there's more to you than this."

"And what makes you say that?" She forgot about trying to be careful. "You haven't been around long enough to find out anything about me. I've been floundering, trying to figure out what I'm doing here. I thought I was supposed to have a mentor to offer some guidance."

"Having a mentor, especially one like me, isn't going to help you find your muse, if that's what you're looking for."

She stood and took her camera back.

"Go ahead. Get mad. Use it. Put it in here." He reached up and tapped her camera.

She turned and crossed back over the rocks the way they'd come, trying not to slip and embarrass herself as she made her exit.

"You're gonna need thicker skin to work with me."

She stopped and spun around, almost losing her footing in the process. She reached out and grabbed a low-hanging limb for balance. "If you remember, I didn't ask to work with you. And since it sounds like you aren't that excited to be working with me, why are you here? Why didn't you just go the other way when you saw me back there on the bridge?"

"A couple reasons. One, I'm the photography mentor at Halcyon. Seeing as you're the only other photographer here, you are my job. Two, Max asked me to watch out for you."

"He did what? When?"

"He called me up and told me a friend of his was coming and asked me to . . . well, just to make sure you were okay."

Unable to wrap her head around Max and Gregory working together to keep tabs on her, Jenna just stared.

"Don't be mad at him. I could tell he cares a lot about you. I told him I'd keep my eye on you."

"That's just perfect." Still holding the limb, she stepped carefully down the rocks to the firm ground.

"You have to find your creative eye on your own," he called. She resisted the urge to turn and toss another barb his way. "If I had to guess, I'd say it's there already and you just need to uncover it. That's why you're here, right?"

seventeen

Jenna

On Monday of the second week at Halcyon, Jenna squatted low among broken, stripped pine trees and thin saplings struggling to push themselves through the thick underbrush of The Bottoms. She'd heard of the place that morning at breakfast. Another artist had mentioned it, an area of the retreat where, a couple of years before, a tornado had ripped through during a summer storm.

"Everything else around here is so lush and alive," Mark, a painter sitting at her table, had said. "I don't know why they don't just clean it up. Or clear-cut it to get rid of the broken tree trunks and let everything start over."

"They can't do that," a woman said. "It's a nature preserve. They have to let Mother Nature do her thing."

Over the woman's left shoulder, Jenna saw Gregory filling his coffee mug a few paces away. His back was to them, but Jenna sensed he was listening. Or maybe he was just taking way too long to fill up that mug.

"Yeah, well, nature hasn't done its thing yet. It's a wasteland."

Jenna rose and picked up her tray. Gregory said her images were amateur. Too pretty. A wasteland should be perfect.

Outside, she'd almost made it to the start of the path when he called to her. She turned slowly, unsure of what to say—or what he'd say—after how they parted at the waterfall a few days before.

"Do me a favor," he said in place of a greeting. He set his coffee down and pulled a camera from his bag. "Play around with this today."

She gasped. "Is that a Rollei?"

He nodded.

She took the camera from him, her fingers finding the familiar crevices and notches. A photographer out in Wyoming had let her use his Rollei and she'd fallen a little bit in love. "Why are you giving me this?"

"Just trying something different." He shrugged. "Have fun with it. See what you think."

She tried to hand it back to him. "I already have a camera. Anyway, I don't think changing cameras is going to fix my problems."

"You're right. It won't. But changing your focus will. Just try it." He shouldered his bag again and picked up his coffee. "See how it feels."

Now, squatting in the bright sunshine, she was determined to prove him wrong. It wasn't that she wanted to take bad shots—to squander her time, to waste her opportunity—but she kept hearing his words. *"This is amateur. You're taking shots you think you need to take."*

She'd known those shots weren't great before he looked at them—and she hated that those were all she had to show him—but hearing the words out loud made something inside her deflate. And because of that, it made her angry. She'd come here to open herself up to creativity, not have someone squash it.

So she did what she always did when someone made her feel small and inadequate—she pushed in the opposite direction. Here she was in The Bottoms, searching for the muse Gregory said she wouldn't find. Broken trees? Check. Sun-parched grass? Check. A barren space ruined by a storm? Check.

But in what was supposed to be a wasteland, all she saw was life. Yes, much of the area was damaged, but she saw bright-green vines encircling twisted and broken tree trunks, golden wildflowers growing out of a hole in a tree lying on its side, a white-tailed deer bounding over a section of tangled fencing. It was exquisite, so different from the pretty scenes she'd tried to capture the week before.

Though she still wanted to be mad at Gregory, it seemed his harsh words had given her a necessary shove. She wasn't sure if this was the creative eye he wanted her to uncover, but it seemed her eye was better suited for finding the inferior, the unloved, the damaged, and The Bottoms provided an abundance of them all.

She worked for a while with her own camera, capturing the sharp colors and angles of light. When she switched to Gregory's Rollei, which produced square-format black-and-white photos, it was all about texture and shadows. The Rolleiflex TLR was what most people associated with old-time photos. The photographer held the camera at chest level and looked down into the finder instead of holding it to the face and looking straight ahead.

Shooting with a camera like this was a whole different experience than using a standard camera, and it took her a while to get used to it—holding it steady at the correct level, remembering that the mirror reversed the viewfinder image. It also forced her to slow down, to think about a shot before hitting the button. Once she got the hang of it though, she was able to focus on the trees above her, balancing on top of mounds of sand and dirt to get an angle right, taking her time, enjoying the peace.

She wondered about the film though—did Gregory develop it himself? Take it into town to get it developed? Other than the Epson printer that printed digital shots, she hadn't seen evidence of a photo lab or darkroom in any of Halcyon's studios. One thing was for sure—she was glad for the lack of an LCD screen on the camera. No need to waste time seeing how the pictures were coming out. She could continue shooting and just imagine she was capturing things the way she wanted.

When her growling stomach told her lunchtime had come and gone, she paused and ate a granola bar in the shade. As she rested she pulled her phone out of her bag. She didn't even check to see whether she had service, she just wanted to see the photo she used as her home screen, a recent shot of Addie and Walsh. They sat in the middle of their front yard, searching for the one four-leaf clover they were sure they'd find.

Jenna had taken the photo before the girls heard her approach. The late-afternoon light was perfect, almost creating a halo around them, and the girls filled the shot in a way that would have made Max proud. Maybe not Gregory—he'd probably find something wrong with it.

She'd shown the photo to Sam one morning as they drank their coffee together.

"They're beautiful, just like their mother." He set his coffee down and looked closer at the photo. "The blonde one looks like you."

"You just say that because of the hair."

He sat back in his chair and picked up his cup again. "Do they look like their father?"

Jenna's stomach did that uncomfortable clenching thing it did whenever anyone brought up the girls' father.

"Maybe a little." She blew a stray curl out of her eyes and felt his careful gaze on her.

"How long has it been? Since the divorce?"

Jenna stared at him a moment without speaking.

"I'm sorry, I . . ." He inhaled. "I just assumed you were divorced. Is he . . . ?" From his pained look, she knew she had to say something quick before he got the impression she was a widow.

"No, no, that's not it. It's fine. It's been, uh . . . I've been on my own for a few years now."

By the sweet and well-timed grace of God, Mario waved at her then, allowing her to sidestep any more questions she didn't want to answer.

A bird chirped nearby and brought her back to the present. She shifted her position against the rough bark of the tree and stretched her legs out in front of her. What she'd said to Sam was mostly true—as long as five, going on six, years was still considered "a few." It was just easier to gloss over the truth than spill it across the clean table in the back corner of Full Cup as Carrie Underwood blared on the speakers.

Her girls had had no choice in who their father was, even who their mother was. Whenever she wished she could pack up and head west again, or north, or anywhere but where she was, she thought of her girls, touched their skin, listened to their laugh, and reminded herself that they only had her. They depended on her for everything. So what she was doing now—these two weeks—it was all for them. She owed them at least that much.

That evening she stopped by her cabin to change into clothes that weren't damp with sweat and speckled with sandspurs. Outside, the air was alive with warmth and the scent of something sweet. Around the edge of the lake, canoes in various faded colors jostled against each other, tied by thick ropes to nearby trees as if someone had been afraid they'd drift away. One of them—it looked like it used to be painted red—had slipped from its rope and was trailing away from the others.

She looked around. After a moment, she slipped her shoes off and walked to the edge of the lake. The water was warm as bath-water. She lifted the hem of her skirt and took a couple more steps until she could grab the canoe to pull it up to the shore.

It wasn't until something rough bit into her fingers that she noticed the tattoo of jagged, rusty holes on the sides of the hull. The hole at the front where the rope had been tied was rusted out, leaving sharp edges and splotchy orange patches. The pads of her fingers were coated in the same orange rust, and a spot of blood seeped out of a shallow cut. She swished her hand in the water around her knees, but when she pulled it out and examined her finger, blood bloomed in a small dot.

So much for trying to do a good deed.

As she pressed her thumb and forefinger together, her gaze settled on the offending canoe. Maybe it had once held a load of laughing, frolicking kids, intent on pushing each other out. Or maybe they raced their canoe against others, seeing which team could skim across the lake the quickest. She imagined the little boat gleaming cherry red in the sun, tanned arms and legs tumbling from the sides, excited voices carrying over the water. Now it was nothing more than a mass of rust and danger.

But there was something about it. The mix of former glory and present decay. She tilted her head and caught a glimpse of the bright-green grass at the edge of the lake through a hole in the side of the canoe. Just a sliver of green against the orange rust and faded red metal. Life against death.

She tapped her fingers on her camera hanging around her neck, then pulled it up to her eye. She snapped and snapped again. After a moment, the light changed as a cloud skirted the sun. Shadows and glare, light and dark. Then, without bothering to check the outcome of her efforts on the LCD screen, she stepped out of the water, slid her feet back into her sandals, and continued to dinner.

On her way out of the dining hall, Casey called to her. Expecting to be urged to join the workshop, Jenna continued down the steps, just turning her head to speak. "I have a few things I wanted to wrap up from my work today. I'll try to make it tomorrow night."

"I was just going to let you know Gregory asked for you to meet him in the barn. And to bring his camera."

Jenna paused and looked back at Casey standing at the top of the steps. "Why?"

Casey shrugged. "I'm guessing he wants to discuss your work. He is your mentor, so that's his job."

"Yes, as I keep being reminded."

Casey raised an eyebrow.

"Sorry. Thanks for letting me know. I'll head that way."

The path down the hill toward the barn took her away from everything else, past the lake, to a part of the preserve she hadn't seen yet. After stopping at her cabin to retrieve Gregory's camera, she wound her way across a low bridge that spanned a muddy creek and through a tunnel of oaks and hanging vines. Palm branches pressed in from the sides of the dirt path, which opened to a clearing. A crisp white barn sat a couple hundred feet off the path, its upper casement windows open to catch the breeze.

There was no sign of life until she noticed Gregory sitting in an Adirondack chair to the side of the barn. His head was tipped back, his eyes closed, his boot-clad feet propped in another chair pulled up in front of him.

"You're not making me clean horse stalls, are you?" Jenna called as she approached.

He opened one eye. "Funny."

"Why are we meeting way out here?"

He dropped his feet to the ground and heaved himself out of the chair. "Come with me."

From the outside, the barn looked like most every other barn she'd seen in the hills of Tennessee: peaked roof, weather vane on top, vertical wood siding. Even a fenced horse corral to the side. But when Gregory grabbed the handles of the double doors and slid them open, any chance of this being a standard barn evaporated. Inside, it was around the same size as Ty's barn, but with the individual stalls taken out, the space seemed larger. No ropes hung on the wall. No straw on the floor. No animal smell.

Instead the area was sleek and modern, the faint scent of vinegar and chemicals both sharp and familiar. The floor was covered in clean, cool tiles that made Jenna want to take her shoes off and walk barefoot. The lights were low, but gallery spotlights shone on the art on the walls. A few paintings here and there—bold, impulsive jabs of color—but most were photographs. Some black and white, some color, all striking.

"Are these . . . ?" Before she could finish her thought, a particular photo caught her eye.

Gregory continued across the room toward a door at the back, but Jenna moved closer to the photo. It showed a woman and two children—obviously hers by the way she draped her arms around them. They sat on a defeated couch in a dingy room. Behind them, a wooden board covered most of a window. Black metal bars covered the rest. All three had smudges of dirt on their arms and faces. It was poverty—the kind that scared her and made her stomach hurt—but it was also joy. The children, a boy and a girl, were caught in a laugh, their faces open. The mom's eyes were tired, and the lines around them made her look older than she probably was, but her smile was soft. Their joy—even if just temporary—radiated outward, pushing back the bonds of their bleak life.

Jenna paused to make sure her voice wouldn't break before she spoke. "Did you take this?" She'd never seen any of his work, and yet she felt sure it was his. That he'd been the one to draw such life and light out of this family's impossible situation.

He joined her in front of the photo. "I did."

She pointed to a group of acrylics. "What about those?"

He shrugged. "I paint every now and then. It loosens me up. I'm not very good though."

She snorted. "Yes, you are. All of this is . . . Tell me about them." She gestured to the photo of the family.

"A few years ago *TIME* magazine did a story on fracking in the Appalachians. The woman's husband was killed in an accident on the job, leaving her with five kids and no income. These are the two youngest." He scratched his bearded chin. "They could barely keep the lights on, but she offered me tea and a homemade biscuit. The kids played marbles with me."

Painful things made beautiful.

She made a slow turn, taking in the array of photos. People, landscapes, old buildings, street scenes. "Are they all from *TIME*, or . . . ?"

"No, that one's *National Geographic*. That's *Travel + Leisure* . . ." He started to point to another photo but let his arm fall. "It's just a random assortment. They asked me to bring some to leave on display this summer while I'm mentoring."

"I didn't realize you were so . . . Are you famous?"

He laughed.

"I'm serious. Are you some famous photographer I should know about?"

"What difference does it make? I'm just a guy who takes pictures and gets paid for them. At least that's the goal."

"These are more than just 'pictures' though. They're incredible. Why are you wasting time at this little art retreat when you could be out winning a Pulitzer or something?"

"Now you're just embarrassing me." He stepped back from the wall. "I don't know. You've seen how well I fit in." He cut his eyes to her and she smiled, then remembered she was supposed to be mad at him. "For some reason, they keep asking me to come back and I keep saying yes. I guess one day maybe I won't, but it works for now. And Halcyon isn't just some 'little art retreat.' It's a big deal to a lot of people in the art world."

He turned toward a door at the back of the room and pulled his boots off. "None of this matters though. What I really wanted you to see is in here. Take your shoes off, if you don't mind. I like to keep it clean." She dropped her sandals next to his boots, then followed him as he opened the door and turned on the light. A counter along one wall held bins, trays, and bottles. A thin metal wire dotted with clips was strung across one wall.

"A darkroom? How come no one told me about this?"

"It's my job to let the photographers know about it."

She stared at him.

"Well, I'm telling you now. And you haven't needed a darkroom until now."

He reached in front of her and flipped another switch on the wall. The main lights went out while another one clicked on, coating the room in a soft red glow. "Let's see what you got today."

She passed his camera to him. "I haven't developed film in a while."

"Don't worry. I'll walk you through it." His voice was low, as if excess noise would damage the film as much as light.

He pulled the film out of the camera and loaded it into the spiral developing reel.

"The reel goes into the processing tank here." He picked up a bottle of developer and poured the liquid into a clear beaker, along with water from a bucket on the counter. "It has to be the right temperature or it'll ruin the film. Hand me that thermometer, will you?" She gave it to him and he slid it into the beaker. "Perfect. Now, I want you to pour the developer into the tank and we'll start the timer."

The red light offered enough light to see shapes and forms, but not enough to see small details. When she had trouble finding the hole at the top of the tank to pour the developer, he reached over and moved her hands to the right place. "There. Pour it in, then hit the timer."

They inverted the tank to make sure the developer coated all the film inside, then repeated it twice more, waiting a minute or so between movements.

"Next is stop bath, fixer, and holding bath, in that order." He held a pair of tongs out to her. "Use these, never your fingers, although I'm sure you remember that. And don't forget to rinse them off before you move them to another solution." He turned the sink faucet on, and she rinsed the ends of the tongs before moving the photo paper to the next tray.

The manual process was fickle and each movement, no matter how insignificant it seemed, could have a huge effect on the outcome of the photos. She hardly knew this man—wasn't even sure if she liked him very much—but in the soft light of the darkroom, he was kind, helpful. A surprisingly gentle teacher.

As they waited for the final wash, he hopped up onto the edge of the metal counter behind her. "I owe you an apology."

"Oh?" She leaned against the table and faced him. "What for?"

He glanced down at his bare feet and leaned forward onto his hands. "Calling you an amateur. Saying you weren't taking the right shots. It was too much."

Part of her wanted to make a joke out of it, to brush it off as nothing and move on to something easier, but instead she nodded. "It was hard to hear. You made me mad."

"I know and I'm sorry." He gave a small half grin. "People don't always like me very much. I'm sure you can see why."

She shrugged. "You won't win any etiquette contests, I'll give you that. But I get it. And your push helped me, I think."

"Then I'm glad I could help."

She smiled. "Don't take all the credit. Yes, I wanted to prove you wrong—and maybe prove myself wrong too. Prove that I really am supposed to be here. But I also just needed to find my footing. Something about The Bottoms—the ugliness, the desolation—it worked for me."

"Like I said, you didn't need to look far to find your creative eye. I knew it was in there. It just gets buried by life if you let it."

She sighed. "Tell me something I don't know."

"Okay, here's something you don't know." He sat up straighter and ran a hand through his hair, leaving bits sticking up in tufts. "I almost gave up photography five years ago."

Jenna raised her eyebrows. "Why?"

"Why else do men make bad decisions? For a woman."

"Ah. We do tend to mess things up."

"Granted, she wasn't trying to mess anything up—she just wanted me to stay."

"And you wanted to go."

He nodded. "I've been a photographer since my early twenties. I don't put down roots. I never stay long in one place. I have an apartment in Atlanta, but I'm usually only there to catch up on sleep and pack for my next gig. I love to travel, so the life fits me well. But it's hard on relationships, family and otherwise. Callie wanted me to stop traveling, to stay in Charleston with her." He rubbed his forehead. "She actually wanted me to work for her dad at his investment firm."

Jenna wrinkled her nose. "You don't seem like the investment firm type."

"Exactly. But I considered it. I figured Charleston had enough opportunities for photography and maybe I could travel some on the weekends."

"So what happened?" She turned to the tray behind her to check the progress of the photos.

"Be patient."

She faced him again.

"I was asked to mentor here for the summer. Then I was offered a freelance spot with *National Geographic Traveler.* I realized what I had going with work was too good to give up to sit in an office all day wearing a suit and drinking scotch with old men."

"But you had to give her up too."

He gave a slow nod, his gaze unfocused. "Haven't talked to her since the day I told her I was leaving. I tried to call her a few times after I left, but she never picked up." After a moment, he blinked and focused on Jenna. "All this to say I understand the pull photography has. Any art, really. Anything that lets you capture the world as you see it and say things you can't say with words. Sometimes it's more important than anything else."

He hopped off the counter and peered into the trays where the photos floated in solution. The images were suspended somewhere between undefined blobs and what she hoped would turn out to be not terrible.

"Tell me something about you." He set the dripping tongs back onto the towel.

"What do you want to know?"

"Anything. I just bared my soul."

"I don't like talking about myself. I'm better if you ask questions." She leaned against the counter and crossed her arms.

"Okay. You're not married."

"That's not a question."

He smiled. "Okay. You're young, you're talented, you seem like a nice girl—why are you not married?"

"Why aren't you?"

"I just told you. I'm elusive. Hard to pin down. But this isn't about me anymore. And you told me to ask questions."

She took a deep breath. "It's kind of a long story."

He gestured to the trays behind her. "We have nothing but time."

She tilted her head side to side, stretching her tight neck muscles as if preparing for battle. "I'll give you the abbreviated version. I moved to Wyoming with some friends after my freshman year of college. Worked, played, took pictures. Fell in love."

Gregory shrugged. "It happens."

She closed her eyes, then opened them again. "Jeremy was a photographer too, and a musician. Probably a better photographer, but he decided to make music his thing."

When he packed up to join his band back home in Asheville, North Carolina, he'd asked Jenna to come too, and with nothing tying her to Wyoming, she went with him. Her camera continued to be good to her in the Blue Ridge Mountains. She sold her prints in galleries up and down the Blue Ridge Parkway and had a robust Etsy business, shipping her prints across the country, even some internationally.

"Etsy?" Gregory asked. "What's that?"

"Are you serious?" She peered at him through the dim light. "It's a website where people sell things."

"Like Amazon?"

"No, not like Amazon. Just . . . look it up."

"Okay. So you were in Asheville with your boyfriend and your thriving photography business. What happened?"

She held up her hands, then let them drop. "I got pregnant."

She discovered she was pregnant on a Tuesday morning via a Clearblue Easy in the restroom of the Asheville Folk Gallery where she worked. Jeremy's band had hired a publicist after a run of good shows, and the publicist had lined up a long string of gigs in the Northeast. Jenna waited until he returned from the tour before telling him. She was already three months pregnant by then, although still another month or so away from showing. He was a little excited but more hesitant. She saw it in his eyes right away: a baby didn't have quite as much pull as the road did.

After that, his band went on longer and more frequent tours—up the East Coast, as far west as Texas, and even up to Boston. She moved out of his apartment and into a house with some friends so she wouldn't be alone. Her roommates told her she was crazy for hanging on, but she thought being a few months away from holding an infant in her arms was a pretty good reason to hang on. Her only other choice was to do it alone, which was what ended up happening when Jeremy moved with the band to New York City.

"Did you ask him to stay?"

"I didn't want to have to ask. So no. He left and I watched him go." She hadn't meant to tell him the whole story, but once she started talking, the story flowed.

"What'd you do?"

"I called my sister in the middle of the night. I hadn't told her I was pregnant, so it was a bit of a shock. But Betsy just . . ." Jenna paused, remembering the silence on the phone when she blurted out the news to Betsy with no warning. "I know she wanted to say a lot, but she didn't. She just showed up at my door the next night with a car full of diapers and baby gear and stayed until a couple weeks after Addie was born."

"You have two kids though, right?"

She ran her hands across the smooth counter surface and nodded.

As luck would have it, she ran into Jeremy again soon after moving to Nashville. She hadn't talked to him in over a year so she didn't know he'd moved there to work with a new studio. He was happy to see her—and Addie—and Jenna desperately wanted her child to know her father.

"Deep down I knew he couldn't have changed much, but I ignored that instinct and we gave it a shot anyway. It was good at first—the three of us together. But then I let my guard down. In every way." She peered at Gregory to see if he understood. "Who would have thought I'd get pregnant a second time?"

She rubbed her eyes. "That pretty much ended things. He made himself scarce, and I just let him slide out of the picture again. It was easier that way. Well, it wasn't easy, but at least I wasn't trying to force something that obviously wasn't supposed to work."

It was quiet in the room. Too quiet. She wanted him to say something, but he was silent.

She laughed to cut the tension. "Clearly I have terrible taste in men and have no business trying to date anyone."

Gregory shook his head and rubbed his cheek. "Geez, kid. You're breaking my heart here."

She stood up straighter and brushed her hair back from her face. "That was a very long answer to your question, but that's why I'm not married. I might have said yes if he'd asked, but it's probably better for all of us that he didn't."

He nodded. "If he had, you might not be here."

"True," she said, then pushed off the counter and turned to the trays, cutting off more questions and any possible sympathy she didn't deserve. "Are they ready yet?"

It was a moment before he spoke. Finally, he stood next to her. "Pull them out and let's see what we have."

She gripped the edge of the first photo, holding it a moment to let the last of the water drip off, then clipped it to the wire.

One by one, she lifted the photos and hung them up to dry. When she'd clipped all twelve photos, she stood back and studied them.

Not terrible, just like she'd hoped. New, vibrant life pushing against the barren and wasted. Promise seeping into the dark places. Not terrible at all.

"See what you did? You were patient. Rather than shooting the first scene you came to, you waited until you saw something of worth. And because of that, I see it too." He moved down the line. "Without color as a distraction, the contrast between light and dark is the focus. Look at the pattern here on the leaves." He pointed to the repeating stripes on a palm branch. "You angled the shot just right to draw our eye here. And this one—this one is different."

He paused in front of a shot Jenna took of one of the other artists, Terry, standing under a towering oak, his face tipped up and just catching the light. "Adding the human element here increases the emotional impact of the scene. It also gives us some perspective as to just how massive the tree is." He turned to her in the dim light. "How do you feel about these?"

She heard the smile in his voice, and she smiled too. "Good. I feel good."

"I think you've found your place, kid. *You* did all this. Own it. Enjoy it."

eighteen

Ty

Between an important South Alabama Dairy Farmers' Association meeting, working with Carlos to keep the pump from giving out again, and a weekend lightning storm that temporarily took out power to the milking barn, it was early the next week before Ty could take a breather.

Roger Daily had his grandchildren for a few days, and not knowing what to do with three kids underfoot, he brought them to Ty's place to play with Addie and Walsh. His wife, Linda, came too, the five of them piling out of Roger's ancient blue-and-white truck like clowns at a circus. Addie and Walsh were playing on the big swing when the Dailys arrived, and the grandkids ran straight for them.

Roger trudged over to where Ty stood next to the fence of the holding pen. He took off his cap and brushed his hands through his stiff white hair. "I can take 'em for a few hours, but all weekend?" He laughed a little. "Little ones just wear me out."

"I know what you mean," Ty said with a smile, although he

173

didn't really know. Being so busy in the barn, the burden of keeping up with the girls had fallen mostly on Betsy's shoulders. Not that they were much of a burden. He'd liked having them around this week—their laughter, their excited faces peeking around the barn door, their loose and limber joy.

He was starting to think he'd miss them a little when they were gone.

"I know you heard the reports from the weather center." Roger slapped his cap back on his head and squinted into the sun. "There's already one storm out there. Only June and they're lining up like dominoes."

Ty laughed. "You always so gloom and doom, Roger? You and I both know those things come and go as they please. Active season doesn't always mean it'll be active around here."

"That's true. But we're nothing if not prepared, right?"

"You're right about that. I already got your plywood on my upper windows."

"Farmers help each other out. Your grandfather would have been the first to say that."

"Yes, sir."

"I think I'll go check out the placement of those boards, if you don't mind. I'd hate for water to seep in somewhere, ruin your hard work."

"I don't think I missed any holes, but you're welcome to check for me."

"I do it for your grandfather. He'd want me to keep an eye out for you."

Ty smiled. "I appreciate that." He didn't need the help, but Roger and Ty's grandfather had been close, and if the man wanted to take care of him, it was best to just let him.

Down in the yard, most of the kids were horsing around on the grass under the big tree, but Addie stood a few yards away, near the house. Hide-and-go-seek, maybe.

Betsy and Linda stood next to what used to be Betsy's garden. Now it was barely more than a briar patch. The soil was hard and untilled, and any vegetables still buried in the earth must have been hard rocks by now. It was a shame, really. Betsy had enjoyed that garden when they first moved to the farm. She worked it every day, coaxing everything from potatoes and carrots to marigolds and roses to grow just a little bit higher, a little bit fuller.

It had been a long time since he'd seen her out in the garden. A year, maybe two? She stood next to it now, one hand shading her eyes, her other hand on her hip. Linda tugged on a limp stalk that leaned sideways against a fence post. Betsy shrugged and Linda shook her head. When Linda pointed at something else in the garden, Betsy patted her on the arm and motioned for her to follow. Away from the garden, away from her forgotten mission.

Linda waved to Ty and followed her husband out to the barn. Together, they walked around its perimeter, pointing at who-knows-what and nodding like they knew exactly what Ty was doing wrong on his grandfather's farm, making a list of what he needed to do to fix it.

Betsy crossed the yard, dodging running children, and climbed up on the fence rail next to where Ty stood, hooking her toes under the board below her. She tilted her face up and closed her eyes. Late-afternoon sunshine filtered through the big oak and cast long shadows on the grass.

Ty reached up and propped his elbow on her knees. "What insightful wisdom did Linda share with you?"

"That I'm a miserable gardener."

Ty laughed. "Really?"

"Mm-hmm. No gardener worth her salt would start something like that and then just let it all go. She offered to come over and help me whip it back into shape."

"What'd you tell her?"

Betsy sighed and stretched her arms out in front of her. "I told her I'd let her know if I needed help."

Ty nodded. "Think you'll ever get back out there? It seemed like something you enjoyed."

"Oh, I did enjoy it. I just . . . It got out of hand, and the longer I stayed away, the worse it got. Maybe one day."

Down in the yard, Roger's grandkids—ages seven, nine, and eleven—had circled around Walsh, who was happy to be the center of attention. While the older kids watched, she performed trick after trick—sloppy headstands, rolls on the grass, jumps, leaps. The kids cheered and hugged her. Walsh beamed.

"Where's Addie?" Ty looked to the corner of the house where he'd last seen her.

Just then, the screen door to the back porch opened and Addie tiptoed down the steps. As Walsh's laughter rang out and her antics became even more animated, Addie took careful steps toward the group in the grass. At the last minute she darted off toward the henhouse, where she paused in the shade along one side of it, her eyes still on the other kids.

"What is she doing?" Ty asked.

"I think she's nervous around the bigger kids. She wants to play, but she's scared to join in."

"Why? Look at Walsh out there. No fear."

"Come get me," Walsh called to the kids, and she darted off to the side of the yard. Addie took a few steps out of the shadows, but not enough to join in the game.

"Jenna was like that when we were little," Betsy said. "I was more like Addie. I used to be jealous of how Jenna was so brave and daring."

"Daring. Yep, I'd say that's a good description of Jenna."

"But it was more than just that. She'd jump in the middle of a group of kids and start playing with them like it was no big thing. I was always too scared. I'd wait until someone asked me to play. I was Addie, tiptoeing around the edge, wanting to be a part of things. Jenna never tiptoed."

Betsy shifted on the fence, straightened out her legs, then tucked them back under the rung. "I remember I had a slumber party once. I think it was for a birthday. My twelfth or thirteenth, I don't remember. It was the same thing. They were my friends, but Jenna was the center of attention. She had bought some nail polish with her allowance money. It must have been the one time she actually did enough chores to get her money for the week. She showed the polish to my friends and they were goners." She laughed. "I still remember what it looked like. Purple with glitter in it. Very Jenna."

"You didn't tell her to leave? Kick her out of your room or something?"

"I couldn't. Even though she made me mad, borrowed things without asking—and usually returned them broken or stained— she was . . . magnetic. I remember watching all my friends watch her, their eyes glued to her. I wanted to be mad, but really, I just wanted to be more like her."

Ty shook his head. "And now? Do you still wish you were like her?"

Betsy was quiet, studying her feet on the wooden board. She

shrugged. "Parts of her, I guess. I'm not sure I'd want to spend two weeks in the Florida wilderness, but there's something appealing about having the courage to jump at opportunities as they come. To not think twice."

"I don't know, Bets. Maybe she should have thought twice about it. She has two good reasons to have thought long and hard before she booked this retreat on barely a moment's notice." He gestured toward the girls out on the grass.

"That's not exactly what happened. You know that. *We* had barely a moment's notice, but that's just because she didn't find out she got in until a few days before she was supposed to be there. She didn't just drop the kids off on a whim."

"Well—"

"She didn't. Or that's not what she meant to do. Anyway, she's my sister. We're family. We help each other out."

Ty clenched his lips together to keep from saying more. No sense arguing over what had already happened. Out in the yard Walsh hung off the swing while Addie picked dandelions in a shaft of sunlight. He squeezed Betsy's knee. "They are kind of fun to have around though, aren't they?" As the kids' laughter bounced around the yard, he leaned his shoulder against her hip. "But we get our house back soon."

Betsy smiled and nodded.

"Think you'll miss 'em?"

She shrugged. "A little."

Ty watched her carefully, trying to catch a chink in her armor, but she gave nothing away. She rested her arm on his shoulder, but her eyes remained steady on the girls. Addie had left her plucked dandelions in a pile and now approached Walsh on the swing. She whispered something to Walsh, and they both laughed.

"We keep talking about getting away, but I'm going to call tomorrow. Maybe check into that little place in Perdido Key with the wooden boardwalks and the sunsets over the river."

Betsy looked at him. Raised her eyebrows. "My field trips can't pay for that kind of place."

Ty wrapped his arm around her waist. "Don't worry about that. I have a little money put away for something like this. Something for us."

"You do?"

She seemed so surprised that he wanted to kick himself for waiting so long before taking her away somewhere. He should have done it months ago.

"Okay then," she said.

"Yeah?"

Betsy nodded. "I could use a vacation."

nineteen

Jenna

On her last night of the retreat, Jenna walked toward the barn to meet Gregory, her mind somersaulting with mixed emotions—hope and dread, nerves and confidence. She readjusted the camera strap that hung across her shoulder, as if the camera were heavier with all the photos it held. She'd taken hundreds during her stay at Halcyon. Not even half of them were worth showing anyone, but some—a few dozen—gave her hope. Maybe she was even a little proud of them.

That morning he'd caught her on her way out of the dining hall and asked her to meet him in the barn after dinner. "We both know you won't show up at workshop, but it's part of my job to make sure you get the most out of your time here. Why don't you meet me in the barn? We can go over your work there."

The lights in the barn were dim, except for the gallery spotlights shining on the photos on the wall. When her eyes adjusted to the light, she saw it—her own photo on the far wall. It was a shot of a tall, thick cypress tree on the bank of a bayou in The Bottoms wrapped in the "arms" of a strangler fig. Also called a love tree, the fig both embraced and strangled its host. A flyer in the dining hall detailing plant life around the preserve noted that the host trees often died, their life snuffed out by the determined fig.

She'd been struck by both the sadness and the determination of the two intertwined trees. At some point, the fig would likely win the battle, absorbing all the available light and water, leaving the cypress to wither and die. But right now, they were balanced, both sporting bright-green leaves and healthy bark. Both determined to thrive.

And now, that moment was housed in a black frame, standing out from the pale wall behind it, only Jenna wasn't the one who'd framed it.

"I didn't hear you come in." Gregory entered the gallery from a room in the back. He dropped his bag on the floor and sat on one of the chairs across from her photo on the wall. "What do you think?"

"You did this?"

"It's one you left hanging to dry. I had an extra frame in a closet . . ." He shrugged. "Just thought you might like to see it."

Snappy comebacks and sarcastic brush-offs skirted through her mind, then leaked away. "Thank you. It's hard to believe I took it, really."

"It's all you. You have a knack for getting just the right angles, but you also see things others might not notice. Like that tree there." He nodded to the picture. "A lot of people, myself included, probably would have walked right by it in search of something less . . . mangled. But you saw a different kind of beauty. Sometimes perspective is more valuable than technical skills. You've got that instinct."

"I'm not so sure." She sat in the chair next to him.

"Trust me. I've been doing this a while." He leaned forward in his chair and propped his elbows on his knees. "Let's see what you brought."

She reached into her bag and pulled out a manila folder. It was the first time she'd used the Epson printer in the main studio, and she'd been excited to see how her photos came out. However, while the Epson printed her photos in perfect, crisp color, she missed the almost spiritual process of developing the black-and-white film in the dusky red light of the darkroom.

He sifted through the stack of photos, pausing to look at one or another, then slipping each one back in the stack. When he got to the end, he flipped them back and started over again from the beginning. As she waited for his reaction, she smoothed the bottom of her shirt, pressing it flat with her hands, then rolling the bottom edge in her fingers.

Her second week at the retreat had been drastically different from the first. She'd walked nearly every path, bridge, and sandy mound in the preserve, some with Gregory at her side but often alone. She stayed out all day, often forgetting to stop and eat, shooting until the dusk swallowed the light. Though she felt out of her element when she had first arrived at the retreat, unsure of her ability to capture anything meaningful from trees, leaves, and darting geckos, she now felt as adept shooting nature scenes as she did people. She felt electric, her creativity burning through her as it hadn't since her time in Wyoming, alone and free.

She was beginning to think she could do this—could find a way to fit her art, her creativity, into her routine life of kids, work, bills, and housework. The task seemed impossible—her life at home was so tight, her free time doled out in such small chunks, she didn't know how to add these new urges into her normal, day-to-day world. But her new sense of purpose was hard to ignore.

"Tell me about this." His sudden words jolted her from her thoughts. He flipped through the stack and pulled one out. It was the shot of the canoe she'd rescued by the lake. Ugly and rusted, with a shaft of fuzzy sunlight beaming through the jagged hole. "When did you take it?"

"A few days after you took me to the waterfall and blasted me about my amateur photo skills."

"Blasted? I prefer to think I inspired, but whatever I did, it was worth it if it pulled this out of you. The first images you took were bland. Then—*wham*—you come out with something like this."

Relief flooded through her. She loved the shot too. "I was on my way to dinner when I saw it. I wasn't even thinking about what I was doing."

"That's when the best stuff happens—when we're not over-thinking. It's a good way to live, really. Don't overthink, just do. Works in a lot of situations. It's already working for you." She inhaled, the corners of her mouth pulling up into an involuntary smile. "But you still need practice. Let me show you a few things."

He spent the next few minutes dissecting a handful of photos, pointing out where she'd missed her angle or lost perspective. She was glad for the critique—to grow as a photographer, she needed the honest feedback—but it was hard not to hear his words as marks against her hard work. Against her.

"Do you agree?"

He was watching her, waiting for an answer, but she'd missed the question. "I'm sorry. Do I agree with what?"

He reached forward and dropped her photos on the low table in front of them. "All right. What's going on?"

"Nothing. Please, continue." She swallowed back the annoying lump in her throat. "You were talking about how I got the shadows wrong, I think."

He sighed. "Jenna, this is your critique, just like if you'd been in the workshop. If you're an artist, you can't react like this."

"I'm not . . . I'm not reacting in any way. And I'm not an artist."

"Then what are you?"

"I'm a photographer, right? Isn't that what you want me to say?"

He leaned forward, close enough that she could see gold flecks in his brown eyes. She looked down at her hands. "But what is a photographer if not an artist? Are you not creating something beautiful, something that will make the viewer feel, or escape, or dream? Something that challenges the way we see the world, or encourages someone, gives them hope or direction? That's what art does. Isn't that what you're doing?"

"I'm trying to." Her words were clear and as sharp as his, but she still couldn't look in his eyes.

He reached forward and tilted her chin up with one finger, forcing her to look at him. "Don't guess. Know it. You are an artist. Get it through your head now or when you leave this place, you'll go right back home and pick up your life as if this experience were nothing more than a blip on your radar."

He sat back in his chair and gazed at her photo on the wall. "Look, there will always be people who criticize your work. I'm trying to help you, to make you better than you think you can be, better even than you're trying to be. But those people who truly criticize, who belittle—their words don't matter. What matters is that *you* can't be the one to drag yourself down, okay? You have to carry on, regardless of whether anyone—me, another mentor, or some idiot walking down the street—understands or appreciates your art. It is yours alone and your approval of it, your acceptance of it, has to come first."

Outside, the world was alive with nighttime sounds, but inside, other than their breathing, it was silent.

"Do you understand what I'm saying?"

She nodded, buoyed by his intensity and the fire in his eyes. "I get it."

"Good. You are a photographer, Jenna Sawyer. Even more than that, you're an artist. A good one. And you have the potential to be even better."

She waited for more, but he stood and looked at his watch. "I have a mentor meeting at nine, so I need to get back. You're welcome to stay here if you want."

"I need to get back too." She gathered her photos. "It's been a long day. And I need to call my sister and let her and my girls know I'll be heading back soon."

"So they're staying with your sister?" He flipped the lights off and held the door open for her. Outside, the steamy air was quieter than before, as if the humidity were cotton in her ears.

She nodded. "She and her husband live on a farm in Alabama. Lots of room for kids."

"Bet they're having a blast."

"Oh yes. Betsy sent me a photo today of the girls sitting on top of a cow out in the middle of a field. They had such big smiles." She couldn't admit it, but seeing Addie's and Walsh's carefree, easy smiles had been hard. Did they miss her at all?

Their feet made soft sounds on the leaves covering the path through the trees. Their only light was the moon, full, round, and unobstructed by clouds.

"It's good they're with family. Sounds like you don't have to worry about them."

"I'm not really worried." She gave a small laugh. "Betsy's good at everything. She probably figured out the whole mom thing in about five minutes. Five years in and I'm still trying to get it."

He glanced at her. "Seems like it'd take a while to get the hang of parenting. It's probably not something that comes naturally—giving up your wants and needs for someone else."

They came to the bridge over the bayou, the water hazy with moonlight.

"You know you can stay longer if you want."

She thought she'd heard him wrong. "Excuse me?"

"You can stretch out your retreat. Stay."

She stopped where she was on the bridge. "What are you talking about?" When he realized she'd stopped, he backtracked. "What about those hundreds of people who apply for each session?"

He shrugged. "If you want to stay, we try to make it work. As long as there's space, of course, and in this case, we just found out a writer had to back out of his session. He was planning to stay to the end of the eight weeks, so that spot is wide open. If no one here takes it, Casey will call the first person on the waiting list sometime tomorrow."

"You'd have to know tonight?"

He nodded and looked at his watch again. "We're talking about it at the meeting."

"I can't stay. They're waiting for me."

"Okay." He said it so simply, so without care, it aggravated her.

She exhaled and pushed her hands through her hair. "Why are you just telling me about this now?"

"I didn't find out about the spot until late this afternoon. I figured I'd see what frame of mind you were in before I told you. That's the thing—it's not a blanket offer to the whole group. A mentor has to make the case for one of the current artists. Why he or she should be asked to stay, how it will benefit them, how they've grown, how much further they have to go."

"And you think I'm a good fit?"

"Wouldn't be asking if I didn't. I convinced the others to hold off on offering the spot to anyone until I talked to you."

He turned his face toward the creek as if to give her a moment of privacy while she deliberated. She studied his profile in the moonlight, her mind swimming.

Could she? Was it possible? She'd just found her footing here, and leaving before she really even got started would be disappointing.

He turned back to her. "Keep in mind that if you stay, I'd expect you to work hard. I'll help you put together a solid portfolio. You already have a decent head start, but we need to flesh it out. Show what you can do. And I may have some contacts I can share with you. Help you get your foot in the door at a few places."

She clasped her hands together across her middle to keep them from shaking. "Why are you doing this for me? There must be other artists here who'd jump at the chance to extend their stay. Why me?"

He held up his hands, then let them drop. "Maybe it's because I see a little bit of myself in you. Whether that's a good thing or not is anyone's guess." He took a breath and leaned against the rail of the bridge. "Max couldn't have known it, but he did me a favor when he asked me to keep an eye on you. The way you see things—your perspective—it challenges me to be better. To work harder. Maybe we can help each other." He looked at her. "I think you're a worthy artist. I think you need more time here. I want to give you that chance."

Finally, he pushed off the railing. "Come on. I'll tell them you need the night to decide. Just let me know in the morning."

twenty

Betsy

Betsy stood over the kitchen sink Magic Erasing mud off the girls' shoes so they could wear them to church. Whenever Jenna arrived, Betsy was sure it would at least be after the eleven o'clock service let out.

Jenna hadn't given her a firm time, but Sunday was the day she was supposed to return, the day that had glowed red in Betsy's mind for two weeks, since the minute she'd opened the gates she'd thought were shut tight. Having the girls in the house had required a delicate dance of exposure and protection. Life spilled on the rugs and countertops, laughter echoing off the walls, small dirty footprints on her kitchen floor. Some of it had felt natural, like slipping into a perfectly shaped second skin. But other parts had been almost unbearable, and she fought the urge to pull her gates closed again, lock them, and hide the key.

While Betsy scrubbed, Addie and Walsh zoomed around the house like they had wheels for feet. Their excitement was catching. As if something bigger than just Jenna's return was imminent.

"Do you think she bought me something? Something big?" Addie asked on one of her passes through the kitchen.

"Well, I don't know," Betsy said. "What if it's something tiny?" She bent down with her hands on her knees, face-to-face with Addie. "What if it's small enough to hold in your hand?"

Addie's eyes grew wide and she peeled off behind Walsh. "Walsh, what if Mommy brings us a fairy?"

Ty finished the morning milking by ten thirty, which left him only a few minutes to shower before Betsy piled them all into her car—Ty's truck didn't have space for the girls' car seats—and sped down the highway to Elinore United Methodist Church. The parking lot was full of pickups and other sturdy, practical vehicles, most flecked with mud. Betsy parked under a tree at the side of the oyster-shell parking lot so the car wouldn't be so hot after church.

They unloaded the girls and headed for the front doors with Ty carrying Walsh and Addie's small hand firmly locked around Betsy's. Betsy smiled hello to families in the parking lot while Ty shook a few hands and made the usual comments about the weather. Hot, getting hotter. Tropical Depression 5 had just been given a name—Dawn—which added extra pep to their small talk.

As folks poured out of the double doors from the nine-thirty service, Betsy saw Anna Beth standing to the side in a bright-pink pantsuit and struggling to button her son Jackson's collar. He kept batting her hand away as only a thirteen-year-old boy could. When she spotted Betsy, she dropped her arms, gave him a hard stare, and marched toward Betsy.

"That boy." She blew a lock of hair out of her face. "First he wanted to wear shorts to church—shorts! I talked him into long pants, but he refuses to button that top button." She shook her head.

"I'll let you two ladies chat." Ty let go of Betsy's hand and joined Anna Beth's husband, Tom, by the wall, uncomfortable in his Sunday best. Ty still carried Walsh in his arms, as natural as if he were carrying a newborn calf. Addie clung to Betsy, creating a pocket of heat between their hands.

Behind Anna Beth, Jackson yanked on his collar, then noticed Betsy watching him. She smiled.

"It is about 90 percent humidity out here," she said. "It has to get hot under those tight collars."

"It's church!" Anna Beth said. "It's not about comfort—it's about reverence. Oh, there's my new boss." She smiled and waved at Duncan Burgess, the new principal at Elinore Elementary. "Better go make nice."

As Anna Beth worked her way toward Mr. Burgess, Betsy and Addie waited for the rest of the congregation to file out of the church. When the crowd cleared, Ty waved at her and she and Addie joined him at the front doors.

They took bulletins from the ushers and made their way to their regular seats—left side, five rows from the front. The girls began to fidget as soon as they sat down, turning around and staring at people in the row behind them, bouncing up and down on the cushioned pews.

"I'll be right back," Myrtle Davis, who sat at the end of their row, said. She appeared a moment later with children's coloring sheets and crayons. "You won't make it through the service without these." She winked. Betsy thanked her, embarrassed for not thinking to get them herself.

The organist started and Betsy opened her bulletin. Being in church usually calmed her, took her outside her own head and into another place, somewhere higher than her usual day-to-day frustrations. But today she was antsy. She crossed her legs and her foot bounced up and down, quick and hard. Ty rested his hand on her knee and she stopped. Took a deep breath and tried to concentrate.

During the pastor's prayer, she bowed her head like everyone else, but she kept her eyes open. She always did that. Something about closing her eyes while praying made her feel too loose, like she might float away if she wasn't anchored by the sight of the wooden pew, the red hymnals, Ty's leg next to hers. Instead of Ty's leg, it was Addie's knee and a fistful of crayons, but it helped.

After another hymn, the pastor began the sermon. Next to them, the girls' crayons quietly scratched across the paper. Walsh asked Ty to draw a unicorn and he took on the task with his usual focused attention. He was adding a flowing mane and pointed unicorn horn when Betsy saw a glow from the side pocket of her purse on the floor. She glanced at Ty, then leaned down to check the screen, although she already knew who it was.

She pulled the phone out of her purse, covering the glowing screen with her hand, then ducked her head and walked quickly down the center aisle. By the time she exited the double doors into the breezeway, she'd missed Jenna's call, of course. She tried to call her right back, but it went straight to voice mail. She typed out a quick text.

Sorry, in church. Call back.

She paced the breezeway while she waited. The only other person outside was a young mother holding a fussy baby. The mother rocked on her feet, gently bouncing the baby in her arms. When Betsy passed her, she heard the woman singing "You Are My Sunshine." She tried not to stare, but the baby's cheeks were so pink, her eyelashes so long. Her dimpled chin so perfect.

She turned so the woman wouldn't think she was crazy and stared at the phone instead, willing it to ring. Instead of ringing, she got a *ding* that meant Jenna had left a message. She walked to the edge of the breezeway, sensing the need for privacy, and held the phone to her ear.

"Hey, Bets." Jenna paused, then sighed. Betsy could almost see her sister, her fingers fiddling with something, her hair a mess of curls, her blue eyes big and round. "I really don't want to leave this in a voice mail, but I'm afraid I might not get cell service again for a while. Something's come up. My mentor here gave me the option of extending my retreat and I . . ." She took a deep breath. "I took it."

Betsy closed her eyes.

"It sounds crazy, I know. It's just that I've only now had a sort of breakthrough to where I can . . . I don't know, see straight, I guess. I've finally gotten to the place where things are clicking. The first two weeks barely scratched the surface." She paused. Betsy crossed her free arm across her stomach, holding herself tight. "I know this is so last minute and I'm being irresponsible, but, Betsy, I just can't . . . I'm so sorry to ask this of you. I can't leave now, and I don't know how else to explain it." Jenna exhaled and so did Betsy. "I know the girls are having a blast. I hope they're not too much trouble and . . . I hope you can understand this. Please understand. I'll call again as soon as I can. And tell . . . please tell them I love them."

Betsy pulled the phone away from her ear and tried to call back, but no answer. She closed her eyes again and touched the phone to her forehead. Behind her, someone stopped. "Are you okay?"

It was the mother with the baby. Betsy nodded. "Thanks."

"Just checkin'." The woman swayed to keep the baby asleep on her shoulder. "You looked a little faint. Thought I might have to find a chair or something for you."

Betsy took a breath and pulled open the door. From the back of the sanctuary, she could see between other heads and shoulders to where Ty, Addie, and Walsh sat, their heads bowed, all probably still working on their crayon masterpieces. Next to them was the empty space reserved for her. Fingers of emotion squeezed her heart and tears prickled at the corners of her eyes.

She strode back to their pew. When she sat, Ty looked over at her and raised his eyebrows. *Jenna?* he mouthed.

Betsy nodded and turned her gaze to the front of the church where the pastor was wrapping up his sermon. Ty reached across the back of the pew and laid his big warm hand on her shoulder.

twenty-one

Ty

Tropical Storm Dawn has made a sharp curve
to the north, heading north/northeast at
40 mph. It is expected to continue on this
track over the next 2—3 days. Residents of
the central Gulf Coast should take proper
precautions in the event Dawn gains speed.

The radio spit out Dawn's coordinates as Ty opened the gate for the
remaining forty cows to exit the barn. When the last one trailed
out, swishing her tail as if waving good-bye, he grabbed the water
hose. Aiming it at the floor of the milking parlor, he turned the
faucet on full blast.

To his right, fifteen curious faces pressed up against the wide
window of the observation room. A group of YMCA summer
campers had come early today to watch the milking. They were

the second field trip this week, which was probably a good thing. Something to distract Addie and Walsh from the fact that their mom did not, in fact, show up as she was supposed to with their promised treats and a ride back home to Nashville.

As soon as Betsy sat back down in church on Sunday after receiving the phone call, he knew something was wrong. She filled him in as they made the girls' lunches after church. Ty took a deep breath to keep his anger in check.

"Did you ask her when she's coming back?"

"I couldn't ask her. It was a voice mail."

"Did you try calling her back?"

"Of course I did. She didn't answer. Or it didn't go through. Or something."

Ty laughed low. "Of course she calls you while you're in church. Where else would you be at eleven thirty on a Sunday morning? Leaving a quick message is much easier than explaining yourself." He dragged his hand through his hair.

"I don't think she purposely called while we were in church."

He gave her a look and rolled his eyes.

"You're not getting mad at me, are you? This is not my fault."

Their whispers had grown harsh—not what he intended, but he couldn't help himself. With one call to the Betsy Franklin Rescue Service, Jenna was off the hook. Again.

"I know it's not your fault. I just don't like the way she uses us. Uses you."

"I'm her sister, Ty. I don't have a choice."

"Yes, you do. You do have a choice, though it looks like you're dead set against using it." He stood from his kitchen stool. "Let's go talk to them then." They had to tell the girls something. Well, mainly Addie. Walsh seemed happy as a clam no matter what she was doing, but Addie was sensitive. Aware. Betsy had wanted to make it sound simple, like Jenna's car broke down or she had to make an extra stop before coming back, but Ty pushed for the truth.

"I can't tell them I don't know when she's coming back," Betsy said.

Ty nodded at Addie, whose face was pressed up against the window in the living room, watching the driveway. "Twenty bucks says she'll know you're lying."

Finally, Betsy told them Jenna just needed some more time. It was a version of the truth, at least.

Since their "discussion" in the kitchen, they'd danced around the subject of Jenna. They didn't bring her up, but her presence—the *lack* of it—filled up their house anyway.

"Whatcha think about the weather report?" Carlos wrenched Ty from his thoughts, bringing him back to the barn. "It's headed for the sweet spot."

Ty looked up just in time to see Betsy smile from the window in the observation room, the kids in a swarm all around her. Ty lifted his chin in response, then remembered she hated the "cool guy nod," as she called it, and held up a hand instead. Addie and Walsh were mixed in with the other kids—two innocent, wide-eyed faces in the sea of middle schoolers, all equally as enthralled as the girls.

Ty turned back to Carlos. "Too early for the sweet spot. And she's still just a tropical storm." He directed the stream of water to the remaining hay and sawdust on the floor.

The "sweet spot" was a very nonscientific method Ty used to predict which storms would affect them—either by a direct hit or by putting coastal Alabama on the east side of the eye, pounding them with the worst of the wind and rain. When storms hit a certain path in the Gulf of Mexico, they often seemed to get caught in a current that funneled them north toward the Mississippi-Alabama border. No meteorologist worth his suspenders would put stock in Ty's "sweet spot" method, but he'd been right so many times, he'd lost count.

Carlos grabbed the wide broom and pushed the standing water out of the barn. "Here's hoping you're right. I'm taking Gloria to Panama City next weekend. Donna—"

"Dawn."

"Whatever. She better not mess up my plans."

Ty turned off the faucet, then curled the hose around the hook. "I was supposed to take Betsy somewhere like that soon. A vacation." A bead of sweat dripped from his forehead into his eye as he wound the hose. He swiped his face with the back of his hand.

"And? What's stopping you? I can take care of things here."

Ty nodded to the window. Betsy had directed the kids' attention to the old black-and-white photos lining the walls of the observation room, but Addie and Walsh remained pressed against the glass. They both grinned when he looked their way.

"Yeah, I've been meaning to ask you about that. Didn't want to pry. How long are they staying?"

Ty chuckled. "The million-dollar question."

Behind the glass, the kids trailed out of the observation room toward the door. Betsy led them over to the side yard where a cow had wandered over to the fence, likely suspecting small hands full of sweet treats. Without even seeing the characteristic diamond-shaped spot on her nose, Ty knew it was Rosie. She was the most affectionate of the whole herd. She pressed her cheek against the wooden posts, and the kids reached through the fence to pet her face and back.

Ty kept four bulls on the farm, and the Grantleys up in Stapleton had a herd of fifteen. When Ty's four hadn't had success with Rosie, they tried several of the bulls from the Grantley farm. Ty had done all he could do for her—all he could stomach. Rosie couldn't seem to get pregnant and the vet had no answers for them. But the girl was maternal and nurturing to everything she saw, whether cow, person, or barn cat. She licked, she nuzzled, she even cleaned other cows' calves.

After a moment, Rosie walked away from the kids' curious hands and fingers to visit another heifer, number 046. Forty-six was easy to spot because she was all white except for the black on her tail and her legs below the knees. A year younger than Rosie, 046 had been successfully impregnated three months ago. From the looks of it, they'd have a Christmas calf. Rosie sidled up to 046 and rubbed her cheek against the other cow's neck.

That evening after a quick and chaotic dinner with Betsy and the girls, Ty retreated to the barn to put away the extra bags of feed and hay he'd bought that afternoon. Some might think that after being in the barn all day, a farmer would relish closing the door behind him at the end of the workday and leaving it behind. The truth was, nighttime was Ty's favorite time in the barn. While the sky outside grew dark, the barn was lit with warm light. The cows were well fed and content, moths fluttered in the lights, and industrial fans on either end of the barn swirled lazily, taking the edge off the heat. The aroma of the cedar beams and rafters filled the air.

As he pulled out a half-used yellow legal pad to note which supplies he still needed to add to their stock, the screen door slammed, then Addie's and Walsh's voices carried through the dark. He looked up to see Betsy following the girls to the barn.

"I thought y'all would be asleep by now," he said as Walsh ran to him and hugged his leg. He looked up at Betsy and she shrugged.

"They weren't even close to settling down. They begged to come see you, so here we are."

He stood and pried Walsh's arms from around his legs. He patted her on the back, and she ran off to the other side of the barn with Addie. "How are you?" he asked Betsy. He shoved his hands into his pockets. "Sorry I had to come back out here. I wanted to get this stuff put away before we need it." He gestured to the pile of bags behind him.

"You getting ready for Dawn?"

"Well, not her necessarily. She won't be too bad. But there'll be more."

"She's in the sweet spot," Betsy said.

Ty laughed, rubbed a hand over his eye. "That sweet-spot business is ridiculous. You know that, right?"

"No," she said with a smile. "If Farmer Ty says it's real, I believe it."

She looked so beautiful in her black sleeveless top and white shorts. Her long legs had the first hints of a summer tan. Wisps of brown hair brushed her cheeks.

"What is it?" She looked down at her clothes, then back at him.

Why did he all of a sudden feel uncomfortable around his own wife, this woman he'd been married to for eight years, known for a decade? He was fidgety, nervous. Words bounced around in his mouth, but the right ones refused to come out.

"Have you talked to Jenna?" he finally asked, his voice quiet so the girls wouldn't hear.

The smile that played at the corners of her mouth disappeared. She shook her head. "Texts mostly. Nothing substantial."

"Nothing about when she's coming back?"

Betsy shook her head.

"And you're okay with that?"

"What can I do? She's six hours away, at least. I can't sit her down and force her to talk to me."

"Did she tell you any more about this extension? Or what she thinks is going to happen when it's over?"

"I don't know any details. Just that she had a breakthrough and wasn't ready to pack everything up and leave just yet. They gave her the chance to stay longer and she took it."

Ty sat back down and picked up his legal pad again. Crossed out a few words, wrote them again. Pulled his cap off. "What are we supposed to do?"

"Nothing. We can't kick them out. It's not their fault." She reached up and tucked a loose strand of hair into the knot at the back of her head. When it fell down into her eyes again, she swatted it away.

"That's not what I mean. I know we need to take care of them. I *want* to do that. It's just . . . It's frustrating that she only thinks about herself. Not about how this affects anyone else."

Their whispered conversation stopped when Addie ran back into the barn. "Can I feed one of the cows?"

Ty exhaled and stood. "I think I know of a girl who needs a late-night snack. Come on." He glanced back at Betsy, then led the girls to Rosie's stall along the back wall of the barn. Rosie stood facing out to the barn, as if she'd been expecting guests. Ty dipped a cup into a bag of oats hanging on the wall and handed it to Addie. "Here. Hold this up to her mouth." Addie giggled when Rosie stuck her tongue down into the cup.

Ty tugged on Betsy's arm and they moved a few steps away from the girls. "I know she's your sister and we need to help," he whispered. "There's just got to be a limit to how much we can do."

She took a deep breath and exhaled through puffed cheeks. "Fine. If you want them gone so bad, I'll tell her she has to come back. Now. Tomorrow."

Ty slapped his cap against the side of his leg. "That's not— I don't know what else to say, Bets. I'm not the bad guy here."

"I know," she said, her words clipped, her mouth tense.

He shoved his cap back on his head and pulled it down low. He was done trying to fix this tonight.

What he and Betsy had put back together in the months since they last left the clinic was like an eggshell. A fragment of what they used to have. He wanted his wife back—he wanted it all back—and he wasn't sure they could continue to build it with the girls here. It had been hard enough with just the two of them. Well, the two of them, five farmhands, two hundred cows, and assorted knobby-kneed schoolkids darting around, making a mess of his barn.

Maybe that was the problem. Too much intrusion, not enough privacy. Maybe if things could just settle down for once—be calm and still and easy—they could get each other back.

But he was a smart enough man to know life wasn't like that.

twenty-two

Betsy

Dawn rolled into Mobile Bay as a Category 1 hurricane, confirming Ty's theory that the Gulf waters weren't yet warm enough to sustain a strong storm. Despite the low rating, however, Dawn arrived at high tide, resulting in downtown Mobile covered in five feet of floodwaters. Thankfully, flooding wasn't an issue in Elinore, twenty-five miles east of Mobile, but the gusty winds and heavy rainfall made for a rough night of sleep.

While the winds blew and rain pounded, Walsh slept and Addie cried. Ty spent the night downstairs, ready for action in case the house or barn sustained damage, and Betsy spent most of the overnight hours in and out of the girls' room consoling Addie.

"When will it stop?" Addie sobbed as a strong gust of wind lashed the side of the house.

"Soon, soon," Betsy murmured. She sat on the edge of the bed, rubbing what she hoped were comforting circles on Addie's back. "Hurricanes blow hard for a few hours, but eventually they just run out of steam. Then morning will come and it'll all be over."

"What about the cows?" Addie sniffed. "Are they okay?"

"They're just fine. Uncle Ty put them out in the back pasture so they're away from trees or anything else that can hurt them."

"I hope so. Oh, I hope Rosie isn't scared." Thoughts of Rosie caused a new gush of tears. Betsy grabbed a tissue from the dresser and wiped Addie's nose. Just a few feet away, Walsh slept in peace, as if all was right with the world.

Did Addie always react like this to bad storms? Granted, this wasn't an average thunderstorm, but Betsy and Ty had encountered much worse. Then again, Addie was only five, and hurricanes didn't make it all the way up to Nashville. Still, Betsy wondered how often Jenna had sat up late at night with one of the girls, knowing she'd have to be at work early the next morning.

Finally, sometime after midnight, Addie lay still, exhausted by her tears and the late hour. When Betsy's own eyes began to droop, she brushed Addie's hair back from her face and stood to leave.

"Could you stay with me?" Addie's voice was quiet but pleading. Betsy paused. The last time Addie had asked her to stay, she'd woken up with both girls tucked in next to her and her heart thumping.

"Please?"

Betsy sighed. "Of course I'll stay." But instead of lying down next to Addie, she sat on the floor next to the bed, one arm raised over her head to hold Addie's hand. She could handle the floor, her arm falling asleep, her hand sandwiched between Addie's small, warm ones. She woke the next morning with a crick in her neck and shoulder, but her heart felt okay.

Two days later, Betsy stood at the washing machine staring at a pile of small, damp, dirt-streaked clothes. As the wife of a farmer, Betsy had all kinds of stain-removal methods in her arsenal—Tide bleach pen, OxiClean, Fels-Naptha, vinegar and lemon juice, hair spray, salt crystals—but after stomping in puddles and exploring the rain-soaked farm for hours the previous day, the girls' clothes were covered in mud and Betsy was at a loss. How in the world had Jenna kept their clothes so clean? Betsy made a mental note to ask if there was some miracle stain-stick she'd yet to discover.

Behind her, Addie lay sprawled out on the floor coloring while Walsh explored the dark recesses under the couch. Betsy shut the door of the washing machine and turned it on. One more try wouldn't hurt, but they needed new clothes.

"Hey, girls," she called. "How about a trip to Target?"

Addie scrambled off the floor fast as lightning. "Mommy lets us pick something from the dollar bins."

"Oh yeah?"

Addie nodded. "If our hands don't get too grabby in the store."

Betsy smiled. "I think we can make that happen."

The rain had fizzled, so Betsy rolled down the windows in the car to take in the water-cleansed breeze. Dark clouds zipped across a mottled sky. No sunshine yet, but it would come soon, heating the moisture to a steamy wall of humid heat.

"What are those birds, Aunt Betsy?"

Addie pointed out the window to three spindly legged, long-necked birds soaring over Highway 35.

"Those are blue herons. They fly over water looking for fish to eat."

"But there's no water here. It's just a bunch of grass and cows."

"Well, we're not too far from the Gulf. And we have the creek. Remember where you and Uncle Ty threw sticks?"

"Yeah."

"The creek is full of little minnows and fish, so the herons like to stick around. One time I found a mama heron sitting on a big nest down by the creek."

"Did she have eggs?"

Betsy nodded. "She did. Pretty ones."

Betsy had been cutting overgrown brush at the back of their property when she'd spotted a blue heron perched on a pile of sticks and leaves on the other side of the creek. It was nestled in the tree line next to the water, almost camouflaged. The heron's head was turned to the side, but Betsy knew it was staring at her with that one tiny eye. When she took a careful step backward, away from the creek, she stumbled over her pile of brush. She caught herself before falling but the noise spooked the heron and it flew off, revealing eggs in the nest. Five blue ones about the size of a child's fist.

Betsy came back every day after, hoping to see the heron on the nest, but the bird never returned. The eggs remained in the nest until one day, the only thing left was a mess of shells and wispy gray feathers stuck to the leaves. She read somewhere that once a heron has been disturbed while sitting on eggs, she will deem the area unsafe and abandon the nest and the eggs. When that happened, predators—dogs, alligators, hawks—would often get the eggs.

Betsy chose to believe the heron came back for her babies and Betsy just missed seeing her. She imagined five little baby herons poking along behind their mother down the creek, miles away from her meddling eyes.

Just before Betsy pulled onto Highway 59, the main thoroughfare through Baldwin County, her phone rang. Thinking Ty might be curious about where they'd gone, she grabbed it out of her purse.

"Betsy? Hi." Her sister's voice was quiet, a little cautious. "How are things going?"

"Well . . ." Betsy turned and glanced over her shoulder. Addie was airplaning her hand out the open window and Walsh was playing with Addie's stuffed elephant. "The girls are fine. I wish you'd talked to me about all this first though. It's . . . it's a lot." She tried to keep her voice low.

"I know. I'm so sorry to have dropped it on you like that. It's just that I had to give a quick answer or they would have offered the extension to someone else."

"Would that have been a bad thing? Don't you need to get back to work?" *Or see your kids?*

Jenna paused a beat. "Well, technically I'm between jobs right now, so staying here a little longer won't affect my work."

"What do you mean, 'between jobs'?" Betsy's heart picked up speed in her chest.

"They could only hold my job for the two weeks I told them I'd be gone. I talked to my boss yesterday and he said since I couldn't give him a firm answer of when I'd be back, he's going to have to fill the position, which I totally understand."

"Wait—but you . . ." So many questions bounced around in Betsy's mind, she struggled to form words to ask any of them. She took a deep breath. "You don't know when you're coming back?"

"Not . . . specifically. They've left it up to me how long I stay. The whole thing wraps up August 15th, so I guess that'd be the very latest."

"Jenna, this is . . . You can't lose that job. You have insurance with it and they've been so good about giving you time off when you need to take care of the kids. How are you going to find something like that again? And what will you do for money while you're looking?" She hated sounding like the mom, but someone had to ask the right questions.

"I have some money saved up, believe it or not. It won't tide me over for too long, but it's enough to cover rent and bills while I'm here. We'll be fine. I'm very good at being frugal. And about the job, I have manager experience, so I should be able to pick up a job at another coffee shop with no problem. Anyway, I'm hoping I don't have to go back to making coffee. That's kind of the whole point of being here."

Betsy recognized the familiar determination in Jenna's voice, and she bit back the avalanche of words threatening to pour out.

Jenna sighed. "I know it seems like a spontaneous, flaky thing to do, but trust me when I say I've put a lot of thought into this. I've worked hard to take care of my girls, and there's no way I'd leave a steady job if I didn't think what's happening here could put me in the position to make a better life for them. For us."

"You're putting a lot of stock in this place. Are you sure it's going to be able to give you what you want?"

"Am I *sure*? No, I'm not. But I've been given a shot—maybe my only shot—at providing something good, something meaningful for me and the girls. For them to see me pursuing a dream for myself. Shouldn't I take it?"

The haze of anger and frustration that had clouded Betsy's brain since the Sunday-morning phone call cleared for a minute, providing space to breathe and think. On the surface, giving up her job seemed crazy, staying at this artists' retreat all summer seemed crazy, but knowing Jenna and her fierce determination to forge her own path, it made a strange sort of sense.

"Gregory—he's my mentor—he's helping me with contacts and building up my portfolio of work so I can use it as a résumé. Lots of artists leave this place and land jobs because of their time here. It could happen for me too."

Betsy nodded slowly. "So August 15th. That's, what, a little over a month away?"

"It could be less than that, but I don't want to leave until I've squeezed everything out of this place that I can."

"I hope you get what you want. I really do. I . . . can't say I totally agree with all this, but I know you, and I know you put your heart into whatever you're doing. If anyone could squeeze something meaningful and life changing out of all this, it'd probably be you."

Jenna exhaled. "Thanks."

Betsy glanced in the rearview mirror. Addie was watching her. "Addie wants to talk to you. I'm going to hand the phone over. Check in again soon, okay?" She reached behind her seat and passed the phone into Addie's waiting hands.

Addie wasted no time when she put the phone to her ear. "Mommy? When are you coming home?" After a pause, she gave a small, "Okay." Betsy waited for the tears, the pleas for her mother to come back, but instead, Addie smiled. It was small, but it was there. Then she launched into an explanation of the new hen Linda Daily had brought by for them.

Betsy rested her elbow on the window ledge and ran her hand through her hair. How was it that Jenna was allowed to slide her responsibilities onto Betsy—again, as Ty had reminded her—yet Betsy was the one feeling like she'd done something wrong?

"Her feathers are all different colors and we named her Rainbow Shine. Do you like that name? She's going to lay some eggs soon. Maybe you can meet her when you come back."

꩜

At Target the girls spotted a red shopping cart the size of a small bus and scrambled up into it. Betsy was used to seeing women pushing these carts through the store, expertly angling them around displays and racks without incident, even with children crawling in, around, and all over the carts. Today, Betsy learned that kind of maneuvering took skills she didn't possess.

She wheeled between racks of kids' clothes, bumping here and there, drawing raised eyebrows and sighs from other shoppers until she finally abandoned the cart behind a wall of Disney princess pajamas. She was pulling Walsh out of the seat when she heard a deep rumble of laughter behind her.

"I don't envy you, having to push that thing through the store," a man said.

Betsy set Walsh down and turned. Mr. Burgess, the new principal, smiled back at her. His gently lined face and kind eyes soothed a bit of the tension in her shoulders. She kept a hand on Walsh while Addie looked through a rack of Little Mermaid bathing suits. She smiled back at him. "That was a first for me, and I don't plan to try it again."

He laughed. "I'm Duncan Burgess." He reached out his hand. "And you're Mrs. Franklin, right?"

"I am, but it's just Betsy."

Walsh pulled out of Betsy's grip and raced to where Addie stood in front of a floor-length mirror trying on sun hats.

"I've been hoping I'd run into you, actually. You do the field trips, right? To your farm?"

Betsy nodded. "Fewer in the summer, but we still have them."

"I think it's a great program and I want to try to send a few more classes this next school year. I'd love your input on how to coordinate the trips with lessons on healthy eating, maybe community support. You can probably give the teachers some pointers for lessons that'll tie in well."

"I can try to help, although your teachers will know more than me. I can adjust the regular talk I give to the kids if they want me to focus more on a certain aspect of the process. Make it more science-based or more health-oriented. Whatever they want."

Mr. Burgess was nodding. "Wonderful. I figured you'd have some good ideas. Once we get a little closer to the start of the year, maybe we can sit down and talk through the details."

Over his shoulder, Betsy spotted Addie and Walsh between the racks. They'd left the mirror and now ventured toward the toy section. "Sorry, I'd better . . ." She gestured toward the girls.

"Right. Go grab 'em. You'll be in here all day if they make it to the toys. They're adorable. Your older one—she's about six?"

"That's a pretty good guess. She'll be six in December."

He held his hands up. "I've been a principal for thirty years. Comes with the job."

"I guess so. Well, they're my nieces."

"Ah, babysitting. I have three grandkids, so I do quite a bit of that myself. And I suppose being a school principal is a little like babysitting too. For the biggest family you can imagine." He laughed. "I do love children, but I'll tell you what—one of the best things about having kids is seeing the change in your spouse. I loved Carol in a whole new way after we had our first daughter. Children change people. They change everything." He shook his head, lost in memory. "Do you have kids?"

Betsy shifted her bag on her shoulder. "We don't. Not yet."

"Then you understand that particular beauty of babysitting.

You get to be around kids all day, then go home at night and enjoy the peace and quiet."

She just smiled.

⚭

Betsy and Ty met in early fall of her junior year. By Christmas, she was ready for him to meet her parents. She had friends who took every college boyfriend home to meet the parents, but Betsy hadn't dated anyone she wanted to put through the particular agony of dinner around the Sawyers' antique walnut dining table. For the life of her, she didn't know why she'd chosen a farmer as the first boyfriend to bring home. She could imagine her father's glances at Ty's callused hands, so different from his own milky-white hands that floated through the air each night as he conducted symphonies and concertos. She imagined her mom taking in Ty's tan, freckled skin, a clear indicator in her mind of inevitable skin cancer.

But she brought him anyway. Ever since their first date—he'd taken her to church at Auburn United Methodist, then to lunch at Amsterdam Café—she hadn't been able to shake the peculiar sensation that she no longer wanted to do life without him. That she needed him. That his singular strength, solidity, and masculinity was tied to her—knots and tangles that probably began long before she was born.

When she brought up the idea of him coming to her home over Christmas break, he agreed without a second of hesitation. The day after Christmas, he pulled up the driveway to her parents' house in his Chevy truck that rattled a little too loudly for her dad's taste.

"What is that racket?" Her father lowered the newspaper an inch and peered around the edge of the Arts and Culture section.

Jenna, a freshman at Alabama and eager for any kind of excitement, jumped out of her seat and ran to the front door just as their mother walked out of the kitchen drying her hands on a dish towel.

Ty barely had a chance to knock on the door before Jenna flung it open. Betsy imagined the scene from Ty's point of view: Jenna's blonde curls springing out everywhere, clunky black Dr. Martens, white sweater that looked appropriate until she turned around and you saw it was open in the back all the way to her waist. Their dad still in his chair, polishing his glasses with the end of his silk tie. Their mom standing poised in a pristine white apron—pristine because she'd ordered their meal from Highlands instead of attempting to cook something presentable for their first child's boyfriend. Betsy could almost hear her mother's thoughts. *Highlands for this guy?*

Dinner went as she'd expected it to. Food delicious, silences awkward, conversation stilted. But under the table, Ty gripped her hand, his thumb rubbing small circles into her palm. With his hand wrapped around hers, he answered her parents' questions as well as he could. They asked about his parents and his major. His grandfather's farm and how he'd make it profitable again after his grandfather's death two years before. He spoke of the dairy industry as a whole, and his family's farm in particular, with obvious pride.

"I knew I was going to be a dairyman before anyone even asked me what I wanted to be when I grew up." He took a sip of water and sat back in his chair. "It's been in my blood my whole life."

Her dad merely nodded, sipped his wine, and set the glass down. "I imagine it'd be hard for your livelihood to depend on something as fickle as the weather. Unpredictable animals. Crop prices."

Ty nodded. "It's an understandable concern. But honestly, sir, cows are pretty predictable, as far as animals go." He smiled. "Once you have a herd that's reproducing regularly, you milk 'em twice a day. That's the thing about cows—rain or shine, heat or cold, hurricane or drought, you've got milk coming twice a day. When milk means money, it's just a matter of getting that milk ready to sell. And I plan to grow most of our own crops in the fields, so we won't have to buy them. That eliminates the problem of fluctuating crop prices."

Her dad raised his eyebrows. "You seem to have it all figured out." He turned to her mom. "Maybe I should have been a dairy farmer, honey."

"Not sure you're cut out for such a rustic life, dear," her mother responded.

"I'm not sure anyone in this family is," her dad said.

Betsy folded her napkin into a neat square. "I can decide that."

From the other side of the table, Jenna winked at Betsy and smiled.

Ty cleared his throat. "Obviously there's a bit more involved, but that's the gist of it." They spoke like Ty was dense, but Betsy knew he picked up on their dismissive attitude. It rolled across the table in waves.

That night Betsy and Ty sat in her father's garden, wrapped in a blanket she pulled off the couch in the living room. Dozens of rosebushes, meticulously groomed by Jenna and their father, towered over the bench where they sat. "I'm sorry about my parents. They can be terrible sometimes."

"Not terrible. They've probably just never met anyone like me."

"I've never met anyone like you."

Ty laughed, low and quiet. "Is that a good thing?"

She nodded, aware—almost painfully so—of his leg pressed against hers, the heat from his hand pouring into her shoulder, her neck. Every nerve danced on edge, ready to jump.

"What do you think about my life? The life I'm going to have? Is it something you want?"

"I wouldn't be here if I didn't. *You* wouldn't be here if I didn't."

Ty smiled. "All this? The house, the fancy food, that Mercedes in the driveway?" He looked up at the house—two stories, Tudor-style, historic marker with an old family crest on the bricks by the door. "I can't give you all this. I'll give you everything I can, but there's no way it'll be like this."

"I didn't choose all this." She placed one finger under his chin and turned his face to hers. "But I did choose you."

twenty-three

Jenna

Jenna squatted on a fallen tree and tried to capture the lacy layer of mint-green fungus covering the bark. Gregory stood a few feet away. "Take it like that and you'll flatten out the texture." He stepped closer and pointed. "See what I mean?"

He'd been by her side instructing her for most of the week since she'd made the decision to extend her stay at Halcyon, sometimes snapping his own shots, other times stopping to give her a quick lesson on lighting, balance, composition. It was as if he'd taken her decision to stay as permission to actually teach her the more technical aspects of photography. His tutorials reminded her of excursions with Max back in Nashville.

Max would chew his lips to keep from giving her unsolicited tips or pointing out where she messed up. Sometimes she'd give in and let him say his piece, but other times she'd ignore his agitation. He was always a gentleman, albeit a grumpy one, never giving advice unless asked. Gregory, on the other hand, didn't care whether she wanted to hear his opinions. He just gave them anyway. That both thrilled and annoyed her.

"I'm trying it anyway," she responded. "Can I experiment or does that break one of your rules?"

Exasperated—both from the stifling heat and from Gregory's insistence on getting everything just right—she sat back on her heels and pushed her hair out of her face. As she did, the tree trunk she was perched atop shifted and sent her to the ground hard.

"Good save on the camera." He chuckled and reached down. She ignored his offer of help and pushed herself up with one hand, holding the camera away from the sand and dirt.

She stood and wiped her hand on her shorts. Though she was satisfied with the shots from the morning, the midday heat was wearing on her. "This isn't working. I think I need to stop and just try again tomorrow. Or at least later when it cools off."

"Cools off? It's Florida in the summer. It doesn't cool off." He looked at his watch. "I have an idea though."

Twenty minutes later, Jenna sat in Gregory's old Jeep Wrangler as he drove them away from Halcyon and toward the beach.

"I can't believe you've been here three weeks and haven't seen the Gulf yet." The top of the Jeep was open and the wind carried his words into the humid afternoon air.

"I almost forgot we were so close. Halcyon makes it feel like there's nowhere else to go."

He nodded. "That's the point. But it is good to get away sometimes." He grinned. "And you need a break."

She leaned her head back against the seat and closed her eyes. As they exited the preserve and crossed into cellular civilization, Jenna's phone began dinging with texts. After a quick look at the screen, she smiled.

Mario: Where are you, girl? No one can run this line like you can. The new manager is an idiot and we NEED you back here. So does your boyfriend ;)

Max: Heard through the grapevine you decided to extend your stay. Halcyon must be treating you well.

Delores: Hi dear. I don't want to bother you, but I noticed you're not back from your trip yet. Just making sure you're okay.

Betsy: Meet Rainbow Shine. And the girls send kisses.

Betsy's text included a photo of the girls staring through the fence of the henhouse at a huge hen with black-and-white polka-dotted feathers. Walsh's hand was up in a wave and Addie gripped Walsh's other hand.

"Everything okay?" Gregory looked over at the phone in her hands.

Jenna scrolled through the texts again, lingering on the photo of the girls. Her desire to touch them—to be with them—was so strong, she had to bite her lips to keep from asking Gregory to turn around and take her back so she could pack her things. "It's fine."

A few minutes later, he pulled off the road next to a long walkway leading to the beach. When their feet touched the sand, they went separate ways. Gregory set up his tripod near the edge of the water, and Jenna headed toward an abandoned lifeguard stand. Even from far off, she could see the splintered and broken boards on the side of the tower. With no houses or condos nearby, the beach was deserted, but she was still surprised no one had come by to repair the damage.

Bits of driftwood, shells, and damp seaweed littered the sand below the tower. It reminded her of an old *I Spy* book she and

Betsy had read as kids. They'd both loved studying the pages and picking out a marble or lollipop or domino from the tangle of miniature objects the photographer had painstakingly set up and photographed.

She knelt in the shade below the tower, the cool sand scratching her bare knees, and pulled her camera to her eye to capture the array of marine life stranded dozens of feet away from its home in the calm, blue-green water. Pastel-colored coquina clams, still closed tight, were nestled against sharp splinters of wood and clear blobs of jellyfish. She nudged a piece of seaweed with the back of her hand and uncovered a chunk of green sea glass. She picked it up and ran her fingers across the smooth, tumbled edges. Veins of dark blue threaded through the green. She slid the glass into her bag and lifted her camera again. Time slipped away as she shot the remains of countless high tides and all they'd left behind.

Sometime later, she glanced up at the sound of feet squeaking on the sand behind her. Gregory shaded his eyes from the sun's glare and set his bag and tripod down on a log of driftwood set back against the dunes.

"Looks like you've given up."

Jenna looked around her and smiled. "It seems so." Her camera rested on top of her button-down shirt where she'd peeled it off earlier, leaving her in a gray cotton tank top and shorts. Her legs were stretched out in front of her in the sand and she leaned back on her elbows. She'd done all she could today.

He sat down in the shade a couple feet away. Sand covered his calves and coated his forearms up to his elbows. She sat up and hugged her arms around her knees, absently twisting the purple-and-blue pipe-cleaner bracelet around her wrist. She'd worn it every day, just like she promised Addie.

They were quiet for a moment before he broke the silence. "What's going on in that head of yours?"

She hesitated, but the warm air and gentle breeze invited honesty. "I don't know if staying here was the right decision."

"Okay."

"As soon as I get it in my head that it was the best thing, I start to feel guilty about it. I keep going back and forth. It's just . . . I've worked so hard to show I've changed from who I used to be, but then here I go making yet another impulsive, selfish decision."

"Impulsive, maybe, but selfish? You really think being here is selfish?"

"I don't know. Maybe." A sand crab dashed across the hot sand in front of them. Jenna moved her foot and it darted in the other direction.

"Tell me why you're here. Why did you decide to stay?"

"I'm here for my girls. And for me too. To try to make things better for all three of us."

"And what about that is selfish? You're away from home, away from your children, away from work, all so you can focus on this talent—this *incredible* talent—that you hope can help give your family a leg up. And if it allows you to do something you love, then all the better. That's not selfish. Seems pretty selfless to me."

Jenna wiggled her feet under the sand until it felt cool to her toes. "I don't know. I don't know if Betsy sees it that way."

"You need to decide now—today—to trust that the decision to stay was a good one. It was the best thing because it allows you to keep working toward your goal of pursuing your passion and providing for your family. You have talent and you have drive—that combination can take you a long way in this industry. Connections don't hurt either, and that's where I come in handy." He grinned and she smiled in return.

"When it's all over and done, everyone will understand why you came here. Though I don't particularly care what anyone else thinks about why you came or why you stayed. It matters to me that you believe in yourself. If you do that, your girls will too."

"Who knew you were such a motivational speaker?"

He laughed. "Seriously. I don't think I've ever been so . . ."

"Encouraging? Uplifting?"

"I was going to say sentimental and sappy, but your way sounds better."

"I think you're in the wrong profession."

"Maybe so." He leaned back on his elbows and stretched one leg out in the sand. "I'll let you in on something else about me: I disappointed everyone in my life when I chose photography over a steady, stable job. My dad's a doctor, his dad was a doctor, and they all expected me to follow in line. It hurt them deeply that I didn't. But I couldn't abandon my dream for theirs. It would have been like giving up the best part of me, and I wasn't willing to do that."

"That sounds familiar."

"A retreat like this makes you feel refreshed. Energized. It's easy to expect everyone else to have changed because you have, but reality is still out there churning away. Your time away changes you, but it doesn't change anyone else." He sat up and brushed sand off the backs of his legs. "That's why I just keep going."

She smiled. "You just keep taking the next job? Keep moving forward?" She was kidding, but then she saw that he wasn't.

He reached down to where the sand crab raced back toward them, then disappeared down a tiny hole in the sand. "I've been offered a job in California. UC Berkeley. I'd be the head of the photography department. It's the only full-time job I've considered in twenty years of being on the road."

"Wow. That's big. Are you're taking it?"

He shrugged. "Thinking about it."

"You should take it. Who knows? Maybe you'll enjoy staying in one place for a while."

He stared out at the water as slow waves crept up the shore. "It'd be an incredible deal for me. I'd get an assistant to help with paperwork and some of my classes. I'd still be able to travel some for freelance gigs." He shrugged. "I don't know though. It'd be a big change, to have something regular. To have a boss. That might not go over well."

She imagined what it'd be like to have a job where she could challenge herself, excel, help others find their own creative eye. To work in the field that excited her, that made her feel alive. It was too much to contemplate.

She stood and brushed sand off her shorts and legs. "You'd be an idiot not to take it."

He laughed. "Do you always say exactly what you think?"

She nodded. "About as much as you do."

He stood and picked up his camera bag, then turned toward the Jeep. "We should get back. Tonight's fried chicken. I need to get all the Southern food I can get if I'm going to head west."

"What's the start date?"

"*If* I decide to take it, the job starts the beginning of fall semester. But I'd probably need to get out there a little early to settle in."

She tied the shirt around her waist as they stepped across the hot sand toward the road. She couldn't even think about fall.

When she opened her door and climbed in, she noticed her

phone sitting on the seat. She hadn't meant to leave it behind. She scooped it up and checked the screen for any missed messages or calls. One voice mail. As Gregory cranked the engine and pulled away from the beach, Addie's voice trailed out of the phone.

"Mommy! Walsh caught a fish! Uncle Ty took us fishing in the creek behind their house. I didn't catch anything. We threw Walsh's fish back so it could go back to its family . . . What? . . . Aunt Betsy wants to talk to you."

After a moment of muffled voices, Betsy came on the line. "Walsh is quite a good fisherman. She pinched off a piece of hot dog, stuck it on the hook, and dropped the line in the water like she'd been fishing her whole life." She let out a small laugh. "Anyway, hope things are going well. Give us a call when you can."

Jenna dropped her phone back into her bag. She propped her elbows on her knees and leaned her head into her hands, then turned her face to him. "My kids are having a lot of fun. They sound happier than ever."

"That's a good thing, right? You can concentrate on you."

She nodded, then sat back in her seat. The wind whipped through her hair and fluttered her shirt against her skin.

"Ever been to California?" he asked.

twenty-four

Betsy

"Aunt Betsy?"

Walsh's voice was a whisper at the edge of Betsy's consciousness. She had her laptop open and papers—a calendar, QuickBooks printouts, notes from three dairy association meetings, and a YMCA summer camp flyer—spread all over the heart-pine kitchen table. It was only ten o'clock, but with the girls up before six, the morning had been a long one.

"Aunt Betsy?"

Five minutes ago, when Walsh had called her name multiple times, Betsy had jumped up and walked to where Walsh sat in the window seat only to find that Walsh's big toe itched and could Betsy please scratch it?

Fool me once, Betsy thought with a tight smile. This time she tuned out Walsh's calls and kept her eyes on her laptop. She'd been going back and forth with the director of Forsythe Ranch, a horse farm a couple miles away that hosted children's camps throughout the summer. The director was hoping to find a regular field trip slot for the rest of the summer. A set group coming each week would be a chunk of extra money for the farm.

"Aunt . . . Bet . . . sy."

"Hang on just a sec," Betsy mumbled as she clicked to open the latest e-mail from the director.

"Aunt Betsy, I have to go *potty!*" Walsh's voice rang out, her voice louder with each word. She stood right next to Betsy, her dark hair a messy halo around her head, her face twisted in frustration.

Betsy sighed, then smiled and snapped her laptop shut. "Okay. Let's go." She shuttled Walsh down the hall to the bathroom.

While Walsh sat on the toilet and sang, Betsy perched on the edge of the tub, her chin in her hand. As someone who liked things to be on time and in order, having two kids in the house with no concept of or desire for a schedule was difficult. Plans and routines helped keep Betsy's mind from wandering to painful places, and while she tried valiantly to stick to those routines, the girls were just as eager to mess them up. They didn't do it on purpose, but knowing that didn't make it any easier.

Once Walsh finished her business and Betsy helped her wash her hands, they found Addie on her stomach in the den, rolling a pink bouncy ball to Etta, whose whole body was under the couch. Only the cat's arms stuck out, batting at the ball. Walsh joined in and Betsy crossed through the room toward the kitchen. On the way, she caught a glimpse of Ty outside. With a large bale of hay in his arms, he walked around the side of the barn and disappeared in the back.

Betsy filled a glass with water and took a sip, then grabbed a damp rag and wiped at a sticky spot on the counter. Behind her in the den, Addie and Walsh whispered, their voices growing louder as they disagreed on something, then settled down. Then footsteps crossed the hardwood floor into the kitchen.

"We're playing house," Addie announced. "I'm the big sister and she's the baby sister. You can be the mommy."

"Girls, I need to finish up some work on the computer. I'm sorry. Can you be the mom and let Walsh be the sister?"

"But I'm not big enough. We need someone big."

"I'm sorry. I can't do it right now. You'll have to figure it out on your own."

Addie's lip stuck out, and a swift wave of irritation mixed with Betsy's guilt, creating a stifling blend of unfamiliar emotion.

"Mommy always plays the mommy for us."

"That's because she is your mommy." Betsy's voice was testy as she tossed the damp rag into the sink.

Addie paused for a moment and Betsy braced herself. But then Addie turned to Walsh. "I'll be the fancy lady and you be my puppy."

Walsh promptly dropped to her hands and knees, barked, and crawled off to the den. Addie followed behind holding an imaginary leash.

Just as Betsy sat back down at the computer, she heard the back door open and two sets of feet scurrying outside. She took a deep breath. Maybe she could finish her work now. It was so peaceful, twenty minutes passed before she thought to check on the girls. She glanced toward the backyard, then reluctantly closed her laptop.

Outside, she found Addie sitting on the grass next to the henhouse, making quiet clucking noises to Parsley, a sweet Speckled Sussex hen pecking near the fence.

"Addie? Is Walsh with you?"

Addie kept clucking but shook her head.

"Do you know where she is?"

Another head shake.

Betsy peered around the edge of the henhouse and scanned

the backyard. She checked Walsh's usual hiding spot behind a big hydrangea near the porch steps. Nothing.

"Walsh?" she called. "Walsh, come on out!"

After a quick walk through the house in case she'd missed Walsh coming back inside, Betsy's heart started to beat a little faster. Logically, Walsh couldn't have gotten far, but telling herself that didn't slow down her heart. She focused her eyes on the entrance to the barn and the sheds surrounding it. No movements small enough to come from a tiny Walsh.

"Walsh? Walsh!"

Picking up on the panicked decibel of Betsy's voice, Addie crossed the yard and wrapped her arms around Betsy's leg. "Where is she?"

"I don't know," Betsy said, peeling Addie's arms from her legs. "If you'd kept your eye on her—" She stopped herself—had she really expected a five-year-old to babysit her three-year-old sister?— but the damage was done. Addie's chin trembled and her eyes filled.

Betsy knelt in front of her. "I'm sorry. I didn't mean that. It was not your job to watch your sister. It was my job. But we can find her together, okay?"

When Addie sniffed and nodded, Betsy took her hand and half led, half pulled her toward the barn. Ty rounded the corner just as she made it to the barn door. He smiled but stopped when he saw Betsy's face. "What's wrong?"

"I can't find Walsh."

"What do you mean, you can't find her?"

"I mean, I don't know where she is. I was inside working and I thought they were both out in the yard. When I came out, Addie was with the hens and Walsh was nowhere." She took a breath. "I've looked all around the house. Inside and out."

"Okay, well, she's got to be somewhere. Walker's in the barn. I'll check with him."

Inside, Walker was adjusting dials on the tanks, getting the morning's milk ready for transport. He shook his head when Ty asked if he'd seen Walsh running around. As Betsy passed him on her way to the other side of the barn, she heard him mumble, "Didn't know babysitting was part of my job description."

Back out in the sunshine, she and Ty called for Walsh over and over, looking in every small space they could imagine Walsh might want to inspect. Tears were pricking the backs of her eyes when she saw Carlos strolling toward the barn with Walsh by his side. Betsy exhaled.

"I found someone out in the side pasture," Carlos called. "This little lady was pretending to drive the tractor. Good thing the keys weren't in it. From the looks of her, she'd have figured out a way to drive off with it if given half a chance."

Betsy squatted in front of Walsh, who grinned, her cheeks still smeared with jelly from breakfast. Betsy wanted to ask her what in the world she'd been thinking, but that was just it—Walsh hadn't been thinking. All she knew was she wanted to explore, so she did. She hadn't meant to do anything wrong.

"Please don't leave the backyard unless someone is with you. A *grown-up* someone. Deal?"

"Deal."

Betsy rubbed jelly from the corner of Walsh's mouth, then stood. When Addie and Walsh scampered off toward the backyard, with Addie pulling Walsh's hand and telling her about Parsley the hen, Betsy turned to Ty.

"That could have been bad."

Ty ran his hand over the top of his head and sighed. "Jenna's got her work cut out for her with that one." He squeezed Betsy's hand. "Sorry, but I've got to get back to it. Milk truck's gonna be here any minute."

Betsy nodded and followed the girls toward the house. Back inside, they went right back to their antics, bouncing the pink ball around in the den, oblivious to the panic that had just ripped through Betsy's morning. She was beginning to see why Jenna wanted to get away for a little while.

Just as she sat back down to work, the pink ball bounced into the kitchen, ricocheted off the fridge and Betsy's shoulder, and knocked over her glass of water. Etta followed, looking frantically for the ball, her claws skidding on the hardwood floor. The girls were close behind in a fit of giggles.

Betsy jumped up and mopped the water with a dish towel before it could reach her computer. She picked up the dripping YMCA flyer and dropped it into the trash can, then shut the laptop. *Not gonna happen today.* She gathered her papers, set them on top of the computer, and put the whole stack on the washing machine, the only place she could be sure the girls wouldn't find it. On the way back through the kitchen, she grabbed her phone.

"Hey, you," Anna Beth boomed. "How's it going?"

"Uh, fine, just losing my mind. And Walsh.

Anna Beth laughed.

"You think I'm kidding. I lost her. Carlos found her sitting on the tractor in the pasture. All I wanted was to get a tiny bit of work done this morning, but between trips to the potty and spilled drinks and missing children, I still have a million e-mails to send and phone calls to return. Is it always like this?"

"Pretty much. But that's when you just give up and get out of the house. It's not any calmer over here, but you're welcome to come by. I have wine in the fridge and a glass with your name on it."

Betsy smiled. Anna Beth actually did have a wineglass with Betsy's name on it, a holdover from when Anna Beth hosted a monthly book club at her house. The club was never really about the books though. "Thanks, but some adult company's all I need. We'll be there in ten."

Anna Beth's house was a hive of activity. Jackson and his friends were upstairs playing video games, their voices careening down the staircase. Lucy and a neighbor were spread out at the kitchen table making beaded bracelets. "Everyone wears them," Lucy explained when Betsy asked. Addie stood still as a statue next to the table, watching the older girls with focused attention.

"If you want, I can make you one too," Lucy said.

Addie nodded. "But you have to make one for Walsh too."

"She watches out for little sister, doesn't she?" Anna Beth said to Betsy. The two of them sat on the couch, their legs propped on the coffee table.

Betsy nodded. "For the most part." Recalling the events of the last hour, she wanted to add that it would have been nice if Addie had been watching out for Walsh this morning, but she bit back the pointless thought. "They fight too—and over such silly things—but Addie takes her big sister job seriously, I think."

"Still no word from Jenna?"

"Oh, there's word, just nothing definite. The retreat shuts down in mid-August, and she's not sure if she'll stay until the end or leave early. They left it up to her to decide. She wants . . . She feels she still has more work to do before she wraps up."

"And you're just hanging on until then."

Betsy shrugged. "We're doing okay."

Anna Beth shook her head and readjusted the pillow behind her back. "I can't imagine. You're taking to it so well. If my sister dropped her kids off at my house, I'd be hot on her trail, tracking her down and yanking her back here to take them home. Granted, her kids are full-blown teenagers and as sullen as the day is long. Nose rings, black clothes, the whole bit. Your two are a bit easier, I'd imagine."

Betsy gave a small laugh, her fingers busy working a knot out of a long plastic necklace. When she loosened the strands, she handed the necklace back to Walsh, who quickly tied it back together. "I don't know. In some ways, it seems kids who did their own thing might be easier."

"Maybe. I guess there are pros and cons for all the ages."

Betsy waited until Walsh scampered back to the kitchen table. "They're just so . . . They *need* so much from me all the time. I feel like I'm constantly running on all cylinders. I'm not used to it. And losing track of Walsh? That was scary. I don't know how Jenna does it."

Anna Beth's eyebrows scrunched together. "Sorry to tell you, but everything about parenting is scary. It's good, but scary too. When you're thrown into parenthood—whether it's planned or unplanned—you just learn to figure things out. And feeling like you're running around all the time? That's part of it, but when it's your own kids, it's a little different. It doesn't make it a total cinch, but I know Lucy's and Jackson's quirks and habits almost better than I know my own. When it happens for you, it won't feel so chaotic." She paused, listening to the thump and roar of the group of boys playing upstairs. "Well, that's a lie. It'll always feel chaotic. But you'll be up to the task. You'll be great."

Betsy lifted a corner of her mouth in a sad smile. "I think you're the only person who still thinks it'll happen for us."

"If you don't believe it, then it's my job to believe it for you. That's a job I take seriously."

Betsy sighed and smiled, thankful not to have to pretend with Anna Beth.

"I remember those days like they were yesterday," Anna Beth said. "Not being able to get anything done without someone needing something *right now*. The potty, a snack, a Band-Aid, whatever. These days, the requests are just more expensive. This morning Jackson storms into my bedroom and tells me he needs four hundred dollars. Four *hundred* dollars. I asked him what in the world for, and do you know what he said? He said he needed it for a new PlayStation. I mean, the nerve."

Jackson bounded down the stairs then, his buddies just behind him, all of them sounding like a herd of cattle thundering down the hallway. As he pleaded with Anna Beth to drive them up to the gas station for Slurpees and the girls at the kitchen table burst into laughter, Betsy closed her eyes. Just a five-second moment of nothingness. When she opened them, Walsh was digging in Betsy's purse.

"Walsh, what do you need, honey?" She rose from the couch to pull Walsh's curious hands out of her purse.

"My snack," she replied. "I'm hungry."

"Me too," Addie called from the table. "What'd you pack for a snack? And I'm thirsty too."

Betsy swiveled her head toward Anna Beth, one eye squeezed shut. "I forgot snacks."

Anna Beth hopped up off the couch. "Don't worry a thing about it. I have enough snacks to feed the neighborhood."

After dinner that night, Walsh wanted to see the hens. "Can we go?" she begged, her brown eyes round and hopeful. A cookie crumb clung to her cheek despite a quick swipe with a handful of napkins. Betsy reached down and brushed it off.

"Please?" Addie was already shoving her feet into her shoes.

Betsy thought of her computer on top of the washing machine, where it had sat untouched since earlier in the day. An array of dirty dishes lay on the counter and table.

"I'll take 'em." Ty set his plate and glass in the sink. "Let's go, girls." He opened the back door and waited while they zipped under his arm and down the porch stairs. "You want to come too?" he asked her.

Outside, the light had softened into that perfect twilight hour when everything seemed easier, lighter, like anything was possible. The light crept in the kitchen windows and filled the room with a pink glow.

She shook her head. "You go ahead. I'll finish up in here. Don't keep them out long though. They need baths, then bed."

"They do or you do?"

"Very funny."

As she stood at the sink with her fingers under the faucet, waiting for the water to heat up, she watched the girls running around, using every bit of energy left in their little bodies. Ty pretended to chase them, then fell down as if asleep.

"Uncle Ty! Wake up!" They crawled all over him, their laughter floating across the yard and through the open back door.

He finally straightened up and unlatched the henhouse door. The girls crept in, hoping, Betsy knew, for little brown-and-white speckled treasures.

All at once, the water flowing from the faucet was scalding. No buildup, just a quick scorching. She slapped the handle, turning it to cold to stop the burning in her fingers. After a moment, she set it to warm and got to work, washing pots and loading the dishwasher.

A few minutes later, Ty led the girls back into the kitchen. They smelled of outside—evening heat, thick grass, fresh straw from the henhouse. A mixture of nature and childhood. Not her childhood, but someone else's.

"Go ahead and show her," Ty whispered to the girls. He patted them on the back, then turned to Betsy. "I'm going to jump in the shower. I'll start their bathwater for you." He headed up the staircase, peeling off his T-shirt as he went.

Addie and Walsh stood in front of Betsy, their hands behind their backs. She dried her hands on a dish towel, then bent down to their level. "You didn't find anything interesting out there, did you?"

They beamed. "We did!" They pulled their arms from behind their backs and presented their treasures. Both of them held a single egg in careful hands.

"Can we save them so they'll turn into chicks?" Addie asked. "We can keep them safe until it's time for them to hatch."

"I'm sure you would keep them very safe, but these eggs won't turn into chicks. They're for eating, not for babies."

Walsh peered at her egg, shook it, and held it up to her ear. "No baby chicks?"

"Nope. No babies. Just food. But that's an important job. Our hens help feed us."

"I guess so," Addie said. "Baby chicks would've been more fun though."

They handed her the eggs before bounding up the steps. Betsy placed them in empty spaces in the egg carton in the fridge.

Commercials on TV always made bath time with kids look like the highlight of any parent's day. Bubbles and giggles. Sweet smiles. Soapy hairdos. Maybe Betsy just wasn't doing it right. The laughter and bubbles lasted for a few minutes, then things usually devolved into warfare.

"She splashed me!"

"That's *my* cup!"

"*I* had the soap first!"

Tonight Betsy had one hand on Walsh's shoulder and one on Addie's to stop a splashing war when her phone rang behind her, high on a shelf so it wouldn't get wet. "Okay, you two, freeze!"

The girls stared at each other, then dissolved into laughter. Crisis averted for the moment.

She swiped a damp lock of hair from her forehead and grabbed her phone. Jenna.

Not now.

The tension headache that had begun when she realized Walsh was nowhere to be found now throbbed in her temples, dull and persistent. She sat on the closed toilet and shut her eyes for a second. "What's up?"

Addie looked up sharply from the tub where she'd been pouring water back and forth between two cups. Betsy smiled at her.

"Not much," Jenna said. "I drove into town to pick up a few things at the drugstore. I'm on my way back for dinner now."

"And things are okay?" She forced brightness into her voice.

"Yeah, yeah. Things are good. Really good, actually. I'm working hard and sending résumés out left and right."

"Résumés. Wow." Betsy realized then that a part of her hadn't expected Jenna to follow through with her plan to change things up in her life. She thought this would be a good experience for Jenna but that she'd return to Nashville with the girls and pick right back up where she left off. "So you're really doing this?"

"Trying to. Gregory has connections all over the country—and some are with big names in the industry. I just . . . I'm excited, Betsy. I mean, not much has happened yet, but the potential is there. Who knows where this could take me?"

"You? You mean you and the girls."

"Of course. The three of us."

"Because this isn't all about you." Betsy turned away from the girls so they couldn't hear her words. As if they could hear over their own squealing anyway. "This trip of yours involves other people. Four of us, actually."

"I know that. I—"

But Walsh and Addie began to kick their legs like mermaids, drowning out Jenna's voice. Water splashed everywhere—the walls, the floor, Betsy.

"Girls. Please." She grabbed a towel and wiped her arms and the front of the cabinet. "Give it a rest for just a second."

"Oh, they're in the bath?" Jenna asked. "Walsh gets so wired at bath time. You'll have to make sure she's calmed down before you put her to bed."

"Thanks. I'll make a note." She struggled to keep the sarcasm out of her voice.

"I'm sorry. You've probably already figured that out. You've probably figured it all out by now."

"Not really. I'm just winging it here. And I can't . . . Look, I do want to talk to you and hear more about these plans . . ." She lowered her voice to a whisper, although with the girls busy playing yet another loud, splashy game, the whisper was unnecessary. "But this just isn't the best time. It's been a long day and they're wet and riled up. I don't want them to know—"

"It's fine, I get it."

"Unless you want to talk to them. They'd love that," Betsy said as she wiped water off the wall with the damp towel. "I can hand them—"

"You know what? Let's try it another night. Or tomorrow. They're having fun and your phone will get wet . . ."

"Well, if you don't . . . I mean, I can . . ." She exhaled hard, frustrated by feeling like she needed to convince her sister to talk to her own kids. She stuck her head out the door into the hallway. "Ty, could you come in here for a minute?"

Back in the bathroom, Addie's eyes were focused on her.

"So is that it?" Betsy stayed by the door, her back partially turned but her eyes on the girls. "I mean, I'm glad to hear things are going well, but I kind of have my hands full here."

"Is that Mommy?" Addie asked.

"It's . . ." Betsy froze. "What do you want me to say?" she whispered.

Ty tapped on the door to the bathroom. "Whatcha need?" His hair still dripped with water from the shower.

"It's . . ." She pointed to the phone. *Jenna*, she mouthed.

"Betsy, I'll just let you go," Jenna broke in. "I'm sorry for calling at a bad time."

"No, wait—"

"I'll call again soon. I promise."

When the line went quiet, she set her phone on the counter. It hit a puddle of water and slid right to the floor. She pressed her forehead to the wall a moment, then leaned down and turned the phone over. The cracked screen looked like a spiderweb.

Ty knelt next to her and took the phone from her. "What'd she say?"

"Oh, not much, except that she's trying to find a new job and who knows, maybe it'll be across the country. That and I shouldn't be bathing them so close to bedtime." She laughed, even though it wasn't funny.

"Why don't you take a breather? I can . . . I'll do something in here while they play."

"No, I'm fine." Betsy turned back to the bathtub and grabbed a washcloth. "Who wants to get clean first?"

"Was that Mommy on the phone?" Addie asked again.

Betsy nodded. Pumped Aveeno baby wash onto the washcloth. "It sure was. She said she'd call again soon so you can talk to her."

"Why didn't she want to talk to us now?"

"I don't know, honey. I guess she was busy." Betsy squeezed the washcloth to get it soapy, then rubbed it on Addie's arms, the back of her neck.

"Wait!" Addie screeched. "Mommy always washes our hair first. Then she does the soap. Not soap first!"

"We'll just do it like this tonight."

"No! This isn't how she does it."

"Well, Mommy isn't here right now, is she?"

She caught the decibel, the hard edge to her voice a second too late. Addie dropped the cup she'd been holding and Walsh's bottom lip quivered.

Behind her, Ty cleared his throat. "Why don't you take a second, babe," he said, one hand on her shoulder. "I can take over here."

"I'm sorry, I—"

"I got it. You need a break," he whispered.

She dropped the washcloth into the water. On her way out the door, Ty grabbed her hand and gave it a squeeze. She pulled away and left the steamy bathroom. Down the stairs, one foot in front of the other, she finally made it out the back door into the yard. The air around her wasn't exactly refreshing—the night was warm and still, without even the slightest breeze rustling the leaves—but the openness felt like coming up from a pool of water after being under for too long. She inhaled deeply, big gulps of air that helped relieve the suffocating helplessness she'd felt in the bathroom.

All she wanted was to not hurt. Before Jenna showed up with the girls, she'd been so close to getting past it all. She reached up and pulled her hair down from the knot at the back of her head. She ran her hands through her waves, untangling snarls with her fingers, and smoothed it back into a bun.

From the bottom porch step, she surveyed the land that stretched beyond the backyard. The barn was dark, its edges sharp against the navy sky. Faint lowing from the cows, sleepy within their stalls, trickled across the grass.

The fence that separated the backyard from the pasture beyond had stood strong for nearly a century. Ty, and his grandfather before him, had mended it from time to time, replacing rotted or cracked wood when necessary, but on the whole, it was the same fence Ty's great-grandfather had built in the 1920s. It was the same with the house and parts of the barn.

When Betsy thought of the longevity of those wood boards, the bricks and mortar and rafters that held their physical life in place here, she felt so small. A farmer's wife. Just one woman in a line of them, their joys and sadness, hopes and hurts mixing together and settling within the cracks and folds. Ty's grandmother had suffered two late-stage miscarriages before giving birth to Ty's father—her only child. His great-grandmother had lost her first husband to tuberculosis. Betsy's hurts and losses were nothing in comparison. Insignificant pains in the face of such tragedies.

And yet her hurt remained. Maybe it always would. Her one constant dream for herself—that of giving and nurturing life, of spending herself for the sake of her own—had yet to be realized. According to Dr. Fields, future prospects didn't look hopeful, but a tiny ember of hope deep in her heart refused to die away.

Upstairs, Addie's and Walsh's voices seeped out through the window Betsy had left open a crack. A moment later, Ty's voice—growling like a bear—drowned them out, sending shrieks and laughter into the dark night.

Betsy stood, one foot on the ground, one on the porch step, caught between two worlds. One of old hurts and pain that she desperately longed to escape and one of laughter and lightness, promise and new dreams. She yearned for that one with an impatient heart.

The girls were wrapped in fluffy white towels, their wet hair clinging to their cheeks and shoulders. Ty was stooped over next to Walsh, holding her footed pajamas up next to her, visibly confused about which end to start from.

"I'll take over," she said from the doorway. Both girls looked up and Ty exhaled, dropping the pajamas on the bed.

"Thank the Lord. I'm out of my league here. I'll be downstairs if you need me."

"Thanks," she said as he passed by. "I needed that."

"I know. You okay?" He paused and leaned against the wall just outside the doorway.

She shrugged. "Better." She offered a small smile.

"Aunt Betsy, I need you!" Walsh called.

Betsy took a deep breath and ran her hand across her forehead. Ty leaned over and gave her a soft kiss. "You're a good woman, Betsy Franklin."

He headed downstairs and she paused before entering the girls' room. Jenna's words ran through her head. *"Connections all over the country. Potential. Who knows where this will take me?"*

She knocked softly and sat on the bed. The girls were on the floor, their towels drooping as they worked to get dressed.

"Can you help me?" Walsh fumbled with the feet of her pajamas. Betsy leaned over and gathered the material so Walsh could fit her feet inside. Once her legs were in place, Walsh grabbed the pajamas and pulled them up. "I can do it myself." She pulled the zipper over her pale belly and up to her neck.

Next to her, Addie yanked her shirt over her head, then jabbed her fist around trying to find the armhole, her face pink and determined. "There," she said when her hand slipped through.

After brushing their hair, Betsy folded back the sheets on the bed and helped the girls climb in. When they settled, she looked at them, right in their eyes. "I owe you both an apology."

Walsh held a Beatrix Potter book in her hands, flipping the pages back and forth, but Addie stared back at Betsy. "For what?"

"I lost my temper earlier in the bathroom and I'm sorry."

"I'm sorry too." Addie lowered her eyes and fiddled with the edge of the knitted blanket.

"What are you sorry for?" Betsy asked. "You didn't do anything wrong."

"I'm sorry about the soap."

Betsy smiled and cupped her hand on Addie's cheek. "The soap doesn't matter at all. Next time I'll wash you however you want, in whatever order you want. Deal?"

Addie grinned. "Deal."

"Will you read us this book?" Walsh held out *The Tale of Jemima Puddle-Duck.*

"Sure." Betsy leaned back against the pillows and opened the book. Before she could read a word, the girls rearranged themselves, the weight of their heads resting against her chest, their legs warm next to hers. Finally, they settled and were still. "We're ready," Addie said.

As their breath came and went, their chests rising and falling, something in Betsy shifted, like tectonic plates bumping and sliding into each other, forever changing the landscape above. Instead of moving them off her, instead of pushing away both the pleasure and the pain, Betsy let herself relax. Rested. Pretended, for one selfish moment, that they were hers.

twenty-five

Ty

A few days later, in the stillness of a hot afternoon, Addie and Walsh appeared in the barn. By now, Ty knew the girls' schedule well enough to know they should have been napping. Instead, Walsh tromped around the barn, saying hi to the cows and trying to feed them anything she found on the floor, while Addie just stood and watched.

Holding Walsh back from feeding a handful of straw to number 051, he glanced up to the house where Betsy stood on the porch steps. He pointed to the girls and held his hands palms up.

Okay? she mouthed, then gave a thumbs-up sign.

Before he could call back that they weren't exactly okay, that the girls would just be a distraction—to both him and the cows—she waved and retreated into the house.

Ty took off his cap, brushed his hand through his hair, and settled it back on his head. "Okay, I guess y'all are with me. Stay where I can see you. Got it?"

The girls nodded.

"And you know if you're out here during milking time, I'm going to put you to work."

Walsh's eyes lit up, but Addie looked unsure. "Work how?" She watched Carlos hook a cow up to the milking machine. "Does that hurt them?"

"Nope. It's very gentle. Almost the same as milking them by hand."

He walked the girls to the end of the line where the last ten cows were waiting for their second milking of the day. He handed Walsh a brush and showed her how to brush along the length of the cow's side and avoid the tail. She got to work, taking her job seriously.

"Where's my brush?" Addie asked.

"You're not brushing. You're milking." Addie's blue eyes grew wide and Ty laughed. "Don't worry, it's not hard." He grabbed two buckets off a set of hooks on the wall, turned one over next to number 073, and set the other one underneath the cow. He patted the overturned bucket and Addie sat down.

He'd chosen this particular cow because her milk supply was low. If it was high, the cow would be too uncomfortable to put up with the slow release of hand milking.

"Watch my hands." He grasped an udder and used his thumb and forefinger to pull down, drawing the milk out. It sprayed into the bucket, startling Addie. She jumped back. "It's okay, that's how it comes out. You try."

"I don't know." She covered her mouth with her hands. "I don't think I can."

"Sure you can. Just try."

She took a deep breath and gingerly pulled on the udder, but nothing happened. Ty rearranged her hand and fingers and she tried again. This time a steady white stream shot into the bucket and Addie gasped. "I did it!"

While Walsh brushed and Addie milked, Ty went along the line and hooked the rest of the cows up to the machines. When he finished, he sat on a bench along the wall just behind Addie and took it all in: the old barn that had been worked by men before him—better men, stronger men. The cows that put food on his table, a roof over his home with Betsy. Carlos and Walker at the other end of the barn, waiting by the door to the pasture, ready to herd the cows out at the right time. And Addie and Walsh, happily absorbed in their own "work."

He couldn't remember a time when he hadn't been aware that he'd be the next Franklin man to work the farm. His grandfather had made it official when Ty was fifteen, but he'd known long before then that his future would be tied to Franklin Dairy. His father had chosen accounting over the family farm and had hoped his only son would make a similar choice. To *not* link his livelihood to cows, milk, and land. But Ty had been determined, going against his father's wishes and instead following his dream down the same path his grandfather had walked. After college Ty returned to the farm, worked the land hard, coaxed it into obedience, tended to the cows until they trusted him. He and Betsy had built a solid life here.

Addie and Walsh's presence reminded him there was only one thing left that they hadn't done. One dream they'd yet to fulfill.

Number 073 had grown tired of Addie's tugging, so Ty stood and patted Addie on the back. "Let's give her a rest, okay?" Addie backed away while Ty hooked the cow up to the machine to finish the job. Walsh was still brushing, so Ty looked around for another brush to give to Addie.

"Uncle Ty?" Addie sat on the bench. "Why do your cows wear earrings?"

"They're not earrings, they're ID tags." He sat next to her and stretched his legs out in front of him. "You know how dogs wear tags on their collars?"

Addie nodded.

"These tags tell us the cow's birthday and who her mother was."

"Does she forget who her mother was?"

"Well, no, I don't guess she does. But when the mothers and babies are separated, the ID tags help us keep them all straight."

Addie swung her legs back and forth, her shoes scraping across the wooden floor. "Why do you separate them?"

"It's just our process. After the moms give birth, they go back out into the pasture and the babies—we call them calves—go into a special pen so they can get stronger. We feed them and take care of them . . ."

He could explain it away, but the truth was, the act of separating calves from their mothers was the one part of dairy farming that still, after all this time, made Ty uncomfortable. Most farms separated calves from their mothers within hours, but he often gave the calves two or three days, allowing them to drink the nutrient-rich colostrum directly from the mother and to soak up as much of her attention as possible before he moved them to another pen. The separation was necessary to get the amount of milk they needed, but whenever a calf was born, he dreaded interrupting those natural routines of early life.

"Are the babies sad?" Addie's eyes filled.

"I think they're just fine," Ty said. After all, the calves were happy as long as they had food coming. Whether from their mom or a bottle didn't matter. It was the mothers who had the hardest time. Some of those cows mourned for their absent babies for days, moaning and stomping in their stalls. Ty swore he could hear those moans in his sleep at night. Others went right back to eating and grazing after giving birth. When Ty moved their calves, those cows hardly noticed.

"I bet the babies are still sad." The tears that had welled up in the corners of her eyes spilled over. "Don't they want their moms?" She leaned her head against Ty's arm.

"Addie," Ty said quietly. "Hey, hey." He pulled his arm around her and held her close. With her face turned in toward him, he felt her hot breath against his shirt. "Shhhh."

"Why isn't Mommy coming back?" she cried, her voice muffled. "Doesn't she want us anymore?"

Across the walkway, Walsh turned at the sound of Addie's cries. She dropped the brush and ran to her sister. "Addie?" She craned her head to see Addie's face, still buried in Ty's side.

Ty closed his eyes and bumped his head against the wall behind him. He'd feared this moment, when his and Betsy's breezy explanations of Jenna's absence would fail them. And it had to happen when he was alone with them, without Betsy's words to soothe the rough edges.

"Your mom is . . ." How did he explain to a five- and three-year-old that at that moment, he didn't know exactly where their mom was or why she wasn't at home. In Nashville. With the two of them.

"Are we going to stay here forever?" Addie looked up at him with wide, wet eyes, her nose red and running. Walsh's little face was both cautious and curious. Alert.

He took a deep breath and blew the air out in a thin stream, thinking fast. "I think you can stay here as long as you need to. Then your mom will be back."

Addie nodded, wiped her nose with the back of her hand. "I like it here. But I miss Mommy."

"I know you do. But you know what? I could use an extra helper around here. You see Mr. Carlos over there?" He pointed in Carlos's direction. Addie nodded. "He's not as good a helper as you are. Would it be okay if I ask for your help from time to time? Just for special projects? You too, Walsh."

Addie nodded again, sniffed. Offered a small smile. Walsh grinned and bobbed her head up and down.

They heard a rustle, then one of the barn cats zipped through, chasing an unseen menace. Addie and Walsh both hopped off the bench and ran, chasing the cat and laughing. Ty exhaled. It was the grace of childhood that allowed kids to change course in a split second. He almost wished he could go back to that place where emotions and concerns only lasted until the next new thing came along. He knew the break was temporary, that the questions would come again the longer Jenna stayed away. He hoped the next time, he and Betsy would have a better idea of what to say to them. What to say to themselves.

With the girls distracted by the cat, he and Carlos finished the last group of cows and sent them out to pasture. Ty shooed the girls from the barn so they could clean up. On their way back to the yard, the girls spied Ty's Gator parked under a shed. He promised them a ride when he finished his work, so that evening, once the barn was clean and the cows were fed, he piled Addie and Walsh on the seat in the back and put it in gear.

"Can you make it go fast?" Walsh asked.

Ty laughed. "It'll go pretty fast, but I think we'll keep it nice and slow."

They puttered around the field for a few minutes until Ty saw

Betsy on the back steps of the house. She sat down and stretched her legs out in front of her, then leaned her head back against the screen door.

Something had changed in Betsy this week. Like something tight inside her had loosened. Smiles came easier and she'd been laughing more. The change was nice, even though part of him still felt like he was walking on ice around her, afraid a wrong step would send him sinking into the chill underneath.

Ty took his cap off his head and pushed his hair back from his forehead. They were going slow, but the light breeze was better than the hot, still air he'd worked in all day. He set the hat back on his head and pointed the Gator toward the house. As they approached, Betsy lifted her head and smiled. Ty jumped down and opened the back gate and drove the Gator right up to the steps.

"Your carriage, ma'am."

The girls giggled.

"Come on, Aunt Betsy, before it turns into a pumpkin."

"Where are we going?" she asked.

Ty patted the seat next to him. "We'll find out when we get there."

She climbed onto the seat and sat down. Her dark hair was pulled up at the back of her head with wisps falling around her face, and she wore a white T shirt and cutoff blue-jean shorts. He laid his hand on her knee. She covered his hand with hers and squeezed, then stretched her arm across the seat behind him.

A few hundred yards from their driveway, a small creek flowed under the highway. Ty pulled under a tree and stepped on the brake, then reached around and lifted the girls out of the back.

"I'll show you what I used to do when I was a kid and spent the night with my grandparents here at the farm," he said to them. Betsy sat on the concrete wall overlooking one side of the creek.

Ty took Addie and Walsh to the other side of the road and reached down and picked up a couple of small sticks. "Watch this." He dropped the sticks into the flowing water, then took the girls' hands and hurried them back across the empty road to where Betsy sat. He leaned over the wall and pointed down. "Wait just a second . . . There they are." His sticks floated downstream.

"Can I do it?"

"Sure."

Back and forth they went, dropping in sticks, flowers, and leaves on one side, then running across to see them reappear on the other side. They had to pause a couple times for cars, but at this time of evening, they had the road mostly to themselves. The sun was low in the sky, but sharp rays sneaked between the pines, turning the girls' faces pink.

Ty sat next to Betsy while the girls searched for more items to throw. He kept one hand on Walsh's back to keep her from launching herself over the wall, and he wrapped his other arm around Betsy's waist. Her fingers nimbly tied clover flowers together into small bunches.

At one point in her search for perfect objects to toss, Addie jumped up and ran to Betsy, stopping in front of her with her hand outstretched. "This is for you." In her hand was a small heart-shaped rock. It was dirty, little clods of dust and dirt crumbling into Betsy's hand, but the lopsided heart shape was there.

Betsy curled her fingers around it. "I love it. Thank you."

Addie nodded and ran back to Walsh. Betsy slipped the rock into her pocket.

When it was time for dinner, Ty loaded the girls back into the Gator and pulled it up to the side of the road. He waited for an old pickup to rumble past. The man in the driver's seat stuck his arm out the window and waved. Ty tipped his cap and pulled the Gator out onto the road behind him.

"Wow," the girls breathed when they saw the load of watermelons in the back of the truck.

A little down the road, the driver slowed and pulled over to the side. He motioned for Ty to do the same. When they stopped, the old man pushed open his creaky door and lumbered to the bed of his truck. He thumped a few melons, then chose one off the top and carried it back to the Gator.

"For your family." He handed it to Ty.

The man walked back to his truck, then paused. "Sun-warmed, straight outta the ground. Best way to eat 'em. Maybe a little salt sprinkled on top, if that's your thing."

Back at the farm, Ty spread newspaper across the picnic table under the big oak and split the watermelon open. Inside, the deep-red flesh was flecked with seeds, and sweet juice dripped onto the table. Betsy brought out a bowl of cold pasta salad and a pitcher of lemonade on a tray with two tall glasses and two small plastic cups. She bustled around the table, setting everything out, making sure they had everything they needed. Ty took her hand and eased her onto the wooden bench next to him.

"We're good," he said. "Let's eat."

The girls ignored the pasta but ate slice after slice of watermelon.

"Ah well," Betsy said. "Watermelon has vitamins, right?"

Ty smiled. "There's gotta be something good in there."

When their mouths and cheeks were bright red, Ty taught them how to spit the seeds. Addie couldn't quite get the hang of it, but Walsh hit the fence post on her first try. Betsy took Addie over to the swing and pushed her under the thick canopy of dark-green leaves. Addie tipped her head back and let her hair fly behind her as she swung back and forth, higher and higher, all traces of earlier sadness long forgotten. Ty smiled when Betsy's laughter joined Addie's.

Later, as the sky turned orange and the temperature dropped a couple of degrees, the four of them lay back on the grass and watched fireflies. The sky deepened in color and stars began to pop out.

Addie held her arm straight up and pointed. "I see the first star!"

"Actually, that one's a planet," Betsy said.

Ty turned his head to her. "You sure about that?"

She nodded. "It's Venus," she said, her voice quiet.

"I think it's a star," Addie said. "We should all make our wish."

"You're right," Betsy said. "We should."

Ty turned to Addie when he heard her whispering, "Starlight, star bright, first star I see tonight." Her eyes were squeezed tight, her hands clasped in front of her.

Ty smiled and turned to Betsy to tell her to look at Addie, but he stopped. Betsy's eyes were closed as well, her mouth moving with her own silent wishes.

twenty-six

Betsy

Elinore hosted a Summer Festival every year in late July. At one time, it was a Fourth of July celebration, complete with a potluck picnic on the grass and a fireworks display that tried, but usually failed, to compete with nearby Gulf Shores' fireworks. That tradition ended when the fireworks went haywire six years ago and caught an empty field on fire. Smoke spread throughout the town, scared cows, sent flocks of birds to the sky, and terrorized Elsie Roberts's schnauzer. Elsie, then-president of the Friends of Elinore, had left her windows open that night before leaving for the celebration. She said her schnauzer, Terry, was never the same.

No one was physically hurt during the fireworks mishap, but Elsie ended the fireworks show right then and there. And since the Friends all agreed they couldn't very well host a Fourth of July celebration without fireworks, they moved the party to later in the month and called it the Summer Festival. Same potluck picnic, but without the side of danger.

The day of this year's festival was hot and humid—not so

different from most days, but this day was extra damp, a clear indicator of wet weather ahead. Betsy could almost sense Elsie's panic, even though Ms. Roberts lived three miles away in downtown Elinore.

Knowing the girls would be up later than normal with the picnic and games afterward, Betsy put them down for a late nap. Their clothes were covered in dirt and grass from the morning outside, so she peeled them off and helped the girls into clean T-shirts and pajama pants. Walsh was asleep in minutes, and Addie lay quietly in the dim room with a handful of books. Betsy tiptoed out, leaving the door open a crack.

While the girls rested, Betsy straightened up, did a load of wash, then made potato salad for the picnic. She pulled out her favorite white mixing bowl and all her ingredients—red potatoes, hard-boiled eggs, dill pickle relish, mayo, mustard, paprika. The first year she brought it to the festival—Ty's and her first summer on the farm—the Friends of Elinore came over and shook their hands, welcoming them to town. Elsie said they were welcome at the festival every year as long as they brought that potato salad. Betsy had brought it every year since.

She could make the dish with her eyes closed, automatically reaching for the right ingredients, her hands doing the work on autopilot, but today she concentrated on the simple act of stirring. Mixing separate ingredients together to make something new, something whole.

After a final stir, she covered the salad in plastic wrap and slid it into the fridge for later. She checked the pitcher to see if there was enough tea left for Ty to have a glass when he came in to get ready.

It had been a month since he had told her he wanted to take her on a trip. When he first mentioned it, she was hesitant, but then she allowed herself to get excited about it. Lazy naps on the beach, as much fried shrimp as they could eat, fruity frozen drinks. Maybe if they pretended things were like they used to be—free, easy, unencumbered—they would be.

But Jenna hadn't come back, Ty never booked the vacation, and now it was as if a distance—not angry, but obvious—had crept between them while they weren't looking. Or maybe they had been looking but hadn't had enough energy to do anything about it. With the longer hours Ty worked to get more Franklin milk on store shelves and prepare the farm for the hurricane season—not to mention the girls' constant needs, wishes, and curiosity—the two of them had been mostly in survival mode.

But that happened, right? After almost nine years, no marriage could keep up the passion and excitement of those first few. That's what the pastor had told them during their premarital counseling sessions as he sat across from them, chin in hand, nodding and squinting.

At the time she scoffed, unable to see her passion for Ty fading in five decades, much less one. And now, approaching the end of that first decade, she still loved Ty with her whole heart. She appreciated his hard work, tried to be a good partner, slept with him, laughed with him. Looking at the big picture of their eight married years, she'd have to say things had been good. She did as well as she could, but at the edges of her mind—the far reaches of her consciousness—something told her it wasn't enough.

As she worked tension out of her head with her fingers, a soft noise came from the second floor. She tiptoed upstairs and peeked into the girls' bedroom through the open inch. Addie and Walsh were sitting up in bed playing with their ponies.

As she watched them, their soft words a balm to her tense spirit, she heard the back door open downstairs. Ty crossed the kitchen floor to the fridge. A glass on the counter, the pitcher of tea, silence. Then his feet were on the stairs.

"I'm here. I just need a few minutes to shower, then we can head out."

Betsy turned to him, but he'd already entered their bedroom and pushed the door closed behind him. She bit her lip, then knocked on the girls' door. They both looked up.

"Is it time to get ready for the festival?" Addie asked.

"Yep. Let's get you dressed."

When they were dressed and ready, she told them to wait there. "Let me check on Uncle Ty and I'll be back in just a few minutes to get you. Okay?"

Across the hall, she opened their bedroom door just as Ty slid the shower curtain open. Steam billowed out of their bathroom. Betsy made the bed and picked up a stack of folded clothes from the bench at the end of the bed. She sat and waited.

A moment later he walked into their room, a white towel wrapped around his waist, his blond hair wet and dripping on his shoulders. He pulled on boxers and a pair of clean blue jeans and sat on the bench next to her. "Are the girls ready?" he asked, his voice end-of-the-day tired.

"They've been ready since last night."

"Did you make the potato salad?"

"Of course." She smiled.

"Good." He rubbed the towel across his head, his face, then tossed it onto the bed. "Wouldn't want to get on Ms. Elsie's bad side." He pulled on his shoes, then sat up and stretched his back. He stood and crossed the room to the chest of drawers and pulled out a collared shirt. His hair made small damp dots on the back of the shirt.

It was just her husband getting dressed after a shower—his cheeks still red from working out in the heat, his muscles stretching and pulling under his shirt, his strength coupled with his visible fatigue. All of it chipped at Betsy's heart and she ached with tenderness. Desire and regret.

She walked to him, reached her arms around him, and pressed her cheek to his back. He froze. She thought he was going to pull away, but then he covered her arms with his own, turned to face her, and pressed his forehead to hers.

"What's all this?" he whispered.

"Aunt Betsy!" Addie called from the other room. "Is it time to go yet?"

Ty closed his eyes. Betsy stood on her tiptoes and kissed his lips softly. "Later," she whispered back.

Ty drove to the picnic with his hand on the gearshift, as he always did. At the beginning of their marriage, as soon as Betsy would slide into her seat next to him, she'd cover his hand with her own, and his fingers would lift and curl over hers. It became habit, their hands finding each other like two puzzle pieces. It had been a while since she'd done that, so she did it now.

It felt good, memory meeting reality. Ty looked over at her and she didn't look away. Without a word he lifted his fingers and curled them around hers. Behind them, the girls chattered and giggled. A warm breeze and the sharp, fresh scent of grassy fields entered the car through the lowered windows, filling the air like a promise.

The community park was abloom with banners, balloons, and tables of food stretching across the grass. The high school jazz band had set up under a small pavilion, and folks were splayed out on blankets and folding chairs. Elsie Roberts hurried around to each group warning of the coming rain and urging them to eat first, talk later. No one listened, this being the only time in the whole year everyone in town came together. When it began to sprinkle a half hour into the picnic, no one cared but Elsie.

Addie and Walsh ran nonstop with dozens of other kids whose combined feet made a giant mud pit on one side of the damp field. After a few minutes of keeping her eyes on the girls, Betsy relaxed, eating and chatting with other farm owners and neighbors. When Walsh crossed the field toward their blanket—crying, tears dripping off her chin—Ty jumped up and ran to her, dodging paper plates and cups on his way.

When he reached her, he knelt low and put his head close to hers. She pointed to her knee and cried fresh tears at the sight of whatever scrape was there, real or imagined. Ty blew on her knee, then whispered something to her that made her laugh.

Linda Daily, sitting next to them, tapped Ty on the shoulder and held out a Band-Aid she'd fished from her purse. Ty smiled his thanks and spread the bandage on Walsh's knee. Walsh responded with a teary smile, then bounded off to rejoin the other kids.

Back at their blanket, Ty sat down and exhaled.

"You're good at that," Betsy said.

"What? Putting on Band-Aids? Same as putting it on me or you."

"Not that. Calming her. Making her feel better."

Ty shrugged. "She's a kid. Just needed a little attention. Someone to tell her she'd be okay."

It never rained hard, but the steady sprinkle ensured no blanket, plate, or article of clothing stayed dry or clean. By the time the band packed up their horns and drums and Betsy tossed their empty plates and cups, everything was mud streaked, especially Addie and Walsh. Betsy and Ty herded them toward their car.

"Do we have to go?" Addie squirmed in Ty's arms.

"Yep, we do," he said. "You two are splattered head to toe with mud, and Walsh has potato chips in her hair. It's time to take this party home."

The girls had been wound tight right up until Betsy buckled them into their car seats, but as soon as they were secured, their energy leaked out, leaving wet noodles behind. During the silent drive back home, Betsy glanced behind her. Walsh was already asleep, and Addie's eyes were at half-mast.

The heavy rain they'd been looking for all evening finally began as they pulled down the driveway. Ty carried Walsh inside and Betsy ran with Addie through the downpour. Even in the rain, the cicadas' wild vibrations in the trees sounded electric. Addie stuck her fingers in her ears, but Betsy had always loved the sound. Their loud, scratchy symphony made her feel almost hopeful. It was the sound of summer, familiar and safe.

After cleaning up the girls and settling them into bed, she pushed open the bedroom door expecting to find Ty, but the room was empty and dark. Downstairs, only a single lamp was on, the TV off. Through the back window above the kitchen sink, she saw light in the barn. She took a deep breath and opened the door to the porch, slipped her shoes back on. She held the screened door so it wouldn't slam shut behind her and ran through the rain that fell harder by the second.

That evening, during the picnic, laughter, and conversation, the air between them had been tense. Not unpleasant but taut. Waiting, wondering. As she stood in front of him in line for Solo cups of iced tea and sat next to him on the blanket, their shoulders close but not touching, the space between them felt warm and thick, almost alive. All she wanted to do was reach over and touch his cheek, his neck, his hair. Anything to bring him closer, to erase their separation, to prove they were okay.

The prospect of being alone with him now, though, was unnerving. She'd pushed away so much, for so long, she wasn't sure how to pull closer now. But she had to try.

By the time she got to the barn door, her skin was wet, her hair damp, her clothes soaked with rain. She tried to wipe some of the water off her face and hair, then gave up the effort and looked around in the dim light for a clean towel.

"Hey."

Betsy looked up. Ty stood at the back of the barn, the light from his office glowing out from the open door. In the half-light, he was only curves and angles. Shapes and shadows. Her heart was a knot of wires in her chest, each wire coming alive in succession.

She forgot about the rain on her arms and face and crossed the floor toward him. A moment later she was in front of him and all thoughts of speaking, of explaining herself, escaped into the night. She pulled him close and pressed her lips to his. Expecting to feel his arms around her, his lips moving in response, she was surprised when he gave her a small kiss, then stepped back.

"What's wrong?" she whispered.

He gave a brief smile. "Wrong? Nothing, I just . . . I was working on . . ." He glanced behind him toward his office. "I was kind of in the middle of something. Can we talk later?"

"I . . ." Betsy stammered and no more words came. Heat crept up her cheeks and her heart hammered in her chest.

"Oh, were you wanting . . . ?" He chuckled, but stopped when she put a hand to her forehead. "I'm sorry. It's been a long day and I'm exhausted. I don't think I can . . ." He smiled. "Were you thinking we'd just . . . ?" He gestured toward the open door to his office. "In there?"

"No, I—I just thought . . ." Her whole body, fingertips to toes, tingled.

He waited, eyebrows raised in confusion. The fatigue, the strain, was right there on his face, but at the moment, she didn't care. Anger ripped through her desire, and all thoughts of intimacy, of connection, evaporated. They might as well have been on opposite cliffs staring at each other across the divide.

"Forget it." Without meeting his eyes again, she turned and strode through the barn and out into the rain.

"Betsy, wait," Ty called behind her, but in her embarrassment, she didn't stop. She stomped across the grass and pumped her arms, pushing against the downpour to get away faster.

On the porch, she kicked off her shoes and took the stairs inside two at a time. At the top, she remembered the girls sleeping in the room across from her bedroom and slowed her steps in response. She entered her bedroom and leaned against the counter in the bathroom, calming her racing pulse, trying to slow her hot, angry breaths.

Downstairs, the porch door opened. She closed her eyes and waited. A quick moment later, Ty blew into the room, wiping water off his face and breathing hard.

"Why'd you run? We need to talk about this."

"Talk about what? How I came out there and you completely embarrassed me?"

"I embarrassed you? How?"

"Well, I . . . but you didn't . . ." She was so frustrated, she couldn't even form a sentence.

"Babe, this is not me rejecting you. But you've been all over the place lately. Now you decide you want me and you expect me to just drop everything? I have stuff going on too."

She exhaled hard and covered her face with her hands, then pulled them down again. "I don't get why you're making this so difficult."

"I'm the one making it difficult?" His voice was tinged with a brittleness he rarely, if ever, directed at her. "I'm trying here, Betsy, but I cannot figure you out. I don't even know how to just *be* with you anymore. Lately, it seems like you're happier around the girls than me, like I've done something wrong, but I have no idea what that is."

He inhaled and turned around. Paced a few steps away, then came back and faced her. When he spoke, his voice was low and controlled. "I'm out there working every day, trying to provide for us, fixing broken machines, watching for storms, and now I've taken your sister's kids in—what else can you possibly want from me?"

"You're going to make this about the girls?" But she knew he was right. Not just about the girls—about all of it. She turned and grabbed a hand towel off the hook by the sink. She pressed it to her face, breathed in and out, then wiped her shoulders and arms.

"Well, I wasn't going to, but sure. Let's talk about them. I love them, you love them—we agree on that. But you should have asked me about keeping them here for the summer. Don't you think I at least deserved a chance to think it through first?"

She tossed the towel down and turned back to him. "I didn't know it would be this long. You know that. It was supposed to just be two weeks. And you think this is easy for me—to spend my days accompanied by two little reminders of what my body can't do? My sister, who didn't even want kids in the first place, can do it perfectly. You think I wanted that thrown in my face all summer?"

She pushed past him into the bedroom. Rain slapped the windows and pounded the roof like a thousand tiny fists. She stood in the center of the room with her back to Ty, her hands clenched, her fingernails digging into her palms.

"I'm sick of wanting," she said. "I want to be able to go through my days like you do, with all the crap from the last two years gone and behind me. I'm tired of wanting something I can't have— wanting it so badly I can't breathe sometimes."

A sharp cry from the girls' room pierced the air and they both stopped, waiting. Betsy pleaded in her mind for the cry to come again so she could escape the suffocation of the room and the storm swirling in her heart and mind, looking for a place to make landfall. But nothing came. Just quiet.

She sat on the bed, tucked her hands under her thighs. Neither of them spoke. The quiet stretched so long she finally looked up at him, but she couldn't read his face.

"That's what all this has been about?" he asked. "Us not having kids?"

Betsy made a sound that was supposed to have been a laugh, but it came out somewhere between a cry and a snort. "All? You say it like it's nothing. Like it's not everything."

Ty knelt on the floor in front of her so their faces were at eye level. "That's the thing, Bets. It can't be everything. I get it. It's disappointing, it hurts, it's not what we imagined for our life." He stopped, looked down, and swallowed hard. "But whatever happens or doesn't happen in our life, I'm here to stay."

He reached up and ran his hand through his wet hair. "When

things get rough, we have to deal with it. We talk, we fight, then we make it okay. We make it better. That's what we do. But it has to be both of us together."

In the glow from the lamp on the other side of the room, Betsy could see every tired line around Ty's eyes, each freckle across his nose, the patch of gray hair at his temples. She wanted to believe his words. Wanted to soak in his strength and pain, his joy and sadness, and let them carry her.

He rested his forehead on her knees for a moment, then sat on the bed next to her. "You have no idea how much it kills me not to be able to give you children, to do something to make it happen for you. For us. But I wanted you long before kids were even a thought in my mind, and that hasn't changed." He put his hands on the sides of her face. "It doesn't matter if we have a dozen kids one day or if in forty years it's just me and you, sitting in our rocking chairs out front. You are enough for me."

She breathed in all of him, deep into her lungs. "I'm sorry," she whispered. "I should have asked you about Jenna and the girls. And I should have talked to you about all this before it boiled over."

He shook his head. "You said you were good, and it seemed like things got somewhat back to normal." He stopped, hung his head, and rubbed his forehead. "You know what though? I knew you weren't okay. Deep down, I knew. But it seemed easier, better for you somehow, if I just let it go. Or maybe that's a cop-out too. Maybe it was just easier for me."

"It's better that you did let it go. Before tonight, I probably would have said I was fine. I thought everything *was* good. In my mind, I'd moved on, but having Addie and Walsh here . . ."

"I know."

"But it's been good too, in a way. Hasn't it?" She looked up at him.

He nodded. "We're going to be okay."

She leaned her head on his shoulder and he wrapped his arm around her, kissed her head.

"It's late," he whispered after a moment. "Let's go to bed."

Under the sheets with the lights off, they remained on their own sides of the bed, as if separately digesting their argument, mentally rehashing all that had been said. It felt good to let some things out in the open, but Betsy knew there was more to come. She wanted to turn to him, to curl herself around him, but she didn't. Finally, she turned to her side and closed her eyes. Sometime later, he rolled toward her, the warmth of his body radiating into her back. Then she could sleep.

twenty-seven

Jenna

Jenna sat at a corner table and rested her laptop on her knees. Out the window the afternoon sun glimmered on the Gulf waters, just across the street from the coffee shop. Halcyon may not have offered Wi-Fi, but that didn't stop the artists from seeking it out on their own when necessary, and Sunset Coffee was the closest place that offered a steady stream of Internet connectivity.

She tapped her fingers on the smooth cover of her laptop. Since mentioning her old Etsy shop to Gregory that first week in the darkroom, she hadn't been able to quit thinking about it. She'd once had several hundred people following her site—both loyal customers who came to her whenever they had a specific idea in mind for their home or office, and new customers who found her through the site or heard of her through word of mouth. Back then, she'd been an entrepreneur, a shop owner, even if that shop was just online, and enjoyed a decent side income from her prints.

She used to daydream about where her photography could take her. Maybe a celebrity would find her site and order one of her prints, setting off a firestorm of orders. Or maybe a travel magazine would notice her work and give her an assignment to some exotic locale. She'd had so many ideas, so many desires. So much possibility. But it had all changed with the appearance of two pink lines on the plastic stick, the boyfriend who hit the road, the life that had altered so dramatically within such a short span of time.

She hadn't checked her Etsy page in years. A few of her frequent customers had continued to contact her after she stopped posting new inventory, asking for more prints or new arrivals. She'd wanted to say yes, but exhausted and scared and trying to keep life going for herself and her new daughter, she had no spark left to offer to her photography or her customers. Finally, the requests dwindled, then stopped, and she set her camera on a shelf in the closet.

But that was then, and possibilities were again opening themselves up to her. Since she'd been at Halcyon, she had amassed a collection of photos she loved, shots she could hardly believe she'd captured herself. It seemed the longer she was here, the more she saw the unexpected dignity and grace of the world around her. Not the "beauty shots" she attempted when she first arrived, but the grit and strength of life that refused to be snuffed out.

Gregory was just as pleased with her progress—more even, if that was possible. A few days before, he'd contacted editor friends of his and talked up the "new talent" he'd discovered. They'd all been interested and said they'd take a look at her new online portfolio.

"Good things are coming for you," he'd said.

And she believed him. But at the same time, she didn't want to sit around and wait. Etsy was familiar to her, a way to ease back into the art world without diving headfirst. She chewed on a fingernail as she waited for her computer to power up. Would she have any followers left, or had they all moved on to other photographers who regularly posted new product? When she arrived at her page, she scanned until she saw the number next to the little heart. Seventeen.

It doesn't matter. You're starting now.

The first thing she did was change her shop description, noting that she'd been gone for a while but was back and posting a new collection called Ray of Light. She'd thought about it a lot this week, the idea that light can seep in—through cracks and around corners—at the most unexpected times. The idea comforted her. Then she scrolled through Etsy's "Top Tips for Shop Success" and read the new seller rules and follower etiquette, Google analytics and search engine optimization. It was enough to make her head hurt, so once she posted her new collection and added prices, she pressed Save and closed her laptop. A smile crept up her cheeks. Who knew what could happen?

Her cell, practically bursting with phone service, sat in the side pocket of her bag. She pulled it out and walked to the front porch swing. As she sat down and pressed the button, a brisk gust of wind rattled the palm fronds along the edges of the porch. That morning she'd overheard the kitchen staff talking about a storm out in the Gulf. Apparently it didn't have a name yet, and therefore wasn't anything to worry about. She breathed in the scent of salty sea spray and a faint hint of coconut on the breeze.

"Let me guess," Max said when he answered. "You've decided to stay forever." They'd sent some texts back and forth, but this was the first time they'd actually spoken.

"Ha. Not quite. But I am still here."

"Well, go ahead. Tell me all about it."

She recounted the highs of the previous weeks—from her initial awkward shots to The Bottoms, the canoe shot, the darkroom, and even helping some of the new artists get settled when they arrived for their own retreats. When she finished, he laughed. "What is it?"

"I've just never heard you like this. You're almost giddy. It's like a vacation high and a creativity surge all rolled into one big ball of energy. I'm a little jealous, I'm not going to lie."

"What do you have to be jealous about? You have all the time in the world to focus on your photography. It's your passion *and* your career. That's my goal. It's why I stayed."

"I get it. I do. I think you'll get there one day, and this is a great first step. How are your daughters doing with your sister?"

"I think they're doing just fine." The day before, she'd talked to Betsy from that same porch swing. Betsy had been taking a nap when Jenna called. She could hear the fatigue in her sister's voice, even though Betsy denied it. She'd said the girls had been up extra early that morning, asking for chocolate milk and tractor rides.

"That's good," Max said. "How are you doing without them?"

She stretched her legs out on the coffee table in front of the swing. Another strong breeze lifted the hair from around her face and blew a stack of napkins to the ground. Jenna closed her eyes. "I miss them. A lot. But I'm trying to be someone they can be proud of. And I'm doing good things here, Max. You'd be proud too."

"I'm always proud of you, sweetheart. You can't do a thing to change that."

twenty-eight

Betsy

Everything Betsy knew about gardening could fit into a teacup, but even she knew late July wasn't an ideal time to plant anything other than maybe some heat-tolerant petunias and hope for the best. Still, she kept finding herself standing in the middle of her long-abandoned garden at odd times, imagining clouds of pink and red, mounds of white and yellow, stalks of green. Soft petals, smooth leaves, a sweet aroma of life and jasmine on the breeze. She had an urge to dig her hands in the dirt, to rip the dead roots and twiggy stalks from the earth and start over.

Unable to sleep once her mind began churning with ideas and the day ahead, she rose early one morning and padded to the kitchen. She was at the kitchen table with a pile of old *Southern Living* magazines and a thick stack of gardening books when Ty shuffled into the kitchen.

"Morning," he mumbled, then kissed her cheek, his face still warm with sleep.

Ever since the night of the festival, they'd been polite with each other. Kind, gentle—casual, even. But there'd been a vein of tension running through all their interactions. They'd yet to go back to the conversation they'd had that night. Conversation, argument, fight—she didn't know what to call it, only that it felt like they'd stuck their toes into untested waters. The morning after, he'd slipped out of bed early, and neither of them had brought up the topic again. Now, almost a week later, she wondered if they should just let it drop altogether.

His eyes scanned the table, taking in the array of books she'd dog-eared and pages she'd ripped out of the magazines: "Flowers for Southern Home Gardens," "Plant These Now to Reap a Fall Harvest," and "Planting in the Dog Days of Summer? It Can Be Done!"

Ty smiled.

"Don't laugh."

"I'm not laughing," he said. "I think it's great. It's about time."

"What do you mean?"

He poured coffee into a mug. "I've seen you poking around out in the garden. I figured it wouldn't be long before you decided to give it another go."

"I don't know what I'm doing, but I can't stop thinking about getting in there and getting my hands dirty."

He smoothed his hand down the back of her head. "Whatever you decide to do with it, it'll be great." He opened the porch door and slid his feet into his boots. "What about peas? Is it the right time to plant those?"

She leaned over and pulled a book toward her. *Southern Vegetables for Every Season.* "I don't know, but I'm sure this will tell me."

"I'd love some field peas. Oh, or purple hulls." He closed his eyes and she knew he was imagining the meals his grandmother used to cook. He'd told her about them—piles of field peas, collards, butter beans, fried okra, thick hunks of cornbread. She'd never cooked like that, but maybe some late-season peas would be a good place to start.

After a field trip from ABC Daycare that afternoon, Betsy buckled the girls into the car and drove up the road to Sweet Peas Nursery. She could have driven farther to a big box garden center, but she preferred the smaller garden shop that only folks in Elinore and the surrounding small towns knew about. Plus, the owner, Marjorie Clarke, was an old friend. She and Marjorie had grown close back when Betsy worked in the garden often. She used to visit Sweet Peas at least once a week to purchase plants or seeds, or sometimes just to chat. Marjorie had lived in Elinore for seventy-five of her eighty-two years. She knew everyone and, in Betsy's estimation, everything about both gardening and life.

Betsy parked in the dirt parking lot and helped the girls out of the car. A tire swing and a small plastic slide were set up in the shade under the low arms of a live oak to the side of the shop. The girls made a beeline for the tree, squealing and yelling.

"Y'all be careful on that swing," Betsy called. "I'll be just inside."

She stepped onto the creaky front porch of the shop. Inside, Marjorie was ringing up a customer while her great-grandson Malik, who was at least a foot taller than the last time Betsy had seen him, slid a pallet of butter daisies into a brown paper sack. While Marjorie finished up, Betsy walked through the shop, trailing her fingers on pots of ivy, small hand-painted birdhouses

Marjorie's husband, Moses, made, and delicate wind chimes that clinked together in the blast of air from the window AC unit.

Behind her, Marjorie sent the customer out the door with one of her customary strong-armed hugs that belied her age and small stature and a few last words of wisdom. "Now, don't forget to water those sweet things. They're not fussy, but they might rebel if they get too thirsty. Just like Mo if I don't keep enough sweet tea in the house." She laughed and patted her friend on the back, then turned to face Betsy.

"My dear." She held her arms out. "It has been much too long."

Enveloped in Marjorie's soft arms, Betsy smelled fresh soil and the faint aroma of Bengay. It was a familiar scent she'd missed. "It's good to see you, Marjorie."

"Mm-hmm, it is." Marjorie pulled back and held Betsy by the shoulders, looking her up and down. "You don't look any worse for the wear, although with those two young'uns running around out there, you have some explaining to do. It's been a while, but not that long."

Betsy smiled. "They're my nieces. They've been spending some time with us this summer."

"Well, that's nice. Always good to have family around. Isn't that right, Malik," she called.

The young man popped his head up from behind the counter and slyly hid his iPhone behind his back. "Yes, ma'am."

"Your daddy's out on a delivery, but when he gets back, I imagine he won't want to see you sitting there playing on that phone."

"Yes, ma'am." He sighed and grabbed a spray bottle of Windex and a roll of paper towels. "I'll be in the back if you need me, Nana."

"Good boy." Marjorie rolled her eyes at Betsy. "Those phones, I tell you. Now, I know you didn't come out here just so those girls could play on that old tire swing. What can I do for you?"

"Well, I let my garden go, which is probably obvious since I haven't been here in ages. I know it's not a great time to plant, but I'm ready to get back in there. I was hoping you could help me."

"Honey, it's always a good time to plant. God gave us enough variety that we can always find something to stick in the ground and grow. It may take extra work in this heat, but you're not afraid of a little hard work, are you?"

"No, ma'am."

"I didn't think so. Come on, let's see what we can find."

Marjorie took Betsy's elbow and led her through the shop toward the back door. On the way she gave Betsy's arm a gentle squeeze. "Last time you were in here, you mentioned going to see a doctor."

Betsy smiled. Marjorie wasn't one to beat around the bush. She thought back to the last day she'd visited Sweet Peas. She'd come in for some marigolds to keep rabbits from eating her flowers, but instead she sat in Marjorie's back office and cried. After a year of trying to get pregnant on their own, she'd just called to book an appointment for her and Ty with Dr. Fields.

Marjorie had tried to get her to look at it as a step in the right direction. "He'll get you fixed up in no time. Healthy girl like you, you shouldn't have any trouble at all."

But even then, weeks before they started any kind of real treatment, Betsy had sensed it would be an uphill battle. She just didn't realize her garden would be an accidental casualty.

"Did you end up going to see him?" Marjorie prodded.

"I did. We spent a lot of time in his office over the last two years. Can't say it did any good though. I don't think we'll be going back."

"Mm-hmm," Marjorie murmured. "In my experience, no time spent on a worthwhile goal is ever wasted, even if you don't get what you want right then." She patted Betsy's hand before pushing open the screened door to the greenhouse. "You never know what may happen down the road, my dear."

The walls of the greenhouse were lined with shelves of terra-cotta pots, some empty, some bursting with blooms and herbs. Marjorie had a green thumb like nothing Betsy had ever seen. In even the driest, hottest summers or the coldest winters—cold for south Alabama, anyway—Marjorie coaxed blooms from the ground, pots, even old feeding troughs. She never used commercial fertilizer, just natural, organic fertilizers she mixed herself. She said she used the same recipes handed down from her grandmother and great-grandmother, all plant whisperers just like her.

She led Betsy to a table in the courtyard outside the back door of the greenhouse. "Now, remind me, how sunny is your garden? All day sun, a few hours, dappled shade . . . ?" Marjorie poked around in various pots and containers, checking tags and markers as she spoke.

"It's full sun until about midafternoon. Then it's partly shaded by our big oak tree."

"And you're wanting flowering plants or edibles?"

"Both? I was thinking flowers, but Ty asked for peas. Maybe I could plant some flowers in with some vegetables?"

"Yes, this'll work well." She pulled a few pots out and set them on the ground. Then she crossed the courtyard to a rack of seeds inside the greenhouse. She spun the rack until she found what she was looking for and pulled a handful of packets down. A few minutes later, the ground by Betsy's feet was covered in pallets and pots of various sizes.

"Let me tell you what we've got." Marjorie handed her the seed packets. "Pinkeye purple hulls for your husband. An inch deep, two inches apart. Winter butternut squash, some Champion collards. These General Lee cucumbers are good for salads. And carrots— it's a little early, but you could try them. I grabbed the Thumbelina variety. Figured your little nieces might have fun with those, and they'll be great for roasting and stews in the fall.

"Now for flowers, these mix just fine with veggies and take the heat pretty well." She nudged each pot with the toe of her Nikes. "Lantana, salvia. Your sweet potato vine might get a little leggy in the heat, but you can just pinch it back. Make sure they get enough water. I have hibiscus and mandevilla. You could use either one, but make sure they have something to climb up on—a trellis or porch rail. Even some fishing line strung up tall would work."

Betsy reached down and touched the bright-orange hibiscus petals. "They're beautiful."

Just then, Addie and Walsh came running around the side of the shop. "Aunt Betsy?"

"I'm out here, girls," Betsy called.

"Wow." Walsh peered down to sniff the flowers.

"None of these have much of a scent," Marjorie said. "But go try those big white blooms over there." She pointed to a large gardenia bush planted at the side of the shop. The girls ran over and stuck their faces up to the blooms.

"That bush came from a single cutting of my grandmother's gardenia," she said to Betsy. "I planted it there when Moses and I first married and we started this nursery. I gave it a little plant food here and there, but I mostly left it alone and let it do its own thing. Never could have imagined it'd still be here sixty years later. Just goes to show good things can happen even when you're not looking for them."

Malik helped Betsy load up the plants in the back of her car.

When Betsy called the girls to come back to the car, he ran inside and brought out a bowl of lollipops. The girls each chose one—red for Addie, blue for Walsh—and gave him shy thank-yous.

Betsy hugged Marjorie before she climbed in. "Thank you. For the plants and the chat."

"You know you always have a friend here, my dear. As long as I'm still ticking along, you're welcome anytime. Oh, I almost forgot." She reached into her back pocket and pulled out two pairs of kid-size gardening gloves. "Give these to those two sweet girls. And let me know if you have any questions about your seeds. Best to plant them early morning or late evening, when the sun's not too strong. No need to burn them up when they're just getting started. And please tell your husband I said hello."

Betsy smiled. "I'll do that."

After a bright start, the afternoon grew overcast, and now, in this space between dinner and the girls' baths, thunder rumbled in the distance. Betsy was glad for the reprieve, even a slight one, after a week of relentless heat.

"Okay, girls, are you ready? Everything's gotta go."

"Ready," Addie said, her eyes on the dirt.

"On your mark, get set . . ."

"Go!"

And with that, Addie and Walsh were off, tearing through the abandoned garden wearing their new gardening gloves. Betsy had instructed them to pull out everything but the dirt, and for a few minutes, they took the job seriously. Addie knelt over a patch of daylilies that had long ago dried up and pulled with glee, flinging clods of dirt as she went. But when she dropped the first pile of weeds and plants into the wheelbarrow, she grabbed its handles and pushed it through the yard, her mission forgotten. Walsh yanked fistfuls of weeds before discovering a line of roly-polies in a muddy spot at the back of the garden.

As the girls played and yanked a few weeds here and there, Betsy did the real work. Remnants of her years-ago project—nurturing a garden that would produce both a bounty for their kitchen table and blooms they could sell in bouquets to farm visitors—fell away beneath her fingers, loosened by the roots.

She'd once been determined to carry on the gardening tradition passed on from Ty's grandmother, a woman known for her luscious blooms and vegetables she shared with neighbors. As the newest Franklin woman to live on the farm, Betsy had felt the pressure to be the best farmer's wife she could be, and that meant doing things just as they'd been done before her.

Much to her surprise, she discovered she enjoyed gardening: the immediate satisfaction of pulling weeds, creating a clean space for plants to thrive. Seeing tiny sprouts pop up where the day before there had just been small mounds of soil. Bright green in spring, deeper emerald green in summer. Gardening had been a comforting outlet, a distraction from monthly disappointments.

Yet the pressure remained—an internal drive to work hard, to bring forth life out of the hard ground, to not fail the women who had come before her. When she resorted to making an appointment with Dr. Fields, the garden became too much life, too much vitality, and she'd walked away.

This time around, she'd work the garden for herself, no one else. Maybe they'd end up with some vegetables later in the year, maybe not. Maybe they'd have flowers, maybe they'd have nothing.

Betsy would do what she could to claim her own green thumb, but it wasn't up to her, and this time she was okay with that. It would depend on the generosity of the hard-packed dirt, the summer rain and sun, the survival of these plants in this garden.

For Betsy, it was already a success. Her hands in the dirt, the quiet twilight around her, new life waiting to be sunk down into the ground. Just doing something purposeful—something solely for her—felt good.

As she pulled the last of the old plants from the ground, the porch door slammed. A moment later, Ty called to Addie and Walsh and handed them watermelon Popsicles. While they raced against the heat—trying to lick the Popsicles faster than they melted—Ty joined her by the garden.

She stood, then laughed when her knees popped. "I guess I'm not as young as I used to be."

Ty picked up a pot and inspected the label, then placed it back on the pallet. "A lot has changed since you were last out here."

Betsy stared at the fresh plot of earth, her mind on the past, her heart drifting toward the future.

"You done for the night?" he asked.

She shook her head. "I want to get all this in the ground before I head in. The garden deserves to be full again. And as you can see, Marjorie loaded me down today."

"Do you want any help?"

"I don't think so. It shouldn't take me long."

"I'll take the girls for a spin then. Let you finish up here in peace."

He whistled and pointed to the Gator sitting in its shed by the barn. The girls cheered and ran ahead of him through the gate and out to the field beyond. By the time the engine roared to life a few moments later, Betsy had begun digging the first set of holes—one inch deep, two inches apart, just like Marjorie said—and dropped in the purple hull peas. Collards came next, then carrots and squash.

When she finished the vegetables, Ty was just walking back into the yard with the girls, their cheeks sticky and their hair curling around their faces from the humidity in the air. Fireflies winked in the low limbs of the oak tree and hovered in the grass around their feet. He paused to wait for her, but she waved them on, wanting to finish before dark.

After loosening the lantana and salvia from their pots and settling them into the ground, she sat back on her heels to survey her work. Everything was ready for sunshine and afternoon rain showers. Over time, the blossoms and leaves would fill the empty space next to the split-rail fence Ty's grandfather built around the garden so many years ago. New hope growing next to old dreams.

twenty-nine

Ty

Tropical Storm Ingrid nearing hurricane
intensity. Center of the storm located
southeast of the Lesser Antilles moving
west at 18 mph. Gradual turn to the west-
northwest expected in next 24 hours.

Ty considered it a good day if he made it back into the house before
dinnertime with Betsy. Prior to this summer, most days were good
days, but with the arrival of Addie and Walsh and their five-thirty
dinnertime, he couldn't make any promises. Often he was still in
the barn—filling his notebooks with notations and checkmarks,
cleaning, preparing for the next day—while Betsy fixed the girls'
dinner, fed them, started their baths.

This evening, though, he wrapped up in the barn earlier than
usual and entered the kitchen while Betsy was still stirring pasta

on the stove. The girls were huddled on the den floor with a five-hundred-piece puzzle.

"Planning to keep them busy for a while?" He rested his hand on the small of her back and nodded in the girls' direction.

"I don't even know where they found that. They were running around chasing Etta, and the next thing I knew, puzzle pieces were all over the floor."

"You remember the puzzle though, right?"

Betsy smiled and nodded. "I remember."

When Ty and Betsy had first started dating, he brought a puzzle to her apartment one night. She'd been surprised, but he knew it'd be a way for them to talk, to get to know each other. He also knew it'd give him something else to concentrate on when all he wanted to do was tangle his fingers in her hair and kiss her all night. The puzzle was his attempt to be a gentleman.

"I had good intentions, you have to admit." He stuck a spoon in the sauce simmering on the stove. "Are those capers? Think they'll like it?"

Betsy shrugged. "I hope so. It'd keep me from having to make two dinners."

Ty sat on one of the stools at the counter and stretched his legs out in front of him. He needed to run upstairs and shower, but it felt so good to just sit for a minute.

Betsy tapped the spoon on the edge of the pot and laid it on the spoon rest. "I may have some peas for you in the fall. If everything goes well."

"You have Gran's cast-iron skillet, don't you? We could make cornbread to go with them." His grandmother had made cornbread with almost every meal when Ty was young. And she'd served it on the same kitchen table he and Betsy used now.

Betsy wiped her hands on a dish towel, then sat on a stool next to him. "Maybe after all these years I'll finally turn into the wife who'll cook meat-and-three dinners." She poked him in the chest. "You'd love that, wouldn't you?"

"If I just wanted someone to make me meat-and-three meals, Ollie's is right up the road. I'd be happy there." He grabbed her finger and pulled her closer. "I have you for other reasons."

"Oh, is that right?" She smiled and he relished the lightness on her face.

With her hand still in his, she shifted on her stool and turned toward the den where Addie and Walsh were still sprawled on the floor with puzzle pieces scattered everywhere. "The girls are happy here."

Ty nodded. "They seem to be."

"I think if we could pack Rosie up in a suitcase, Addie would take her everywhere. She's crazy about that cow."

Ty laughed. "I think you're right."

"And the hens, the swing, the creek. This is what childhood is supposed to be like—barefoot and dirty, going to bed exhausted."

"That kind of describes our days too. Except the barefoot part for me."

Betsy smiled. Other than the sauce simmering and the water boiling, the kitchen was silent. "Jenna's looking for jobs, you know. She has it in her head that this place, Halcyon, is going to open all kinds of doors for her."

"And you don't think so?"

"I have no idea. She's just pinning a lot of hopes on this retreat and what it can lead to as far as jobs. She said her mentor has his foot in the door at places all over the country."

"Hmm," Ty murmured. "I guess it wouldn't surprise me if at the end of all this, she decides to shake things up."

A squeal came from the den. "This is it!" Addie yelled, holding up a single puzzle piece. She handed it to Walsh, who dropped it and went back to rolling a small stuffed ball to Etta.

He smiled and turned back to Betsy, but she was looking down, oblivious to Addie's elation, her brow creased in concentration.

"What is it?" he asked.

"We have good schools around here," she said after a moment.

He straightened up in his seat.

"The elementary school. It's good."

"And?" he said slowly.

"Jenna hasn't said when she's coming back. And you said it yourself: she could go on from the retreat to something else."

He willed himself to nod, his mind working to come up with the right words, and quick. "I was thinking more along the lines of her finding a new job—not that she'd stay gone. She has to come back for her kids. She knows that."

"I know. I just . . ." She shrugged. "It's already August. What do we do if school starts and she's not here?"

"Betsy, I . . ." He stopped, pressed his lips together. "I think it's a little early to be thinking about that. The kids have their own school and friends in Nashville. They'll want to get back home."

She gazed in the direction of the girls, but he feared that instead of seeing them, she looked past them, through them, to other possibilities, other dreams. Finally, she turned back to him. "You're right. I know you're right. It was a crazy idea."

"Is it time to eat yet?" Addie yelled from the den.

Betsy swiveled her head to the girls, her face caught somewhere between disappointment and relief. "Yes, it is," she said after the briefest pause. She hopped off the stool and touched Ty's arm. "Iced tea or water?" she asked, her voice casual.

⌒

All through dinner, Ty's mind whirled with their fractured conversation. Betsy didn't seem affected by it. In fact, she seemed lighter somehow, even more animated. She laughed at Walsh's impersonation of Walker falling off an overturned bucket and indulged Addie in a lengthy session of "One Hundred Questions."

An hour later he was about to step in the shower—could already feel the hot water loosening his muscles, washing away the heat and stress of the day—when Betsy's phone vibrated on the dresser. She'd left it there before taking the girls into the hall bathroom to bathe them before bed.

He left the water running and crossed the room to check the screen.

Jenna.

He sighed and ran his hand through his hair. He wanted to just let voice mail pick up, but at the last second he answered. "Hang on," he said in place of a greeting. "Let me get Betsy."

Without waiting for an answer, he took the phone across the hall to the bathroom. He peered in through the half-closed door, just enough to see Betsy with one hand on a wet, wiggling Walsh and the other hand trying to cover a shivering Addie with a towel.

He crossed back into his room and closed the door behind him. "Give her a few minutes to finish up what she's doing." With reluctance he turned the shower off in the bathroom and sat on the bed. "How are things going?"

"They're going really well."

He raised his eyebrows, surprised to hear the confidence in her voice. "That's great, Jenna."

"I can't imagine what you must think of me, staying gone this long. But I'm making some real progress here, so . . ." She paused. "Thank you. For taking care of the girls, for letting me work on . . . well, on me."

"Yeah, well, your sister really loves you." He squeezed his eyes closed and ran his hand over the top of his head. "I do too, of course, but Betsy wanted to do this for you. She's thinking something big is going to come out of your trip down there."

Jenna let out a gentle laugh. "But you think otherwise?"

"I don't know, Jenna. I'm just not sure what's going on. Remind me what you're doing at this art thing."

"I'm trying to build something different for our life. For my life with the girls."

"How so?"

She paused, then sighed. "My job is to make coffee for people who spend as much on their caffeine habit as I do on groceries. I train employees. I clean up messes and defuse hot tempers and give away free drinks when a barista makes a mistake. Day in, day out."

"But—"

"I come home to the girls exhausted, but I haven't done anything all day that I'm proud of or that they can be proud of. I don't want them to see me as someone who's given up her dream just for a paycheck." Her voice rose as she spoke. "Even if nothing comes of this, I want them to know I worked for it. That I tried to follow my calling. Does that make sense?"

Despite his frustration, it did make sense. He followed his heart to the farm instead of accepting the life of relative ease that an accounting job would provide. But he wasn't ready to admit that to Jenna. "There's nothing wrong with steady work. I have the same schedule seven days a week, every week of the year. And you want to talk about exhausted? How hard is it to pour coffee?" He leaned forward and propped his elbows on his knees. "I'm sorry. It's just . . . What you do brings in a paycheck. It pays your bills. Not everyone has that."

"I get that. I do. And I appreciate that steady paycheck. But I want to get to a place where I can try to pay bills with my art. Or at least make it a bigger part of my life. This place is opening my eyes to how I may be able to do that." Through the phone, he heard a door open, then a chorus of loud nighttime noises.

"I thought you didn't get cell reception there."

"I don't. I called from my cabin. I had to charge it to my credit card, but I didn't want to worry about the call dropping." The chains of a porch swing creaked. "Things are changing for me, Ty. My mentor has talked to some magazine editors to see if I can start as a freelancer. And I've opened my Etsy shop back up. I posted a new collection of photos I've taken here and I've already had two orders." Pride filled her voice.

Part of him was glad for her, but his frustration made him keep pushing. "That's great, but what comes next? What happens if another too-good-to-miss opportunity comes on the heels of this one and you just have to take it? Do we keep the girls indefinitely while you keep following your true calling?"

He was being harsh, but he couldn't stop himself. His and Betsy's life had changed with the arrival of the girls. While Betsy was leaning into the unknown, even welcoming it, Ty was getting nervous. And Betsy's comments about school had only increased his tension. Sure, she agreed that it was a crazy idea to think about enrolling them in school, but he knew her ache was still there. The unmet desire.

"No, Ty, that's not it." Jenna exhaled forcefully. "I don't think I'm explaining myself very well."

287

"Well, while you're figuring it out, don't forget we have two little kids living in our house. *Your* kids."

"I know that, and I know I'm walking a fine line staying away from them for this long."

"I think you may be right on that."

"But they sound happy every time I talk to them. Like they're having the time of their lives. Like they don't mind that I'm still gone, because they're with fun parents now."

"That's ridiculous. You're the parent. We don't know what we're doing. We're just stand-ins until you get back." As he said the words, he thought of all he and Betsy had learned about parenting during their six-week crash course. Then he thought of Betsy in the other room getting the girls ready for bed. "Look, it's late. I don't want this to turn into a fight."

"Do you think I'm a bad mother?" Her voice was quiet. "That I can't take care of my kids? I want to hear it if that's what you think."

"No one's saying that, Jenna. To be honest, Addie and Walsh seem to be happy, well-adjusted kids, and that probably says a lot about your mothering skills. It's up to them to decide what kind of mom you are, but I have to tell you, your sister skills could use a little work."

Jenna was silent. Ty continued.

"You pack up your kids and drop them off with Betsy—the sister who for five years has been unable to have her own children—and expect us to just accept it. To kick back and wait for your little adventure to end so you can blow back in here whenever your time is done and whisk these girls away. Then you get to return to your life with Addie and Walsh while your sister—*my wife*—is left with a silent house."

Ty rubbed his hand across his eyes, pushing hard until colors exploded behind his eyelids. He glanced toward the bathroom—steam still fogged the mirror from the hot water running only minutes ago. He wished he were in there now, scalding water pounding his back, beating the tension out of his shoulders.

"I didn't know," she stammered. "About Betsy. And you. Five years?"

"She'd been off the pill for six months when you called and told her you were pregnant."

"Oh," Jenna breathed. "I had no idea. I just figured y'all were . . . I don't know, waiting. So when she stayed with us last summer, she was talking about some tests . . . I didn't ask for details. I should have asked."

"We'd just done our first IUI. It's where you . . ." He cleared his throat. His anger had leaked out, leaving him drained. And his head was pounding. "Anyway, it didn't work and we found out the day before she left. She'd been hoping . . . We'd both hoped it would turn out differently."

Jenna groaned. "I can't believe she didn't tell me. Why wouldn't she say anything?"

"Would it have made a difference? Would you have skipped the retreat if you'd known?"

"I don't know, I . . ." She exhaled.

Ty scanned the perimeter of their bedroom. Their wedding photo framed on the wall, their clean, folded clothes mingled together on a side chair, a pair of Betsy's sandals on the floor. His eyes rested on a glass jar sitting on her nightstand, next to a glass of water and a paperback she read every night before bed. The jar had a smattering of debris at the bottom. It took only a moment to realize what it was. After Addie found the first heart-shaped rock at the creek and passed it to Betsy, it became a game between the three of them—Betsy and the girls. Whenever they came across anything heart shaped—mostly rocks, but leaves and pieces of bark too—they'd stick it in their pockets. Ty didn't know Betsy had saved them.

"I don't think it was the easiest thing for her to talk about. But knowing Betsy, even if she had told you what was going on, she still would have wanted you to go on this trip. To do what you needed to do. But she's my wife and it's my duty to protect her. I'm sure you plan to come back here at some point, but until then, we have a life, a farm to take care of, and two kids to try to love and entertain while you're gone. Just do me a favor and give us a heads-up before you come back this way."

He waited for Jenna to explode back with as much force as she could muster, but she didn't. "Are the girls still awake? I'd like to talk to them."

He wanted to say no, but she was their mother. "I can check."

Ty crossed the hall and tapped on the door. Addie and Walsh were in bed but still awake. Betsy sat on the edge of the bed talking quietly to them. "Girls? Your mom's on the phone."

Betsy moved to make room for Ty, and he handed the phone to Addie. "Hold it out so you both can hear."

"Mommy?" Addie asked.

"Hi, baby. How are you?"

Sitting so close to Addie on the bed, they could hear Jenna's voice coming through the phone as clear as if she were sitting right there with them.

"Good."

"What have you been doing?"

Addie shrugged.

"Addie?"

Betsy leaned down and whispered, "Tell her about the henhouse."

"We get to check the hens for eggs every morning. Yesterday I found four all by myself."

"I found two," Walsh added.

"You did? That's so cool. Will you show me the hens when I get there?"

"Are you getting here tomorrow?"

"No, baby, I won't be there tomorrow. But I'll be back soon. I promise."

"But that's what you said last time."

"I know. You just have to trust me, okay? I love you both so much. When I see you, I'll hug you in the tightest hugs you've ever had. How does that sound?"

A smile played on Addie's lips. "Super-duper tight?"

"Super-duper-duper-duper tight. How about that?"

"Good," Walsh said.

"Okay, sweet girls. I'll talk to you soon."

"Okay. I love you, Mommy."

"I love you too."

Lying in bed, Ty wanted to tell Betsy about the call with Jenna—the longing he heard in her voice, but the determination too. The things that worried him. But when it came to Jenna, he didn't know how to navigate the sore places in Betsy's heart.

Her impossible idea of enrolling the girls in school still weighed heavy on his mind, and he knew he wouldn't sleep with so much unspoken between them. He rolled onto his side and looked at her, her profile sharp in the light coming in through the window. "You awake?" he whispered.

She opened her eyes, her gaze on the ceiling. The quiet moment before she spoke seemed to last an eternity. "You know what I need? New gardening boots. For my birthday."

Ty exhaled and tried to make it sound like a laugh. "Really? That's what you want for your thirtieth birthday?"

She nodded. "The toe in one of mine is busted. I got a boot full of dirt today."

"Boots for your birthday. I can handle that."

He waited for more about the girls, Jenna, school—something—but Betsy turned in silence and reached her arm across him. Ty smelled the lemon scent of her shampoo when she rested her head on his chest and closed her eyes. Instead of bringing it all up again, he closed his own eyes. Finally, he felt the rhythm of her breath deepen.

Boots for your birthday, he thought before sliding into sleep. *You deserve so much more than that.*

thirty

Jenna

Jenna's phone rang while she was still several steps away from her cabin. She hurried to open her door, fumbling and dropping her camera bag, though thankfully her camera still hung around her neck. She'd spent the morning shooting one of the artists, a painter who had set up his easel in the bow of a canoe and rowed it to the center of the lake so he could better observe the reflection of the trees' canopy on the water.

Jenna was fascinated by his concentration, his determination to angle the canoe in just the right position to study the reflection and transpose it onto his canvas. She was so enthralled, in fact, that she hadn't realized until now that she'd left her cell sitting on her kitchen counter instead of sticking it in the pocket of her bag before she left her cabin.

Once inside, she grabbed the phone without looking to see who was calling.

"Oh, Jenna dear. It's Delores. It sounds like I caught you at a bad time."

"No, no. It's fine." Jenna flopped down on the small love seat and kicked off her shoes. "I was just hurrying to get to the phone. How are you? It's been a long time."

"It has and I'm better now that I hear you're okay. I started to worry when I didn't see you and the girls back at your house. Are you still at the art retreat?"

"Yes, ma'am. And I'm sorry for not calling to let you know my plans changed."

"It's no worry. I would have called sooner, but I didn't want to be a bother. Now, tell me all about it. What happened to make you stay longer?"

"Well, the first two weeks were hard. I wasn't even sure why I'd come. But things started to pick up for me toward the end, and when my mentor offered me the chance to extend my stay, I took it. All the first two weeks did was tell me I needed to be here longer." She ran her hand through her tangled curls, then grabbed a clip out of her bag and pulled her hair back, away from her face. "It's been great, being able to focus on my work and really push myself to try some new things."

"That's wonderful. The time away must be a good thing. I know you miss your girls though. Are they still with your sister?"

"They are. They're turning into little farm kids. But I do miss them." She shifted in the love seat to lie with her legs hanging over the arm.

"I'm sure they miss you too. This is turning into a long trip. I'm glad things are going well for you there though."

Jenna sighed and closed her eyes. She'd been focused on her work, adding quality shots to her portfolio and soaking up instruction from Gregory, but she hadn't been able to shake the phone conversation with Ty. He was an honest and forthright man and she'd always appreciated that about him, but when the brutal honesty was directed at her, the words stung. She struggled to push his words away, but at the same time, maybe they were the exact ones she needed to hear.

"Hon?"

Delores's voice was so concerned, so gentle, Jenna had to struggle to hold back tears. "You must have some kind of miracle phone powers." She sat up and put her feet on the floor. Forced a small laugh. "I get terrible reception here, but your call came through with no trouble."

"Oh, I don't think it's any kind of miracle. Just good timing. I've been thinking about you and figured one phone call wouldn't disrupt your muses too much."

Jenna smiled. "Is your computer close by? I'll show you a little of what I've been working on."

She gave Delores the address of her Etsy shop, then listened as Delores's fingers tapped on her keyboard.

"I've almost got it . . . there." She paused. "This is your work?"

"Some of it. I have a lot more to add, but I wanted to get my shop back up and running now that I'm shooting again."

"These are beautiful. I'm impressed, though I'm not surprised. Those photos of Addie and Walsh on your living room wall told me you were talented, but I didn't know you had all this in you."

"I didn't either, to be honest. But I'm building my portfolio to show more of a range of work. I've been researching jobs—event photographers, photo assistants. Just entry-level jobs right now. And I've applied for a few freelance positions. I know I won't get them, but it's good to get my name out there anyway. It's hard to get picked up if no one knows who you are."

"That all sounds wonderful. I'm curious though—now that you

know what you can do, will coming back home to Nashville feel like small potatoes?"

Jenna laughed. "I don't know about that, but it definitely would be hard to put the photography on the back burner again and go back to just making coffee. I don't think I could do it. Not now."

"But why would you need to? Women were born to multitask. You're already a mother, a friend, a strong woman—a *talented* woman. You can work your job and raise your kids and do your photography too. It doesn't have to be one or the other."

Jenna stood and paced the small cabin to have something to do, a way to relieve the anxious energy coursing through her limbs. "I don't know." She paused by her camera on the kitchen counter. When she'd first arrived, it had felt as mysterious to her as a book in another language. Now it was familiar, an extension of her own hands and fingers. According to Ty though, that familiarity—that gift—had come at a cost. "I don't know. A better mother would have packed up by now and headed back home to her kids. It's just . . . It feels like if I don't do this now, I won't get another chance."

"I understand the feeling," Delores said, her voice soft. "But you're a fine mother and pursuing your dream is something you *can* do, no matter where you are. Even if you're back home."

Jenna thought of her little house full of blankets and Barbies. Her girls' laughter, their feet pounding the floor. Her camera gathering dust on the shelf. She felt like a different person now—would her life back home be different too?

"You may be right. You're usually right about most things."

Delores laughed. "I wish Willard were around to hear you say that. Now, I have one more question. This is another subject entirely, but I'm curious. Have you spoken with that nice boy from the coffee shop since you've been gone?"

"Sam?" Her smile was involuntary. She thought of how he looked sitting across the table from her in the mornings. Brown hair a touch too long for a corporate job, button-down shirt rolled up to his elbows, charming grin.

"Yes, that's the one. You were seeing him pretty much every day before you left, right? I'd imagine he's pretty disappointed to be missing his dates with you."

"They weren't dates, they were just coffee. We texted a bit soon after I got here, but we haven't talked since the last day I was in the shop. I'm sure he's found someone else to have that cup of coffee with."

"That's too bad. From what you said about him, he sounded . . . sincere."

"That's a good way to describe him."

"Trust me when I say in the long run, sincerity is a good quality to have in a man. Much better than those flashy bozos I see strutting down the street when I go out to get my hair done."

Jenna laughed. "I'm not really in the market for a man, sincere or otherwise, but I'll keep that in mind."

"I've said this to you before, dear, and I'll say it one more time. You're young and smart and you have your whole life ahead of you. Don't make the mistake of thinking there's only one road you can take, only one life you can live. You'll figure out how to make the different parts of your life come together. I have all the faith in the world in you."

thirty-one

Betsy

```
Hurricane Ingrid advisory 28. A hurricane
warning is in effect for Jamaica and the
Cayman Islands. This is a dangerous storm
that could reach Category 4 before land-
fall. Maximum sustained winds are 145 mph.
Ingrid is moving west-northwest at 15 mph.
```

The morning of her birthday, Betsy woke to giggling coming from the door to her bedroom. Then shushing, then more giggling. Outside, a soft rain fell, tapping on the windows. She kept her eyes closed, feigning sleep, until she felt a tap on her shoulder. She cracked one eye open.

"Happy birthday, Aunt Betsy!" Addie and Walsh yelled.

Ty stood behind them, his expression displaying both apology and amusement. "Told you it'd be a good day for you to sleep in." He leaned down and kissed her lightly. "Happy birthday," he whispered.

She smiled and stretched, then sat up against the pillows. "Is this all for me?" She eyed the tray tipping precariously in Addie's hands. Ty reached down and straightened it.

Addie nodded. "Blueberry muffins, orange juice—"

"And chocolate chips!" Walsh added.

"Walsh insisted on those," Ty added.

"Well, why not? Chocolate chips go great with breakfast, in my opinion." Betsy winked at Walsh.

"And coffee." Ty handed her a large steaming mug.

"Thank you," she murmured, her lips already on the edge of the mug. "What time is it?"

He checked his watch. "Seven thirty."

"You need to go, don't you?"

"I do. Carlos and Walker covered the milking for me, but we've got a load of straw bales coming later this morning. I need to get ready for that." It was part of the farming life—weekends were just like regular days. Cows still needed to be milked, fields tended to, barns repaired. None of that stopped just because everyone else took a two-day break. Or because a storm was brewing in the Gulf.

"Go on then. It's fine. The girls and I may move this party downstairs, turn on *Curious George*, and do some more lying around."

Ty smiled. "Whatever you want. It's your day. Little rainy"—he eyed the window—"but not too bad. I was thinking later on, why don't you leave the girls with me for a few hours? You could take off and do something on your own."

Betsy shrugged. "I don't have anything I need to do." She

glanced at Addie and Walsh and lowered her voice. "And what about Ingrid? The news last night sounded pretty bad. Is there anything you need to . . . prepare, just in case?" She didn't want to be too specific with Addie listening, especially not after her fears the night Dawn came through.

He shrugged. "Nothing that can't wait until tomorrow." His voice was light, but it didn't hide the tension on his face. "Look, it's your birthday. Go out and do something you want to do. Get your nails done or something."

"Do you know who you're talking to? When's the last time I had a manicure?"

"I don't know. Don't all women like those?"

She laughed. "Sure. Maybe I'll get my nails done." She held her hand up and studied her fingernails. They were smooth and rounded, despite the week's gardening, but nail polish felt like a foreign concept. "I did read about a master gardener seminar at the library this weekend. I can look it up and see when it is. Maybe I'll learn a few tricks to keep all these new plants alive."

"Perfect. Just bring the girls out when you're ready to leave."

"If you're sure."

He smiled. "Girls, I'll see you a little later on, okay? Thanks for helping me with breakfast."

Walsh reached over and grabbed a chocolate chip from Betsy's plate and turned to Ty. She flung her arms around his leg and squeezed, then reached up and handed him the chocolate chip. "For you."

He popped it in his mouth, grinned at Betsy, and waved good-bye.

When Betsy and the girls came out later that morning to bring Ty the leftover blueberry muffins, the barn was unusually silent. Instead of the regular music pumping from the barn speakers, brooms and hammers and machines moving and working, the space was still. While the cows grazed in the pasture, a knot of men huddled around the laptop on Ty's desk, the tinny voice of a meteorologist floating from the speaker.

Betsy didn't know how he did it—if it had something to do with his "sweet spot" internal hunch or if it was something else more science based—but Ty had always known which storms to concern himself with and which ones to ignore, regardless of what the weathermen said or how other farmers in the area chose to prepare.

He'd predicted the ferocity of Hurricane Mabel six years ago with startling accuracy, even when the storm was still more than ten days out. He moved the cows to the middle of the back pasture, away from the buildings and tall trees, even when other farmers thought he was overreacting. They preferred to err on the side of hope—a flimsy thing in the face of Mother Nature's fury—but Ty chose to be realistic.

After Mabel blew through, leaving fallen trees, dead animals, and busted houses in her wake, Ty and Betsy found their cows munching wet grass in the pasture, only a few skittish heifers in the whole bunch. Their barn survived with minimal damage thanks to his preparations—a few missing shingles, some loose boards—and they didn't miss a milking. Few doubted his instincts after that.

Seeing Ty hunched over that laptop, his lips a thin, straight line, his hat flung carelessly on the desk, she knew it was serious.

"I don't know about you, Terry, but this reminds me a lot of how Ivan started way out in the Atlantic," the voice from the computer said. "Maybe even Frederick. No one's really talking about it yet, but I'd say—"

When Ty saw her and the girls, he closed the laptop. "I'd say we've heard enough for now, boys."

The guys straightened up and looked around, as if coming out of a dazed sleep. They blinked and rubbed their heads and beards, smiled at her and the girls.

"Hey there, Bets," Carlos said. He bent down to Addie and Walsh. "I'm going to need some help later this afternoon. Think I can count on the two of you?"

The girls nodded with enthusiasm.

"How's Gloria doing these days?" Betsy asked. "I haven't seen her in a while."

"Oh, she's good. She'll be happy to see you—"

Ty cleared his throat and Carlos stopped. "I'll tell her you said hello."

Betsy smiled. "Okay then." She glanced at Ty, but he'd lowered his gaze to his desk, straightening a pencil and a stack of paper.

When the guys dispersed, Ty grabbed his hat and slapped it back on his head. "What's this?" He nodded to the basket under Betsy's arm. "Those were supposed to be for you."

She looked at him another quick moment before handing the basket over. "The girls were concerned that you farmers get hungry during the day and don't have enough food out here to munch on. They said I really should share."

"And we had extras," Addie said. "There's one for you, one for Mr. Carlos, one for Mr. Walker . . ." She called out each man's name like they were special friends.

Ty leaned against his desk. "I'm sure they'll appreciate it. Why don't you run and catch them before they get too busy?" The girls trotted out into the barn with the basket.

"What's going on?" She nodded to the computer.

Ty sighed. "Ingrid. It's looking like she could turn ugly. Already is for some places."

"What's your plan?"

"We're in pretty good shape here. We did a lot of prep at the beginning of the season so no need to cram now. I need to check the shutters on the house, make sure they close tight. And you may want to take a trip to the store in case we lose power like last time. Better to do it now before panic sets in. We still have a few days."

She glanced through the open door. The girls handed Walker a muffin, then ran to the fence for the next delivery. "So it's coming this way?"

He shrugged. "No way to tell for sure. But we're due."

"And you have a feeling."

He nodded, his gaze on the floor. Then he turned to her. "So, time for you to head out?"

"I checked online and that class is at two."

"Great. What else?"

"I . . ." She shrugged.

"Don't worry about us. Walker is working long hours this weekend—I think he's saving for a car. I have extra hands around, so we'll be fine."

"Okay, but what about naptime? It's getting close, and I don't think Walsh should—"

"We'll be fine." Ty placed his hands on her shoulders and turned her around. "Really. They can take a quick nap after they've burned off some energy, then I have their whole afternoon planned. All you have to do is relax. And don't come back before dinner. The girls and I are going to cook you up something special."

"Okay," she said, still unsure.

"Why don't you call Anna Beth? See if she can meet you for a drink."

"In the middle of the afternoon?"

"Why not? It's your birthday."

Betsy kissed him and waved to the girls. On her way back to the house, she walked past her garden. The earth was still freshly turned and deep black where she'd mixed fertilizer in with the soil. The fledgling plants were ready, waiting. She said a little prayer that their shallow roots would soon take hold so if the storm came, they'd be grounded.

The gardening seminar lasted an hour and a half. Betsy planned to stay for only a little while, just long enough to ask about aphids on her cucumber plants, but the speaker, a spry woman of about seventy, was so enthusiastic and knowledgeable, Betsy didn't have the heart to duck out early. She took Ty's advice and let herself relax, enjoy the absence of Goldfish crackers and myriad questions, and the company of other adults, even if those adults were all at least three decades older than she was.

During the talk, the woman in the seat next to Betsy leaned over and whispered, "Have you heard the talk about the storm? It's still way out in the water, but it's coming."

Betsy nodded. "Yes, ma'am, I just—"

"It makes me nervous as a June bug. Sylvia's up there talking a blue streak about the beauty of our native azaleas and pitcher plants, and all I can think about is that darn storm coming and ruining everything."

When the seminar was over, Betsy gathered her things and

picked her way to the door, dodging tight knots of folks discussing both Sylvia's talk and the meteorologists' gloomy forecasts. Betsy was on her way to the exit when she heard laughter and an animated voice coming from the children's department. She paused, then backtracked and peeked her head in.

In one corner of the room, a young woman in pigtails danced across a small stage, acting out scenes from Goldilocks. A group of moms sat on the floor in front of her with children in their laps. The kids laughed when the woman jumped out of a too-small chair. The moms smiled at each other—knowing smiles, tired smiles. *We're-in-this-together* smiles. Afternoon story time. The camaraderie of parents, members of the mom-club. Betsy felt something twist in her chest.

"Are you looking for anything specific?" A librarian reshelving books paused and looked up at Betsy.

"Oh, uh . . . maybe something about flowers?"

"Sure." She stood and motioned for Betsy to follow her to a shelf across the room. "This is our nonfiction section. Books about flowers and plants are right down here."

Betsy stooped and ran her fingers across the spines. Titles jumped out at her. *A Seed Is Sleepy. Planting a Rainbow. The Curious Garden.* Nothing like her vintage *Henderson's Book of Fanciful Flowers*, but she grabbed a handful anyway. She smiled thinking of Addie and Walsh curled up in bed with these books.

Out in her car Betsy tapped on the steering wheel, trying to decide what to do next. Manicures weren't her thing, but she didn't want to disappoint Ty by coming back too soon, making him think she didn't trust him to take care of the girls on his own for just a few hours. The truth was, this summer had shown her what she always suspected but just hadn't seen in action—he would make an amazing dad. In acting as a stand-in father to Addie and Walsh, he was everything she knew he'd be. Gentle and caring, firm when he needed to be, a good partner, a strong guidepost.

She clenched and unclenched her hands around the wheel. She knew Jenna was trying her best. Her sister was always full of good intentions. With their mom no longer around—not that she was ever very present even when she was alive—Betsy saw Jenna as mostly her responsibility. If that extended to her children, then so be it. But she'd been as accommodating to Jenna as she could. She backed out of her parking place and turned onto the road, trying not to think about where she was going, what she was doing.

The sign for Elinore Elementary School, painted in bright red-and-blue stripes, beckoned from the side of the road. The long red-brick building was shaded by overhanging oaks and Spanish moss, and its U-shape welcomed like outstretched arms. A handful of cars sat in the parking lot. She got out and dashed through the light rain, hurrying so she wouldn't lose her nerve.

Just inside the front door, the secretary sat behind a computer, her phone pressed between her chin and shoulder. She held up a finger to Betsy. "That's right," she said into the phone. "Teachers come back on the 15th and students begin on the 20th . . . Okay, you just let me know. Bye now."

After replacing the phone, the woman looked up at Betsy. "Can I help you?"

"Yes, I'm looking for Mr. Burgess?"

"I'm afraid he's busy at the moment. If you leave your name, I'll let him know—"

"Betsy?"

The woman and Betsy both looked down the hall. Duncan

Burgess walked toward them, his hands in his pockets, a smile on his face. "Did I forget a meeting?"

"No, no. I just stopped by on the chance that you might be here."

"Well, you found me. I came in to go through some student files. Just trying to get things squared away before the chaos starts." Betsy smiled. The woman at the desk cleared her throat. "Mr. Burgess, I've been holding your calls like you asked. I have several messages." She held up a handful of small pink slips of paper.

"Thank you, Mrs. Kline. I'll take those." He held out his hand and Mrs. Kline passed him the messages. "Mrs. Franklin and I will be down in my office if you need anything."

Mrs. Kline cocked an eyebrow in Betsy's direction. "Yes, sir, Mr. Burgess."

Betsy followed him to a small office overlooking the playground at the back of the building. "It's good to see you again." He cleared off a stack of manila envelopes from the chair across from his desk. "Sorry it's such a mess in here. Sit, please." He sat in his desk chair and motioned for her to sit as well.

A coffee mug on his desk held ballpoint pens and one red pencil with an eraser shaped like Mickey Mouse ears. The mug read *World's Best Grandpa*. Betsy shifted in her seat.

"Is there something I can help you with? Or did you come to talk about the field trips? You know, I thought about talking to the kindergarten and first-grade teachers to see if we can link the trips to the farm with a lesson on health—you know, nutrition and where food comes from. That's a little different than they've done it in years past, but I think it would be interesting. What do you think?"

Betsy nodded, her head fuzzy. "Sure, that . . . that sounds great. I do have one other thing I wanted to talk to you about. It's not about the field trips though."

"Okay." He leaned forward and propped his elbows on the desk. "I'm all ears."

She took a deep breath. "Would it be possible for me to enroll a child in the school when she's not technically mine?"

There it was. The urge she couldn't even explain to herself, much less to her husband. She tried the other night in the kitchen, but when she voiced the idea, it didn't sound the same as it had in her mind. Ty thought it was crazy. And it was crazy—the idea of the girls staying, settling—but it kept dancing through her mind at inopportune times. In and out, here and there, but she kept forcing it away. Then it went and burrowed its way into her brain and hung on tight. It didn't make sense, it was impossible, but it was out now.

"By 'not technically yours,' you mean . . . ?"

"It's my niece. The older one. You saw them when we ran into you in Target."

He gave a slow nod. "I remember." He exhaled and sat back in his chair. "Is that . . . Are they going to be staying with you and your husband? Permanently?"

"I'm not sure. Maybe." She kept herself from wincing at the lie. But she'd heard Mrs. Kline. School started in mere weeks. It was likely the same for the girls' school in Nashville, and Betsy still didn't know exactly when Jenna would be back. She shut off the competing voices in her head. "If they do end up staying with us— for the school year—what would I need to do to enroll Addie in kindergarten?"

"Well, timing isn't the big issue. You can enroll a child anytime during the year. The real issue would be showing that you're her legal guardian, and that may take a while. You'd have to fill out paperwork to file for guardianship." He ticked items off on his fingers. "You have to get a letter of consent from the child's parents, interviews with the court, usually a home visit to establish living conditions. It's a lot to tackle, especially before the August 20 start date."

He paused, straightened a notebook on his desk. "I was under the impression that you were just keeping the kids for a little while. Babysitting." He looked up at her. "I guess plans have changed?"

"Something like that," Betsy said, unable to explain further. Her head felt like it was underwater.

"My suggestion would be to talk to your sister. If she agrees the kids should start school here, then get the paperwork started. I'll take care of enrollment."

Betsy rubbed her hands up and down the top of her thighs, then picked up her bag from the floor. "Thank you. I'm not sure about everything, but I'll let you know if we decide something firm."

He nodded. "Okay."

She was halfway down the hall when Mr. Burgess called her. He met her in the hall, glancing behind her toward Mrs. Kline's office, then spoke quietly. "I have to tell you, these things often don't work out well. If you have both parents' consent, then fine. The process should be pretty smooth. But if not, then you have to prove abandonment, and if the parents don't agree, going against their wishes is hard. I've seen families ruined over this."

Betsy swallowed hard. Nodded.

"Just make sure this is really what you want to do."

In the privacy of her car, Betsy threw her bag down on the passenger seat and let out a shaky breath. What had she just done? She hadn't meant to say the words out loud. Not really, anyway. Yet she'd let her guard down for a minute and they'd come. But then Mr. Burgess's last words—abandonment. Ruined families. An intrusive whisper in her mind told her she'd gone too far, but on the other hand, life had to go on for these girls, right? If that meant getting them in school when everyone else started, how could that be a bad thing?

Rainwater dripped off trees onto the windshield and pulled her from her thoughts. The rain had finally let up but the clouds were still thick, making it feel later than it was—only five o'clock. Betsy's stomach rumbled in protest of her skipped lunch. She rolled down her windows on the way home and savored the breeze on her cheeks that almost felt cool—nothing like the usual stifling humidity after a summer rainstorm. She let the wind carry away her thoughts and quiet the noise in her mind.

thirty-two

Betsy

She saw the lights before she pulled into the driveway—hundreds of tiny white orbs set against the blurred gray sky. A handful of extra trucks lined the edge of the driveway, and stretched between the back door and the oak tree was a huge banner. *Happy Birthday Betsy* spread across the top in big, blocky letters, the rest decorated with Magic Marker polka dots and squiggles.

Betsy let out a laugh, then ran her hands through her hair and checked her reflection in the rearview mirror. "Of course," she murmured. "Of course he did."

She took a moment to gather her bag and books, her stomach fluttery with nerves, then thought better of it and left the books in the car. As she climbed out she took a deep breath and pushed the last hour from her mind.

Friends were scattered throughout the yard. Carlos and Gloria stood by the picnic table loaded with bowls and trays of food; Linda and Roger Daily watched their grandkids on the swing with Anna Beth's Lucy; Anna Beth and Tom and a sullen Jackson, who

311

probably would rather have been anywhere but an adult's birthday party, stood near the cooler. A few friends from church and neighboring farms completed the gathering.

Ty leaned against the fence near her garden wearing a wide smile. He pushed off the fence and made his way toward her. As he passed a metal tub, he stuck his hand in and pulled out a bottle of Blue Moon, uncapping it as he walked.

"Happy birthday, Aunt Betsy!" Addie and Walsh yelled, running across the yard. "We made the sign ourselves!" Addie said. "Uncle Ty helped with the words, but we did all the drawings."

She leaned down and rubbed their backs. "I love it." The girls beamed.

Ty handed her the bottle and kissed her. She wrapped her arms around his neck and pulled him close.

Behind them, Carlos whistled. "Get a room, kids," he called. Gloria slapped at him and let loose with a string of rapid-fire Spanish. "Sorry, sorry," he said.

Betsy laughed. "I can't believe all this."

"Come on," Ty said. "Get yourself a plate. Anna Beth and Tom brought barbecue."

She let Addie pull her toward the food table and point out all the offerings. Mounds of barbecue, macaroni and cheese with bread-crumb topping, potato salad that looked very familiar—"Ty gave me your recipe and asked me to make it," Anna Beth said. "My lips are sealed, I promise"—fluffy biscuits, broccoli salad, and enough desserts to feed double the crowd. A *tres leches* cake courtesy of Gloria, banana pudding, chocolate brownies, and a pecan pie that was missing a few pecans along the edge. Linda and Roger's grandson stood nearby licking his fingers.

Friends milled around in various stages of eating and relaxing.

Ty had packed the metal tub full of beer and a few bottles of wine—juice boxes for the kids—and music flowed from the back porch. The combination, plus the early-evening air that still held that bare hint of coolness, was just enough to loosen laughter and hips. Betsy caught a glimpse of Linda doing a little shimmy under the oak tree, her lips moving to the Eagles' "Take It Easy."

"This is too much," Betsy said, adding a scoop of macaroni and cheese to her plate.

"Not enough, I'd say." Ty reached across the table and grabbed one more bite of barbecue.

"I don't mean the food. Everything. It's perfect." She sat on one end of the bench and balanced her plate on her knees. Ty sat next to her and leaned back against the table behind them.

Before he could speak, Roger appeared before them, a plate of banana pudding in one hand, a fork in the other. "Ty, we need to talk about the storm," he said around a bite of pudding.

"Right now?" Ty's arms were stretched out on the edge of the table, a picture of ease. "I hate to talk shop after hours."

"You know as good as I do farmers don't have 'after hours.'"

Ty grinned. "I know, I know. You're right." He sat up straight and tipped back the bill of his cap so he could see Roger clearly. "What's up?"

"It's already changed directions from the two o'clock report."

Ty's face clouded. "West?"

"North-northwest. Warnings up for Cuba now." He finally swallowed his last bite. "Blasted thing just keeps getting bigger."

"Do they have any idea where it'll make landfall here?" Betsy asked.

Roger shook his head. "Right now, much of the northern Gulf Coast has a target on its back."

Ty's knee bounced up and down, shaking the entire bench. "Y'all go talk," Betsy said. "I'm fine here with my food."

He shook his head. "No, this is your party. I can check all that later."

"It's fine. Go check it out and I'll see you in a bit."

He set Betsy's drink down on the table behind him, kissed her on the cheek, and stood. "I'll just be a few minutes."

Roger and Ty headed toward a cluster of men on the other side of the yard, one of them holding an iPad. Just a few feet away from them, the kids ran and tumbled in a scrambled version of hide-and-seek. A moment later something bumped her leg. Betsy looked down to see Lucy peeking out from under the picnic table. Lucy held her finger up to her lips.

As Betsy surveyed the crowd and worked on her plate of food, Linda slid onto the bench next to her. "I saw your garden. It's looking good."

"Thanks."

"A few things you could have done different. For example, I never would have planted carrots next to cucumbers. My experience is they mix well in a salad, not in the ground. But it's your garden. Who knows? Maybe it'll work out for you."

Betsy hid her smile. She knew Linda well enough to know the woman would burst if she wasn't allowed to share her opinions. "If it doesn't work, I'll try something else next time."

Linda nodded. "They've got shallow roots, all of them, since you just planted. If this storm comes our way, you may end up having to replant some of them. But that can be done."

"You worried about the storm too?" Betsy asked.

Linda shrugged. "I try not to get too worried until the thing's knocking on our door. I've been around long enough to see 'em change directions at the last minute, and I'm left with a pantry full of canned beans and D batteries doing nothing but taking up space. Roger, on the other hand, probably needs anxiety medication at the start of every hurricane season. It's all I can do to get him to turn off the Weather Channel.

"As far as your garden, sometimes storms can be helpful," she continued. "All that wind and rain shows you which plants are the strongest. Those are the ones you keep, plant more of next season. But the ones that break under the force of the storm—well, you just toss those and pretend they never set foot in your garden in the first place. Eventually you learn to choose strong ones from the get-go. You know how it is around here. Everything needs to be strong. Plants and people." She patted Betsy's knee, then made her way to the dessert table.

As Betsy watched her go, she imagined the roots beneath her new plants growing and spreading, holding the delicate new blooms and fledgling plants firm in the soil, preparing them for the storms to come.

When the men finished their huddle, Ty and Carlos took the Gator out into the fields with a pile of kids on the back. Afterward, Ty closed and latched the gate, then grabbed Betsy's hand. It wasn't completely dark yet—a line of bright orange still illuminated the western horizon behind the pines in the distance—but stars had already popped out in the indigo sky.

"Do you hear it?" He nodded toward the music flowing from the porch.

She smiled and nodded. Van Morrison's "Moondance" always reminded them of a particular chilly October night in Auburn.

They'd danced under the stars on the outskirts of town, music from his truck pouring into the cool night air. They'd only known each other a few weeks.

Tonight he led her to a spot away from everyone else in the backyard and wrapped his arms around her. She nestled her head under his chin, and his shoulders relaxed. Together, they swayed to the music, neither of them bothered by the side glances and broad smiles of their friends. Betsy had the sense they were alone on an island of calm, but the words from the principal—*"guardianship, abandonment"*—cascaded through her mind and told her the moment wouldn't last. Real life was calm and chaos, fights and forgiveness, that delicate dance of marriage.

But for right now, the moment was enough.

"It's a good night," she said.

"It is."

She looked up at him. "I can't believe you kept all this such a secret."

"Carlos almost blew it this morning. I thought you'd suspect something was up."

She shook her head. "How'd you keep the girls quiet?"

He laughed. "I didn't tell them. I knew they wouldn't be able to keep their mouths shut. I waited till you left this afternoon. Anna Beth and Tom came early to help set up, and everyone else came a little before five. I'm glad you stayed away long enough. We cut it close as it was."

He pulled away and took her hand, spinning her slowly before reaching for her again. His arms settled around her hips, his hands on her lower back. Their friends still mingled under the twinkle lights and stars, the sky now clear after the day of clouds and rain. "Where'd you go today? Did you get your nails done?"

She smiled, swatted him on the rear. "I told you I wasn't going to do that. I'm not that kind of girl."

"I'll tell you a secret." Ty leaned down and put his mouth close to her ear. "I'm kind of glad you're not," he whispered. "So you didn't pamper yourself, you didn't go shopping—what'd you do all afternoon?"

Her stomach clenched with nerves. "I went to that gardening meeting I told you about. At the library. And I stopped in the children's department and got some books for the girls. I think they'll like them."

"That's great."

She took a deep breath. A little voice in her head told her to stop, but she ignored it. "I also stopped by the school."

With her arms around his shoulders, she felt his muscles shift and tighten. "Why?"

"I was just curious. What it would take to enroll the girls there. I mean, if we decided to do it."

He pulled away from her and dropped his arms. "If we decide to do what?" he asked, his voice hard.

"To—I don't know. If Jenna doesn't come back and we—"

"Betsy, they're not puppies. We can't just take them in."

"But isn't that what we're doing?"

"This is temporary. They already have a mom."

She inhaled, sharp and involuntary. "I know that."

"Then why? You can't go around making choices for our life without talking to me about it."

She held her hand up. "I'm not making any choices. I was just getting information."

"But even going to the school . . ." He raked his hand through his hair and released a long, tired breath. "Who'd you talk to? Some secretary who's going to blab to everyone in town that we're taking in your sister's kids?"

"No, the principal. He won't say anything." She reached for his hand, but he didn't move. "I just needed some answers and figured he'd be a good person to talk to."

"You're taking this too far." He shook his head, took one step back, then another.

"Wait a minute. Ty, please."

He shook his head again. "No. I need a minute." He started to walk away, then paused and turned back to her, his hands out at his sides. "I'm never going to be enough for you, am I?" Then he turned and crossed through the grass toward the barn.

Across the yard, Roger stood and circled his hand around his mouth. "Ty?" he called. "You going to check the weather?"

"No," Ty yelled, before softening his voice. "I just need to grab something. I'll be back in a minute."

Betsy reached up and lifted her hair off her neck. She pulled an elastic band from around her wrist and tied her hair back. Ty's words buzzed in her ears. *"Never enough."*

The kids had started to slow down, their jubilant voices a notch quieter, their games less frenzied. Parents began rounding them up, shushing their protests and carrying the ones too tired to walk all the way to the driveway. Betsy said her good-byes and thank-yous on autopilot, apologizing for Ty not being there to offer his thanks. Out in the barn, the lamp in his office lit up a small rectangle of light on the grass. Soon, everyone was gone except Roger, Linda, and Anna Beth and her crew.

Linda and Anna Beth picked up stray forks and plates and tossed them in a trash can next to the picnic table. When Roger dumped his third scraped-clean plate of banana pudding in the trash, he called to Linda, who wiped her hands on a napkin and waved good-bye.

"Tell Ty to give me a buzz tomorrow," he said. "No doubt things will worsen overnight. We'll need to make sure all the farmers in the area are ready, even if they don't think they need to be."

Betsy nodded. "I'll do that, Roger. Thanks."

Anna Beth motioned for Betsy to join her by the table. "Everything okay?" she asked as Betsy sank onto the picnic bench and sighed.

"I think I screwed up."

"What happened?"

"I talked to the principal today."

"Mr. Burgess? About what?"

"About the girls. About possibly enrolling Addie in school."

Anna Beth's eyes grew wide. "What? Why? Did something happen with Jenna? What'd she say?"

"No, nothing happened. It's what *hasn't* happened."

Anna Beth narrowed one eye. "What did Ty say? He didn't look too happy on his way to the barn."

"He's mad I didn't talk to him first. We did talk about it once, but . . . we didn't get very far. And he's right—I should have told him before I went today."

Anna Beth chewed on her bottom lip, a sure sign she needed to say something Betsy wouldn't like.

"I know it sounds nuts, but I'm just planning ahead," Betsy said before Anna Beth could speak. "Ty's doing the same thing—all his preparations for a hurricane that may or may not even come this way."

"Honey, planning for a hurricane and planning to keep your sister's kids are two different things. They're whole different universes."

"But why can't it work? Why does it have to be ridiculous? It's

August! School starts in a couple weeks and Jenna's not here. What else am I supposed to do?" Her voice rose like stair steps, carrying across the lawn to where Addie and Walsh sat on the back steps, polishing off the last of the brownies.

"These girls, Betsy, they're . . . they're not your kids."

Betsy stared at the ground as the sting of her friend's quiet words sank in deep. "I have to get them to bed." She stood abruptly. "Thanks for helping Ty with the party." She turned and walked toward the girls on the steps.

"Betsy, wait. Don't be mad at me."

"I'm not mad." Betsy dug the heel of her hand into her eyes. Embarrassed was what she was. She'd shown her hand to the two people closest to her and she'd been turned down. Probably for good reason, but that didn't make her feel any better.

That night Ty stayed outside putting the tables and chairs away in the storage closet while Betsy settled the girls in bed. Expecting him to be back inside any minute, she sat on the bed and waited. From the window, she could see light in the barn.

She curled her fingers over the edge. *Stay up or go to sleep?* She knew it was never good to go to bed angry—or let your husband do so—but tonight it seemed better than the alternative. There was still so much left to say, but what good would it do? Jenna was a mystery, Betsy was planning ahead, and Ty didn't like it. Nothing they could say to each other would change any of that.

Finally, she reached over and turned off her lamp, pulled the sheet up over her legs. The bed felt emptier tonight than other nights when Ty had to work late. Tonight it felt cavernous, a deep and uncharted territory, and she didn't have the tools—or the energy—to examine it. She tried to relax, but Anna Beth's words continued to tumble through her mind. *"They're not your kids."*

thirty-three

Betsy

Hurricane advisory 31. Hurricane Ingrid
lashes the Cayman Islands. Interests in
the northern Gulf of Mexico should closely
monitor the progress of this storm.

The morning Ingrid reached the Cayman Islands, Betsy woke to an empty bed. Ty hadn't rolled over and kissed her cheek as he usually did, waking her just enough to make her smile, before tiptoeing out of the room. This morning, just like the two before it, he left without a kiss, word, or touch.

It had been three days since their fight. Squabble, as Anna Beth would have said. Three days since they'd had a real conversation. Granted, Ingrid, now a dangerous Category 4 hurricane, was taking much of Ty's time. With talk of the destruction she'd flung onto the western edge of Haiti and Jamaica, coupled with his regular farmwork, he was coming in at night long after the girls were asleep. He'd fall onto the bed, still damp from the shower, barely awake enough to mumble good night.

It was still early, at least an hour before the girls would wake up. Thank the Lord they were late sleepers. Downstairs, she poured herself a mug of coffee, then slipped her feet into shoes and crossed the dewy grass to the barn.

"Hey, Betsy," Carlos called. "What's up?"

"I just need to talk to Ty for a minute. Is he out here?"

Carlos pointed toward the pasture. "He'll be another hour at least." Ty's tractor had just emerged from behind a stand of trees. "He's preparing the back pastures in case we need to send the herd out there. Walker and I are handling the milking today."

"Will you tell him I'll have breakfast for him when he's ready? You, too, if you're hungry."

"Thanks. I'll tell him."

Back in the house, she turned on the *Today* show for distraction, then clicked over to the local news for a weather update. The rosy-cheeked weather girl on Channel 9 pointed out the predicted track of Ingrid—continuing through the Caribbean and over the extra-warm waters of the Gulf of Mexico. Landfall, expected somewhere between New Orleans and Pensacola, was estimated at midweek.

Betsy's phone buzzed with a text. She turned off the TV and checked the screen as she headed to the stairs to check on the girls.

Ty: Sorry, can't make breakfast. Busy day. Will see you tonight.

She checked the time. Eight fifteen.

Upstairs, the girls' room was dim and cool, the ceiling fan rustling a pile of coloring pages on the dresser. Addie lay curled in Betsy's grandmother's white knit blanket. Walsh had flung all her covers off and lay stretched out flat, arms overhead. Betsy stroked the girls' arms and faces until they woke.

"How about a trip to the beach today?" she whispered.

With a note left on the counter—as cool and impersonal as Ty's text—Betsy and the girls left with a cooler of food and two bags stuffed full of towels and sunscreen.

The public beach in Gulf Shores was packed, umbrella to umbrella in some spots. Sand buckets, beach towels, foldout chairs, and Yeti coolers filled every available inch of white sand. It was only a matter of days before the parking lots and high-rise condos emptied out, everyone chased away by the threat of screaming winds and fierce undertow. But today, the sun was still bright.

Betsy took one look at Addie and Walsh, the glee on their faces when they saw the sparkling blue water, and packed them back into the car.

"We're leaving?" they asked, verging on tears.

"Just moving down the beach a ways."

Betsy drove through Orange Beach, past the Flora-Bama, then onto the narrow two-lane road that ran through Perdido Key only a few hundred yards from the Gulf. She pulled off the road onto an oyster-shell parking lot. A long walkway led to the beach, and the crowd was lighter here. It wasn't empty, but tourists were no longer jostled together like pickup sticks.

Betsy and the girls gathered their bags and began the walk past mounds of sand dunes, some topped with waving sea oats, others covered in gnarled shrubs and oaks. The salt-tinged breeze whipped around their faces, sharp and damp, stronger than usual. As they approached the water, the walkway dissolved into sand, sugar white and powder fine.

Addie and Walsh dropped their towels and buckets and darted toward the water. They squealed when the water touched their toes, then backpedaled to dry sand. After a few excited minutes, they settled down, Addie with a bucket and shovel, and Walsh squatting low watching coquina clams burrow into the wet sand after each wave receded.

Betsy flagged down a teenager renting beach chairs and paid for two long padded chairs with a large umbrella between them. With the girls happy in the sand, their pale skin slathered in sunscreen, Betsy sank into the soft chair. It had been a while—a year at least—since she'd been to the beach. Living just twenty miles from the Gulf, it was a shame, regardless of how the farm and field trips took up her time. Knots of tension in her shoulders and neck began to loosen, one knot at a time.

Time passed quickly as the sun made its arc through the sky. When it was overhead, Betsy called to the girls and pulled from the cooler their Ziploc bags of sandwiches, apple slices, and crackers and three bottles of water. Addie and Walsh sat in the shade of the umbrella with their legs crisscrossed, a thin layer of sand covering much of their skin.

Betsy watched the water as she ate. On such a clear day, it was hard to imagine a storm swirling almost directly south of them. The waves were still slow and lazy.

"Why don't you come here every day?" Addie asked around a mouthful of Ritz crackers.

"It's a little far to come every day, but I should come more often," Betsy said.

"I think Uncle Ty would like it," Addie said.

"You do?"

Addie nodded. "Maybe you could come on a date."

"A date? What do you know about a date?"

"It's what you do when you love someone."

"Oh, I see," Betsy said. "Have you ever been on a date?"

Addie nodded. "Mommy takes me on dates sometimes. She picks me up from school and takes me to the park for Mommy-Addie dates. She does it with Walsh sometimes too, but not together. We each get our own dates."

Walsh nodded. "We eat cookies and swing and slide."

"That sounds like fun," Betsy said.

"Yep." Addie chewed thoughtfully for a moment. Betsy watched them. They so rarely talked about Jenna, even when Betsy knew they were thinking of her. It was like a plug kept their words in tight.

After lunch and making drip castles in the wet sand, Walsh climbed up on the chair next to Betsy and laid her head down.

"Are you tired, sweetheart?"

Walsh shook her head no.

"If you want to close your eyes, you can. I'll wake you up if I see a dolphin."

"Okay," Walsh said, her eyes heavy.

Addie joined her not long after. "I'm not tired, I'm just going to rest a little bit." She sat back against Betsy's shins. After a few minutes, Addie dozed next to her sister.

Betsy pulled out her phone to check the time. Half expecting to see a text from Ty, she was disappointed to see only a red banner at the bottom of her phone alerting her to the hurricane watch in effect for the coast. She tucked her phone back into the bag and closed her eyes.

Ty was the proverbial man of few words, but when he spoke, what he said was important. Each word measured and careful. Because she'd been on the receiving end of such sweet, thoughtful words from him, the absence of his words now felt like a knife twist.

While the girls slept, she returned to a conversation she'd had with Ty a few days after their last appointment with Dr. Fields back in January. She'd canceled two field trips, unable to muster the energy necessary to keep the kids' attention. Ty had found her lying in bed at noon, fully clothed, with the lights off. He sat next to her.

"I just need a few minutes." She wiped tears off her cheeks. "I'll be fine."

"I'm worried about you, babe."

"I'm fine. I'll be fine." Why couldn't she be more like him? Somehow he was able to pick up and continue on, seemingly unfazed by the prognosis the doctor had given them.

"Anything's possible," he'd said. *"You could always try praying."*

"I was thinking," Ty said, taking his cap off and rubbing his head. It was unusually cold this January, and the chill clung to his clothes. Temperatures had dipped into the twenties and thirties for long stretches, downright frigid for south Alabama. "He didn't say it couldn't happen. Or that it would never happen. We'll just keep trying."

"I'm tired of trying. I'm tired of looking at my calendar, counting days. Of having to be so careful and exact. It's exhausting."

"So let's not do it like that. Let's just get back to me and you, minus the calendar. Like it used to be."

Betsy sniffed and wiped her cheeks again, unsure if it was possible to go back to that carefree, casual place they'd been before they decided to start a family. Maybe for him it was. But it wasn't a possibility for her. Not yet.

"There's also adoption," he said.

She looked at him. He held his hat in his hands and smoothed a frayed string at the edge of the brim.

"Do you even know how much that costs? Way more than IVF."

"Not always. I've done a little research." He took a deep breath and let it out slowly. "If you go international, yes, it's expensive, but adoption within the U.S. is less, maybe even more so if you stay within the state. And there's even a program where you can foster a child first, then apply for adoption. That brings the cost down more."

Betsy blinked hard and pushed herself up until she was sitting. "Is that really what you want? To adopt?"

"Betsy, I have what I really want. Do I want children with you? Absolutely. But *you* are who I want. I know you want this more than anything, so I'm trying to figure out a way to make it happen."

She'd known it then, even in her haze of grief and disappointment. Deep down where it mattered, she knew now. He loved her. *Her.* He was reserved, but forthright. Calm, but decisive. When he spoke, she knew she could trust him. They'd chosen each other, above all, and she'd make the same choice again every time.

Three days of silence was long enough. She pulled her phone back out of her bag and tapped out a quick text.

Will be home for dinner. Let's talk tonight. ❤

When the sun had lowered in the sky and clouds bloomed from the horizon in the south, Betsy followed the girls to the water's edge to look for shells. The wind had picked up and the tide was higher now, creeping up past the soggy mounds of their sand castles, inching toward beach chairs that had been on dry ground hours ago. As they walked, eyes on the sand, the warm water rippled over their feet.

They came to a stretch where the shore flattened out, revealing a wide strip of damp sand not yet covered by the tide. It was speckled with shells, none of them deemed beautiful or special enough for the stream of shell-hunting vacationers to have picked up earlier in the day. To Addie and Walsh, they were a treasure. Soon their hands and sand pails were full of broken shells in tan, yellow, pink, and blue.

"Look!" Walsh called, her voice high with excitement. "A heart!" She bent down low over a pile of shells and picked up one with a small hole at the bottom. Half the diameter of a pencil eraser, the hole was jagged, making the delicate outline of a heart. "It's for you," she said. "You keep it."

Betsy thought of the Mason jar by her side of the bed where she'd deposited all the heart-shaped items the girls had collected over the course of the summer. The faded yellow shell would fit right in with the others.

"And look at these." Addie peered down at a spread of coquina shells with both halves still attached. "They look like butterflies." She picked up a handful and passed them to Betsy. "These are for you too."

Betsy laughed, her hands full. "I don't know if I can hold any more. You're filling me up with too many pretty things."

As they continued their walk, clouds overtook the sun. Betsy found a tan-and-white spiraled shell half buried in the sand. Wide at the top and twisted to a fine point at the bottom, it fit snug in the palm of her hand. While Betsy rinsed the shell to rid it of sand, Addie ran to her holding something in her hand.

"Look," she said, hushed and reverent. A quarter-size sand dollar, bleached white by the sun, sat in the center of her palm.

"Wow," Betsy breathed. "I can't believe no one picked it up already."

"It was hidden under another shell."

"Well, it must have been there just for you to find. Want me to add it to my bucket?" She held out the pail so Addie could place it inside.

Addie shook her head. "No, this one's for Mommy. I'm going to give it to her when she comes back." She held the sand dollar with one hand cupped under the other one and stared down at it. Her long blonde curls, frizzed at the edges by humidity, flared out around her face, just like Jenna's used to in the heat of the summer. Walsh stood on tiptoes next to her sister, her damp hair clinging to her cheeks.

There was a photo at Betsy's parents' house—probably stuck in a box somewhere—of Betsy and Jenna on a beach trip in elementary school, before boys and cameras and textbooks became priorities. In the photo they both wore swimsuits, Jenna's thin, reedy body nestled up against Betsy's, already a little fuller, curvier than her little sister's. Betsy had flung her arm around Jenna's shoulders. Their heads tilted at the same angle, but in toward each other, their cheeks inches apart.

Closing her eyes, Betsy could feel the warmth of her sister's cheek, smell the fruity scent of her hair, feel the wet sand on their skin.

She opened her eyes when Addie spoke. "Careful, Walsh. It'll break." Addie lowered her hands so her sister could peek inside, their heads close. "No touching. We're going to give it to Mommy. She's going to love it."

Addie and Walsh were Jenna's, no doubt—they both looked like her in different ways—yet something in Betsy's blood ran in those two girls too, linking all four of them together despite time or distance. But life had already laid down its blueprint, already mapped out the roads and detours, disappointments and accidents that had brought them this far.

Betsy breathed in deeply, then out, like a rushing tide. It was time to get them home.

After shoving their sandy towels, plastic shovels, and buckets into the bags, Betsy picked it all up and they started back toward the boardwalk. They rinsed their feet at a water hose propped up on the railing, then slipped their feet into their flip-flops. Walsh turned around as they walked, waving behind her. Betsy turned, but nothing was there but the water and sand.

Just before they made it back to their car, a Perdido Key State Park worker waved to them. "Hope y'all had a good time!" she called. "You're seeing the calm before the storm." She was coiling a long rope in a loop around her hand and elbow.

Addie held up her bucket. "We found shells!"

"Ooh, that's my favorite thing to do at the beach." She crossed the walkway toward them. Her cheeks were pink. and she'd tucked her gray hair under a bright-yellow baseball cap with *PK* emblazoned in blue letters. *Honey* was embroidered on the pocket of her shirt. "What'd you find?"

Addie pulled out the sand dollar.

"Well, looky there. You found yourself a dollar. Not everyone's that lucky. Whatcha gonna spend it on?"

Her brow wrinkled, Addie looked at Betsy.

Honey laughed. "I'm just kidding with you." She turned to Betsy. "And did Mom find anything good?"

Betsy held out the tan-and-white spiraled shell still clutched in her hand like a talisman. "The girls found most of the good stuff. I just have this."

"Hmm," Honey muttered, stepping forward to take a closer look. "That there's a paper fig. Kind of a funny name for a shell, but see how thin it is?" She ran her finger along the shell's fragile edge. "Most of the time they break apart in the waves. Somehow this one made it through in one piece."

Honey slung the coil of rope up on her shoulder and brushed her hands on the sides of her canvas shorts. "Glad you enjoyed your day." She stared at the water a moment, then turned to her pickup idling in the shell lot a few spaces away from Betsy's. "Couple more days, no telling what the beach will look like. We're planning for the worst, but hoping for the best. It's all we can do." She climbed in the truck and stuck her arm out the window in a wave. Addie and Walsh waved back.

They crossed the white shells to their car. After loading the bags and empty cooler in the trunk, Betsy strapped the girls into their car seats, then laid a towel over their laps so they could spread out their shells on the ride home. Addie still held the fragile sand dollar in her hand, her fingers clamped around it.

"You know, it might be safer if you put it down. It could break by accident with you holding on to it so tight."

Addie shook her head. "I can take care of it."

"Okay." Betsy tucked a strand of hair behind Addie's ear.

She climbed in and buckled her seat belt, the lowered windows ushering in a gentle breeze and easing the heat in the car. Before she put the car in drive, she turned around to the girls. "I had fun with you today."

Walsh nodded, leaned her head back against the headrest of her car seat. Addie cleared the rest of her shells off the towel and made space for the sand dollar. She placed it in the center, then looked up at Betsy. Betsy nodded once and winked. Addie smiled, her cheeks like two round, pink crab apples.

Betsy set her own shell in the cup holder next to her, then held her arm out the window. As she pulled out onto the road, she stretched her fingers in the wind. Ahead of them, the pink and orange sky beckoned.

thirty-four

Jenna

"What am I supposed to do with no cell service?" Micah asked. "No one told me it would be this bad."

Jenna bit her lip to hide her smile. Micah was part of a group of artists from UT Austin here for the last week of the retreat. With Gregory gone on a quick trip to St. Augustine for his Lost Florida project, Jenna was helping Micah, the lone photographer in the group, get settled. They'd just finished breakfast and were waiting for the welcome meeting.

"You'll get used to it. It's hard at first, but if you just accept that you're going to be a little out of touch for your time here—"

"A little? I'm totally cut off. I can't get any news, no sports, nothing." He scrolled his thumbs across the surface of his phone, his distress increasing by the second.

She laughed, then reached over and took it from him. "Trust me. Just leave it alone and focus on what you came here to do." When Casey stood in the center of the group to get everyone's attention, Jenna leaned toward Micah and whispered, "There's a spot by the lake where you can get a little service if you stand in the right place. I'll show it to you in a little bit." He smiled.

Jenna looked around the room as Casey began the meeting. The group was mostly seniors about to embark on their last year of college. Fresh, eager, ready to dive into their work. She was both happy for them and a little jealous. Their only responsibility was to their work and studies, nothing to dictate where they should go from here. The world was open to them. She remembered what that felt like.

After the meeting, she walked Micah around the preserve. He lugged two camera bags, a tripod, and a backpack full of supplies with him. She tried to get him to leave everything but his camera behind, but he refused. When they neared a pond with bright-yellow wildflowers poking their faces above the water, he stopped to set up his tripod.

"This is perfect. I have to get this before the light changes. See how the sunlight plays on the petals?"

She nodded and watched. His equipment was expensive, spotless, probably purchased specifically for this retreat. She thought of her twenty-year-old Canon sitting on the counter in her cabin.

"Just remember," she said as he set up his shot, "your first idea of what's photo worthy isn't always the best. Think of the body of work you want to create while you're here. The feelings, the themes. What do you want to say?" She couldn't believe she was repeating the same lines that had made her cringe when she first heard them from Casey and the others. Back then, she'd thought they were empty clichés, but now she knew they held some truth.

"So you're telling me this isn't photo worthy?" Micah asked.

"I'm not saying that. I just think you might be surprised at the photos you're taking by the end of the session. When Gregory gets back, ask him to take you to a place called The Bottoms."

He shook his head. "Why would we go there? Isn't that the ugly part of the preserve?"

She smiled. "Yeah. It is."

Gregory called her name as she left the dining hall after grabbing a quick lunch. Her shoulders relaxed when she saw him coming toward her. Halcyon had somehow felt incomplete without him.

"When did you get back?" she asked.

"Late last night. I was supposed to be gone a few more days, but I was ready."

Together they walked out of the dining hall and into the thick, warm air outside.

"I'm glad to be back. It feels different here this summer." As they walked he bumped her with his elbow. "How's the new group?"

"Fresh as little daisies. Eager to take the art world by storm."

He laughed. "They're always that way. Although maybe not you though. When you got here, you were more . . ."

"Surly? Oh wait, that was you."

"No, I was going to say you were tentative. Thoughtful. Maybe a little defiant, but that's better in the long run."

She needed to get back to her cabin and pack some of her prints for shipping, but when Gregory sat in the shade under a sweeping oak tree, she sat next to him. The mess in her cabin could wait.

The other artists filed out of the dining hall, ready to gain as much new ground as possible on their works in progress. Jenna waved at Micah. He held up a single camera bag that hung from his neck. She smiled and gave him a thumbs-up.

"You must be teaching him well," Gregory said.

"I'm not teaching. I'm just trying to help him make good decisions. Like not hauling three bags and a tripod around the preserve every day."

"You're a good assistant then. How about that?"

She shrugged and leaned her head back on the chair. "I'll accept that." A breeze kicked up and rustled the sunlit leaves overhead.

"I'm taking the job in California."

"Good for you." She kept her gaze on the trees, holding her breath tight in her chest. The last few weeks with him had felt different. The push and pull, the conversation, the comfortable silence as they worked. It was both enticing and unsettling. She sensed his gaze on her but she didn't turn her head.

"You could come with me, you know."

She laughed to mask her thudding heart. "Me, in California?"

"Sure. Why not?"

She finally glanced at him and something in her shifted, as if she'd just stepped into a boat bobbing in the water. His voice was casual, his body relaxed, but his gaze was firm and unwavering. She rubbed her forehead. "Gregory, you can't just ask me to come to California with you."

"Why not? I just did." He gave her a half grin.

"It's too big." She shifted in her seat to face him. "I can't just . . . I have kids and a life and . . ."

He sat up and leaned toward her. "I know you do. And we'll figure all that out. Look, you've been trying to decide what to do in your life, right? Halcyon was a gift and you took it and look where you are now. Maybe California is another gift and all you have to do is take it."

"California is a gift for *you*. It's your job. I can't just follow you there. I've followed a guy across the country before, and it didn't turn out too well for me. I can't do it again."

"I'm not asking you to follow me just for the fun of it. It's a job for you too. The dean said I get an assistant—an official, well-paid one—and I get to choose who it is. You'd be helping me with grading and paperwork, but you'd have plenty of time to do your own thing. California's a beautiful place for photography. It could be a fresh start."

She closed her eyes. It couldn't, wouldn't work. When she opened her eyes, he was watching her.

"What do you say?"

"Hey, guys," a voice called from up the path. Jenna looked over Gregory's shoulder and saw Casey walking toward them, a bright-red envelope in her hand.

"Will you come to my cabin later?" Gregory asked, his voice quiet. "We can talk there."

She nodded and he stood.

"How's it going?" Casey said when she reached them.

Gregory nudged a rock on the ground with the toe of his boot. "Just catching up on what I missed while I was gone."

She nodded toward Jenna. "Your mentee has done a great job with Micah."

He smiled. "I knew she would." He shoved his hands in his pockets. "I need to get going. I have a lot to do tonight. I'll see y'all later." He looked back at Jenna once before turning and walking through the trees.

"Sorry for interrupting," Casey said when Gregory was out of earshot.

"It's fine. I was just telling him about Micah."

"This came for you in the mail." Casey held her hand out. "It looks important."

Jenna took the envelope and turned it over in her hands. She smiled when she recognized Addie's drawings. Addie always drew extra-long eyelashes on her smiley faces and hearts on their cheeks. Betsy had written Jenna's name and the address, and the girls had decorated the rest of the envelope with faces, dots, and flowers.

"From your kids?"

Jenna nodded. She slid her finger under the flap and pulled out a sheet of pink construction paper. She took a deep breath.

"How are they doing with you being gone?"

"I think they're doing okay," Jenna said, her gaze on the drawing.

"That's good." A strong breeze whipped around the lake, carrying the scent of pine needles and salty air. "I wonder if this wind is coming off the storm."

Jenna looked up. "What storm?"

Casey raised her eyebrows. "Ingrid? Big hurricane?"

Jenna shook her head. "I haven't seen any news in a while."

"I can tell. It's a big one, out in the Gulf. The predicted track keeps wobbling, but they're thinking Mississippi. We should stay clear of it, but if it moves east at all, there's a whole list of things we have to do to get ready. Including getting all the artists out of here."

Jenna thought of the girls at the farm. They weren't too far from Mississippi. She reached into her bag on the chair and pulled out her phone. One bar of service.

Casey tucked her hair behind her ears. "I heard about Gregory's job offer in Berkeley."

Jenna nodded, her attention on her phone as she scrolled to Betsy's number. "He's taking it."

"Wow, I hadn't heard. That's—well, good for him."

"That's what I told him."

"What about you?"

Jenna looked up. "What about me?"

Casey shrugged. "I don't know. The two of you seem to work well together. I know there's the assistant position . . ."

Jenna shook her head. "There's no way that would work."

"Yeah, you're probably right. Plus it's scary to uproot your life."

Casey's voice was soft, but Jenna heard something else, as if she was saying two things at once.

"Anyway, I just wanted to make sure you got your mail." She headed back up the path, then turned her head and called back to Jenna, "It's sweet to know your girls miss you so much."

Jenna checked her phone again for that single service bar, but it was gone.

❦

That evening, when she knocked on Gregory's door, he opened it dressed only in blue jeans.

"Sorry, I just hopped out of the shower. Let me . . ." He ducked into what she assumed was his bedroom. "I figured you weren't coming," he called, his voice muffled. When he came back, he wore a wrinkled plaid shirt with the sleeves rolled up. His hair stuck up in damp spikes, like he'd just run a towel over his head. She remained on the porch, her feet rooted to the hard floor.

"Do you want to come in?" he asked slowly.

She nodded and he held the door open for her. All around the room sat open boxes. On the floor, a chair. Through the bedroom door, she spied an open suitcase on the bed. "You're packing."

"Yeah, I got a call that they want me out there sooner than I thought. This storm is causing a mess at the airports already, so

I'm heading out tomorrow. I have to pick up a few things at home before I go."

"What about the artists here now? What about Micah?" The poor kid needed a mentor.

"Casey called another photographer, a guy from Birmingham who's worked here a few sessions. He'll take my place this last week."

"They didn't take long to replace you."

"I think they knew I'd take off eventually. They've probably had a replacement lined up since I got here."

Jenna walked through the cabin—larger than hers, but still simple and rustic—and peered into one of the boxes filled with books.

"Jenna." His voice behind her was close, then she felt his hand on her shoulder.

She moved away from his touch and sat on the couch with her back against the arm. He sat facing her and waited. With the front window open, the room was warm, and she was glad for the ceiling fan sending down a cooling breeze.

"I thought Max was kidding the first time he mentioned this place to me. I laughed when he suggested I apply for it."

"Why'd you laugh?"

"Because it sounded so ridiculous. Managing the time off, figuring out what to do with my kids. And the idea of being on my own for two weeks with my camera . . . I never thought it'd work."

"Yet here you are."

"Here I am. Little longer than I planned to stay though."

He nodded. His jeans had a hole in one knee and he pulled at a fuzzy string. "Are you glad you stayed?"

She hesitated. Everything racing through her mind made it hard to think straight. "I think so. But . . ."

He propped his elbow on the back of the couch. His hand hung down and grazed the top of her knee.

"I don't know how to put these two parts of my life together. I love my children, but I also don't want to give up all this . . . this . . ."

"You. You don't want to give up on yourself."

"I guess that's it. It's like I've rediscovered this fundamental part of my life that's been missing and I don't want to lose it again."

"Then don't lose it. Don't give it up." He took her hands in his and squeezed. "Come to California with me. You can have the creative life you want and nothing will get in the way of it."

"But I have the girls. I can't uproot them too. I can't do that to them."

"You've done it once already. They've been at your sister's for what—going on two months now, right? And you've said it yourself—they're happy there. What if . . . ?" He paused, closed his eyes, then took a breath. "You made the choice to give up a life in the arts when you had your children. And that was a good choice for you at the time. But now you have a chance to make another choice. You can choose not to leave that life behind."

"That's crazy," she murmured. But as she sat next to him, staring at their hands together, she let herself imagine what it could look like—another life, the life she'd once wanted so badly. A new but not unfamiliar sensation pulsed from their hands, up her arms, through her body.

He shook his head. "It's not that crazy." He looked down a moment, then back at her. "I've worked with a bunch of photographers over the years. Most of them were good. A couple were really good. But you're different. You have the skills—you know composition and balance and lighting. You've learned patience and waiting for the right shot. But you also have an eye most people don't have. You're able to see worth and goodness where others just see something broken and ugly."

He chuckled and his vulnerability surprised her. "I don't usually have trouble moving on, but I don't want to leave you behind. We can make a life in California, however you want that to look. Travel, work, art." He leaned in close, brought his face close to hers. "Come with me," he whispered.

When he brought his lips to hers, she didn't pull away. For a minute—just a little slip of time—she let herself get lost in his hands and his touch, the scent of his skin, the way his muscles moved under her fingers. It was easy, natural, and she remembered what it used to be like. What she used to be like.

Don't do this again, Jenna. The voice in her head was insistent. Then Gregory's words came back. *"A life in California. However you want."*

"No. Stop." This time she spoke the words out loud.

She put her hands on his shoulders and forced herself to sit back. When she did, she heard the crinkle of paper in the front pocket of her bag and remembered Addie and Walsh's drawing she'd tucked inside. She'd memorized every scribble and line on the pink sheet of construction paper. It was the three of them—their family—sitting around a table. Addie had drawn their hands linked with so many fingers wrapped together, it was hard to tell where one hand stopped and another one began. All three of them had hearts for eyes. "Hearts are for love, and we love each other," Addie always said. At the top of the paper, Addie had written, in her large, exaggerated print, *When are you coming home?*

Jenna squeezed her hands together and imagined holding their hands, their fingers pressed against hers. She breathed in deep and for a moment forgot Gregory was sitting there in front of her.

She had plenty of jagged places inside her, but Addie and Walsh were smooth. Soft, tumbled edges, like sea glass. They were her light. She'd made a choice for them once because she had to—she chose them over the life she thought she'd live. But she was in control of her own life now. If she wanted to go to California with Gregory, she could do it. Maybe that's all she needed—just to know she *could* make that choice if she wanted to. She didn't doubt that she'd made the right decision all those years ago—to love her babies, to put down her camera and take on motherhood and all its beauty and limitations. And she'd do it again. But this time, she'd keep her camera with her.

All of a sudden, going home sounded like the simplest thing in the world. Her girls. Home. Nothing else mattered. Not California, not Gregory, not even her own fears. With the decision made, extricating herself from this temporary life was just a matter of leaving. She was good at that—leaving one place when her time there ran out—but this time was different. Instead of leaving, she was returning.

Gregory still looked at her, studying her.

"I can't do this." Jenna stood, pulling her bag onto her shoulder. "I'm sorry, I shouldn't have—"

"No, it's not you. It's just . . . I have to go home."

"At least let me walk you back." He rose to stand next to her.

"It's okay." She moved to the door and opened it. "I know my way."

She left him standing on the porch, moths fluttering around the bare bulb hanging over the door.

"Jenna?"

"I'm sorry," she called, her feet quick on the trail back through the trees. "I just have to go."

And then she ran. Heat lightning flashed in the distance but she kept running. Finally the glow of her porch light appeared through the trees. Instead of going straight to her cabin though, she stopped at the spot by the lake where she usually could find a whisper of cell service. Her phone screen lit up the dark, attracting two moths that danced in the light. She brushed them away and held up her phone. When the one service bar appeared at the top of her screen, she typed out a text to Betsy. Just a few words to explain, then she'd call tomorrow.

I'm finished here. Will be there tomorrow. I miss you and the girls so much.

In the cabin she flung her bag onto the tiny kitchen table and pulled the girls' drawing out, scanning it with her eyes, taking in the hearts and hands. The love they poured onto the page. She'd been gone for almost two months, yet there they were, still thinking of the three of them together. Upstairs in her bedroom, she tucked the note under her pillow, and she imagined seeing them, holding them. She'd never wanted anything more.

thirty-five

Betsy

Back at the farm, the girls ran inside and emptied their buckets on the kitchen table, sand and bits of shell going everywhere. They talked over each other, telling Betsy everything about each shell as if she hadn't been there all day with them.

"Where's Uncle Ty?" Addie asked. "We have to show him all this."

Betsy dumped the pile of wet towels in the laundry room, then noticed the remains of Ty's dinner—or maybe a late lunch—in the sink. The TV was on in the living room, tuned to the Weather Channel. Ty didn't usually trust "the big boys," as he called them, much preferring the local meteorologists. She peered out the window toward the barn. All the lights were blazing, Carlos's and Roger's trucks parked in the grassy lot by the barn.

When she opened the fridge to find some dinner, she saw his note pinned to the door with a smiling cow magnet.

Working on the back fence. I'll be in as soon as I can. Please wait up.

"I think he's still going to be a while," Betsy said.

While she pulled together a quick meal for the girls, they organized their shells into piles—big ones and small ones, pale and bright, smooth and bumpy. They instructed her to leave the piles on the table so Ty could see them when he came in. "Don't even move them an inch," Addie directed. "They might break."

"You got it," Betsy said. "But you'll have to help me move them tomorrow. We'll need our table back."

"Yeah, before the storm comes for sure. I'll need to put them somewhere really safe then."

Betsy nodded, surprised. She didn't know the tension brought on by the approaching Ingrid had trickled down to Addie and Walsh. What else had they picked up on when the adults around them thought they didn't understand?

After dinner and a quick bath, she put the girls to bed. Fatigue from the full day in the sun hit her as she closed their bedroom door behind her. A shower perked her up enough to head back downstairs and grab the laundry basket full of the girls' clean clothes. She paused by the kitchen window, straining her eyes to see whether the guys' trucks were still parked in the dark driveway. It was hard to tell, but she assumed they were still hard at work preparing the fences and property. Regardless of where on the coast Ingrid made landfall, they were all in for high winds and heavy rain at the very least.

On her way out of the kitchen, she spied a bottle of wine left over from her birthday party. She wasn't afraid to choose a bottle of wine for its label, and this one featured a shoreline, a setting sun, and a set of footprints in the sand. She smiled, poured herself a glass, and took it upstairs with the laundry basket.

She'd just set the basket down on the floor when her phone

lying on the dresser buzzed with a text. Thinking it'd be Ty giving her an update on when he'd be finished, she grabbed it and opened up her messages. She froze, wineglass halfway to her lips. Jenna.

Just a few words and her world shifted beneath her like sand.

Half an hour later, the porch door opened downstairs. She heard Ty drop his boots by the back door, then climb the stairs. He pushed open the bedroom door and stopped in the doorway, taking in the small stacks of folded clothes, the girls' duffel bag on the floor, partially filled.

Confusion crossed his face. "What are you doing?"

"Jenna's coming back," she said quietly.

He exhaled and pushed the door closed behind him. Crossing the room toward her, he put his hand on her shoulder and squeezed. "Are you okay?"

She set down a stack of shirts and turned to face him. "I'm good."

He stared hard, not speaking.

"Really. I'm good. It's okay, it's time." Then with no request made or permission given, the tears came. She covered her face with her hands and he wrapped his arms around her.

"I'm sorry for going behind your back and talking to the school. I went too far." With her face buried in his chest, her voice came out muffled, but she knew he heard because his arms around her tightened. "My head has been turned around for so long, and I know I haven't treated you very well. I'm the one who pulled away, not you. You've been standing in the same place, waiting for me to come back. And I've missed you so much."

Fresh tears fell as he ran his hand down her hair, rested his cheek against hers. "I've missed you too," he whispered.

She pulled back and looked in his face. "You are such a good man. You're more than enough for me, more than I could ever deserve."

He shrugged. "Well, you have me. Can't do much about that." A corner of his mouth pulled up and she brushed her thumb over that little half smile. "I'm sorry too. Not for being mad, but I over-reacted. It was childish of me not to come back and talk to you about it after the party. I just . . . I didn't have the words. I didn't know what to say."

"I know. I don't blame you. Not about anything. Let's just . . . Can we start over? Start from right here, tonight?"

When she kissed him, his response was immediate. His lips on her face, his hands on her back, his body melding to hers was all she knew. Together, the two of them were more than enough.

Afterward, they lay next to each other, still and quiet, her cheek against the soft place just below his shoulder, their legs intertwined. Outside the window, a barn owl hooted somewhere in the darkness. After a moment, a second call answered it. Back and forth the calls went, a mysterious language she would never understand. She found Ty's hand on his chest and covered it with hers. He lifted his fingers and curled them around hers, wrapping her hand tight.

thirty-six

Jenna

Halcyon was whisper quiet the next morning as Jenna loaded her suitcase, binder of prints, and camera bag into her car. Even the cicadas and tree frogs were silent. Down at the lake, streaks of dark purple in the sky reflected on the calm water.

On her way out of the preserve, she made two stops. At the main studio she tucked two envelopes in the edge of the doorway. One held her cabin key and a note to Casey apologizing for her quick departure. The other envelope contained a note for Micah. She smiled as she thought of the words she'd written to him, basically repeating the instructions Gregory had given her when they'd first met: *Find your creative eye. Keep your skin thick.*

Her last stop was Gregory's cabin. She knew it was a risk to come—he could already be awake. Could be on the front porch waiting. But he wasn't. His cabin was dark, the curtains inside pulled tight against the strong morning sun that would soon hit them.

She set her last envelope on the chair by the door. In it, she'd tried as best she could to capture her feelings on paper. Her gratitude. Her appreciation. What twisted and turned in her heart. Despite her rambling words—she was never very good with those—somehow she felt he'd understand.

It was 6:30 a.m. when she pulled down the preserve's long, winding driveway through the trees. Moss and vines hanging from tree branches looked ghostly in the glow of her headlights. As she turned north and headed for the interstate—no slow two-lane highways this time—the barest tinges of fuchsia and violet swept the sky.

It was too early to call Betsy, but Full Cup would already be open.

"It's a beautiful day at Full Cup Coffee. How may I help you this lovely Tennessee morning?"

Jenna smiled. Mario answered the phone with a different jingle every day. "It's Jenna."

He whooped. "Girl, it's about time. Please tell me you're coming back."

"I will if there's a job for me."

"Hallelujah. The imbecile they hired to replace you threw his apron down yesterday and quit. It was that Rich woman. You're the only one who knows how to handle her."

"What about Melissa? She was doing well before I left."

"Oh no, she quit too. Couldn't handle the pressure. Things fall apart when you're not here. Oh, and your boyfriend still comes in every day. He's a sad little puppy."

"He's not my—"

"Yeah, yeah. So when are you coming back?"

"I have a stop to make on the way, then I'm coming home."

thirty-seven

Ty

Hurricane advisory 33. Winds from Hurricane
Ingrid continue to increase. A gradual turn
to the north is expected today. Ingrid is
expected to make landfall within 24 hours
as a dangerous hurricane with winds of at
least 150 mph.

Ty awoke to news that the world had changed. Well, not the whole
world, just their little corner of it. While they were sleeping,
Hurricane Ingrid had charged ahead like a freight train toward the
northern Gulf Coast.

When he reached the barn at four forty-five, his radio was
already on, tuned to the local weather. For all of the previous
day, the cone of uncertainty had shifted between the Louisiana-
Mississippi coast and the Mississippi-Alabama coast. Now it

appeared it was zeroing on extreme western Alabama, putting Elinore squarely on the stronger east side of the storm. Basically the worst place to be.

Carlos sat in Ty's office, his hat in his hands. Ty leaned against the desk and sucked in a mouthful of hot coffee. As it scalded the back of his throat, eliminating any remnants of sleep, the phone in his pants pocket buzzed. He pulled it out and checked the screen.

"Mornin', Roger."

"Just making sure you'd heard the news. It's headed this way."

"Sounds like it. But we've suspected it for a while."

"Yeah, well, this is the one we hoped wouldn't come."

When he finished with Roger, assuring him he'd take all the necessary precautions, he turned to Carlos.

"Well?" Carlos said.

Ty shrugged. "We get to work. Cows have to be milked, hurricane or no hurricane. We'll adjust the last milking time to make it as late as we can, then put the herd in the open pasture. Glad we got those fences fixed already. We'll move the tractors and equipment out there too." He rapped his knuckles on the desk. "We need to check water pumps and the ID tags on the cows."

"Pray," Carlos said.

Ty nodded. "Already a step ahead of you." He nudged Carlos's foot with his boot. "Go ahead and refill your coffee. It's gonna be a long one."

While Carlos and Walker double-checked the generators and fuel supply, Ty walked through the field, taking stock of the herd. He didn't know if it was some acute sense of smell or hearing, but the cows always seemed to know when bad weather was coming. They'd skitter around, startling easily and generally acting like nervous old women. Today was no exception.

He ran his hands down their backs and murmured soft words to them the way his grandfather had taught him all those years ago. He scratched their ears while he made sure their ID tags were in place and legible. Nevertheless, they remained nervous and jumpy, not calming at his touch as they usually did.

The sky was cloudy from stem to stern, no differentiation in any direction, so the casual bystander with no knowledge of hurricanes might think it was just another cloudy day with impending rain. But Ty sensed the coming storm as his cows did—tasted it, smelled it. He could almost feel it, like his skin was extra sensitive to the barometric pressure and electricity in the air. A strong wind already whipped through the trees.

By noon he was tired. The humidity made the air feel heavy, pressing on his shoulders, weighing him down. He worried for his herd, but more than that, he worried for the three girls waiting up in the house. And the fourth—Jenna—who was on her way.

After receiving the news last night that Jenna's return was imminent, Ty wasn't sure what Betsy's state of mind would be this morning. Last night she'd fallen into what appeared to be a peaceful sleep. She got up once during the night to check on one of the girls who was having a bad dream, and when she crawled back into bed, she wrapped her arm around Ty's middle, a band of warmth seeping down deep. He'd slid out of bed at four thirty, kissed her on the forehead, and tiptoed out of the bedroom.

Early afternoon he made the trek across the windswept yard to the house for a quick bite to eat. He was surprised to find Betsy alone in the house making peanut butter sandwiches. The girls were upstairs playing.

"She's not here yet?"

Betsy shook her head. "She just texted from Pensacola though, so she won't be long. Says the roads are packed." She gestured to the sandwiches on paper plates in front of her. "Want one?"

"Sure. Thanks." He washed his hands at the sink, then opened the fridge for something cold to drink.

"Everything going okay out there?"

"As well as it can. Ingrid's wobbled a little farther east. Now they're saying somewhere near Bayou La Batre."

Betsy set down her peanut butter–covered knife and faced him, her hip pressed up against the counter. "That's bad for us."

He took a long swig of lemonade. "It could be. Then again, it could keep moving east. They have all these predictions, but I'd rather watch the storm and see what it's doing. Once it hit the Gulf, it's been pretty steady north-northeast. If it stays that way, it could skirt past us and hit Florida." He set his glass down and rubbed his eyes. A few dozen miles could make a big difference in destruction to this town or another one. "I'd rather it not be us, but . . ."

"I know." Betsy picked up the knife again and spread jelly on the other slices. "You don't want it to hit anyone."

"That'd be my preference, yes. It's gonna be bad somewhere."

They ate lunch in bursts, interrupted by phone calls and texts from friends and neighbors checking on each other. Before heading back to the barn, Ty found the girls in the den playing with Etta.

"You know what?" he asked.

Addie glanced at him as she rubbed the cat's back. "What?"

"I think you two are my favorite little people in the whole world."

Addie grinned but Walsh jumped up to her feet. "I'm not little. I'm strong." She held her arms up in a muscleman pose.

He kissed them both on top of their heads.

A band of light rain and rumbling thunder was moving through as he descended the back steps. "Let me know when she gets here," he called back to Betsy, who stood on the porch with one arm holding the screen door open.

She nodded, then glanced up at the rolling sky. With her hair loose around her shoulders and her hand on her hip, she reminded him of a woman carved onto the bow of a ship charging through open waters. Solid, firm, sure. A fixed point.

thirty-eight

Betsy

Hurricane advisory 36. Hurricane Ingrid
continues northward toward the Gulf Coast.
A warning is in effect from Grand Isle,
Louisiana, to Apalachicola, Florida. Conditions will deteriorate rapidly within
the next 24 hours. Fluctuations in intensity are possible prior to landfall.

Two months ago, Betsy had sat on her front steps unsure of
what the arrival of her sister would bring. She'd been nervous, waf-
fling between her desire to love and her fear of withholding love at
the same time.

Today was different. Today she knew what Jenna's arrival would
mean.

Anna Beth had come over that morning to sit with the girls for
a bit while Betsy helped Ty secure a tarp over the henhouse.

"If I ever meet your sister, I'm going to give her a good talking-to," Anna Beth said on her way out the door.

"Oh yeah?" Betsy smiled. "And what would you say?"

"Just a good woman-to-woman talk. I could say things you can't because she's not my blood. Anyway, you rarely say what you mean and I always do."

Betsy laughed. "You're right about that. But I'm trying."

Anna Beth hugged Betsy and kissed her cheek. "I know you are."

She walked toward her car in the driveway with a plan to head home and bake cookies. "It's what I do when these storms come in. I bake till the power goes off, then I eat. It keeps me calm. And fifteen pounds over my goal, but calories consumed during acts of God don't count. I'll bring some by if we're all still here after this thing blows over." She pulled open her car door and a strong gust of wind blew it closed again. "I still can't believe your sister is driving here today of all days. She has some timing."

The air was always the same in the hours before a hurricane hit—strange and swirly, the sky a creepy combination of yellow and gray, the clouds zipping past each other in their constant counter clockwise motion. Bands of wind and rain kicked up, then tapered off, driving up the dense humidity.

Ingrid was still hours away, but late that afternoon, the farm was like a beehive. Carlos and Walker and a few of the other guys helped Ty move vehicles and equipment out of the barn and sheds and to the open fields. Betsy knew they were waiting until the last possible moment to milk the herd before the other men headed out in high winds to their own homes.

Just as a clap of thunder sent the girls running through the drizzle to the cover of the porch, the gravel at the end of the driveway crunched and Jenna's car finally appeared around the curve. Behind Betsy, the girls gasped and darted back down the steps.

"Hold on." Betsy put a hand on their shoulders. "Wait until the car stops."

Jenna opened her car door and stood, then eased it closed behind her. The soft raindrops made dark spots on her blue tank top. Betsy scanned her little sister top to bottom, trying to detect something—a hint of doubt, a whisper of uncertainty. Any second thoughts. But Jenna seemed resolute. Stable. Sure. She gave Betsy a small smile, then turned to the girls, her eyes damp and bright.

Betsy's heart brimmed with emotion—a desire to both hug her sister and chastise her. Love her and punish her. But then Walsh flew down the steps with Addie close behind. Jenna bent down and held her arms out. The girls wrapped themselves around her, arms and legs like the sweet potato vine that grew up and over the garden fence.

Jenna laughed and kissed their cheeks, their foreheads, their noses. The girls talked nonstop, over and around each other so their words formed an unintelligible noise. While Jenna tried to take it all in, Betsy turned and walked to the end of the porch. She turned her eyes to the sky as if studying the clouds, but really she wanted to give them—their little three-person family—a moment of privacy. Or maybe it was she who needed the privacy.

After a moment, Jenna straightened. "Let me talk to Aunt Betsy for a minute, then I want y'all to show me everything."

Jenna approached Betsy, a flicker of hesitation in her eyes. When she reached the top step, Betsy hugged her. It felt better than she expected, both of them letting their shoulders relax and drop.

"You have impeccable timing, you know, driving here the day of a hurricane." Betsy sat on the swing at the end of the porch, and Jenna sat next to her. The girls climbed onto Jenna's lap and she pulled them close. The fast-moving rain band had already passed, though the winds were still strong and steady.

"I thought I'd get here hours ago, but so many people were on the roads. I knew the storm was out there, but Halcyon is pretty cut off. No TV, no newspapers. Terrible phone service, as you know. I just didn't know it was so big or so close." She pushed her curls out of her eyes. "Florida was okay, but the closer I got to Alabama, the crazier things got. I stopped to fill up and the first place had already run out of gas. I had to sit in line at the next station for twenty minutes."

"I'm not surprised. The thing keeps moving around, so everyone from New Orleans to Florida is on edge. They're thinking Mississippi now, but lots of folks have left already, just in case. You were probably the only person driving toward the storm."

Jenna nodded and readjusted Walsh on her lap. "Highway Patrol stopped me as I was exiting I-10 to come here. They asked me where I was going and why, then strongly suggested I reconsider my destination. I promised them I would."

Betsy gave a small laugh. "And they just let you go?"

"I told them I had two little girls waiting for me." She turned to Betsy. "And my sister. I told them I understood the risks, but I was willing to take the chance."

∽

The next few hours were chaotic. Ty finished the last milking and blew in the back door as the winds intensified. "The cows are in the pasture and the men have all headed home. Nothing to do now but wait."

Betsy helped Ty close and latch the shutters on the sides and back of the house while the girls flitted from one toy to the next, one lap to the next. Having woken up early and skipped their afternoon naps, they were keyed up on hyper energy and lack of sleep.

Jenna waffled between the weather reports on TV and trying to play every game the girls came up with—I Spy, hide-and-go-seek, and hopscotch. They brought her coloring books, crayons, and puzzles. It was as if they were trying to fit two months' worth of playing into one frantic afternoon. Betsy and Ty stayed glued to the TV and the front windows as the rain bands lengthened and strengthened.

When the third NWS bulletin flashed at the bottom of the screen, issuing a piercing alarm and stern words, Ty stood and motioned for Betsy to follow him to the stairwell. He put his head close to hers. "Either we're all sleeping on the floor, or we'll have to bring mattresses downstairs. I don't feel comfortable with us spending the night upstairs. Not with these old trees in the wind."

Jenna took the girls upstairs to get ready for bed, and Ty and Betsy pulled a mattress and a few sleeping bags into the living room. They tucked the mattress against the wall below the stairwell, and Betsy piled it with blankets and pillows, hoping to make it look like a fun way for the kids to sleep and not a safety precaution.

As she tossed down the last pillow, Ty came up behind her. "How are you?" His hand was warm on her back.

"I'm good, I think. The flashlights are ready and we have plenty of extra batteries. We have candles too, if we need them." She ticked the items off on her fingers. "While you were in the barn, I did as much as I could for the garden. And we'll just have to hope for the best with the hens. I wish I'd been able to—"

Ty put his hands on her shoulders and turned her to face him. "Bets, we've done all we can. I meant how are *you*?" His words were slow, deliberate.

She took a shaky breath and let it out. "I'll be fine. I just want to get past tonight, then we'll be able to see a little clearer. This all makes me nervous." She waved her hands around, as if to encompass the storm, the house, and the people in it.

He kissed her forehead as hard rain pelted the windows. "I know. I'm anxious to see what tomorrow will bring." He pulled her close and rested his chin on her head. "And whatever it is, you and I will be okay."

She turned her face up to him. "I know."

Through the evening hours, Betsy watched Jenna. She saw how gentle she was with Addie and Walsh, how she laughed with ease, touched them often. Her body was relaxed, her tough, defensive exterior gone. Then again, maybe it had been gone for a while. Betsy had expected Jenna to be the same girl she'd been years ago, the last time they'd spent any substantial time together, but maybe she'd changed over time without Betsy realizing it. Or maybe the summer had changed her.

In fits and starts around the activity in the house, Jenna told Betsy about Halcyon—her cabin, the lake, some of her photos. Betsy told Jenna about the girls' explorations of the farm, their obsession with Rosie, their rides on the Gator. But Betsy knew they were both leaving out parts—likely the most important parts—of the last seven weeks.

The unsaid words and misunderstandings sat between them like a living, breathing thing. She had no doubt some of it would remain unspoken, settling quietly into each woman's heart, but she feared if they didn't find a way to put at least some of those thoughts and feelings into words—and do it now, tonight—something would slip between the cracks and they'd lose their chance.

When the girls were hungry, Jenna asked if she could make them some dinner. "Just sandwiches or something easy."

"I can do it." Betsy pulled open the fridge door.

"No, let me. Please."

Betsy backed away. The girls climbed up on the stools and watched as Jenna pulled out bread, turkey, apple slices, and carrot sticks.

Occasionally Jenna's phone rang or buzzed with a text. She'd check the screen but then go back to whatever she was doing, undisturbed by whomever was trying to get in touch. When the girls finally began to tire, exhausted from their excitement over the storm and their mom's return, Jenna settled them on the mattress near the stairs. She kissed their faces and whispered in their ears until they were calm and still.

Despite the increasing strength of the storm outside, Jenna seemed at peace.

Ty was still awake at eleven o'clock, pacing through the house and watching the red spiral symbol on the weather map moving steadily onward. Outside, the winds had begun to howl, whipping through the trees and sending small limbs and branches to the ground. At one point, Betsy heard a meteorologist say that while the storm's track continued to wobble, it seemed to be tilting farther to the east, causing them to readjust their landfall predictions.

About this time, Ty's eyes closed, then jerked awake. Betsy laid a hand on the side of his face. "Why don't you go ahead and lie down? I'll wake you up if we need you."

"You know I can't sleep on nights like this."

"At least get some rest then. You need it for whatever tomorrow brings."

He swung his legs up on the couch. "Are you going to try to sleep?"

She turned and looked back at Jenna, who sat on a stool in the kitchen, a mug of tea in her hands, her gaze on Addie and Walsh across the room. "Maybe later. I'll keep an eye on things for now."

The windows that looked out over the porch were the only ones not covered by shutters. Betsy stood next to them, peering into the dark to try to make sense of the swirling chaos outside. Bright staccato bursts of lightning illuminated the blue plastic tarp over the henhouse, one corner of it flapping in the wind. She could only hope the hens were tucked in their nests inside the main structure of the house. If the rest of the tarp held, it was possible they'd make it out just fine. She didn't even want to think about the cows, their livelihood, huddled together in the back pasture. But the herd had made it through hurricanes before.

The red spiral on the TV weather map was still offshore, but judging by the relentless winds pushing against the house and making it creak and moan, Ingrid seemed to be just next door. And angry. But there was nothing any of them could do now. They were safe inside while the storm raged and cast its ominous gray-green light over the farm.

Despite the rushing noise from the wind, the girls slept. Ty remained awake on the couch for a while, but he finally nodded off, his head slumped sideways on the couch cushion. When the power went off, only Betsy and Jenna noticed.

thirty-nine

Jenna

With the house dark, the pounding wind outside sounded even louder than before, louder than any storms Jenna had been through in Nashville. Betsy gathered a few candles from the counter and set them in the middle of the table along with a box of matches. With the scrape of the match and the accompanying glow of burning candles, Jenna sensed the barriers between them slipping away.

Betsy pulled a bottle of wine from the cabinet and poured two glasses. "I figure we may need this." She passed one to Jenna, then sat on the stool across the counter.

Jenna pulled her glass toward her and ran her fingers up and down the stem. It was cool under her touch. She glanced up as Betsy took her first sip and closed her eyes a moment. Sadness, regret, and affection bumped around in her heart as she watched her sister. It was the same as the night she'd overheard Betsy and their parents discussing Jenna's trip to Seattle. Back then, she didn't have words to express how she felt—words to explain her jumbled emotions.

Tonight, so many years later, she still wasn't sure if she had the words, but she knew she had to try.

"I have something for you." Jenna reached into her bag and pulled out a thin silver picture frame she'd bought at a shop near Sunset Coffee. Inside the frame was a five-by-seven photo of two cypress trees twined together. Like the purple-and-blue pipe-cleaner bracelet Addie had given her, the two trees were wrapped around each other, each the same size and thickness. The trees had essentially become one, neither able to survive on its own without the support of the other.

"Jenna, this is gorgeous." Betsy ran her fingers over the glass. "You took this?"

Jenna nodded. "I missed your birthday. I wanted to get you something special, but . . ."

"This is special. It's perfect. Thank you."

Outside, something heavy hit the porch roof. They paused, waiting to hear if the noise would rouse the girls, but they slept undisturbed.

"Are you glad you went to Halcyon?" Betsy sipped her wine and watched Jenna from across the top of her glass.

Jenna nodded slowly. "I am. If I hadn't gone, I'd still be thinking the best of me had already come and gone."

"And now?"

"Now . . . now I see what I'm capable of. This will sound crazy, but I'm kind of proud of myself." She bit back a smile. "I know it was hard on y'all to have the girls here for so long, but I think that extra time there is what helped me settle into myself. It showed me who I am. That I'm more than just a girl who got knocked up—twice—and works at a coffee shop."

"Is that how you saw yourself?"

Jenna smiled. "Well, with no evidence to the contrary . . ."

"Jenna, I've always known you were capable of so much more."

"Even though Mom never did?"

"I think she . . ." Betsy sighed, propped her elbow on the counter, and rested her chin in her hand. "I don't know what she wanted."

"I know what she didn't want. She hated that I took photography and art theory instead of marketing and statistics like you. She made it clear you were the one who made good life decisions. I was the cut-rate, disappointing second child."

Jenna hated the sound of her voice, the words coming out of her mouth, but it was now or never. She wanted these thoughts and feelings out and gone, to clear the air between her and her sister so they could move past it. She wanted them safe and close, like they used to be.

Betsy pulled the rubber band from the messy knot at the back of her head and raked her fingers through her hair. "You've got it all wrong." She twisted her hair back up.

"What do you mean?"

"After you moved to Wyoming, she used to call me to see if I'd talked to you, if I'd checked on you, how you were doing. I think she knew she'd handled you wrong but was too proud to just call you up and fix it. She cried a lot."

"Mom cried?"

Betsy nodded. "I could hear it through the phone. She was heartbroken, both over the fact that you left and that she played such a part in your leaving."

"I don't . . . I can't . . ." Betsy could have been talking about a different woman altogether, not their cool, distant, scientific mother. Why did Jenna never see this side of her?

"It's true. You were special to her."

367

"But you did everything right. You had all the grades and accolades and the nice boyfriend who always brought you home ten minutes before curfew. That was you, not me."

"You think I was the golden child, but it wasn't always that way." Betsy laughed. "That job I was supposed to have after graduation? With Prescott Branding? The summer internships, the informational interviews . . ."

"Sure. You were practically on their payroll before you even graduated high school."

"Right. I gave it up for Ty."

"You . . . what? I thought that was your dream job."

Betsy nodded. "It was my dream—when I was willing to choose a career based on what would please Mom and Dad and impress their friends. I realized one day the path was laid out in front of me and all I had to do was follow it, so that's what I did. I chose the right major, scheduled the right classes, made good grades, worked at Prescott every summer. It would have been a fine job, but my heart was never in it. And when I met Ty, giving it up was an easy choice."

"Wow," Jenna breathed. "What did Mom and Dad say? And how did I never know any of this? I just assumed the job didn't pan out or was filled in-house."

Betsy shrugged. "You were off on your next big adventure. I didn't think you cared that much about what was going on back at home."

"That's not true." But it was, wasn't it? She'd been so focused on doing what *she* wanted, on flaunting their parents' expectations, but she did it at the expense of knowing what was going on in her sister's life.

"Anyway, they were livid, as you can imagine. Good little Betsy daring to rock the boat. And to marry a farmer, of all things." She gave a half smile. "You know what though? That one moment—telling them I wanted a life with Ty more than the job in Birmingham—it was liberating. I remember thinking, This must be what it feels like for Jenna. To forget the rules and follow your heart instead."

She paused and slowly twirled her wineglass. "I think I've always been a little envious of your ability to do exactly what you want without feeling the pressure to do the right thing. I wish I'd done that more."

Jenna propped her chin in her hand. "And here I've been, most of my life, jealous of how perfect you seemed. Of how Mom and Dad adored you."

"There was no adoring going on for a while. I even thought Mom might skip the wedding, but Dad talked her down."

Jenna shook her head. "I feel like I'm seeing a whole side of our family I never knew. I guess that's what I get for trekking across the country and leaving everything—and everyone—behind."

Betsy leaned toward Jenna and tapped her finger on the counter. "But you see, all my rule following, all my doing the right things—it was the only way I knew to get her attention. Of course, I didn't realize it at the time, and even if I had, I never would have admitted it, just like you probably wouldn't admit that all that sneaking out and coming in late and moving to a commune in Wyoming was just to get her attention, to try to make her *see* you. We were both doing the same thing, just in a different way. You rebelled; I tried to be perfect."

"Until you weren't."

Betsy nodded. "Until I wasn't. And that one little break from the rules felt so good."

A sharp crack of thunder exploded outside, causing them both to jump. The candle between them flickered, making the shadows on the wall of the kitchen jump and shake. Lightning flashed, illuminating the emotion swimming across Betsy's face.

Jenna opened her mouth to speak, to try to make sense of it all, but another deep rumble of thunder rolled across the sky and Walsh cried out, her voice a scared whimper. In an instant, Jenna was out of her seat, crossing the room to the mattress. "Shhh." She smoothed Walsh's hair away from her forehead. "You're okay." Her daughter's eyes never opened, but when she shifted and resettled on her side, Jenna could tell the fear was gone. Walsh's face was calm.

The back door was open and she followed the brush of cool air coming through the doorway. Rain fell in a soft cascade, a stark contrast to the pummeling deluge of the last few hours. Betsy was sitting on the porch in the dark, and she turned when Jenna's foot bumped something. "Your eyes will adjust after a minute." She patted the seat next to her and Jenna sat down.

"Is it over?" Jenna asked

Betsy shook her head. "This is the eye. It gets strangely calm before the other side of the storm hits. But that side's usually not as strong as the first push. Everything okay inside?"

"They're fine. And Ty's asleep too."

"Good. He'll have a lot of work to do tomorrow. He'll need his rest." She rubbed a hand across her eyes. "We probably do too."

In the distance a siren blared, and a couple of cars zoomed down the highway. "That's a good sign. At least the road is still open."

Through the gauze of clouds covering the moon, it was impossible to tell the extent of the damage. Jenna could see big branches in the yard and a wide piece of what looked like metal sheeting pushed against the side of the henhouse, but that was just what was close to the house. Who knew what lay beyond? "It doesn't look too bad right here. Think everything else is okay?"

"It's hard to tell. At least the trees stayed off the house. Ty was worried about that."

Jenna stretched her legs out on the ottoman and leaned her head on the pillow behind her. The air smelled like rain and damp earth. And a little salt.

"So what's next for you and the girls when you get back home?"

"Well, I talked to my boss on the way here. The guy they hired to replace me just quit and they need a shift manager. I told them I could start as soon as they put me back on the schedule." She glanced at Betsy. "I asked for a raise too."

"You what?"

"I know. I ditch my job for two months, then have the nerve to ask for a raise. But I was feeling bold. And he said yes."

Betsy chuckled.

"I think it was strategic on his part, to keep me from leaving again. But I don't care why he agreed to it, just that he did."

"Good for you."

Jenna nodded. "But I'm going to look for something else part time too. Maybe in an art gallery or a photo studio. Something I can fit in while the girls are in school. I can start there and see what happens."

Betsy smiled. "That'd be great. It sounds like things are mostly going back to normal." She paused. "Is that what you wanted?"

Betsy wanted to ask more, Jenna could tell. And she understood it—when she'd left for Halcyon, she'd been almost breathless in her desire for change. Now here she was, appearing to go right back to life as it was before.

"At first, I wanted everything to be different—me and everything around me. I wanted something to shake me up and spit me out in the life I once thought I'd be living." She hesitated, but the time for hiding truths was over. "And I had a chance to do it. To leave and start over somewhere else."

Betsy looked at her. "What do you mean, start over?"

"Gregory got a job in California and asked me to come as his assistant." She swallowed hard. "I considered it, but it didn't take long to realize the best part of me, the only part I don't want to change, is what I have with Addie and Walsh. They're the only good things I've ever done and I don't want to let them down. Everything I do is for them. So, to answer your question, I think some things will go back to the way they were before, but I'm not the same person I was when I left Nashville. So maybe it's something in between."

They were silent for a moment.

"I see the change in you. I saw it when you got out of the car this afternoon. When you arrived here in June, you seemed conflicted. Nervous. You made me nervous."

"I was. But I'm not anymore."

"I'm not either. And I'm not worried about the three of you. You're a good mother. If I've learned anything this summer, it's that. Well, that and I had no idea what it took to keep two kids alive."

Jenna smiled. "I think you did just fine. The girls seemed great every time I talked to them."

"I just didn't tell you everything. I lost Walsh. I almost caused the girls to choke on whole grapes because I didn't know you had to cut them up. I had no idea what to do when they refused to go to bed. I realized how much you do on your own. How challenging it must be for you."

Jenna shook her head and laughed. "You lost Walsh?"

"She was out in the pasture trying to drive the tractor. And I thought she was in the yard playing with Addie. She's a sneaky little thing."

"Yes, she is."

"My point is you think you've done a poor job with these kids, but you haven't. You've established routines for them. Order and structure. They're happy and kind and compassionate. They're *good*. And so are you."

Jenna squeezed her eyes closed, her sister's words like a comfort, a cure, and a release all at once.

Overhead, a lone cicada chirped in the dark tree branches as the rain fell harder. Jenna stood and followed Betsy back into the house, then closed the door softly behind them. While they were outside, Ty had moved to the floor next to the girls' mattress. He had one hand on the mattress holding Walsh's hand, the other hand under his head as a pillow.

Betsy grabbed the sleeping bags and pillows from the end of the couch and Jenna spread a blanket on the floor on the other side of the girls' mattress. They unrolled the bags and set their pillows side by side. Jenna lay on her stomach, her chin on her hands. Betsy did the same and they peered at each other in the dark.

"We need chocolate pudding," Jenna whispered. Betsy laughed softly. When Addie stirred, Betsy leaned up and pulled her blanket a little higher. Jenna's heart ached for her sister. Betsy had always been her rock. An oasis—a safe place to find rest. She'd make the best kind of mother.

"Betsy," Jenna whispered. "I didn't know about you and Ty. About the doctors. Ty told me on the phone a few weeks ago."

Betsy lay her head down on her arms, her face to Jenna.

"I just . . . I'm really sorry. I probably shouldn't have asked you

373

to keep the girls. I shouldn't have just expected you to take that on for me."

Betsy shook her head. "It's okay. This time with them has been good for me. For me and Ty."

"You're an amazing woman, you know that, right? When I grow up, I want to be just like you." Jenna scooted over and laid her head on Betsy's pillow.

"You're crazy, you know that, right?" Betsy laid her head next to Jenna's, their faces close together.

Jenna smiled. "I do know that."

forty

Betsy

When Betsy's eyes opened, she wasn't sure what had woken her up.
A voice? A knocking? Her alarm clock? She sat up when she heard
a rustle and a groan. On the other side of the girls' mattress, Ty sat
up too, rubbing his eyes and rolling kinks out of his neck.

Addie was still asleep on the mattress near Ty, one leg flopped
over the edge. Next to Betsy, Jenna lay on her side curled around

Walsh, who must have crawled in her mother's sleeping bag during the night. Her head fit right underneath Jenna's chin.

Betsy and Ty looked at each other over the mattress. At this early hour, before trucks began rumbling down the highway and the whine of chain saws filled the air, everything was quiet. The only sounds were Walsh's light snoring and the whir of the ceiling fan in the den. At least the power had come back on while they slept.

"I'll make coffee," she whispered.

While they waited for the coffee to brew, the heady scent curling through the kitchen like incense, Ty wrapped his arms around Betsy and she leaned into him, inhaling deep. With the shutters closed, it was impossible to tell what damage Ingrid had left for them to discover. After a moment, he pulled away. "It's not going to get any better the longer we wait. Might as well go check the damage."

Ty opened the back door and they descended the steps with trepidation. Betsy counted at least four trees down, a kayak that didn't belong to them lying on its side in the driveway, and strips of roof shingles dotting the yard. Though tree limbs and branches covered the grass like carpet, the big oak in the center of the yard appeared to have survived the onslaught with minimal harm. Only the swing was missing, its ropes frayed at the ends where the wood had ripped away in the wind.

From where they stood in the yard, the barn looked structurally okay, but she knew Ty would inspect every inch of it when he got there. "I need to get out to the pasture." He turned to her. "Tell Jenna she can't leave yet. Not until we find out what the roads are like."

"I already thought of that. I'll tell her."

"I'll be back in when I can, but it may be a while. What are you going to do?"

She raised her eyebrows. "Well, I'm not going to sit around drinking coffee while you work."

"Okay, I . . . I just figured you might want to take it easy today . . ."

She smiled. He was fumbling, trying to say the right things and avoid the wrong ones, the hidden emotional mines that might set her off.

"Put me to work, Boss. I'm ready."

"You got it." He held his hand out to her and together they headed toward the barn to assess the damage, their boots making wet squelches as they stepped through the debris.

The next day Betsy followed Jenna's little blue car up Highway 59 toward the interstate. They'd said their good-byes at the farm, each trying to get in as many hugs and last words as possible. Betsy had fished two heart-shaped rocks out of her Mason jar full of bittersweet summer memories. She painted them gold and, once dry, pressed them into the girls' hands. "You can use them to start your own collection when you get back home."

Addie smiled, her eyes round and damp. "Then we'll pick out the best ones and send them back to you."

"That sounds perfect."

There was so much more to say to these girls, so much she wanted to thank them for, but they were young, happy to be with their mom, happy to be going home. There was no need to burden them with a grown woman's heart, even if it did feel whole for the first time in years.

Ty hugged Jenna, then bent down low to the girls, his voice steady and quiet. A tear slipped down Betsy's cheek. She flicked it away with her finger, then reached out to hug her sister. "You know I'm going to follow you out of here, right?"

"You don't have to do that. We'll be fine."

"I know you will, but I just want to make sure. My mind's made up."

Jenna smiled. "Thank you. For this, for them." She nodded toward the girls who were climbing into the back of the car. "For everything."

Jenna's car stopped at the light to turn onto I-10. Betsy sat behind in her own car. When the light turned green, Jenna beeped the horn and three arms stuck out of the windows and waved wildly. Betsy waved, then made a U-turn and headed back home.

Out in the barn Ty was in the middle of the morning milking. The day before, he'd found 216 of his cows in the pasture where he'd left them before the storm. Two were missing and he'd yet to find them. It would take the herd some time to calm down and settle back into routine, but considering all they'd been through, they were doing fine.

"It's later than I'd like to be doing this—definitely later than they'd like—but they're happy now," Ty said. "We should be back on the regular schedule tomorrow."

He stood and kissed her head, pulled her in close, as if he thought by holding on tight to her, he'd keep her from coming apart. That was the thing though—she didn't feel like she was coming apart. Instead, it felt like bits of her were returning, strands and wisps settling back into place after a long time away. Still, she let herself melt into his arms. He felt rock-solid.

forty one

Jenna

A few weeks later, Jenna sat in her car outside the Nashville Gallery of Arts trying to get up the nerve to open the door. She'd applied for the job—as photography assistant—on a whim just days after returning from Halcyon, not thinking she had a chance but feeling just brave enough to try.

"Good for you," Delores had said. Once Jenna had returned to Nashville, she and Delores had picked right back up with their nightly visits after the girls went to sleep. Delores clinked her wineglass to Jenna's. "I'm proud of you, dear."

Jenna had been proud too. And a little giddy, which only intensified when she received an e-mail the next week asking her to come in for an interview. But now, staring at the sleek glass building, she was wracked with nerves. What had she been thinking? Jenna Sawyer—no college degree, only one summer of intensive photography instruction under her belt, and applying for a job like this?

She smoothed her hair from her face and pulled her shoulders back. *Do it, Jenna. Get out of the car.* Before she could second-guess herself, she pushed open the car door, grabbed her bag, and entered the cool, temperature-regulated air of the lobby.

"Thank you for agreeing to come in so early for your interview," the museum director said as he led her down the hall to a large, airy office in the back. "We're hanging a new installation later this morning, and this was the only time all day I could guarantee a few quiet minutes."

He sat and gestured for her to sit in the chair across from his desk. "Halcyon Art Retreat?" he mused as he scanned her résumé over the top of his glasses.

"Yes, sir. It's in central Florida, near the coast."

"Oh yes, I'm well aware of it. A few of our artists on display here have spent time at Halcyon. And I see you worked with Gregory Galloway." He tapped his pen on the desk and looked up at her. "A lot of people would love a chance to spend the summer under his mentorship. I bet you learned a lot."

She took a deep breath and nodded. "I did. Much more than I expected to. It was . . . life-changing."

The director raised his eyebrows. "I see."

Half an hour later, she walked out of the gallery into the morning sunshine with a grin on her face. The interview had gone well. Very well. And who would have thought Gregory would have played a part in it?

On a whim, she swung by Full Cup on her way home. She was off today, but she hadn't yet had a chance to catch up with Mario and a few other baristas she used to work alongside. Her shifts started at ten now, and by that time, business was in full swing and there was no time for chatting.

She found a space out front and checked the time before

she hopped out to pay the parking meter. Nine fifteen. As she approached the glass door, she saw Mario standing at the counter handing a whipped cream–topped drink to a lady with white hair and cowboy boots. A barista she didn't recognize was ringing up a customer. Another one stood in the back on tiptoes pulling a syrup bottle off the top shelf. Jenna pushed open the door, prepared to go straight to the counter to talk to her friends, but almost involuntarily, her eyes searched the room.

Or maybe not involuntarily. If she was honest, she'd have to admit he was the person she most hoped to see.

After a quick scan, she determined she'd missed him. Maybe he grabbed his coffee to-go now. Or maybe he didn't even come here anymore.

Just as she was waving to Mario, a group of ladies in the back stood to leave. As they made their way to the front of the store, tossing leftover bits of pastry and lipstick stained napkins in the trash, she saw him. His back was to the door and his thumbs were busy typing out a message on his phone. Other than his phone and a sheaf of papers, his table was empty.

Mario cleared his throat. Jenna held up her hand and mouthed, *Sorry.* He rolled his eyes, and Jenna made her way to the back of the store.

She hesitated before speaking. His back was still turned—she could leave now and he would never even know she'd been there. But even from behind, he felt good. Safe. A little like home.

"Sam?"

He turned. A slow smile stretched across his face.

"Can I buy you a cup of coffee?"

forty-two

Betsy

In the weeks after the storm, Betsy had mostly ignored her garden. There was so much else to do around the farm—clearing debris and hauling trash, finding the two missing cows and the owner of the rogue kayak. Helping neighbors whose homes or property hadn't fared as well as theirs had. A tree had fallen clear across the garden during the height of the storm, crippling the split-rail fence on three sides and coating her carefully planted rows in splintered bark and wet leaves. With everything else going on, it seemed easier to just leave it and come back to it later.

But today when she passed the garden on her way back up to the house, the rich, dark soil called to her. What she thought would just be a quick walk down the rows to see what, if anything, had survived had turned into a half hour on her hands and knees in the dirt collecting handfuls of sticks and acorns and tossing them away from the garden.

She'd just paused in the shade of the oak tree when she heard the screen door open, then slam shut. She smiled. Ty was coming to check on her. When he reached her, he handed her a glass of ice water. "Remember what the doctor said. Don't try to do too much."

"I know." She took a long sip of water. "He said to keep my stress level low. Gardening is about as low stress as it gets. And you're going to have to stop worrying about me. It's not like this is the first time we've done this."

"I know, I know." He reached over and brushed dirt off her cheek. "I want you to rest if you need it."

"I will. You have my word. Now let me get back in there and fix my garden."

"Yes, ma'am."

She still couldn't believe she'd had the nerve to go back to see Dr. Fields again. Or that Ty had been the one to suggest it.

"A lot has happened since we were there last," he'd said. "We're stronger now. Maybe we give it one more shot."

She'd been hesitant to go back to that waiting room of muted colors and hushed voices, the blood draws, the urine specimens, everyone's cautious optimism. But Ty had a feeling, so they tried one more IUI. It was as strange and awkward as it had been the other three times they'd done it, but this time they laughed as they left the office, their hearts not heavy as before. Ty took her out to an early dinner at LuLu's and they celebrated with shrimp po boys and dancing to a bluegrass band.

They wouldn't know the results for at least another week, but unlike last time when she chewed through her fingernails while waiting on the call, this time she felt calm. Whatever happened, she knew they'd be okay.

She was walking down the last row of the garden when sunlight filtered through the high clouds and something caught her eye. Approaching carefully, she saw a bright-green shoot pushing up from the earth. It was next to the trunk of the fallen tree they'd yet to clear away—a few more inches and the bud would have been flattened. As it happened though, it stood proud and tall, unscathed by the storm, having pushed itself through the mangled vines and splintered wood of her garden.

She knew what it was. She and the girls had planted the autumn crocus bulb a few weeks before the storm. Addie had set the bulb down in the shallow hole and Walsh covered it with a layer of dirt.

The bud looked so vulnerable—a lone spot of life in the wreckage. She was tempted to protect it, to pluck it out of the ground and bring it inside the house where nothing could harm it. She imagined the green stem and delicate purple bloom perched in a milk glass vase in the center of her kitchen table, reminding her daily of life, precious and sweet.

But when her fingers closed around the shoot, she paused. Having weathered and survived the storm's fury, the stalk felt strong and healthy beneath her fingertips. It had already proved itself. She pulled her hand away. It would do just fine on its own.

That night after dinner, she and Ty sat on the swing together on the back porch. Fireflies blinked in the darkness and cicadas scratched out their nightly concert. As they rocked back and forth, Betsy thought of the hurricane that had flung itself so mercilessly at the Gulf Coast. Weeks before landfall, the storm had begun as a puff of air, a gentle breeze that floated across Africa, picking up dust and dirt and red Saharan heat. It coasted to the ocean where it spread out over the water like milk from an overturned bucket.

The warm water of the Atlantic agitated that formerly gentle breeze, particles mixing and mingling, until it became a cauldron. A tempest. An angry, steaming force to be feared. It unleashed its fury at the point of landfall, then moved inland, leaving a trail of damage and upheaval in its wake.

Yet it also left behind unexpected beauty and bursts of new life. A tiny green shoot pushing through the garden soil. Hope shining like a beacon in the dark places.

Acknowledgments

I understand now, more than ever, how it takes a village—an enthusiastic, generous, and savvy village—to launch a book into the world.

Thank you to the entire Thomas Nelson family, especially Amanda Bostic, Allison Carter, Paul Fisher, Kristen Golden, Jodi Hughes, Kristen Ingebretson, Karli Jackson, and Becky Monds. Thank you to Allison and Kristen G. for answering my million questions and helping me navigate this new world of publicity, marketing, and general author business! Thank you to Karli for your incredibly wise and insightful reading and careful editing of *Hurricane Season* and to Jodi for jumping into *Hurricane Season* in Karli's absence and taking care of me. Thank you to Kristen I. for another gorgeous cover. Thank you to Julee Schwarzburg for another round of careful and fun edits. Thank you to the entire sales team who works so hard to get my books into the hands of bookstores around the country. Thank you also to my sharp and savvy agent, Karen Solem, who is always quick with encouragement and can tamp down my anxiety with just a few calm words.

Thank you to my friends in Alabama Writers Connect:

Acknowledgments

Doug Bullock, Michael Calvert, Nancy Dorman-Hickson, Anna Gresham, Chuck Measel, Denise Trimm, and Jennifer Walker-Journey. Thank you for throwing the yellow flag when necessary. You all helped me dig deeper than I thought I could, and *Hurricane Season* is much stronger for it. I'll bring the wine next time.

Thank you to friends who read this story in the early stages and gave helpful feedback: Anna Gresham, Ella Olson, Sara Beth Cobb. A huge thank-you to Will Gilmer of Gilmer Dairy Farm in Lamar County, Alabama, and Kerra Middleton and Robert Middleton of Middleton Farms in Moss Point, Mississippi, for answering my questions about cows, storms, and dairy farming. You all provided such helpful feedback, and if I got anything wrong, it's on me, not you!

Thank you to all the book bloggers, book communities, and book reviewers who helped spread word about *The Hideaway* to new readers. You're a tremendous help to authors, especially new ones like me, and I was honored time and time again by the welcoming embrace you all gave me! Thank you especially to Kristy Barrett, Barbara Bos, Jen Cannon, Dena Charlton, Danielle Feliciano, Kellye Garrett and the 17 Scribes community, Holly Hamblin, Lisa Munley, Jenny O'Regan, Laura Rash, Kristen Swanson, and Jessi Tarbet. Thank you also to bookstores and librarians all over the country who put *The Hideaway* on your shelves. I hope you and your readers enjoy *Hurricane Season* just as much.

Thank you to Eric Holsomback for answering a pile of questions about cameras and darkroom procedures. Thank you to Laura McLeod and my mom, Kaye Koffler, for being my south Alabama publicists! Thank you to Anna Gresham for the brainstorming, laughter, and conversation that continues to be a lifeline. So glad you Facebook stalked me.

Acknowledgments

Thank you to my sweet little family: Matt, Kate, and Sela. Thank you for putting up with papers and Post-its spread all over the house, for letting me escape when necessary to figure out the characters and other worlds in my head, and for sharing in my excitement and joy over this crazy book-writing thing. I love you and am so thankful for you. Thank you to the rest of my wildly supportive, funny, and loving family: Randy and Kaye Koffler, Joe and Charlotte Denton, Jake and Leigh Koffler, William and Connie Seale, and assorted Kofflers, Rolls, Handwergers, Cranes, and Kirbys. Thank you to everyone who read *The Hideaway* and took time to tell me you enjoyed it, and thank you for telling other friends about it!

Thank you to writer Dani Shapiro for the enormous encouragement and wisdom found in her book *Still Writing*. Her essays about the struggles and joys of writing helped pull me through the "I can't do this" sections of *Hurricane Season*.

Even though I've been breathing in books like air for as long as I can remember, this is a "job" I never imagined I'd actually be doing. Thank you, Lord, for the opportunity, and I pray I can continue to write stories that entertain as well as allow readers to feel a sense of connection and of being heard.

Discussion Questions

1. At the start of the book, Jenna loved her children but she also longed for a way to pursue her creative impulses. Did you understand her feeling of not knowing how to balance motherhood obligations with the need/desire to pursue her art and live a creative life? Or was it frustrating to see her making choices you wouldn't make?

2. Betsy longed to have children, but when it looked like pregnancy wouldn't happen for her, she closed the door on that dream. Do you have any experience with having to mentally move on from something you desired that wasn't totally in your control to achieve?

3. As much as he could, Ty tried to understand Betsy's feelings and choices. Do you agree with how he handled her dealings with Jenna and her decision to talk to the principal about school? Should he have responded or handled the situations in a different way?

4. Is there one character you connect with more than the others? Maybe because of his or her actions, inaction, hesitations, or desires?

5. If a woman takes time off from work or family obligations to pursue something she enjoys, do you think our society's reaction to that mother's choice is different from a man wanting the same thing? Would a man receive comments like "You're a parent—you really should be home with your children"? Would it be easier for a man to pursue his passions and hobbies because he doesn't have mom guilt? Or do you think parents across the board battle guilt and pressure when trying to balance family obligations with personal desires?

6. It's often difficult for people who experience no trouble having children to understand the internal feelings of those whose path includes infertility. What was your reaction to how Betsy handled her feelings of failure and inadequacy? If you feel comfortable sharing, have you or has someone you know ever dealt with infertility?

7. Toward the end of the book, Jenna had the option to continue pursuing her art by moving to California and taking the job as Gregory's assistant at Berkeley. Do you think she could have made that option work? What about her children? Ultimately, she decided all she needed was to feel she had a choice in the matter but that she didn't need to take the job and go to California to feel fulfilled—she could do that at home with her children in the life they'd made for themselves. How did you react to her choices at the end?

8. What was your reaction to Gregory? Did you understand the connection between him and Jenna? Did you see him as trying to get her to make bad or selfish choices or as honestly trying to help her pursue the creative life she desired?

9. Over the course of the few months before Jenna left Nashville, Sam Oliver became a constant in her life by showing up every

day (except Friday) to have coffee with her. What do you think he represented to her? What do you think he saw in her that kept him coming back? Was he just a distraction for Jenna or do you think they could have developed a deeper connection once she returned to Nashville?

10. Jenna's two friends were Max and Delores, both much older and wiser than she was. Why do you think she developed such important relationships with these two people? How did they affect her throughout the book?

the
hideaway

LAUREN K. DENTON

With great love, thanks, and admiration,
I dedicate this book to my parents, Randy and
Kaye Koffler, my biggest and earliest fans.

1

MAGS

MARCH

Sunsets in Sweet Bay have always made me feel a little like a child. I think it's all that vast, open water. I expect something to come rising out of the deep at the last minute, something huge and unexpected. I'm always waiting, anticipating. But each night is like the one before—a frenzy of color, the disappearance of the sun, the dusk settling in like an old friend getting comfortable.

Earlier this evening, when I left the house to come out here to the garden, Dot was standing by the microwave waiting for her popcorn while Bert washed his cast-iron skillet with just the right amount of gentleness. Business as usual. We'd had a pleasant dinner—good food, lively conversation—but everyone knows after dinner is my time in the garden. They stopped asking me long ago to join them in their nightly routines—a television drama, a jigsaw puzzle, Glory laying out her quilt squares. Late evenings belong to me and my memories.

I sit here on my old bench, made by hands that once held mine.

The bench isn't much, just cedar planks and peeling paint, but it's been a friend, a companion, for almost as long as I've lived in this house. My fingers curl under the edge of the bench, a habit formed over the years. I close my eyes and breathe in deep. So much has happened. Sometimes it hurts to think on it all. Other nights, like this one, the memories are sweet.

Next to me is the latest issue of *Southern Living* that came in the mail today. Sara and her shop are featured on page 50. I like having her photo close. This way, I can pretend she's sitting here next to me. Just as I'm about to open the magazine, I get that hitch in my chest again. A tightness, like a little fist squeezing closed, then a fluttering. Then it's gone.

I reach down and pull off my shoes so I can feel the dirt under my toes. That always makes me feel better. My doctor suggested I wear these ridiculous white orthopedic walkers even though I much prefer my old rubber boots. Good Lord, I loved those things. They were practical, hardworking. Same with the waders and hats. You can't fix a busted boat motor or change the oil in a truck wearing a fussy dress and teetering heels. My Jenny never seemed to mind my getups—she felt right at home in our unconventional life—but Sara was a different story. I saw how she looked at me, like she wondered how in the world her grandmother, not to mention a house as grand as The Hideaway, could have turned out so strange.

I've wondered from time to time whether I should sit Sara down and tell her my story. By the time she moved in with me, she was already at that tender point in every young girl's life where friends' opinions mean more than anything else, and I knew my existence in her life didn't help her climb the ladder of popularity. But I always wished I could find a way to help her see The Hideaway, and me, in a different light.

Truth be told, I think she's a stronger woman now because of who I turned out to be. If I'd remained under my parents' thumbs, always worrying about how others perceived me, I would have been a wispy shadow of a real woman. And I have to think that somehow my refusal to bow to the norms helped shape Sara—even if she hasn't consciously realized it.

Maybe the time is now. She's no longer a fickle teenager but a grown woman. And a smart one too. She'd do well to know my story, know how it changed me from quiet to bold. Weak to strong. I'll tell her. I'll sit her down and tell her everything. One of these days.

2

SARA

APRIL

I love the smell of New Orleans in the morning. Even now. The city's detractors say it smells like last night's trash or the murky water dripping into the sewer drains, but I know better. It's the smell of fish straight from the Gulf—not stinky, but briny and fresh. It's the aroma of just-baked French bread wafting through the Quarter from Frenchmen Street. It's the powdered sugar riding the breeze from Café du Monde. Sure, there's the tang of beer and smoke and all the sin of Bourbon Street, but when you mix it up together, the scent is exhilarating.

I walked out the front door of my loft at nine fifteen and inhaled the crisp air. It was April, which in New Orleans—and anywhere else in the Deep South—could mean anything from eighty degrees to forty, depending on the whims of God and the Gulf jet stream. This day had dawned cool and bright.

Instead of slipping into my Audi, I walked to the corner of

Canal and Magazine to catch the bus to my shop. It was more of a walk than I preferred to do in wedge heels, but Allyn was always telling me I needed to break out of my routine and "do something unexpected." I smiled. He'd be proud of me for ignoring the time—and my feet—and enjoying the morning. After all, no one would mind if we opened up a little later than usual.

In the Big Easy, businesses were always opening late or closing early for one reason or another. It wasn't the way I preferred to operate, but it was the way of life here, and I'd gotten used to it.

"Hey there, pretty lady," a deep tenor voice called out from the shady depths of Three Georges Jewelers. This George was always trying to hawk CZ jewels and faux baubles to unwitting tourists. I never bought into George's ploys, but I couldn't avoid him. He was too charming.

"Hi, George. Planning to cheat anyone out of their hard-earned dollars today?"

"All day long, my dear. One of these days, you'll have one of my beauties shining on your finger. Send your beaux my way and I'll set them up with something perfect."

"I'm sure you would, but there is no beau for me today."

"A pretty lady like you? I'm shocked!"

He called everyone a pretty lady. Even some of the men.

I wound my way through the Quarter to where the bus picked up shoppers and business owners and shuttled us to the middle of Magazine Street. Everyone I encountered was in a jovial mood, and I remembered why I fell in love with New Orleans.

As I twisted the key in the lock at Bits and Pieces, balancing a tall to-go cup of coffee in the crook of my elbow, Allyn roared into the driveway on his Harley.

"You're late." He gracefully dismounted the bike. "Pull an all-nighter like me?" His Hollywood starlet shades covered half his face. His hair was orange today.

"No, I didn't, thank you. You're one to talk—you're late too."

"Can't make an entrance if I'm always on time." He hopped up the front steps and grabbed my cup of coffee just before it slipped from my arm.

I pushed the door open and the welcome scent of gardenias drifted past us. We carried a line of hand-poured soy candles in the shop with such pleasing fragrances. Light, not overpowering. I designed Bits and Pieces to make people want to stay for a while. We even kept a Keurig in the back and pralines in a dish by the cash register.

I was in love with everything I'd tucked into the old shotgun house—from restored furniture to antique silver to vintage linen pillows embroidered with the ever-present fleur-de-lis. I'd found much of it at antique markets and estate sales. Even a few garage sales. I didn't limit myself to specializing in one particular type of item—that's why I named it Bits and Pieces. A little bit of everything.

Invigorated by the sunshine and the freshness of the spring air, I propped open the front door and we began the day. I set the music to Madeleine Peyroux while Allyn tinkered with one of the vignettes he'd set up in a side room. In deference to his constant harping that I needed to allow a bit of Southern Goth into the shop—to appeal to the legions of Anne Rice and voodoo fans in the city—I gave him some leeway.

I figured New Orleans had enough mix of high and low, uptown and downtown, that I needed to relax my rules a bit. However, I did draw the line at voodoo dolls. Instead, he scattered tiny white porcelain skulls throughout the shop. Several of my customers bought them to use as unconventional hostess gifts.

The day went on as it usually did. Being the middle of the week, most of the customers breezing in and out were locals. Weekends were for the tourists. A few regular clients had hired me to redecorate their houses, and one popped in to show me photos of sideboards she wanted me to look for the next time I went scavenging. A student from the New Orleans Academy of Fine Art brought by a selection of framed photographs for me to display. Allyn picked up sandwiches from Guy's Po-Boys.

As we neared closing time, Allyn ducked into the back office to check a few voice mails that had slipped in while the shop was busy earlier in the day. After a moment, he motioned to me from the hallway.

"Some lawyer called. He said he needs to talk to you about a Mrs. Van Buren?" He shrugged. "Asked you to call him as soon as you can."

It had been over a week since I'd talked to Mags. We usually talked on Sunday afternoons, but I'd missed our last call because of a water leak at the shop. Instead of hearing the latest Sweet Bay gossip, I'd spent the entire day with buckets, soaked towels, and a cranky repairman. By the time I made it back home and showered, it was too late to call. She left a message on my phone the next morning, but we had yet to catch up with each other.

My customer glanced at me, then at his watch. Not wanting

to appear distracted, I shook my head. "I'll have to call him back a little later."

"Sure thing, Boss."

As the customer slowly circled the shop, scratching his chin and considering his purchase, I fought a strange urge to jump in my car and drive back to Sweet Bay to see Mags. I laughed under my breath at the impulsive idea. I couldn't just drop the strings holding my life together and take a break, but I still longed to hear her voice with a force that surprised me.

An hour later, after selling the circa-1896 dining table and packing it into the back of a truck, we finally closed for the day. All I could think about was calling the lawyer. Maybe Mags had gotten herself into hot water with someone in town. I smiled at the thought. It wasn't out of character for my grandmother, but wouldn't she want to tell me about it herself? Or, at the very least, Dot could have called to fill me in. Why would a lawyer call for something trivial?

Allyn and I stayed in the shop until seven checking the register, straightening furniture, and tidying up in preparation for the next day. I often didn't leave until much later, but I headed out early with him.

"Want a lift back to your place?" he asked when we paused in the driveway. "I have an extra helmet."

"Thanks, but I think I'll take my time getting home. I still have to call the lawyer back."

"Right. What was that all about?"

"It's Mags. Van Buren is her last name."

"Ah, Mags from Sweet Bay, Alabama." Allyn attempted an exaggerated Southern drawl. "Impressive last name for your eccentric little grandmother." He was quiet for a moment. "Lawyers don't usually call with good news, Boss." He fit his helmet over his head.

"I've already thought of that."

"Did she mention anything when you talked to her on Sunday?"

"I missed the call. I was here with Butch and the gaping hole in the roof, remember?" I pinched his elbow, and he pinched me back.

"I still don't understand why you don't go back to Sweet Bay more often. Or why not bring her here for a visit sometime? I make a killer White Russian. Don't old people like those?"

I laughed. "I have no idea if she likes White Russians. And I do visit. I told you all about my Christmas trip—Bert almost burned the tree down trying to decorate it with lit candles. Mags had to douse it with the fire extinguisher. It was total chaos as usual. Our Sunday phone calls work just fine."

"Maybe for you. I bet Mags would love to see your face more often. Who wouldn't?" He patted my cheek and slung one leg over the seat of his motorcycle. "It's not like you have to make a cross-country trip to get there."

I bit the inside of my cheek and glared at him, but he was right. I may have left Mags and my small hometown for the greener pastures of New Orleans, but Mags was my only family—I owed her more than I'd given her.

"Okay, okay, I'll shut up. Go ahead and make your phone call.

I'll see you tomorrow." Allyn lifted his helmet to give me a quick kiss on the cheek, revved the engine a few times, and sped away.

Instead of heading for the bus to take me back to Canal, I took a left on Napoleon and walked toward St. Charles. On the way, I pulled out my cell and thumb-swiped to my voice mailbox. Five or six unanswered messages stared up at me from the bright screen, Mags included. She'd rambled on about nothing in particular so with the ongoing roof problem that week, I hadn't made time to return her call. I touched her name on the screen and the sound of her voice filled the air around me.

As I heard it a second time, the tone of her voice struck me as unusual. I must not have noticed it before because of the chaos surrounding the water leak, but she didn't sound as chipper as she usually did. Just after she gave me a rundown of the squirrels uprooting her geraniums and the bats in the chimney at The Hideaway, she paused and sighed.

"I know it's not a holiday, or even close to one, but I'd love to see you, dear. Sometimes, the sight of your face is all . . . well." She cleared her throat and laughed a little. *"Things are busy over there, I know. It's not like I'm going anywhere, so you just come whenever you can. Don't change your plans for me."*

Her message finished just as I approached the handful of other folks waiting for the streetcar on St. Charles. I sat on a bench away from the group and fiddled with my phone, switching it from hand to hand. I wanted to call Mags—to check on her, to apologize for not calling earlier—but something compelled me to call the lawyer first. I pushed the button, and my stomach knotted as I waited.

"Ah, Ms. Jenkins. Thank you for calling me back. I was just about to walk out the door."

I heard him settling back down in his chair, then a file folder slapped the desk. "I'm Vernon Bains, Mrs. Van Buren's lawyer. Has anyone contacted you?"

"No. What is this about?" I asked, ignoring the gentle sadness in his voice.

"Your grandmother passed away this morning. I'm sorry to be the one to tell you, but Mrs. Ingram didn't feel she could handle speaking about it yet. She asked if I would break the news to you."

I closed my eyes and turned my back to the other people waiting for the streetcar, then covered my eyes with my free hand, pressing my temples until it hurt.

"You'll be happy to know she didn't suffer. She complained of some chest pain, so Dot brought her in to the doctor. They couldn't have known it before, but Mrs. Van Buren was at the beginning of what turned into a major heart attack. The doctor called for an ambulance, but she died on the way to the hospital. Dot said it looked like she just closed her eyes and fell asleep."

I thought of the streetcar rumbling down the tracks toward me as it picked up and deposited people at various points on the line. Three and a half more minutes and it would stop for me.

I cleared my throat and sat up straighter on the bench. "Thank you for calling, Mr. Bains. I appreciate you letting me know."

"We'll have a reading of the will on Friday afternoon here at my office."

"And where is that?"

"I'm in Mobile. Just across the Bay."

3

SARA

APRIL

That night, I took a glass of wine into the courtyard. My building and several others on the block, all duplexes formed out of circa-1850 carriage houses, backed up to a small patio ringed by bougainvillea, sweet jasmine, and palms. Someone had stuck a wrought-iron table and a jumble of chairs in the middle, creating an open area in the lush oasis. On nights when the humidity wasn't 200 percent, a cluster of neighbors and friends of all ages and varying degrees of quirkiness congregated to toast the end of another day.

On this particular evening, Millie and Walt, the couple who lived in the other half of my duplex, were staring each other down across a chessboard. Everyone knew better than to disturb them until one—usually Millie—cried checkmate. I settled down onto a glider and took a slow sip of cabernet.

I had roughly forty hours before I needed to head east on I-10 toward Alabama. I'd have to start early the next morning to move appointments, make phone calls, and write notes for Allyn. He'd probably resent me for assuming he couldn't do my job alone for the week, but I couldn't help it. The shop was my baby, and I didn't take lightly leaving it even for just a few days.

I pulled out my phone to check the time. Eight o'clock, a good time to call. Dinner would be over, and if everything was as it had always been, Bert would be putting the last of the scrubbed pots and pans away. Dot would gather her crossword book and a big bowl of popcorn and retire to the back porch for the evening. Mags would head to her garden in her dirt-caked rubber shoes.

Mags always spent the late evenings there, sitting on one side of a well worn cedar bench. Not gardening, not reading, just sitting. When I was a child, I'd try to keep her company there, but she always shooed me away, saying she needed to be alone with her memories.

My finger hovered over the number for The Hideaway. What would happen to the house now that Mags was gone? It hadn't been a proper bed-and-breakfast since I was a kid. Could it be again? Should it be?

When I was young, the house had been a fun, if bizarre, playhouse to explore. As I got older, I became more aware of the unusual living arrangements the house offered. It might have been a legitimate B and B at one time, but over the years it had become a senior citizen commune with a revolving door, a long layover for people on their way to Florida retirement glory.

Maybe Dot and Bert would stay on and run the place, although it couldn't have much life left in it. The house had once been a true beauty—Victorian turrets, white gingerbread trim, French doors opening up to a wide wraparound porch—but it had deteriorated over the years. By the time I left for college, it was hard to ignore the peeling paint, dislodged bricks, and window screens covered in wisteria and kudzu.

Even still, no one could deny it had a peculiar charm. Somewhere, in some forgotten, dusty travel guide, The Hideaway was still listed as a "Southern Sight to See." Every summer, some unwitting family would stumble in, bleary from travel, and be shocked to find the B and B was decidedly not what the guide made it out to be. Mags and the others would fuss over them and usher them up to their rooms, excited to have real guests again, convinced it was the start of "the season."

Somewhere in the first couple of days, the guests would inevitably cut their vacation short, saying something had happened at home and they needed to get back. Even though they couldn't wait to leave, something about the place, or the people, would have charmed them. They were always apologetic about leaving. It was a strange conundrum—guests fleeing, sometimes in the middle of the night, but always thanking Mags for her hospitality.

Aside from the true guests who came and went, the B and B was always home to a wild assortment of folks who had checked in years back and never left. Some took jobs at the house, helping with gardening or cooking, and some just lived. Mags's friends Bert and Dot Ingram had been there for decades, and Major and Glory Gregg moved in not long after them. The Hideaway was always a hodgepodge of flabby arms, gray hair, housedresses, and suspenders.

"Good evening, The Hideaway."

I smiled at Dot's familiar voice. "It's Sara."

"Sara, hon. I've been waiting for you to call." She put her hand over the phone and called out in a muffled voice, "It's Sara." Then she said, "Vernon must have called you. I just couldn't bring myself to say it out loud. How are you?"

I sighed and rested my head against the back of the glider. "I'm okay. How are you?"

"Oh, you know It all just happened so fast." Her voice broke and she paused. "You'd think a seventy-two-year-old woman would have another decade of good living left, if not more. At least a woman like Mags. And her heart of all things. She was healthy as a horse."

"Did she mention anything at all about feeling bad? Had she been having any pain? I didn't have a clue."

"Believe me, I've gone over this a million times in my head," Dot said. "She did mention being a little short of breath a couple times over the last week, but I blamed it on those awful cigarettes she snuck every now and then when she thought we wouldn't notice."

Dot blew her nose. "She'd slowed down a lot since you saw her at Christmas. She just wasn't up to her usual speed, cruising around on her bike and banging through the screen door at all hours. I should have realized something was going on."

Mags had sounded a little weary the last time I talked to her, but I chalked it up to normal fatigue. She was seventy-two, after all.

"She must have had a hint that something was coming though, even if we missed it," Dot said. "Last week, out of nowhere, she said if she ever got really sick, we were under strict orders to pull her out of the hospital and bring her back to the house. She said she'd rather spend her evenings in her garden instead of a cold, sterile hospital room. Can't you just hear her say that? As we pulled down the driveway to go to the doctor this morning, she had the presence of mind to ask Bert to check the garden for berries, because she wanted a slice of his strawberry pie."

Dot's tissue crinkled over the phone.

"There's no way you could have predicted this was coming." I said it as much to myself as to Dot. "I wish somehow I had known though. Maybe I could have done something."

"Not much you can do from three hours away."

"I could've come back for a visit to help."

"She never would have asked you. Regardless of what I think, she wouldn't have wanted to be the reason you left your life there, for any length of time."

"You think differently though?"

Dot sighed. "I just think it was hard for her not to see much of you, even if she never said it."

"But we talked every week. And I came to Sweet Bay as often as I could. It'd have been different if I had more staff at the shop who could take over for me. I only have Allyn."

"I know, I know. You're probably right."

I mentally shushed the voice in my head—maybe it was Allyn's voice, come to think of him—that asked if things really would have been different if I'd had a full roster of staff at my disposal. Would I have gone back more often? I wanted to say yes, but I wasn't sure. I had grown comfortable with the distance between Sweet Bay and me.

"She always told me she understood," I said.

"Sure she did. She was so proud of you over there. She never wanted to be a burden to anyone, especially you. You know Mags. She hardly ever asked for help and she was private until the end."

Of course Mags wouldn't have called me up and begged me to come for a random weekend. That's not who she is—or was. She wanted me to come on my own terms. I just waited too long.

"No sense in worrying over it all now," Dot said. "How could any of us have known? She was Mags—we took it for granted that she'd be around forever."

By the time we finished our call, the courtyard had emptied out. Only Millie and Walt remained, peering at each other and pondering their next moves on the chessboard. I could just barely make out the early evening sounds of Bourbon Street a few blocks away, quiet as a house cat compared to the frenzy that would ensue in the coming hours.

"You're a million miles away," a familiar voice called out. "What's going on?"

Bernard, an artist who lived in one of the duplexes across the courtyard, settled down in the chair next to me. He twisted off the plastic top of a dented Nalgene bottle and took a long sip.

"Just watching Millie and Walt. Married sixty eight years and still embarrassingly in love."

We watched them in silence for a few moments.

"Gone out with the fellow from the law firm again?" he asked.

"We've gone out a few times." A slow grin crossed Bernard's bearded face. "What's that look for?"

He held up his hands in mock surrender. "I'm not saying a thing. He just appeared to have a fat wallet for someone so young."

Mitch was a lawyer at one of the oldest firms in New Orleans. He made partner when he was thirty, a record in the firm, maybe even in the city. We'd been out a handful of times since he booked the chef's table at Commander's Palace for our first date, but it wasn't exclusive and definitely wasn't serious—which is exactly how it had been with most of the men I'd dated in New Orleans. And I was just fine with that.

"He's nice, believe it or not. He asked me to go with him to some gala tomorrow night, but I have to cancel. I'm going back to Sweet Bay, actually. My grandmother died."

Saying the words out loud gave my new reality—that I was now family-less—a weight I didn't quite know what to do with.

"I'm so sorry. Were you close?"

I hesitated. "We were and we weren't. There was always some part of her she kept away from everyone else, including me."

"So that's where it comes from."

"Where what comes from?"

"You're a private person yourself. Locked up. You don't lay all your cards out like most everyone else around here."

I considered that for a moment. "Maybe Mags and I were more alike than I realized."

"Was she a typical 'fresh-baked cookies and soap operas' kind of grandmother?"

I laughed. "Not quite."

"Mine made the best potato-chip cookies in Butler County, Mississippi."

"Potato-chip cookies?" I rubbed my eyes. "Now, that does sound like something Mags would have cooked up. But no, she wasn't typical, that's for sure. She used to embarrass me like you wouldn't believe."

"Isn't everyone embarrassed by their grandparents to some

degree? Come on—potato-chip cookies? No one actually ate them—we just shoved them under our napkins until we could sneak them to the dog."

I smiled and thought of the woman who didn't think twice about picking me up from school in a men's smoking jacket and plastic flip-flops. She walked or biked everywhere she went because of constant floaters in her eyes. When Mom and I would drive her to get her hair done, I always slumped down in my seat. With fuzzy gray curls peeking out from under a bird's-nest hat complete with baby-blue eggs perched on top, Mags was oblivious to my humiliation. At least she pretended to be.

But she was my only true family. Probably my biggest fan. And now she was gone.

I stood and squeezed Bernard's shoulder. "I should get on to bed. Allyn will be giddy at the prospect of running the shop for a few days without me. I need to have his instructions ready to go."

Inside my loft, everything was in its place: overstuffed down pillows on a couple of linen slip-covered couches, vintage silver vases of fresh flowers, a few tasteful pieces of artwork. I'd decorated the loft in the same vein as Bits and Pieces, although I was rarely home long enough to enjoy the flowers or the soft comfort of the couches.

As I went through my usual preparations to get ready for bed, my mind was on Mags. Occasionally, she'd flutter through The Hideaway in a burst of energy, saying she was going to clean out and declutter. She'd poke through closets, check desk drawers, eye various pieces of furniture as if she'd actually have the nerve to get rid of any of it. She never did. It was as if once things—or people—found their way there, she couldn't bear to force them out.

I, on the other hand, hated clutter and chaos, and my home and shop were evidence of that. I hadn't consciously developed a taste so different from what I grew up with, but that's how it turned out.

Across the room my eyes fell on two side chairs I'd recently refinished but hadn't had the nerve to part with yet. I'd run across them on a rainy Saturday trek to an estate sale at a decadent, moss-covered home on St. Charles. Water dripped from the ceiling into silver buckets discreetly tucked around the opulent parlor of the eight-bedroom, prewar home. Mildewed silk curtains covered the ten-foot-tall windows. A tarnished, silver-encrusted mirror hung in the downstairs powder room. It was shambles like these that had made me fall in love with old, forgotten things in the first place. I came away from the sale toting the pair of French side chairs with busted cane bottoms that now sat in my living room, proud and beautiful. My shop was full of similar rescued and restored beauties.

Maybe I wasn't as different from Mags as I'd thought. I'd spent years all but running from her and The Hideaway, but there I was, inviting other old and tattered things into my life by the armful.

I sat up against the bed pillows and gathered my hair into a braid to keep it neat while I slept. On the bedside table was the bottle of Jo Malone hand lotion I rubbed into my fingers and cuticles, the last item to check off my list before turning off the light. But tonight, I paused with my hand on the chain. Instead of pulling it, I opened the drawer of the small table and reached all the way to the back.

The photo was still there, though I hadn't pulled it out in a while. Mags and my mother smiled up from the yellowed Polaroid, while I, a busy eleven-year-old, laughed at something outside the camera frame and tried to bolt. My mother's hand on my shoulder was a feeble attempt to keep me in place long enough to snap the shot.

I focused on Mags. The ever-present bird's-nest hat was missing, and her hair—salt and pepper, heavy on the salt—was loose around her shoulders. It must have been a day with low humidity, because her hair fell in gentle waves instead of frizzy curls. Her face was soft, and her eyes crinkled into a smile at the corners.

I'd never thought much about Mags as a younger woman, but in this photo, it was easy to peel back the years and see how she must have looked at my age, or even younger. I'd held this photo in my hands many times, but I'd never seen past her fifty-four-year-old face into the person she may have been before my time, before my mom's time even. As far as I knew, she'd always been the same strange, frustratingly dowdy woman I'd always known her to be. But those eyes. And her smile—it was tilted higher on one side, as if a smirk was in there somewhere, trying to sneak out.

I held the photo a moment longer, then put it back in its place at the back of the drawer and turned off the light. I could feel the storm brewing—my throat burned and my eyes stung. I'd held myself together all day, but with the room dark and quiet, the tension in my chest and sadness welling in my heart overflowed. Tears spilled over my cheeks unchecked and made damp spots on my pillow.

While my chest heaved with quiet sobs, I had a fleeting memory of my grief after my parents' death. It was different back then—not better or worse, just different. A twelve-year-old with a grandmother and four live-in "grandparents" grieves much differently than an adult who knows she's now alone in the world, regardless of how she's tried to tell herself she doesn't really need anyone else.

I rode out the storm until it ended. Exhausted and shaky, I reached over and pulled the photo out again. I propped it up against a book on the table and took a deep breath. The murky yellow glow from a streetlight outside my window illuminated Mags's face in the photo. I sank farther into the pillows and closed my eyes, content to know that Mags, wherever she was, was sending that half smile my way.

4

MAGS

I was going to leave him, but he beat me to it. My bags were packed, stuffed into the upstairs closet ready to go when the right moment presented itself, but then I found his note. I couldn't believe he left a note.

> Margaret, I have business in Tennessee. I'll be gone a while.
>
> Robert

As if I didn't know what his "business" was. Mother kept telling me to ignore everything. Of course she did. She said if I kept busy at home, doing what I was supposed to do, my husband would end up back under our roof where he belonged. I took her advice through gritted teeth for most of the three years Robert and I had been married, but I just couldn't do it anymore. And I didn't even get the satisfaction of leaving him, because he was already gone.

Once everyone found out he'd gone out of town on "business" again, they'd surely think I left to escape the embarrassment, eyes rimmed in red, hair a mess, vowing to do better, to be the wife who would keep him home. But I wasn't worried. No one in that town knew me very well anyway.

After I read the note, I took a pencil from the drawer in the kitchen and poured myself a gin and tonic from the stash Robert never bothered to hide because he never thought I'd want to drink it. I took the drink, pencil, and note into our tidy backyard. I sipped the cocktail, thinking, massaging Robert's note in my fingers. When the glass was empty, I took the pencil and wrote "Good riddance" underneath his words. Then I grabbed a box of matches from next to the grill and lit one. I held the note over the fire until the flames licked the bottom edge of the paper and engulfed it.

I was just about to pull out of the driveway when Daddy careened down the street in his silver Chrysler, landing like a pinball in front of our house, one tire up on the grass. When he climbed out of the car, he was red-faced and out of breath, as if he'd run the whole two blocks from their house instead of driven.

"Margaret, I'm so glad you haven't left."

I hadn't told anyone I was leaving.

"I know you, my dear," he said, as if he'd heard my thoughts. "I knew what you'd do as soon as Robert told me he was going away."

"You talked to him?"

"I was supposed to have a meeting with him at the bank today, but he called and canceled. I saw through the lie right away. If he had business in Tennessee, I would have known about it."

When I opened my mouth to speak, he did instead. "I'm not here to talk you out of it. I just wanted to give you this." He handed me an envelope. "For whatever you need."

"I don't even know where I'm going."

He nodded. "You'll find the right place. When you come back, everything will have straightened itself out. You'll see. Some time away will be good for you."

So he didn't know me that well after all, but I appreciated the effort. I took the envelope. I didn't need to open it to know what was inside. "Yes, the next time you see me, things will be much different."

For one thing, I wouldn't be wearing my wedding ring, although I hadn't had the nerve to take it off just yet.

He took a step closer to me—still too far away to put his arms around me, but close enough to warrant some sort of physical touch. In the end, he patted my shoulder awkwardly. We stood there, two statues full of emotion, neither able to make the first move. I was always more my father's daughter than I cared to admit. Better than being my mother's daughter though.

After all, it was Daddy standing there in front of me, concerned about me. Mother was probably at home trying to come up with a reason to call me. A new recipe I needed to try for Robert since he was so tired of my tuna casseroles. ("I bet a good juicy Steak Diane would bring him home from the office earlier.") Or maybe she found out I skipped my Camellia Ball dress fitting with Mrs. Trammel, and she wanted to call and chide me. Forget the fact that I was a twenty-two-year-old adult with my own home and husband, and I could make my own dress-fitting appointment if I needed one. Which I didn't.

I opened the car door, tossed my bags in the backseat, and turned back to face Daddy.

"I'll see you soon?" he asked.

I shrugged. Smiled.

"What should I tell your mother?"

I thought for a moment. "Tell her the truth." His version of the truth was all she needed to know.

"Good-bye, Daddy." I lowered myself into the car. He put a hand on the door and helped me close it. It always stuck, something Robert promised many times to fix. The door shut with a dull thud.

Finally.

"I'm gone," I said out loud.

I rolled my windows down when I reached Mobile Bay. Warm air laced with the scent of just-caught fish and soft muddy banks whipped around my face. I ripped out my hair band and let the wind have its way with me.

Along the edges of the Causeway, old men stood in clusters, each holding a cane pole with the line dropped into the marshy waters along the shore. A shrimp boat bearing the name *Miss Carolina* in sweet cursive pulled away from a dock while a deckhand threw nets over the side.

I pushed the gas down a little farther, even though Robert always cautioned me to stay below the speed limits. "There's no need to draw attention to yourself, Margaret."

Funny, he never wanted his *wife* to be the center of attention.

On the other side of the bay, I drove through the familiar towns—Daphne, Montrose, Fairhope—until I reached a deserted road lined with pecan trees and open fields. I'd gone over the bay many times with Mother, shopping for clothes or getting a bite to eat at Central Café. Robert and I stayed a long weekend at the Grand Hotel in the first year of our marriage, back when things were mostly peaceful and I could still close my eyes to his indiscretions. But I'd never been off the main roads and thoroughfares of the quiet "over the bay" communities. This was unfamiliar territory.

The last marker I remembered seeing was one for Sweet Bay. I needed to pee ("Oh, don't be crass," Mother would say) so I began looking for a place to stop. A faded sign directed me to "The Hideaway—the South's Best-Kept Secret." The driveway was long and curved. I assumed there was a house at the end of it, but I couldn't see it through the trees. My heart beat faster the farther I went down the driveway.

When I emerged from the canopy of trees, I put my foot on the brake. A gorgeous old Victorian house sat bathed in the sun's last remaining rays. An old woman stood in front of the house unwooping an Oriental rug with a straw broom and yelling at a feisty black-and-white dog. The dog played a game of chase, darting on and off the rug as the woman worked. They both stopped and turned when they heard me approach.

The woman directed me to a parking spot under a large oak tree. When I opened the door, she asked, "Parker, four nights? I wondered where you were. I thought you may have changed your plans without letting me know."

"Excuse me?"

"Are you Parker? Mrs. Helen Parker? Double for four nights?" She peered around me into the car. "You're by yourself? What do you need the double room for? I have a full house tonight–I could use that double elsewhere if you can take a single."

I could be anyone I wanted to be.

"A single would be fine."

The woman told me to wait in the foyer while she got my key. Inside, people were scattered everywhere. Miles Davis floated from an unseen radio. In the large room to my left, a man sat at an easel in front of a tall window. A few others sat around him, lounging on various couches and chairs. Some smoked, one sipped on brown liquid in a highball glass. They all gestured wildly, pointing to the man's canvas and out the window. The artist laughed and flicked a bit of paint at one of the women.

Down the hall in the kitchen, someone stood at the stove singing. Her back was turned, showing off dark hair hanging all the way down to her bottom.

The woman came back down the hall with a key in her hand.

"I'm Evelyn DeBerry. I'm the owner here, and I'll give you a rundown of the rules." She glanced at my gray-checked Christian Dior dress and black peep-toe heels. "Although it doesn't look like you'll give me any trouble." She smiled at me, then gestured toward the group of people on the couches and rolled her eyes. "Beatniks."

I knew I looked like a dutiful housewife. It was what I was expected to look like, and I'd never questioned it. Not really, anyway. But I was no longer dutiful. I had escaped, and my sense of liberation was powerful. Now, I felt more of a connection with the beret-wearing crowd on the couch than I did with Mrs. DeBerry, who sported pearls and rolled hair like mine, despite the age difference. I could feel the stares from those on the couch. "*Oh, how sweet. June Cleaver in the flesh,*" their smirks seemed to say.

As Mrs. DeBerry rattled off a list of rules, I looked past her into the living room again. A man I hadn't seen at first sat among the artists. He wore dirty blue jeans and a long-sleeved plaid shirt. No beret, no cigarette, no brown liquid. But his blond hair was long. To his shoulders. For some reason, it caught me so off guard. I had to stop myself from crossing the room to touch it.

As I watched him in my peripheral vision, he turned to me. In response, my whole body turned toward him without my permission. In that never-ending moment, everything about me was reflected in his face—the way I looked on the outside and everything roiling around inside me that didn't match my appearance. It was as if I'd been hollowed out.

Then the moment passed. He gave a small smile, pulling just a corner of his mouth upward, and rejoined the conversation around him. The encounter left me disoriented. I took a deep breath to slow my heart.

"Mrs. Parker, are you okay?"

It took me a moment to realize Mrs. DeBerry was talking to me. "I'm fine."

I struggled to regain my composure. I glanced at the man again. His back was to me now. For all I know, I had imagined it all

5

MAGS

Mrs. DeBerry led me upstairs to my room. It was large and filled with stuffy antiques—a mahogany rolltop desk, a Chippendale curio cabinet, and enough occasional tables to hold a dinner party's worth of drinks. Mother would have loved it. Mrs. DeBerry stood at the door waiting, so I thanked her and told her it was lovely. Satisfied, she turned to go, then paused and stuck her head back in the door.

"The arty types just keep filling this place up. The worst part is, they don't pay half the time! They feed me lines about money coming in—I know it's all lies, but the bills keep coming, so I have to take whoever shows up. Henry never would have let this happen . . ." She trailed off, staring out the window.

I longed to finish unpacking, crawl into bed, and disappear for a while, but I didn't want to be rude. I sat on the edge of the bed and waited.

"Let me know if anyone gives you any trouble. Mr. DeBerry

may be gone—he passed away last year, God rest his soul—but I'm no pushover. I'll kick them out in a heartbeat if they cause any problems for a regular guest." She smiled at me like we were in this thing together, then left the room.

Mrs. DeBerry had taken one look at me and lumped me in with the "regular" people. I knew I looked the part, but I also knew what stirred deep in my soul. I wasn't "regular" if it meant socializing only with those who had money and the right appearance and peering down my nose at anyone who fell outside the lines. Or if it meant sticking with a marriage that had crushed any dream I ever had about what marriage could be. Not anymore.

The next morning, with nothing to do and no responsibilities, I stayed in bed until nine, then made my way downstairs for breakfast. I took in more of the house than I had seen the night before. It was grand, if a bit run-down. The dust was thick on tabletops and the rugs needed a good airing out. Cigarette smoke hung thick in the air, despite no morning appearance of the crowd from last night.

Outside, Mrs. DeBerry sat at a white wrought-iron table in the backyard overlooking the bay. She nursed a cup of tea, adding to it from a porcelain teapot. Limoges. The same pattern Mother had selected as my wedding china.

I walked down the steps, and Mrs. DeBerry turned.

"Have a seat. I'd love company." She gestured at the extra teacup, as if she'd expected me to appear. "How was your night? The riffraff didn't make too much noise for you, did they?"

"They were fine. I slept well."

"That's good. Sometimes lying in bed at night, listening to them cut up for hours, I think of how it used to be around here. Much more civilized, that's for sure." She sniffed and looked at me out of the corner of her eye. She wanted me to ask. Hearing stories about her more proper and civilized clientele was the last thing I wanted, but I indulged her. I looked out at the water as she spoke.

"We bought this house as our summer home, but Henry decided to open it to paying guests when we realized its income possibilities. It took off immediately. People came from all over the South to stay for weeks at a time. Magazines used to send their editors out here at least once a summer, sometimes twice." She sighed.

"It was perfect—the lawn dotted with ladies in hats and gloves. And such dashing men. Henry would take them out on the boat, and they'd come back windblown and glowing. And the dinners—oh, the times we had. Guests filled the table, and our staff served gumbo with the most succulent shrimp you've ever tasted. Fresh bread. Pies so good they'd make you cry. Mrs. Parker, I wish you could have seen this place then."

I smiled, but it felt stiff on my face. It sounded just like dinner parties at Mother's house, the ones she insisted Robert and I attend, if for no other reason than to show her friends we were a happy couple. "What happened?"

She shrugged. "Henry got sick, and we had to stop taking on so many guests. He'd long stopped working—the house was our only source of income, and it more than paid for what we needed. But with fewer guests, money got tight. We had to let the kitchen staff go, then our cleaning staff. I'm sure your trained eye could see the state the house is in. Our old Bertha would have an apoplectic fit if she saw how I've let things go." She refilled her teacup and mine.

"After Henry died, I needed the money, so I had to be less selective about who I allowed to stay here. Hence, the artists," she said with a flick of her wrist. "I just don't know how long I can keep this up. I can always move back to Mobile, but I've been gone so long, I don't know anyone there anymore. If I did go back, I'd be the outsider, and I assure you, I have no desire for that. Imagine me, an outsider. It's preposterous."

She fanned herself with her hand, then rose from the table. "I need to get on with my day. You enjoy yourself, now. I can't offer you a boat ride, but there are games in the main parlor—the artists break those out later in the day. Heavens above, I don't know how they get by in life. No jobs, no money . . ." She continued her rant as she walked back up the steps and into the house.

Alone, I breathed in the cool air. It was January, but it felt more like early spring. I leaned my head back in my chair, untroubled for the first time since learning of Robert's indiscretions. Sitting in that chair with the sun on my face, miles away from the center of the storm, I finally felt free.

I awoke sometime later to a man sitting at the table opposite me. I sat bolt upright, patted my hair—an automatic gesture—and smoothed my hands down my dress.

"It's okay. You look fine."

When I chanced a look at him, I realized he was the man from the night before, the one who stood out from the crowd. I hadn't noticed how defined his jaw was, how thick his fringe of eyelashes. He was so close, it was hard to breathe. He seemed to take up all the air in the entire world.

"Pardon me for saying so, but you look a little out of place here," he said.

I looked down at my dress and put my hand up to my hair again. His scrutiny reduced me to half my size.

"I don't think it's me who's out of place," I said, surprising myself. He wore a flannel shirt, dungarees, and scuffed boots. "Where's your black turtleneck and beret?"

He let out a soft laugh. "Touché. Your name's Helen, right?"

I reached up to scratch the back of my neck. The collar of my dress felt warm and too tight. "That's right. Helen Parker."

He stood and held out his hand. "Want to take a walk with me?"

Under the table, my wedding ring sat heavy on my finger. I had yet to take it off. I rubbed the ring with my other fingers, considering his offer. In the end, I took his hand.

And that one little decision changed everything.

6

SARA

APRIL

I spent Friday morning going over last-minute details with Allyn. As I'd suspected, he was ecstatic about having the place to himself.

"No more French café music, for one thing." He walked around the shop, ticking items off on his fingers. "I may move some of these sconces to the back to make room for a few paintings a friend of mine dropped by. Oh, and I saw some great old masks sitting by the curb in front of the Funky Cat last night. I may stop by and see if I can pick them up before the garbage truck comes. They might make a nice vignette somewhere."

"I'm not deeding the shop over to you. I'll be back by next Friday at the latest. I figure that gives me time to go through Mags's things and tie up any loose ends with the lawyer. Don't think I won't notice if this place looks like a Mardi Gras float when I get back."

I thought he'd tease me as he always did about running too tight a ship, but instead he hugged me. He'd been doing that a lot. He sniffed and I pulled back to look at him.

"It's okay, Allyn. Why are you upset?"

"I always wanted to meet her. The way you described her, I thought we might have been kindred spirits or something. Her having African American roommates in the 1960s? In the Deep South? If she loved people on the fringes, she would have loved me. Anyway, she was the last family you had left. Doesn't that make you the slightest bit sad?"

"I'm fine. Really." To avoid meeting his eyes, I turned away and straightened my dress. Allyn eyed me, assessing me. I raised my eyebrows in answer.

"Whatever you say." He looked at his watch. It was a couple hours before I had to leave town. "Get out of here. Finish packing, put on something comfortable, and pick up a large coffee on your way out. When you get to Sweet Bay"—he affected the drawl he liked to associate with Alabama—"call me if you need me. You keep your emotions stuffed in a drawer somewhere, but your grandmother died and you're going home."

Home. I hadn't thought of Sweet Bay as home in over a decade. The word unsettled me a little.

"I can get Rick to come and take over if my services are needed," he continued. Allyn's friend Rick annoyed me—constantly misting his face with lavender water (to keep his complexion young) and boasting about his ability to fit into women's skinny jeans—but he had a killer eye for what customers liked.

I took Allyn's advice and was now zipping across Lake Pontchartrain headed toward Alabama. I rolled down the windows and let the breeze play with my hair and soothe my frantic mind until the car got too warm and my hair began to frizz.

On the way, I mulled over what Allyn had said about burying

my emotions. My first reaction was to blow it off and blame it on his constant attempts to psychoanalyze me. But he wasn't the first person to tell me I had a tough exterior. When I'd called Mitch to cancel our date on Saturday night, he called me unreadable.

"You break our date to one of the biggest events I have to go to all year, and you don't even seem sorry about it."

"I told you, my grandmother died. I'll be wearing my black dress for a much more somber occasion than a fund-raising gala at Galatoire's."

"I don't mean to slight your grandmother's death, but you've hardly mentioned her to me. We've been going out for I don't know, a little while—and I still can't read you. I don't know what makes you tick or what's important to you."

Maybe Mitch and Bernard were right. Maybe I was too private. But it didn't bother me. Allyn was one of the few people—okay, the only person—who knew what I was really like on the inside. And that wasn't even by my choice. Early in our friendship, he more or less kidnapped me one night after work and whisked me away to a party in a courtyard much like the one behind my loft. We hung out with his friends for hours, talking and laughing. I was more comfortable in the company of his strange, colorful friends than I had been with any other group of people I could remember.

Around midnight, someone popped in an old VHS tape of *Xanadu*, and most everyone flocked to the TV inside. Allyn and I stayed outside and talked. Actually, I did most of the talking, answering every one of his myriad questions about my life and childhood as honestly as I ever had.

The next morning, nursing a grating headache, I opened Bits and Pieces an hour late, much to a snickering Allyn's delight. He admitted there had been a boatload of vodka—cleverly disguised as pineapple juice—in the punch he'd been handing me all night.

"How else was I going to get you talking? I had almost no idea who you were until last night. I never would have pegged you as a former Bourbon Street bartender in hot pants."

I smacked him on the arm and pretended to be put off all day, but he knew better. "You had fun and you know it. You should let your hair down more often. You're much more fun to be around when you're not working so hard to keep all those balls up in the air. Let one fall now and then."

The rest of Louisiana and all of Mississippi passed in a blur of concrete, casino billboards, and occasional lingering hurricane damage. When I crossed the state line into Alabama, something clenched in my stomach. I had no idea what the next few days would hold. Being twelve years old when my parents died, I didn't have to take care of anything related to the business of death. Mags had been there to talk to the doctors, the lawyer, the funeral home. I was insulated from the ugliness of it all, except for the savage hole in my heart. When Mags took to her bed after the funeral, Dot stepped in as my surrogate mother. She sent thank-you notes to those who had sent food, returned casserole dishes, delivered the funeral bouquets to the hospital, and packed lunches for me when I went back to school.

As the only surviving member of our tiny family, I'd likely be responsible for all those particulars. But this time, there wasn't a twelve-year-old child in the mix. She had grown into a thirty-year-old woman more than capable of taking care of the details.

I arrived at Mr. Bains's office ten minutes before our scheduled meeting. I approached the door to his office on the sixth floor with a mix of nerves and determination, certain I'd be walking away with nothing more than a few dusty boxes of old clothes and maybe some items belonging to my parents.

"Excuse me. It's time to . . . um . . . ahem." Mr. Bains cleared his throat to get our attention. Dot, Bert, Glory, and Major had spent the last ten minutes oohing and aahing over me.

"Your hair is so pretty. It's longer since we saw you last." Glory examined a dark lock between her fingers. Her short dreadlocks stood up at jaunty angles. "I just got a new shade of red in last week. Maybe you'll let me try it out on you? Fix you up nice for the funeral."

Glory Gregg was the hairdresser at The Hideaway. At one time she kept the residents' hair in the latest dos deemed acceptable for senior citizens, and a few that would look better on skateboarding teens. Did Ms. Mary Lou ever forgive Glory for the bad dye job that left her hair eggplant purple instead of dusky midnight? Major was Glory's army veteran husband. I never knew if Major was his given name or just his title.

"I'm making Mags's favorite chicken à la king tonight in her honor," Bert, the chief culinary officer, said. All the residents knew they needed permission before entering the kitchen. Bert was soft-spoken and gentle, but the kitchen was his domain and he'd let you know if you overstayed your welcome when he needed to start a meal. "You'll be at the house for dinner, right?"

"Sure she will," Dot said. "I've already gotten the blue room ready for you, dear."

Before I could speak, Mr. Bains stood up behind his desk. "If I could have everyone's attention, we'll get started. This shouldn't take long, but I don't want to waste anyone's time." He looked down at his watch before he sat and opened a slim folder.

"As you all know, I've gathered you here for the reading of the will of Mrs. Margaret Van Buren, better known as Mags. In typical cases, as the estate attorney, I would mail a copy of the will to beneficiaries. However, Mrs. Van Buren specifically requested I gather the five of you to hear the will together. Being a longtime friend of hers, I intend to follow her wishes to the letter."

Instead of speaking of the house itself, Mr. Bains began with a list of mundane items. When he started outlining which kitchen items would go to Bert and which quilts Glory could have, I tuned out. My mind drifted back to the day I became a permanent resident of The Hideaway. My parents had dropped me off so they could do some Christmas shopping. It was only September, but they liked to spread the expenses over a few months rather than end the year in the red. As owners of the only diner in town—famous for their loaded cheeseburger and a darn good catfish pie—they made enough money to pay the bills and keep me in My Little Ponys and then Converse sneakers, but not much extra rattled in their pockets.

It was raining that day. I had curled up in the window seat in the downstairs den, tracing raindrops trailing down the window with my finger, when someone knocked on the door. I paused, waiting to hear movement in the house. No one came, so I rose and peered out the window next to the door.

Sergeant Burnside, the chief of police in Sweet Bay—and a frequent Jenny's Diner customer—stood on the porch shaking water off his cap. As he settled the cap back on his head, he noticed me standing in the window. His eyebrows crunched together and the worry lines on his forehead deepened.

When Mags appeared behind me and opened the door, Sergeant Burnside asked if he could talk to Mags in private. I knew it was something terrible.

A little while later, Dot found me in my room and gave me the details: the rain, my parents' 1975 Volvo, a huge water oak, slick roads, and flashing lights. The police found a toy store shopping bag a hundred feet away, sitting in a horse pasture like someone had set it down and left it for a child to find, like a present.

I hadn't noticed the quiet in the small office overlooking downtown Mobile until Mr. Bains said my name. Now everyone was looking at me.

"I'm sorry. What did you say?" I asked.

He looked down at the paper in front of him and read.

"'To my granddaughter, Sara Margaret Jenkins, I bequeath The Hideaway and all its contents, save for those already speci-fied for other people. She is to take possession of the house effective immediately. I request that she use her talents and skills to reno-vate the house and property to its fullest potential, hiring help as necessary, and live in the house during renovations to keep a close eye on the work. Don't let anyone bungle this job.' Her words, not mine." Mr. Bains looked up at us.

"'My friends can stay in the house as long as Sara owns it,'" he continued. "'After renovations are complete, she may do with the house what is in its and her best interest.'"

Mr. Bains rummaged in a desk drawer, then handed me a manila envelope closed with a metal clasp. "Enclosed is a letter she said will explain things in more detail. There's also a copy of the will for your records. I trust any questions you have will be answered fully by the contents therein."

We sat in silence as he gathered his things. "If no one has any questions, I have a four o'clock meeting I need to get to. I'm only a phone call away if you think of anything later."

"Wait, wait." I held my hand up, unable to grasp what he had just unloaded and not ready to be alone with the others and their questions. "That's it? That's all it says?"

"Well, there's the letter . . ." He motioned to the envelope in my still-outstretched hand.

"But I don't understand. I only planned to be in Sweet Bay a week. I can't . . . She's giving me the house?" I looked around at the familiar faces next to me. "Did any of you know about this?"

"Know she'd leave you the house, you mean?" Dot asked. "No. Although I suppose it's silly to think she would have left it to anyone else—especially us."

Bert cleared his throat and Major shifted in his chair. "Silly? What's so silly about it?" Major asked.

"We're old!" Dot said. "Why would Mags leave it to us when we're probably not far behind her? It belongs to Sara, as it should."

"Maybe, but we've all lived there for decades." Major's voice grew louder. "She could have at least given us a say in what happened to the house."

Glory rested her small dark hand on Major's beefy one. "We're lucky Mags made any plans at all. She loved us, so of course she wants to take care of us. She would never want us turned out on the street." She glanced at me as if looking for confirmation.

I opened my mouth, then closed it. My mind was a chalkboard

wiped clean. My fingers found the edges of the folded letter inside the envelope.

"Thank you, Vernon." Dot stood. "It's time for us all to go home. We'll eat, then we can talk about everything." She looked at me. "We'll see you at the house."

I pried open the manila envelope before I even closed my car door. Aside from the copy of the will Mr. Bains mentioned, there were two sheets of paper. The first sheet was letterhead from First Coastal Bank with an account number stamped at the bottom. The other was Mags's letter. I peered inside the envelope, expecting it to be empty, but it wasn't. I turned the envelope upside down and a key slid into my open hand. It was small, the color of an old penny, and almost weightless.

Dot and the others were still moseying across the parking lot toward their cars. I pulled the letter out and started reading.

Dear Sara,

You're probably wondering why in the world I decided to leave you the bed-and-breakfast—my refuge, my own hideaway for fifty years—when you've spent years building your own life in New Orleans. But aside from my dear roommates, you are my entire family. Who else could I give the house to? I'm sure at least one of them (probably Major) will disagree, but it's my house, my choice.

As Mr. Bains read in the will, my hope is that you will do what you must to make The Hideaway beautiful. It was once, long before I stumbled on it, and it's high time someone restored it to what it should have been all along. I let it go to make a point, but my anger has long since dried up. The place deserves to shine again and you, my dear, are the person to tackle the job. I don't care how you do it, just give the house back its glory. After that, you can do whatever you want with it. If you decide to sell it, please give my friends enough time to make alternate plans.

Don't worry about money. I have an account at First Coastal with your name on it. Use the money to do whatever you need.

To say The Hideaway is important to me is an understatement. I'll go to my grave carrying memories of both sweet, miraculous love and deep, aching loss in my heart, and the house has been a witness to it all. My highest hope is that somehow, it can give you the love and strength it's given me over the years.

I trust your vision for the house and for your future. Just remember the two don't have to be mutually exclusive.

Love,

Mags

7

MAGS

His name was William. He told me a little about himself on our walk: woodworker. Had some pieces in local shops and galleries. Good at it, but didn't make much money. Never married.

I gave him similarly scant details about my own life. Society life in Mobile. Balls and parties. Married. Husband huddled up in a chalet with his lover.

"Puts you in a bit of an awkward position, now, doesn't it?" he asked.

"Awkward?" I laughed. "Of all the positions it puts me in, awkward doesn't come to mind."

He just smiled.

"What are you doing here?" I asked. "At The Hideaway, I mean. You don't live here, do you?"

"I do. For the moment, at least. I've moved around with buddies the last few years. We were up in Asheville for a while, then

441

down to Florida. I landed in Sweet Bay last year but just moved in with the charming Mrs. DeBerry a couple of weeks ago."

We walked on. Down the path in front of us, a family piled into a motorboat, arms overflowing with jackets, blankets, and fishing poles.

"And you? What brings you here?"

"I told you. My husband left. So I did too."

"There's more to it than that. There always is."

"You want to hear the whole sad story?"

"I don't have anything else to do or anywhere else to be." He smiled, then his brow creased. "But if it's not something you want to talk about, I understand."

I took a deep breath of the damp, cool air and blew it out. "I think it's okay. Being here makes everything that's happened seem . . . well, a little less crushing. It started before we were even engaged, so I guess you could say we got off on the wrong foot. Robert and I had been going steady for a while when he asked me to be his date to the biggest Mardi Gras ball in Mobile. A mutual friend had seen him downtown weeks earlier outside Zieman's Jewelers, shaking hands with Mr. Zieman himself. Naturally, I expected a ring to come soon, maybe even the night of the ball."

Just then, the boat with the little family roared to life. We paused and watched the man back the boat out of its spot alongside a covered pier, then zoom off toward deeper waters.

"Let me guess—the ring didn't come," William said, resuming our walk.

"Not exactly. I knew Robert was very popular—especially with the girls—but I chose to ignore the rumors. I was content knowing he'd asked me to be his date when he could have asked anyone.

In hindsight, I should have paid a little more attention to those rumors."

"It's always easier to ignore the things we don't really want to know."

"Yes, well, it would have saved me some tears if I'd listened."

In my mind, I saw the twinkling lights hanging from the ballroom rafters as if they were etched in my brain. The men at the ball were in high spirits, drunk on liquor, excitement, and the look of their ladies in floor-length, sparkling gowns. Every so often, Mother would catch my eye and smile like everything was right with the world.

And it was—until AnnaBelle Whitaker entered the room.

"What happened at the ball?" William asked.

I shrugged. "He had a problem being faithful. Even back then."

"So you left."

"It took me a while, but yes. I left."

"And you could have gone anywhere. Gotten in that car and put a thousand miles between you and your cheating husband. But instead you ended up here, walking beside me. Life's a funny thing, isn't it?"

"Funny?" I asked. "I'm not quite sure that's the right word."

I married Robert Van Buren. Handsome Robert, who came home from Korea and wanted to get to know his neighborhood pal again. But by that time, I was a woman, no longer the childhood buddy. He courted me, romanced me, and asked me to the ball, then humiliated me in front of all of Mobile. But I married him anyway! Then he did just what I, and probably everyone else in town, expected him to do—and I kept staying! After all, good wives didn't leave their husbands, however unfaithful they were.

Without warning, a snort of laughter escaped me. William stopped walking and stared at me, but I kept laughing, unconcerned with whether I was being proper. I laughed until my stomach ached and tears dripped from my chin. I wasn't altogether sure whether those tears were from humor or grief.

"Feel better?" he asked when my fit was finally over.

"Tons." I wiped my eyes.

"I think this place will be good for you." He took my hand.

I instinctively tried to pull it away, but then I thought of Robert and AnnaBelle on the dance floor at the ball, his hand on her lower back, both of them oblivious to the openmouthed stares all around them. William's hand was large and warm and it felt good.

"You can hide out while you figure out what to do next. But I should warn you: The Hideaway tends to make people want to stay."

He squeezed my hand, and to my surprise, I squeezed back. Life already felt different.

Before heading back into the house for dinner, William took me to his workshop to show me a table he was building. "I'd love to know what you think about it," he said as we crossed the grass between the house and the small woodshed where he did his work.

I looked up at him in surprise. Robert rarely asked my opinion about anything other than the doneness of a steak or whether the housekeeper had cleaned the kitchen well enough. The simple fact that William wanted to know what I thought about his work sent a spark of longing through my chest.

"You seem like someone who appreciates nice things. It's not perfect, but I think it's kind of nice." He grinned at me and pushed the door open.

A table stood in the center of the room, lit by a single light hanging from a cord in the ceiling. I inhaled sharply. With his rough, calloused hands and joking manner, I'd expected something practical and useful, not such beauty.

The table was long and slim with oak boards stained a rich, dark brown, but the best part was the legs. Delicately carved vines and leaves snaked around each one. I knelt and ran my hand down one leg, my fingers following the shallow curves and twists of the carving.

"This is beautiful." I looked back up at him.

"You sound surprised."

I shook my head. "No, I—"

He laughed. "It's okay. I've heard it before. I learned carving from my grandfather. He used to whittle sticks into little creatures—bears, dogs, cats. I tried it one day on a scrap piece of wood and discovered I was good at it." He shrugged, then looked around the shop. "I didn't realize it was so messy in here until now."

Sawdust covered the floor like dew, and his tools were in disarray on his work surface. In the corner, broken pieces of wood sat in a jumble.

"I can help you straighten up, if you want."

"You don't have to do that. I wouldn't want you to get your clothes dirty."

I raised an eyebrow.

"Suit yourself." He reached behind him and grabbed a broom, then held it out to me. "You can start with this."

We got to work. I swept piles and piles of sawdust—the stuff seemed to multiply the more I swept—while he gathered loose boards and stacked them along one wall. It wasn't long before we both grew warm and William pushed open the door to allow in a breeze. I paused in the open doorway and slipped my feet out of my heels, kicking them to the side.

"You'll ruin those in no time." William pointed at my legs covered in pantyhose. "You might as well take them off too."

"What? My stockings?"

"If you haven't noticed, you're the only one here who wears those things. Well, you and Mrs. DeBerry."

I looked down at my stocking feet. I could see the indentations on the top of my toes where the heels had dug into my skin. My heart beat a little faster as I reached down and pulled the thin silk off, one leg at a time. Then I dropped them in a pile on top of my shoes.

Lord, if Mother could see me now.

With the sweeping finished, I helped him organize his tools in his tool bag and on little hooks stuck into the wall. We worked in easy silence at first, then we began to talk. About his family and mine, about Robert and our marriage.

"I remember the night he arrived home from the war," I said. "My parents and his were having dinner at the Battle House Hotel. Robert had his family's chauffeur bring him to the dinner. Mother said when he pulled her to the side and asked about me, she knew he was going to propose. She burst into my bedroom late that night and told me all about it. She was so excited about the prospect of marrying me off—especially to the Van Buren family."

"What makes them so special?" William asked.

"The Van Burens own Southern National Bank downtown. My father is an executive in the shipping industry. It helps my family to have a friend in the banking business—even better if we're married to them."

"I see. And did the proposal come quickly?"

"Not as quick as Mother would have liked." I smiled. "We'd been friends before, but it wasn't romantic. We had to get to know each other again. But something about him was different, more serious than I remembered."

"I'd imagine war will do that to a man," William said.

"I don't know if it was the war or just that he decided it was time for us to be together. Everyone knew it would happen. I was never too comfortable with the idea that his parents and mine decided a long time ago that we'd be a perfect match for each other. I guess I just let myself be pulled along by everyone's excitement. And the fact that Robert was quite charming didn't hurt matters either."

"Was it ever a perfect match?"

"I suppose in some ways it was. Just not in the way I wanted it to be."

"And what way is that?"

I laughed a little and smoothed my hair with my hands. "My, you are direct, aren't you?"

"I'm just curious about you. That's all."

I didn't answer his question—after all, how could you explain true love, the kind that nurtures and respects, that honors and cherishes? That's what I'd hoped for when I married Robert, even though all the signs pointed to him being unfamiliar with—and uninterested in—that kind of love. But I hardly knew William, and it felt silly to try to explain my heart.

"You wanted to be treasured."

"I-I guess you could say that," I said, stammering. "Instead, I got this life—and a husband—I hardly recognize. It's not what I pictured, that's for sure."

I looked up to where he stood in front of the window, framed by the fading daylight outside. His gaze on me was so intense I had to turn my eyes away. I pushed off from the worktable where I'd been scraping spilled paint off the handle of a hammer. I wasn't sure where to look or what to do with my hands. William crossed the floor toward me. When his fingers touched mine, I closed my eyes and exhaled.

Big and warm, his hand wrapped around mine. I wanted to close the distance between us with one more step, but propriety held me back. He dropped his gaze to our laced fingers. Just as he opened his mouth to speak, someone called from the house.

"Dinner!"

He leaned around me and peered through the window toward the house, then sighed and looked back at me. "I think it's time for us to go," he whispered. He held his elbow out to me. "May I escort you?"

I raised an eyebrow and smiled, then bit it back. I nodded and slipped my arm into his.

Dinner was a loud jumble of laughter and conversation, dishes passed down the long table, a wineglass spilled, chairs scraping against the hardwood floor. I tried to keep up with the conversations as well as I could, but William's steady presence next to me scattered my thoughts. My fingers still tingled where he'd held my hand earlier, and I both wanted him to touch me again and was afraid of what might happen if he did.

After dinner and dessert, guests drifted away from the table, some to the back porch, some to the parlor where easels had been abandoned almost midstroke, and a few to bed. When a couple of women grabbed the remaining plates and dishes and carried them into the kitchen, I pushed my chair back and stood.

"I should probably go help." I gestured to the open door of the kitchen. I picked up a scraped-clean casserole dish and followed the women out of the dining room. If they thought it strange that a woman they didn't know was helping with the dishes, they didn't say anything.

As I washed and wiped, I tried to calm my frenzied mind and racing heart, but it didn't work. Compared to Robert's charm and swagger, William was substantial and strong. Still confident, but there was no boasting. No bluster. But it was more than that. We'd only spent one afternoon together, and already this man knew me in a way Robert never had. I'd been acknowledged—*seen*—maybe for the first time. The sensation was dizzying.

Fifteen minutes later, I walked out of the kitchen drying my hands on a towel. William still sat at the dining table, alone. At that moment my heart stilled, calm and sure. He smiled and pushed my chair back a few inches with his foot. Instead of sitting down next to him, I turned toward the stairs and began to climb. More than hearing him on the stairs behind me, I felt his presence staying close. When I walked into my bedroom, I left the door open.

The next morning, I woke with the sun on my face. I'd left the window curtain open to catch the breeze when the room grew warm during the night. I stretched and smiled, remembering, but I froze when William stirred next to me in bed.

Good Lord, Margaret, what have you done?

But then he wrapped his arms around me and pulled me close to him. Whispered into my hair. Kissed my neck. Things Robert never did. In that moment, it was easy to forget the previous three years had even happened.

I felt bold. Eager. Yet I was scared to speak, scared to break the silence between us that felt almost sacred. I waited, a complicated knot of tension and contentment in my chest.

A few minutes later, I couldn't wait any longer. I rolled to my other side and faced him. "I have to tell you something."

"Mmm?"

"My name isn't Helen Parker."

He smiled, his eyes still closed. "I know."

"What do you mean, you know?"

"I saw you through the window when you first arrived here. You hesitated when Mrs. DeBerry asked for your name. I thought, 'Now there's a girl who's running from something. Or someone.' Makes sense that you'd give a different name."

Was that what I was doing? Running? It didn't feel that way. It felt more like I was arriving.

"So what's your name?" he asked.

"Margaret."

"Margaret," he repeated. Just when I thought he'd drifted back to sleep, he spoke again. "Can I call you Maggie? Margaret's a little . . . stuffy."

I laughed. "You can call me whatever you want."

"Okay, Maggie." He propped himself up on one elbow. "Remember what I said yesterday about you being in an awkward position? This is what I meant."

"You'll have to explain that."

"It's awkward because you're going to fall in love with me. Don't laugh, just wait—it'll happen. Then when people hear that you left your husband, they're going to say you're getting back at him by being with me. You'll have to defend yourself to them— prove to them that this is something other than a rebound." He lay back down next to me.

"I am not going to fall in love with you," I said, our faces inches apart.

"You're not?" He moved his lips closer to mine.

"Nope," I murmured.

He smiled. "Now it's my turn to tell you something. From the moment I got here, I felt like this was where my life would start. My real life. I've done a lot of things and gone a lot of places, but when I arrived here, something felt different." He reached up and stroked my cheek. "I wasn't sure what to look for, but then you showed up. I think you're what I've been waiting for."

Silence stretched between us, but it wasn't uncomfortable. Rather, it was a space for dreams. For possibility.

8

❧❧❧

MAGS

William and I quickly became an item. Everyone in the house saw it and no one questioned it. Only Mrs. DeBerry thought it improper.

"Mrs. Parker—or whoever you are—it is 'Mrs.,' isn't it?"

I nodded.

"Mrs. Parker, he's a bum. They're all bums. They don't do anything. You're a young girl. What would your father think?"

"He'd probably be shocked, Mrs. DeBerry. Just like you are. Even I am, a little. But William isn't a bum. You should know that."

She shook her head and walked away, mumbling about ladies and gentlemen and indecent things.

William introduced me to his friends as Maggie. He looked at me when he said it the first time, as if asking for belated permission. I nodded. Maggie felt good. It felt light.

A woman in the house, Daisy, lent me some clothes when she saw me adjusting the waistband of my slim skirt. "Here, this will be more comfortable." She pulled a long tunic dress out of a bag.

I smiled—Mother would definitely not approve. I stopped rolling my hair that day. I let it fall around my shoulders, free and unruly. That night, I shoved my bobby pins, pearl necklace, and foam rollers into a side pocket of my suitcase. I went ahead and dropped my wedding ring down there with them. Lord, it was a sad, expensive little collection.

The days were long, with nothing concrete to mark the passage of time. Most mornings William and I sat among the other guests in the dining room, munching on croissants and idly reading the newspaper. No one had real jobs to hurry off to, so the mood in the house was one of utter relaxation. It wasn't hard to slip into a routine of ease.

As the painters painted, the sculptors sculpted, and the yogis practiced their moves in the grass, I learned the routines of the house and became a part of them. Since I didn't have a creative endeavor to take up my time like everyone else, I wanted a job to do—something to make me feel useful and productive.

Starla, the woman I'd seen in the kitchen the first night I arrived, asked me to help with food preparations. She just needed an extra hand to help pull meals together, but I took it a step further. I made a grocery list every few days with ingredients for each meal plus extra items for the house—toilet paper, matches, soap. I organized the pantry by food type and size. I scoured the oven and cleaned out the refrigerator. As a wedding gift, Mother had hired a woman to clean our house in Mobile twice a week, so I rarely had anything to clean or straighten at home. The hard work felt good, and I relished my sore muscles and dirty fingernails.

William and I spent most evenings sitting on the back porch, huddled together on the glider. He'd massage my feet and tell me stories of working in orange groves in Florida and selling his tables and benches from a roadside shack in Asheville. My privileged prior life was sedate and sheltered compared to William's hard-earned wisdom and tales from the road. I soaked him up, every word, laugh, and touch.

He knocked on my door early one morning before the sun was up. He stuck his head in the room when I answered.

"Come with me," he whispered, holding up a mug of coffee. "Outside, five minutes."

Curious, I dressed quickly. Following the aroma of coffee outside, I found him waiting in his truck, the passenger door open for me.

"Where are we going? It's still dark."

"I know. You'll see."

He drove fast down Highway 55. When he turned onto a side street, I grew lost in a maze of dirt roads and creek beds. Finally, we went around a bend and the path opened into a cove overlooking Mobile Bay, isolated except for a blue heron standing on thin legs in the shallow water. It was still dark beneath the cover of trees, but directly in front of us, the sky had exploded in streaks of orange and pink, with violet clouds scattered like pebbles. Just above the waterline, the horizon remained a deep indigo blue. Seagulls gliding in the air provided the only movement other than the quiet waves creeping forward and back along the shore.

We watched the sky change colors without speaking. At some point during the show, we walked to the edge of the water and sat down, a blanket over our shoulders and our toes just touching the water. I leaned my head on his shoulder.

"What do you think?" he asked once the sky was a solid fluorescent orange.

"It's breathtaking. How did you find this place?"

"It's mine. I bought this plot of land from a buddy who moved to San Francisco. It had been in his family for generations, but he didn't plan to come back and said he didn't need ties here. I've done nothing but move around, and I guess ties are what I'm looking for—something to anchor me to a place I can call my own."

We sat close and still, watching the gulls overhead and the water's gentle movement. In the distance, the double masts of a shrimp boat interrupted the perfect line of the horizon. He took my hand in his and traced the skin on my palm and wrist, up to the crook of my elbow. The light touch sent chills up my arms and down my back. He laced his fingers between mine and I pressed myself into his side. It had been a little more than a month since we met, but already, I felt connected to him in a way I'd never felt with Robert.

"This thing that's happening between us—it's fast." I was scared to say the words out loud, so I whispered them.

"Too fast?" He turned to face me.

I shook my head. "I don't know. I don't even know how this sort of thing works. I've never been with anyone other than Robert, and we'd known each other for years. Is it possible—rational—for us to feel so much so quickly?"

"Sure it's possible. Rational? I don't know and I don't care. I care about us and where we're going."

"How do I know this isn't a rebound, like you said?" I touched the tip of his nose. "And how do I know you're not just taking advantage of the only woman at The Hideaway not dressed in black and ranting about Kerouac or Ginsberg?"

He didn't laugh or even smile. "I'm not taking advantage of you. You know me well enough by now to know that."

"That's the thing—sometimes I feel like I don't know you at all."

"You do know me." He pulled away a bit. "What else do you need to know? My life before you wasn't that interesting, then you showed up and my world cracked open. Isn't that enough?"

"It is—or I want it to be. But you have to understand how it feels to open the door to a world that's entirely unknown to me. And . . ." I stopped. I didn't want to remind him. Or me. As if either of us could forget.

"And what?"

"I'm still married. I have a husband."

"You're right," he said softly, his gaze on the water. "Do you have plans to return to him?"

I shook my head.

"Then this new world—I know it makes you nervous, but isn't it also a little exciting?" He cupped my cheek with his hand. "We can make our future anything we want it to be." The corner of his mouth pulled up—the same half smile he offered as a life preserver the first evening I arrived at The Hideaway.

It almost made me mad—that smile that seemed to belittle my fears of linking my future to someone—and somewhere—else. But at the same time, I wanted to cling to that smile, to wrap myself around the unknown and not ask questions.

"And as for this just being a rebound for you," he continued, "a way to get back at Robert for his lady friend, you'll have to judge that for yourself. I don't think it is though. I think this is . . . something else."

I nodded and he took my hand.

"Let's not mention Robert again. I don't want him to be a part of this," I said.

"Suits me just fine."

I nestled back down beside him under the blanket. He pulled me closer and kissed me.

"I told you, you were going to fall in love with me," he said with a grin.

I pushed him away and laughed. "What makes you think I'm in love with you?"

"You are, aren't you?"

I was a new woman—risky and adventurous. It felt foreign and perfect at the same time.

"I guess you'll have to wait and see."

9

SARA

I pulled down the long gravel driveway in front of The Hideaway and began the slow trek through the trees. When I reached the house, I parked my car under the big oak. Nerves stalled my hand on the car door handle.

My parents' deaths and the lonely years after had left a wound deep in my heart. Although the wound had healed, it was still tender. I didn't let myself think of their deaths often—it was too painful, like pressing on a bruise. Thankfully, my scrambling to open Bits and Pieces and make a name for myself in New Orleans occupied almost all my mental energy. Their absence was always present, but most of the time, I was able to keep it tucked under the surface of my life. I was comfortable with that. I could live with that. But here I was, back at the place where it all happened.

When I finally exited my car, I stood in the driveway holding my suitcase and picking rocks out of my open-toed sandals. I heard the crunch of gravel and turned around to see Major's car slowing to a stop behind me. I waited by the door while the four of them climbed out.

"Go on in," Major said. "You don't need to wait for an invitation."

"I still can't believe y'all leave the doors unlocked."

"It's not New Orleans, honey," Dot said, before kissing me on the cheek and walking past me into the house.

I took a deep breath before following them in.

Major pulled out my chair at the table before I sat down. Dot and Glory must have done a number on him on the ride over from Mobile. He seemed calm, but I could only imagine the rant he probably unleashed in the car. I glanced around, trying to gauge the tension level, as Bert filled our glasses with iced tea.

"We're real glad you're here," Glory said to me, spooning out a serving of green beans.

I laughed a little, but her calm, delicately lined face told me she was serious. "I thought y'all might fight over who got to kick me out the door first."

"You're like a daughter to us," Glory said. "Kicking you out would never cross our minds. All we can do is look to the future of the house, whatever that may be."

Four pairs of eyes shifted in my direction. I took a long sip of tea.

"I meant what I said earlier," Dot said as I set my glass down. "The house belongs to you now, as it should. Mags asked you to take care of this place, and no one could ever argue with her once she got an idea in her head. Regardless of what you decide to do with the house in the end—"

"She's not going to sell the thing, that's for sure," Major's deep voice burst out. "It needs to stay in family hands." He shot to his feet, his chair squeaking on the hardwood, and stomped to the other side of the room. So much for him cooling off in the car.

He stood at the window overlooking the driveway for a long moment before he turned back to us. When he did, most of the anger had drained from his face. "I know we don't deserve the house. Blood's thicker than water, and all that. But after living here so long and being with Mags every day, I'd say we're a little more than just water. Now she's gone and given our house to someone who only visits a couple times a year." He lifted his glasses and rubbed the bridge of his nose. He sighed. "I know it's not *our* house, but it feels that way."

"It does feel that way, but Sara grew up in this house," Dot said. "It's more hers than ours. Mags let us stay here so long out of the kindness of her heart—and because she loved us. But she's not forcing us out. She wouldn't have given the house to Sara if she didn't trust Sara to make the best decision. I agree with her on this."

Silence fell in the room as Major shuffled back to his chair and we all started eating. Forks clinked against plates and a breeze from the open window ruffled the curtains.

Dot looked at Bert and tilted her head toward the kitchen. Bert raised his eyebrows and nodded. "I'll be right back." A moment later, he returned carrying a bottle of wine and a tray of glasses. "Nothing like a little wine to loosen the lips and calm the nerves, right?"

"I think someone's lips are already loose enough," Glory said.

Bert started to laugh but stopped when Major glared at him.

"Okay, let's all just enjoy our dinner," Dot said. "We need to speak words of love to each other and celebrate who Mags was, not second-guess her actions. It's her life, her house, her decision."

I looked down at my lap and smiled. Dot was Mags's best friend in the world. It made sense she would echo what Mags had said in her letter to me.

"Everybody agree?"

We all nodded. Glory winked at me from across the table. I smiled back at her. Everyone watched as Bert uncorked the bottle and poured a couple inches into each glass. His calm movements soothed our frayed nerves. One by one, everyone reached over and took a glass, even Major.

I waited until everyone had taken a sip before I spoke. "It means a lot that Mags trusted me with her home. In all of our conversations, she never said anything about leaving the house to me. If she wanted to surprise me, she did it. I have a lot going on with my shop and—"

"Yes, your shop," Glory said. "Did you see the binder by the couch when you came in? She always kept it in her bedroom, but we brought it out so you could see it. She has every magazine article that has ever mentioned you or Bits and Pieces. She showed that binder to everyone who came through the door. She was so proud of you."

I always told Mags when a magazine writer or reporter came into the shop with a voice recorder and a notebook, telling me we'd been noticed again by another editor somewhere. Sometimes I worried she'd think I was flaunting my success, but she always celebrated with me. I had no idea she'd gone to the trouble of tracking down the magazines and clipping the articles.

"Sara, you have quite a talent and we"—Dot bored a hole in

Major with her eyes—"think you'll be the perfect person to whip this place into shape. I, for one, am glad for it. A few cans of paint and a hammer or two are just what we need around here."

From the little I'd seen before dinner, painting and hammering were the least of my concerns. If I decided to sell the house—and living three hours away, did I have another choice?—I'd have to do a lot of work just to get it ready for the market. Talking about selling right now was premature, but finding a good contractor wasn't.

"I'll check everything out, put a plan together, and start calling around," I said. "I'm good at cosmetic updates, but I'm no expert on plumbing, wiring, any of that."

"Now, don't get too ahead of yourself, dear," Dot said. "The house doesn't need that much work. She's still a beauty, much like your grandmother. She just needs some spit and polish."

"We'll start there and see how it goes," I said carefully.

"And have you thought of your plans for the house aside from the renovation?" Glory asked.

I knew what she was really asking. "I haven't thought about much, honestly. It's been a quick couple of hours."

"Just give us some warning if you decide to pull the rug out from under us," Major said.

"Mags specifically asked me to do that. Even if she hadn't, you know I wouldn't do that to you."

With dinner mostly over, Bert stood to get the dessert. "Someone dropped off a hummingbird cake this morning. I've been holding myself back all day."

"So many people have been bringing food by," Glory said. "Such kindness."

"I didn't know Mags had so many friends," I said.

"Most everyone in Sweet Bay has been helped by Mags at one time or another," Bert said. "Either that, or their parents were. Anyway, this is what Southern people do, whether they know the deceased or not. You know that." He set the cake down in the center of the table as if he made it himself.

"If it's okay with you, I'm going to pass on dessert," I said. "I think I'll walk around a little before heading upstairs."

"You sure you don't want any? You're not one of those girls who never lets herself eat sweets, are you?" Bert asked. "If nothing else, that's what grief is for. You can stuff yourself silly and blame it on the person who died."

"Bert! That's terrible," Dot said.

"I'm just kidding and Sara knows it. But we do have a counter full of cakes and pies in the kitchen. Someone will have to eat it all."

"I'll have a slice tomorrow," I said as I stood.

"Let us know if you need anything," Dot said. "Your room is all ready, but I may have forgotten something. Feel free to look around, go on down to the dock, whatever you want. The place is yours."

"Sure is," Major said under his breath. "She's got the keys to prove it."

I spent the next hour walking around the house and yard to get a sense of what a renovation would entail. Of course I'd seen the house each time I'd come back for visits, but I hadn't taken a hard look at it with a critical eye.

Inside, it was hard to get a sense of the space because most of the rooms were overstuffed with furniture, as if each person who'd moved into the house over the years had added a treasured chair or table to the mix. The resulting hodgepodge of furniture matched neither each other nor the style of the house. A few pieces stuck out though, and for good reason—an oak pie safe with hand-punched tin covering the bottom shelves, an armoire with delicate scrollwork carved into the pine at the top and bottom, and a corner hutch covered in peeling white paint and doors with squares of wavy glass. These had been in the house for as long as I could remember, but before, they'd just been part of the overall chaos of the house. Now, I saw they bore the handmade, vintage charm so many of my customers craved.

The main living room had floor-to-ceiling curtains that, when opened, revealed beautiful windows reaching almost to the ceiling. I tied the curtains back on their hooks and peered through the salt-crusted glass. Past the lawn, the bay stretched out flat and calm. As I turned to cross through the room, a blur of blue on the floor caught my eye. I knelt and ran my fingers across the splotch of what appeared to be blue paint just inside the front door. I scratched at the edge with my fingernail, but the paint was so old it had almost blended in with the wood.

Across the hall from the living room, the kitchen had last seen an update in the 1980s. The countertops and backsplash still boasted the cheery yellow Mags had loved so much. Laminate cabinets with faux-wood trim and ancient appliances rounded out the dated look. Baskets hung everywhere, adding a country feel that must have been Bert's doing.

Despite this veneer of age, the house had great bones. I couldn't help but feel a ripple of excitement as I walked the wide center hallway from the front door straight through to the porch in the back. Twelve-foot ceilings, tall windows, hardwood floors, curved staircase—these were the things of a designer's dream.

I moved outside to the yard. The house had been built with boards salvaged from an old barn in Virginia, or so the story went that I'd heard as a kid. Mags used to tell me if I looked hard enough, I could find places in the wood where goats had rubbed their horns or chickens had pecked, leaving small holes and dings. I never did find those places, but I spent whole afternoons looking for them. Mags probably told me that story just to occupy me while she worked in her garden, but now, as I looked at the façade of the house, it wouldn't have surprised me if it was true. Most of the wood was pockmarked with holes the diameter of a No. 2 pencil, although they were probably due to industrious carpenter bees, not farm animals.

A thin layer of peeling paint covered the grass at the base of the house. Fungus-green peeked out where the paint had peeled from the weathered wood. Kudzu, that great Southern beast, covered the entire chimney and one upstairs window. On the chimney, crumbly bricks at both the base and top made use of the inside fireplace impossible—or at least dangerous.

Much of what I saw remained exactly as it had been for as long as I could remember. The house had always been a little disheveled, but I was used to it and didn't question it much. Now, standing in the grass facing the house, I wondered about the general sense of deterioration and neglect that covered the house like a shroud. Mags had let the house slip into disarray for a reason—she'd said so in the letter—but any hint of anger in her had been lost on me.

Whatever her reason, my fingers itched for a paint scraper, sheet of sandpaper, or bottle of wood glue.

If I didn't have a life in New Orleans and a business to get back to, I knew I could make something of The Hideaway. Mags was right. The beauty was there—it just needed someone with a trained eye and good taste to uncover it. But the project would require a much longer duration in Sweet Bay than I had anticipated. What would happen to Bits and Pieces if I stayed away for too long, unable to offer input on items purchased and sold, decorating decisions, and customers' urgent requests?

Later that night, I sank into bed in the blue room without changing clothes or even washing my face. The crisp sheets were cool against my legs, and a breeze through the open window lifted the curtains. Dot called it the blue room because everything in it was in varying shades of blue—the bedding, curtains, rugs, even the framed prints on the wall. Each of the bedrooms in The Hideaway had its own color scheme—my blue room, the yellow room, the pink room, and a red room that I had always thought was a little creepy.

I bunched up the pillows behind my head and surveyed the room where I spent so many nights as a kid. It still felt familiar despite having spent only a handful of nights here over the last several years. I'd already checked the closet. It still held some of the clothes I hadn't gotten around to packing up and taking back to New Orleans with me. Earlier, I'd run my fingers across the polo shirts and too-small blue jeans.

Despite making a life for myself elsewhere, I felt like the last eight years in New Orleans hadn't even happened. Except now I was Sara Jenkins, owner of Bits and Pieces, with a client list as long as my arm. I wore Nanette Lepore and Tory Burch instead of cutoffs and flip-flops. I'd been intentional for nearly a decade, working my butt off to be successful, but back in the blue room, it felt like nothing had changed, like all my hard work had just been "spit and polish."

Allyn will know what to do. He loved to dole out advice to anyone within earshot whether she asked for it or not. Occasionally, his words of wisdom were too risky (or downright scandalous) for my taste, but underneath the sass, his pointers were always spot-on. Working together for four years, six days a week, eight hours a day gave him the ability to home in on all my insecurities, insufficiencies, and flaws. In a loving way, of course.

Allyn had been with me since the very beginning of Bits and Pieces. He breezed through the door the day before I opened, and all the revelry and cheekiness of New Orleans blew in with him.

"Honey, you better be doing something special here because there are a million and one home décor shops in this city. What's your hook?"

I was busy typing on my laptop, trying to get a press release out to *New Orleans* magazine, when he entered. I'd spent the morning rearranging furniture and dusting in the heat. The AC repair guy was late, and I was sweaty.

"Sorry, we don't open 'til tomorrow." I barely looked up from my work.

"You may open tomorrow, but you won't have any customers with this boring old stuff. You need my stamp on the place."

My fingers paused on the keyboard and I looked up. "I'm sorry, can I help you? If you're looking for a job, I'm not hiring yet. And this stuff isn't boring, it's tasteful."

"What's that you're working on?" He sat next to me and peered at the screen. The smell of his cologne was thick as cake batter.

"A press release, if you must know. Like I said, we open tomorrow."

"Who's the 'we' if it's just you?"

"It's a figure of speech." I closed my laptop and stood. I knew enough of New Orleans by then to know he didn't necessarily mean trouble, but I was still a little wary of this colorful stranger in my shop. The place was full of small items I'd picked up here and there, and he could grab something and run off with it in a heartbeat if he wanted.

"I'm Allyn." He extended his hand. "With a y."

"Sara. No h. And the shop isn't officially open yet, so if you could come back tomorrow . . ." I stood by the front door and gestured through it with my free arm.

"You need me. I can make this place sing."

"It looks pretty good already, if you ask me." I glanced through the front room I'd so carefully decorated.

"It needs something. More Southern Gothic flair. I'm your man for the job. Or I can be your woman for the job, whichever you prefer."

I raised an eyebrow.

"Just kidding," he said. "But seriously, I'm an out-of-work hairdresser waiting for Hollywood to call, and I have time on my hands." He paused and looked down at his feet. "People used to live in this house, you know. A lot of people. I was one of them, and I know every nook and cranny of the house and the neighborhood. I can help you."

I started to speak but he continued, confident again and

grinning. "And anyway, seeing as you're the one writing press releases and shopping for inventory, you're going to need some help. Who's going to make coffee runs? Get the air conditioner fixed? Open up in the morning when you have a late night?" he said with a smirk.

"First off, I've already called the repairman. He's just late. And second, I don't have many late nights, except now that I'm trying to get this place up and running. I would have opened quicker, but it's been a chore getting people to show up on time and do the work. Like this AC." I fanned my gauzy top away from my body in an effort to stir up a breeze. It was June, and the heat was already intense.

"You must be a transplant. We natives know how to get things done. Just give me a shot."

For the first time I took him in from top to bottom. Movie star sunglasses perched on his head. Acid-green hair with blond roots showing. Red tank top tucked into black skinny jeans. Black Chuck Taylors.

"You look like a Christmas nightmare," I said.

"I can get the AC fixed in an hour."

I hired him on the spot, and it was the best decision I could have made. I discovered early on that he was being truthful when he said he'd lived in the house. A decade before, when he was young, scared, and desperate to figure out who he was, he'd run with a slew of other kids from the dirtier parts of the city. Without welcoming homes to return to, they'd lived in the empty house on Magazine Street for months. It became their refuge, and Allyn still felt welcome in the space—hence his attitude of ownership the first day he'd strutted into my shop. I never would have thought we'd still be together four years later. He may have been flamboyant, keeping odd hours and even odder company, but he was a true friend to me.

Backed into a corner, I did the only thing I knew to do. I picked up my phone from the nightstand and called him. I had to shout so he could hear me over the pounding house music.

"Just a minute," Allyn said. "Let me go outside."

"Where are you? That music is terrible."

"No, it's great. You should see the people here. It's Margaritaville meets Marilyn Manson."

I told him about the will, the house, and what Mags had done. He wasn't as shocked as I'd been.

"Who else would she have left it to? The old folks? You're her family. You obviously care about the place, or you'd have stuck a For Sale sign in the yard the minute you got there."

"I guess so. I just wasn't prepared to come here and start the biggest house-rehabbing project of my career. Especially not in Sweet Bay."

"It doesn't have to be that big, does it? Make a few tasteful changes and bring it up to date. Why the drama?"

"A few tasteful changes wouldn't even scratch the surface of what's necessary to turn this place around. Plus, it is Mags's home and she loved the place. I wouldn't feel right doing it halfway. She said it deserved to be beautiful again, and I have to honor that."

"Then there's your answer."

"But I don't live here," I said. "My life—my job—is in New Orleans. I can't stay here and direct a renovation. Dot, Bert, and the Greggs would all be under my feet, trying to micromanage everything. Plus, I miss you."

"Are you done? First, your life here in the city isn't going anywhere. Just because you stay there a little longer than you originally intended—"

"A little longer? This could take months. Lots of them."

"—that doesn't mean you can't pick right back up when you get back," he continued, undeterred by my outburst. "I can manage the shop and Rick can help when things get busy. Plus, it's not like you'll be across the country. Sweet Bay is, what, three hours away? You can come back for an afternoon or a whole day if necessary. It's not a long drive.

"Second, you always talk about how you set people up with beautiful houses and things, then you leave and never get to enjoy the beauty of what you created. The house is yours now. You won't have to hand the keys over and never come back, unless that's what you want to do. Regardless, you'll own the results and you won't have to bow to what anyone else wants. Sounds like a no-brainer to me."

"What am I going to do with a bed-and-breakfast in Sweet Bay even if it is beautiful again? If I keep it, I'll have to hire people to run it, and if I sell it, I'll have my head on a plate carried by Major Gregg." Even I could hear the petulance in my voice.

"I don't know who Major Gregg is, but Mags left the place to you, no one else. Remember, you called for my advice, so listen to it. You have to do this. This is your project, and I think you know it. Yes, it's happening somewhere other than here, but you're good at what you do. And anyway, you need to make peace with Sweet Bay. We'll all be here when you get done."

I was quiet, digesting, listening to the muffled bass and manic voices in the background. I gripped the phone in my hand.

"Third," he said, "I miss you too. If you do this, don't think I won't drive over to check things out. I think I need a little Sweet Bay in my life too."

I laughed. "This town wouldn't know what to do with you. You'd stop people cold."

"Darling, I'd be offended if I didn't."

After the call, I didn't feel total relief, but I did allow that tingle of excitement and anticipation to bubble back up to the surface. I wanted to pull out my computer and notebooks where I'd sketched and mapped out ideas, but my eyelids were heavy. I pulled the blue quilt up to my chin and surrendered.

10

SARA

APRIL

The funeral was a quiet affair, almost an afterthought—no real ceremony, no tearful eulogies, not even a funeral parlor. The five of us just met the funeral director at the cemetery. He shared a few words about the meaning of life and loved ones who had passed on, then pushed a discreet button and the coffin slowly descended into the ground. It was simple, just as Mags wanted it. I found out later that Mags gave Dot clear instructions for her last hurrah.

"You don't have to put me in a pine box, but you get my drift," she'd said. "And don't anyone go crying over me. We've all had enough years together to be happy we knew each other at all. Just skip the hoopla and take me straight to the grave."

Dot couldn't resist adding a couple of extra details. She laid an armload of cheery sunflowers on top of the casket and propped an eight-by-ten framed photo of a smiling Mags on an easel next to our chairs.

473

I'd never noticed the resemblance between us. In this old photo, it was unmistakable. I had the same dark, unruly curls, although I tamed mine with a flat iron and extra-hold spray. But I saw something else, something in the shape of her light-blue eyes or the slope of her nose. I saw me in there. Even more than I resembled either of my parents.

Mags was young in the photo, early twenties at most. Her curls tumbled out of a messy ponytail and one shirttail hung free. Her eyes crinkled into barely visible laugh lines. I recognized pieces of the Mags I had known, but I'd never seen her smile like that. She was holding her arm up, trying to get the camera away from who-ever was taking the photo, but that smile—no one had ever made me feel that way.

As the funeral director spoke of the glorious light (he must have missed his calling as a revival preacher), a small blue car approached a little ways off. A man climbed out of the car, his face shaded under a cap. He stood still and glanced over at us a few times. After a little while, he sat back down in the car and slowly pulled away.

When the service was over, I helped Dot and Glory gather the flowers while Bert and Major talked to the director. In the hurry to get everyone into their cars and back to the house, I didn't notice the man drive back up to the gravesite. As I pulled out of the ceme-tery, I saw him in my rearview mirror. He stood by Mags's grave as the cemetery workers carried off our chairs. He brushed his hands against the sides of his pants as if he was dusting something off, then reached over and touched her headstone.

Back at the house, the driveway was already full of cars. Word had spread quickly, and old friends of Mags, some neighbors, mostly former "guests," came to pay their respects. It was a good thing, because the house was stuffed full of food, like Bert predicted.

Mr. Eugene Norman, the glassblower who used to make all the neighbors nervous with his raging furnace in the yard, sent a towering bouquet of lilacs that Dot placed on the table in the entryway. Mr. Crocker, who owned a farm up Highway 22, dropped off a mason jar stuffed with gardenias. Tiny Bernadette Pierce hobbled up the front walk with the help of a gold-tipped cane. Bernadette, or Bernie, as everyone called her, checked in a few weeks after my parents' wreck and stayed a while, long enough for her husband to think she really had moved to Tahiti with the gardener. She moved slowly and painfully up the walkway. I took her arm, fearing she might topple over before she got to the dessert table. The grin on her face when she turned to see who I was proved me wrong.

"The cane is just a prop," she whispered. "I may be eighty-four years young, but I can move just fine. And this." She gestured to the gray bob on her head that wasn't moving in the breeze. "This is a wig. Luis and I may not have gone to Tahiti, but we did get out of Dodge. This is my first time east of the Mississippi since I moved out of The Hideaway and we went to California. My former husband, Harry, is still alive and living somewhere in the South, so I have to be careful." Her eyes were bright and wild. Crazy maybe, like a fox.

Other folks came and went throughout the day, many more than I'd expected. Those who remembered me talked about what a sweet girl I had been, as if I'd turned out to be someone wearing black lipstick and studs in my chin.

"That's not what we mean," Hattie Caldwell said when I joked about it to a small group of ladies gathered on the back porch. "It's just that after all you'd been through, you were still a polite, gracious child. I was a therapist in my former life, and believe me when I say you could have taken many roads after such tragic deaths in the family. From the looks of you, you've taken the right one."

Hattie hadn't been back to the house in at least twenty years, so she may not have known I no longer lived in Sweet Bay. What would she think of the road I'd taken if she knew it had paved my way clear out of Alabama?

That afternoon while most of the guests were out on the porch or sitting around the main parlor, I caught Dot alone in the kitchen. She struggled to open a Tupperware container of pimento cheese. A tray of crackers sat on the counter next to her.

"Dot?"

"Mmm?" She couldn't get the lip of the container to pop up, so I held my hand out and she slid it over to me. "Did you notice the car that pulled up toward the end of the funeral?" I pulled the lid off and handed the Tupperware back to her.

"At the gravesite?" Dot asked, her attention on me now that the pimento cheese was no longer stuck inside frustrating plastic. She dipped a cracker in and took a bite. "I didn't see anyone but us."

"An old man pulled up on the path and watched us for a few minutes. I didn't recognize him, but I think he was there for Mags."

Bert and Major walked through the kitchen door. Bert put his hand on Dot's back and Major pulled open the fridge.

"Who was where?" Major asked.

"Sara saw an old man at the funeral. Someone who had come to pay respects to Mags."

Dot and Bert exchanged a look, but Major shook his head.

"The obituary said the funeral was family only. That's why everyone else came here." He shut the fridge. "He must have been there for someone else."

I nodded but kept thinking about the man. It sure looked like he was there to pay respects to Mags, so who was he?

Later, after all the guests were gone, I came back downstairs for something to eat. Dot and Bert were on the back porch talking. As I moved around in the kitchen, their quiet voices drifted. I took my plate to the door of the porch and watched them.

They sat next to each other in wicker chairs, hands linked in the empty space between them. I smiled thinking of how these two found love at The Hideaway. The house provided the perfect backdrop to their second shot at love when they both checked in on the same day for solo vacations. Bert's wife had died a few years earlier, and Dot was getting over a messy divorce. When it came time for them to go back to their own lives, they decided to stay. They got married on the dock at sunset six weeks later.

I turned, not wanting to disturb their moment, but my foot bumped an overlooked plate from earlier in the day. Dot turned.

"Hi, dear, come join us. We were just telling old stories." She wiped her eyes with a tissue. "The funeral seems to have dragged up all kinds of memories."

"Are you sure? I can take this upstairs ..."

"Nonsense. Come sit. This will give us a chance to talk. The day got busier than I expected. I knew Mags had admirers all around, but I didn't know so many would show up. Many of them were older than she was, not that seventy-two is old."

"If it is, I'm ancient," Bert said.

Dot sniffed and swiped his shoulder. "You're not ancient, just well aged."

"Doesn't make it sound any better." He smiled.

I settled into an adjacent chair and took a bite of my ham sandwich.

"We were just talking about Bernie Pierce," Bert said. Dot still had tears in her eyes, so Bert gave her time to gather herself. He gently tipped his rocking chair back and forth. The wooden boards on the porch floor groaned and squeaked. "Do you remember her?"

I nodded. "She's a hard one to forget. The situation always seemed a little scandalous to me—Mags harboring someone who left her husband. Did Bernie actually run off with her gardener?"

"In a nutshell, yes," Bert said. "But it wasn't that simple. Bernie's husband Harry was a bully. He used to knock her around, and one day Mags happened to be outside their house when she heard a ruckus inside."

"Mags claimed she'd been out delivering tomatoes to some of the neighbors, but I think she was just sneaking one of her cigarettes," Dot said.

"She was in the right place at the right time," Bert continued. "Harry shoved Bernie and she fell through the open doorway and onto the front porch. Mags stomped up the front walk, stepped right up to Harry, and thumped him hard right here." Bert pointed to the space between his eyebrows. "Then she did it again for good measure. Harry was so taken aback, he just let her do it. Then she took Bernie's hand and led her down the steps into the front yard. She told Harry that Bernie wouldn't be coming back and if he ever so much as stepped a toe on her property, she'd chase him down with her oyster knife."

Dot laughed. "Mags never would have actually hurt him, but the important thing was Harry didn't know that. Everyone knew Mags could shuck oysters faster than the men down at the docks, so for all Harry knew, she'd shuck out his heart with her little pearl-handled oyster knife."

"Her gardener, Luis, packed up some of her belongings one day and brought them all over here for her," Bert said. "He handed her the bags and a pink rose he'd plucked from someone's yard on the way over. We saw a lot of him after that, and they finally left for California together. We didn't hear from her again. Not until she walked in here today."

"Sounds like Mags was a good friend," I said.

"Sure was," Dot said. "She was the best."

We were quiet a moment until Dot spoke again. "Have you thought any more about your plans for the house?"

"I've had a chance to look around. I have a few ideas. Nothing too drastic yet."

"I just hate to see it change too much. Mags liked it the way it is," Dot said.

"I'm sure she did in some ways, but she left me with specific instructions to fix it up. You have to admit, the house has seen better days. I'm good at my job, but it won't be worth it if I only use a hammer and a can of paint," I said as gently as I could and waited for Dot's reaction. She had become the mouthpiece for the four still living in the house. I wasn't looking for permission, but if I had her blessing, I knew the others would fall in line.

She took a deep breath and looked at Bert. He raised his eyebrows and held his hands up in surrender. "It's your call, honey."

"We all know I don't have a real say in this," Dot said. "The house is yours now to do what you like. Me? I'm partial to the old place being a little rumpled—just like Mags was—but I understand most people wouldn't agree. You do what you need to do to spiff it up, whatever that means. If you think you might sell it when you're done, just try to give us as much warning as you can. I know you have a life to get back to in New Orleans, but remember we have a life here in this place."

"You took your first steps out here on this porch, did you know that?" Bert asked.

I shook my head.

"That's right," Dot said. "Jenny brought you over here one afternoon before the evening rush at the diner. You'd been on the verge of taking off for a few weeks. She wasn't gone ten minutes before you put one foot in front of the other and toddled clear across the porch. I still remember the look on your little face when you realized what you'd done."

"I've never heard that story," I said.

"An old house can hold on to its memories for only so long," Bert said. "We may hold you hostage at night and spoon-feed you old stories."

"Bert," Dot said firmly. "She does not want to sit around here with a bunch of old folks all night." Dot turned to me. "Mags did ask you to stay at the house while you're in Sweet Bay. Is that your plan?"

"Sure beats the Value Inn on Highway 6," Bert said.

I smiled. "I think I will stay here. Judging by how much work there is to do, it'll be easier if I'm here to at least make sure things start off right. If that's okay with all of you," I said, not wanting to sound, well, like I owned the place.

Dot smiled. "I was hoping you'd stay." She looked at Bert. "Not so we can smother you in old stories, but so you can get a real sense of the life here. This was your home too. It still is. We all need a place to escape real life sometimes."

My life felt fine to me—no need to escape, thank you—but maybe there was something to what Allyn said about making peace.

11

MAGS

MARCH 1960

Just before I left for one of my trips to Grimmerson's Grocery for weekly supplies, the doorbell rang. I left my list in the kitchen and walked to the front door. Mrs. DeBerry came out of the living room just as I arrived at the door, and I stood by as she opened it.

A man in a dark suit and sunglasses stood on the porch holding a briefcase. "Are either of you"—he looked down at the piece of paper in his hand—"Mrs. Henry DeBerry?"

I looked at Mrs. DeBerry.

"I am," she said, turning to me. "Could you put the kettle on the stove for me, dear? I'd love a cup of tea."

"Of course." I started down the hall, though curiosity paused my feet by the staircase where I could still hear them talk.

"I've already asked you people to stop coming to the house. The money is coming if you can give me just a little more time."

"Mrs. DeBerry, this is your second notice. You won't get a

482

third. I understand you have several people living under your roof. I'm sure they wouldn't appreciate—"

"Can you step out on the porch, please?" she asked a little too brightly. "Let's just talk out here, why don't we?" She pulled the door behind her, closing me out of the conversation.

Another man like this one had come to the house the week before, but I hadn't thought much about him. I'd asked Mrs. DeBerry later if we were going to have a new guest at the house, and she laughed. "Oh no, he won't be staying here."

I opened the envelope of cash I was about to take to the grocery store, then ran back to the door. I flung it open, only to find the man climbing into his car and Mrs. DeBerry pressing her hands to her flushed cheeks.

I held the envelope out to her. "We can do without a trip to the store this week. We have leftovers, and Starla and I can rework the meals around what we still have in the pantry. You can use this."

"Don't be silly. Everything is fine. I told Mr. Curtis he must have written the wrong name down. Simple as that. You go on to the grocery and be sure to pick up a box of tea bags for me."

Mrs. DeBerry ambled down the hall to her bedroom and closed the door behind her. I went on to the grocery and tried to put the thought of Mr. Curtis out of my head.

When I wasn't helping Starla in the kitchen or cleaning up after the artists, I sat in William's workshop while he worked. His hands carved rough planks of pine and oak into smooth, practical pieces.

Kitchen tables. Pie safes. Armoires. Buffet tables. Things Mother would display proudly at the front of the house. I told him so.

He nodded as he pushed a piece of sandpaper down the length of a table leg. Up and down. Slow and steady. "Your life at home sounds a lot different from mine."

"What do you mean?" I asked, not as innocent as I sounded.

"I make the furniture people like your mother show off at parties, but I don't actually go to the parties."

"You're not missing much."

He laughed, just a puff of air from his nose. "What are you doing here?"

"You know why I'm here. I've already told you."

He put the sandpaper down and slapped his hands against his pants to rid them of dust. He marched over to me, grasped me firmly by the shoulders, and lowered his head so we were at equal height. "Tell me why you're *still* here."

"I-I've stayed because of you. Because everything feels different with you. I'm different with you." I pushed his hands off my shoulders. "Why are you asking me this? You were the one who said your life began when you saw me at the front door. Have you changed your mind?"

I paced to the other side of the room to escape the uncomfortable intensity of his gaze, but then his hands were on my shoulders again. He turned me around to face him, his face close to mine. I smelled wood dust, turpentine, and something else distinctly William.

"I'm not going to change my mind. I just want to make sure you know what you're doing. You're giving up a lot to be with me. I'll never be able to give you what your daddy has or what your husband could. Do you understand that?"

I gave up my old life the minute I packed my bags and shoved them in the closet of the house I shared with Robert. I did it again when I closed the car door, peering at Daddy from inside the quiet cocoon. And again when I pulled away from the house without a last look over my shoulder. I knew what I was doing, and now that William was part of my new life, it all made perfect sense.

I nodded. "I understand."

He pulled me tightly to his chest, kissing my cheeks, my eyelids, my forehead. "Okay. We're in it. Let's show everyone how far we can go."

Later that day, I bumped into Mrs. DeBerry as she stood bent at the waist, rummaging around in the closet by the front door.

"Can I help you with anything?" I took her arm and helped her straighten up. Her face was red and beads of sweat had formed on her upper lip.

"I'm fine. Just cleaning out a little. I haven't looked in this closet in ages." Around her sat beautiful pieces of clothing I'd never seen her wear. Impractical things, like Chinese satin-soled shoes that would fill with water the first time they touched the dew-saturated grass and a chocolate-brown floor-length mink coat.

I ran my hands up and down the coat. Mother had a mink she only wore during Mardi Gras season. It could be sixty-five degrees on Fat Tuesday and she'd still pull it out. "Luxury is luxury, Margaret, regardless of something as temperamental as the weather," she'd say.

"You can have that old thing," Mrs. DeBerry said when she

saw me touching the mink. "Henry brought it back from a trip to Russia ages ago. It's too warm to wear it in Alabama, but maybe you'll make a trip up north someday. I'm too old to be making trips anymore."

She stopped rummaging and glanced around the house, her gaze pausing on a pair of artists painting at easels in front of the large living room windows. She shook her head. "Henry would turn in his grave if he could see what our B and B has turned out to be."

"Maybe not. It still has a charm."

"It must. After all, you're still here. It's been a couple of months now. How long do you plan to stay, dear?" She tossed items into a box at her feet, but her gaze remained on me.

I picked up the red satin shoes from the floor. The fabric was worn away near the soles, but the embroidery on top was still perfect. I tossed them in her box. "I don't know. Can I let you know a little later?"

She exhaled. "Stay as long as you want. That's what everyone around here seems to do anyway, and it'll probably continue long after I'm gone."

"Are you going somewhere?"

She glanced around the room again. "I'm getting old. I'm probably not the best proprietor for a place full of young folks such as yourself, but here I am. Next to losing Henry, giving up this house would be the hardest thing I could ever do."

She hoisted her box and took a deep breath. She'd avoided my question, but her face was still flushed and damp, and I worried for her.

"Are you sure I can't help you with that? I could take it to your room for you."

"No, no, I'm fine." She turned toward the hallway but paused. "Mrs. Parker, you've been good for this house. You straighten up, clean what needs to be cleaned, help organize meals. You even shooed the artists out of the living room and outside into the fresh air. And you've done it all without being asked. You're taking care of this old place, and I want you to know I appreciate it."

The emotion on her face surprised me. As she eased her way down the hall toward her room in the back, her box tight in both hands, she called over her shoulder, "Are you ever going to tell me your real name?"

I smiled. She'd probably seen through me that first night, but she chose to let me have my time of anonymity, even if I was only anonymous to her.

"It's Maggie. Maggie Van Buren," I said just before she turned into her room.

"Good night, Maggie."

12

◦✦◦

SARA

APRIL

I spent most of the next morning calling contractors I was familiar with in New Orleans. It turned out not many were willing
or able to work two states away. I found a couple with satellite
offices in Alabama who said they'd look into it, but it didn't sound
hopeful. Each one I talked to asked why I wasn't using a local
contractor, but when I asked if they had any referrals for contractors in the area, they all asked some variation of "Now, where's
Sweet Bay again?"

With reluctance I did what I never do when looking for help on
a project. I opened the Yellow Pages. I'd thought the days of thumbing through the phone book looking for a particular business were
long gone—who didn't just type it into Google? But after a lot of
thumb-typing, it was clear Google's long arms hadn't reached
Sweet Bay.

I flipped to the beginning and called the first entry listed under A: A1 Contractors. Clever. Twenty seconds on the phone with Earl Weathers told me all I needed to know about whether local people still talked about The Hideaway.

"You know that place used to scare all the kids around here," he said when I told him I was renovating the house. "Or maybe it was the lady inside who scared us. My buddies and I used to dare each other to go to the front door and ring the doorbell, then run away. We were just kids. Big imaginations." He laughed. "I wondered what would happen to the house now that the old lady's croaked. So they hired you to take care of it? What'd you say your name was, sweetheart?"

"I didn't," I said through my clenched jaw. "It's Sara Jenkins."

"Jenkins," he said, pondering. "Wait, you're not . . . ?"

"That's the one. Mrs. Van Buren was my grandmother."

"Oh, I . . . you—Lord'a mercy," he sputtered. "I guess I spoke too soon."

"Nope, just soon enough." I hung up, cutting off his apologies.

The next two calls were similar. Their eagerness to get inside the house and see what it was like was unprofessional at best, offensive at worst. I thanked them all for their time—although I wished I hadn't given them a reason to think of Mags again—and ignored their protests as I hung up.

I finally found one that looked promising. Coastal Contractors. The logo had a silhouette of a heron standing in front of a sun setting over water. At least they had a logo. And a brick and mortar office. The other ones I called appeared to be working out of their homes. Nothing wrong with that, but I imagined Earl sitting on his back porch, picking his fingernails with a pocketknife, waiting for work to come calling. I couldn't stomach being the reason he folded the knife away, hitched up his pants, and climbed into his work truck.

No one answered at Coastal. Instead, I was greeted with a message on an actual answering machine. The mechanical click at the beginning of the message told me it wasn't a typical voice-mail recording. The message told me if no one answered, they were likely out on a job or working out back. *"Leave a message or feel free to stop by for a chat."* The voice was friendly, giving me hope that maybe this wouldn't turn out to be just another dead end.

When lunchtime rolled around, I made a plate of chicken salad and coffee cake left over from the mountain of funeral food and headed out to the dock. Dot and Bert were in town for groceries, and the house was calm, a stark contrast to the previous day's whirl of activity. I sensed that this quiet peacefulness was how the house had been for much of the time since I'd left. From what Major said, they'd all settled into a tranquil existence here. I remembered the old magazine articles that featured the house as one of the top vacation destinations in the Southeast.

Taking in the house from the long grassy hill that sloped down to the water, I had trouble imagining The Hideaway as anything but a tired, sprawling old home. The house had been a much livelier place when I was a child, but nothing close to the resort featured in the magazines. Fireworks, boat tours, badminton on the lawn—it was more than hard to imagine. It was impossible.

I settled in a chair out on the dock and took my first bite when I heard a voice behind me.

"Well, if it isn't Sara Jenkins, back from the dead."

Clark Arrington. Perfect.

"That's probably not the most appropriate thing to say, considering my grandmother just died," I said in place of a greeting. Clark had always been just socially awkward enough to offend most people, even if he wasn't trying.

"I sure was sorry to hear about Mrs. Van Buren. How are you holding up?"

"I'm fine. I see you still live across the street."

"Yeah. I'm in the apartment above my parents' garage, but I'm moving out soon." I wondered how long he'd been telling people he'd soon be moving out of his parents' home. "You here for long or just for the funeral?"

"Looks like I'll be here for a little bit. I'll be doing some work on the house."

"I see." He walked to the edge of the dock and peered into the water below. "Tide's coming in." He straightened up and stared at me with an expression I couldn't decipher. "And the owner's okay with you doing the work?"

"The owner? That'd be me now. Mags left me the house in her will and asked me to fix the place up, so yes, I'd say the owner is fine with it." Why was I defending myself to him?

"I'd just be careful if I were you."

"What's that supposed to mean?"

"You haven't been here much lately. A lot has been going on."

I assumed he was messing with me, like he did when he used to taunt me in the yard on his bicycle. I once threw a Coke can at him as hard as I could because he had made fun of Mags. The can fell short, landing feebly in the water at his feet, adding embarrassment to my anger. I ran into the house, the sound of his laugher echoing in my head, and flung myself across my bed in tears. Part of me was mad at Mags for being so easy to make fun of, for having this grand old house but letting it be so shabby, for not caring about rules and the way things were supposed to be, but on the heels of that came guilt for being mad. Mags was my grandmother, kooky but loving.

This time, I didn't have a Coke can to throw at him, but I wouldn't have given him the satisfaction anyway. "Thanks for the heads-up, Clark. I have things to do, so if you'll excuse me." I picked up my plate and cup and headed toward the house.

"You remember Sammy Grosvenor?"

I stopped walking. Sammy was a well-known Baldwin County developer. He'd been sticking his nose into waterfront property owners' business for decades. He used to knock on Mags's door, reeking of body odor covered with strong cologne, mopping his forehead with a damp rag. Each time, he'd say he had been out walking around and admired the property. And each time, Mags told him to get lost.

"It's a lot of money, Mrs. Van Buren," he'd say. "You could turn in the keys and spend your golden years with your feet up and a drink in your hand."

"Do I look like someone who wants to snooze the rest of my life away, Mr. Grosvenor?" She'd spit his name out like it tasted bad. "This is my home, and I'm not selling it. If you were smart, you'd stop sniffing around here."

Sammy was the one thing on which Mags and many of the other townspeople agreed. No one liked the way he scoped out homes and businesses as if he imagined a theme park in their place. Dot always told Mags she should be careful with Sammy, but Mags was never too concerned. If she didn't let wind blowing through a broken glass pane in the kitchen bother her, she definitely wouldn't be bothered by a land developer who had so far been all talk.

Clark's name-dropping let me know Sammy was still on the prowl, still trying to get his hands on the property. I wasn't worried, though. Mags could be a bear when she wanted to, but I had more professional ways of making him get lost. Starting with a court order if necessary.

"Yeah, I ran into him a while back," Clark said. "He started babbling about this old house here. Something about his time finally coming. I don't know what he meant, but it smelled fishy to me. He was excited though. I'll tell you that much."

I kept walking toward the house. This was nothing more than Sammy attempting another dead-end scheme and Clark trying to get in the middle of it all. However, deep down, in some small, hidden part of me, something squeezed. Sammy could be ruthless if he wanted to be.

I walked up the porch steps and made sure the screen door slammed shut behind me.

13

SARA

APRIL

The office of Coastal Contractors couldn't have looked more opposite than what I had imagined. The mental image of Earl sitting on the porch in his dirty overalls quickly dissipated as I turned off County Road 1 at the sign bearing the now-familiar heron and setting sun. The cottage overlooking the water was quaint, its cedar-shake siding weathered to a relaxed gray—the kind of gray that sent people back for paint chips again and again, trying to get the same shade on their walls.

I collided with a mess of black fur and a wet tongue as soon as I walked through the open door.

"Popcorn, down!" a male voice said. "Sorry, she just gets excited. It's been a quiet day, so you're the lucky recipient of her pent-up attention. Here, try this." A towel, dry and mostly clean, appeared in my hand as I held my now-damp dress away from my legs. I wiped at my arms and right cheek, trying without success to remove all traces of the sticky slobber. I had never been much of a dog person. Too much wet, not enough manners.

Giving up the futile attempt, I looked up to see a man pushing the dog out the back door. "Crawford, she's headed your way," he yelled before closing the door on Popcorn's protests.

"Sorry about the commotion." He wiped his hands on his shorts. The room smelled strangely like raw fish. "I'm Charlie Mack. How can I help you? Or do you need directions somewhere?" His gaze drifted down to my dress and sandals, a few notches too dressy for an afternoon on the bay and the affections of an exuberant Labrador.

"Actually, I do need some help. I'm an interior designer in New Orleans, but I'm in Sweet Bay working on an old bed-and-breakfast."

"Is it a tear-down?"

"No. It's an old house and not in the best shape, but its bones are good. It's probably best to consider everything suspect—wiring, gas lines, the whole bit. It'll need a thorough inspection first. From there, I'm thinking about taking down a couple interior walls, updating the kitchen and baths, and a whole lot of painting."

He nodded and scratched out a few notes on a piece of paper he'd pulled out of his shirt pocket. When he finished, he sat back in his desk chair, his heft leaning the chair back almost horizontal. He was two-fifty easy, maybe more. Older than me, but not by much. Did the plural on *Contractors* mean Popcorn and him?

"I can tell you now, we're the right people for the job. We do everything from new construction of massive bay houses to little old ladies who want their bathrooms to look like the one they saw in last month's *Southern Living*. How did you find us, anyway?"

"Yellow Pages. I started with A."

He laughed. "So you called A1 first, got Earl on the phone, and quickly went on to the Bs, then found us. That's how it works sometimes. However clients come in, we'll take 'em."

"So you're a sort of one-man, one-dog operation?"

He laughed again. "No, it's my buddy Crawford Hayes and me. Popcorn's just around for laughs. She's the company dog. Crawford's outside, banging around on something, as he usually is when he's not on a job site."

"Banging around? Should I be concerned?" I peered around Charlie to look out the back window of the office.

"Crawford builds things, or attempts to. He's got a work space out back. He calls it his shop, though it's not much more than a messy hardware store. Right now, he's building me a boathouse. I just bought a twenty-five-foot Regulator," he said proudly. He stood and gestured for me to follow him to the back of the house. "Crawford's the best contractor in Baldwin County, so don't think you're getting a country carpenter."

We walked out onto a deck overlooking a tidy lawn. The scrubby grass mingled with sand at the edge, and calm water lapped the shoreline. He pointed to a shed off to the side.

"I'm lucky he let me join in this operation. It was one-man and one-dog, like you said, before I came on. Now we can take on more work together, although Crawford's probably the one for what you need. Point him to some old, falling-down house and he's a happy guy. I don't have the heart the historic places require, but he's a different story."

Popcorn nosed her way out of the shop just before the door opened wider and Crawford walked out. It was the second time Coastal Contractors had surprised me. I'd expected another big guy like Charlie—well past college years, but still retaining the good-natured frat boy look of too much beer and not enough exercise.

Instead, Crawford was slim, but not skinny, with thick brown hair sticking up in front like he'd pushed it off his forehead with the back of a sweaty wrist. He'd rolled up the sleeves of his checked button-down against the late spring warmth. His khakis had a scuff of dirt at the bottom hem and a small hole near one pocket. A pencil stuck out of his hair, tucked behind one ear. He was a far cry from Mitch's sleek suits and power ties. He looked more like a mad scientist—albeit a cute one—than a contractor.

"Crawford, this is . . . I'm sorry. I didn't even get your name," Charlie said.

"I'm Sara Jenkins." I held out my hand and Crawford shook it firmly. Small calluses at the base of his fingers pressed into my hand. "I tried calling a few times before I drove over, but I kept getting the machine."

"Sorry about that," Crawford said. "I've been out here all day trying to finish up the framing on this boathouse, and Charlie—well, it looks like he's been out fishing."

Charlie grinned, unapologetic. If this was how they spent their days, how did these guys make enough money to afford the nice office and shiny trucks parked out front? As if reading my mind, Crawford answered my question.

"This isn't a typical week for us. I just finished up two big jobs over in Point Clear on the boardwalk, and Charlie is wrapping up a house in Spanish Fort and starting another one next week. We decided to take a few days before jumping back in."

We went back into the tidy office and sat at the table in the middle. I explained again, this time in more detail, what I envisioned for the house.

"I thought we were dealing with just a big house," Crawford said when I finished. "I didn't realize it's a bed-and-breakfast. What'd you say the name is?"

"I didn't. It's The Hideaway. In Sweet Bay."

I waited, but Charlie just kept scratching Popcorn's ear and Crawford wrote the name down on his notepad and sat back in his chair. I couldn't believe I'd found the only two people in Baldwin County who'd never heard of the place.

Then Crawford smiled. "I've always wanted to see inside that house."

Here it comes.

"I saw it a year or so ago by accident. Turned down the wrong driveway looking for another job site. The house was obviously in disrepair, but I could tell it had been beautiful once. I'd seen the sign before but didn't know anything else about it. Then again, I'm not a local. How'd you get the job? Didn't you say you're from New Orleans?"

"I live in New Orleans now, but I'm actually from Sweet Bay. Born and raised."

"No way," Charlie said. "Don't see too many girls around here who look so classy. No offense," he said quickly. "But you kind of stick out like legs on a fish."

I smoothed my still-damp dress over my knees and ran my hand down my ponytail, making sure nothing was out of place.

Crawford's gaze on Charlie was a laser beam, then he shook his head and smiled. "Please excuse my partner. Sometimes he doesn't know when to stop. And he's used to the taste of foot in his mouth."

I smiled, grateful for his easy removal of awkwardness.

"The owner hired you to redo the place?" he asked.

He really doesn't know anything.

I took a deep breath. "It was my grandmother's house, and she just passed away. In her will, she gave me the house and asked me to renovate it. It used to be very different from what it is now. It was written up in magazines and everything. But over the years, I guess the clientele changed. People who checked in usually ended up living there. I know it sounds strange," I said, seeing his eyebrows rise. "I have no idea how she ever had the money to keep the place going."

"Sounds like a beast of a project." Charlie grinned.

"I don't know about that, but I do need professionals to come in and tell me just how bad it is. The place has always been a little wild. Four of my grandmother's friends still live there, and I'm staying there for the time being, so the house will be occupied during renovations. We'll need to work on it in stages, I suppose, rather than ripping it all up at once."

"You're staying in town during the work?" Crawford asked. "I would have expected you to set the plans in motion, then hightail it back home."

I uncrossed then recrossed my legs, uncomfortable with his laser beam directed at me. I smoothed my hair down again.

"I considered it, but there's so much work to do. Rather than spend the next several weeks on the phone checking on things here, I'm treating it like a normal job. I'll see it through to the end, then hightail it back."

Crawford held my gaze for a moment, then looked at Charlie, who nodded.

"We'd love to take on the job," Crawford said. "I'm biased, but I think we're the best ones by far to do the work. As Charlie probably told you, old houses are my thing. I'd love to get in there and peel back the layers on this one. If you'll have us, of course."

Charlie leaned back in his chair, his arms crossed over his considerable girth. Crawford sat closer to the table, fingers twirling a pencil, eyes on me. Popcorn whined at the door, waiting to be let out.

"Sure. Of course. You're hired."

"Okay then," Crawford said, a smile lifting a corner of his mouth. "When can I see it?"

That evening, in the purple dusk after sunset, I strolled out into the backyard. An old streetlight attached to a wooden beam marked the path to Mags's vegetable garden. It wasn't what it used to be—rows of tilled earth straight as an arrow, little markers noting what each row contained, tall wooden spikes to stake the tomato plants—but it was clear Mags had been doing her best to keep the garden up. The rows weren't as obvious and some of the markers were missing, but from what remained, it looked like there'd be a bounty of snap beans, purple-hull peas, and cucumbers later in the summer.

The garden sat adjacent to the house and overlooked the bay. Mags used to say that, sitting in the garden, she could see everything that was important to her—the house, her plants peeking their heads through the soil, the water making its unhurried way to the Gulf. She could listen to the voices of her friends and the laughter of seagulls.

Memories surfaced as I settled down on the worn bench. I used to run barefoot up and down the deliberate rows of fertile soil, flapping my arms to scare away the crows. I'd squat over delicate strawberry vines, the aroma of dirt and life permeating the air, and carefully choose the plump, red berries that Bert would later use in his not-yet-famous strawberry pie. Even as a teenager, I welcomed the chore, eating at least as many berries as would end up in my basket. Sitting there in the falling dark, I could imagine the furry skin on my tongue, the tiny seeds popping, a burst of summer sweetness in each bite.

I ran my hand over the surface of the bench next to me. It was a gnarled, weather-beaten thing, but beautiful in its own way. No frills, just cedar boards fastened with wooden nails and dovetail joints. It still bore remnants of an old coat of green paint.

As my fingers rounded the edge, they found an indentation in the wood on the underside of the bench. I took it for another mark from a carpenter bee, but as I rubbed it, a shape began to emerge. I got down on my knees and peered underneath. As I tipped the bench back, the glow from the light fell across the wood and revealed the engraving of an old skeleton key.

I recognized that key.

Mags's headstone had been simple—it bore her name and the dates of her birth and death. It wasn't until after the graveside service that I noticed the carving at the very bottom. It was a small key, just like this one, along with the words, "You hold the key to my heart."

I never knew my grandfather, though I'd always referred to him as Granddaddy. My mom was only a few years old when he died, so her memories of him were few. Anytime I asked Mags about him, she just repeated that it was a tragic, too-early heart attack but wouldn't offer any more information. She was single my whole life. No other romantic interests that I knew of. It seemed strange that she would have made such a public pronouncement of love for her long-gone husband when I'd never once heard her talk about him, other than the few times I'd asked. The sentiment seemed too romantic for my simple, often stoic grandmother.

But she chose to add a last whisper of love on her headstone. Could it have been for someone other than Granddaddy?

14

MAGS

APRIL 1960

Mrs. DeBerry didn't show up for her usual morning toast and pot of tea out in the yard. A few of us stood outside her bedroom door. I knocked but got no response.

"Maybe she died in her sleep," Starla whispered. "What? It happens," she said when we shushed her. "She was old. Maybe her ticker gave out."

I knocked again. "Y'all were up late last night. Did any of you notice anything? Maybe she fell."

"No, nothing," Gary said.

"You wouldn't have noticed a garbage truck if it had rumbled through the living room," Starla said, laughing.

"I can't help it if—"

I cut off their banter by pushing open the door. Inside, Mrs. DeBerry's small room was neat and clean. And empty. The furniture remained, but every personal item was gone. The dresser top was bare, and pale squares stood out on the walls where frames had hung for decades.

I backed out of the room and bumped into Daisy.

"Oh, Maggie, I was just looking for you. This was on the kitchen counter this morning." Daisy handed me a creamy envelope—heavy paper, fine stationery—with my name printed on it. "That's Mrs. DeBerry's handwriting," she said.

As Starla, Daisy, and the others talked over each other, trying to decide what exactly had happened, I retreated up to my room. On the way, I tore open the envelope and pulled out the card inside.

Maggie,

It just got to be too much. I hope you of all people will understand. I can tell you come from good people and you'll take care of the house as it deserves. The spare key is under the pansies on the back porch and six extra sets of sheets are in the closet in my bedroom. Call Ned Lemon if the pilot light goes out.

I sat on my bed and dropped the card on the quilt next to me. Mrs. DeBerry had said her good-bye to me the night she gave me the mink and I hadn't even realized it. She'd gone through the house, taking what was important to her, and left everything else for us to figure out.

"Who else would she have asked?" William said when I escaped to his workshop to give him the news. "No way would she trust the others around here who float in and out of the house all day and night."

"People don't just go leaving houses to strangers."

"She must have seen what I see in you. You're smart, hard-working, and determined. You do what needs to be done. Think of it this way—you want something different out of life, right?"

I nodded.

"This could turn out to be a very good thing for you. Maybe even for us."

I leaned into him and closed my eyes. "This is insane. What do I know about running a bed-and-breakfast?"

He wrapped his arms around my back. "We'll figure it out together. And anyway, what else do you have to do?"

I could have thrown out a dozen reasons why I wasn't a good candidate to take over the house, but as I stood there wrapped in William's arms, the idea began to take root in my mind. After all, with no husband to support me, no formal job training, and no money other than the check from Daddy, I didn't have much going for me.

But there was something else. This house had offered me a respite, a shelter from the storms in my life. And it had given me William. If taking over the house would allow us to stay safe and undisturbed in The Hideaway's cocoon, then that's what I would do.

That night around the dinner table, William and I told everyone about Mrs. DeBerry's departure and the note she left behind. A stunned silence met us, then everyone began to talk at once. A few were angry and some were distraught, thinking they'd lose what had essentially become the ideal artists' retreat. But most were satisfied and gave me their blessing, just as William had predicted.

"It's okay with me if you run the place," Starla said. "You've turned out to be all right. At least you're not wearing that pillbox hat anymore." She grinned at me and I returned the smile.

"I don't exactly have experience running a business."

"You'll be fine," Starla said. "How hard can it be?"

As the conversation around the table grew lively, I saw what The Hideaway could be under my care. Mrs. DeBerry likely hoped I'd be the one to turn it back into the pillar of Southern hospitality it used to be. True, it would be a place for hospitality, but not the kind she had in mind. No ladies in hats and gloves and no dashing men—not unless they bore wood dust on their legs or carried a paintbrush in their hands.

William carved a new sign for the house. He worked hard on it, making sure each letter was smooth and perfect.

"This could be your ticket to fame and fortune," he said once we pulled off the side of the road next to the old, faded sign. "People will come from all over just to see your Hideaway. You just wait."

I helped him heft the enormous wooden sign out of the back of his truck.

"I'm proud of you," he continued. "You can make something of yourself here—something that's just you."

I stayed silent as we leaned the new sign up against the post of the old one. His insinuation that I hadn't been my own person before didn't sit well. But hadn't I said it myself? Wasn't it true? I'd been fit into a mold before, and I was only now experiencing life with full breaths of air and space to move.

We stood back against the truck to admire the sign. It was perfect. It would guide just the right kind of traveler to The Hideaway. Not those looking for a resort or a game of badminton on the lawn, but those folks who needed a place to stay. A place to call home.

15

MAGS

APRIL 1960

The warmer spring temperatures allowed us to finally stow our blankets and heavy soup pots. When I wasn't working in the house or helping William with odd jobs in his wood shop, we made light meals of sandwiches or grilled fish, listened to music, and spent long afternoon hours in the cove, our pale limbs stretched out on a towel to soak up the spring sun.

One evening, I found a can of bright blue-green paint on a shelf in his workshop. On a whim I grabbed the can, a paintbrush, and a box of sandpapers and carried it all to the front porch. Using a firm hand and long strokes I'd learned from watching William, I sanded the peeling paint off the shutters and door, then covered them with fresh paint. Later, I blew my damp hair out of my eyes and stepped back into the driveway to examine my work.

A woman walking around the side of the house paused and backed up a few steps. She cocked her head and stared at the porch, then turned to me. "Did you do that?"

I nodded.

"Hmm. Not bad."

Over the span of a few weeks, William carved a house for me—intricately detailed, but small enough to fit in the palm of my hand. He presented it to me at the cove on a blessedly warm Saturday. He pulled me away from dinner preparations that afternoon, saying he needed to show me something. I'd been chopping peppers and onions for pasta. I wiped my hands on my apron and followed him, thinking we were headed to his workshop. Instead, he led me to his truck and opened the passenger door.

"I can't leave right now—the pasta . . ."

"Yes, you can. Starla can take care of it. This is important."

I shook my head, frustrated with his spontaneity, but good Lord, he was handsome and so earnest. I abandoned the dinner and climbed into his rusty old truck.

At the cove he took my hand and led me to the water's edge. "I'm going to build a house in this cove one day. Just for us." He held the delicate carving out to me. "Hold on to this for now, and our real house will come."

"Is this your way of proposing to me?" I turned the house over in my hands, trying to cover my smile with a frown.

"No, when I propose, you'll know. This is just my way of saying, hang on, there's more to me than what you see. I can give you more than sawdust-covered hands and an old truck that won't even play the radio for you. I can't build it right now—it might not even be soon—but one day, I will."

"Right now, you're enough for me. Just you."

His eyes searched me, as if trying to decipher something written on my face. Whatever he saw must have satisfied him, because he smiled and retrieved a camera from the bag he'd brought with him. I held my hand up, but he snapped a picture anyway.

"What was that?" I asked as he placed the camera back in his bag.

"Just want to remember this day. Come on," he said and began to remove his pants.

"What are you doing?" I laughed and turned away.

"What are *you* doing? I'm going swimming."

William built other things for me—a sideboard buffet for the dining room, several small occasional tables, and a corner armoire with glass doors to hold dishes. On each of these pieces, just out of sight so no one noticed but me, he carved an old skeleton key. It became his trademark, and he carved it into each piece he made, even the ones he sold to other people.

My favorite piece was a simple cedar bench with practical, sturdy legs and a coat of moss-green paint. I'd started a vegetable garden in a sunny patch of grass next to the house, so he placed the bench there where I could keep an eye on things as they grew. We often went out to the garden together after dinner and sat on the bench while the sun went down, listening to the late-day sounds around the house. I imagined us sitting on that bench at the end of the day for the rest of our lives, listening, watching, loving.

As life with William was smooth and easy, the situation at the house was deteriorating. I didn't know just how poor The Hideaway's finances were until I spent some time in Mrs. DeBerry's account book. It was a mess, but even I could see that she'd fallen behind on house payments the last several months. The bank had sent two letters, the second less friendly than the first. The men in suits must have come after Mrs. DeBerry ignored the letters. With only a couple hundred dollars left in the account at First Coastal Bank and not much coming in from the "guests," it wouldn't be long before we had no money to keep the lights on, much less satisfy the bank.

I still had the check Daddy gave me the day I left home, but I hadn't even looked at it—it was buried in the pocket of my suitcase, along with my wedding ring and pearl necklace. In a way, that check was tied to Robert, and until now, I'd wanted nothing to do with it. I'd planned to save it until it was really needed. Now, it was. With the possibility of losing The Hideaway right in front of me, it made the most sense to use that money to pay down what Mrs. DeBerry owed to the bank. When I cashed the check at First Coastal and asked to deposit the money into the account to pay the house payments, the teller smiled.

"I don't know where you got the money, but I'm glad for it. I would have hated to see that lovely house shuttered. It seems like a nice place."

I smiled back. "It is."

I held a meeting one afternoon—a family gathering of those living in the house at the time. I stuck notes under everyone's doors, asking them to meet me in the parlor at 4:00 p.m. sharp. I wanted the note to express authority and the gravity of the situation.

"Thank you, everyone, for coming," I said, once they all settled down on chairs and couches. I willed my voice to be strong. "As you know, Mrs. DeBerry is gone and she has left The Hideaway with me. You all have an invitation to stay on as guests in the house as long as you like, but I need you to be able to pay somehow."

Most answered me with grumbles and whispers.

"We had an understanding," someone piped up. "With Mrs. D."

"It wasn't exactly an understanding from what she told me. She needed the money, but she didn't have the heart to ask. Now, I need your money, and I'm asking you to pay. Before you all get mad, I understand your professions as artists dictate that your financial . . . statuses may not be steady. I get that. But I need you to pay something. Get a part-time job, find new galleries to show your work, whatever. The bottom line is room and board can no longer be free. We'll all have to pull our weight here or we'll sink. As it is, we're behind on several bills, and sinking may not be far behind. This house is all we have right now. We need it to work."

I took a deep breath, expecting an onslaught of angry voices or overturned easels. Instead, there was silence.

"I just booked a show at Peterson's Gallery next month," said Daisy. "They asked for seven paintings—it'll be my biggest show yet."

"I've been hired to teach yoga at a studio in Fairhope twice a week," said Starla.

"I'm working on two armoires for Tom Grimmerson," came William's smooth voice. "He stopped by last week and asked to see what I was working on."

I scanned the room until my eyes found him leaning against the door frame in the entryway. He wore a red work shirt and scuffed boots. A thin coat of sawdust covered the front of his pants, and he smiled that familiar, slow smile I'd come to love. My body told me to cross the room in one stride and bury my face in his neck. I smiled my thanks.

"He has a friend who may be interested in some of my work too," he said, as if just to me, although everyone in the room watched us. "Good things are coming."

I kept my gaze on him as the room buzzed with talk of up-coming shows and income possibilities.

This could work. But my thought wasn't just about the house. It was William, me, a new life. All of it. Good things were coming, indeed.

Then Daddy showed up.

16

SARA

MAY

The next morning, after breakfast and a quick shower, I pulled the string on the bare bulb hanging in the center of the attic ceiling. It didn't illuminate much, but sunlight trickled in from the eaves on each end of the house. It was a bright day, and the light caught the dust motes my feet stirred up.

I'd decided to start at the top and go down. I had no idea what mementos and clutter previous guests had stored in the attic over the years, but I suspected it would be full to overflowing, much like the rest of the house.

Taking my first look around, I wasn't far off. One end of the attic housed furniture jumbled together—it was dark under the low ceiling, but I could make out the shape of a few small tables and a bench that used to sit in the dining room along one wall. The back of a small chair caught my eye. When I crept closer, I recognized the little red rocking chair I'd been so proud of as a child. I'd gone with Mags to a yard sale and begged her to buy me the broken-down chair—painted an ugly, faded yellow and missing one armrest. I knew I could make it look better.

We hauled it home, and I went after it with sandpaper, wood glue, and paint. I even fashioned a cushioned bottom out of some old batting I found in Glory's quilting box and a few squares of left-over fabric printed with smiling cats. I ran my hand over the dusty cotton and wood. My first restoration job. I couldn't believe Mags still had it.

Bags and boxes littered the rest of the attic, along with a few broken suitcases, an easy chair missing its bottom cushion, and an artificial Christmas tree.

I peered in a few of the boxes—musty clothes, discarded kitchen items, a few ratty teddy bears. Goodwill wouldn't even take this stuff. I opened the trash bag I'd brought with me and tossed in items no one would miss.

When the bag was bulging, I dragged it across the floor to the ladder. As I backed down the narrow steps, I noticed a box I hadn't seen earlier. It was pushed so far under the eaves, I could barely see it, but just enough light bounced off it that I could make out a key-hole at the top. I paused with my feet on the ladder, then climbed back up and pulled the box farther into the light.

Dull green metal, the box was unremarkable except for the keyhole. I remembered the envelope Mags left for me, the small key falling into my hand, weightless. I had yet to come across any-thing in the house with a hole small enough to fit it. I scrambled down the ladder to the blue room and retrieved it.

Back in the attic, I crouched down and slid the key into the hole and turned it. The lid popped open. Inside were several small photo books, a tiny house carved out of wood, yellowed newspaper clippings, and a few loose photographs. Wood chips, still smelling faintly of cedar, littered the bottom of the box.

I paused, hands on either side of the box. It was for me, right? Mags left me the key, and it fit into the lock perfectly. The lid had snapped open willingly. This had to be something she wanted me to see, to have.

I reached in and pulled out the black-and-white photo sitting on top. It was unmistakably Mags, but not the Mags I'd grown up with. Her tiny frame, light eyes, and sharp cheekbones were the same. And her hair—the humidity must have been high, because the edges were beginning to frizz. That was the Mags I knew, but the similarity ended there. This young, unfamiliar Mags wore a shimmery cocktail dress with a rounded neckline, narrow belted waist, and full skirt. A strand of pearls adorned her neck and she wore large pearls in her ears. Her hair, the part that hadn't frizzed, was rolled into gentle waves peeking out from under a white pill-box hat. Lacy white gloves covered her hands, and she carried a small purse with a silver clasp. On her face was just the barest hint of a prim smile, one that didn't reach her eyes.

The date stamped along the edge of the photo was 1957.

I'd been in Mags's closet before—nothing in there even came close to resembling this dress. A dainty and demure Mags? Not a chance. Who was this woman?

The carved house was the length of my hand. It had four rooms, a porch across the front, and a chimney on top. Whoever carved it had exceptional skill with a knife and an obvious love of such fine work. I turned it over in my hands, examining each side. The underside bore the rough engraving of a skeleton key.

The rest of the items in the box begged to be picked up and

examined, but laughter from downstairs floated up into the attic. My watch showed it was after nine, and Crawford had said he'd be here at nine on the dot. I placed the wooden house carefully back in with everything else. That's when I saw the blue velvet box. I pulled it out and gently pried the box open.

Inside, nestled in soft white cotton, lay an exquisite diamond ring. Beautiful not for its cut or size, but in its simplicity. It was breathtaking, perhaps especially because it shone in such opposition to my grandmother's disdain for anything having to do with money or luxury.

Underneath the box was an envelope, the seal on the back jagged as if it had been ripped open. I worked my fingers inside. Instead of finding something whole, my fingers brushed small pieces of paper. I hesitated, then turned the envelope over and poured it all out into my hand.

The bits of paper were torn, with rough edges and angry rips. The pen had faded but words written in a steady, sure hand were still legible. *Maggie, discomfort, your finger, cove.* Seen together, maybe they would have meant something, but in my quick scan of the words in the dim light, they meant nothing. The last bit of paper stopped me though.

Love, William

My grandfather's name had been Robert.

The words from Mags's headstone floated back to me: "*You hold the key to my heart.*"

William? Who are you?

My heart thumped and a bead of sweat trickled down the center of my chest. I carefully slid the bits back into the envelope, then pulled the ring from its home in the box and held it in my palm. I had no way of knowing how long it had been tucked away in the attic, but it sparkled as if it had been cleaned just yesterday.

After glancing at my watch again, I reluctantly put the ring back in its place. I closed the lid on the box and climbed down out of the attic. I'd come back as soon as I could to retrieve the treasures.

When I reached the first floor, I stopped to brush dust off my skirt and pull down my shirtsleeves I'd rolled up. I gathered my hair—still damp from the shower and starting to curl—into a neat bun, took a deep breath, then followed the voices into the dining room.

Crawford sat at the table with Bert, slices of chocolate pie in front of them despite the early hour. They were laughing like old friends. I hesitated at the doorway, not sure how to break up their camaraderie and still trying to slow my hammering heart. Bert noticed me first.

"There you are. Come on in and have some pie. My friend here says it's his favorite."

"It's true. Chocolate pie makes me lose all rational thought," Crawford said with a smile. He forked the last bite into his mouth and dropped his napkin on his plate. "Thanks for the treat. I'd love to talk some more, but I imagine Sara is ready for me to get to work."

"You two have fun." Bert's smile dimpled his cheeks. He picked up their plates and forks and moved toward the kitchen sink. "Let me know if you need anything while you're poking around."

"Looks like y'all hit it off," I said to Crawford once we were out of earshot.

"I can't turn down pie. And he was so eager for me to have some."

"It's the funeral food. He tries to force it on whoever happens to walk into the kitchen." My voice was casual, belying none of the butterflies fluttering in my stomach. Nervousness was rare for me in a professional situation, and I blamed it on my findings in the attic. Even still, something about being near Crawford made me feel flustered.

He laughed as he walked into the hallway, his hand barely brushing mine on his way past. "Why don't you show me around?"

We spent the next hour scrutinizing each room of the house. He made notes in a small notebook as I outlined my ideas. Since the funeral, I'd formed a clearer picture of the new Hideaway. Mags said I could do whatever I wanted with it, and after Allyn assured me everything at the shop would go on without a hitch, I'd begun to enjoy the feeling of freedom—both the time away from my hectic work schedule and the anticipation of diving into a new project.

The house had six rooms and a kitchen on the first floor, each room separated by walls to create choppy, awkward spaces. I wanted fewer walls, more open areas, and more light—both in color palette and in natural light flowing in from the tall windows on the south and east sides of the house.

Upstairs, the bedrooms were spacious but dated and plain— fine for Mags and her friends, but not for a more modern B and B. With only three bathrooms, guests—the few who ever came— had no privacy. I wanted the rooms to be luxurious, each with its own private bath and cozy dining space. A small table, a couple of chairs, a microwave, and a mini fridge would appeal to out-of-towners coming for a relaxing stay.

"How I'll get those out-of-towners to come, I have no idea," I said as we descended the stairs. "My first point of business is to get the house ready for them, then I'll figure out the rest. Or if I end up selling it, someone else can figure it out."

Crawford was quiet as we walked out onto the back porch. I opened the screen door to head into the yard, but he didn't follow. I turned and saw he was still standing in the doorway.

"You know, I see a lot of houses in the work I do," he said. "A lot of *old* houses. I'm not going to say I'm jaded, but I'm also not often blown away by what I see. This one is different though. For one thing, look at these floors." He gestured down the wide center hallway. "These are heart pine planks. They probably came from a single tree. Cut, planed, and sanded by hand. No one makes houses like this anymore."

Charlie was right. Old houses were Crawford's passion. I could see it in the way he stared down the hallway, the way he ran his hand up and down the time-smoothed door frame.

"Even if you do decide to sell, at least you're not tearing it down. A lot of people buy property down here on the water just for the sunset views. They tear down whatever house sits on the land, often before they've even walked through it, and then build an Italian villa in its place. I get it—modern conveniences and all that—but there's something to be said for the character a century of life can bring to a house."

"I'm not much for new." I sat on a wicker chair and tucked my legs under me.

"Right."

I knew what he was thinking. My trendy silk blouse, slim

skirt, and J. Crew ballet flats hardly screamed vintage charm. "I'm serious. Most of what I work with every day is old."

"I thought you were an interior designer. Don't most people want new things when they redecorate their houses?"

"Not always. I am a designer, but I also sell vintage furniture in a shop on Magazine Street. I go to estate sales, yard sales, whatever I can find, and buy gorgeous old things for pennies. Usually the owners don't even know what they're selling. They're just trying to clean out Grandma's house after she died."

Crawford glanced down and my words hit me. I rubbed my forehead with my fingertips. "Well, that wasn't very nice of me, was it?"

"I do a little of the same thing," he said, taking a seat in the chair next to me. "But I make the old furniture instead of looking for it. I pick up old wood—mostly scraps I find on job sites—and turn it into tables, chairs, that sort of thing. It's all pretty haphazard, to be honest, but my mom likes it." He smiled. "I've sold a few pieces here and there, and I'm working on a table for a client now. That is, when I can find time between work and this boathouse Charlie's talked me into building."

"I'd love to see your work sometime."

"I doubt it's anything you'd be interested in. To be honest, it looks like it was made in someone's woodshed in the backyard. And most of it was."

"Trust me, if it looks in any way like it's had a past life, I have customers who'll eat it up."

Glory stuck her head out the back door then. "Can I get y'all anything? Iced tea? More pie?"

Crawford stood. "No, ma'am. Thank you though."

"Don't leave on account of me, now," she said.

"It's time for me to head out anyway. I have a stop to make in Fairhope before I go back to the office."

I walked him back through the house to the front door. He said he'd be in contact soon about prices and materials.

"You really think you'll sell it once you finish all this work?" he asked at the top of the front porch steps.

I picked at a string on my skirt and shrugged. "I haven't decided. It seems like the smartest thing to do. I sure can't stay here and run a bed-and-breakfast."

"That's too bad. Once this house is fixed up, you'll be sad to let it go. Mark my words: it's going to be a showstopper."

Later that afternoon, I waited until the upstairs hall was quiet before I pulled down the creaky attic stairs and climbed up to retrieve the box. After Crawford left, I hadn't been able to focus on anything except the box and its mysterious contents. Part of me felt like I did when I scored a big find at a junk shop or estate sale—excited to dive in and see what I could make of something old—but another part was scared to wade any further into who Mags might have been.

I tiptoed back to my room with the box and closed the door behind me. I reached into the box, gently pulling out the envelope, and emptied it onto the blue quilt, turning each piece over so the words were visible. They were still disjointed, but I moved them around until most of the torn edges lined up and it seemed maybe they were in the right places. There were gaps, sections of the note that had been lost to the years, but what was left was an even bigger mystery.

> Dearest Maggie,
> ... leaving now to save ... the discomfort ...
> is the right choice ... know our time ... your finger ...
> be mine and I ... in the cove, just as we planned ...
>
> Love,
>
> William

I stared at the broken note for several long moments trying to sort out the emotion behind the words. Anger? Frustration? Passion? With the missing pieces, it was so hard to tell.

I pulled the box back toward me and laid everything else on the bed—the ring box, stack of newspaper clippings, tiny wooden house, and handful of photographs, the one of Mags on top. But there was something else I hadn't seen earlier. Stuck down along the edge of the box was a yellowed postcard. It had a picture of Mobile's Bellingrath Gardens on the front. The postscript on the back was dated June 1960. There was no return address, just one line written in small, neat cursive.

> Margaret,
> You made the right choice.
>
> Mother

I heard a faint knock at the door, and Dot poked her head in. I discreetly nudged a newspaper clipping over the ring box.

"We're headed out for dinner. You sure you don't want to come? We're going to our regular meat-and-three over in Daphne. Bert hates to miss the early bird specials, and the food is actually pretty good."

I smiled. "No thanks. I'll find something here."

She gestured toward the assortment on my bed. "What's all that?"

"Just some things I found up in the attic earlier." I almost said more, but something stopped me. I craved more time alone with all I'd found before I brought Dot into the mystery.

She nodded, her eyes scanning the items. "Okay then. See you when we get back. I'll try to bring you some leftovers."

She stepped away from the door but paused before closing it. "Secrets may come to light the deeper you dig in this old place. Feel free to ask me anything. I may not have all the answers, but I can probably come pretty close to the truth."

17

SARA

Crawford and his team worked fast. The electrician came during breakfast the next morning. Glory grabbed her coffee and hurried up the steps, her long nightgown billowing out behind her. Ten minutes later, we heard knocking at the door again. It was the foundation specialist. Back at the table, Dot was folding and refolding her napkin.

"It's okay," I said. "They're just here to see if the house has any major problems, which it probably does. It's better to find out quickly. Remember, this is a good thing."

Dot's eyes filled. "I trust you. It's just hard to see other people trampling around the place."

"But it's a bed and breakfast. That's kind of the idea, isn't it? Didn't it used to be this way?"

"That was a long time ago. And we made friends with the guests quickly. Look at Major and Glory."

"You're welcome to make friends with Larry the electrician,

although I doubt he'll be moving in. He'll be up in that hot attic checking the wiring, but I'm sure he'd love a piece of Bert's pie."

"I know you're poking fun at me, but maybe I'll do just that. At least let them know those of us who live here care about the house and are keeping a close eye on them."

"Just remember they're here doing a job I hired them to do, and I care about the house too."

Dot reached over and patted my hand. "Don't mind me. I'm old and set in my ways. I'm sure whatever you have in mind for this place will be just fine. I'm going to check on that pie."

I hadn't planned to say anything just yet about my findings in the attic, but since no one else was around, I took advantage of our privacy. "Dot, did you ever know Mags to be . . . well dressed?"

She paused in the hallway. "Well dressed?" She laughed a little with her back still turned. "Not unless you count those hideous hats as formal attire. What in the world makes you ask that?"

"It's probably nothing. I just found this old picture of her up in the attic yesterday. She was much younger and looked . . . well, different than I ever saw her."

"Mags was very pretty." Dot walked back to the table. "Even as she grew older, she still had that beauty, but when I first moved in here, she was a knockout."

I nodded. Mags had been pretty—the photo beside my bed in New Orleans showed that. But mentally peeling back the layers to the woman she might have once been and actually seeing that younger woman were two very different things.

I wanted to ask about William and the ring too—the words danced on the end of my tongue—but just then, the front door banged open, followed by the sound of work boots on the hardwood and a tinny radio belting out a Spanish love song. Dot pulled the belt on her robe tighter.

"It's okay," I said. "Go on and get changed."

"I'd love to talk more about this though. Could you show me the photo later?"

I nodded. "It may be nothing. I just thought I'd check."

"You never know. Mags wore some getups in her life, that's for sure." Dot glanced left and right in the hall before hurrying to the stairs, the pie for Larry the electrician long forgotten.

I sat there a minute longer. Dot's reaction seemed innocent enough, but that hesitant pause before she turned around spoke louder than her casual dismissal of the photo. I'd said it may be nothing, but Mags's neat hair and prim smile told a different story.

I spent the rest of the morning taking inventory of all the furniture in the house. So much of it had to go—La-Z-Boy recliners, a velour couch with cat scratches along both arms, at least fifteen water-stained occasional tables, even a strange orb-shaped plastic chair that shouldn't have been allowed out of 1972.

Hidden among the ugliness were a few pieces I could work with. Mags's chair for writing letters sat in a corner of the main living room. It was an old Chesterfield with nailhead trim, its leather in surprisingly good condition. Even after the invention of e-mail—not to mention texts—Mags kept in touch with former guests by writing letters to them. She always used thick, creamy Crane stationery embossed with a breezy, swirly M in the upper left corner.

Such traditional stationery always seemed out of character for her, but she said it was a sacrilege to use anything else. Saturday was her day for writing, and this chair was the place. Her old cat, Stafford, would sit with her, his hind legs on the back of the chair and his front paws draped over Mags's shoulders.

I sat in the chair and ran my hands up and down the armrests. Under me, the cushion gave way just enough to create a scoop of soft leather. I picked at a stray cat hair stuck in the seam of the cushion.

A gorgeous old buffet table stood next to the chair under a bank of windows. It had slim drawers on the front and carvings of vines and leaves snaked up its curved legs. Sunlight glinted off the table's surface, despite the layer of dust. A closer inspection revealed a small key engraved along the edge of one of the drawers. I smiled—the key was becoming a familiar sight—and ran my fingers across the indentation.

Major stuck his head into the room. "What's the order of business today?"

I stared at him. We hadn't spoken more than a few polite words since the conversation at the dinner table my first night at the house.

"Put me to work," he said. "I don't like to see these other people working on the house while I just sit here. Makes me uncomfortable."

"Okay, I was about to move some of these older pieces of furniture outside to take to Goodwill. I won't do much before talking to Dot and Glory, but some of these things are useless." I gestured to an orange plastic love seat. I loved refinishing things, but I couldn't do much with spray-painted plastic.

"I'll give you permission myself. You can't imagine what it's like to have to look at some of this stuff every day. I'm no decorator, but even I know when something's ugly as a three-eyed cat. And I don't like cats."

Together, we moved the most offensive pieces outside. While carrying a bulky coffee table to the driveway, he cleared his throat. "Glory tells me I'm not good with apologies," he said. "The other night at dinner—"

"It's okay, I understand. If I were in your position, I'm sure I'd feel the same way."

"I was just caught off guard." He grunted as we backed down the front steps with the table. "The four of us wouldn't have been able to take care of this house for too many more years on our own, anyway."

"I don't know about that. Y'all have been here so long, the house is a part of you."

"It's a part of you too, even if you don't live here."

We set the table down and surveyed the furniture we'd amassed in the driveway.

"Who's going to want that old thing?" Major pointed to a side chair with springs exposed and fabric hanging off the back.

"We're keeping that one."

"You're getting rid of a perfectly good coffee table" half uphol stery, half glass, there was nothing good or perfect about it—"but you're keeping an old busted chair?"

I smiled. "It's ugly now, but just wait." Whenever I saw chairs like this at an estate sale or garage sale, I couldn't snatch them up fast enough. As long as the wood wasn't too banged up, it was the easiest thing to refinish and recover. I regularly picked up chairs like this one—stuffing pouring out, ugly fabric, scratched wood—for less than fifty dollars and sold them for a few hundred. I wasn't going to sell this one though. "It'll be your favorite chair when I'm done with it."

Major snorted. "Doubt that."

He continued shuffling things around outside while I sat in the gravel next to the frayed side chair. Using a pair of pliers I'd found in the kitchen, I ripped the staples out of the upholstery and carefully pulled off the tattered fabric, laying the strips down by my feet. I'd already decided to reupholster it in a cool graphic print to downplay the fussy Rococo design carved into the wood. After a while, Major paused in the shade, wiping his forehead with a handkerchief.

"You okay?" I asked.

"Of course. Just thinking of Mags. She talked about going down there to visit, you know. She even looked into buying an apartment so she'd have a place to stay."

"In New Orleans?" It wasn't difficult to imagine Mags meandering through the little streets and alleyways of the *Vieux Carré* with her flowered hats and ponchos. But still—Mags in New Orleans?

Major nodded. "Especially if bad weather was coming. If there was even a hint of a hurricane out in the Gulf, she'd keep that darn TV on the Weather Channel all day long." He turned a chair around so it faced me and sat down. "I don't know if she actually would have gone down there. I can't imagine her anywhere but here."

I smiled. She probably would have fit right in, making friends with George the jeweler, Allyn, and all the other misfits.

"She hated being so far from her only family," Major said. "She figured if you weren't coming this way very often, she could go to you. Then at least you couldn't blame your lack of visiting on distance anymore."

I sighed. "It wasn't the distance so much as—"

"I know, I know, your shop. I'm just calling it like I see it."

"Thanks. That hurts," I said. But he was right. Regardless of my reasons—the still-sore memories of my parents, my suffocation at the hands of small-town life, even my childish embarrassment of Mags and her friends—it had been a mistake to allow so much time to pass between visits. The phone calls hadn't been enough, even if they were as regular as clockwork.

"Just speaking the truth, young lady." He folded his handkerchief into a tight square and stuck it in his pocket. "But it's water under the bridge. You're here now, and wherever Mags is, I'm sure she's happy you've come."

He sounded confident, but I wasn't so sure. What kind of ungrateful granddaughter would I have been if I'd ignored Mr. Bains's summons to come to the reading of the will? If I'd stayed away from the funeral? If I'd come back to collect Mags's things long after Dot and the others had moved out?

It hurt to admit it, but those were my first thoughts on the streetcar after talking to Mr. Bains. Of course, they were fleeting—I knew I'd return to Sweet Bay, regardless of whatever memories waited for me. And now, back at the house I thought I'd left for good, I no longer yearned to leave. New Orleans still beckoned, but Mags—the one I never knew—beckoned too.

Later that day, I went into town to buy a few items for Bert.

"Teriyaki? What in the world for?" Major asked when Bert asked me to pick up a bottle for him. "You getting adventurous in your old age?"

"I don't want Sara to think all I can cook is chicken, butter beans, and cornbread," Bert said. "She's used to better things in New Orleans. I've never made an étouffée, but I can make a good roux. In fact, scratch the teriyaki and pick up some shrimp. We'll have gumbo instead." Bert was hunched over a battered church cookbook, thumbing through pages.

"Bert, I'd eat a wooden chair if you cooked it," I said. "I'm sure whatever you whip up will be delicious. Don't make something special just for me."

"Go ahead and pick up shrimp and teriyaki," he said. "Maybe I'll combine the two and come up with something new."

Major wrinkled his nose. "Just stick with chicken and butter beans. You're good with those."

I laughed and grabbed my keys. Outside, the air was light and breezy. I inhaled—cut grass, salty air, and the faint scent of coconut. I smiled. Close by, someone was sunbathing on a dock.

I picked up Bert's ingredients at Grimmerson's Grocery, then paused on the sidewalk. Paint chips hung in the window of Grant's Hardware across the street, practically begging me to dive right into my job at The Hideaway, but the diner next door advertised fresh-squeezed lemonade. The day had grown warm, and my thirst won.

I took a deep breath to steady my nerves before opening the door. The last time I stood outside the diner, Mags had bumped into me from behind.

"What are you standing out here for?" she'd asked. "The lemonade is inside, not out on the stoop. I'm sweating through my shirt. Let's go in."

But I couldn't make myself grab the door handle. My parents had been gone less than a year, and my nerves were still raw and exposed. The diner was *their* place. I'd been afraid to see someone other than my mom manning the register, someone other than my dad slinging plates of catfish and coleslaw across the counter.

In the end, I backed away from the door, bumping into Mags in the process. Red-faced and sweating, and not from the summertime heat, I escaped around the corner and found a bench outside Sandifer's Music Shop. A few minutes later, I felt Mags's small hand on my shoulder. I looked up and there she stood, holding a huge Styrofoam cup of lemonade. Her bird's-nest hat sat askew on her head, one of the birds dislodged from its nest and holding on by a string. With two fingers, she pulled her shirt away from her skin and flapped it back and forth in a lackluster attempt to create a breeze. She kept her other hand on my shoulder, the heat from it radiating into my bones. After a moment, she pointed the straw toward me and offered me a sip.

I didn't make it into the diner that day, but this time, a bell dangling off the doorknob announced my entrance. The cash register sat in the same place, although the counter now sported wood pallets and metal sheeting, giving it a modern, industrial look. It didn't fit with the country décor in the rest of the diner, but it was a step up from the old red laminate counter. The place was quiet with only a couple other customers. I found a booth by the door and scanned the menu sitting on the table. On the back of the menu was a note in memoriam:

"Miss Jenkins?" The voice came from the other side of the diner. I scanned the room until I saw a vaguely familiar man holding a hand up in greeting. He heaved himself out of his booth and lumbered toward me. It wasn't until he stood by my table that I recognized him as Sammy Grosvenor. I smiled, but it was short and tight.

"Condolences for your loss, Miss Jenkins." He wiped his hands on a napkin. Cornbread crumbs dotted the front of his shirt just under the Middle Bay Land Development logo.

"Thank you."

"I remember your grandmother well. Was she still living in that delightful little bed-and-breakfast on the bay?"

"She was, and I'm the owner of the bed-and-breakfast now. Although I feel certain you already know that."

He nodded. "Ah yes, that's right. I do remember hearing that ownership had changed hands. Now would be a great time to sell, you know. Property values in Sweet Bay are on the rise. I'm sure you'd find a willing buyer if you were to ask around."

"Let me guess. You'd prefer if I started with you."

"Only if it strikes your fancy." He smiled sweetly.

"I'm not selling, Mr. Grosvenor."

"I don't give up easily, Miss Jenkins."

"Neither do I."

He balled up his napkin and tossed it in the trash can on his way out the door. I released my breath and sat back in my seat.

"Sara, is that you?" I turned to see Mrs. Busbee, the new owner of the diner, walking toward me, tucking a dish towel into the apron tied around her waist. She hugged me, her doughy arms smelling of fried chicken, and set a glass of lemonade on the table in front of me.

"It's good to see you," she said. "Don't you worry about ol' Sammy. He's always blabbering on about something or another. My opinion is it's always best to just ignore him."

"That's my plan."

"I was so sorry to hear about your grandmother. She was a big part of life around here."

"Thank you. We got your chocolate pie at the house."

"Good, good. Are you here for long, or will you be heading back to New Orleans? I'd sure love to get over there one day and see your shop. I bet I'd find a million things there I'd just have to have."

It was a funny thing about small towns. People knew too much about me when I lived in Sweet Bay, so I left. Years later, people still knew my business, but now I didn't mind as much. It was kind of nice to hear the pride in Mrs. Busbee's voice.

"I'm sticking around for a bit. I'm doing some renovations at The Hideaway that'll keep me in town for longer than I expected."

"That's wonderful. It'll be nice to see your face around here again. I wasn't sure if you'd ever want to come back in this diner. It must hold a lot of memories for you."

Another customer waved at Mrs. Busbee. She tapped my menu with her finger. "Let me know if you want to order anything else." She turned and, after grabbing a tea pitcher off the counter, made her way to the thirsty customer.

A small picture of my parents accompanied the memorial on the back of the menu. I'd never seen this particular photo before.

They stood next to each other behind the counter, red aprons around their middles, my mom holding a metal spatula. Smiling, heads tilted toward each other, they looked satisfied with their life of running a small-town diner, living with a young child, and checking in on the family matriarch and her dusty old house.

They didn't need much extra money—which was good, because the diner didn't bring it in—or prestige, even though they had a lot of that. Everyone who came through Sweet Bay—especially tourists on their way to Gulf Shores—stopped at Jenny's for a bite to eat. Everyone knew them. Everyone loved them.

I was staring into nothing, thinking about my parents, when the bell rang and a group of boys rushed into the diner, all laughs and jeers. They pushed each other around, joking about a teacher. One of the boys came too close to my table and bumped it. My lemonade tipped, and before I could grab it, the sweet liquid spread over the table.

"Oh . . . sorry," the boy mumbled, before sprinting to his group at the counter.

I scooted to the side, but not before some of it dripped onto my lap. I moved farther over and tried to wipe the liquid from the seat.

"You don't seem too upset about it," said a voice from the edge of the table. I looked up. Crawford Hayes stood next to my table, eyes crinkled and smiling.

"Not much I can do about it now." I pulled at the napkin container to keep him from seeing the pink flush creeping up my cheeks, only to find one napkin left in the box.

"Here, let me help." He swiped a box from a neighboring table and dried the table, then grabbed a clean towel from Mrs. Busbee. "For your pants." He handed it to me.

"Thanks. I can't be too mad about it. Aren't kids always jumpy after being cramped in school desks all day?"

He smiled. "Yeah, I remember that. You probably do too."

"Not really." I glanced at the boys now congregated at a booth in the back. "I was more of a homebody. Even though my home was—well, you've seen it."

"You lived there? I didn't realize."

I nodded. "Not always, but I did for a while. My parents died when I was twelve, and I moved in with Mags. Living in a house like that with a bunch of old people is a great way to alienate yourself from people your own age."

He was still standing next to my table, so I gestured for him to sit. Under the table, his legs brushed against mine. I moved my legs out of the way, then slid them back an inch or two.

"Wow, both your parents died? I'm so sorry."

"It was a long time ago."

"So you left town the first chance you got?"

"Something like that. I moved away for college and kept the holiday visits short. I think in my mind, I'd already escaped, so I didn't want to stick around too long."

"Were you afraid you might stay? Because I have to tell you, as an outsider moving to Sweet Bay, this town seems perfect. It's something about being right on the water and . . . I don't know, maybe there's something in the air too. I'm not sure I could ever leave."

I must have sat on the end of Mags's dock as a kid a thousand times while the rest of the world floated away—pelicans gliding overhead, fish jumping, the tide creeping toward the Gulf. Even back then, I couldn't deny its allure.

"Sweet Bay is magical in its own way," I said. "But it wasn't for me—at least not when I was eighteen and ready for more than fish fries and pep rallies. I don't think I worried I'd get pulled back in. I think I felt guilty because I knew I didn't intend to move back."

"And yet here you are, back in Sweet Bay. And you're doing what your grandmother asked you to do. Not everyone would follow through with it."

I shrugged. "Maybe you're right."

I sat up straighter in my seat and smoothed my hand down my hair. "Enough about me. Charlie said you're the best contractor in Baldwin County, and you love old houses the best. Where'd that come from?"

He laughed again, the sound of it calming something inside me. "I told you he sticks his foot in his mouth."

"No, he just sounded proud."

"To answer your question, my parents used to live in a ninety-year-old house back in Tennessee. They worked on it for my entire childhood. That thing was never finished—they were always working on some project or another. Once I was old enough to hold a hammer or use a hand sander, they put me to work. I guess that's where I got my passion for old houses, for loving on them and giving them the attention they deserve. That probably sounds weird."

His eyes turned down a bit at the sides when he smiled, making him look younger than he probably was.

I shook my head. "It's not weird. Or if it is, it describes me too. I get it—it's a passion you either have or you don't."

"Exactly. I did something similar to my house here. It was built in the 1920s as an old fishing house, and it was a train wreck when I bought it. The real estate agent thought I was crazy, but I promised her a gourmet meal in my new kitchen when I finished. She never thought she'd actually get the dinner."

"Did she?"

"Sure did. I'm not much of a cook, so I overpromised. I ended up ordering from a restaurant and serving it on nice platters so she'd think I cooked it myself."

"That's terrible," I said, laughing.

"She wasn't there for the food anyway."

I smiled. "I see."

"No, I don't mean that. She's sixty years old and happily married. She only wanted to see what all I'd done to the house."

"Was she impressed?"

He nodded. "It's a fine house, I have to admit. Now it is, anyway. It took a long time and a lot of patience digging through years of ugly updates. I did most of the work myself, and I'm proud of it. It was a hard time in my life, and I was thankful for the distraction."

He grew quiet and looked away for a moment. The bell rang again and two old men entered. They lowered themselves into a corner booth and one pulled out a deck of cards.

"I need to get back to the house. Bert is waiting on this." I picked up the grocery sack I'd laid by my feet.

We walked out of the diner and I turned toward my car parked a few spaces up. The late-afternoon sun was warm on my face. The air was that perfect spring temperature when it's hard to tell where your skin stops and the air begins. A faint Southern breeze lifted wisps of my hair.

He moved toward his truck parked across the street, then stopped. "We'll probably be seeing a lot of each other at the house with everything that's going on, but . . ." He cleared his throat.

He's nervous. The thought caused a pleasant tightening in my stomach.

"I'd love to see you again like this. Separate from the house, I mean." He jangled his keys in his pocket.

Why not? My life in New Orleans was a flurry of phone calls, customers, and client meetings. I pored over cash register receipts until late at night, mulling over every dollar made and lost. I often ate takeout because I wasn't home enough to go to the grocery store. Mitch was the closest I'd come to having a boyfriend in a while, but my life was so taken up with the shop, I hadn't even stopped to consider whether I wanted him to be my boyfriend.

But here in Sweet Bay, I had nothing taking up my time except the house. No late nights, no early mornings. I had all the time in the world. Plus, Crawford seemed genuine. For one thing, he ate chocolate pie with Bert at nine in the morning because he didn't want to seem unappreciative. And I'd found that people who loved old houses tended to be trustworthy.

I nodded. "I'd like that."

He smiled and headed for the truck, turning once to look back at me over his shoulder.

18

SARA

MAY

Bert still couldn't decide what to make for dinner even after he spread all the possible ingredients on the kitchen counter. He waffled so long, Major put his foot down. "Gumbo, minus the teriyaki. There's your decision, old man. Oh, and use chicken. That shrimp was practically cooked by the time Sara got home with it. I don't want a late-night run to the ER with food poisoning."

"I can make it with chicken, but don't forget, the roux—it takes a while," Bert said, his hands already reaching for the peppers and onions.

"You mentioned gumbo, and now I've got a hankering for it," Major said.

Dot and I watched the exchange from the doorway. "Major's the only one who can get away with pushing Bert around in the kitchen," Dot whispered. "Bert usually won't stand for it, but I think he secretly wanted to make the gumbo to impress you. He just needed a reason to do it."

I followed Dot out onto the porch. Glory was already there knitting and purling, a long strand of red yarn trailing from her fingers down into a basket on the floor next to her chair. Dot sat on the wicker love seat, but I was too jumpy to sit still. Both Crawford and Mags—the one from the old photo—danced through my mind. I stood by the screen door and surveyed the backyard.

After a few minutes of listening to Glory and Dot's conversation, I sat down. I pulled out the old photo of Mags that I'd stuck in my pocket earlier. During a lull in their chatting, I held the photo out to Dot. "This is the picture I mentioned this morning."

Dot pulled her glasses off the top of her head and settled them onto her nose.

Glory leaned over to take a peek. "Gracious. Is that Mags?"

I kept my eyes on Dot. I wanted to see her reaction. If she was as surprised as I was, she didn't show it. She just stared at the photo and gave a slow nod. Then she reached up and wiped the corner of her eye. Glory patted her knee.

"Did you ever know Mags to look like this?" I asked.

Dot shook her head. "I moved in here in '61. By then, she was a little . . . freer. Granted, she was nine months pregnant when I got here, so that might have explained her not wearing nice dresses and expensive jewelry. Even after she had Jenny, though, she never dressed like this. Now, Robert . . ." Dot cleared her throat. "He always dressed as if he could be called away to an important board meeting at any moment—or maybe he just wanted to look that way." Dot rubbed her thumb over the date along the edge of the photo. "Nineteen fifty-seven," she murmured.

She handed the photo to me and leaned back in her chair. She seemed to choose her words carefully. "Mags didn't always dress and act like she did as we knew her. She had a different life before she arrived here—wealthy parents, high society, fancy parties."

She might as well have been talking about some woman I'd never known. Mags in high society? I would have laughed had I not been so surprised.

"She was mostly quiet about that part of her life—quiet about much of her life, mind you—but she let things slip from time to time." Dot smiled and tapped her finger on the arm of her chair. "I remember the first time she mentioned anything about her old life. It was my wedding day, about a month after Mags had Jenny. I'd picked out a beautiful orange taffeta number for her to wear as my one bridesmaid, and she was not happy about it. She had a hard time zipping up her dress in the back, so I helped her get it up the last couple of inches. She moved and twisted, trying to get comfortable in the dress. Finally, she flopped down on the bed and said, 'Lord, I've always hated tight dresses.'

"I laughed, thinking she was kidding. I'd never seen her wear anything other than baggy blue jeans, big tops, and wool socks. What in the world would she have to do with tight dresses? So I asked her.

"'Oh, I used to wear them,' she said. 'Formal dresses, pearls, and an embarrassingly large diamond ring.' You can imagine my shock. Probably much like yours now," Dot said.

I nodded. I thought of the ring in the box in the attic. It was a diamond, but it wasn't large or embarrassing.

"She lay on the bed, fiddling with the boned bodice of that frilly orange dress. She said, 'I thought I was done with these things for good. No offense—it's a nice dress.' Then she hopped up off the bed and pulled me out the door, saying I wouldn't be late to my own wedding on her watch."

"Did she say anything else?" I wanted to hear more.

"Later that night after everything had died down, she told me it had been a perfect wedding. Now, it wasn't much—just the other guests in the house, a few friends from the neighborhood, and Bert's brothers from Florida. I wore a dress from Irene's Dress Barn on Main Street, and Bert and I exchanged rings we bought at an estate sale. I didn't need any more than that, but I was a little embarrassed in light of what Mags had said about that large diamond ring of hers. I figured such a ring would have called for a rather large wedding, much fancier than the one we'd just had. I told her as much, but she laughed and said, 'Dot, you can't imagine the wedding I had.' I started to defend our little wedding, but I'll never forget what she said next. 'I never knew how much I wanted uncomplicated love and a simple wedding until the chance was gone.' I don't know what her wedding was like, but she was so wistful, it made me appreciate what I had with Bert even more."

I picked up the photo of Mags again. It was hard to imagine her life had ever included fancy parties and an elaborate wedding. The ring from the box would have fit in perfectly with a simple wedding and uncomplicated love. Why didn't she get what she wanted?

I pulled the postcard out of my pocket and handed it to Dot. "This was in the box too."

She read the words on the back, her lips barely moving.

"You made the right choice."

Dot cut her eyes over to Glory, who leaned forward to see. Dot handed the card back to me. "I don't know what that means," she said, but her eyes said something else.

Somehow, Mags had gone from wearing fancy dresses and

pearls to a bird's-nest hat and rubber waders. Did it have something to do with her parents? Her mother? I wanted to ask, but Dot stood and called back into the house.

"Bert, I'm coming in and I want to taste a roux that will make Major's head spin!" She looked at me over her shoulder as she walked through the doorway and disappeared into the darkness of the hallway.

19

MAGS

MAY 1960

I was out on the dock, staring at the decrepit motorboat suspended by fraying ropes in the boathouse. The hand crank wouldn't budge, so I was trying to figure out how to lower the thing into the water to see if it would still float. There were no obvious holes in the hull, but I knew even pinpricks could sink it. Years before, Daddy gave me boating lessons on summer mornings. He spent a small fortune on a wooden Chris Craft and stored it in Point Clear. In the absence of a son to teach these things to, I was going to be his sportswoman—only I wasn't very good. The first time I took a turn at the wheel, I ran straight into a sandbar in Mobile Bay, damaging the motor so badly that Daddy had to jump in and pull the boat back to shore.

"I need rubber boots," I said under my breath. If I stood in the shallow water right under the boat, I'd get a better look at the bottom, as well as the motor, a rusty Evinrude.

"Don't tell me you're going to try your hand at boating again."

I spun around. Daddy stood on the grass at the edge of the dock, shielding his eyes from the sun. It was as if I had conjured him out of the still Sweet Bay air.

I waited for his image to float away, but he walked down the dock toward me, smiling. "I've missed you. Your mother made shrimp cocktail last night. Since you weren't there to share, I had to finish them off myself." He patted his round stomach. "I didn't mind so much."

"Daddy, I . . ."

"So, this is The Hideaway, huh?" He looked behind him at the house overlooking the bay. "I've read about it but never actually seen it. Looks like it could use a paint job—or two—but it's nice. Can I have a tour?"

He sounded friendly, but there was tension in his casual smile. I had no way to tell what he knew, and I didn't want to give too much away before I figured that out.

"Sure. Let's take a walk." I led him around the house to the front door. When we walked up the front steps, a group of three black-clad women passed through the door on their way out. Daddy turned to watch them climb into a waiting car, driven by yet another woman in black, this one sporting sunglasses and a black-and-white knit scarf. She waved at me and I waved back. Daddy raised his eyebrows but didn't comment.

Inside was surprisingly quiet, and I was thankful. Gary stood at an easel at the front window, his paintbrush suspended in air, apparently waiting for the muses to tell him what to paint. Starla was in the kitchen humming under her breath, preparing the evening meal.

I walked him around, showing him some of the artwork

hanging on the walls and propped up against door frames. He nodded and smiled when appropriate and poked his head into each room.

"Oh, this is nice," he said when we got to the back porch. He sat in a glider facing the lawn. "I can see why you like it here. It's peaceful."

We sat silent a moment. Daddy settled into his seat, his arms stretched over the back, a picture of relaxation. I waited as long as I could.

"How did you know where to find me?"

"I didn't at first. When you left, I thought you'd bunk with a friend for a week or so, then get back home where you belonged. But when the weeks kept coming with no word from you, I grew concerned."

"I was going to call. I—"

"Then I remembered the check I gave you."

I inhaled sharply. *The check.*

"After a couple of weeks, I called my bank and asked them to alert me the minute you cashed it. I was relieved you were still close by. A simple call to First Coastal in Sweet Bay told me you were here. The teller I spoke to was terribly complimentary about this place. I wanted to wait for you to come home on your own, but it's tearing your mother apart not knowing what's going on with you."

I gave Daddy a look. "If it's tearing her apart, then why isn't she here with you?"

"Now, Margaret, that's just not fair. Your mother loves you. And so does your husband."

When I didn't respond, Daddy cleared his throat. "So this is a bed-and-breakfast, right? Did you check in for an extended stay?"

"You could say that."

"What have you been doing this whole time? I know you haven't just been working on that old boat out there."

"Actually, I'm managing the house now. The owner had to leave and she asked me to take over. I think the job suits me." I smoothed down my pants—wrinkled and linen, so different from the pressed pencil skirt I'd be wearing back home.

Just then, Daisy crossed the backyard in yoga attire, her mat slung over her shoulders. "Hi, Maggie," she called out.

I held up a hand in greeting.

"I just ran into William," she continued, unconcerned with the strange man sitting on the porch with me. "He said to tell you he'll be a little late for dinner tonight."

My breath caught in my throat and heat crawled up my cheeks. I kept my eyes on Daisy making her way around the side of the house, even though I could feel Daddy's stare.

Finally he broke his gaze and laughed to himself. "When you were born, I suggested we call you Maggie, but your mother refused. She said Maggie was the name of someone in pigtails and bobby socks. She said there was power in a name, and Margaret held the kind of power and influence she wanted you to have." He shook his head. "I still think Maggie's cute." He paused. "Is William a guest here?"

I closed my eyes. "Daddy—"

"You know what? Whoever he is doesn't matter. You've had your time away. I even gave you a little money to help you out, but you've made your point. It's time to come on back."

"What?"

"People are starting to talk, and you know how your mother

feels about that. I don't particularly care for it either. I know you've had a hard time with Robert, but we've let you stay gone long enough."

"You *let* me stay gone?" I fought to keep my emotions under control. "You didn't let me do anything. It was my choice to come here, and it's been my choice to stay."

"Okay, fine." He held his hands up in surrender. "You've stayed gone as long as you needed to. But enough is enough. It's time to get home."

"Home? I don't even know where that is anymore."

"What are you talking about? Your home is with Robert, your husband. Where else would it be? Certainly not here." He gestured toward the house with his hand, casually dismissing the place that had become my entire world.

"I don't belong with Robert anymore—not in his life and definitely not in his bed." Daddy's mouth dropped open. I'd shocked him, but I didn't care.

"Margaret," he whispered. "Do not disgrace yourself by speaking of such matters."

"Oh, Daddy, you sound like Mother. We're both adults. Can't we speak that way?"

"You want to speak like adults? Okay, you're holed up here in this secluded hotel when all of Mobile is talking about how you packed your bags and left your war-hero husband. You may feel slighted by Robert's actions, but you're not coming out on the right side of this."

"If I cared what side I came out on, I wouldn't have left in the first place. And anyway, Robert left first, if you remember. Funny how no one mentions that. You knew it wasn't business—you said so yourself. His leaving just showed me it was my time to leave too. He opened the door and I walked through it."

"Tell me about this William, why don't you? You talk about the speck in Robert's eye, but what about you carrying on with another man?"

"What makes you think I'm carrying on with William?"

"Your red cheeks when that gal over there mentioned his name told me all I needed to know. If he's here in this hole-in-the-wall hotel, he's no one you need to be associating with. Does he even have a job?"

"Of course he has a job."

"He does know you're married, right?"

I sighed while Daddy drummed his fingers on the seat next to him.

"Let's just forget about him for a minute. What about a job for you? A real one. You can work for me and I'll make sure you're paid double. Your own spending money in your pocket—that'll give you the freedom you want without having to make your point living and working at a place like this."

I shook my head slowly. "You don't get it, Daddy. I'm not here because I want a job. This job fell into my lap and I took it, simple as that. I'm here because I couldn't stay back home any longer. Not as the person I was. I've been forcing myself into molds for too long. I need to make my own life, and it's happening here."

"I don't understand what you mean by needing your own life. Your own life is all you've ever known." He threw his hands up. "I've worked hard to make sure you and your mother never have to go without a single thing. Do you mean to fling that in my face and tell me it was unnecessary?"

"No, I appreciate all you've done for me. It's just that what I want—what I need—can't be bought and paid for. Not with money, anyway."

We both turned when we heard a noise coming from the doorway into the house, but no one was there. He took a deep breath before speaking again.

"Robert may have left, but he's back now." I raised my eyebrows and he nodded. "That's the real reason I came to get you. He's back in Mobile and he's sick. He needs his wife by his side. If he's a decent man, this William should understand."

"Sick? Robert doesn't get sick," I said with a laugh. "He's never even had a cold in the three years we've been married."

"I don't know why you're laughing. Death is not a laughing matter."

"Death? What are you talking about? Robert is not dead or about to be. He's been in the mountains with AnnaBelle. If folks are talking about anything, they should be talking about that."

"He may have started there, but he's been in a hospital these last few weeks. He had an episode—some sort of shock or mental break. From the war. He's home now and he needs you."

I shook my head. "This is crazy. If he's really sick, then all he needs is someone to nurse him back to health. That could be any woman with a cool washcloth as far as I'm concerned. He doesn't need me."

"Listen to yourself! You said 'in sickness and in health.' Yes, he did wrong, but Margaret, you have to understand that sometimes men do things to test those marriage vows. If you stand firm, he will see your strength and integrity and renew his commitment to you. It will happen. Believe me, I know."

I wanted to question him, but I was also afraid that would take us down a path I wasn't sure I wanted to go.

"This is one of those times when you need to put aside your differences and your . . . your stubbornness, and just be his wife. For the sake of your family. Your future family." He tilted his head, then looked down at his shoes and sighed. "I know nothing is perfect, but it's worth a shot. If something happens later and you still want . . ." He raised his hand and gestured to the house. "What comes is what comes. But right now, you need to stand behind the vows you took. I've talked to Robert and he sees the error of his ways. I believe him. He's ready to give you 100 percent."

I heard a rustle in the hallway again. I got up to look, but by the time I got there, the hall was empty and the front door to the house was just closing. Probably just someone going out for the day. I took a deep breath, my hand shaky on the smooth door frame.

"This is a life-changing decision you're asking me to make," I said. "I've already changed my life once by coming here. Why would I do it again when the end result isn't a sure thing?"

"Is what you have now a sure thing? This house? This William? You've only been here a short time, and you've been married to Robert for three years. Has your time here had that much of an effect on you?"

I thought of William moving his hands expertly across pieces of wood. Wiping the dust from them before crossing the workshop to push my hair out of my face and kiss my lips. I thought of the tiny house he carved for me. Then I thought about Robert's and my house back in Mobile. The gleaming countertops, the perfectly manicured lawn, the cushioned window seat in the living room that looked out over our treelined street full of ante-bellum homes.

He stood and smoothed the creases out of his pants. "I think you've already made your decision. You need to get home to it." He nodded, then walked down the hallway and passed through the front door.

20

SARA

Over the next week, renovation work started in earnest, and stress levels in the house increased accordingly. When the team arrived to repair the cracked and water-stained ceiling in the parlors and dining room, Major and Bert were hard at work at the dining table, Bert looking up new recipes and Major balancing his checkbook. Bert hopped up and moved his cookbooks onto the back porch when the men brought out the plastic sheet to cover the dining room table. Major, in keeping with his nature, grumbled.

"This is my home, people. Why does no one understand this but me?"

"We all understand it," I said, trying to soothe his irritation. "I know it's inconvenient, but it won't last forever."

He slapped his checkbook closed and pocketed his calculator. "I don't know what I'm even going to get out of all this." He trailed behind Bert toward the porch.

"You'll thank me for it later, Major," I called after him. I surprised myself by assuming Major would still be living in the house after renovations were over. In truth, I didn't know what would happen with the house when everything was finished, so I hoped I hadn't lied to him. If I had to ask him, and everyone else, to move out, no one would be thanking me.

On Friday evening of the first full week of work at the house, Crawford picked me up twenty minutes late for our first date. When I answered the door, he held out a creamy white rose as a peace offering.

"I'm sorry," he said. His still-damp brown hair curled around the bottom of his ears. He smelled faintly of cedar and fabric softener. Oddly, a splotch of mango-yellow paint stained the front of his khaki pants. The edges of the paint blurred, like he'd tried to wipe it off but only made it worse.

"Don't laugh. I had to go to a client's house in Daphne before I came this way. The woman said it was an emergency, so I dropped what I was doing, thinking my guys had taken out the wrong wall or something. Turns out, the painter used the wrong color on her dining room wall." He held his hands up. "She was mad."

"Looks like it," I said, biting back a laugh. I ducked inside and found a vase for the rose, then followed Crawford out to his truck. He opened my door for me, then closed it gently once I settled in.

My stomach had been bothering me for much of the day, and as I got dressed after my shower, it hit me that I was nervous. Had I crossed a line by accepting a date from a man I hired to work for me? I'd never done that with any of the contractors or builders I'd worked alongside back in New Orleans—it went against my nature to mix work with my personal life. But something about Crawford made me want to break the rules. As he pulled out of the driveway and onto Highway 55, the quivering nervousness in my stomach settled.

"I'm glad you said yes," he said.

I looked over at him. He'd left his window down a couple inches and the breeze ruffled his hair. I took a deep breath and exhaled. Tension slipped away and in its place was peaceful relaxation mixed with a surprising amount of anticipation.

"Me too."

We drove until we reached the mouth of Sweet Bay where it flowed into Mobile Bay. Turning south, we continued until Crawford pulled down a hidden driveway, much like the one at The Hideaway. At the foot of the drive, a tin-roofed, plank-walled restaurant appeared before us. Crawford pulled into a parking place up front just as a dog nosed its way out of the front porch screen door.

"Don't worry, it's better than it looks," Crawford said.

Inside, the hostess grabbed two menus and wound us through the tight quarters of the dining room and out onto the spacious deck in the back. Settled at our table, I leaned back in my chair. The bay was bathed in the bright pinks and deep purples of the late evening sunset.

"I've missed this," I said.

"Missed what?"

I looked out to the bay. "The water, the sunset, all of it."

"Correct me if I'm wrong, but there is water in New Orleans, right?"

I laughed. "Yes, of course there's water. The Mississippi River swims right through the city, but I spend most of my time at my shop or at home in the Quarter. I can easily go days, or even weeks, without seeing the water at all."

"That's a shame. Seems like a girl born near the water would want to stick close to it."

I smiled. "Sometimes on slow days at the shop, I'll close up for lunch and head for the levee near the park. I just sit and watch the barges go up and down the river."

"That's more like it."

"It sounds strange, but I usually end up closing my eyes and pretending I'm back on the dock at The Hideaway, the sun dancing on the water. No sound except the wind in the trees and the water lapping up against the dock. But then I'll hear a tugboat horn or smell someone's crawfish boil and I'm back in New Orleans."

I'd never told anyone about my Hideaway daydreams—especially not Allyn. He'd work his own brand of psychoanalysis on me, and I had no time for that.

It took me a second to realize Crawford was studying me, smiling.

"What?" I lifted my hand to check my face and hair.

"Nothing. You just look exceptionally relaxed. And beautiful. Like a picture in a magazine."

"Oh, come on now." I looked up at the waiter who appeared at just the right moment, providing distraction from Crawford's compliments.

We placed drink and appetizer orders and sat back to watch the sun dipping toward the horizon. On the other side of the deck, a man with a ponytail and dark sunglasses set up his guitar and a couple of speakers. Around us, couples and small groups filled the tables, as if everyone in Sweet Bay recognized the perfection of this South Alabama evening.

With fried crab claws and cocktail sauce on the table in front of us, we dug into both the food and typical first-date chitchat. Instead of boring, it was comfortable, fun even—a stark contrast to most of the first dates I'd been on with lawyers and businessmen in New Orleans. We talked about our childhoods and professional lives, dream vacations and things we'd do for a million dollars. I told him about Allyn and asked him about his partnership with Charlie.

"I knew Charlie in college. He was always the guy drinking too much at parties and ripping his shirt off at football games. You can see it, can't you?" Crawford said when I laughed. "We ran into each other down here a few years after we graduated. I had a lot of jobs going on at once, and I needed someone to man the office while I was out on-site. I hired him just hoping he wouldn't burn the place down, but he's been great."

He looked down at the table for a second. "He took over for me when I needed to bow out for a little bit. He's a true friend, and I don't take that lightly. He'd have to mess up pretty badly for me to let him go. Even then, I don't think I could do it."

"He must have really saved you."

He nodded but didn't offer any more, so I didn't ask.

"Tell me about your parents," I said. "You said they worked on your house a lot while you were growing up."

He smiled. "They were DIYers in the truest sense of the word. They never wanted to buy anything they could grow, build, or create on their own. It was annoying as a kid and embarrassing as a teenager, but now I appreciate it. They made me want to do things for myself rather than take the easy way out."

"I'm guessing it'd be easier to build something from scratch on an empty piece of property rather than take something crumbling to pieces and try to turn it into a gem."

"Exactly. And there's nothing wrong with building new houses. We do it all the time. But I'd much rather take a house that already has a life and turn it into something beautiful. You encounter all kinds of problems you don't have to deal with when you build new, but I get a lot more satisfaction at the end when I see something solid and real where before there had only been hope."

Just as the waiter asked if we wanted to try dessert, a couple came up to our table. The man put his hand on Crawford's shoulder. Crawford looked up.

"Peter, Janet," he said, standing up. "Good to see both of you."

"You are a lifesaver." Peter shook Crawford's hand. "In fact, it's possible your little redo of our kitchen saved our marriage."

"I wouldn't go that far," Crawford said.

"Oh yes," Peter said. "My wife is wonderful, but even she won't argue that she can be a handful at times."

"It's true," Janet said. "And he's right—our kitchen saved our marriage. Now I can fix my coffee and he can make his green-tofu-whatever smoothies, and we're not bumping into each other the whole time. Crisis averted, thanks to you."

While they caught up, I finished my wine and watched Crawford. He conversed easily with Peter and Janet as he re-enacted having to calm their dog down when he arrived at their house early one morning. Peter clapped him on the shoulder and thanked him for not shooting the dog when it burst out of the gate. Crawford laughed.

Back in New Orleans, Mitch was always "on." He was loud and overconfident in front of other people and never wanted to miss an opportunity to impress. Crawford put everyone—even dogs—at ease. Being with him was as easy as the tide going out.

Crawford turned to me and introduced me to his friends. Peter shook my hand while Janet eyed me up and down. "You've done well for yourself, young man," Janet said to Crawford. "She's very pretty."

I swallowed and fumbled for a smile, but Crawford defused my embarrassment.

"She is—and she's also a great client. She told me exactly what she wanted on the redo of her house. She practically did all the work before she even hired me. All I had to do was get the guys in and follow her orders."

Peter laughed. "Sounds like she'd be a good one to keep around." He winked at Crawford.

Crawford laughed and kept his gaze on Peter, but he wrapped his warm hand around mine and squeezed it gently.

"Now if you'll excuse us"—Janet pulled on Peter's arm "my husband promised his handful of a wife a dance before we leave. Crawford, the next one is yours." She winked at him as they wound through the tables to the open corner of the patio where others had gathered to dance. The man with the guitar had just started a slowed-down version of James Taylor's "Country Road."

"How about it?" Crawford held out his hand. He was confident in his own way, easy in his khakis and untucked button-down. I put my hand in his, and we found an open space away from the others. He put his other hand on my back and we began to move. The couples dancing, the waiters and tables, even the music all receded. It was only Crawford and me, the water behind us, and the sky, now dark except for a faint orange glow just over the horizon.

21

MAGS

MAY 1960

I didn't say anything to William that day about Daddy showing up. He knew me well enough to know something was wrong, but thankfully, he didn't press. The next day, I couldn't keep it from him any longer. I didn't like deceiving him, especially when it had the potential to destroy all the plans we'd made, however casual they may have been.

"William?" I sat in his workshop with him as he brushed long strokes of stain onto the armoire for Mr. Grimmerson. The earthy scent of newly cut boards tempered the sharp tang of turpentine in the air.

"Hmm?" He was concentrating on his work—eyebrows furrowed, brush moving evenly up and down the wood.

"I need to talk to you about something."

His hands went still, then he grabbed a ragged bandanna he used as a hand towel and wiped the stain off his fingers. He knelt

563

on the floor in front of me where I sat. "Don't say it. I don't want to hear the words."

I couldn't move. I couldn't have spoken if he'd asked me to.

"Let's just discuss it later, okay?" He kissed me on the lips, then stood and went back to his work.

He didn't show up for dinner that night or later when everyone gathered for a game of backgammon in the living room. I kept an eye on the door all night, not wanting to miss his entrance, but he never showed up.

I awoke at some dark hour of the night to William slipping into my bed and tucking his arms around me. I repositioned, fitting my body snugly against his. He touched my hair, smoothed it, tucked it behind my ear. He raised up on one elbow and traced the side of my face with a finger, then my neck, then my collarbone. He leaned down, kissed me on the cheek, and lay back down behind me. A breeze kicked up the curtain at the window, and a touch of fresh air caressed my face.

The next morning, he was gone. In his place on the bed next to me was an envelope with a note inside.

My dearest Maggie. I'm leaving now to save you the discomfort of having to explain yourself to me. Or maybe it's to keep from hearing you say the words. But you are a good woman and this is the right choice for now. I'm not worried—I know our time will come. When it does, I hope you'll wear this proudly on your finger. For then, you will be mine and I will be yours. We'll spend our years in the cove, just as we planned.

Love,

William

Next to the note was a small blue box. I cracked it open. Inside was a perfect ring. A small, solitary, sparkling diamond on a simple gold band. I thought of the ring Robert had given me when he proposed: six diamonds clustered busily together on a gold filigree band. The comparison between the two, and the obvious perfection of the one that came from the man who understood the real me, would have been laughable had the moment not been so heartbreaking.

I threw the covers off and raced downstairs, still in my pajamas. Voices in the kitchen grew quiet as I hurried down the hall in my bare feet and slammed open the screen door on the porch. I crossed the grass to his workshop and found what I already suspected. All the wood was gone, all the tools. The only thing left in the room was an empty sandpaper box.

Back in the house, I bumped into Daisy. She'd been watching me from the back porch.

"I was up early this morning," she said. "He was packing his truck before the sun came up. I didn't ask where he was going. I assumed you'd know."

I shook my head and turned toward the stairs. Back in my room, I crawled under the covers, my feet still wet from the grass. I laid my head on his pillow with his note clutched in my hands, trying to detect any of his scent. I stayed there the rest of the day.

22

SARA

Crawford stopped by frequently after that first date, adding a sense of humor and order to the blur of paint fumes, trash bags, and plastic sheeting in the house. One afternoon, he showed up with the plumber to check on the sewer line in the backyard. When he parked his truck in the driveway, I was on the front porch in a rocking chair going through some of Mags's mail, trying to decide what was junk and what was important.

"Do you have big plans for the morning?" Crawford asked, climbing the porch steps. When he got to the top, he walked over and squeezed my knee.

"Just deciding whether to go on a Caribbean Disney cruise or order this turbocharged commercial-grade juicer." I held up two brochures from the stack of mail on my lap.

He laughed. "Mickey Mouse or spinach juice. That's a tough call. Think I could pull you away from all this for a bit?"

"I think I could be convinced."

"I need to go over a couple of things inside, but my next appointment isn't until three. I could show you what I've been working on in my shop. If you're still interested."

"I'd love to."

"Great," he said, exhaling.

While he finished up in the house, I retreated to the blue room to find something to wear. When I'd left New Orleans two months before, I planned to spend a week in Sweet Bay and as such had packed mostly business casual clothes, appropriate for the funeral and meeting with the lawyer. I'd spent the last few weeks in running shorts and old fraternity T-shirts I'd found in the closet in my bedroom—not ideal attire for spending the day with someone I found increasingly charming.

I miraculously unearthed a clean pair of black capris and paired them with a thin sleeveless top. My only options for shoes were dressy sandals or heels. I opted for the black wedge flip-flops I found in the bottom of my closet. I twisted my curls up in a clip to ward off the humidity and hoped for the best.

Downstairs, Crawford was just finishing up. When I got to the bottom of the stairs, he looked up from the clipboard he and the electrician were poring over. He smiled and held up one finger. I nodded and slipped out to the front porch. He came out a few minutes later and gave a low whistle. "Quite a change from a few minutes ago."

"What? With the house?"

He laughed. "No, you. You look great. Way too nice for a ride in my work truck."

"Don't worry. I've seen worse."

He escorted me to the truck and opened my door. "After you."

"My workshop's not much," he said on the way. "It's really a glorified garage. And not that glorified, actually. But it gives me the space I need to work off some energy."

"When I started refinishing furniture, I did it on the sidewalk in front of my apartment with a stack of old newspapers and a can of spray paint."

"I bet your work space is a little more upscale now though."

"Well, I don't work on the sidewalk anymore, but it's still not fancy. I have a small space at the back of my shop, but I still pull pieces out into the courtyard sometimes when I need more room to work."

"I'd love to see your shop sometime," he said. "And have a guided tour of New Orleans."

He pulled off the highway at the sign for Coastal Contractors. The driveway was empty, and inside, the office was quiet. In the small kitchen area, Crawford pulled a small bone from a box under the sink. "For Popcorn."

Opening the back door, he whistled a quick tune and the same black fur and wet tongue flew at us from the left. Crawford got down on a knee and scratched under the dog's chin, then tossed the bone out into the yard. Popcorn leaped on it, wagging her tail. By the time we descended the creaky stairs leading down to the yard, Popcorn had settled in the grass, happily gnawing away. I leaned down and smoothed my hand down her soft head.

"Not much for dogs, right?" Crawford asked.

"They're fine as long as they're not directing their wet mouth at me." I massaged Popcorn's ears and snout, her fur soft as velvet. I stood and Crawford gestured to his shed. We crossed the small yard, and he pulled the door open for me.

Inside, the still air was laced with the scent of turpentine and fresh wood. "This smell is so familiar. When I was younger, there was an old shed off to the side of The Hideaway. It always smelled like this."

I walked to the other side of the workshop, trailing my fingers across the top of his worktable. A couple of old doors were propped up along one wall and various electric saws and routers lined another. A bookshelf in the corner held how-to books mixed with well-worn paperbacks. He reached over and pulled a window open, allowing salt-scented air to trickle in.

He pointed out some of his unfinished work, then took me out to the dock and showed me the boathouse he was building for Charlie. The morning had been overcast, but the clouds were just beginning to part, letting bright sunshine peek through the haze. It was quiet on the dock, no sounds but the water lapping at the pilings and a sailboat at a neighboring dock creaking on its lines.

When his cell rang, it cut through the quiet and startled us both. He checked the screen and groaned. "I'm sorry, I've got to take this. I'll be quick."

I nodded and walked to the end of the dock where a hammock was strung up under a covered section. I kicked my shoes off and leaned back onto the thick strings, listening to Crawford's side of the conversation—something about not being able to move a garage to the other side of a house once it was already framed out. Before long, the gentle movement of the water against the pilings and the call of the gulls overhead lulled me.

I hadn't been able to stop thinking about the box in the attic and its treasures. Not to mention the key engraved on Mags's headstone and everywhere else. They remained at the edges of my mind, and I pondered the mysteries in every idle moment.

I was sure Dot knew something about the postcard from Mags's mother, but it was clear she hadn't wanted to say anything in front of Glory.

What choice had Mags made that so pleased her mother? And could it have anything to do with the words on the headstone?

It seemed the longer I stayed in Sweet Bay—and the more I uncovered of Mags's life before she came to The Hideaway—the more confused I was.

Soon I heard Crawford's footsteps approaching. "I'm so sorry. This client calls me every time she opens another issue of *Southern Living*. If she doesn't stop changing her mind, her house is going to be a mash-up of every house they've featured in the last year."

"Don't worry about it. This hammock was about to put me to sleep."

"Yeah, it'll do that to you. You look pretty relaxed."

I repositioned myself so I was sitting up, cradled by the strings under me, and he sat down on the bench opposite the hammock. He slung an arm up over the back of the bench and looked out at the water. "Coming from my landlocked hometown, I still get a kick out of living here. I don't think I'll ever be able to live anywhere I can't see the bay from my back door."

I breathed in. "It is special. I'm glad to be back, for however long I'm here." I surprised myself, but it was true. I was very glad to be right where I was.

We were both quiet a moment before he spoke.

"Tell me more about your grandmother. What was she like?"

I smiled. "She was a character. She was her own woman and didn't care a thing about what other people thought of her."

"That must be one of the perks of getting old. Just not caring what people think."

"I guess so." I laughed. "Mags had the craziest collection of clothes—things like huge embroidered caftans and floppy hats embellished with flowers she'd picked up at the craft store. But she also had this gorgeous, long mink coat. I never knew where she got it, but it always seemed a little magical to me, like it came from another era. As you know, it rarely gets cold enough in Sweet Bay to actually need something like that, so she'd wear it as a bathrobe instead."

"She sounds like someone I'd liked to have met," Crawford said.

I nodded. "People who knew her well—her friends, folks in town—really thought a lot of her, but back when I was young, I just saw her as my strange little grandmother. There was this one . . . incident—it probably won't sound like much, but at seventeen, it felt like the end of my world."

"What happened?" Crawford leaned forward, resting his elbows on his knees.

"I was at a party the summer after I graduated from high school. It was in an empty barn on this guy's family property outside Sweet Bay. I'd missed my curfew by a mile, but I wasn't driving and I didn't want to ask someone to drive me home. It must have been one or two o'clock in the morning, tailgates down, music blaring from every truck, a huge bonfire. I was talking to this guy I'd had a crush on for all of high school when here comes Major's rusty orange van rumbling down the driveway."

"No way," Crawford said.

"It gets better. The van stopped before it got to the barn, but then it pulled right up next to where I was sitting. Mags hopped out of the van and walked over to me. I remember being so glad she'd skipped her bird's-nest hat and boots, but the four gray heads peering out the windows of the van was spectacle enough."

Crawford buried his face in his hands. "Stop," he said, laughing. "That's terrible."

"If you've never been the one whose grandmother and her friends shut down your party, it's a special feeling."

"I can only imagine." His laughter died down. "So, were you and Mags close? Or did you just bide your time until you could move out?"

"We weren't on bad terms by any means. She was my grandmother, and I loved her. But . . . it was complicated. It was hard to be really close to someone who seemed to try to be as eccentric as possible. I just didn't understand her."

"Is that why you left?"

I stood and walked to the edge of the dock. Out in the distance, a dolphin fin sliced through the calm water. "It was a lot of things. My parents' accident, then living with Mags and her friends. The barn party was just the last straw. Plus, I knew if I did stay in Sweet Bay, the only designing I'd be doing would be helping Staci at Tips and Tans decide the best layout for her tanning beds and foot baths, or maybe decorating the principal's new office at Baldwin County High if I was lucky. I wanted to design houses and beautiful spaces, and I didn't feel I could do that in Sweet Bay where everyone saw me as just Mags's granddaughter.

"After college, I moved on to New Orleans and started

working two jobs to save money to open my own shop. I came back often at first—at least every couple of months. But as I got busier, the amount of time between visits got longer. Once I opened Bits and Pieces, all my time went into the shop. I always came back around the holidays, and maybe once in the summer, but that's all I've been able to manage. But you have a business—you know how busy it is. How often do you get up to Tennessee to visit?"

He shrugged and gave a half smile. "Honestly? As often as I can. It's a long drive but my mom's alone, and I don't like to go too long without checking on her."

I looked out at the water and sighed.

"I'm sorry," he said. "That's probably not what you wanted to hear."

"No, there's no reason for you to hide that. You're a good son, and you take care of your mom. I should have done the same thing with Mags. It hurts to think . . ." I turned my head when my eyes started to fill.

He stood and crossed the wood planks toward me. When he put his hand on my shoulder, I leaned into him, and he wrapped his arms around me.

After that day, Crawford always came bearing gifts, climbing the front porch steps with a half grin on his face. He'd offer up a box of cinnamon rolls from the diner or a bag of cleaning supplies once I started tackling the years of grime on the porches and dock. Dot and the others loved it. Whenever he'd stop by, especially if it was after work hours, they'd make a big show of leaving the room.

"We'll give you two some privacy," they'd say, tripping over each other to get out of the way.

One night when Crawford had a late meeting in Mobile, Bert requested we all gather around the coffee table after dinner for a game of Monopoly.

"You only like that game because you cheat," Major said as Bert set up the board and divvied up the silver game pieces.

"I don't cheat," Bert said, aghast. "Is it even possible to cheat at Monopoly?"

"If there's a way, you'll find it, I'm sure."

"Major," Glory said. "That's enough. No one cheats. You're just not very good. But that doesn't mean you can't close your mouth and indulge the rest of us."

We were an hour into the game when a car pulled up out front. Dot lifted a corner of the window curtain and peered into the dark night. "It's a truck. Let's see, it's black . . . the door is opening now. It looks like a man . . ."

"Thanks for the play by play," I said, hiding a smile. "I think it's Crawford."

"Oh heavens. My hair's a mess." Glory shot like a dart toward the stairs.

"Wait, Glory, you don't have to go," I said. "Crawford probably won't even notice your hair."

"Well, why not?" she asked from the bottom stair. "It's a new color and I think it's quite lovely." Dot joined her on the stairs.

I opened the door so Crawford could see their frantic exits.

"Where's everyone going?" he asked.

"I have no idea."

"We're old and in the way," Bert said. "You two don't need us cluttering up your evening." He stood from his place on the couch next to Major. "Come on, Major."

Major didn't budge. "I don't see why I have to get up and ruin a perfectly good lead in Monopoly just because this young fella decides to show up."

"Don't quit on my account," Crawford said. "I'll just join in."

Major narrowed his eyes.

"Or sit and watch," Crawford said.

"Don't you worry a thing about it," Bert said. "We'll continue our game another time, Major, you're coming with me." Bert bumped Major's outstretched legs with his knee, urging him to get a move on.

Major grumbled and stood. "All right, all right, I'll go, but I don't like it."

We watched helplessly from the front door until the room was empty and quiet. Crawford started laughing, then I did too, relieved that everyone's swift escape hadn't rendered the evening too awkward.

"What do you say?" He gestured to the game still spread out on the coffee table. "I've been known to win a game of Monopoly."

"You're on."

He settled down on one side of the table and waited for me.

Getting involved with a man in Sweet Bay was the last thing on my mind when I left New Orleans. In fact, I was almost embarrassed at the thought of telling Allyn about Crawford not because anything about him was even remotely embarrassing, but because I'd been so focused on doing what needed to be done in Sweet Bay, then getting back to New Orleans.

Now not only had I met someone, but I actually craved his

company. More than that, I missed him every time he closed the door and walked away from me.

"Well?" He patted the floor next to him.

We picked up the game where the rest of us had left off. Crawford took over Major's spot in the lead. Amid conversation, walking through the house to look at odd mementos and souvenirs, and occasional game playing, I beat him by five thousand dollars and three hotels.

23

MAGS

MAY 1960

I let Robert move into The Hideaway. Maybe it was the shock of William leaving. I actually preferred to think that was it and not that I was still able to be swayed by my parents' wishes for my life. Whatever it was, I agreed to my father's plan to keep us together— although I knew it would only be an illusion. I did put my foot down at the idea of returning to our home in Mobile. It was out of the question. If they wanted us to have the look of a happy marriage, he had to come here, because I wasn't leaving.

The day he moved in, I sat him down in the living room when everyone else was out.

"Margaret—"

"It's Mags." I hadn't planned that, but it worked. I was no longer Margaret, but I also couldn't bear to hear William's nickname for me coming from Robert's mouth. I shortened it to the least proper thing I could come up with on the spot.

"Mags?" He laughed, then went silent when he saw my face.

577

"Don't speak. If you're going to live here, we will have rules."

He nodded and waited, a grin still struggling to escape his lips.

"First, you are never to mention AnnaBelle's name. Or any other woman you may have . . . met . . . since we married. I won't have the guests in this house thinking I am a ridiculous woman for taking you in. They know nothing about you or where you've been. They'll believe me when I tell them you've been away on business. Because that is where you've been, right?"

He rubbed a hand over his face. "Marg—"

I held a hand up.

"Two, you are not to ask any questions about how I've spent my time since I've been gone. Not a word of it. It is mine and mine alone. Three, you'll have your own bedroom and I'll have mine."

"Wait a minute, you mean to say I'm sleeping alone every night? When my wife is in the same house?"

"I'm your wife in name only. I know how this works—it benefits both our families for this marriage to work out. Or at least look that way. I'll hold up my end of the bargain, but don't expect me to forget everything that's happened. And not just AnnaBelle. All of them. For all three years."

He drummed his fingers on the armrest.

Suddenly exhausted, I sat in the chair behind me. I sighed and rubbed my temples with my fingers. "Also, I'm pregnant," I said with my eyes closed. "If this is a problem, you can go ahead and leave."

I'd known for a few weeks—ever since I vomited in the kitchen sink one morning not long after William left. I'd just reached for my usual cup of coffee, but the smell left me reeling and retching into the sink.

Starla's eyes had widened as she handed me a dish towel. "Gary had it last week." She backed away from me. "I can't get sick—I have yoga to teach. Sorry. Let me know if you need anything." She hurried for the door of the kitchen.

"I don't think—" I began.

"Oh, you have the bug, all right. Either that, or you're pregnant."

I was carrying William's child. It was both perfect and absurd. Laughable and heartbreaking.

Robert fired back at me. "So you skewer me for my indiscretions when—"

I shook my head. "You have the option to leave. Believe me, the door is wide open."

He stared at me, his jaw clenching. "Okay, I won't ask. You're right—I have no right to do that. You're my wife. I'll help take care of you while you're . . . sick . . . unwell. Whatever happens when you're carrying a baby."

I smiled in spite of myself. "You don't have the first clue what to do around a pregnant woman."

"I've taken care of wounded soldiers on the battlefield with bullets whizzing two feet past my head. I think I can handle a vomiting housewife."

"We'll see about that. And just so we're clear, you are the convalescing housewife in this situation. I have a house to run."

Robert was true to his word over the next nine months. For the first time, he did exactly what I asked him to do. He brought me saltines and ginger ale when I needed them, answered the telephone when I couldn't get to it fast enough, and mopped the floors to a shine. He learned to peel shrimp when the sight and smell of the slippery little things sent me running to the toilet. He grew handy with a vacuum and even got the motorboat up and running again.

Dot and Bert checked into The Hideaway when I was a few weeks away from giving birth. They had no reason to think the baby's father was anyone but Robert. That is, until the night Dot found me in the garden. I'd been going out there most evenings. Sitting on William's bench made me feel closer to him—thinking of his hands on the wood and on me, smoothing us and turning us both into something sturdy and beautiful. The fact that I was about to have his baby without him in my life made me feel like I was carrying much more than an extra thirty pounds.

In the garden, with the dark covering me like a cloak, I let myself cry. Since William's departure, I'd been able to hold back the threatening tears, resolutely going about the business of keeping the house in order and finding new ways for guests to pay for their stay. This time, with no one around to watch, I stopped holding back.

I didn't know how long Dot had been standing there, but by the time I looked up, I knew my face was a wreck. She sat beside me, took my hand, and rubbed circles onto my palm with her thumb. The gesture—and the lack of questions—not only calmed me, it solidified our friendship. I knew I could trust her.

She sat with me as my tears came and went. When I was done, spent from the energy of letting out all my closed-up emotions, she handed me a tissue.

"I could have used this about an hour ago," I said, wiping my damp face and hands.

She laughed.

"You're not going to ask what that was all about?"

She shook her head. "Don't need to. That baby isn't your husband's, is it?"

My mouth dropped open, but I quickly closed it, then shook my head. "How'd you know?"

"Just a hunch. You and Robert don't seem exactly friendly toward each other. Is the father here?"

"He left. But I think it was partly my fault."

"You're pregnant, he left, and you think it's your fault?"

I sighed. "I—my father came and . . ." I didn't even know how to explain. "Anyway, he didn't know I was pregnant. I didn't know it then either."

"I see."

But I knew she didn't. She couldn't have. It sounded like any other misdirected love story—two people in love, someone gets hurt, and one leaves, never to be seen again. Love stories end like that every day, but ours was different.

"It's just temporary. He's coming back." I willed my voice to sound sure, but to me, it just sounded tired.

"What about Robert?"

I shrugged. Was it wrong to wish for him just to disappear? He'd done it before—with AnnaBelle and others before her—maybe he'd do it again.

"What are you going to do?" Dot asked.

"I guess I'm going to keep waiting."

I still loved William, and he had to love me too. What we'd started here hadn't been a dream, that much I knew. We would be together again. Those truths were the only things that kept me going and allowed me to go through the motions of my life.

One day, I told myself again and again, *he'll come back.*

24

MAGS

As my body grew larger to accommodate William's baby, my heart grew as well. I cried over everything. Everyone attributed my weepiness and mood swings to the pregnancy. Only Dot and I knew the real reason for my tears. I assumed she told Bert what was going on, although he never let on that he knew. Bert was a loyal friend and a wonderful partner to Dot, but "women problems" weren't high on his list of topics to discuss.

My water broke early one foggy morning as I stomped around in the vegetable garden, trying to remember where I had planted the carrots. All the little rows of upturned earth looked the same. For some reason, it became important that I knew exactly where they would grow that fall. Okay, perhaps I was also letting off a little steam—mild contractions had rolled through my body all night, and anger was hot on their heels. I was furious with Robert for being in the house, with William for not, with my parents for conspiring to keep me from the man and the life I so desperately wanted. To be honest, I was mad at myself too. After all this time, I still couldn't stand up to Mother and Daddy.

At the hospital, Dot waited in the room with me while Robert stood with a handful of other husbands in the waiting room. He was likely the only man in the room about to greet a child who wasn't his.

Everyone assumed Robert was the father of the baby struggling to free itself from my body. A nurse by the name of Yolanda was the only one who found out the truth. Dot had left the room between contractions to find me some ice chips, leaving me alone with Yolanda.

In a burst of pain, I cursed Robert with all the strength I had in me.

Yolanda murmured and patted my hand. "Baby, I know it hurts, but you can't lay all that blame at your husband's feet. Sure, he put that baby in there, but this little one will make it all worth it. You'll be kissing Robert's face in no time."

"Robert may be my husband, but he did not put this baby in me," I spat out between clenched teeth. Finally, the contraction released its grip on me and I exhaled. "I should be raising this baby with William in our little house in the cove." I turned my head toward her. "But we're not, are we?"

Lord have mercy, Yolanda had no idea what hit her.

"That man out there didn't father this baby?" Yolanda's eyes grew wide.

I shook my head and wiped sweat off my face, waiting for the next contraction.

"Where's the baby's daddy?"

"I don't know." I didn't have the energy to explain.

Jenny was a sweet, beautiful baby, and I took easily to mothering. Perhaps it was because so many people had warned me of colic, diaper rash, and every other potential pitfall of a new mother's life. Jenny had none of that—she offered only gummy smiles, infectious laughter, and plump cheeks and fingers.

It was hard at first—having Robert around without William—but there were good times too. We had a picnic in the backyard for Jenny's second birthday. It was a sparkling fall day, brisk and sunny. Starla and I set up the long picnic table next to the house, and we scattered various toddler toys on the grass for Jenny to play with. The adults sipped apple cider and laughed at Jenny's antics with a two-foot-tall plastic Mickey Mouse. Bert found it on the side of the road "in perfect condition," he said. Dot disagreed, but Jenny loved her new Mickey.

After gifts and cake, everyone went back inside except the three of us. I sat at the wrought-iron table—one of Mrs. DeBerry's leftovers—to rest my feet in the shade while Robert picked up wrapping paper and empty cups. Jenny sat in the grass and dumped blocks from one box into another. When Robert finished cleaning, he picked Jenny up in the air and swung her around and around.

She squealed and laughed, her voice carrying through the quiet air. As soon as he put her down, she ran to me and threw her arms around my neck with the force of a tiny hurricane. I hugged her little body, and she ran happily back to her blocks.

Robert sat beside me and said, "What a great day. Jenny's

happy, you seem to be happy—at least you have a smile on your face. I'm happy as a lark. See, we can make this work."

I looked over at Jenny. With her blonde hair and small round nose, she looked so much like William. I closed my eyes and pretended he was there.

25

MAGS

I reread William's letter trying to find something I'd missed. He said he'd come back for me, but I didn't know how to reach him to tell him I was ready. Lord, I'd been ready since the day Robert arrived, since I discovered just how wrong it felt to share a house with a man I didn't love, regardless of any sense of duty or obligation. But life didn't slow down for my wounded heart, and our big, strange family at The Hideaway—cobbled together by circumstances, accidents, and varying degrees of luck—charged ahead.

Robert needed care, as Daddy had said, but not all the time. I didn't know exactly what was wrong with him, but he'd have these nightmares. I never knew when they would strike. He'd wake up screaming, sweating, and rolling in his bed, but I was never able to calm him down. It'd take a while before he was fully awake enough to hear me telling him it was just a dream. When the nightmares came, he usually spent the next day in bed. He wouldn't eat, wouldn't shower, and definitely wouldn't talk about it.

The following day, he'd hop out of bed as if nothing out of the ordinary had happened. If I asked about it, he'd respond with "What do you mean?" or "I just didn't feel well. No big deal." Bert, who'd fought in France, said it was common to most soldiers who'd seen time in battle.

The episodes were scary but infrequent, and I soon realized Daddy had exaggerated Robert's sickness. Sure, it helped to have someone around to look after him when the nightmares came, but he was far from death's door. When I mentioned to Robert what Daddy had said about the severity of his illness, he laughed.

"He did what was necessary to make sure you stuck around. I can't say I blame him. If Jenny ever ran off with some kid who wouldn't amount to anything, I'd do whatever it took to set her on the right path too."

It was the first time Robert had referred to William. A kid who wouldn't amount to anything? I stood up so fast the chair behind me fell back with a clatter, and I left the room.

Around the others Robert and I were mostly amicable, but I was simmering on the inside. I resented the way Daddy had manipulated me into taking Robert back, and I resented Robert's presence in my life when I thought I was done with him for good. All this had pulled me from William, so I fought back in whatever ways I could.

The house had never been perfect—not even when Mrs. DeBerry was in charge—but now I saw the imperfections as badges of honor instead of problems to fix. I was done with trying to make everything look flawless just for the sake of appearances. The house was warm and comfortable, if not magazine-ready, but no one living there really cared about that anyway. I loved that the place was a little off-kilter, and the quirkiness only solidified its charm.

I hoped the same was true for me when I spied a bird's-nest hat in the front window of Irene's Dress Barn on Main Street while shopping with Dot. I bought it and it became my favorite accessory.

My new eccentricities bothered Robert, especially since I'd been neat and organized before, but he knew better than to speak of me or the house like he owned either of us. He wisely took it as a trade for me allowing him to live in the house. This allowed him to keep up appearances to his friends, who thought it terribly romantic that he and his wife ran a bed-and-breakfast in Sweet Bay. He never bothered to give them the correct facts, and for some reason, I let him keep that bit of his pride intact. Anyway, I didn't care what his friends thought of him, or us.

26

SARA

JUNE

I was taking framed photos and prints off the walls and stacking them in a back bedroom for safekeeping when Allyn called. I'd been meaning to call him for days, but something—or someone—interrupted me every time I sat down to do it.

"I see how it is," he said when I picked up the phone. "You get back to your roots and forget all about me."

"That's not it, and you know it."

I was out of breath from carrying too large a load with the phone sandwiched between my shoulder and my ear, so I paused and sat on an ancient couch. This one had escaped a fatal trip to Goodwill because of its clean lines and still-firm cushions.

"So what's going on?" he asked as I stretched my sore neck muscles. "Are you becoming a permanent Sweet Bay-ite?"

I laughed. "That's not how you say it."

"Well, what is it then?"

"I don't know, but it doesn't matter. I'm not becoming a

permanent Sweet Bay anything. It's just a big job and it's taking a while. You were the one who said I needed to relax and dive in."

"I know, and I'm glad you are. Things are just fine here, thanks for asking."

I smiled. "Tell me—how are things going with you and the shop?"

"Everything is still in one piece, if that's what you mean."

"It's not."

"I know, I'm just kidding. Everything is good. We had a busy weekend—oh, we sold the grandfather clock."

"Really? I wasn't sure that thing would ever find a home."

"Whatever. You find perfect homes for even the strangest little trinkets. Anyway, a man came in Saturday looking for something for his study. I showed him the clock and told him it would make him look professorial."

"Professorial?" I asked.

"I don't know where it came from, but apparently it was the right thing to say. He took it home that afternoon."

I laughed. Allyn could sell the shirt off someone's back and make him glad to see it go.

"Now tell me what's going on with you," he said. "I know something's up. The last time we talked, you drilled me with questions about every item in the shop, and now you've hardly asked a thing. Spill it."

"It's funny you should ask. I've . . . well, I've sort of met someone." I held my breath, waiting for his reaction.

"I knew it!"

"You—what?"

"I just had a feeling you'd get down there and meet someone.

You're away from your rigid schedule and routines, you have time on your hands—it's the perfect situation. And it's the only reason I can think of that would make you loosen up and actually trust me with your shop. Now you just have to convince him to come back to New Orleans with you."

"Hold on, we're not that far along. We've only been out a few times."

"I'm glad for you," he said. "You need something like this. What's his name?"

"Crawford."

"Hmm. Sounds sexy."

"I'd hit you if you were sitting here next to me."

"I know. That's why I said it—because I'm over here and you can't do one thing about it."

The bell on the doorknob in Bits and Pieces jangled in the background.

"I need to run. Gotta go make some money for my absent boss."

"You sure do," I said, ignoring the drop in my stomach at the thought of life at Bits and Pieces carrying on without me. "Thanks for calling. I'm glad to hear your voice."

"Have fun with Crawford. Call me soon and give me more details. Or better yet, maybe I'll pop over there for a visit soon."

We hung up and I stared at the dark screen before dropping the phone on the couch. I tried to keep my mind from drifting to all I was missing at the shop as I scanned the wall across from me. Several small prints still hung on the wall along with a huge map framed in wood trim with no glass. I stood and walked over to take them down and place them with the others, but the map was too big for me to carry. Closer up, I could see it showed the

Eastern Shore of Mobile Bay from Fort Morgan all the way up to the Tensaw River Delta. I scanned the shoreline, taking in the familiar towns, rivers, and bays. My eye stopped at a tiny hole pricked into the map, just south of Sweet Bay. Probably from a thumbtack.

But something else was there. A small hand-drawn arrow pointed at the little hole. I quickly scanned the rest of the map for other holes or marks, but it was clear.

The map showed no specific town or park at the marked spot, just a stretch of green along the shore where Sweet Bay met Mobile Bay. I tried to visualize that area but came up blank. The restaurant where Crawford had taken me on our first date was near there—we must have passed right by that point, but nothing stuck out in my mind as particularly noteworthy.

But it must have been important to someone.

It could be nothing—just a piece of real estate someone was interested in at one time or maybe a prime fishing location.

I chewed on the end of a fingernail and stared at the map.

Since finding the box in the attic and learning about Mags's previous life of privilege, I was curious about her in a way I had never been before. It seemed like everything I found in the house was part of the mystery of Mags. I'd always taken for granted that she was exactly who she appeared to be and nothing more, but I was beginning to see there had been much more to her beneath the surface.

I headed toward the kitchen to find someone who might be able to help. Dot and Glory were out for the afternoon, but I thought Bert or Major might be around somewhere. A quick trip through the first floor and a call up the stairs from the landing proved me wrong. The only other person in the house was a man kneeling on the floor in the upstairs hallway, patching a spot on the wall with Spackle and singing along with the radio.

Then the front door opened and Crawford breezed in, a binder of paint chips under his arm and his cell pressed to his ear. I hadn't realized how dusty and quiet the air in the house was until the open door ushered in a wave of fresh air tinged with the smell of new blossoms and freshly cut wood.

I stopped where I was on the bottom step and smiled. He finished his phone call and looked up at me, returning my smile.

"You look happy," he said.

"It's a good day." I motioned for him to follow me, then showed him into the room where I'd found the map. "What do you make of this?"

He stepped closer and squinted. "It's a map of Mobile Bay and Baldwin County. Why?"

"No, not the map itself. Look at this little hole." I pointed to the spot marked by the arrow. "What do you think that is?"

"Hmm. Sure looks like someone wanted to remember this place." He scratched at the faint stubble on his chin. "I think I may know where this is. I could take you there sometime if you want."

I looked at my wrist, but I hadn't worn my watch in weeks. "You couldn't—you don't have time to take a drive now, do you?"

"With you? Absolutely. Let me just drop this stuff off in the kitchen."

A few minutes later, I walked with him toward his truck, then stopped. "Wait, don't we need to bring the map? I may be able to get it out of the frame."

He chuckled. "Don't worry about the map. I can find my way there."

All I knew was the spot was just south of where the two bays met, but Crawford seemed to know exactly where to go.

"I know most of the landowners around the mouth of Sweet Bay, but I've always wondered about this one stretch of empty land. It's not marked from the road, just a long, twisting driveway like all the others." He peered through the trees on either side of the road as we drove.

He'd taken my hand as we pulled away from the house, and it was still wrapped in his. His hand was sturdy and warm, and I liked the sensation that our hands fit together like two paired objects that had found their way back together again.

"It's hard to believe there's still undeveloped land around here," he said. "Most people wouldn't dream of letting a coveted piece of property by the bay sit empty, you know?" He slowed as he approached a dirt road leading toward the water. "I think this is it."

We went around one bend, then another. Finally, the tree-covered dirt path, just wide enough to accommodate Crawford's truck, opened up into an inlet of some sort, protected on three sides by craggy old oak trees. Spanish moss draped across low-hanging limbs.

The place was more than undeveloped—nothing marred the mix of sand and grass except a pair of seagulls picking through a clump of wet seagrass next to the shoreline. The sun shone overhead and reflected off the water, a brilliant prism. I pulled my sunglasses down from the top of my head.

Crawford parked the truck along the path and we stepped out into the soft sand. I tossed my sandals on the floorboard before I closed the door.

"I can't believe no one has built here," he said as we picked our way through the prickly grass and then sand to the water's edge. "It's gorgeous. I don't know anywhere else around here that's so private and tucked away like this. The owners probably field offers left and right from people wanting to buy."

"If they haven't wanted to build, I wonder why they haven't given in and sold it. They'd make a fortune."

"Who knows? Maybe some things are still more important than money." He turned and walked back toward his truck. "Maybe they're hanging on to it for a reason," he called over his shoulder.

He opened the passenger side door and pulled out a drop cloth from behind the seat. Back on the sand, he spread it out next to me as a makeshift blanket.

"So what's the deal with the map?" he asked. "Was this the first time you'd seen it?"

I shook my head. "I vaguely remember seeing it on the wall when I lived at the house, but I never paid much attention. I was taking pictures down earlier today when I noticed the little hole and the arrow."

"If this is the right place, it makes sense someone would want to remember it. It could be a great private retreat. And it's off the main roads—you have to know where you're going to get here."

I ran my fingers through the sand next to me. If this even was the right place, had Mags been the one to mark the location on the map? So many other people had come through The Hideaway's doors over the years, that map could have belonged to anyone. But the place where it hung—centered on the wall and directly across the room from the couch—made me think she put it there so she could keep an eye on it, like a tiny speck on a map could get up and walk out of her life.

As if reading my mind, Crawford asked, "Do you think this has anything to do with your grandmother?"

I inhaled and blew the air out slowly. Maybe I was reminiscing about things so long forgotten they didn't even matter anymore. Mags was gone, and whoever else knew anything about this stretch along the bay was probably long gone too.

"I don't know. I'm wondering if this place played a role in her life before I was born. Maybe even before my mom was born. I feel like I'm trying to put a puzzle together without all the pieces."

"Isn't that always the case? Especially with grandparents," he said.

"Maybe so."

"We tend to know a lot about our parents' lives, but our grandparents? The big events of their lives happened long before we were born. By the time we're old enough to be curious about what made them who they are, they're old and forgetful. Or not even around anymore."

"Sounds like you're speaking from experience."

"My grandfather died when I was ten. I was sad when he died, but the sadness passed, as everything does when you're that young. It wasn't until much later, after college even, that I began to wonder more about his early life. But by then, I'd long missed any chance to ask questions."

"That sounds about right." I thought of the ring and jumbled note from the mystery William. One part of it stuck out to me more than the rest—something about a choice. And that it was the right one. It was similar to the postcard from Mags's mother, which I still knew nothing about. I wanted to know what the stakes had been. What effect did this choice have on Mags's life? Her mother and William were of the opinion that it was the right choice. Did Mags think so?

And why couldn't I have found these bits of information while Mags was still alive? But I knew the answer. Everything I needed to know—including Mags—had been right in front of me my whole life. I just never chose to look.

"I think Mags may have dealt with a lot more in her life than I ever gave her credit for. I always knew she was self-sufficient and determined, but I never gave much thought to what made her that way. The kicker is I had almost thirty years to ask questions, and now, like you said, I've missed my chance."

"Maybe just the fact that you're here matters, that you're even trying to figure some things out. Not everyone would care. Most people would sell the big house they'd just inherited, make some money, and get back to real life."

I shifted my legs. My "real" life in New Orleans had beckoned so loudly when I first arrived in Sweet Bay. It had been a siren call until I met Crawford. And Mags.

"But you're still here," he continued. "I bet that wouldn't be a small thing to your grandmother. It's definitely not a small thing to me." He tucked my hair behind my ear and traced my cheek and jaw with the back of his fingers. "This thing with us has . . . well, it's caught me by surprise." He laughed a little. "I wasn't expecting someone like you to show up in my life."

"Someone like me?" I smiled. "I can't tell if that's good or bad."

"It's good. I know you have a life—not to mention a business—to get back to, but for some reason, I'm not worried about that. Am I crazy, or do you feel the same way?"

"You're not crazy." We sat near enough that his leg pressed against mine. His warm breath was so close and the wall around me was falling down, brick by brick.

He traced long strokes down my arms with his fingers, and my skin prickled in response. When his lips met mine, something inside me landed. I hadn't been aware that part of me hung loose and disconnected, but now it slipped into place, anchored and safe. The heat that started in my belly flooded my brain and escaped into the air, becoming part of the water, the sky, and the sunshine.

Crawford forgot about any work he had to do at The Hideaway, or anywhere else for that matter. We stayed on the beach all afternoon, our only company the occasional skittering sand crab or stilt-legged heron. Only when the sun began to descend did we shake the sand off the drop cloth and make our way back.

27

SARA

JUNE

The workers were packing up for the day when we arrived back at the house from our trip to the mystery beach. Crawford stayed a bit, going over checklists with the workers and double-checking the position of recessed can lights planned for the kitchen ceiling. After he left, I took a glass of wine out to the garden and sat on Mags's bench. The evening air felt cool on my skin, which was still a little pink from our afternoon in the sun.

I'd been there a few minutes when the screen door slammed on the back porch. I turned to see Dot strolling across the yard toward me.

"Good heavens, from behind you look just like a young Mags sitting out here on this bench."

"I do?"

She nodded. "You sure do. Except that smile on your face is brighter than a lightbulb." She sat next to me. "I could see it even with your back turned."

I bit my lips, trying to wipe away the smile.

"It's okay," she said. "You have permission to be happy with that boy. He seems like a good one."

I nodded. "I think he is."

"Did the two of you have a nice afternoon? You were gone when Glory and I got home."

"We took a drive. Have you ever noticed that big map on the wall in the front parlor?"

"Of course. It's been there for decades. Why do you ask?"

"I noticed a hole in it today—a place near Sweet Bay that someone had marked with a thumbtack or something. And there was a little arrow drawn on it, pointing toward the hole."

"What in the world? I've never noticed that."

"I saw it when I was taking the pictures off the wall. Crawford and I drove out to the spot to see what was there. Or at least, I think we were in the right place."

"What was there?" she asked.

"Nothing more than sand, grass, and water. It's beautiful though. I'd love to know what was so important about that little cove."

Cove. The word triggered a memory. Someone else had used that term, but I couldn't remember who it was.

"You think it was Mags who marked it?" Dot asked.

"Maybe," I said, my mind in high gear. All afternoon, I hadn't been able to shake the feeling that the stretch of beach was more than just empty sand. Something about the seclusion and the barrenness of it felt significant.

We sat in silence a few moments. I was about to ask Dot again about the postcard I'd found, but she spoke first. Her voice trembled in a way I'd never heard from her.

"Now that we're alone, I have something I need to tell you."
She paused before continuing. "I've held it in a long time out of
respect for Mags, but with her gone, I think I'm the last person
around who can tell you the truth."

I exhaled. "I have some questions too, but you go first."

She smiled. "I told you earlier you reminded me of Mags sitting here on this bench. I came out here one day, a long, long time
ago, and found her crying. She wasn't making a big deal about it,
no drama, just big tears making tracks down her face and dripping
onto her shirt."

"What was she crying about?"

"Did Mags ever say anything to you about a man named
William?"

My heart started to pound. "No, she didn't, but there was a
note . . ."

That was it. William was the one who mentioned the cove. It
was in the note he wrote to Mags: *"in the cove, just as we planned."* I
still didn't know what it meant, but at least it validated my feelings
about the place.

"A note from William?" Dot prompted.

I nodded. "Pieces of it, at least. It was in a box up in the attic.
I found it when I was cleaning. The box was full of all these little
mementos. That's where the postcard from Mags's mother came
from. The note was in pieces, like someone had torn it up, but I
put it together as best as I could. There was . . ." I couldn't bring
myself to mention the ring. It felt too sacred. "It was signed, 'Love,
William.'"

She nodded. "Yes, I do think a lot of love was involved."

"Who was he?"

Dot put her hand on top of mine. Her skin was thin, the back of her hand and her wrist speckled with brown age spots.

"William was your mother's father."

"No, my grandfather's name was Robert. You know that. Wasn't he here when you moved in?"

"That's true, Robert was here. But he was not the father of Mags's baby—of your mom. That was William."

I swallowed hard, then shot to my feet. Dot pulled her hand back to her lap, her eyes patient. I walked a few paces away, then turned around. "That's not possible. I don't even know this man. Do you? He can't be Mom's—my grandfather. It's impossible."

"I know it sounds that way, but it's true. William and Mags met here after she left Mobile. Things between them escalated quickly, and she got pregnant."

"Did Mom know about this?"

"I don't think so. I know it sounds bad. I think it was hard for Mags to talk about."

"What about Granddaddy? Was she married to him at this point?"

"Yes, she was. But before you jump to conclusions, you need to know a little about Robert. He was not a faithful husband. Mags didn't tell me much, but she told me that. He had other women over the years, one in particular. When he went away with this woman and left Mags in Mobile, she decided to leave too. She started a new life here, and William was a big part of it."

"So Robert was just her first husband? Did Mags and William ever marry?"

My head was exploding, but I tried to ask rational questions.

"No, they didn't. I was never sure exactly what happened. I

moved in after William left and Robert was back. Mags was weeks away from giving birth to your mom. She told me William was the father and he had left. She was heartbroken. At first, she said it was her fault, but I found out her parents had something to do with it. The way they saw it, Robert was a more appropriate husband for a woman of means, like Mags had been."

Dot snorted. "Appropriate in the wallet, maybe, but money doesn't guarantee happiness or loyalty. To my knowledge, Mags and Robert slept in different bedrooms every night he lived here. Robert thought it was a big secret, but we all knew. She may have been willing to allow him back into the house, but not into her bed."

"William left even though Mags was pregnant?"

"He didn't know. Apparently, he was supposed to come back. Maybe they had some plans that never worked out."

"That postcard from Mags's mother . . . ," I said.

"Right. I didn't want to say too much on the porch with Glory. She and Major moved in well after your mom was born. They don't know anything about William. I'd never seen that postcard before, but her mother must have been talking about Mags choosing Robert over William. Although I'm not sure it was exactly a choice—her mother was likely the one pulling the strings. It was very important to her that her daughter marry the right last name."

Pictures flew through my head like an old movie reel. The photo of Mags at the funeral, her smile blazing, so unlike the photo from the box in the attic with her hat, pearls, and forced smile. The unspoiled sand and beauty of the cove, hidden among the trees and moss, safe from a world of rules and propriety. The little hand-carved house, complete with a porch, fireplace, and bed-rooms for children.

Mags had ended up with a cheating husband over what sounded like an uncomplicated love that had produced my mother and, in a way, me. Why?

28

SARA

JULY

Once Crawford began making frequent visits after work, I found myself listening for the crunch of gravel signaling his arrival, his footsteps on the porch, his quiet knock. Each time he came, he stayed a little longer, leaving the house late, the dark night alive with a cacophony of cicadas and crickets.

He came by one evening with a box of fried chicken in one hand, a six-pack in the other, and a bottle of 409 cleaner tucked under an arm. "I'm here to work. But first, you have to eat dinner with me."

I smiled. "Let me run upstairs and get cleaned up first."

"Don't do a thing."

I looked down at the dirt-smeared T-shirt and blue jeans I'd found in an upstairs closet. My usual neat ponytail was now a messy bun at the back of my head, curls escaping everywhere.

He reached over and rubbed a smudge of dirt from my cheek. "You're kind of sexy right now."

I laughed. "And you're kind of crazy."

He took my hand and led me to the kitchen. I put the chicken on paper plates while he searched for a bottle opener.

"So have you discovered any more mysteries we need to decipher?" He rummaged in a drawer of kitchen utensils. "Another old map, maybe a hidden door?"

I poked him with a plastic fork. "Very funny."

Balancing our plates and beer bottles, we walked down the back steps toward the dock.

"Actually I have found out a little more about Mags," I said, unable to keep quiet about it.

"Really? Fill me in."

We settled on the dock with our makeshift picnic. Crawford took a sip of his beer and looked at me expectantly.

How much should I tell him? Would he be interested in the life of my eccentric grandmother? What I'd found out had the potential to change the foundation of my entire world, but to anyone else, it would probably just be stories of an old lady's life.

I hesitated. "We can talk about it later. Let's enjoy our dinner first."

"No, tell me." He leaned toward me. "I want to know."

Back in New Orleans, Mitch's eyes would glaze over anytime I tried to talk about something deeper than city politics or the New Orleans Saints. His hands would fumble in his pockets until he found his phone and pulled it out, at which point he'd relax. "Go on," he'd say, his fingers busy tapping on the screen. "I'm listening."

But Crawford kept his eyes on me. He seemed sturdy enough to take on the murky waters of my life without buckling, and I wanted to let him in, to push open that iron door in my heart that Allyn always bugged me about. So I told him everything I knew—about the Mags I'd known my whole life and how I'd gotten her wrong all those years.

He shook his head when I finished. "That's a lot to take in."

I picked at the cold chicken on my plate. "I know. All I ever knew about the man I thought was my grandfather was that he died of a heart attack. I wish I could ask her about everything. She was a lot tougher than I ever knew."

"Do you think things would have been different if you'd known this part of her life all along?"

I'd already asked myself the same thing. If I'd known the Mags who had the courage to leave her home and a bad husband to search for something better, who had such a deep capacity for love and heartache, would my life have been different? Would I have still left? Or would I have stuck close by her side to absorb that rebellious iron will and courageous strength?

When we finished our chicken, Crawford ran back up to the house to see if Bert had left any pie on the counter. He returned a few minutes later with half a cheesecake on a silver pie plate. "It's not chocolate, but it'll do."

While we finished the cheesecake, I told him about Clark and the Coke can incident in the backyard and the short period in middle school when I wanted to be a rock-and-roll singer.

"You can sing?" he asked.

"Not a bit. I just thought Eddie Vedder was sexy. I figured if I wanted to snag a guy like that, I needed to sing in a band."

"Did you wear plaid and stop washing your hair?"

I laughed. "Well, I didn't go that far. I had too much polite Southern girl in me to go full-grunge. Plaid didn't look good on me anyway."

"While you were singing to Pearl Jam, I was the biggest Garth Brooks fan in Tennessee."

"No!" I laughed.

"Oh yes. I was proud of my 'Thunder Rolls' concert shirt. I wore it until it fell apart and my mom threw it away."

"Probably best that we didn't meet back then."

"We would have been oil and water." He sat back in his seat and propped his long legs on the railing at the edge of the dock.

"So you have a hidden love for Garth Brooks and your business partners include a slobbery dog and a fisherman."

"And a bad fisherman at that."

"Tell me something else," I said. "You mentioned that Charlie took over for you at work for a little while. What happened back then?"

I couldn't help myself. I wanted to know.

He sat up and rested his elbows on his knees. I worried I'd pressed too much, but when he turned to look at me, his face was calm.

"My dad died, for one. He'd been sick for a while, so it wasn't a surprise, although that didn't make it much easier. Soon after, my girlfriend left me. That one was a surprise. We'd been serious, but she found some other guy—actually found him before she left me. Those two events back-to-back were hard to handle. Charlie stepped in while I pulled myself back together."

He balled up his napkin and pushed it down into the neck of his empty beer bottle. "That was two years ago, and I haven't dated anyone since. I've kept myself busy with clients and making some furniture here and there. Things have been good. But the day you came into my office, you sort of kicked things into gear for me. I couldn't get you off my mind. I realized I hadn't thought about that old girlfriend in ages, and the old wound doesn't hurt anymore." He let out a small laugh. "Something about you makes me want to spill my secrets." He leaned back in his chair and turned to me. "What about you though?"

"Me?"

"Look at you. You must have a trail of broken hearts in your wake."

"Nah. I'm too busy to break hearts."

"Sure," he said.

"I'm at the shop all day and usually don't leave until at least eight. If I have a client appointment at the end of the day, that pushes me getting home even later." I wasn't giving the best impression of myself: a workaholic with no time for anything but battered furniture and wealthy patrons. Crawford owned his own business too, so I couldn't use that as an excuse.

"What about now? Am I taking you away from anyone?"

I shook my head. Mitch and all his inconsistencies and indifference didn't count next to Crawford, the first man who'd made me *feel* anything in so long.

"I would have figured you'd have all the single men in New Orleans lined up at your door."

"Allyn would love that. If it were up to him, I'd go on dates every night of the week. But the last thing I want to do at the end of a long day is go to some noisy bar for a first date with someone I'll probably never see again."

"Good thing this isn't some noisy first date," he said.

"Yes, very good thing." I leaned over and rested my cheek against his shoulder. I breathed in. The scent of the water was always the same. I imagined Mags and William on this same dock, planning for a future that never came to be.

"You know, you're different from the girl who walked into our office and wiped dog slobber off her fancy clothes."

I picked at a string on my cutoffs and shrugged.

"Now look at you. You're covered in dust and dirt, and you have fried chicken grease on your fingers."

I looked down at my hands, my last manicure a distant memory. "I bet Mags would be proud."

Crawford was right. I was a different person here. I liked having bare feet most of the time. I didn't mind wearing clothes I'd picked up from the five-and ten store in town. I had no use for my suitcase of silk tops and skinny pants, and I hadn't pulled out my flat iron in weeks. I missed the shop and Allyn, but I was getting used to being back in Sweet Bay.

When we thought we saw a dolphin fin cut through the water, we moved to the end of the dock and sat on the edge to get a closer look. The wooden boards were still warm from the day's heat. After a moment, I looked over at the man sitting next to me. Moonlight trickled across the water and grazed his cheek. His shoulder rubbed against mine as we dangled our legs over the edge of the dock. When I arrived in Sweet Bay, I was counting the minutes until I could leave. Now, the leaving part wouldn't be so easy. We'd both avoided talking about what would happen when the house was complete and I had to get back to my real life in New Orleans. Maybe now it was time.

"As fast as your workers are going, the house will be finished soon," I said.

"And . . ." He waited for me to continue.

"If we try to pursue this, we'll be stuck with a long-distance thing we haven't even figured out and too many hours spent on I-10 wading through coastal Mississippi." I hated the words even as they left my mouth.

Crawford raised his eyebrows and pushed my hair back from my face.

I looked down. "I could just save you the trouble now."

"Trouble of what?"

"Of leaving later. Of finding out that the driving back and forth isn't worth it. That I'm too busy, too remote, too attached to my work." I'd heard all the lines before.

"That won't happen."

"Why not?"

He took my chin and turned my face toward him. "It won't happen because you won't be too busy. Not for this. And I won't be either. If making the drive is the way I get to see you, I'll do it. I spend a lot of time in the truck anyway. Might as well make it worth my while. And as for pursuing this 'thing,' we've passed the point of choosing not to pursue it, don't you think?"

I nodded and he kissed me. It was soft but urgent, all traces of hesitation gone.

"I thought I'd be in and out of Sweet Bay in a week. And now here you are. And the house, and Mags . . . I thought I was done with this place."

"Mags and I were conspiring all along. We wanted to mess up

your plans so you'd come back where you belong." He kissed me again. "We'll figure it out," he whispered.

We stayed on the dock long after the last lights had gone off inside The Hideaway and on down the bay. We finally picked up the remains of our picnic and walked around the house to his truck parked in the driveway.

"I would've made time for you," I said, pushing that heavy door in my heart open even farther. "If I'd met you in New Orleans, I mean. Even if you'd stumbled into Bits and Pieces on a day with clients swarming all over the place and deadlines staring me in the face, I wouldn't have been able to say no to you."

"That's good to hear. Because I sure don't want to hear you say it now." He stood with his back against the truck and took my hand to pull me toward him. "I'm all in, and I want to see where this can take us."

I nodded. "Me too."

"Okay then." He put his forehead to mine and kissed me, then climbed into the truck and rolled the window down. "We're not going to talk again about what happens down the road. Let's get the house finished, then we'll discuss the impossibility of you leaving."

"Deal."

"And anyway, these guys work for me. I can slow them down as much as necessary to get you to stick around here longer." He winked and pulled away.

29

MAGS

NOVEMBER 1963

Jenny turned three in October, and we were cruising toward Thanksgiving when the brakes hit. Everyone in the house gathered around the television to watch the newscasts about President Kennedy's assassination. Even the men were emotional. The women cried in clusters, but I tiptoed around the sobbing as much as I could.

Robert found me standing in front of the kitchen sink one night after dinner. The only light in the room came from a small lamp sitting on the telephone table. I didn't realize I was crying until he walked over and brushed the tears away from my cheeks. At the rare physical touch, I leaned my cheek into his hand, then remembered. I shrugged his hand away and turned off the faucet.

"I was just . . . I just wanted to help," he said.

"Thanks, but I'm okay." I busied myself by drying a few cups sitting by the sink.

"I'm sorry. I just thought after all this time . . . Do you think we'll ever be able to go back to how it used to be? We have Jenny now, we—"

"How it used to be?" I said softly. "You must remember that time more fondly than I do."

"I don't mean all that. I know I made mistakes. But you've stayed with me. It must mean something that you haven't kicked me out." He chuckled as if he'd lightened the mood.

"Maybe I should have done that a long time ago," I said, my back still turned.

"What's that?"

I turned around to face him. "You're right. I haven't kicked you out, although sometimes I wonder why. You've been great with Jenny and with the house, but I still can't forget everything that happened before. Everything that drove me here in the first place."

"But I still love you. I wouldn't be here if I didn't." He said it so simply, as if the fact that he loved me—or thought he did—erased everything else.

It had been almost seven years since Robert got down on one knee and proposed to me, promised me it would never happen again, that he wanted me and me only. He was still as sharp and handsome as he was back then, only now he had some gray at his temples and a track record of breaking promises.

"You only think you love me," I said. "I understand it—being married to me makes sense. Our families together makes sense. But I could never trust you again. Don't you see that?"

"I've been here three years now and I'm still trying to make it up to you. You can't see that? We can make this work. I'll never want anyone else, I promise."

My composure burst like a delicate bubble on a sharp blade of grass. "You promise? Your promise to love and cherish me was still rattling around the church the first time you decided to sneak off with God knows who. I'm not the same woman who sat at home waiting for you to walk back in the door."

"Good," he said, surprising me. "I don't want you to be her anymore. You're different now, and I like it. You're strong and focused. You have opinions and you're not afraid to let people hear them."

"Do you know what made me this way—this strong, opinionated woman you like so much? This house. And William." Neither of us had spoken his name—at least not around each other—since Robert moved in. "If I'd stayed with you, I'd still be that sad, passive woman standing in the kitchen, waiting on her husband to come home and eat her chicken dinner."

"Margaret, I will never cheat on you again. There will never be any other women. How many ways can I say it?" His voice rose along with the color in his cheeks. "I don't see why you won't just forgive me."

"Because you're not him!" I yelled, fresh tears spilling over.

"And how is that my fault?" he yelled back.

And with that one question, everything that was boiling inside me stilled, like a pot pulled off a hot burner. Years of pent-up anger and resentment flooded out, loosening the tight heat in my chest. It wasn't his fault. Yes, he cheated—that was on him. But our marriage, the culture that pushed me toward a certain type of husband and away from another—Robert had nothing to do with it.

I leaned back against the counter and pressed the heels of my hands into my eyes. "You're right. It's not your fault."

He moved toward me, but stopped before coming too close. "I'm sorry," he said, his voice brimming with emotion.

Robert cheated, I cheated, William left—all of this was true and couldn't be erased. But even still, the three of us had been mostly innocent bystanders, caught up in a society that dictated the who, what, and when of young people's lives.

He took a step closer and I leaned my forehead on his chest.

"I wish it had all gone differently," he said. "If I could go back . "

"I know." I straightened up and looked at him full in the face. "And my forgiveness—you have it."

On his way out of the kitchen, he paused with his hand on the door frame. "For what it's worth, I'm glad you came here. This house, this mysterious place—it turned you into a different woman, and we're all the better for it. I'm just sorry I don't get to be the man who . . ." He looked out the window, then back at me. "Well. Anyway, good night."

He let his arm drop and left the room. I remained in the kitchen with my arms hanging loosely at my sides. Then I folded the dish towel I'd used to dry the dishes and turned the lamp off.

The soft glow from the light in the garden filtered through the windows and made everything look watery. We were all floating in the semidarkness—me, Robert, maybe even William, wherever he was.

30

MAGS

1964

Significant exits in my life were always preceded by me finding a note. A small, handwritten piece of paper, either hurriedly scrawled or carefully written. Either way, a note was a note, and it meant someone was leaving.

This time, the departure was inevitable.

Four long years after moving into The Hideaway, Robert left a note saying he couldn't stay. He gave some details, but I didn't pay much attention. Deep down, I knew the day would come. He'd spent all that time promising he'd never leave again, but in the end, he was never a man of his word.

After Robert's exit from my life, joy came a little more frequently. William was still a barren place in my heart, but I had Jenny, I had my own slice of waterfront paradise, and I lived with my best friends. Things could have been worse. While part of me still longed for William to come back, another part of me—the part

I showed to everyone else—was willing to move forward into whatever my life would hold.

I heard on the six o'clock news one evening that a vet in Daphne had rescued a flock of Canada geese from a pond between two busy highways, and I knew they were meant to live at The Hideaway. For some reason, the vet let me take them home in Major's orange van. I expected him to put his foot down and demand that I find a more suitable vehicle, but I think my yellow rain slicker and captain's hat threw him for enough of a loop that he just watched me waddle the geese out of his office and into the van.

He held his hand up for a moment like he was going to wave me down before I pulled away, but he let it drop, so I tooted the horn and drove off. Those geese saved me from irritating solicitors and salesmen peddling everything from penlights to kitchen knives. They'd take one look at those birds walking around, unchecked by gate or fence, and take off in the other direction. Lord, it was funny to see them run.

Eugene Norman, a self-taught potter, moved in not long after the geese arrived. His only request was that he be able to practice his trade while living in the house. He pulled his potter's wheel out into the backyard and made all sorts of odds and ends while staring at the water. He probably should have kept a closer eye on what he was making. After presenting me with several sets of misshapen and unusable dinner plates and coffee cups, he hung up his potter's apron.

Next, he tried glassblowing. He and Bert constructed a furnace on the empty lot next door, where he built fires so hot the flames turned blue. He'd found his niche though—he made green-glass paperweights by the dozen and actually sold some at a gallery in Fairhope.

Less than a year after Robert left, I got another note, this time from AnnaBelle. I wondered if she still fit into that tight Mardi Gras dress. She wrote to tell me Robert had died at her house in Tennessee. She heard him yell out in his dreams, which wasn't unusual, so she shushed him and went back to sleep. In the morning, he was dead.

As his wife I was asked to write his obituary. His parents tried to change my words, but I'd already sent it to the newspaper to be printed by the time they read the proof.

Mr. Van Buren died in the arms of his lover, AnnaBelle Whitaker, in Tennessee. His wife, Mags, can now rest in peace.

31

SARA

JULY

As the days went on, I dug through drawers and closets, cleaning out forgotten cardboard boxes, duffel bags, and file folders. Drywall dust, paint thinner, and wood polish swirled around me to create a headache-inducing fog, but I kept searching for anything that held meaning. Someone had saved stacks of newspapers and crates of plastic egg cartons, but I didn't care about those—I wanted to find things that would show me more of who Mags had been.

While sorting through the drawers of an old rolltop desk in the parlor, I found a thin photo book in the back of the bottom drawer. When I pulled it out, a portion of the back page disintegrated in my hands.

The swirly, vintage script on the front read "Picturewise Vantone Prints Are Better!" A sticker on the back said "Mann's Photo Supply—The Gulf Coast's Top Photo Finishers." The photos showed random people in various states of work and relaxation. Each black-and-white photo bore a date stamped along the white edge—June 1960—and a handwritten name.

There was a young and handsome Mr. Norman standing next to a rock-faced furnace built into the grassy slope next to the house. He held a long tube into the fire with a clear bulb of glass attached to the end, the flames just reaching the bottom of the bulb. "Nella" sat in what appeared to be her bra and sturdy underwear out on the dock, a bottle of Johnson's Baby Oil next to her on the chaise. "Daisy" stood before an easel in what I recognized to be the front parlor, her paintbrush poised over the canvas. Several pages of the book had been torn out, leaving just jagged edges behind. Who had filled those pages? And what moments from The Hideaway's past were captured in those photos, now forgotten forever?

As I stood to place the book into my shoe box of items to keep, two photos fell to the ground. I leaned down to retrieve them and crouched back on my heels to look closer. The first one showed a man standing on a beach, the shoreline just visible at the edge of the frame. I'd seen one photo of Robert in my life, and this was not him. Robert had been young in the photo, clean-cut, dressed in a serious suit, and carrying a briefcase.

This man had shoulder-length light hair that looked damp at the ends. He wore blue jeans and an unbuttoned plaid shirt. I felt sure I was looking at the face of William, my real grandfather. With his eyes closed and his mouth just barely open, he seemed to be caught in that moment just before laughter takes over. I brushed my fingers over the photo, trying to find bits of me in his face. A wave of longing pulsed through my chest.

The second photo was similar to the funeral photo of Mags that Dot had placed next to the casket. It had the same huge, moss-draped oaks in the background, and she wore the same button-down shirt, one tail hanging free. Her eyes still crinkled in happiness, but her angle was different. In this photo, she didn't hold her hand up toward the camera, as she had in the photo at the funeral. She'd crossed her arms lazily in front of her body, and her stance was confident, flirtatious even.

I held the two photos next to each other. Even though the images were gray and blurred with age, their faces spoke of love and desire.

The front door opened and Dot and Glory's animated conversation filled the house. Glory walked past the living room toward the kitchen without seeing me, but Dot paused in the doorway.

"Finding anything interesting in here?"

I held up the two photos.

She walked closer and peered over my shoulder at them, then fumbled a hand on top of her head searching for her glasses. "Never have 'em when I need 'em," she said under her breath. She took the photo of Mags and held it out at arm's length.

"This one, I've seen—or at least one like it." She tilted the photo to look at the date. "A little three-by-five of Mags smiling this same unbelievable smile was in the junk drawer in the kitchen for as long as I can remember. Whenever I'd ask Mags about it, she'd just say it was a long-ago happy day. That's why I wanted to use it at the funeral. I didn't know there was another photo from that same day. Now this." She took the second photo. "I'm guessing this is William. I've never seen a picture of him." She rubbed her thumb over William's face. "I can see why she was so smitten."

I stood and stretched my sore legs. Dot patted my shoulder and moved back toward the hallway, then stopped.

"I know I told you a lot the other day—William and Robert and all. Are you disappointed? Do you wish I hadn't told you?"

"No, I'm glad you told me. It was shocking, and still is, but I'm glad I know the truth—or at least parts of it."

"Good. I was so worried I'd ruined the picture you had in your mind of who Mags was."

"Well, you did, but the picture I had in mind wasn't the right one. I'd rather know the truth than forever think she was just a woman who liked to wear caftans and weird hats and poke fun at the neighbors."

"She was all those things," Dot said, "but it was just her armor. Underneath, she was tender. Not as unbreakable as everyone thought."

"But why did she keep it all such a secret?"

"You know how most women tend to talk a lot about feelings and emotions?"

I nodded.

"Mags wasn't that kind of woman. I was her best friend and she didn't even give me all the details. She told me a little, but I had to string most of it together as best as I could. I think it was too hard for her to talk much about William."

She paused for a minute. "William's shadow followed her all those years. She never fully admitted it, but I could see it. Even as an older woman, his presence was still very much a part of her."

"Those nights she'd sit in the garden ..."

"Oh yes. William made her that bench. He made a lot of the pieces in this house. I'm not exactly sure which pieces, but I know he made some of them." She squeezed my hand. "I'm not sure I answered any of your questions."

"You did. Thank you."

She padded away to the kitchen, leaving me in the parlor with the photos in my hand. I placed the photo book in the shoe box but stuck the two loose photos in my back pocket. Those were staying with me.

I continued my rummaging that afternoon. In the downstairs coat closet, I found a black leather jacket with laces on the arms and braided tassels hanging off the bottom. It had been pushed all the way to the back for who knows how long, hidden by more useful raincoats and light winter jackets. Allyn would snag something like this from a cluttered vintage shop and wear it until it fell apart.

I laid the jacket across the back of the couch and picked up my phone. He answered on the first ring. "Bits and Pieces, how may I help you?"

"It's me."

"Hello, you." I could hear the smile in his voice. "Checking up on me?"

"Nope, just calling to check in. I'm following your orders."

"We're doing fine. I got that order of linen pillows we ordered months ago. They got a piece of my mind, and we got a 10 percent discount on our next order."

"Good for you. Go ahead and call—"

"I'm all over it. Mrs. McMurphy has already picked them up. I can't talk long, but fill me in. How's it going with Mr. Sexy?"

"It's Crawford. And he's wonderful." I couldn't say it without smiling.

"Mm-hmm. I know that voice. You're happy."

"So what? I'm always happy."

"Not like this, you're not. So you two have been out again?"

"We're not exactly going out. He's just spending a lot of time at the house. After work."

"You scandalous woman! Sneaking around with the boss after hours."

"He's not my boss. I hired him."

"Even better. Sneaking around with a hired hand. I love it."

"Allyn, I love you, but you're making this sound dirty."

"Of course I am. I'm happy you've found someone. Now don't screw it up. And before you get all testy, I just mean don't let your head into the game too much. That's when you start to back off. Let it go and see what happens."

"That's my plan." I could hear commotion in the background, so I hurried. "I've found some of Mags's things in the house as I've been cleaning out."

"What kind–? Oh, hang on a sec."

I waited while Allyn answered a customer's question. I could hear the soft hum of voices in the shop, the tinkling of Allyn's music of the day coming from the speakers. Things were just fine, as he'd said.

"I need to run," he said when he picked up the phone. "Barb here is interested in the sofa."

"*The* sofa?" I asked. Over the winter, I'd refinished a Victorian-style sofa from the 1800s with curved walnut arms and a tufted back. It was in mint condition and the most expensive item in the shop.

"That's the one. I'll let you know how it goes. But I do want to hear about Mags. We'll talk soon."

With a click, he was gone. I put the phone down on the desk and sighed. My presence at Bits and Pieces wasn't as necessary as I'd thought. Everything was running like clockwork even in my absence.

32

SARA

JULY

I'd just sat down on the front porch after dragging a trash can to the road when a car approached. The small blue sedan came to a stop in the middle of the driveway. I couldn't see the driver's face through the shadows of the trees overhead.

The man who eased out of the car had a full head of thick white hair under a plaid cap, and he stretched each leg out in front of him as if relieving them of stiffness. I'd seen that same white hair and plaid cap in my rearview mirror when I drove away from Mags's grave. When the man stepped away from his car and turned toward me, I knew. This was William.

He shuffled to the bottom of the porch steps. I would have spoken first had my mouth—my brain—not been so empty of words. My heart thudded when he finally spoke.

"My name is William Cartright. I'm looking for—well, I'm not sure what. Is this . . . are you . . . ?"

"I'm Sara Jenkins. This is The Hideaway."

He nodded and looked up at the house. "I couldn't forget this place," he said, before turning to me again. "I was . . . I knew Mag–Margaret–Van Buren. It was a long time ago. I read her obituary in the newspaper. It took me a while to get up the nerve to come back here." He ran a hand across his stubbly cheek.

It was hard to speak over the lump in my throat, full of both affection and sadness. "I'm her granddaughter." My voice broke, but he was so caught in his memory I wasn't sure if he noticed. I swiped my finger under my eyes.

He offered a small smile. "I thought you might be. You look a lot like she did. The paper said her one survivor was a granddaughter, but I didn't think I'd have the luck to run into you. I don't mean to be presumptuous, but would you have a few minutes to talk to me?"

I gestured to the rocking chair next to me, and William began the climb up the steps. When he settled into the chair, he took a breath and seemed to relax a little. I couldn't take my eyes off him.

Even in his old age, it was obvious he had been handsome once. He had an angular jaw and chocolate brown eyes framed by still-full lashes. I tried to imagine him with hair to his shoulders, as it had been in the photo of him at the cove. His hands—large, dotted in age spots, and mottled with purple veins—pulled at the zipper of his jacket. They were strong, useful hands.

"Thank you for talking to me. You probably haven't even heard my name." William ran his hand over a small Band-Aid on his chin. A dot of blood showed through the bandage right in the center, as if he'd nicked himself shaving.

"I have," I said quietly. I didn't know how much to tell, so I went with the truth. "I found a note you wrote to Mags."

He raised his eyebrows and gave a slow nod but didn't speak.

"It was in pieces in a box with some old photos and a few other things. I didn't understand what it meant—I still don't, really—but I've been piecing bits together. Mags's best friend Dot still lives here. She's told me what she knows."

I wasn't ready to mention the biggest fact I'd discovered—that William was my grandfather. It was still outlandish to me, and I suspected it would be even more so to him if he didn't know, and according to Dot, he didn't.

"Then maybe you can tell me a little of what I missed," he said. "Again, if I'm not asking too much. I know she must have had a full life after I left—she has a granddaughter, after all." He smiled. "So life must have treated her well. I don't want to pry, but I've always been so curious . . ."

"It's okay. She lived here until the very end. She was always surrounded by friends. The ones who live here now lived with her for years. The house made her happy. I think she had a good life."

Despite the fact that you left her heartbroken and pregnant.

I couldn't argue the facts, but this gentle man didn't seem like the kind of person who would have done that. I wanted answers but I didn't know how to venture into those waters. Turns out I didn't have to. William dove right in.

"I came back a year or two after I moved out." He took his cap off and placed it in his lap. "I saw her sitting at the table where I first spoke to her—a fussy little wrought-iron table Mrs. DeBerry left behind—and she was laughing. A man was swinging a little girl around in a circle in the grass. When he put her down, she ran and threw her arms around Maggie's neck."

William paused. "I knew it had to be her husband, and the

little girl was theirs. I couldn't bring myself to barge in. Especially not when I saw the girl. I suppose that was your mom?"

I nodded even though he didn't have the story right. "Why did you leave?" The question tumbled out before I had a chance to censor myself. "The first time, I mean. Where did you go?"

He shifted in his chair and recrossed his legs.

"I'm sorry. Maybe I shouldn't have asked that."

"Yes, you should have. I knew coming here that if I wanted answers about Maggie, I'd likely have to answer for what I did." He slid his hands up and down the arms of the rocking chair. "Maggie's father showed up at The Hideaway soon after she took over the house. I was looking for her when I overheard them on the back porch. Her dad was scolding her about staying here instead of being back home with her husband." He stopped and looked at me. "Forgive me. I don't know how much you know, and I don't want to be the one to— Well, I don't want to change your view of your grandmother."

"It's all right. I know about you and Mags. Some of it, at least. I need to know the rest."

He nodded. "We fell for each other quickly. I knew what we were doing—all I had planned for us—was wrong, but I couldn't help myself. That is, until I heard her talking to her father. I realized then that he was right."

"And you just gave up? If you really loved each other, couldn't you have made it work somehow?"

"Not then, we couldn't. I saw exactly what I was up against. Who was I to be carrying on with another man's wife and trying to plan a future with her? Aside from the fact that what we were doing was wrong, I was nobody—I couldn't pay to put gas in my truck half the time, and her husband was a wealthy socialite with a steady job. Maggie was used to nice things, even if she had turned her back on her old life. I wasn't sure she'd really thought of what it would mean to stick with me and turn down a life of money and ease. I knew I had to get myself together and make a real plan before expecting her to stick with me."

I thought of Mags sitting on her bench crying to Dot, missing William. I shook my head. "Knowing Mags and who she turned out to be, she probably wouldn't have cared about the money."

"You have no idea how many nights I've laid awake thinking that same thing. I made a mistake leaving like I did, but I always planned to come back for her. I thought I'd spend some time away, make a decent amount of money, and then return to whisk her away like a knight in shining armor." He chuckled.

"What happened?"

"I came back a few weeks after I left. I'd wanted to give her time to settle things with her parents and her husband, but it was so hard for me to stay away. I stopped at Grimmerson's first to pick up some flowers. I'd made some furniture for Tom, and he knew Maggie and I were—well, together. He sold me the flowers but advised against taking them to her. He told me her husband had moved in. I didn't go see her that day, but I was just young and headstrong enough not to give up." He shook his head.

"I did stay away for a while then. I worked hard, made some money, and I came back again, but I guess I waited too long. When I saw them in the backyard, I didn't have the nerve to wreck what she'd built with Robert and their little girl."

My heart caved inside of me. I closed my eyes and worked the tension out of my forehead with my fingers. I wanted to tell him the truth about that little girl, my mother, but I couldn't. Not yet.

"I didn't see any mention of Robert in her obituary," he continued. "Did he . . . did they stay together?"

"He died of a heart attack when Mom was just a few years old. But I don't think . . ." I paused, unsure of how much to explain. "I think their situation was complicated."

"I see," he said quietly.

"You don't seem surprised."

He shrugged. "I just worried about her, is all. He'd already left her once."

"Seems a lot of people left her. The only ones who stuck by her are the ones who still live here."

"So she never remarried?"

"There was never anyone else."

We rocked in silence for a few moments. "What about you?" I asked. "Did you ever get married?"

He nodded. "Twice."

I raised my eyebrows.

"I tried to forget her, but no one could ever measure up. In their defense, they were good women. Both times, it was my fault it didn't work out. I compared everyone to Maggie. I was twenty-eight when she arrived here with a red coat draped over her arm. She was stunning. I've been in love with her ever since."

In the photo of Mags at the funeral, and the other one I'd found in the desk, she'd had such a radiant smile. Her hair was messy and free, and even the sand and sky around her seemed ripe with life. William had been the man to make her so happy. He'd been her heart and soul. Regardless of how he and Mags had ended, I felt a sudden closeness to him, an appreciation that he'd drawn so much life and joy out of her, even if I never got to see that side of her.

"I've taken up enough of your time." He straightened in his chair. "I appreciate you talking to me."

"I'm glad you came." I wanted to say more, but it was still a little strange to be sitting next to my grandfather—one, he wasn't named Robert, and two, he wasn't dead. But despite the oddity of the situation, we had an undeniable connection and I wanted to know more about him.

He rose from his chair and began the walk back to his car.

I stood and walked to the top of the steps. "Would you mind if I called you? Maybe we could meet again."

He smiled. "I'd like that."

I put a hand on the door behind me. "I'm going to get some paper and a pen. Don't go anywhere."

He chuckled and stopped on the bottom porch step. "Don't worry. I'll stick around this time."

I sat in the rocker watching the taillights on William's car disappear in the trees. Not a minute later, the front door opened and Dot's gray head popped out. "Is your friend gone?"

"He is. Although he wasn't a friend."

"Well, I wondered." She sat in the chair William had just vacated. "I didn't take you for a woman with gentleman callers as old as Bert."

"Aren't you and Bert the same age?"

She waved the thought away. "Don't tell him that. So who was the visitor?"

"It was William."

Her rocking chair creaked to a stop. "William?"

I nodded. "He saw the obituary in the paper. Remember me telling you I saw a man at the cemetery after everyone else left? That was him."

"The thought crossed my mind, but it seemed unlikely. It's been so many years."

We rocked in our chairs, each lost in our own thoughts. Around us, crickets practiced for their evening serenade, stretching their legs and testing instruments.

"What was he like?" she asked.

"Amazingly, still lovestruck. He's been married twice, but he's still in love with her—or at least, who she used to be. It was sad to hear him talk that way about her, especially since she's not here to see him again. Do you think she still loved him at the end?"

She shrugged. "On the one hand, Mags was a smart woman— I'd like to think she wouldn't have let her heart stay tied to a man she met in her early twenties, but the head and the heart rarely agree. A woman never fully forgets her first love. And I'd imagine that's especially true if she never finds love again—not to mention if she carried his child. I know she loved him, but I always had a hard time swallowing the fact that he left and never came back."

I told her about William overhearing Mags's conversation with her father and how he planned to come back with the means to compete against Robert's wealth and status.

"Then why didn't he? Mags would have gone back to him in a heartbeat—especially after Robert died."

"That's the thing—he did come back, but he saw Mags and Robert in the backyard with a little girl—Mom—and he assumed it was Robert's and her child. He didn't want to disrupt their life or hurt the child."

"My goodness."

"It's terrible, isn't it? It would have been so easy for them to be together again, but neither of them knew." I sighed. "I wish Mags hadn't held on to her secrets for so long. I wish I had known all of this." I cradled my chin in my hand. "I wish I had known her."

33

SARA

JULY

At the house, the construction team took out the wall dividing the kitchen and dining room and the one between the foyer and the main parlor. Even with everything covered in dust and plastic tarps, I could tell the decision to remove the walls was a good one. Despite the noise and dust, it was easier to breathe in the house with the rooms opened up.

The new bathrooms upstairs were framed out, and the old ones were updated to include spa baths and separate showers. Major was the biggest fan of the new bathrooms.

"Have you seen those bathtubs?" he asked Bert one morning over cowboy coffee on the back porch when the electricity had been temporarily turned off. "They're huge. I'm not too keen on men soaking in tubs, but these may change my mind."

Downstairs, the kitchen floors went from yellowed tile to hardwood and the counters from ugly linoleum to butcher block. I walked in the kitchen one day to find Bert leaning over the new counter, his ear an inch from the wood and his eyes closed. Major stood in the corner of the kitchen, just out of Bert's line of sight, doubled over in quiet laughter. I gave Major a stern look and walked over to Bert.

"Bert?" I whispered. "Are you okay?"

He straightened up and smoothed his hand across the surface. "I'm just fine. And Major, I see you over there laughing. I read that some butcher block comes from ancient trees, and if you listen hard enough, you can hear the sound of wind in the branches."

Major couldn't contain himself any longer. "Ancient trees? Wind in the branches? Did you forget to take your pills this morning?" He laughed and grabbed a dish towel off the counter to wipe his eyes under his glasses.

"I'm not crazy," Bert said. "You know how you can hear the ocean in a seashell? It's the same thing."

"I do know about the seashells," I said, hiding my own laughter. "And you may be right about some butcher-block wood, but I ordered these from Ikea, so I don't think they're ancient. More like Swedish."

"Sweden? I bet they have ancient trees there."

I chose creamy white paint for the cabinets and a soothing pale gray for the walls throughout the rest of the house. It would make the spaces feel even larger and pop against the new white crown moldings. Everything was coming together just as I'd imagined. My favorite change was in the center hallway, which had previously been lined with built-in bookshelves, making it seem slimmer than it was. I asked Crawford to rip them out, and what a change it made. The hallway was now ten feet across, and when I opened the front and back porch doors, the breeze floated through the house like a cool whisper.

I ended each day a hot, sweaty mess, but I was satisfied. Exhausted and bleary, but satisfied. It was early evening on such a day when a car pulled up in the driveway. I smiled. Crawford was coming over for dinner, and he must have decided to come early. The last of the workers would be out of the house soon, and he'd said we needed to celebrate my victory.

"Victory?" I said when he asked me about dinner.

"The house is incredible. I may have coordinated the actual work, but it's all your plans. You made this house what it's becoming. Your phone is going to be ringing off the hook with people wanting to book their vacations when it's finished."

"What vacations?" I asked. "No one even knows about this place anymore, other than the neighbors who probably don't care."

"You know how word spreads. Once it gets out that there's a fancy new bed-and-breakfast in Sweet Bay, they'll start coming. You haven't said it, but I think this is what you want. Otherwise, why go through with the renovations?"

Is that what I want?

"It's settled," he continued. "I'm bringing dinner and wine, and you don't need to do a thing. I'll be there by seven."

"Okay then. As long as you don't mind hanging out with a girl who's spent all day cleaning the bathroom floors."

"There's no one I'd rather spend my evening with. As long as you keep your hands to yourself."

I laughed. "Thanks."

"On second thought, forget I said that. I'll just need to check them for germs first."

I was still smiling when I heard the crunch of gravel in the driveway. I welcomed the pleasant clench in my chest as I thought about Crawford—his warm eyes, his slow grin, his rumpled clothes and hair. How was it possible that in this small space of time in Sweet Bay, my life had changed so remarkably?

Every time my mind crept back to New Orleans, I forced myself to focus on what was in front of me rather than what waited for me in my real life. It was a trick I'd learned since I'd been back at The Hideaway—pretend to be the spontaneous, go-with-the-flow person I wished I was and I could almost forget that I was going against the grain of my cautious, orderly life.

He knocked and I jumped up off the couch. When I got to the front door, I pulled it open and held my hands out. "They're so clean, you could eat off them."

But it wasn't Crawford.

"Miss Jenkins. I hoped I'd find you here."

Sammy Grosvenor. Middle Bay Land Development. My stomach dropped.

"I haven't seen you around the diner again, so I thought I'd come by for a little chat. Do you mind?" He put his hand on the door and pushed.

"I do mind." I held on to the door firmly. "If you need to talk to me about anything, we can do it out here. Although I can't imagine that we have anything to say to each other."

"Oh, there's plenty." He peered around me into the house. "Clark was right. He said a lot's been going on around here and I can see it. Looks good, Miss Jenkins. I hate to tell you it's all about to change."

I crossed my arms over my chest.

He raised an eyebrow. "Allow me to explain. You're the owner of one of the choicest plots of waterfront property in Sweet Bay. I tried to tell you this when we spoke at the diner a couple months ago. Only one other piece of property rivals yours in terms of desirability, but the owner has proven to be quite stubborn. With the unfortunate death of your grandmother and your refusal to sell, I've informed Mayor McClain that it's high time we get ourselves in gear and make some necessary changes."

He trained his eyes on me, his round face red with heat and exertion, his hair matted down on top. My stomach tightened into a ball of knots waiting for him to explain, but I wouldn't give him the satisfaction of appearing interested.

"I'll cut to the chase. My case to the mayor shows that this stretch of property serves no one but The Hideaway's cornucopia of senior citizens. The area will better serve Sweet Bay, and the entire county, if it is developed into something a little more upstanding. I've always liked the idea of some fancy loft apartments. You know the kind—industrial look, exposed pipes, metal railings. Maybe some shops and restaurants underneath and a nice boardwalk along the water to connect it all.

"With my plan in the works, Sweet Bay could rival other tourist destinations along the Gulf Coast. I've assured the mayor's staff that these changes would move us up substantially in the eyes of folks looking to spend vacation dollars. The mayor couldn't say yes fast enough."

"Mr. Grosvenor—"

"Please, call me Sammy."

"*Mr. Grosvenor*, you've been trying to get your hands on this house for years, and my answer is the same as it was at the diner. You're not getting the house. Now if you'll excuse me, a friend is coming over soon and I'd prefer it if you didn't ruin our dinner."

I tried to close the door, but he stuck a foot in the doorway. I opened it back up and sighed. He was a bothersome bug, a pest that wouldn't go away.

"You misunderstand me, Miss Jenkins. I don't want the house. I have no use for it. I want the house gone."

"Gone?" I laughed. "You can't do that. It's not your house to take."

My voice sounded light, but inside, bells were going off. Sammy had come around many times, but he'd never had a real plan, just a desire to take land out from under an old lady's nose. This time, it sounded like he'd done his homework.

"The mayor agrees with me that eminent domain is the right road to take. It's the first step in paving the way for our new Sweet Bay. I'll allow time for the residents to collect their things and make some plans, but do inform them that they should be quick. I don't have time for the Ingrams and Greggs to sit around and bemoan their misfortune. We're all adults here and this is how the world works. I'll stop by again with the necessary papers, but I wanted to let you know what's going on."

"That's—this is impossible."

"I'm afraid it is very possible," he said with less bravado. "You know, Miss Jenkins, many of the residents in this town think I'm slimy. They think I do nothing but twiddle my thumbs and wait for someone to die or run out of money so I can swing in and take the house."

I raised an eyebrow.

"It's true, I do work that way sometimes. But this time it's different. This is all in the name of bettering our town of Sweet Bay."

It was a lie and we both knew it. He didn't care about Sweet Bay—all he cared about was the money a hot new development would put in his pocket. Inside, I was seething, but I couldn't let him see it. I had to talk to Mags's lawyer first.

"Are you finished?"

"Yes, I . . ." He cleared his throat. "I'm finished. Do you have anything to add?"

"Not a thing. I'll have my lawyer contact you in the morning."

With the door closed, I let out a shaky breath. I pressed the heels of my hands over my eyes, then grabbed my phone off the dining table and walked to the back porch to call Crawford. The night couldn't have felt less like a victory if I'd walked off the end of the dock and fallen into the water.

"I'll have to take a rain check for tonight," I said when he answered.

"Why? What's wrong?" I heard the concern in his voice. Mitch—or any of the men I'd dated in New Orleans—would have been on his phone the minute I bailed, looking for other friends to meet up with. Instead, Crawford gave me a chance to lighten the load Sammy had just dumped on my shoulders.

I took a deep breath. "What do you know about eminent domain?"

In the backyard, the sky was solid lilac, the sun long gone below the trees. The sun-warmed grass poked the bottoms of my bare feet.

Without thinking, I did something I hadn't done since I was a young girl. I stretched out on the grass on my back—toes pointed, arms stretched over my head—and stared up at the sky.

After my parents died, I often came out into Mags's backyard just to lie down and think. As the stars popped out, I'd imagine they were holes, and my parents were up there peeking through the sky at me. I thought if I only stayed still long enough, I could catch all the love they dropped down.

As Crawford had told me on the phone, there was no reason to jump to conclusions. "Wait until you talk to Mr. Bains. See if Sammy's plan even holds water, then we'll figure it out, whatever it is."

"But what about all your work on the house? The painters are coming tomorrow, and the electrician is coming back in the afternoon to—"

"Let me take care of the house. We can pause the work if necessary until we figure out what's going on. Most of the heavy lifting has already been done. The rest can wait."

I hoped it would just be a simple wait and not a permanent ending.

I rolled onto my side and looked up at the house. The lights inside gave the rooms a welcome glow. It sure didn't look like the neglected relic it had been when I first arrived.

Was it possible Sammy could take it all away from me?

34

SARA

JULY

I walked into Mr. Bains's office in Mobile the next day to find him swimming in paperwork. File folders and papers covered his desk and the floor surrounding it. His face, mottled and damp, showed the day had been a rough one. When he saw me in the doorway, he gestured to the paper-covered chair across from his desk.

"I wondered when I'd hear from you."

I sat down, desperate for him to tell me Sammy had it all wrong.

"My buddy over at the courthouse called me late yesterday and told me the news," he said before I could speak. "He knew I'd been Mrs. Van Buren's lawyer and thought I'd want to know. It's harsh, but this type of thing does happen. Granted, usually it's to make way for a road expansion or railroad tracks, not something as trivial as condos and a boardwalk. But Sammy has the mayor's ear on this one. When he started chirping about tax dollars coming into the county and how that could change the face of Sweet Bay, the mayor turned to mush."

"So he can do this? It's really going to happen?"

"Looks that way. Unless of course . . ."

"Unless what?"

Mr. Bains sat back in his chair and clicked the end of his pen. "You can try to challenge Sammy's right to take the property. We can go to trial, show them that The Hideaway can be more than just a home for five—now four—people that doesn't do much for the town."

"Would it do any good?"

He shook his head. "I doubt it. It sounds like Sammy's nailed down all the loose ends. He's acting on the mayor's behalf, so it's legal for him to do it. His plan is to use the property for the good of the public, which always sounds good to a judge."

"Is making Sweet Bay a tourist destination a good thing for the public? Is that what the people want?" I couldn't imagine Sweet Bay becoming glitzy and high class any more than I could imagine Mr. Bains sprouting horns on his head.

He shrugged. "People in small towns like to talk about keeping things the way they've always been, but when you start talking about what the influx of money could mean—better schools and parks, a beefed-up police department, things like that—you'd be surprised how quickly some people can give up that idea of small-town charm.

"Now if you're up to it," he continued, "you could try to convince them that the work you're doing on the house could better the town in similar ways—attracting vacationers from around the South or what have you. That doesn't have quite the same punch as multiunit condos and high-end boutiques, but it's something, and it would appeal to the residents who will stand against anything Sammy tries to do just on principle alone. I must say, though, I was under the impression at the will reading that you were less than thrilled at being named the beneficiary of that place. I would think this might be a good thing for you—Sammy coming in and giving you a reason to let the house go."

"I wasn't thrilled at first, but . . . things are a little different now."

He nodded. "I can see that."

I closed my eyes and took a deep breath. Despite how I felt about the house now, was this a sign that Mags's death—and Sammy's timely plan for the area—was supposed to usher in the closing of The Hideaway?

"Could anything make Sammy change his mind?"

"It would have to be out of the goodness of his heart. And Sara— I'm not sure there's much good in there. I wish I had something different to tell you. I'd advise you to begin making your exit plans."

On the drive back to Sweet Bay, my phone buzzed in my purse. I pulled it out with one hand and saw Crawford's name. Blood pumped in my ears as I pressed End and dropped the phone on the passenger seat.

Don't push him away now, Sara.

But I didn't know what else to do. It felt like The Hideaway was slipping through my fingers, the path in front of me leading back to my real life.

At the house, so many trucks filled the driveway that I almost missed the motorcycle parked to the side under the oak. Two men with *Sears* stamped on the backs of their sweat-stained shirts struggled to fit the new stainless-steel refrigerator through the front doorway. They'd taken the door off the hinges, but it still wouldn't fit. I avoided the commotion and walked around the side of the house.

I found Allyn reclining in a wooden Adirondack chair on the dock, a drink in his hand, his black boots and socks in a pile next to him. He'd propped his pale, skinny feet up on the railing. Glory sat next to him, laughing.

Allyn turned when the boards on the dock squeaked under my feet.

"Remind me why you ever left this place. It's so relaxing. I think I might move in. If that's okay with you, of course," he said to Glory.

"Of course it is. You can stay as long as you like." She patted his hand.

I tried to smile, but my throat was tight.

"Oh dear," Glory said, noticing.

Allyn stood to get a better look at me, and I hugged him hard. "I'm so glad you're here," I whispered.

He took a step back, then tightened his arms around me. "Whoa, what's wrong with you?"

I let him go and wiped the corner of my eye. "Nothing, I'm fine. I'm just happy to see you. What are you doing here?"

"At the moment, Glory and I are getting acquainted. She told me a fascinating story about cutting Dolly Parton's hair back in Georgia."

Glory held her hands up. "I'll let you two kids talk. Let me know if you need anything, Allyn. I'll be right inside."

She walked back to the house and held the screen door so it wouldn't slam behind her. I turned back to Allyn. "I can't believe you. You've already got her eating out of your hand."

"It's the hairdressing bond. We're two of a kind." He sat back down in his chair and picked up his glass. "Tell me what's going on."

"You tell me what's going on. If you're here, who's manning my shop? You didn't just close up, did you?"

"I wouldn't do that to you. Don't worry, it's all taken care of. Rick was more than happy to hold the fort down until I get back tomorrow. Now, spill it. You're not a hugger, so something's up. Plus, you're about to cry and you don't do that either."

I sighed and sat down in Glory's chair.

"I just left the lawyer's office. It appears the VIPs of Sweet Bay feel that some fancy condominiums and a shiny new boardwalk would serve the people of Baldwin County better than The Hideaway. So much better that they actually want to take the land and the house from me."

"VIPs of Sweet Bay?" He shook his head. "Who are they and how can they make that kind of decision?"

"It's called eminent domain. The government—in this case, acting under the urging of a land developer—can take this property, no questions asked, and turn it into something else 'for the good of the public.'"

Allyn waved his hand around until I stopped talking. "Way over my head. I'll ask Jaxon about it."

"Jaxon? Who's that?"

"He's a new friend."

I raised an eyebrow.

"He's a lawyer. Very smart. Maybe he can help."

I pinched the bridge of my nose with my fingers. "Unfortunately, I think it's a slam dunk for the developer. Legally, he can do this, although ethically, it's pretty dirty. Plus, Mr. Bains has already looked into it. I don't need another lawyer. What I need is something to make this guy go away."

"He's actually taking the house from you? And what—tearing it down?"

I nodded.

"How long do you have before all this happens?"

"I don't know yet."

We sat in silence. Allyn handed me his glass of tea and I took a sip.

"Everything was going so well." I laughed, but it was only to keep the tears at bay. "The house is coming along and it's going to be gorgeous. The thought had even crossed my mind that I might be able to run this place as a B and B. I'd keep Bits and Pieces, obviously. And I couldn't move here—not fully anyway—but maybe I could do both. Crawford and I . . . well, like you said, Sweet Bay and New Orleans aren't that far apart."

I leaned back in the chair and tilted my face toward the sun. "So much has happened here, I just can't imagine it all ending now—and at the hands of Sammy, which makes it even worse."

I closed my eyes and forced my thoughts of William, the house, and all those pieces of furniture engraved with a skeleton key into a deep pocket in the back of my mind.

"It's probably a good thing this happened now," I said, willing my voice not to shake, "before I make any big changes in my life to accommodate this house. Sammy will raze it, throw up some atrocious condo building, and that'll be that. I'll head back to New Orleans and do what I'm supposed to be doing, and things will go on in Sweet Bay like they have been for years—except now it'll be filled with snowbirds and spring breakers."

Even with my eyes closed, I could feel Allyn staring at me. I sat up and took another sip of tea, forcing myself to look calm.

"What about Crawford?" he asked.

"He said we'd figure it out."

Allyn waited, but he dropped the subject when I didn't offer any more.

"It's beautiful here. A little . . . quaint"—he glanced around— "but I could sit on this dock all day. It's so quiet I think I can hear the fish breathing."

"That's just because the construction guys are wrapping up for the day."

"Construction guys?" He grinned. "Maybe you need to show me around."

After a ten-cent tour, during which Allyn was disappointed to discover that most of the workers had indeed left for the day, we ended up in the driveway next to his Harley. He handed me a helmet.

"I brought an extra in case I needed to rescue you."

"Rescue me from what?"

"Doesn't matter. You don't need to be rescued. You're doing just fine, and we'll figure out what to do about the house—and your man. I just need to do it over something stronger than sweet tea. Hop on."

With no energy to argue, I did as he asked. I directed him to the Outrigger Lounge, the only white-tablecloth place in Sweet Bay. The tablecloths were white vinyl, but in Sweet Bay, that counted. We sat at a table on the patio overlooking the bay. Allyn ordered white wine for both of us, along with fried pickles and a plate of Oysters Bienville.

"What?" he asked when I looked at him over the top of my menu. "If you're going to stay here, I need to make sure the food is up to par."

"Stay here? Did you not hear me tell you everything about Sammy?"

"I heard you. Tell me about Crawford."

"Crawford is wonderful. Almost too wonderful, considering."

"Considering what?"

"Even if I had considered staying in Sweet Bay—which I haven't—I might not even be able to. If the house falls through, I wouldn't have the option of staying."

"Of course you have the option. You're a big girl—you can do whatever you want. More than that, I'd say he gives you a pretty good reason to stay."

A reason to stay—was that what I was looking for?

"But what am I supposed to do—go buy a house? I have the shop and clients and the Broussards' house coming up. It's not like I could just forget all that and move to Sweet Bay."

"You're overthinking this. We don't know how it all will play out."

I dipped a fried pickle in ranch dressing, then dropped it and leaned back in my chair.

"What?" he asked.

"I haven't been back home that long, but Sweet Bay was starting to feel—I don't know what it was feeling like, just something differ-ent than it did when I was younger. I think I was starting to like it."

"Did you hear what you said? You just called Sweet Bay home."

"I did?"

Allyn nodded.

"Hmm. Maybe it's that it feels like life here could be different a second time around. But you know how much I love the shop. And you. And New Orleans."

"Of course I do. But you've opened the door to a whole other part of your life. The house, your memories of Mags, those crazy old people living in the house now. Crawford," he said, tilting his head. "This isn't small stuff. And it's okay to feel pulled in two dif-ferent directions."

"Sounds like my therapist just jumped in the conversation."

He waved the thought away. "That's why you pay me the big bucks. But you never finished telling me about Mags's things you found in the house."

I pieced everything together as best I could—Mags's privileged life and marriage to Robert, Robert leaving to be with another woman, and Mags moving to The Hideaway and meeting William.

"For reasons that made sense to him at the time, and I think due in part to Mags's parents, William left. He planned to come back for her, but it never happened. And he never knew she was pregnant."

"So little Mags had some secrets."

"Yes, but it's more than that," I said. "By the time she was my age, she was a widow and in love with a man she'd never see again. But despite all that, she was content. Or she seemed so. She loved her friends and her old house, gave the neighbors something to talk about, and never cared about how 'a woman of her age' should live her life. She was brave."

"Sounds like it," Allyn said.

"Maybe she worried I would have thought badly of her if I'd known all this."

"Would you have?"

"No, just the opposite. It would have shown me there was a reason for her oddness, that she was more than just the strange old lady I always thought."

"You think she was strange because of what happened with William? I don't get it."

"Not William, but Robert. And maybe even her parents too. From what I'm gathering, Mags was raised to be proper and lady-like, to always do the right thing, even to marry the right man. I'm thinking maybe she got to Sweet Bay and ditched all that. Maybe she went in the total opposite direction from what her parents and Robert represented."

I thought of her crazy hats and bright yellow ponchos that made me want to crawl under the nearest rock when I was a teenager. What if all that quirkiness had just been her way of pushing back against a lifestyle and culture that had crushed her dreams? "It all makes perfect sense now."

I flagged the waitress and ordered another glass of wine. The sun was setting. Long, thin clouds, now dark purple against the orange sky, draped across the sky like streamers.

"I drove by my old house last week," I said. "My parents' old house." We'd started on our entrées–blackened Gulf snapper for Allyn, grilled mahi wrap for me.

"How did that feel?" Allyn asked.

"Strange, I guess. I hadn't seen it in a really long time. Ten years, at least. It's white now—it used to be light blue. But my old wooden swing was still hanging from the oak in the front yard. Two kids were playing on it. My mom always hated that swing. I busted my forehead on it when I was little." I pointed to a spot above my right eyebrow. "Had to get four stitches right here."

Allyn smiled. "You've never told me much about your parents. Your mom. What was she like?"

I sat back and readjusted the clip in my hair. "She was kind. Soft-spoken. It was like she was put on earth to do exactly what she was doing—being my mom, Ed Jenkins's wife, owner of the side-of-the-road diner. And she was always good at accepting people and situations for who and what they were. Like with Mags. She had to have known her own mother led an unconventional life, but she took her for who she was without being bothered by any of it."

"Or maybe she was bothered and you just never knew. You were still young when she died, right?"

I nodded.

"Maybe she kept that part from you."

"Maybe." I remembered Mom's calm demeanor, her contentment with her life and everything around her. With me beating a trail out of Sweet Bay as soon as I could, maybe I was as unlike Mom as I was Mags.

"You're the same way, you know," Allyn said after a pause. "Or at least you were with me. I walked into your shop with green hair and a ring in my nose and you didn't even flinch."

I squinted an eye and held up my thumb and forefinger a centimeter apart. "Maybe just a little."

He laughed and nudged my chair with his foot. For a moment,

we ate in comfortable silence. From a table across the deck, laughter came in bursts. A flock of pelicans coasted overhead.

"You're not really going to leave, are you?" Allyn asked. We'd finished our meal and were waiting to pay our bill. I traced my finger along the top of my empty wineglass—my third, two more than I usually drank. "It seems like you have a lot of unfinished business here," he continued. "You've only just met William, you have a hot romance of your own to deal with, and you need to look further into this emergent domain thing."

"Eminent domain."

"Whatever. See if it's a done deal."

I sighed. "I told you, Mr. Bains has already figured it out. It would take a change of heart for Sammy to give up the property, and that's not going to happen."

"Maybe. It's just a shame to lose such a fabulous house. I wish we could relocate it to New Orleans. It could be our hideaway when we need to escape annoying customers."

It was an attempt to lighten the mood, but I didn't feel light. My head throbbed and I was exhausted. He looked across the table and saw it.

"Let's get you home." He pulled me to my feet.

At the house, Allyn dropped our helmets in the yellow room, the one he had picked out during our earlier tour of the house. The painters hadn't yet reached the bedrooms, so they still boasted those original lovely color schemes.

He helped me to the blue room, and I curled up on the bed

while he tugged off my shoes. Just before he turned the light off, my cell phone rang. He fished it out of my purse and looked at the screen.

"Crawford," he said.

"Not now. I'll call him in the morning."

He sighed. "Does he know about the house?"

I nodded, my eyes already closing. "I told him last night."

"You're going to involve him in all this, right? If this thing between the two of you is as meaningful as you say it is, you can't just ditch him and slip out of Sweet Bay. That would be the easy road, and you can't take the easy one this time."

"This time?" I opened my eyes. My brain was foggy, but his words cut through the muck.

"Something has changed in you since you've been here, and it's more than just Mags. I think Crawford is part of it. Don't cut him out yet."

"But what did you mean about 'this time'?"

He shook his head and stood up from the bed. "Look, you left Sweet Bay a long time ago when things were hard. Believe me, I'm glad you did, but you do have a tendency to skip out on the rough parts. It'll be messy if Sammy goes through with his plan and you have to figure out what to do with everything you've started here. But don't cut and run."

I pulled the sheets up tighter under my chin, fending off his words. It annoyed me to admit it, but he was right, as usual.

"One more thing," he said from the end of the bed. "You shut your heart down too much, which is infuriating, but when you do open up, all of us—me, Crawford, Glory, and her gang downstairs—we can't help but love you. You're magnetic in your own twisted little way, and I think you got that from Mags. These people attached themselves to her and her house, and all these years later, they're still here because they still love her. Listen to Mags—to who she really was—before you make any decisions about the house. And about your life."

He patted my feet under the blankets, then clicked the light off and closed the door behind him.

35

MAGS

We rented cabins at the state park in Gulf Shores after Hurricane Lorraine blew through. Lorraine didn't hit us dead-on; she rolled ashore in Biloxi—close enough to call for evacuation notices in our area (which we ignored, as usual) and to take down much of the electricity in Sweet Bay, but far enough away that the beaches were back to normal after a few weeks. We were all exhausted after the cleanup efforts in Sweet Bay, what with all the downed trees and closed businesses. When we got our heads above water, I suggested the vacation.

There were seven of us—Jenny and me; Dot and Bert; Major and Glory Gregg, who checked in for an extended stay not long after Robert died; and Eugene Norman, the potter-turned-glassblower. Starla, Gary, and Daisy had long since moved on. After a quick call to secure the cabins, we packed a few things and piled into the Greggs' orange van to drive the half hour it took to get to the sugar-white

659

sand of Gulf Shores. It was late August, the last weekend before Jenny started third grade.

Jenny and I sat in the back row of the van with Glory. Dot and Eugene sat in the row in front of us, with Bert and Major in charge of getting us to the beach in one piece. Jenny had just finished telling us a long story of how she and her friend from school, Doreen, had slipped an earthworm into the school bully's desk during recess. Jenny laughed out loud and looked back and forth at Glory and me until we laughed too. It was hard to be around Jenny and not feel lighter.

Glory took Jenny's soft face in her hands and smoothed her hair back. "Child, you are a beautiful creature, but I must say, you look nothing like your mother." Glory looked at me. "She must have her father's look. Was he as blond and fair as this?"

Dot turned sideways in her seat so she could make eye contact with me. She raised an eyebrow and waited for my answer.

"Mama? Was he?" Jenny asked.

The first time Jenny asked about her father, I couldn't have forced the right words out even if I'd wanted to—which I didn't, because she was too young. I gave her the same easy answer I gave everyone—that he died from a heart attack when Jenny was only three. I'd tell her the truth one day, when she could handle it. Or maybe when I could handle speaking of it.

What Glory said was true—my child looked nothing like me. She was the spitting image of her father. She had William's fair coloring, wheat-colored hair, and full eyelashes. She also had my daddy's tall forehead and Mother's strong nose. She deserved to know the truth about her father and her family, but not at the tender age of nine.

"He sure was, sugar." I patted Jenny's hand, my eyes turned out the window, looking at nothing in particular.

We arrived at the park to discover there had been a mix-up, and only one cabin was available for rent. Several had been damaged in the storm, and it seemed lots of other people had the same idea we did—it was the weekend before Labor Day, after all.

"It's a fine cabin," the woman at the front desk told me. "It's one of our larger units, so you won't feel too cramped." She eyed our ragtag group as if she didn't believe the words she was saying.

"Cramped? Seven people in a two-room cabin will be more than cramped."

"Major, don't make a scene," Eugene said. "We drove all the way here. We can't turn around and go home now."

"Home is thirty minutes away. We'd be back before *Columbo* starts."

Before Major and Eugene could continue arguing—or worse, compare the merits of *Columbo* with those of *Hawaii Five-O*, a favorite pastime at The Hideaway—I spoke up.

"Enough. We already live together, so what's the problem with sharing tighter quarters for a few days? We won't be in the cabin much anyway. Mark it down," I said to the clerk. "We're staying."

Once the decision was made, everyone got into the spirit of the vacation. Bert emptied the coolers of food supplies he'd brought for the weekend and set out ingredients for a feast, Glory retrieved her suitcase of board games and beach toys, and everyone relaxed enough to enjoy the last real weekend of summer.

At some point during our stay, I took a notebook and a plastic lounge chair to the edge of the shoreline. I nestled the chair down in the sand, pushed my toes under the thin layer of seashells, and started to write. A little later—fifteen minutes or an hour, I couldn't be sure—Dot appeared and sat in a chair next to me. Baby oil glistened on her shins and she smelled like a coconut. She'd bought her bathing suit—a perfect yellow polka-dot bikini—especially for this trip, and she'd hardly taken it off since we'd arrived. She felt good in it, and it showed.

"Does that have anything to do with Jenny?" she asked.

I looked at her. "It's a letter. How'd you know?"

"I knew that conversation in the van got to you. Then here you are writing away in your little notebook—I just put two and two together. When are you going to give it to her?"

I shrugged. "One day. When the time is right." I could feel her stare, but I kept my eyes on the water. "She's the best part of us. He would have loved her so much."

"You sure about that? Why hasn't he come back?"

"I don't know, but he must have a good reason." Dot didn't believe me—I could see the pity in her eyes despite the oversize sunglasses. I knew what she was going to say before she said it.

"What if he met—?"

I cut her off quick. "Don't say it. You didn't know him. You didn't know us."

"Okay, fair enough." She took a breath as if to speak but paused. "What if he's dead?"

"He can't be. I'd feel it."

Dot held her hands up in surrender. "I'm just trying to help you figure this out. You say the two of you were in love, but I still see a man who abandoned you for no good reason."

I sighed. "And I still say it wasn't totally his fault."

"Right, your parents and all that. Then where is he?"

Who knows? I shrugged again.

"Do you regret loving him?"

"No." My voice was firm. "The only thing I regret is that I never actually told him I loved him. I never said those words. If I had, maybe he would have stayed and fought for me."

That was the truest thing I'd said about William since he left, and the admission left me sore in my chest and a little angry.

"Regardless, it's been more than ten years." I slapped my notebook closed. "Whatever the reason, he hasn't come back and I have no way of knowing if or when he'll return. I have to make sure Jenny doesn't go through her whole life thinking her dad was a fine chap who just happened to die of a heart attack."

"Are you going to tell her about AnnaBelle?"

"No, there's no reason. Robert's actions don't affect her—he wasn't her dad, and at this point, she hardly remembers anything about him. Her real father was—is—kind and good. That's what she needs to know. He never would've wanted to do anything to hurt his family."

But he did. He hurt me.

I pushed that thought away, just out of arm's reach.

The water lapped farther and farther up our ankles each time it rolled in. To our left, a cluster of gray-and-white sandpipers nibbled at tiny clams as they burrowed into the soft, wet sand. The sun had inched down in the sky while I'd been writing, and only a few brightly colored umbrellas dotted the beach. Dot leaned her head back on the chair and stretched out her legs. She was long and lean and brown as a berry.

"So when are you going to let Bert get you pregnant?"

Dot let out a half laugh, half snort. "You don't beat around the bush, do you?"

"Sounds like someone else I know." I flicked a few grains of sand at her with my fingers. "Anyway, it's about time. You've been married a while, and we could use some more little ones running around the house again."

"What? And ruin my figure?" Dot wiggled her hips. Grains of sand stuck to the baby oil shimmering on her skin. I laughed and handed her a towel.

"What about you?" She brushed sand off her legs and re-positioned herself on the chair. "You could quit with those crazy hats and outfits and men would line up out the door for you. You know they would."

"Yes, those Sweet Bay men really ring my bell."

"It's a big world out there, that's all I'm saying."

"If there's more outside Sweet Bay, I don't need it. And I'm done with men. I gave it a go twice, and you see how far that got me. At thirty-three, I'm long past the age of letting myself get swept up by a man, no matter how handsome or charming he may be."

The words sounded believable—even to me—but I knew my heart. If William had walked onto that beach right then and there, I would have run to him and thrown my arms around him, no questions asked. I probably would have hit him too, but where my heart was concerned, it would always belong to him.

I leaned my head back on the chair. The sun, still strong even in the late afternoon, baked my legs. The searing heat felt good and cleansing. I gave in to the pull of sleep until the rising tide skimmed the backs of my legs. At the same time, Bert's voice drifted to us from farther up the beach.

"We're going to have to toss out life preservers if y'all don't move back," he called. Jenny trailed behind him, a sand bucket in one hand and a stringy clump of seaweed in the other.

"Come on back to the cabin," he said. "I have grilled shrimp and West Indies salad waiting on the deck."

He turned to Jenny and said something we couldn't hear, then the two of them took off, running back the other way. My sweet girl ran as fast as her legs would carry her, beating Bert to the cabin by a nose. She gave him a high five and climbed the steps to the cabin.

Lord, I love that girl. I tightened my grip on the letter in my hands, the letter that would one day tell Jenny everything she needed to know about her father—nothing more and nothing less.

36

SARA

JULY

I didn't roll over until ten the next morning. As soon as I did, the pounding started, reminding me why I always stopped with one drink. With the shop to run and clients to please, I didn't have time to sleep in and nurse hangovers.

My phone was on top of the blanket next to me. I took a deep breath and called Crawford.

"Are you okay?" he asked in place of a greeting.

"I'm fine. I'm sorry for not calling earlier. Allyn came to town, and . . ." It was a limp excuse, but it was all I had. I hadn't deciphered anything else going on in my head yet.

"I'm glad you got to see him. I'll back off now that I know you're okay. I was just worried."

"Thanks. What do you mean 'back off'?"

"Look, I know you've got a lot going on and you have decisions to make. I want to help you with this, but I understand if you need to do it alone."

Whether I did it alone or had help, deciding what to do would not be easy. The situation had already tied my stomach in knots.

"And this should go without saying," he continued, "but if you have second thoughts about us—about me—just be honest."

"No, I'm not . . ." But was I? Thoughts swirled through my head like a tornado, but I couldn't put my finger on which ones were about the house and which were about Crawford.

"Come on, Sara. It's the first time you haven't taken my calls. This big thing happens—Sammy and his news about the house—and all of a sudden you pull away."

He'd been nothing but caring and concerned about me, and here I was trying to avoid the hard part, just like Allyn said. What kind of person did that?

"I'm sorry. I'm not having second thoughts about you, or about us. I just feel like the rug was pulled out from under me. Before, everything felt so . . . possible. Now, I don't know. If I'm not here in Sweet Bay, how would we . . . ?"

He exhaled. "We'll figure it out, just like we said. Sammy may have pulled the rug out from under you, but I'm still here and I'm not going anywhere. And that will stay the same whether or not Sammy goes through with his plan. Okay?"

I couldn't speak over the lump in my throat, so I just nodded, even though he couldn't see me.

"Can I come see you?" he asked.

"Yes, please. I don't want to do this alone."

After we hung up I turned over to find a glass of water and two Tylenol on the nightstand. As I swallowed them down, the sound of laughter found its way up the stairs and into my room. Downstairs, Allyn was holding court in the kitchen while Dot,

Bert, Major, and Glory all drowned in laughter. Major laughed so hard he spilled his coffee. Allyn grabbed a dish towel and helped him clean up. Bert clapped him on the back. Not the sight I expected to see.

"Good morning," Dot said to me quietly when I entered. She put her arm around me and I patted her hand.

"Your friend fits right in. Mags would have loved him."

"You're right. She never would have let him leave. Can I talk to you for a minute?" I gestured into the adjacent dining room.

"Sure, hon."

We sat down at the table. In the middle was an arrangement of small vases. I reached over and ran my finger across the thin porcelain lip of a vase with tiny painted flowers.

"Mags loved having fresh flowers in the house." Dot picked up one of the vases and turned it over in her hand. "I found a box full of these in the mudroom the other day. I was going to add them to our Goodwill pile, but I thought better of it. These happy things deserve to be displayed." She wiped the dust off the vase with the hem of her shirt. "You wanted to talk to me about something?"

"Yes," I took a deep breath, then let it out slowly. "I have some bad news."

She waited, all the lightheartedness from the kitchen gone from her face.

"Sammy Grosvenor visited me a couple of days ago."

"Good grief, what does he want now?"

I didn't want to overwhelm her with details, so I just gave her a brief rundown of Sammy's plan.

"But I don't understand," she said. "He can't just swoop in and take the house, can he?"

I shrugged. "I've already talked to Mr. Bains, and it sounds like my options are slim."

Dot stared absently out the bay window, her chin propped in her hand. Her bottom lip trembled and I had to look away. Finally, she reached over and took my hand. "What are you going to do?"

"I don't know. I'm not sure there's much I can do. I keep asking myself what Mags would do if she were here. How would she deal with Sammy?"

Dot smiled. "Mags always knew just what to do in difficult situations. When it seemed there was no way out, she'd always find one little sliver of daylight and scratch herself out. But I'm not sure even Mags could get out of this one."

"All this work," I said, looking around. The room smelled like fresh paint and wood polish, and through the hall I could see a worker in the parlor coiling an extension cord around his arm. The renovations were turning The Hideaway into a pearl instead of a crusty shell.

"Well," Dot said. "If nothing can be done, this may force Bert and me to grow up after all." She chuckled. "It's probably time, any-way. We've been talking for ages about needing to make the move down to Florida where his kids are. I know Major and Glory have family back in Georgia. Maybe it's time for us all to move on." Her words were confident, but her eyes were sad. She patted my hand again, then rose and walked back to the kitchen. I followed her.

From the doorway, we watched the scene before us. Bert mimed Major struggling to reel in a fish, while Glory narrated for Allyn an episode that included Major falling in the water only to discover it was an alligator on the end of the line. No one had ever seen him swim so fast.

"Y'all go on and laugh," he said. "But let's see how fast you swim when a six-footer is snapping at your legs. Ah, there's Sara, thank the Lord. A diversion."

"Feeling okay?" Allyn asked with a grin.

"Fine. Thanks for the Tylenol."

"I'm glad you two had a chance to catch up last night," Glory said. "You must have missed him. He's a hoot."

"Come on." Allyn linked his arm through mine. "Help me pack up. I need to get back to New Orleans and run your shop."

I trudged back up the front porch steps after seeing Allyn off, but the approach of another vehicle stopped me before I made it to the top. I turned as Crawford's truck rumbled down the driveway toward me. Tension slipped off my shoulders like silk. He parked, crossed the gravel to the steps, and folded me into his arms. I pressed my cheek into the soft space under his ear and tightened my arms around him. When we pulled away, he smiled. "Better?"

I took a deep, cleansing breath. "Yes. Thanks for coming."

"I want to be here. We have work to do. I can make some phone calls and see if we can dig up anything that would make Sammy rethink his decision. There has to be something."

I nodded. Tears threatened to fall, so I turned away. Crawford tipped my face back toward him. "It's all going to be okay, whatever happens."

"It almost feels like everything would have been better if I hadn't come here. I fixed up the house and got everyone's hopes up for a great future for the house. Now I'm letting them down."

"You're not the one letting them down. It all would've happened the same way whether you were here or not. But by coming back, you got to know your grandmother—the real one. And you've reconnected with the folks here in the house who love you like you're their own granddaughter."

"But the house and all our work . . ."

"Don't give up on it yet. The Hideaway is a part of you," he said. "It's your past regardless of what Sammy tries to do. And who knows, it could even be a part of your future." I nodded and he took my hand. "Now, let's get to work."

37

SARA

JULY

We spent the rest of the morning and most of the afternoon on the back porch, my laptop practically burning a hole in the cushioned ottoman and both of our cell phones buzzing with activity. While Crawford called friends in town he thought might be able to pull some strings, I researched eminent domain, property laws, and anything else I could think of that might give us a loophole. I even called Mitch.

"This isn't really my thing," he said when I told him the situation. "I mean, if you go to trial with it, I'm your guy, but I'm not sure I'm the right person to talk to about saving an old house."

As he spoke, Crawford paced the back porch with his cell to his ear and a notebook in his hand, scrawling notes as he listened. He'd postponed a morning meeting and canceled plans to attend an important General Contractors Association meeting in Mobile. "You know what? Don't worry about it. I'm sure things here will be fine."

"Are you sure?" Mitch asked. "I can probably ask around at the office and see if anyone is willing to take it on."

"I'll take care of it."

Crawford looked at me when I tossed my cell into the chair next to me.

"Was that a friend?" he asked.

I shook my head. "Just someone I thought might be able to help. Dead end."

He leaned against the door frame and crossed his arms. "That's most of what I've gotten too. Don't worry though, I still have a few people I can talk to." He looked at his watch. "I'm so sorry, but I've got to run. Missing my morning meeting wasn't a big deal, but I can't put off Mrs. Webb. She'll eat my apologies for dinner."

I laughed. "You've done enough. Thank you."

I walked him out and returned to my seat on the porch. Although the sun glinted off every shiny surface like a spotlight, without Crawford there to keep the sadness at bay, it crept back in. He seemed buoyed by the possibility of finding just the right loophole to fend off Sammy, but I wasn't as confident. Sammy may have been harmless years before, but it was only because he'd been busy laying the groundwork for what was happening now. I was glad Mags wasn't around to see it.

⚷——⚜

That evening, I found Dot at the dining room table. Bert puttered around in the kitchen behind her, putting away pots and pans from dinner.

"I'm turning in, girls," he said when he stuck his head in the doorway. He crossed the room to kiss Dot on the cheek. "Don't stay up too late, dear. We don't have to work it all out tonight."

Bert walked into the hallway and disappeared up the stairs. I looked at Dot.

"It's nothing," she said. "We're just talking about our next steps." She squeezed my hand. "It's been a big couple of days for you. It's a lot to digest."

I sighed and shook my head. "I think I've hit my limit, for sure."

"You'll figure out what to do. You're Mags's granddaughter. You have spunk running deep in your veins."

I bet William had some of that too. Maybe it came from both of them, their DNA mixing and marrying, passing on down the line to me.

Dot closed the magazine she'd been flipping through and pushed her chair back from the table. She stopped on her way out of the dining room. "I almost forgot to tell you. Bob Crowe called today."

I shrugged. "Who?"

"Bob Crowe? The Roving Reporter? Honey, you have been gone too long. He breaks all the big stories. From the *Mobile Press-Register?*"

I shook my head.

"It's a big deal for him to call." She seemed disappointed that I didn't hold him in the high esteem he obviously deserved. "He said he wanted to talk to you about The Hideaway. I wrote his number down—it's by the coffeepot in the kitchen. Maybe he can help you with Sammy. That's what he does—he finds dirt on people that no one knew was there."

"I'm sure there's plenty of dirt on Sammy, but I don't see what a reporter can do to fix this mess."

"Just call him. See what he has to say."

In lieu of responding, I smiled, which satisfied her.

After she left, I picked up a few stray mugs from the dining room and carried them into the kitchen, the weight of the last couple days bearing down hard on my shoulders. I made my way toward the stairs but stopped when I saw light coming from the reading room in the back of the house. I walked to the doorway and peeked in.

Glory was asleep on the couch, her legs propped up on an ottoman. Her glasses had slipped down her nose, and she held a half-empty mug of tea that tipped precariously. I reached over and took the cup from her hand, careful not to wake her. I picked up the magazine lying facedown on the cushion next to her and saw the title: *Georgia Land and Real Estate*. She'd underlined several houses for sale and made notes in the margins. *Could make this work. Part-time job at the armory?*

Everyone in the house was scrambling. I thought of what Crawford said earlier, that The Hideaway was in me—it was my past, maybe even my future. Something clicked and the heaviness in my brain and body receded for a moment.

I grabbed Bob's phone number off the counter in the kitchen and took it upstairs with me. Before crawling into bed, I called and left a message at his office.

"Mr. Crowe, this is Sara Jenkins from The Hideaway. I'd like to talk."

38

SARA

AUGUST

I woke a few days later to the sound of excited voices and footsteps in the downstairs hallway. The house didn't usually have that kind of activity until at least midmorning when Bert would flip through recipes for the evening meal and Major would chide him for whatever choice he made.

I dressed quickly and headed for the noise, but the doorbell rang before I reached the first floor. As I crossed the foyer to the front door, I saw the newspaper lying on the console table. "A Sneaky Deal in Sweet Bay?" the headline blared. I smiled. Mr. Crowe must have done his job.

"I hope you don't mind that I spoke to that reporter," Mrs. Busbee said in a rush as soon as I pulled open the door. "I've got to get up to the diner, but I just had to talk to you first. When Mr. Crowe told me this place might be torn down because of Sammy, I couldn't help myself. Who does he think we are? The Sunset Strip?" She shook her head and glanced at her watch. "I'd hate to

THE HIDEAWAY

see anything along this stretch of the bay except The Hideaway. Please let me know if there's anything else I can do."

Neighbors came by and called throughout the morning, all of them offering their support. Mr. Crocker from the farm up the road shyly approached the house just as I was closing the door behind Norm Hammond, the town barber. Mr. Crocker said Mags had let him and his wife stay at The Hideaway for a long weekend soon after the birth of their fifth child.

"'We needed some time away from the demands of the farm, not to mention the kids, but we didn't have an extra dime in our pockets. The next thing we knew, your grandmother was on our doorstep telling us to pack our bags. She knew we'd had a tough year with the drought and adding an extra mouth to feed, and she wouldn't accept payment from us. Not in money, anyway. I left her fresh milk and eggs every morning for a mouth after that. I hat was forty years ago and I still haven't forgotten. Your grandmother was a gem and this house was a lifesaver."

Later, Mr. Grimmerson stopped by and told how after Hurricane Lorraine blew through in the seventies, Mags's home was one of the only places that didn't lose power—something about being on a separate power grid. "I had supplies in my store that people needed, but no one could drive anywhere downtown with so many trees down. Your grandmother rode her bicycle all the way to my store, helped me load supplies onto a wagon she pulled behind her bike, and then brought it all back to The Hideaway. This became my temporary outpost. She opened her doors to people who needed a place to stay or just needed batteries and flashlights. She was always helping people in the most unexpected ways."

During a lull in the action, Crawford pulled down the drive-way with sausage biscuits from the diner for everyone in the house. "I figured you'd be busy, being famous and all," he said to Dot and Glory as they helped him clear the dining room table of newspapers so he could set out the food.

"Famous isn't what we want to be," Glory said.

"Yeah, but 'not homeless' is," Major said. "So if it takes Mr. Crowe and the *Mobile Press-Register* drumming up support for the house, I'll take the fame. I'll be upstairs shaving if anyone needs me."

"No one's coming to take your picture, Major," Glory called as he left. She turned to us. "I'd better go talk some sense into him. He'll be down here in his Sunday best before long." She hurried up the stairs behind him.

With the room blessedly empty, Crawford pulled me to him. "I've missed you," he said into my neck, his lips tickling my skin. He put his hands on the sides of my face and kissed me.

"You're in a good mood for someone whose hard work may be about to meet the wrecking ball."

"Not gonna happen. I have a feeling for these things."

"Oh, you do?" I asked.

"Mm-hmm. I also have a feeling we need to get out of here soon. I love your roommates, but—"

Bert rounded the corner from the hall, his gaze down on yes-terday's mail, and walked right into us. "Don't mind me," he said, disentangling himself. "I'll be out of your hair in a jiff."

"See what I mean?" Crawford whispered.

He kissed me again, soft and quick, then called out to Bert. "I brought enough food to feed an army, Bert. No need to run off." He handed me a cup of coffee, but before I could take a sip, the doorbell rang again. "No rest for the wanted," he said. "Better see who it is."

—⚷—

I was just starting back up the front steps after chatting with a man from the Baldwin County Preservation Society when I heard a rustling in the azalea bushes at the side of the house. Clark Arrington pushed his way through, carrying a pair of loppers in his hand.

"Oh, hey," he said when he saw me. "I always tried to keep these bushes from growing too tall for Mrs. Van Buren. I just figured I'd keep cutting them back until someone tells me to stop. But if you'd rather me not . . ."

"No, it's okay." Before, I probably would have told him we could take care of the bushes ourselves, but in light of everything that had happened, I appreciated Clark's desire to continue this trivial means of keeping The Hideaway in shape.

"I'm sorry about what's happening to this old place," he said, his hands busy in the bushes along the edge of the porch. "Sammy's been talking about it for a while, but I didn't think he'd actually go through with it."

So this was what Clark had been dropping hints about on the dock. And I'd just thought he was being a nuisance.

"Thanks," I said.

"Yeah, I've been doing some work for him here and there over the last year or so. He wanted me to help him on this deal, but I just couldn't do it. Not if it meant tearing down your grandmother's house. I kind of liked the old bird."

I laughed. "I'm glad to hear it, Clark. I wasn't sure, to be honest."

"She was nice to me. She used to pay me in vegetables for my work around the yard. And if they ever had any leftover pie, she'd bring a slice across the street and leave it on the steps leading up to my apartment. She always covered it in plastic wrap to keep the ants away."

Clark bent down to pick up the branches he'd cut, then without saying good-bye, retreated through the space in the azalea bushes.

By lunchtime, a banner had been erected at the end of the driveway facing Highway 55. "Sweet Bay Supports The Hideaway!" it said. Several smaller, homemade signs dotted the grass: "Protect Our Town!" "Go Away, Sammy!" and "Save Sweet Bay!"

The flood of neighbors and well-wishers slowed in the afternoon. I sank down in a chair at the dining table next to Bert, who was folding dish towels. "I can't even wrap my brain around what's happened today," I said.

"It's been a big day," Bert agreed. "I think it's been successful though. Maybe Sammy will pull the plug on the whole deal."

"Sammy won't do it, but if the mayor fears he's angered too many people, maybe he'll back off." I reached over and grabbed a towel to fold. "I never thought people in Sweet Bay cared anything about this place or even liked Mags that much. So many people made fun of her. I can't believe they're stepping up now and giving us—giving her—support."

"You don't have it quite right," Major said from the kitchen. He walked into the dining room. "If you hadn't been stuck inside that teenage head of yours all those years ago, you might have figured that out."

I opened my mouth, but he continued. "I'll be the first to say Mags was a little odd—she wore strange clothes, never picked up a mop for as long as I knew her, and she had a strange affinity for sitting in the garden late at night—but she left her mark on Sweet Bay, and people won't soon forget that. Take me and Glory. We arrived here in south Alabama at the height of the sixties—two black faces in a whole town of white. She didn't bat an eye about opening her doors to us. Not only that, she talked us out of leaving when we thought we'd overstayed our welcome. She was a strong woman a step ahead of the times.

"Sure, some people made fun of her—small-minded people will do that. And kids—kids laugh at anything different from them. But most of the adults in town knew she was a necessary part of life here in Sweet Bay. A necessary part of our lives, for sure."

"Major's right," Bert said. "And like Mrs. Busbee said in that article, Mags was the town matriarch and she took care of people. She never seemed to have extra money to put into the house, but money would show up when someone needed help. I stopped trying to figure her out a long time ago. She is who she is—or was—and we loved her for that. End of story."

That was just it though—they had all known there was more to Mags than she let on, and the townspeople respected her for her help in times of need. I, on the other hand, took her for exactly who she was on the surface, never bothering to consider that a full, rich life had been waiting just underneath. I realized I loved her life, her spirit. I loved who she had been all along.

39

MAGS

1976

I wasn't normally a churchgoing woman. Back in Mobile, we attended the Episcopal church, although I always got a feeling it was more because of the beauty of both the stained glass and the congregation. The Methodist church right down the street would have been fine, but it didn't have glass brought in from Europe and couldn't claim the mayor of Mobile and the head of Bay Imports as members.

Dot and Bert had been going to Baldwin Baptist since they moved in, and they asked me to accompany them every Sunday. And every Sunday I declined. The house was quiet on Sunday mornings, and I usually spent those hours on the dock or in my garden. Why mess up a perfectly good morning with fire and brimstone and a healthy heap of guilt to go on top?

"You should try it just once," Dot said to me one Saturday evening as I tiptoed through my garden picking bell peppers. "What can it hurt? It might even help."

"What makes you think I need any help?"

"Just think about it," Dot said. "No one's going to make you walk the aisle if you don't want to, and it may make you feel better to let go of—well, anything you may be holding on to."

Dot was many things, but subtle wasn't one of them. "Why do you think I need to feel any better than I do right now? I'm fine."

Dot moved closer to me, sidestepping a tall pepper plant. "I've been here for sixteen years. That's sixteen years of watching you walk around with a weight on your shoulders that you never talk about and pretend isn't there. And watching you love someone who is never coming back."

I drew in a quick breath and stepped back.

"Don't get mad, just listen to me for a minute. You are a strong woman in every area except one—William. You've told me a thousand times that you're over him, but it's just not true. I know he came in here and set your world on fire, but it was a long time ago, and life goes on. After all these years of being your best friend, I think I've earned the right to say this: You need to let him go."

So much for trying to look strong.

I wasn't ready to give up, but would it free me if I did? I wasn't sure if I even wanted to be free. What if, miracle of miracles, he did come back one day? If I'd already shut my heart off and let him go, I might not be able to kick it into gear again.

I put my arm around Dot. "I'll think about it."

Surprise crossed her face. "I thought you'd slap me for sure."

"Have I ever done anything to make you think I'm a violent person?"

She smiled. "Maybe not, but after Robert left, I told Bert to hide the oyster knife just in case he ever came back."

Not long after that conversation, I gave in.

"I won't even ask what changed your mind. Just be ready at eleven," Dot said. "And try to wear something normal."

I didn't tell her, but what made me change my mind was a simple question from Jenny that literally stopped me in my tracks. She and I had taken a stroll before dinner, and after chatting about her biology homework and the roses growing outside Grant's Hardware, Jenny took a deep breath. I knew something was on her mind, but I also knew just enough about teenagers to know if I came out and asked her what was wrong, she'd never tell me.

"Mama, how did it feel when you and Dad fell in love?"

I was so unprepared for that question, I stopped putting one foot in front of the other.

She turned. "What are you doing? We're in the middle of the street."

I followed her to the sidewalk, trying to come up with an answer.

"I know you don't like to talk about him," she continued. "I just—Mabel told me Mark Kupek is in love with me. She asked me if I'm in love with him, but how am I supposed to know? What did it feel like with you and Dad?"

Which one? The man she thought was her dad or the real one? I still hadn't given Jenny the letter I'd written on the beach in Gulf Shores, even though she was now approaching high school. Every time I gathered the courage to pull the letter out of its hiding place and take it to her, I lost the nerve. She'd be rocking on the back porch with a paperback in her hands, or laughing with friends on the end of the dock, or playing checkers with Bert. She was content with her life and the family she had at The Hideaway, and I couldn't bring myself to shatter the peace.

Her question about love made me realize I'd put myself—and her—into a bind by not laying out the truth and letting her decide how to feel. Instead, I'd chosen the lens through which she'd view her family. But my daughter had asked me about love, and the only true love I knew was William, so I told her the truth.

"It was electric, like a thousand butterflies in my chest or a thousand balloons flying free. Sometimes being apart was even better than being with him, because I could anticipate seeing him. When we'd finally see each other again, the air between us would crackle and snap, and I couldn't cross the room fast enough to be next to him."

It had been a long while since I'd thought of those first weeks with William. Was that all love was? Electricity, excitement, and anticipation? No, not all.

"That's how it felt, but love is a choice you make in your head too. I knew I was in love with your father because I couldn't imagine my future without him, I didn't want to imagine it. He became such a part of me that I knew if he wasn't there, I'd lose a part of myself too."

"Did you? Lose a part of yourself?"

"A small part," I said. "But I had you, and you opened my heart up in ways I never expected. You, my dear, were a balm for that wound. So were our house and our friends. I have a lot of good things in my life. But I still haven't forgotten him."

We walked in silence a few moments before she spoke. "I'm

definitely not in love with him." She might as well have said, "I'd rather not have chicken for dinner tonight." My Jenny, so uncomplicated.

"Who is Mark Kupek?" I asked.

"Just a boy," she answered.

I laughed and put my arm around her thin shoulders. *My sweet girl.* "That's how it is—they're always 'just a boy,' until they're not."

The church service was much like I expected it to be—lots of flowered hats, big smiles, hand-clapping hymns, and a good old fiery sermon peppered with "Mm-hmm" and "Preach it" from the congregation.

But something happened during the prayer time. After lifting up every injury and ailment in the congregation and the tribulations of every possible extended family member, the preacher stopped and called for a time of silent prayer. His voice lost its showman's edge and grew raspy and honest.

"I'm sensing there are folks here who need one-on-one time with God. No sweaty preacher up here spouting off about everything they should be thinking or feeling—just you and God. If that's you, I encourage you to close your eyes right now and listen." The organist started up with a melancholy tune that drew congregants to the front altar like a magnet. My butt stayed planted on the pew. "If you hear God's still, small voice, don't worry about me or anyone sitting around you. I just ask you to listen to what He might have to say to you this morning."

The church was quiet except for the organ. I closed my eyes

and tried to listen for that voice. Since the day Jenny asked me about falling in love with William, I'd been more aware than usual of his shadow trailing me. He'd been gone for years, yet he was still a very real presence in my life. Dot let me know in no uncertain terms that the weight I'd thought I'd hidden well still sat on my shoulders in full view of everyone around me.

I wasn't always on the best terms with God, but I was thankful He had given me William at all. If William hadn't been living at The Hideaway when I moved in, there was no chance I'd still be there now. I would have stayed a few nights, felt the heavy weight of that fancy ring on my finger, and probably gone right back to Mobile and to Robert, continuing to scratch out an existence in the thing we called a marriage.

But William had been there. And my life was profoundly different because of him and my time at The Hideaway. I was thankful, but Dot was right. I was no longer the twenty-two-year-old I was when I met him. I was almost forty and my right to be a lovestruck girl had passed its expiration date. He was not coming back.

With my eyes squeezed shut and that organ droning on, I pulled my shoulders back and lifted my chin. *God, I know we haven't talked in a while, but–*

The preacher clapped his hands. "Thank You, Lord, for that time of prayer and silence. Can I get an amen? Mrs. Betty Jo, how about 'Onward, Christian Soldiers.'"

Betty Jo fired up the organ again. Mouths opened in song and hands lifted in praise, the time of prayer finished.

Fine then. I looked up at the rafters and winked. *I wasn't ready to let go anyway.*

40

MAGS

1980

My Jenny found love at eighteen—too young in my eyes, but I quickly realized I had no need to worry. Ed Jenkins was no Robert Van Buren. Ed doted on Jenny, but he also pushed her to challenge herself. At his urging, she enrolled in a culinary program at the community college. She was always helping Bert in the kitchen, but I'd never thought of culinary school. Ed took a bite of her seafood gumbo one night and said, "You need to open a restaurant, Jenny."

The idea for Jenny's Diner grew out of that early evening dinner, consumed on the dock at sunset surrounded by our friends. Once darkness overtook the sun, lightning bugs popped out in the shrubs and trees. From the dock, they made the place look alive.

Jenny and Ed married less than a year later, and little Sara Margaret arrived ten months after that. Sara had the good fortune of loving, attentive parents and a multitude of "grandparents" who doted on her day and night. As Jenny's Diner grew in popularity, our job as stand-in parents grew in importance. Bert learned how to operate an Easy-Bake Oven, I became proficient in the rules of Go Fish, and Glory's knitting needles became fairy wands in Sara's little hands. Back then, Sara thought The Hideaway was a magical palace, and I never corrected her because, in a way, it was.

Sara looked a little like Ed, but a lot like me. She had my skin coloring and dark, rebellious curls. That hair flew behind her as she ran from room to room through the house. She'd flee from anything resembling a brush or hair band, so her hair grew long and wild, especially during the summers when she was out of school and spent most of her time at our house. I sometimes tried to imagine what Sara would look like as a young woman or as an adult, but I couldn't see anything other than the carefree child before me.

I got to where I couldn't allow myself to imagine William coming back for me, or even Jenny, especially once she became a woman with her own family, her own roots. For some reason, it was easier to think of him coming for his granddaughter. Occasionally I'd allow myself the luxury of imagining Sara and William together. I'd give myself over to an afternoon's worth of a daydream about the two of them finding each other later in life and knowing immediately that something connected them—something potent and essential. They'd be drawn to each other, and they'd trust it, even if they didn't know why.

Jenny's death on the rain-slick highway shattered me. It was unspeakable. Not only had I lost my daughter, but I'd lost the last tie I had to William. I'd loved my daughter for the person she was, and she knew that, but I'd also loved William through my love for her. When Jenny was gone, it felt like he was finally gone too.

But the real truth was William was gone the minute he made the decision to leave The Hideaway all those years ago. I should have accepted that fact much earlier, but it was easier to hang on. After all, I hadn't decided what exactly I was going to tell him in his workshop that day. I wasn't going to ask him to leave—I don't think I was, anyway. I suppose I thought we'd figure it out together, like he'd said about so many things. I may have made the choice by not outright refusing my father all those years ago, but William took the decision out of my hands by leaving on his own. I don't know how he knew Robert was back in the picture, but I suppose he did what he thought was honorable.

All I had left of him were the few things he made for me during our short time together—the pieces of furniture, the bench in the garden, the tiny replica of the house—the one that should have been ours, built into a quiet cove on the bay, undiscovered by anyone but us. But life doesn't always work out the way it's supposed to, does it?

41

⊷❦⊶

SARA

I called William at the number he gave me, and we made plans to see each other the next day. He said he'd make a day of it and visit some friends from his days at The Hideaway, Gary and Starla.

"Starla?" I asked.

"She gave herself that name back when she wore all black and smoked twenty cigarettes a day. It's a miracle she's still alive. I think her real name is Betty."

When he arrived in town, I directed him to The Outrigger for lunch, where we found a table on the deck overlooking the water. I wanted to tell him about the possible fate of the house—not to mention our family connection—but I was nervous about his reaction to both. To stall, I told him about leaving Sweet Bay, landing in New Orleans, and opening Bits and Pieces.

"But couldn't you have opened your shop here? I've dreamed about Sweet Bay since I left fifty-some years ago. It's a special place, you know. And the house—it has a pull."

691

"I get it now," I said. "I think my time away finally showed me that. But after living with Mags for a decade, I guess I needed a break. Back then, she was a little odd."

"What do you mean, odd? Maggie was many things, but I wouldn't describe her as odd."

"I think it happened after you left. I understand more now, but as a clueless teenager, I just wanted out. And in coming back, I'm finding pieces of her life that I never knew existed."

He smiled, but it was halfhearted. "If it took her passing on for you to come back to your home and understand more of who she was—and who you are . . . well, maybe something good can come from something so sad."

I shrugged. "Maybe so."

Bubble gum snapped as someone approached behind us. "Y'all ready to order something?" the waitress asked without looking at us. I recognized her as the same waitress from my dinner here with Allyn.

William glanced over the menu and ordered a fish sandwich. I chose the grilled shrimp salad, and we both ordered sweet tea.

"You sure you don't want a glass of wine? Or three?" the waitress asked. I looked up at her and she winked.

"No, thanks. I'm fine."

"I'll have that out to you in a few." She snapped her gum as she wrote our orders on her little notebook and walked away.

I took a deep breath. "I left something out the last time we talked. I wasn't ready to tell you then, but I don't think I can keep it in any longer."

"Then you'd better tell me."

"That little girl you saw the day you came back to The

Hideaway?" William nodded and I swallowed hard. "You're right that she was my mother. But she was not Robert's daughter."

William's brow creased between his eyes.

"Mags and Robert never shared a bedroom once he moved in," I said, making my point clear.

"Then who . . . ?" He turned his eyes to the water and clenched his jaw. "She . . . that little girl wasn't mine, was she?"

I nodded.

His mouth opened and closed, then he shook his head as if shaking away a dream. "Are you sure?"

"Yes."

"In those last couple weeks before I left, something about Maggie was different." William dragged his hand across his face. "She looked and sounded the same, but she *felt* different to me. I even wondered . . ." He shook his head again. "So all this time . . . and that day, behind the house wasn't . . ." He exhaled, blowing the air out with force.

I looked away. Whatever his feelings were, they were private. When I glanced back at him, his head was down and he'd put his hand over his eyes. Finally, he sniffed and pulled a handkerchief out of his pocket.

I'm sorry," he said. "This is such a surprise. Where is she now? My—the little girl?"

I hated to deliver another blow. "Her name was Jenny. She and my father died in a car wreck almost twenty years ago."

William took his cap off and held it in his hands, pulling at the edges with his fingers. This man had lived most of his life under a wrong presumption, and I'd just thrown open the shutters, letting in the light of truth. Should I have kept my mouth closed?

He turned back to me. "Up until I met Maggie, I'd lived much of my life without a family. My parents died young, like yours did. When I met her, I thought that would all change, that I'd finally be a part of something bigger than myself, but it wasn't to be." He shrugged. "Not then anyway." He pulled the corner of his mouth up in a small smile as he wiped his eyes again. "This must be strange for you too. But I'm glad you're here—does that make sense?"

"It does. I understand."

The waitress brought our food and we ate mostly in silence. I began to dread the silent car ride back to the house, but then William began to talk about his life after he left Sweet Bay.

Despite the failed marriages, his life had been mostly good. When he left The Hideaway, he moved around for a while, finding odd jobs to support himself while he worked on his furniture.

"I was constantly on the road in my old truck, the bed filled up with planks and boards I pulled out of abandoned houses. I was always covered in sawdust. Still am, really." He looked down at his hands and dusted them off on his pant leg, even though they were clean.

He found a few shops that agreed to carry his pieces, and business took off. After coming back and seeing Mags and Robert together, he settled in Still Pond, a small farming community an hour north of Mobile, and had been there ever since.

"It's a nice town. I've had friends over the years, I have a church, people who look in on me. Most of the town eats at a dining table or sits on a bench I made for them or their parents or even grandparents. I know most everyone there. It's been a good life," he said, nodding. "Lonely at times, but a solid life."

"Sounds a lot like mine."

"You mean you don't have a fellow down in New Orleans waiting on you?"

I shook my head. "Not in New Orleans."

"Here?"

"For now, I suppose."

"I don't have much recent experience dealing with young people's relationships, but I can listen. If you want."

I wasn't in the habit of talking much about my relationships.
Allyn knew most of what was going on with me at any given time,
but it had taken me a while to feel comfortable sharing my life with
him. For some reason, I felt okay telling William about Crawford.

Talking about Crawford naturally led to talk of the house and
how beautiful it was becoming. I rounded it out by giving him the
blow-by-blow of Sammy's plan.

"Sammy Grosvenor. The name rings a bell, but . . ." He shook
his head. "Can he do it? Can he take the house?"

"I wish there was a way out, but Mags's lawyer has gone over
it and checked with the mayor's office. Sammy has had his eye on
the property for a long time, so once he convinced the mayor the
time was right, he jumped on it."

William sighed. "All in the name of progress, I suppose."

I nodded.

"So much life in that old house," he said.

"Sammy used to come around The Hideaway every once in
a while. He'd tell Mags he could set her up nicely for the rest of
her days if she'd only sell. Every time, she'd practically chase him
off the porch. I don't think Sammy ever understood what kind of
woman Mags was."

William chuckled. "So she wasn't interested in passing her time with shuffleboard and sudoku?"

"Not quite. The only time I ever saw her sit down and relax was when she went to the garden at night to sit on your bench. Otherwise, she spent her time working on something—the boat motor, her vegetables, replacing a missing board on the dock."

"Sounds a lot like me," William said. "Keeping busy—making things with my hands—is the only way I know to live. It's the only way for me to keep Maggie with me. Well, that and the keys."

"The engravings," I said slowly. "You made those."

He nodded. "It's my trademark. I've carved that key into everything I've made since I met her. But it's more than my mark, it's my inspiration—or more accurately, she's my inspiration. She held the key to my heart back then, as well as now. As much as it meant to me though, I didn't think she'd ever thought about it again. Seeing it carved into the marble on her headstone . . . Well, I wasn't sure what to do with that. I guess that's why I finally made myself come back and ask some questions. I sure am glad I found you."

"I am too."

We were both quiet a moment.

"Can I ask you a question?" I said.

"Of course."

"Why do you call her Maggie?"

He smiled. "It seemed like she was making a fresh start in her life, so I gave her a new name to go with it. And you call her Mags?"

I nodded. "I guess somewhere along the way it was shortened."

He sat back in his chair and crossed his hands over his middle. "So Sammy is taking the house."

I looked out at the water but kept an eye on William.

"Memory is a powerful thing," he said. "My memories of Maggie have kept me going all these years even though I hadn't seen the house, much less her, in decades. But the house isn't the keeper of memories for me. Mine are up here." He tapped his forehead. "You're different though. Losing the house will be a bigger blow for you, I imagine."

A year ago—six months ago even—losing the house probably wouldn't have even registered on my radar. But now? Everything about this new, unexpected chapter of my life was tied to the house in some way. Losing it felt like losing a part of my body I'd just learned how to use.

After lunch, William drove me home. We made no immediate plans to see each other again, but I wasn't worried. We had a lifetime of absence to make up for. I hugged him before I left his car, and he patted my cheek.

That night, long after Dot and the others had gone to bed, I walked through the house, dark except for the light in the kitchen. In the downstairs hallway, I paused in front of Mags's bedroom door. Dot and Glory had done a little cleaning out, taking bags of odds and ends to Goodwill and Sweet Bay United Methodist for their annual rummage sale. They told me they were leaving Mags's clothes and personal belongings for me to go through.

I turned the knob and the door creaked open. I'd requested that Mags's room be the last one to undergo renovation, so everything looked as it always had—single bed pushed up against one wall, a dresser along the opposite wall, chair and ottoman in one corner.

Her vanity sat under the window that overlooked the backyard and the bay. I turned on a lamp and sat on the small stool in front of the mirror. A pot of Pond's cold cream sat on top next to a tube of Jergens lotion, a couple prescription bottles, and an old, silver-handled hairbrush. I twisted the top off the Pond's and inhaled. It was Mags's scent. Granted, the scent was usually mixed with something else—dirt, brackish water, motor oil—but the Pond's was always underneath.

The top drawer of the vanity held a variety of hairpins, travel-size shampoo bottles, a box of needles, and small spools of thread. In the middle of all these trivial items, a pearl necklace gleamed in the lamplight. I smiled. Most people would have wrapped something like this in tissue and protected it in a jewelry box, but not Mags. She just dropped it in with everything else.

The bottom drawer appeared to be empty, but when I pushed it closed, I heard something inside skid across the wood. I pulled the drawer back open and leaned down to peer in. Way at the back was an envelope. I reached in and pulled it out. My mother's name was written on the front. I turned the envelope over—it was still sealed, never opened.

I moved my fingers over the envelope and felt a folded piece of paper inside. It wasn't for me, but it had been for my mom, and for some reason, she'd never read it. *Should I?*

I slid my finger under the flap and opened the letter.

My dear Jenny,

As I write this, you are a lovable nine-year-old running around the beach with salty air in your face. The thought of telling you what I'm about to share on paper is unfathomable—that's why I plan to give this to you when you're much older. Hopefully by then you'll be able to better understand the complexity of the human heart and how it can clutch both hope and pain in the same tight fist.

Up until now, you've been told that your father, Robert, died of a heart attack years ago when you were a toddler. It is true that a man named Robert Van Buren died when you were three, and of a heart attack, but this man was not your father . . .

When I finished the letter, I ran my fingers across my mom's name on the front of the envelope. Then I wiped my cheeks and replaced the letter inside. It was late, and I was tired, but instead of going upstairs, I lay down on Mags's bed. I slid the envelope under the pillow and closed my eyes.

42

SARA

AUGUST

Despite the signs and pleas from Sweet Bay, Sammy and Mayor McClain did not relent. The mayor sent a firm but apologetic note explaining that we would be compensated for the value of the house, which none of us cared about. Sammy showed up on the doorstep two days later with a court order in his hands.

"You have thirty days to vacate the premises. You don't want to be here after that."

He backed down the steps and walked to his car, but he stopped before he opened the door. "Miss Jenkins, this doesn't have to be all that bad. You'll get on back to New Orleans and go about your business. I'll set things in motion here and move on to my next acquisition." He opened his car door and sat down. "Life goes on."

Later that evening, hours after Sammy had dropped off his court order like an unwanted fruitcake, the five of us sat in the living room together.

"I'm proud of you," Dot said. "You turned this house into

something magnificent, which is exactly what Mags wanted. You should be proud of yourself too."

"What are you going to do?" I held a mug of Lady Grey tea, but it had long grown cold.

"We're moving down to Florida," she said. "We should have done it years ago. If you'd told me when I first moved in here that I'd outlive Mags and still be here at this age, I'd have told you to go jump in the bay. This place gave us a wonderful life, but everyone has to join the real world sometime . . ." She paused and shook the ice cubes in the bottom of her glass. "I suppose our time has come. Almost fifty years later."

"Just like that?" I asked. "It's such a quick change."

Dot looked at Bert and he nodded. "It's not so quick," she said. "We've talked about it off and on for years, but just never put the plan in motion. But it's time now. And we're okay with it. Don't worry about us." I thought I heard a wobble in her voice, but her face remained calm, almost cheerful.

"What about you?" I searched Glory's face for any indication of panic or sadness. If I'd seen even a hint, I'd have crumbled.

"Major and I have had our eye on some property back in Georgia for a while. It's still on the market, so I think we'll put up a nice little house and dig in roots. We may even try our hand at farming."

"Farming?" Major laughed. "A trendy chicken coop is not a farm, my dear."

"We'll start there and see what happens." Glory winked in my direction.

"Your turn," Dot said. "What's next for you? For a little while, we thought you might stick around here." She glanced at Bert. "We weren't sure at first, but it seemed like you and Crawford . . ."

"What she's trying to say is it was nice to see some young love under the roof again," Bert said. "And he seems like a gentleman. Knows how to treat a lady. That goes far in my book."

"I'm sure she can rest easy knowing she has your approval," Dot said. "Crawford put a lot of work into this house. He must be devastated that it's all going to be for naught. How is he handling everything?"

My mind went back to something he'd said in the dining room the day the newspaper article came out. We'd finished breakfast and he was about to leave.

"Most of the houses I work on are just jobs to me," he'd said. "Occasionally I get asked to work on some great old house and it becomes more important, but when I finish the job, I move on to the next one without a hitch. This one was different from the start."

"That's probably because you had your eye on the owner before you even saw the house," I said.

"I got lucky. I heard she almost went with Earl and his overalls." He smiled. "The thing is, I've come to love the house too. When I first saw it, I loved that you weren't taking the easy road and unloading it as quickly as possible, which probably would have put it right into the hands of someone like Sammy. Yet here we are staring demolition in the face." He ran his hand through his hair, leaving it sticking up in tufts, and leaned toward me, his elbows on his knees. "Regardless of the house, you come first. I can find another old house to fix up, but I don't want to lose you."

Dot looked at me, still waiting for an answer. Crawford was so kind and good. He'd probably never left anyone in the dust, as I had with Mags. He wouldn't know how to do that. I shook my head and answered the question she hadn't asked. "I don't know what's going to happen."

In the last weeks, I spent as much time as I could soaking up the essence of the house and Mags—I walked down the long, curved driveway, watched the sunset from the dock, rocked on the porch, and sat in Mags's bedroom. I wanted to pack up the memories and take them with me, even if only in my mind.

My last night in the house, I found myself in the garden at dusk. Cicadas serenaded me from their hidden places as I sat on Mags's bench, my fingers automatically finding the skeleton key on the underside. A light breeze blew in from the south, the sky darkened to a range of purples and pinks, and I let my tears fall without holding them back.

I stayed in the garden long after darkness fell, covering everything like a warm, thick blanket. Sometime later, the screen door creaked open. "Sara, honey?" Dot asked. "You okay out there?"

I pulled myself up off the bench and took one last look around. In the dark, everything was a little out of focus. I saw myself as a child, scrambling through the garden, trying to snatch up as many strawberries as I could before Mags came around with her basket. Then as a teenager, sitting next to Mags on the bench, not understanding why she came out here every night in the dark to do nothing but think. Then me at eighteen, packing my suitcases and pulling away from The Hideaway, leaving a smiling, waving Mags behind.

It seemed everywhere I looked—every surface I touched, every sound I heard—reminded me of how I'd misunderstood perhaps the bravest woman I'd ever known. With my mind and heart full to overflowing, I turned and left the garden.

The next morning, I stood in the driveway packing and repacking the trunk of my car. It all fit fine, but I kept rearranging items so I wouldn't have to look Crawford in the face. Everything William had made, and as many other pieces as we could haul, sat in a storage facility in Fairhope. The box containing Mags's most precious items sat up front on the passenger seat.

Finally, Crawford put his hand on my arm. "I think it's fine." His voice cut through the quiet.

Thunder rumbled in the distance, but the sun shone brightly. I exhaled and leaned my forehead on his chest. He wrapped his arms around my back and his hands went to my hair, lifting the curls off my neck. I raised my face toward him and he pressed his palms to my cheeks.

"I'll miss you," he said.

I nodded, not trusting my voice to speak.

"I'm going to give you some time to get back in the swing of things at work. Pull Allyn back in line, get your shop in order, whatever you need to do. I'm not going to bother you, but if you decide you want me there, I'll hop in the truck that minute. I mean it. I'll even bring Popcorn if you want."

"I don't need Popcorn." I leaned my cheek on his chest. "Besides, who would take care of Charlie while you're gone?"

"Good point."

We were both quiet, then he cleared his throat. "I could say so many things right now, but I'm not going to. You know how I feel about you, and I think I know how you feel about me."

"You think?"

He sighed. "I can't help but think if you felt the way I do, you wouldn't be about to drive back to New Orleans."

He's right. What am I doing?

"But my shop, everything . . ."

His shoulders tensed.

I closed my eyes to keep the tears from falling.

I want my life to be here. I'm more me here than I've ever felt before. My life has changed and it's because of you and Mags and this place. I wanted to say it, but I couldn't push the words out of my mouth.

Crawford squeezed my shoulders and I turned to open my car door. I didn't want to hurry away from him, but I needed the silence of my car to let my emotions go. I could feel another storm coming—it was lodged somewhere in my throat—and I preferred that it happen in private.

I faced him for one last good-bye. His now-familiar smell of cedar and fresh laundry, and something else vague but distinctly Crawford, filled my senses and muddied my thoughts. His lips were warm and soft, his faint stubble tickling my skin. I put my hand to his face and turned to climb in. He leaned down to the open window.

"Sara? Please don't wait too long."

43

SARA

SEPTEMBER

Later that day, I opened the door to Bits and Pieces and inhaled the familiar scent of gardenia. I walked through the shop, running my fingers across chair backs, plump down pillows, and dustless tabletops. Allyn had been hard at work.

I walked behind the counter into our makeshift office. Allyn was hunched over the laptop with his head in his hands. The glow from the screen made his face appear pale and sickly.

"Hey," I said.

Allyn jumped, almost toppling his can of LaCroix on the table. "I didn't hear you come in. I've been trying to figure out all this QuickBooks stuff. Couldn't you just use a notebook and a calculator?"

He nudged a chair out to me with the toe of his boot. I sank into it. "So, you're back," he said.

"I'm back." I laid my head down on the table in front of me. He

706

patted my shoulder, then reached into the mini fridge and pulled out a beer.

"It's only two o'clock. Is this what you've been doing since I've been gone?"

"Calm down, Boss. It's not for me."

He opened the bottle and handed it to me. I hesitated, then took a long swallow.

"William?" he asked.

"He's back home in Still Pond, swimming in all the memories I dredged up for him. He wants me to come visit him one day." I smiled. "He still makes furniture, you know."

Allyn nodded. "Maybe you can sell some here."

I pushed back from the table, but Allyn stopped me with a word. "Crawford?"

"He's giving me some time to get settled in. He's waiting on a phone call telling him I'm ready for a visit."

"That's a phone call that'll never happen," he said, partly under his breath.

"What?"

"You'll get back to work here, pick up some new clients, take off on salvaging trips, do what you do—and just not be able to find a free weekend for him to come."

I shook my head. "No, I don't think that's what will happen at all. I—"

"You and I both know how this will go." Allyn cut off my babbling. "The same thing happens every time you meet someone."

I thought of Mitch and others before him. Mitch had lasted longer than most, but our mutual understanding got us both off the hook when our lives were too busy to connect.

"Am I talking to Allyn the therapist or Allyn my friend?"

"They're one and the same. I just know you better than you know yourself, so I'm obligated to warn you of what's to happen."

We sat quietly until the bell on the door announced a customer and voices filled the room.

Allyn took me out onto the floor to show me some new mercury glass vases he'd brought in and a line of hand-painted ceramic dishes. They'd already sold out once and he'd had to place a second order. Allyn moved confidently through the shop, picking up a stray feather, brushing off a cushion with his hand.

"Allyn, this is . . . Thank you for taking care of everything. I appreciate it. And you."

"Don't mention it. Anyway, I didn't expect you to come back, and I didn't want to be the reason it went under without the captain at the helm. Bits and Pieces is your baby, but you know how I feel about this place. It feels partly mine too."

"You didn't think I'd come back?"

He shook his head. "In all our years together, I always thought if you ever left New Orleans, it would be because you finally answered the call from that old house. Once you got settled there, I heard something different in your voice. You didn't sound like the girl who plans her day out to the last second and chafes when something interrupts the schedule. You sounded happy, and not in an 'I just scored a table for Mrs. Broussard' kind of way."

"I don't chafe." My voice betrayed both my irritation and guilt. "And I guess you don't know me as well as you think you do. I didn't stay, did I?"

"No, you didn't."

I sighed and stretched my arms over my head. "You obviously

have things under control here. I'm going back to the loft to unpack. I'll see you in the morning?" I turned and headed for the door.

"Oh, no you don't. For better or worse, you're back in New Orleans, and we're going to celebrate. You're not sitting home and pouting on your first night back. Let me make a few phone calls. I'll pick you up at eight."

I didn't bother arguing. I knew I wouldn't win.

At eight on the dot, Allyn picked me up on his motorcycle. He handed me a helmet and I climbed on, hitching my skirt up to my knees. I felt awkward back in my usual clothes. I thought I'd relish straightening my curls into submission and slipping my feet back into summery wedges, but my toes were cramped, and my work with the flat iron was no match for the thick humidity in the air. I missed the cutoffs, T-shirts, and air-dried hair that had become my staples in Sweet Bay.

We sped through the Quarter's tight streets and back alleys until we reached the restaurant. Allyn's friends waited outside for us, a colorful menagerie of laughter and hugs. On the way in the door, Allyn pulled me to the side. "Are you sure this is what you want?"

"Sure. It'll be fun."

"I don't mean tonight. I'm talking about this—New Orleans. Leaving Sweet Bay. Coming back."

"I—yes. I went to Sweet Bay for Mags. She's gone, the house is gone. This is where I belong."

As I said the words, I thought of all I was giving up, but

something told me I'd made my decision. I didn't let myself think of the implications.

"Whatever you say." Allyn took my hand and led me inside.

Dinner was as raucous as I'd expected it to be. After several rounds of after-dinner shots, most of which I politely declined, someone touched me on the shoulder. "You're back."

Mitch.

Under the table, Allyn nudged my knee.

"I didn't hear from you after you called about the house," he said. "Did everything go okay?"

"It was fine. I actually just got back today. I stayed a little longer than I expected."

He nodded, unbothered by the fact that I'd been gone for more than four months instead of a week as I'd originally planned.

The lively conversation at the table carried on without me, and no one looked our way—except for Allyn, who kept one eye on us as he bantered with the group about a recent photo of Lady Gaga dressed as a drag queen.

Mitch sat in the chair next to me, emptied when the previous occupant excused himself to go to the ladies' room.

"You look good," he said. "Rested."

Of all the things I looked, I knew rested was not one of them. Maybe it was what he thought I wanted to hear. He was the one who looked good. Sleek charcoal suit, white shirt unbuttoned at the throat, confident smile. It wasn't Crawford's torn khakis and wrinkled cotton, but it was nice.

Just then, a wispy blonde with legs too long to be real sauntered over from the bar and put her hand on Mitch's shoulder.
"Your drink is ready, baby." She gave me a once-over, then glided
away to a small table in a dark corner. Mitch and I both watched
her as she settled herself in her chair and gazed back at us with a
look of amusement on her smooth face.

"It's not what it looks like," he said.

"It probably is. And it's okay."

"I'd love to call you. Or better yet, what if I stop by later
tonight?"

"I don't think that's a good idea," I said.

"Tomorrow then. I'm free after three. I can pick you up and
take you somewhere quiet. I know you don't like places like this."

I thought about it. I could slip back into my life like nothing had
changed. Go back to the shop, back to fancy dates with Mitch every
two weeks, back to my routine. It was tempting, if only because I
knew I could bury myself in it. But everything had changed, and
I'd be cheating everyone—Crawford, William, Mags—to pretend
otherwise.

I looked up at Mitch. His body was turned toward me, but his
eyes were on the blonde. I cleared my throat and he turned back
to me.

"What do you say?" he asked.

"Go on." I nodded toward his date. "Enjoy yourself."

He kissed me on the cheek and followed his date's path to the
corner table, leaving a musky scent in his wake.

Allyn pushed my drink closer to me, but I nudged it away.

"Sad to see him go?" he asked.

"Not really."

"So small-town Alabama woodworkers are more your thing now, huh?"

I smiled. That covered both Crawford and William—sort of. "Something like that."

Allyn dropped me off at my loft past midnight. I'd let him and his friends talk me into a dash to the revolving Carousel Bar at the Hotel Monteleone after dinner. Thankfully, Allyn whisked me away after one round, much to the dismay of the rest of the group.

I dismounted at the curb in front of my loft and handed Allyn the helmet.

He was about to pull away when I stopped him.

"Was there a part of you that hoped I wouldn't come back? You would've been the 'captain at the helm' after all."

"No, I—"

"Don't worry, I'm not mad," I said. "In fact, I totally get it. You can run Bits and Pieces with your eyes closed just like I can. It's your baby too."

"I'd never wish for you not to come back. Understand that first. But if we're being honest, sure—I thought it'd be fun to have the run of the place. That is, if you even left it in my hands. You could just as easily have sold the shop and gotten a nice chunk of money out of it. I wouldn't have blamed you a bit."

"I couldn't sell the shop. There's too much of me in it. And you."

"Same thing with The Hideaway," he said. "You could have sold that, but you didn't because there was too much of you and your family in it. You're funny that way—you hang on to things that mean something to you, but you have a hard time hanging on to the people who do the same. Other than me, of course. I know you could never let me go."

I pinched his shoulder. "You're right. We're stuck at the hip, lucky for both of us."

"But unlucky for Crawford." He revved his engine, but before he pulled away from the curb, he pulled his helmet back up. "You may think you have nothing left in Sweet Bay, but you're wrong. You do have something, regardless of the house. You have love. And you have family now—William, Dot and Glory and their old men. You can't tell me that's nothing."

He snapped his helmet back into place and sped off.

44

SARA

SEPTEMBER

The next day began like so many others before it. I had my usual breakfast of yogurt and fruit, showered and dressed, and was out the door at nine fifteen. The last time I'd left my building on a regular workday, it was a crisp April morning. Now it was early September, cloudy and so muggy you could almost wring the air out like a sponge. I hopped into my car and zipped through the Quarter and down Canal toward Magazine. Along the way, other shop owners opened their doors, swept the detritus of the previous night from their sidewalks, and watered thirsty window boxes.

I jiggled my key into the lock at Bits and Pieces, holding on to my purse and to-go cup of coffee. Allyn roared into the driveway behind me.

"Morning, Boss." He tucked his helmet into its place under the seat.

Inside, I flipped the lights on, powered up the computer, and

714

switched on the Keurig in the back. When I checked the dish for pralines, I found squares of dark chocolate. The CD player held Michael Bublé rather than the usual Madeleine Peyroux or Diana Krall.

"Just small changes," Allyn said, noticing my tension. "You can handle it."

And I did. That day drifted into the next, and before I knew it, I'd been back a week. My skin prickled anytime I thought of Crawford, but I tried to get through each day without thinking too much. I still felt restricted in my heels and smooth hair, but I fit my surroundings, and the shop was thriving. Nothing—and yet everything had changed.

The Saturday shoppers came early, reminding me why I loved retail in a tourist town. Whether they were from Louisiana or Minnesota, they all wanted to buy something embellished with New Orleans's famous fleur-de-lis. Thankfully, Allyn had amped up our supply of pillows and knickknacks featuring the symbol.

I was blessedly busy all morning, my mind occupied with customer questions and client requests. I visited the site of Mrs. Broussard's new house to ensure the builders remembered to include the east-facing bay window in her walk-in closet/dressing area—at her special request—and I squeezed in a quick trip to an antique mall in Metairie. Allyn and I passed each other in the back hallway once, both hurrying to meet a demand somewhere.

"Glad you came back to this?" he asked with a smile.

LAUREN K. DENTON

"I haven't sat down since I ate my breakfast this morning and my feet are killing me, if that tells you anything."

"Do you still love it?"

I nodded. "I think I do. I just may have to take these heels off and go barefoot."

"That's the Sweet Bay coming out in you." He continued down the hall to a waiting customer.

Early afternoon business slowed enough for me to take a short break on the front porch. I sat in the swing as folks passed by on the sidewalk. I was fine until I saw the little girl. She was probably four or five, with dark curls and still-plump arms. Her daddy grabbed her and spun her around, her delighted squeals making everyone around them smile. When he brought her back to the ground, she ran straight into her mother's outstretched arms.

All the sadness and longing I'd packed into the most remote pocket of my mind when I left Sweet Bay came flooding back. I thought of Mags. Of William's old, gnarled hands and Crawford's sturdy, capable ones. Of The Hideaway and all that had taken place there. The force of my longing almost doubled me over.

Allyn chose that moment to stick his head out the front doorway. "You okay?"

I managed a nod. He kept his eyes on me a moment longer before closing the door.

Back on the sidewalk, the little family was gone. I stood and peered over the edge of the porch rail for a better view, but I didn't see any sign of them. I ran shaky hands over my hair and straightened my dress, then opened the door and walked back in.

After a quick snack, consumed in stolen moments in the back office, my cell rang. I was busy with a customer, so Allyn answered.

716

A moment later, he mouthed something to me from across the room. I shook my head in confusion. He crossed the room and whispered, "It's Vernon Bains. The lawyer?"

I took the phone and left the customer in Allyn's care.

"Mr. Bains, this feels like déjà vu with you calling me here at work," I said as I stepped into our tiny courtyard and pulled the back door closed behind me, "Last time you had bad news."

"Ah, Miss Jenkins, a common misconception. A lawyer on the phone doesn't always mean bad news. In this case, I have very good news for you. At least, I think it's good."

"I'm listening."

"It appears Mr. Grosvenor has withdrawn his plan to take over The Hideaway's property."

"Excuse me?"

"He called me early this morning and said he was going in a different direction. When I pressed, he said he bought another piece of property near Mobile Bay. He's scrapping the boardwalk idea and building his condos there instead. For better or worse, it appears Sweet Bay is destined to remain the secluded town it's always been."

"I—but I don't . . ."

"I know," Mr. Bains continued. "I was speechless too."

I forced my brain into gear. "So if Sammy isn't taking it, does it just . . . ?"

"Everything goes back to normal. I can't say the mayor won't one day try to run with the plan again, but without Sammy badgering him about it, and seeing as how most of the town of Sweet Bay was against it, hopefully he'll let the idea die."

Allyn stuck his head out the door. "Everything okay?" He

walked into the courtyard and sat next to me. *What is it?* he mouthed. I shook my head.

"I don't know what to make of Sammy's change of heart," Mr. Bains said. "I'll let you know if I find out anything else."

"Tell me," Allyn said as soon as I put down the phone.

"Sammy isn't taking the house."

"What happened?"

"I have no idea."

Allyn sat back in the wrought-iron rocker and crossed his arms. "You said you needed something to make Sammy go away. I guess that something happened."

A grin pushed at my cheeks. I couldn't wipe it away.

"You're excited," Allyn said.

"I don't know what I am." I stood and took a deep breath. "But I think I have to go."

"Of course you do. Get out of here."

"Wait." I sat back down. "I can't do this. Mrs. Girard is coming at four and I have a shipment—"

"Don't worry about it. I'll take care of everything," he said.

"But what about—?"

"Stop. It's fine. You can go."

"I don't even know what I'm going there to do."

"Yes, you do. You've already started a life there. Now you're going to go back and pick up where you left off."

"You make it sound so simple," I said.

"Things aren't always as difficult as you make them out to be. Sometimes you just have to turn your brain off and dive in. This may be the last time Sweet Bay tries to pull you back."

I chewed on the end of a fingernail. "Crawford?"

"Only one way to find out."

I hugged Allyn and went inside to grab my purse. On my way through the shop to the front door, I trailed my fingers on table-tops and chair backs. Pausing at the door, I turned to look through the room. Two women stood in the corner near an armoire, contemplating the big purchase. Allyn joined them, and within seconds he had them laughing and moving toward the register. Bits and Pieces would be just fine.

On my way out of the city, I rolled my windows down as far as they'd go and dropped my heels on the floorboard next to me. I didn't know exactly what I'd find in Sweet Bay when I returned, but I wasn't going to let my last chance slip away without a fight.

I called Dot from the car and told her I was on my way home.

"Well, it's about time. I guess Vernon called you?"

"He called this afternoon. I was going to give you the news, but it sounds like you already know."

"Oh yes." She chuckled. "A lot has happened since you've been gone. Let's wait and talk when you get here though. I need to make a phone call."

She hung up before I could ask what was going on.

A couple hours later, I pulled down the long driveway and shaded my eyes from one last sharp ray of light. Two people sat in rocking chairs on the porch, and one of them stood as I approached the house.

Crawford. But it wasn't him.

When my eyes adjusted to the shadowy light on the porch, I

recognized William's slightly stooped figure. Dot sat in the chair next to him. I parked under the big oak and climbed out. Without stopping to grab my bag, I headed for the porch. William and Dot were both smiling.

"What in the world is going on?" I asked. "How do you two . . . ?"

"It's been busy around here," Dot said.

I looked at William. "I took care of Sammy," he said.

"You—what?"

"A long time ago, I bought a piece of property down at the mouth of Sweet Bay. I didn't think much about it until I decided that's where I wanted to build a house for me and Maggie one day. It doesn't have a name—we just called it the cove." I glanced at Dot. She winked. "I never built the house, but I kept the property all these years in the hopes of—I don't even know. I just couldn't bear to part with it."

"And you're giving it up now? But how did you know . . . ?"

"It was Crawford," Dot said.

William nodded. "He worked hard for this house after you left. He found me after digging through old land records looking for anything that could fend off Sammy. He was the one who put it together that the cove could be the thing to save the house."

Crawford did it?

"But why would Sammy want the cove?" I asked.

"He visited me years ago and asked me about it. Turns out it's quite a coveted piece of property. I told him back then I'd never let it go, but now that Maggie . . . Well, once I met you, I realized I have no reason to hang on to it. All it took was a phone call. Sammy bought the property from me on the spot and signed The Hideaway back to you."

"I can't believe you sold it," I said.

"I hope it's okay." His face clouded with concern. "I could tell how much you loved this house, and I hated to see you lose it."

"Okay?" I laughed. "It's more than okay." I didn't have the right words, so I hugged him, and Dot too.

"William and Crawford just couldn't give up on this old place," Dot said. "Or you, it seems."

"I don't know about that. We haven't . . . I haven't talked to Crawford since I left."

Dot arched an eyebrow. "And yet he's been here doing all this work. Honey, he didn't do it for us."

"I got to know him a little this past week," William said. "He builds things, you know."

I nodded. "I know. You have that in common. And you two." I pointed at William and Dot. "Looks like you've sparked an unexpected friendship."

Dot looked over at William. "We had a lot to catch up on, that's for sure." Then she turned to me. "Let's get you inside. I apologize in advance—it's a mess in there."

I followed her through the front door where boxes and suitcases spilled in disarray all over the sparkling hardwoods. Despite the mess and the remaining old furniture, the house felt new. Even unfinished, the open floor plan, extra space, and fresh paint gave it life and new legs. Excitement fluttered again in my chest.

"We meant to be all packed up by now, but it's taking longer than we expected," Dot said.

I put my hands on my hips and inhaled deep. "Maybe you should just stay here then."

Openmouthed, Dot stared back at me. "What?" she asked, just

as Major called down from the landing on the stairs, "Thank the Lord. We're all old. Our kids can come visit us."

I smiled and patted Dot on the arm, then headed for the kitchen to look for a celebratory bottle of wine. "Go ahead and unpack your bags. You're not going anywhere."

45

SARA

DECEMBER

I stood in The Hideaway's gleaming new kitchen pouring a cup of coffee when Major stomped down the stairs.

"Sara! Where's my Gillette? And my toothbrush? I can't find anything in this blasted house."

"It's all in your new bathroom, the one attached to your room. You know you don't have to keep using the hall bath. That's why I built you and Glory your own."

Major trudged back up the stairs, grumbling the whole way, until Glory called out to him. "Stop your whining, Major, or you'll be brushing your teeth on the dock."

I took my coffee into the light-flooded dining room and sat at our new heart pine table. I ran my hand across the top, my fingers finding the indentations of the skeleton key at the edge.

"See? You'd have missed all this if you'd stayed in New Orleans," Bert said from across the table, working on his second

723

apple scone. "What would you do without Major's presence in your life?"

"For one, I wouldn't have someone yelling at me about a toothbrush at seven in the morning."

I heard a tentative knock and looked up to see Mr. and Mrs. Melman.

"Breakfast is at seven, right?" Mrs. Melman asked.

"Yes, please come in and make yourself at home," I said. "Scones and coffee are just in the kitchen there, and muffins and fruit are on the table."

"Thank you. This place is wonderful," she said. "Has the house been open long?"

Bert and I looked at each other.

"It's recently reopened," I said.

Mrs. Melman touched her husband's elbow. "We'll have to tell Maylene and George. They just love quaint places like this."

As the Melmans shuffled into the kitchen, Bob Crowe and his wife entered the dining room. Bob booked a weekend right after we opened for business. "You've outdone yourself." He pulled a banana out of the basket on the table. "I know I talked this place up in the newspaper article, but I still had doubts it would make it."

"You and me both," I said.

"How'd you get Sammy to back off, anyway?"

"It wasn't me. Someone offered him a better piece of property and he took it."

"You sure got a lucky break. There's no chance anything Sammy could build would be half as classy as this."

The Crowes followed the Melmans into the kitchen in search of steaming coffee and pastries. The air smelled of cinnamon and apples mixed with a tang of salty air from the open windows. The sky was bright, the sun sparkled, and my heart was full. My new Hideaway. My new life.

It wasn't lost on me that if it weren't for Mags drawing me back to Sweet Bay, I wouldn't have had any of this. I'd still be churning away in New Orleans, thinking I'd found all I was to do with my life. I'd thought I was done with The Hideaway forever, but family was the magnetic pull that drew me back. I may have given up on Mags a long time ago, but in her own unorthodox way, she was the one who saved me in the end.

The phone in the hall rang, and I jumped up to get it. "The Hideaway, this is Sara." I loved the words as they left my mouth.

"Hey, babe," Crawford said.

"Hey, yourself. Why didn't you call my cell?"

"I know you love answering the house phone."

I smiled even though he couldn't see me.

"You're out early this morning," I said. The background noise told me he was in his truck with the windows down.

"I'm on my way to the McCaffertys' house in Lillian to meet the floor guy. You'd love this place. It's a rambling old Creole full of antiques. I mean *antique* antiques."

"What are they doing to the house?"

"Adding on. Again. They need room for the grandkids. Although I don't know how kids and all these antiques will mix. How did the night go? Was Major on his best behavior?"

"I didn't hear a peep out of him until he got feisty this morning about his toothbrush. But he's fine. It's all perfect, actually." It had been a few weeks since the last construction worker left, but the newness had yet to wear off for me.

"I can't wait to see you," he said. "I have a few more stops to make, then I'll head your way. Need anything?"

"Just you."

At ten, after giving the Melmans a map of the Eastern Shore of Mobile Bay and suggesting a few places they could grab lunch, I went next door. It was a beautiful thing, my business being forty feet from my home. Sometimes I missed the clattering streetcars and morning "rush" of traffic in the Quarter, but you couldn't beat walking next door with your coffee mug to flip the Open sign around and begin the day.

In the three months I'd been back in Sweet Bay—for the second time—renovations on The Hideaway had wrapped up, and Crawford and his team built a small cottage on the empty lot next door. We were fortunate to have a long stretch of good weather in early fall, and the builders made quick work of the cottage. It now housed my new shop, Lost and Found. Allyn was the one who'd convinced me I could do it.

"You started the first shop from scratch. Why can't you do it again? Alabama surely has just as many estate sales and old barns to salvage as Louisiana does. They'll eat your stuff up, just like they do here."

Crawford was on Allyn's side, of course. They met when Crawford and I drove to New Orleans to pack up my loft and bring a few things back home from the shop. Allyn insisted on taking us out to dinner. I picked a sidewalk café near Jackson Square, a place I thought would be just noisy enough to distract us from the fact that Crawford and Allyn would have nothing to talk about. But I was wrong—I could hardly get a word in between them bantering back and forth, first about farming and motorcycles, then about me.

"You're the lucky one who gets all of Sara's pent-up romantic yearnings," Allyn said to Crawford, nudging me with his shoulder.

"That makes me sound like I've been locked up in a tower somewhere."

"You basically have," he said, then turned to Crawford. "No one has been able to break down that wall she built around herself."

"You did the hard work," Crawford said. "All your advice at least convinced her to give me a shot."

"Do I even need to be here? I can scoot out if you two want to keep talking about me and my wall."

Crawford smiled at me. A candle flickered on the table between us, right next to a red glass vase holding a plastic rose. His knee touched mine under the table.

The truth was, I'd had to convince him to give *me* a shot when I got back to Sweet Bay. I drove to his house after I told Dot and the others they didn't have to move out. He didn't believe I was there to stay.

"I can't do this twice," he said. "How do I know you're not going to skip town again?"

"I'm not going anywhere. This is where I need to be—where I want to be. Everything has changed."

Crawford leaned against his kitchen counter, hands in his pockets, and smiled, but it wasn't his usual smile. "Of course it has. You have the house back."

"Yes, I have the house, but it's more than that. I'm sorry for not calling, for not explaining myself to you. Once I got back to New Orleans, it didn't take long to realize I'd made a huge mistake." I stepped closer to him and put my hand to his face. "There's nowhere else I want to be, and no one else I want to be with."

He covered my hand with his own but still didn't speak. Finally, he gave me a real smile. "You're back?"

"I'm back for good."

Despite being a week into December, it was a warm day. Sunlight flooded through the bank of windows facing the bay. Not long after I propped open the front door, a gaggle of ladies entered the shop, all fleshy arms and laughter.

"You'll have to forgive us if we're too loud, dear," one of them said. "We're just excited to be here on a girls' weekend. Our husbands are out hunting and we have a lot of shopping to do."

"You've come to the right place. I have a little bit of everything, so make yourselves at home. Let me know if you have questions."

They were still puttering and gossiping when Crawford walked in. It may sound crazy, but I could have sworn the sun blazed brighter and the breeze turned warmer when he entered. Or at least that's how it felt to me. He walked through the room, stopping to chat with the ladies and make them blush with nothing but his charm and easy smile. It was hard to believe I'd even considered leaving him—and everything else—for my overloaded life in New Orleans.

"This is perfect." One of the women touched a buffet table in the back of the shop. "I'm looking for something just like this to go in my dining room. I love the rustic look. Where did it come from?"

"A woodworker up in Still Pond made it," I said. "He's been making pieces like this for most of his life. He can't handle the workload he used to, so he only makes a limited number of pieces now. I have two tables in here and another handful next door that are also for sale. He does custom orders here and there, if you ask nicely."

She chuckled and smoothed her hand down the length of the table.

"You won't find another table filled with as much love as this one. Look here—see this key engraved into the wood? He cuts the key into every piece he makes. He started doing it fifty years ago when he fell in love with a girl named Maggie. He said she held the key to his heart."

"Well, you don't hear that every day," the woman said. "What happened to them? Tell me they married and lived a happy life together."

"They didn't marry," I said, "but they should have. I'm pretty sure she loved him until she died earlier this year, and he still very much loves her."

"Sounds like you know this woodworker well."

From across the room, Crawford caught my eye and winked.

I nodded. "I do. He's my grandfather."

That night, long after the last customers found their way out of the shop, most with shopping bags rustling around their knees,

Crawford and I relaxed in the rocking chairs on the back porch of The Hideaway. The Crowes were getting ready for a dinner I'd booked for them at the Grand Hotel in Point Clear, and the Melmans were at the Outrigger. Another group of guests wasn't arriving until the next afternoon, so I had the evening off.

I sipped my wine and settled farther into my chair. My legs rested on a blanket in Crawford's lap and he gently squeezed my bare feet.

A scuffle in the house behind us made us both look up to the open doorway. Bert stood with one hand on the door frame, the other caught in Dot's firm grasp.

"Bert, give them some privacy," she scolded, then turned to me. "I'm sorry. I told him you two wouldn't be interested in his silly games, but he's being very pigheaded."

Bert shook his hand free from Dot's and walked out on the porch. "I picked up this new game at Grimmerson's today. George said it's popular with the young people."

"It's *Pictionary*," Dot said, exasperated.

Crawford grinned. "What do you say?" he whispered.

"I can draw a mean crawfish," I whispered back.

"Let's do it," he said. "Here's to another night in paradise."

46

MAGS

MARCH, NINE MONTHS EARLIER

I often went back to the cove. I went on days when I couldn't bear the loneliness of missing William—or maybe I just pined for that short, sweet time in my life when he would hold me, touch me, make me feel as alive as a power line, shooting sparks and electricity out into the universe. I'd sit along the edge of the water and imagine what it would have been like if things had turned out differently. If Robert hadn't had that first episode and landed himself in the hospital, or if I'd never cashed that check, leading Daddy to The Hideaway, William and I might have still been together. We would have spent every evening out on our porch overlooking the water, dumbstruck at our love and how lucky we were to have found each other.

Or maybe that's not true at all. Maybe we would have fizzled as quickly as we began. A bright burst of fire at the beginning and another, dimmer burst at the end, like a firework that never quite made it off the ground. We could have hurt each other a thousand ways, both of us eventually needing more and offering less than we had to give. I would have always wondered if he stayed with me out of a sense of duty, because of Jenny, while he'd worry that I'd only stayed with him to defy Robert and my parents.

I could dream all day long, but at its core, the truth of my life is that I am a lucky woman. I've known real love and true beauty, two things not given to every person. Without Robert, I never would have found my way to The Hideaway or William, and without William, I wouldn't have known the delight of both Jenny and Sara.

While I'm thankful for both of these men in my life, I'm more thankful for the woman they showed me I could be on my own. Not to mention the people they brought into my life. The Hideaway was always full of friends and lovers, mothers and daughters, secret keepers and secret spillers, straight talkers and soft shoulders. We had hurt and we had joy, but I wouldn't have had it any other way.

Things could have turned out better or worse, but I don't dwell on any of that. I have a tarnished old house to live in, a garden to keep my hands dirty, and sunsets to watch. Sitting here on my old cedar bench, my toes dug deep in the earth, herons swooping low over the water, and the sun an orange ball of fire slipping below the horizon, I figure I've had it just about as good as it gets.

ACKNOWLEDGMENTS

Thank you to my agent, Karen Solem, for your patience, kindness, and enthusiasm for this story. Thank you to everyone at HarperCollins Christian Publishing and Thomas Nelson for taking a chance on me and *The Hideaway*. It's an honor to be welcomed into the family with such open arms. I especially want to thank Daisy Hutton, Karli Jackson, Becky Philpott, Kristen Golden, Amanda Bostic, Kristen Ingebretson, Jodi Hughes, and Paul Fisher. Additional heartfelt thanks to Karli, who believed in and championed this book from the very beginning. I truly believe you were just the right editor at just the right time, and I'm so thankful my manuscript landed on your desk. Thank you also to Julee Schwartzberg for her editing prowess and another huge thanks to Kristen Ingebretson for the gorgeous cover. I've spent way too much time just staring at it, wishing I could sit on those rocking chairs in the warm breeze.

I'm grateful to have stumbled on Denise Trimm and her fiction workshops, first held under the Continuing Ed program at Samford

University, then under her own Alabama Writers Connect. The encouragement, feedback, critiques, and laughter have been such a thrill these last several years. There have been various incarnations of the group, but the biggest thanks for help with *The Hideaway* goes to Denise, Barry DeLozier, Anna Gresham, Alex Johnston, and Chuck Measel. I'm also thankful for and indebted to The Cartel, of which we will not speak . . .

Thank you to my friends and family who read various drafts of *The Hideaway* and gave heaps of encouragement and confirmation that the time I spent writing it hadn't been wasted: My mom Kaye Koffler, my husband Matt Denton, friends Sara Beth Cobb, Thames Schoenvogel, Carla Jean Whitley, and Ella Joy Olsen.

Additional thanks to Sara Beth Cobb of Nimblee Design for creating such a beautiful website and logo for me so *The Hideaway* would have a place to hang out online. Thank you too for being so excited about this story from the beginning and for encouraging me in myriad ways. I'm thankful for our friendship.

Thanks to my dear friend Anna Gresham for unending support, laughter, rambling texts and e-mails about how HARD this writing thing is, and long car rides where we never run out of things to talk about. You're a kindred spirit and I'm thankful to be "Anna's friend Lauren."

Thank you to Angie Davis for the beautiful photos and for making me more comfortable than I expected when having someone take pictures of me!

It's a beautiful thing when writers help other writers. A huge thank you goes to author Patti Callahan Henry for launching me from the slush pile to the desk of Ami McConnell, then editor at Thomas Nelson. Thank you for reaching out a hand to help and for thinking enough of my story to pass it along to your friend, and thank you to Ami for handing it off to the fabulous Karli Jackson. Thank you to authors Anne Riley, Carla Jean Whitley, Ella Joy Olsen, Emily Drake Carpenter, and Karen White for being generous with encouragement, support, and advice. Author Carolyn Haines responded to an out-of-the-blue e-mail from me and, over the years, offered encouragement and support as I worked toward publication of *The Hideaway*. I'm a member of the Women's Fiction Writers Association, a group of generous and talented writers who are always quick to offer advice, commiseration, encouragement, and shared excitement. Writing can be a lonely pursuit, and it helps to be able to jump online and within seconds, have friends jumping into conversation.

People smarter than me offered tidbits of info that helped make the details in this book more authentic: Elisa Munoz for insider information on New Orleans levees. Julie Gulledge and David Wallace for help in finding information about Mobile Mardi Gras balls in decades past. Aaron Dettling for lending his legal expertise in the area of eminent domain. Any mistakes are mine alone.

My family is my heart, my biggest and most profound blessing. Thank you to my hardworking husband, Matt, who never complains when I escape to the library to write and come home long after I say I'll be home. Thank you for believing in me and for loving me more than I deserve. I'm so glad I get to do life with you. Thank you to Kate and Sela, my lovebugs who make me want to be better every day and who had such blind faith that my book would be AWESOME! My sweet Kate was the only one with whom I was brave enough to take to the D section of the library and point to where I hoped my book would go one day. Kate was on the receiving end of many of my hopes and dreams—dreams that seemed too far-fetched and naïve to say out loud to any adult. She took those dreams at face value and never doubted that they'd come true. Thank you to all the Kofflers, Dentons, and other extended family members and friends who have shared my joy and excitement as if it were your own. I love all of you.

Every day as I sat down to write *The Hideaway*, I asked God to guide my hands (and words) and to give me continued inspiration. I loved the characters and I was devoted to telling their story, but I was constantly plagued by fears that the inspiration would dry up and this would become one more unfinished story in my overloaded file of unfinished stories. By His grace and some kind of blind naivety on my part, I was able to not only finish this story, but (with much help) hone and polish it into something I am immensely proud of. So, thank You, Lord, for the inspiration, for guiding my words, for allowing me to bear Your creative image through my writing.

DISCUSSION QUESTIONS

1. Sara fled Sweet Bay and The Hideaway as soon as she was able. Do you think that decision had more to do with her parents' death and the pain associated with that time in her life or because of Mags's mystery and eccentricities? A combination of the two?

2. After leaving her parents, husband, and former life, Mags makes a new life at The Hideaway. In essence, her friends at the B and B become her new family. Have you ever found yourself in a situation where you've had to make a new life and family with the people around you?

3. Mags's parents expected her to marry a man from a respectable family who made enough money to keep her in the life she was used to. They also expected her to look the other way when Robert strayed and to wait for him to return to his senses and his marriage. How are marriages in general different today? How are they the same? Do you—or someone you know—have experience similar to Mags's?

4. As Sara peels back the layers and hears stories from Mags's friends, she learns Mags had a full, rich life before becoming the unconventional grandmother Sara knew. Have you ever been surprised to learn something about a family member you thought you knew well? How did your childhood view of this person differ from your opinion once you grew into adulthood? Did the new revelations change the way you thought about the person?

5. In a sense, Mags uses The Hideaway as a way to hide from her life and difficult situation in Mobile. In what way are other characters in the book hiding? Think of Sara in New Orleans, Allyn at Bits and Pieces, and Dot's friends at The Hideaway. Do you have any experience with hiding in a comforting or safe place when things in your life feel out of control?

6. Sara comes to regret that she never took the time to get to know who her grandmother really was. Do you have experience with familial regret? Has someone passed away or otherwise passed out of your life whom you wish you had taken a chance to ask key questions, whether about the past or some event that person had experience with? How do you deal with or make peace with that regret?

7. When we first meet Sara, she is fully devoted to her work and doesn't make much extra time for friends, family, or extra pursuits. How does Sara evolve over the course of the book? What did you think about her decision to return to New Orleans and Bits and Pieces after spending the summer at The Hideaway? Do you understand her?

8. Sammy Grosvenor has a vision of Sweet Bay as a tourist destination. Those who live in Sweet Bay want it to remain

the sleepy town it's always been. What do you think of the tension between progress and the desire to keep things the same? Do you know of a place that has undergone a similar fight with progress?

9. Mags left her parents and husband to escape a life that was suffocating. Would you have had the courage to make a decision so opposite your family's expectations? Do you think Mags made the right decision to leave her home? What about her decision to stay at The Hideaway?

10. If Sara had been able to meet Mags as a young woman, do you think they would have been friends? Would they have agreed with each other's life choices?

The only thing certain is change—even
in a place as steady as Perry, Alabama,
on a street as old as Glory Road.

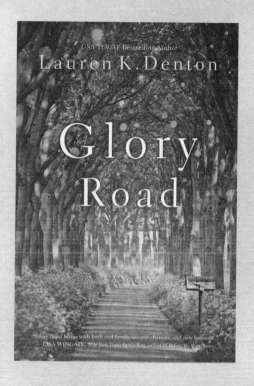

"*Glory Road* brims with faith and family, second chances and
new horizons. Three generations of women may well remind
you of your own as they face transitions and find paths as winding and sweet as those in a lovely garden on a summer's day."

—Lisa Wingate, *New York Times* bestselling
author of *Before We Were Yours*

About the Author

Photo by Angie Davis

LAUREN K. DENTON is the author of *USA TODAY* bestselling novels *The Hideaway* and *Hurricane Season*. She was born and raised in Mobile, Alabama, and now lives with her husband and two daughters in Homewood, just outside Birmingham. Though her husband tries valiantly to turn her into a mountain girl, she'd still rather be at the beach.

∽

LaurenKDenton.com
Facebook: LaurenKDentonAuthor
Twitter: @LaurenKDenton
Pinterest: Lauren K. Denton, Author
Instagram: LaurenKDentonBooks